Buffy
THE
VAMPIRE
SLAYER

3

Read how it all began.

BUFFY THE VAMPIRE SLAYER 1

BUFFY THE VAMPIRE SLAYER 2

Buffy THE VAMPIRE SLAYER

3

CARNIVAL OF SOULS
NANCY HOLDER

ONE THING OR YOUR MOTHER
KIRSTEN BEYER

BLOODED
CHRISTOPHER GOLDEN AND NANCY HOLDER

Based on the hit TV series created by Joss Whedon

SIMON PULSE
NEW YORK   LONDON   TORONTO   SYDNEY

SIMON PULSE

An imprint of Simon & Schuster Children's Publishing Division

1230 Avenue of the Americas, New York, NY 10020

This Simon Pulse paperback edition November 2010

Carnival of Souls ™ and copyright © 2006 by Twentieth Century Fox Film Corporation.

All rights reserved.

One Thing or Your Mother ™ and copyright © 2008 by Twentieth Century Fox Film Corporation.

All rights reserved.

Blooded ™ and copyright © 1998 by Twentieth Century Fox Film Corporation.

All rights reserved.

All rights reserved, including the right of reproduction in whole or in part in any form.

SIMON PULSE and colophon are registered trademarks of Simon & Schuster, Inc.

For information about special discounts for bulk purchases, please contact Simon & Schuster Special Sales at 1-866-506-1949 or business@simonandschuster.com.

The Simon & Schuster Speakers Bureau can bring authors to your live event.

For more information or to book an event contact the Simon & Schuster Speakers Bureau at 1-866-248-3049 or visit our website at www.simonspeakers.com.

Designed by Mike Rosamilia

The text of this book was set in Times.

Manufactured in the United States of America

2 4 6 8 10 9 7 5 3 1

Library of Congress Control Number 2010922985

ISBN 978-1-4424-1211-8

These books were previously published individually.

B orn into a legendary role, Buffy the Vampire Slayer carries the burden of humanity on her shoulders. Her true identity is known only to her Watcher, Giles, her best friends Willow, Xander, Cordelia, and Oz, and her good-hearted vampire boyfriend, Angel. Living in Sunnydale, California, above the Hellmouth, she is a high school student by day and a demon's worst adversary by night. These are her stories.

TABLE OF CONTENTS

CARNIVAL OF SOULS

IN MEMORY OF BELLE'S BELOVED
GRANDFATHER,
GEORGE WAYNE HOLDER.
WE MISS YOU, PAPA WAYNE.

As always, my thanks first and foremost to Joss Whedon; and to Sarah Michelle Gellar, David Boreanaz, David Greenwalt, Tim Minear, Marti Noxon, David Fury, and the many other producers, actors, and staffs of both *Angel* and *Buffy*. My deepest gratitude to my agent and dear friend, Howard Morhaim, and to his assistant, Allison Keiley. Thank you to Patrick Price, who has been such a wonderful editor and a writer's true friend in the publishing loop; and to Debbie Olshan at Fox, whose insights have kept me out of more trouble. Thanks to the *Buffy* and *Angel* fan clubs, Abbie Bernstein, Tara DeLullo, Kristy Bratton; Titan/Dreamwatch; Inkworks; cityofangel.com; litvamp, saveangel.com, IAMTW, novelscribes, SF-FFWs, Persephone, and Buffy Studies gurus David Lavery and Rhonda Wilcox; Ashley McConnell, Monica Elrod, Terri Grazer Yates, Linda Wilcox, Karen Hackett, Barbara Nierman, Elisa Jimenez-Steiger, Ellen Greenfield, Wayne Holder, Amy Shricker, Jennifer and Janice Kayler; and Christie and Richard Holt; Steve Perry; Del and Sue Howison, Lydia Marano and Art Cover, the YaYa's—Lucy Walker,

Anny Caya, Leslie Ackel Jones, Elise Jones, Kerri Ingle, and Belle Holder; Sandra Morehouse and Richard Wilkinson; Bob Vardeman, and Jeff Mariotte and Maryelizabeth Hart. Thanks to Andy Thompson at Family Karate for teaching us to live the black belt way. Lisa Clancy, you are my Termie. Belle Holder, you're my daughter, and I love you. Courtesy, integrity, perseverance, self-control, indomitable spirit.

PROLOGUE

It was Tuesday.

After nightfall.

In Sunnydale.

And Buffy Summers the Vampire Slayer was out on patrol instead of at the Bronze with Willow and Xander (and hopefully Angel) because Giles had figured out that tonight was the Rising.

The Rising of what, Buffy's Watcher did not know, but it was easy to guess that it probably meant vampires. Maybe zombies. Something that rose from graves, anyway.

Something that kept her from the fun other sixteen-year-olds were having.

Sighing, Buffy trailed her fingers over the lowered head of a weeping cherub statue and waved her flashlight in an arc.

"Here, rising guys," she called plaintively. "Ready to play when you are."

She had on her black knitted cap and Angel's black leather jacket, but she was still a little chilly. Maybe it was just because she was walking through Blessed Memories, the graveyard that contained the du Lac tomb, famed in the annals of Buffy's diary as the graveyard out of which Spike and Dru had stolen a fancy decoding cross called, amazingly enough, the du Lac Cross. They had used it to nearly kill Angel. Since then, it was not her favorite cemetery ever.

Blessed Memories also contained a pet cemetery, a little square of plots with miniature headstones that tugged at Buffy's heart. TOBY MY PUP RIP 1898. R KITTIE LUCY 1931. She had no time for pets, not even zombie cats freshly risen from the grave. She had hardly any time for anything, what with the slayage and the studying, okay, not the studying; but still and all, it was Sunnydale that was the problem, with all its death and monsters and standard normal-teenage-girl pressures, like having friends and not getting kicked out of school. . . .

If my best buds and I could be anywhere but here, that would be . . . She thought for a moment. She and Willow were really good at that game. Anywhere But Here was created for high school kids, especially those who had to live in Sunnydale.

. . . in Maui, with Angel. . . . Okay, not. Too much sun for

a boyfriend who would burst into flames if he stepped into the tropical rays. So . . .

. . . in Paris, with Angel . . . and Willow could be with James Spader—I officially give him to her because I'm with Angel now—and we're so not eating snails, but oh, I know! French pastries. And we are shopping . . .

. . . for rings . . .

Buffy stopped and cocked her head. Did she just hear something? Snap of a twig, maybe? A cough?

She listened eagerly for a replay so she could head toward it. She waited. Waited yet more. Heard nothing. Turned off her flashlight. More waiting.

Behold the sounds of silence.

She tried to pick up the Paris thread again. French pastries, okay, maybe too early in the relationship to shop for rings, then for shoes. . . . Truth was, she really *would* be happy to be just about anywhere but here. If only she could just run away, join in the fun-having of other kids her age. Join the circus, even.

Except she didn't like circuses. Never had. What was with those clowns, anyway? She shivered. She was with Xander on that one: They gave her a wiggins.

Send in the clowns.

Six miles away, just past the outbuildings of Crest College, the trees shivered. The clouds fled and the moon trailed after them, desperate to hide.

Sunnydale, loaded with souls ripe for the plucking . . .

Five miles away.

The clowns materialized first, big feet flapping, over-stuffed bottoms wiggling, in polka dots and rainbow stripes, and white gloves hiding fingers that no one should ever see.

A jag of lightning:

A parade of trucks, wagons, lorries. A maroon wagon, its panels festooned with golden Harlequins and bird women plucking lyres, shimmered and stayed solid. Behind it, a Gypsy cart with a Conestoga-style bonnet jangled with painted cow-bells, and beneath the overhanging roof, black-and-silver ribbons swayed. Behind the wagon, a forties-era freight truck blew diesel exhaust into the velvet layers of moonlight. A jagged line, creaking back into shadows, disappearing. Maybe the entire apparition was just a dream.

Thunder rolled, and they reappeared.

Maybe they were just a nightmare.

Spectral horses whinnied and chuffed; it began to rain, and through the murky veil of downpour and fog, the horses' heads were skulls; their heads were . . . heads. They breathed fire; they didn't breathe at all.

They began to rot in slow motion.

The clowns ran up and down the advancing line, applauding and laughing at the flicker-show, the black magick lantern extravaganza.

Skeletons and corpses hunkered inside truck and wagon cabs and buckboard seats. Whipcracks sparked. Eyes lolled.

Mouths hung open, snapped shut. Teeth fell out. Eyes bobbed from optic nerves.

Things . . . reassembled.

A creak, and then nothing.

Two ebony steeds pulled the last vehicle—the thirteenth wagon in the cortege. It was an old Victorian traveling-medicine-show wagon, maybe something that had crisscrossed the prairies and the badlands, promising remedies for rheumatism and the gout when the only ingredients in the jug were castor oil, a dead rattlesnake, and wood alcohol.

Where their hooves touched, the earth smoked. Black feathers bobbing in their harnesses, black feathers waving from the four corners of the ornate, ebony wagon, the horses were skeletons were horse flesh were demon stallions ridden by misshapen, leathery creatures with sagging shoulder blades, flared ears, and pencil-stub fingers. And as the moon shied away from the grotesquerie, the angle of light revealed words emblazoned on each of the thirteen vehicles that snuck toward Sunnydale, home to hundreds of thousands of souls determined to ignore the peril they were in:

PROFESSOR CALIGARI'S TRAVELING CARNIVAL

The wind howled through the trees—or was it the ghostly dirge of a calliope?

Too soon to tell.

Too late to do anything about it.

CHAPTER ONE

What the heck is that? Buffy wondered as she stepped from beneath the shelter of a tomb in Shady Rest, cemetery number eight on her hit parade of twelve. The repeated hollow sounds, which maybe were musical notes, had coincided with the stopping of the rain. They were even stranger than the Hindi songfest she had watched with Willow and Xander, the one about the podiatrist and the water buffalo.

She listened hard. Was it a distant boom box? Did it have anything—*please*—to do with the Rising? It would be so nice if something actually happened before she packed it in, aside from ripping her black leather pants on the chain-link fence she'd hopped to get in there. Plus dropping her big black flashlight, which now no longer worked.

There it was again, kind of a sinister tootling or something. . . . She was already trying to figure out how to describe it to Giles. It was nothing she had ever heard before.

A terrified shriek pierced the darkness.

Ah! But *that* was!

The Slayer brightened. No, no, not brightened—because that would be wrong—so much as erupted into action, racing toward the plea for help. She put on the turbo as the shriek was joined by a cry, this one lower in pitch. A guy and a girl, then.

Without her flashlight, Buffy scrutinized the passing shadows: grave, grave, crypt, tree draped with moss, grave, stone vase of dead flowers, darkness. Naturally whatever was going down, would go down in darkness. It was the way of evil.

From the sleeve of Angel's leather jacket, she pulled out a stake. Well-whittled death, that was the way of the Slayer.

She ran into the black gloom, her gorgeous and, unfortunately, suede boots crunching wet leaves and twigs, and a plastic drink cup—wishing now for Angel's help, because he could see in the dark—and then she stepped on, or rather in, something slippery and gross. Okay, maybe it was okay that he wasn't here to witness that.

"Oh my God! Help!" screamed a girl. She was maybe twenty yards to Buffy's left . . . and she was being pursued by something big—make that a lot of something bigs, judging by the rhythmic thudding of many footfalls.

"Stephanie!" yelled a guy. From the somewhat familiar sound of his voice, Buffy figured him for David Hahn; and that would mean these were the Hahn twins. Sophomores, kind of geeky, definitely not part of the socially acceptable crowd. They both had scraggly teeth, which couldn't really be laid at the door of fault; but no one was forcing them to appear in public with monumentally bad hair, unless they were under a curse or something.

"David!!" Stephanie shouted.

"The Hahns it is," Buffy crowed under her breath as she homed in on their voices.

She did a huge leap across an open grave—*Hmm, the Rising, as in* finally *rising from a grave?*—and landed hard in a pile of leaves.

There they were, two freaked-out figures dashing through a patch of moonlight. They were wearing baggy jeans and badly fitting sweaters with matching diamond patterns. The Hahns were as unfashionable, and therefore conspicuous, as vampires that had stayed underground too long, then tried to pass as regular kids.

The moonlight also revealed that the things after them *were* vampires, with elongated faces, mouths full of fangs, and glowing gold eyes. Not such good outfits on them, either, all dressed in black and thick, heavy boots—the total vamp fashion trend Spike seemed to have started. Maybe it would eventually die along with him.

"Vampires, *so* not a problem," Buffy muttered, gripping

the stake in her fist as she ran toward the terrified twins. Stephanie and David were zigzagging, in an effort to dodge the monsters. Good strategy.

But the tallest of the vampires gained on them. He was scary-bad with tattoos—maybe brands—on his bald head and a motorcycle patch on his jacket that featured a skull wearing a pirate hat. The insignia read DEAD MEN TELL NO TALES, but Buffy knew that was wrong. In Sunnydale, the dead had lots to say.

Sure enough, the vampire caught David's sweater and gave it a good, hard yank. The fabric of the sweater ripped down the back, and the two sides flapped like wings.

"Hey! Stop that!" Buffy yelled, although truth be told, the vamp had done David a favor.

In response, one of the other vampires whirled around and hunched forward in a hulking stance with outstretched arms and slashing nails. Its hair was yellow-white, like Spike's, and it had piercings all over its face. The pose was meant to be menacing, and it would have been if Buffy weren't the Slayer and had therefore seen the same stance a bazillion times before.

"Didn't anyone tell you guys not to play with your food?" she asked the monster. It was a lame quip and she'd used it before, but she doubted the life of a stand-up comedian awaited her.

"The Slayer!" it shouted, maybe hoping to warn the others. Although, frankly, vampires were not usually known for their thoughtfulness.

"*C'est moi*," she said, in a pretty good French accent if she did say so herself. Then she sprang forward so fast that it didn't have time to dart out of her way. It had a second to stare in shock at the thick end of Mr. Pointy's cousin sticking out of the dead-center heart area of its black T-shirt; and then— *whoosh!*—it exploded into a shower of dust.

One down, and she counted five more as she ran through the vampire dust, waving her hands in front of her face to keep it out of her eyes. It looked like none of the others were stupid enough—at least so far—to take up where this guy had left off. The remaining five were all busy dogging David and Stephanie.

Then one of the vamps began to lose ground. It was a female wearing a Sunnydale High School letter jacket, and as it turned to glance over its shoulder at the Slayer, Buffy recognized it. *Her.* Her name was Mariann Palmer, and they both had had Dr. Gregory for science before Miss French the giant praying mantis had decapitated him. Buffy felt a pang that she had not been able to save Mariann from becoming a vampire any more than she had been able to save Dr. Gregory from getting beheaded. But this was not the time for sentimental reunions or regrets. This was the time to deal more vamp destruction.

Buffy used a flat gravestone in her path as a springboard to vault high into the air, and landed piggyback-style on Mariann's back.

Mariann—or, more correctly, the demon now inhabiting

her body—stumbled forward as Buffy shouted, "Ride 'em, cowgirl!"

Mariann whirled in a circle, her arms flailing, trying to grab Buffy's legs and/or throw Buffy off. It was like riding a mechanical bull—or so Buffy imagined.

Although Buffy's thighs were clamped against Mariann's sides and her ankles were locked across the vamp's stomach, Mariann kept trying to grab her arms, which was an indication that this particular evil undead was really stupid. If their positions had been reversed, Buffy would have (a) gone for her feet, which were dangling right in front of her; or (b) tucked into a forward roll, which might have resulted in her rider doing a face-plant as she went over and down.

However, Mariann had yet to learn some strategic moves.

"And time is up!" Buffy exulted. "I win a silver buckle, and *you* win a trip to hell!"

Arcing both arms over the vampire's shoulders, she jabbed the stake toward Mariann's dead, unbeating heart, hard.

The stake hit the mark, and the demon inhabiting Mariann screamed. That's how Buffy had to think of it as the face and body of a girl Buffy had known exploded into dust.

As Buffy landed, the ground beneath her left heel gave way—a little sinkhole, a common problem with Sunnydale cemeteries, on account of all the tunnels and empty graves— and she swayed left and right, straining to maintain her balance.

Vamp number three, a big burly guy in a sleeveless denim vest, with closely shaven black hair and a goatee to match, took advantage of the moment to turn and charge her like a bull, head-butting her just beneath her rib cage.

With an "ooph!" Buffy tumbled backward, landing on her butt, then slamming her lower back against the edge of a low stone border outlining a grave. Her head smacked the gravestone proper. She saw stars and little birdies, but she ignored them as she scrabbled back up. No lying down on the job, especially if she didn't want to die on the job.

Rather than follow through with his attack, the vampire whirled around and caught up with the other three. She wondered why the forces of darkness stopped to take her on under any circumstances. If she were one of these vampires, she would take off as soon as she realized the Slayer had spotted her. Of course, if she were a vampire, she wouldn't be Buffy, who thought like that. She'd be a demon inhabiting a human body, with a whole new set of operating instructions: *Bite, rip, suck, maim, kill.*

The little birdies blurred into a gray haze, and Buffy steadied herself by grabbing on to the monument at the head of the plot—an obelisk topped with a cross—and realized she had let go of her stake. The world took shape again, pretty much; she glanced down and scanned the plot, her eyesight smeary. The dim, watery moonlight didn't help. If only she had some light.

It was *le grand boo-boo*—hey, she was thinking in French!—to have carried only one flashlight. There was so much to keep track of in the exciting world of slayage.

Problem was, while she was still learning on the job, other people sometimes paid the price for her ignorance.

If she didn't get a move on, the other people might be David and Stephanie.

She reached up and broke off an overhanging tree branch, tapping her fingertips along the break to make sure it was good and sharp.

Ouch. It so was.

She broke off another one and slid it inside the sleeve of Angel's jacket.

Buffy resumed her pursuit, down a small hill and into a shallow stream sloshing over smooth, round pebbles. It was artificial, part of the landscaping of the cemetery. Her mom, Joyce, had once said it might be nice to be buried beside the little brook, which gave Buffy a wiggins, because who on earth wanted to think about their mom dying?

Speaking of dying, the twins had stopped screaming, but she was relieved to see that they were still running. That happened; people ran out of breath if they tried to do both. For most people there were usually two reactions to being attacked by vampires: fright—freezing in one's tracks, unable to move; or flight—running faster than you had ever dreamed was possible, usually without any plan for survival beyond putting as much distance as possible between you and the thing that was after you.

For the Slayer there was another option: fight. That was what a Slayer was born to do, lived to do—well, besides shopping and smoochies with Angel—and Buffy knew she was in full kick-ass mode as she burst into a record-breaking sprint after the vampire quartet. She wished Giles could see her. Maybe then he would let up on the training.

"Go to your right! There's a hole in the fence!" she shouted to David and Stephanie. "Go right!"

She had no idea if they could hear her, or if they *would* hear her. Blind panic could turn "Go right!" into "Smarfhsufl!" or make someone completely forget the difference between right and left. It was the adrenaline. It told you to forget everything except being afraid. She knew how that worked. Panic made you do the wacky.

"Go right!" she yelled again. Of course the *vampires* were listening to her, so they started cutting to the right, in anticipation of David and Stephanie's doing the same.

But the twins kept running forward. In fact, they were flying full speed ahead, not seeming to compute that they were about to run straight into the chain-link fence that bounded the perimeter of the graveyard. She grimaced, her mind fast-fowarding to the inevitable collision with the fence, the collapse to the ground, and the vampires either trying to tear out the twins' throats right there or carrying them off like so much delectable takeout.

"Stop going straight!" she ordered them, legs and arms pumping. She wasn't even sure they could put on the brakes in time, even if they could make sense of what she was saying.

Then she heard the weird music again, the weird tootling or organ or whatever—oh, it was a calliope.

A calliope?

And it was closer this time. Or maybe just louder.

She filed that away for a time when she could think about it, and kept running forward. The vampires had figured out that David and Stephanie weren't going to go toward the hole in the fence, and had veered back to the left, hot on their heels.

"Help!" Stephanie screamed.

That told Buffy that Stephanie wasn't completely out of her mind with fear, so she shouted, "Go to the left! Left! Left, left, left!"

But it was too late. Stephanie and David slammed into the fence at the same time, really crashing into it; and Buffy grimaced as she put on a burst of speed in hopes of getting to them before the vamps did.

Then, to Buffy's utter amazement, that section of the fence gave way. Clanging and rattling, it dropped forward just like a drawbridge on a castle. David and Stephanie ran right over it.

And so did the vampires.

Shrieking and clinging to each other—which was slowing them down—the twins disappeared into the dense forest just behind the graveyard. The vampires followed after, and Buffy brought up the rear.

The treetops sucked up the moonlight, and within seconds Buffy was running through pitch-black woods. Tree branches whipped her face and neck as the vampires pushed through them, then let them *fwap* backward. She smelled pine and tree resin.

"Stephanie! David! Where are you?" she shouted into the blackness as she raised her hands to shield her face and kept running.

That was when vampire number three tackled her *again* and the two sailed backward. Buffy kept hold of the vamp as her back slammed hard against a tree trunk. Straightening her arms, she immediately slid downward, hauling the vamp's face against the trunk. It roared in pain as it fell, and Buffy executed a totally righteous snap kick into its groin for good measure.

Then she rolled to the right, extricating herself before the vampire landed on top of her. Twigs snapped beneath its weight. Before it could react, Buffy flipped it over, straddled it, raised her arms above her head, and staked it.

Dustorama!

Three down, three to go.

Then it started to rain again.

"Great," she muttered, getting to her feet as big, ploppy drops tapped her on the head. She *had* to go and buy the suede boots, didn't she. Even after her mother reminded her that they weren't very practical. Joyce didn't know the half of it. But for a few brief weeks, they had been Buffy's pride and joy.

You'd think the Watchers Council would at least give her a clothing allowance, but no. Here she was saving the world and she could actually make more babysitting. No pay, no tips, no rewards, nothing. That was the definition of a sacred duty, she supposed: no gain, all pain.

Oh well, nothing to be done about it now.

The rain muffled sound as she crashed through the dense stands of trees. There were fifty percent fewer vampires to deal with than when she had first given chase, but she figured they had been the slower, stupider ones. The vamps that were left were probably going to be able to run the twins to ground unless she got to them first.

Problem was, she couldn't tell where David and Stephanie had gone. She ran blindly into a thick tree limb and then very nearly got tripped by a root.

She looked upward and squinted into the rain, hoping for a slice of the moon to steer by, but the tree coverage was thick. A burst of helpful lightning, then? Or even the winking lights of a plane bound for Anywhere But Here?

Nada.

She exhaled, trying to come up with a plan B. But all her plan Bs included flashlights.

She listened hard, hoping one of the Hahns would scream. Or not. Not screaming might mean they successfully got away. But few humans managed to outrun vampires. Which was why no one in Sunnydale seemed to know there *were* vampires. City Hall called them gangs on PCP, and everybody bought that, just another example of how hard people around here just didn't want to know.

She couldn't just stand here. She was all about moving

and getting it done. Buffy tried to remember if she had ever seen a map of the forest. It was so hard to pay attention during Giles's stuffy, scone-y lectures. She had been startled to realize that what he called "training sessions"—air quotes there—were occasionally more like study hall, with quizzes on crystals and all kinds of stuff. Instead of whacking at Giles with a quarterstaff, she was forced to *sit in a chair* and memorize useless facts—

—useless facts such as the layouts of the graveyards, the school, and the rest of Sunnydale, including the forest.

Not using air quotes now, are you, Buffy?

She started running. Her boots squished in mud and tufts of grass. Her knitted cap grew sodden and heavy and she whipped it off as she galloped along, wondering if her eye makeup was running. She had gotten smart; she always wore waterproof mascara against just such an occasion as this. A *girl* Watcher would have tips like that for a Slayer. Whoever got to have a female Watcher was lucky.

A bolt of lightning lit up the forest perimeter and she took note of the locations of the trees. Buffy saw a colorful flash of movement just before the shadows swallowed up the light. Purple splotches? Yellowish gray polka dots? She wasn't sure. But neither twin had been wearing busy patterns like that. None of the vamps, either, from what she had seen. But what she had seen *was* a pattern, or something mottled by the play of light and shadow.

That could only mean that someone *else* was in the forest.

She approached cautiously, rain sluicing down her head to drip off the tip of her nose as she kept herself pointed in the direction of the flash. Thunder rumbled and she crossed her fingers for another crash of lightning. She wondered if he or she of the nonconformist outfit had spotted her and was just waiting for her to walk straight into his or her clutches—or his or her tentacles, or his or her huge, gaping maw.

Before I moved to Sunnydale, I thought "maw" was Southernspeak for "mom." And I didn't realize that "exsanguinated" meant "completely drained of blood." Being the Slayer has certainly improved my vocabulary. There's a plus.

She reached a hand forward, grabbing a hunk of pine branch and bending it out of her way.

A few more steps forward, and she realized she was at the same impasse as before. Options, options, who's got the options? Maybe she could climb a tree and—

Then she felt warm breath against the back of her neck, and a low, gravelly voice whispered, "*Boo!*"

Buffy whirled around with her arms outstretched.

There was nothing there, accompanied by a loud flapping of wings, and noisy cawing, like from a crow. Several. Birds were fluttering out of their sentry stations and flying away.

From . . . what?

"Okay, you got me. Very funny. Tag, I'm it," she said, raising a hand. Was it a ghost? Didn't matter, though. The Slayer motto was "Feel the wig and kill it anyway."

"You have my attention," Buffy said. "What do you want?"

As if in response, there was that weird music again. Yes, it was a calliope. The notes sounded off, very . . . very . . . She didn't have a good word for it, like "exsanguinated" or "maw."

Just . . . *weird.*

Cascades of notes, barrels of them, rolled through the trees. The music sounded as if it were coming from the other side of the forest. Maybe whoever was playing it was trying to make some kind of statement. Maybe it was the supersized version of "Boo!" Or David or Stephanie had found the calliope and were sending out a distress call. Or the vamps were having a dinner show bizarro-world style. Someone was playing the hits of Zombie Broadway while the others sucked the Hahn twins dry.

The calliope music rose like a scream. The forest quaked as if every living thing was screaming right along with it.

Lacking any other plan, Buffy kicked it up a notch and ran like a bat out of hell, toward the music.

And voilà! She heard the Hahns screaming again, and they were close. She followed, veering around some large bushes.

Whoa. Where on earth did this come from?

An illuminated white-painted wooden archway stretched about fifteen feet across a clearing. Baseball-size lightbulbs spelled out words: PROFESSOR CALIGARI'S TRAVELING CARNIVAL. Two columns formed an entryway decorated with painted clowns holding balloons.

Brrr. Clowns.

Behind the entrance, wind whipped the canvas flaps of a

trio of two-story, multistriped tents. A darkened Ferris wheel cut a sharp silhouette in the night sky. Where did the twins go?

Inside the carnival, Buffy flew past a silent Tilt-A-Whirl and other rides, surrounded wooden buildings in crazy cartoon colors with garish, hand-painted signs proclaiming DOGS ON A STICK! CONES! COTTON CANDY!

And then she heard Stephanie scream.

Buffy followed the sound, shouting, "I'm right behind you!"

A calliope began to play, slowly, eerily. Up the scale, down the scale, warbling and trembling. The volume made the bones in Buffy's head vibrate.

There was another scream, barely audible above the playing. She followed it toward a large oblong tent. Above the tent flap door, which was popping in the wind, a curlicue sign read FUN HOUSE.

Buffy ran inside and found herself in a narrow, dark tunnel made of wood. Fake cobwebs draped overhead.

As Buffy took a step forward, a green light winked on about two feet above her head, revealing a realistic-looking skull and crossbones. The jawbone dropped open and the skull cried, "Arrr!" Crazy laughter bounced off the walls.

The skull was at the top of a T intersection. She took advantage of the light to consider whether she should go right or left. The light went out. The cackling stopped.

She glanced quickly in both directions, and still had no clue which way to go. On the right: darkness. On the left: darkness too.

She thought she heard another scream, but it was hard to be sure. Still, her Slayer reflexes responded to it the way mothers jump at the cry of a baby, and she resumed her dashing in the dark, hands outstretched. She hated running blind.

"Gah!" she shouted as a light flashed on and a clown hopped from the darkness on long, flappy shoes. Its lifeless eyes widened and its mouth opened in a wicked, spooky grin.

Just a statue, Buffy told herself, and ran on by. A chill ran down her spine. *Stupid clown statue.*

More lights flicked on overhead, dim-colored lightbulbs of blue, green, and red. Buffy spared a thought for the high school boys who would traipse through here and take breaking those bulbs as a personal challenge.

Then she encountered another clown statue, this one with black Rasta braids and an evil, leering grimace that reminded her of Spike. It stood at the end of the next corner, light bearing straight down on it, concealing its eyes while highlighting its mouth.

Just for good measure, she said to it, "Stay."

It stayed where it was, and she jogged on, safe from her childhood fears.

But as for her sixteen-year-old fears, those were alive and kicking.

Another corner—she was in a maze that folded back upon itself, and back again—and then the lights got brighter, although no less colorful, and she put on the brakes when she realized she was running full tilt toward a mirror reflection of herself.

Stop! she told her entire body, but she couldn't slow down fast enough.

Shutting her eyes, she slammed into the mirror with horrendous impact. The breath was knocked out of her and she braced herself for the surface to shatter. But it didn't. She bounced off of it as if it were made of rubber, not glass.

She staggered backward, hitting the wall on the opposite side of the tunnel. It was also a mirror.

In front of her, Mirror Buffy frowned and rubbed her right shoulder.

She realized she had just begun to navigate a mirror maze, which would slow her down, so no joy there.

"Stephanie? David?" she shouted, but the calliope and the crazy laughter drowned her out.

Buffy thought about the kind of life one would have to have to think this fun house was fun.

She tentatively started moving forward and smacked into a mirror. Muttered, "O-kay," and tried turning to the right.

Bingo. She advanced one whole step.

Then she smacked into another mirror. She leaped back through one panel's worth of space and found another empty section to her left. Then to her left again. Then to her right.

In the next reflection, the clown with the black braids appeared behind her.

Oh, God, it is *alive!* she thought, whirring around in a fists-up fighter stance.

It had vanished.

Buffy looked back at her reflection.

The clown was there.

She darted to the left, to look at it in a different mirror.

It disappeared again. Trick?

She didn't have time to find out. She kept one eye on the mirrors as she found a space and moved forward.

And reflected a thousand times in a galaxy far away, Stephanie Hahn's face opened its mouth and shrieked.

Über-bingo!

Buffy darted forward and touched the next mirror. It was solid. The next one, solid.

Her hand reached across the threshold of the next one. Empty space. Yes! Buffy jumped through it.

The next one, solid.

But forty-five degrees to the right, empty space.

Buffy stepped through.

Stepped through.

Solid.

Solid.

Solid.

She moved in a circle, touching a mirrored surface every time.

She groaned. Dead end.

She leaped back through one panel's worth of space and found another empty section to her left. Then to her left again. Then to her right.

The calliope stopped playing.

"Oh my God!" Stephanie cried somewhere offstage. "Help us, someone! Help!"

"I'm here!" Buffy shouted. "Keep making noise!"

"Oh my God! Something's wrong with their faces. Their faces are . . . their faces . . ."

She trailed off. Buffy went superalert, fearing the worst.

"Stephanie?"

"*My* face," Stephanie said slowly.

Uh-oh, sounds like she's going into shock.

The Slayer knew she had to pick up the pace. She flailed her arms as she began to run, crashing into another mirror. She tried to jump straight up, but the mirror reached down from the ceiling.

"Stephanie?"

She heard nothing.

"David?"

Nothing, squared.

Then she whipped around a corner and flew down a straightaway.

Stephanie!

"Okay, you're all right," Buffy told her, coming up behind her and putting her hands on her shoulders.

"Oh my God," Stephanie whispered without turning around.

"I know. It's okay now. Let's go save your brother." Buffy wrapped her hand around Stephanie's and turned to go.

Stephanie stumbled, but she otherwise didn't move. She was staring at herself in the mirror.

"I'm so beautiful," she said. "I am the most beautiful thing I've ever seen."

Wow, she had gone completely catatonic or something. "You are a thing of beauty," Buffy humored her. "Now, come on."

Stephanie turned her head and studied her profile. "I never realized how *perfect* my nose is."

"We have got to go. Now," Buffy said, putting her hands on Stephanie's shoulders and looking hard into her myopic, very ordinary hazel eyes.

"But I'm—I'm so beautiful." Stephanie gazed back at the mirror.

Buffy hoisted Stephanie off her feet and slung her over her shoulder, firefighter style.

"Wait, no, I want to see myself!" Stephanie pleaded, reaching out with both her hands. "Am I still hot? I need to see if I'm still hot!"

"You so do not," Buffy muttered, and picked up the pace. Lucky thing about being the Slayer: Carrying a squirming body didn't slow her down terribly much.

She hustled on, stretching out her right hand as she held on to Stephanie with her left.

And then she found David. One vamp was holding his limp body; the other was diving in for a good chomp. . . .

"Hel-*lo*," one of the vamps said as it turned and spotted Buffy, with Stephanie still over her shoulder.

"Hel-*lo*," Stephanie cooed at it. Oh, God, she was flirting with a vampire.

"Shut up," Buffy said sternly. She set Stephanie down. "Stay here."

"My eyes," Stephanie sighed happily. "Do you see all the gold flecks in them?"

"Glad you're listening," Buffy said. Then she launched herself at the vamp that was holding David, rushing it as she extracted the extra tree branch from the sleeve of Angel's jacket.

The vamp tried shielding himself with David. Buffy reached down and slipped her arm behind David's knees. Then she lifted him up like a curtain, ducked underneath him, and rammed the tree branch through the vampire's heart.

It shrieked as it dusted. Number five came at her, and all she had to do was take another lunge forward and dust that one too.

The other one took off. Buffy let it go as she caught David and set him down. He was only semiconscious, which was a good thing because it would keep the cost of his therapy down once this was all over and he started acting out. There were puncture holes, but the bleeding had already stopped, which was a good sign unless it meant that he was dead. Which he was not.

The dead don't drool.

She tore off a section of his god-awful sweater, breaking the ends, and wrapped it around his neck like a scarf. He was wearing a green-and-brown-plaid button-down shirt beneath the sweater. It was hideous. He looked even nerdier than before, and she honestly had not thought that would be possible.

"David, wake up. We have to go," Buffy said to him, giving him an experimental shake.

"Hey, what?" David murmured, half-opening his eyes. "You're not Stephanie."

"Shh," Buffy urged him. "Can you stand?"

He nodded. She helped him to his feet, but he drooped over her shoulder and she picked him up. Then she turned to Stephanie, who was staring at herself again and said, "Earth to Stephanie Hahn. Your brother is wounded and we need to get out of here."

"Wh-what?" Stephanie blinked as if someone had slapped her. She was coming out of it, whatever "it" was. "Who— Buffy Summers? From school?" She looked around. "Where are we?"

"Somewhere we shouldn't be," Buffy replied. "Come on."

Clearly perplexed, Stephanie took Buffy's offered hand. Her brow wrinkled as she gazed at her brother.

"Where are we? What happened?" Stephanie asked again, stumbling along behind Buffy. Buffy didn't like having her there. It was a vulnerable position. But Buffy had to remain on point, which was even more vulnerable.

No time to worry about it; she hustled along as fast as she could, bumping into mirrors, finding the path. There was a flash of red in the corner of one mirror; of green in another.

"What are you doing here?" a voice demanded. It was low

and deep, and from a darkened doorway about ten feet to the Slayer's right.

Moonlight silhouetted the figure of a man. Tall, thin, and hunched, and wearing a dress? There was some kind of hat on his head.

A harsh fluorescent light flicked on.

His face was thin, and long, and etched with lines like muddy ruts in a road. Long white hair tumbled down over his shoulders. He wasn't wearing a dress, but a black satin bathrobe covered with stars embroidered in black. His red hat was the kind of hat an organ-grinder monkey wore, with a tassel and all that. Not that she had ever actually seen an organ-grinder monkey. But she had read about them during her Curious George period.

His bony hand was on a light switch. Dark, purple veins bulged through the white skin. His fingernails were way too long. This was not a person who was going to stare into a mirror and tell himself he was hot.

"Ah," Buffy said. "Hi."

"Hey," Stephanie added, letting go of Buffy. She sidled toward him. "New in town?"

"Yes, I'm new in town. This is my carnival, and you kids are trespassing," he snapped at her. He crossed his arms over his chest. He had hair on his ears, and the pupils in his eyes were a little too big.

Buffy's jangle vibes were off the charts.

"Sneaking around, destroying my property . . ."

The scrap of sweater had loosened around David's neck, revealing the vampire bite. Moving fast, Buffy covered it with her palm and said, "No destroying—just wacky teen pranks. We came here on a dare and we kind of got lost and now it's time to say good night, and we are *so* sorry."

"This is your carnival?" Stephanie said, drifting closer. "Wow. That's so cool." She actually fluttered her lashes. "I'm Stephanie. Most of my friends call me . . . Stephanie."

You have *no friends,* Buffy wanted to say. Was she actually coming on to this weird guy?

The man swept his gaze up and down Stephanie, grinning with dark brown teeth. "You are very lovely," he said.

"I know," she cooed, smiling at him like smiling at him was doing him a favor.

He seemed charmed, which increased his skank factor. He tore his attention from Stephanie to David and said, "Is he all right?"

"Just too much fun," Buffy said. "He, ah, he goes to bed early because he's a jock. . . ." She winced. There was no way David Hahn could be mistaken for a person who exercised. He was thin and skinny and the destined-to-be-picked-on size.

"I see." He ticked his glance from David to Buffy. "And how are *you* feeling?"

It sounded like a trick question. She kept her eyes wide and innocent as she answered, "Great! Never better. I'm all about staying up late and . . . leaving." She nodded at him. "So, we'll just do that."

At that moment David raised his head and blinked a couple of times. He looked at Buffy, then at Stephanie, and said, "Hey."

Buffy took that as her cue. "And I am feeling so very much all right that I can walk my friends home now. So."

"I was practicing my calliope," the man said, his voice shifting. He was changing the subject. "I would have heard you sneaking around if I hadn't been so devoted to my instrument." He pulled back his lips, which would technically be termed a smile. Lots of dark brown dental problems. "Would you like to stay and listen for a while?"

"Oh, no. No, we're late as it is. We got kind of lost and . . . good fun house," Buffy assured him. She recalled the one vamp getting away. "You might want to lock it up for the night. And maybe go into your . . . where you sleep, because there's other, ah, kids out, you know, mischief-making." *And hang some garlic and crosses on the doors.*

"Your concern is touching," he said. He slid his fingers into the pocket of his robe and fished around. Buffy tensed.

Then he pulled out a handful of colorful cardboard rectangles.

"Here are some tickets. Bring your friends. Tell them they can get in free *legitimately* during our operating hours."

"Oh, you are so nice." Stephanie put her hand on his shoulder. He smiled at her.

Concealing a grimace, Buffy took the passes, glancing down at them and reading aloud, "'Professor Copernicus Caligari's Traveling Carnival.'"

He unpeeled Stephanie's fingers from his shoulder and enfolded them between his hands as he bowed from the waist. "At your service. And you are . . . ?"

"Buffy. Summers," she said. She didn't like telling him. She wished she had told him her name was Cordelia Chase.

"What a lovely name," he said. "It has a certain . . . ring to it." His voice was breathy, fake. She really didn't like him.

"That's nice," Buffy replied. "So now, good-bye." She reached out an arm and grabbed Stephanie's elbow. Then she took a couple of steps forward, making it clear that it was time for him to move away from the door and let them leave.

"Good night, young Buffy. Dear Stephanie. And friend." He indicated David with a nod.

"He's my brother David," Stephanie announced. David bobbed his head. He still wasn't a hundred percent back in the game.

Professor Caligari made a big deal out of moving aside to let them pass. "Shall I walk you off the grounds?"

"Oh!" Stephanie trilled.

"No," Buffy said quickly. "We are going. So, thank you. And seriously, there are some . . . gang members lurking around, and it might be better if you locked up for the night."

He raised his brows and cocked his head. His hair was so

thin that she could see his ears through it. "Such concern. See you soon," he said, waving his fingers at her, one at a time. He was very creepy.

Buffy hustled Stephanie and David out of there as fast as she could without dragging them. Stephanie smiled at Caligari until she was walking backward.

"Come on," Buffy gritted.

They walked back through the silent carnival, which Buffy found no less sinister on the return trip. The lightbulbs over the entrance had been turned off, and Buffy had only dim moonlight to navigate back toward the forest.

"Where do you guys live?" she asked Stephanie.

Stephanie gave an address that was surprisingly only two streets over from Buffy's.

Back onto the main drag, a car whizzed by, and Stephanie waved at it. Buffy figured she was trying to flag down a ride.

A few vehicles later, a truck flashed its brights, slowed, and pulled up beside them. There were three guys in the back in Sunnydale High School letter jackets, and they started hooting and whistling.

"Hi, guys," Stephanie called, waving at them. She wiggled her hips and the guys burst into guffaws. "Can I have a ride?"

"Oh, yeah, baby," one of them shot back. "On the rear bumper!"

"Hey," Buffy said.

But Stephanie didn't seem to understand that she'd been dissed. She just laughed and waved as the truck took off.

"What is your deal?" Buffy said under her breath.

Stephanie's body language did not alter as she said to Buffy, "Try not to be jealous. It's not my fault I was born this way."

"But it is *your* good fortune," David piped up, sliding his arm around Buffy. "I can have any chick I want, and you're the one."

Buffy blinked at him. David had sort of activated—maybe it was the night air—and he had the goofiest smile plastered on his face. He was actually posing, his nose lifted into the air, his lids half-closed, his chest puffed out. It would have been pathetic if it had not been so out of character for him.

He winked at her. "Don't hate us because we're beautiful."

"Okay," Buffy said. "I am walking you both home right now."

She got them home; how, she did not know, because they put on a show for every car that drove past, waving and blowing kisses. Once she had pushed David into the house so he couldn't try to do her another favor and kiss her good night, she realized it was nearly 2 a.m.

If her mom had happened to look in on her in her bedroom only to find her missing, she would be grounded until she was as old and spindly as Professor Caligari. She'd talk to Giles first thing tomorrow morning about the weirdness of Caligari. And of his carnival.

Buffy climbed up the duodera pine tree outside her house

and flattened her hand on the sill. Climbed into the open window.

A handwritten note rested on her bed. His handwriting.

Hey, Buffy,
Stopped by Bronze, then here. Maybe you're out
patrolling.
A.

Dejected, she quickly undressed and got into her pajamas—spaghetti-strap T-shirt and long pink pants with navy blue Japanese writing on them. She climbed under the covers and sank her head back on her pillow, sighing as her sore, tired body began to relax.

Her mind returned to its regularly scheduled dozing: Anywhere But Here. Disneyland. Paris. Bakersfield.

Okay, not Bakersfield . . .

Her eyes grew heavy. She sighed and settled in . . . and she dreamed: of the Eiffel Tower, and Angel smiling; and flower fields spreading across acres and acres of land; and a river, and a valley, and a man with a long, lined face . . . and white hair . . . reflected in a mirror of red-flecked gold and glittering jewels. Caligari, his eyes glowing a deep bloodred.

The calliope played, sinister and strange, the notes rising and falling . . .

And the mirror filled with faces. Men, women, children, stretching in ways that bones could not stretch; eyes pulled wide, narrow, contorted with agony; screaming, writhing, begging . . .

. . . and the calliope wail became their shrieks of terror and despair.

As the Slayer groaned and dreamed on.

CHAPTER TWO

Giles sat by himself at a black lacquer table in the Lucky Pint and drank a black and tan. The Lucky Pint was the closest thing Sunnydale had to a pub, although it more resembled a Chinese opium den than, say, the Plough. The Plough was his favorite pub, all shiny brass and hunter green, located in the Bloomsbury section of London, near the British Museum. Just thinking of it made him homesick. By contrast, the Pint was garish in the extreme, decorated in the scarlet-and-jade-green color scheme Americans seemed to associate with things of the Orient—primarily, Bruce Lee movies and fortune cookies.

He sighed and tapped the table to the rhythm of the song

they were playing. "Piece of My Heart" by Janis Joplin. He used to listen to this very song in London, after he'd gone down from Oxford. That was where he, Ethan Rayne, and the others in their black-magick circle had raised the dread demon Eyghon. They were all dead now, except Ethan; and if Giles had his way, Ethan would be dead one day soon. The sorcerer had tried to kill Buffy, offering her to Eyghon in his place. And Eyghon had possessed Jenny, who still hadn't gotten over the ordeal, and was only now beginning to thaw toward him.

If Ethan's death came tomorrow, it would not be soon enough.

Buffy had not checked in and Giles was a trifle worried. He still hadn't figured out what the Rising was, and he wondered, not for the first time, if both of them were on a fool's errand tonight: his Slayer, out looking for the Rising, and he, here to get information about it. Better to be near a phone, in case Buffy rang him up, than sitting here waiting for an unreliable informant who might or might not show.

He moved his neck in a slow circle. He had a headache, and he was tired. He looked at himself in the mirrored wall beside his table. God, he looked old. Where had that angry young man gone? The one who had worn working-class clothes and an accent to match, and played the guitar like a very demon?

That stuffy and proper man in the mirror had swallowed him up, forced him to be someone else, to grow up.

Ripper, you're not Peter Pan, he reminded himself. *You have a Slayer to guide. You have responsibilities. So get over it, as Buffy would say.*

"Giles," said a voice, although there was no reflection of its owner in the mirror.

"Angel," Giles replied, swiveling his head toward Buffy's vampire boyfriend. He was tall, handsome, and unsmiling. Precisely the sort of bad boy Giles had been in his day. However, when one was over two hundred and forty years old, one hardly qualified as a "boy." And bad men were something else entirely.

"Did you bring Clem with you?" Clem was the name of a demon Angel had located at Willy's Alibi. This Clem had offered to tell Giles about the Rising—for a small price, of course. In this case, it was not too high, although it was rather off-putting: It seemed he was part of a floating demonic poker game that placed bets using kittens.

Angel shook his head. "Said he couldn't make it." He glanced down at the table. "Black and tan. The black is Guinness. That's from my part of the world."

"Have a seat," Giles said, gesturing to the banquette across from him. "We'll order up a round."

Giles gestured the perky, heavily tanned waitress over and ordered two more.

As she left to place their order, Angel leaned forward. "Clem did tell me a few things over the phone."

"About the Rising?"

Angel nodded. "It has something to do with a carnival."

Giles raised his brows. "Indeed? I haven't heard anything at all about a carnival."

"Clem says that's all they're talking about at Willy's Alibi." Although Willy was a human—technically speaking; personally, Giles thought him a bit less than that—his bar was a favorite haunt for demons. More than once, he had provided valuable information that had helped Buffy immeasurably in her slaying duties—not because he was a good man, but because either he got paid for it, or he wanted to avoid the beating Buffy threatened him with.

Also for money or to avoid physical pain, he had just as handily betrayed Buffy or her friends.

"What are they saying?" Giles asked Angel.

Their drinks came. Angel hesitated, took a tentative sip, and looked disappointed. Giles surmised that despite knowing he couldn't taste it, Angel had hoped.

"They're excited about it," Angel replied. "They say it'll tear Sunnydale apart. Bring the Slayer down."

"Oh, well, they say things like that all the time. Bit of false bravado, to deny how much Buffy intimidates them."

Angel wrapped his hands around his beer glass as he leaned forward. "It's real enough to keep Clem from being seen with me. Or you. Not that I'm real popular with demons to start with."

Giles considered. "So, are you saying the Rising refers to the arrival of this carnival?"

"From the sound of it," Angel replied.

"So . . . Buffy needs to stop this carnival from coming here."

Angel nodded.

Giles leaned forward, his Watcher brain going into overdrive. "How?"

Angel shook his head. "That's all I got. He didn't even want to tell me that much. He's scared."

Giles slid out of the booth, gathering his jacket from beside himself on the leatherette.

"Where are you going?" Angel asked.

"To the library. To my books. To look stuff up."

Angel drained his black and tan and set down the empty glass. Then he rose, as steadily as he had sat down.

"Where are you going?" Giles asked him.

"Back to Willy's. See if I can get more information to take to Buffy." He cocked his head. "Did you bring kittens?"

Giles looked mildly shocked. "I didn't realize you were a gambling man."

"I'm not. I was just going to suggest that you give them back, if you can."

They walked out of the Lucky Pint, into cool, but not cold, air. It had rained earlier that evening, but as was usually the case with this accursed land, it had not lasted long.

Angel stopped. He lifted his chin slightly, concentrating; when Giles began to speak, the vampire held up his hand for silence, and Giles complied.

After a few seconds, Angel asked, "Did you hear that?"

Giles cocked his head. "I don't hear anything except the music in the bar." Which was something far more current than "Piece of My Heart" and far less melodious.

"It's a calliope," Angel said.

"I can't hear it," Giles repeated, concentrating. He shook his head.

"I can. It's playing circus music."

"As in a carnival," Giles replied. "So it's already on its way here. Perhaps already setting up."

"I'll skip Willy's and take a look."

"I'll go with you," Giles said.

There was no answer.

He looked to his right, where Angel had been standing. There was no one there.

"I wonder how he does that," Giles muttered.

He decided to take a two-pronged approach to the developments at hand. Angel could look for the carnival. Giles would begin the research.

He walked to his Citroën and drove back to the school library, to do what he did best.

In the backseat his two new pets mewed.

From the backseat of her car with the license plate QUEEN C, Cordelia raised her head and said, "Wait. Stop. You're distracting me."

"*Distracting* you?" Xander asked, peeved.

"Listen." She unleashed her patented you're-existing-when-you-shouldn't scowl. "That is *music*. Meaning that someone else is out here!" She put her hand on the arm-rest, about to wrench open the door and sail out into the night. "This is my place to park! If someone else is tres-passing—"

"There is no one out there," Xander said, urging her back to the make-out zone.

She wouldn't go. She stayed as she was, lifting the tail of Xander's dark blue plaid shirt to wipe the steam off the win-dow. "There is, too. I can hear music."

"We're fine in here," Xander argued. "The windows are all steamed up. No one can see a thing."

She gazed at him as if he were the king of cretins. "Hel-*lo*? How many cars with personalized license plates that read QUEEN C are there in Sunnydale? *One*. And do I lend my car to my friends? *No*. So who would be in here? *Me*."

He reached for her hand. "Okay, but since no one knows we're, um, seeing each other—"

Her glare could have melted him, except she was one superpower short. "We are *not* seeing each other. Okay? There is no seeing each other going on. This, this insanity is not see-ing each other!"

"Okay! I get it! I'm only saying—"

She batted his hand away, hard. "Look, I told you there would be no making out within two hundred yards of any-where anyone could catch us doing . . . this." She shuddered.

"Except somewhere hidden, like a closet. That music means there's someone nearby, and I, for one, have much to lose if anybody sees me with you." She smiled at him without smiling. Back to the melting of his manly self.

"Got it?" she asked.

"Oh, I got it," he said angrily. "I'm just not keeping it. *I'm* not the one who said, 'Oh, what the heck,' and drove up here. I was perfectly happy to wait until we could sneak into your gazebo and go for it there."

"Excuse me?" Now she pulled herself up to a fully upright position and tucked in her shirt. "The gazebo is being painted, remember?"

"Oh, sorry, Veronica Lodge," he bit off. "It's very difficult for me to keep track of all the many home repairs you invent so I won't end up at your house."

She flared. "The only place you're going to end up is in my trunk—"

They stared at each other. There was that crazy moment that happened between them where their blood pressure skyrocketed and their eyes glazed and it was like . . . wow, talk about *lust*. . . .

And then they both shook their heads at the exact same time and said, "No. Too small."

"Besides, we might suffocate," Cordelia offered.

"Great minds think alike," Xander said.

"Our minds have nothing to do with this," Cordelia retorted. "It's just physical, pure and simple. Although when I think about it, when I'm not around you . . ." She looked away and muttered, "I just want to throw up."

"Hey, I feel the same way," Xander said. "It puts me off my snack foods." He reached down and held up a bag of Cheetos. Then he made as if to unroll the window—which he couldn't do, because the windows were electric—and cast the bag out.

"Oh, *please*." Cordelia grabbed the bag from him and tossed it to the floor.

"Ask me again," he urged her.

"What?"

"Say please." He grinned at her.

"I loathe myself," Cordelia said, moaning.

Then she resumed smooching Xander for all she was worth.

Which was, actually—especially if you counted all the money her father had set aside for college—quite a lot.

Angel walked alone.

As he followed the sound of the calliope, he strode down Main Street, past the Sun Cinema and the Espresso Pump. He thought about Buffy, aware that as he passed each storefront he cast no reflection—and equally aware that no one on Main Street noticed.

Even Buffy had stopped noticing.

Ever since the day he had taken her skating, he couldn't stop replaying what had happened. It had shaken his world.

The Master had sent assassins to kill her, and one of the Three had attacked her at the rink. Angel had vamped, and in the ensuing fight he had been injured. She had tenderly touched his cut, and kissed him with such sweetness . . .

Kissed him while he still wore the true face of his demonic nature: fangs, glowing eyes, nothing there for her to love. He'd been overwhelmed with shame. But Buffy didn't care.

He paused.

The feelings raised in him—hope, for himself; and intense fear, for her—had been almost more than he could handle. They still were. It was classic Beauty and the Beast. He had been at his most repulsive—the antithesis of everything she stood for—and she had loved him anyway.

Was it weakness, to have a relationship with Buffy? She was only sixteen years old, a young girl.

But she's the Slayer. She's not just sixteen years old. Her life moves faster; her life is different. Every night she stares death down. Every night she conquers it.

I've conquered death.

She moves in the darkness.

Like I do.

And she loved him.

And I love her. I'm not leaving her alone in the shadows. She tries so hard to have a normal life, but it isn't normal. Her friends think they understand, but they don't.

I do.

So . . . would it be moral to abandon her because of what I am, or what I was?

He didn't know.

He just didn't know. She was still so young and unformed; she moved in a world that revolved around crushes and fashions that changed at lightning speed. Whereas for him, time dragged . . . or had dragged, until Buffy had come into his life.

She was the sunshine that he had not been permitted to walk in for nearly two hundred and fifty years. And to bask in her love, even when he was at his worst . . . it was a gift he had never dreamed he would ever receive.

I have to put this out of my mind, he told himself. *I have other things to do tonight.*

So Angel glided through downtown Sunnydale, brooding, ignoring the occasional smile that flickered over the mouth of a female pedestrian, or two, or three.

A kid on a skateboard barreled past. A woman walked a toy poodle on a pink leather leash studded with rhinestones. The poodle growled at Angel.

He walked on.

Then he heard a scream from the alley to his left.

Putting on a burst of speed, he ran into the alley.

He saw a kid, possibly eighteen, and in the military, as evident by his camouflage uniform and cap. Marine Corps. His black lace-up boots were dangling off the pavement as two vampires in game face toyed with him. One of them had its hands around the soldier's neck, squeezing the life out of him, while the other dove in for a bite—

Angel vamped and rushed them, grabbing the one who was choking the marine, and throwing him against the alley wall. The soldier fell to his knees, coughing and gasping. His cap fell off, and his—*her*—hair tumbled over her shoulders. She was a girl.

The other vamp growled and attacked Angel with a sharp snap kick to the face. Angel staggered backward from the impact, and took advantage of his own momentum to deal the vamp a roundhouse kick. Then he planted his palms on the ground and added a back kick for good measure.

Next he executed a three-sixty backflip and landed on his feet. The soldier, who had recovered, was pummeling the vamp in the face with her fists.

Angel grinned. *Semper fi.*

Then the vamp Angel had thrown across the alley picked himself up and launched at the marine. She saw it coming and thrust the pummeled vampire in front of herself, like a shield. The other vampire couldn't stop in time, and crashed into its partner.

At the same time, Angel body-slammed them both, sending the two flying. While the marine attacked the nearest one again, Angel grabbed a piece of wood off the ground and snapped it in two. Result: two sharp, if jagged, stakes.

He rejoined the fight, to discover that the marine's vampire had gotten the upper hand. The soldier was flat on her back and the vamps were bending over her, fangs glistening as they got ready to tear out her throat. He could smell her fear. Her heart was pounding into overdrive.

Angel grabbed the first vamp around the neck, pulling it to an upright position, and staked it. It dusted.

The second one lunged for him—*what a moron*—and Angel shot his hand through the dust to take it out as well.

Then he turned his face into the shadows and said, "Are you all right?"

"Yessir," the soldier said in a deep Southern accent. She gathered her hair up, feeling around among the curls as if she might be looking for a barrette. "Thank you. What *were* those things?" the young woman asked as she walked across the alley to retrieve her hat.

Angel said nothing. Apparently she hadn't seen his face in vamp mode.

"What's the Rising?" she continued.

"Where did you hear about that?" he asked her.

"Those two. They said this town was going to bleed." She found her cap and popped it back on her head. "Because of the Rising."

"Anything else?"

"No, sir. That was it. What was wrong with their *faces*?"

"Gang," he said. It was what everybody in Sunnydale said to explain away the reality of vampires.

"I thought as much," she drawled. "I've seen the same gang in Virginia. Where I'm from."

Angel hesitated, wondering if she was trying to send him a code. If she *knew* about vampires. He asked, "Are you stationed at the Sunnydale Armory?"

"No, sir. I'm here on R and R." Her answer came so fast, he wondered if she had practiced saying it.

"In Sunnydale?" he asked.

"It's got a beach," she responded casually. "And a nice mall. My cousin lives here. She goes to high school. Melody Nierman. I'm her cousin Claire. Maybe you know her?"

"No."

"I guess it's not *that* small of a town."

"No, it's not." He started walking down the alley, back toward Main Street.

"Thanks again, sir," she said. And then, "Do *you* know what the Rising is?"

"No."

But he sure as hell was going to find out.

Willow Rosenberg was having a hideous nightmare. Others might simply call it a dream, but to Willow it signified much that was very bad. For in it Xander was explaining to her that the reason Ms. Jenny Calendar never taught her any spells was because the pretty computer science teacher at Sunnydale High was afraid of competition.

"See, the only places where she comes out ahead of you are spellcasting and hotness," Xander explained. "And also fashion. But then, she has a lot of money to spend on her appearance because she has a job. Face it, Will, you are job-free."

"I have no job," Willow sadly concurred.

"When it comes to job-having, you're not there."

"Maybe someday I could have Ms. Calendar's job," she said wistfully.

He wagged his finger at her. "Then it wouldn't be her job anymore, would it? Envy's not a pretty color on you, *chica*."

"I'm not envious. I just want . . . her clothes and her job and her . . . hotness," Willow told him.

"All quite understandable," he said, talking through a mouthful of Doritos. He was carrying a bag the size of a Miata, and stuffing his mouth so fast that sometimes she couldn't actually see his hand.

They were walking together through a multistriped tent, just Willow and Xander and his enormous bag of Doritos, like in the old days of elementary school when they had been best buds. Now they weren't such best buds because Xander liked Buffy and not Willow. Not in the bud-liking way, but in the way of sweeties. It put a space between them, only Xander didn't know it.

Now Xander was gorging on Twinkies, cramming them unchewed into his mouth until his cheeks stuck out like a chipmunk's. There were several enormous packages of them cradled in his arms, and it kind of irritated her how he just kept eating. Pigging out. He was such a glutton.

"Buffy also has it over you in the clothing arena," Xander

continued, talking with his mouth full; now he was eating a giant glazed Krispy Kreme doughnut. "Of course, Buffy's mom has more going on than your mom, so that makes sense."

Bits of glaze sprinkled the front of his oversized plaid shirt. Talk about lack of fashion statement. Only on him, it looked so *cute*. . . .

She sighed. Xander was right, of course. She was such a loser. If only she could be more like Ms. Calendar. Or Buffy. . . .

"I'm all about the envy," Willow murmured as she turned over in her sleep.

From the window, calliope music drifted.

CHAPTER THREE

B uffy was the luckiest Slayer ever.

About an hour after she had snuck into her room, she had jerked awake from a deep sleep—nightmare? she couldn't remember now—and gone downstairs in search of a comforting bowl of Cherry Garcia ice cream. There she had discovered that Joyce Summers had fallen asleep on the couch.

Her mother sighed in her sleep, and Buffy got a blanket, covered Joyce up to her shoulders, and kissed her forehead.

In the morning Joyce—who had no clue how late Buffy had come in—was so touched by Buffy's thoughtful gesture that she decided to make an example of it. There was to be a reward involved—a mother-daughter shopping trip to the mall.

Still glowing from the good Buffy behavior, Joyce pulled to the curb in front of the very nice exterior of Sunnydale High and beamed at her little bundle of former juvenile delinquency.

"Have a good day, honey," she said, and Buffy didn't mind the kiss good-bye.

Buffy was halfway up the steps leading to the main entrance of the gulag when Harmony Kendall, one of Cordelia's so-very Cordettes, stepped in her way with a shake of her blond hair and said, "Hi, um, Buffy, right?" As if she didn't spend half of every lunch period gossiping with Cordelia about Buffy, Xander, and Willow. Or maybe that was an exaggeration. Maybe they didn't even warrant that much gossip time.

"Hi, Harmony," Buffy said uncertainly. Cordelia's friends were not famous for being nice to anybody, not even to one another.

Harmony had on a pretty royal blue jacket, black jazz pants piped in navy, and a pair of black boots. She was holding a silver clipboard and a pen with a silver unicorn charm dangling from the eraser end.

"I have to do this thing," Harmony said, sighing, "for extra credit. So I can pass Life Studies." She looked skyward, as if the angels were surely weeping over her fate. "I'm supposed to help the losers on the Student Council with their stupid fund-raising survey."

"I'm all for it," Buffy assured her. "The raising of funds."

Harmony shook her head. "No, I have to ask you what kind of schoolwide fund-raiser we should have. I said blood drive, but apparently we can't charge for that. I don't see why not. After all, this is a free country."

"But we should," Buffy shot back. "We give enough." Seeing Harmony's confused look, she added, "Um, seeing as how they bleed us dry of the fun with too much homework and pointless surveys."

"Exactly!" Harmony pointed her pen at her. "You are so right. See? Blood drive is the best idea." She looked down at her clipboard. "Some people are so lame. Willow wants to have a book fair. Who would spend money on books? I mean, really. They have them for free in the library. And besides, how many books can one person seriously have?"

Buffy pressed her lips together and gave Harmony a very thoughtful look. "Exactly. I mean, why buy books when you can buy shoes?"

"Yes," Harmony said, her voice rising. "That's what I told Willow."

"You have to have a different heel height for every pair of pants," Buffy continued. "That is not the case with books."

Harmony's face was wide with wonder. "Gee, Buffy, you're really not as hopelessly out of it as Cordelia says you are."

"Oh. Thanks." Buffy knew Harmony wouldn't catch the sarcasm in her voice.

"Oh, sure, no problem," she said, with total sincerity. "So, shall I put you down for shoe sale?"

Buffy started reading the list upside down. *Bake sale, car wash, book fair, blood drive, raffle, play, dance* . . . When one got in trouble at school as often as she did, one got very good at reading upside down.

. . . *carnival.*

"Oh." Buffy glanced from the list to Harmony. She kept her voice deliberately casual as she asked, "Who suggested a carnival?"

"Some lame-o named Jonathan." Harmony flashed Buffy a *what-a-dork* expression. Then she grew more thoughtful. "But Cordelia said that might have possibilities, if we made sure there was a carnival queen and her royal court."

Yeah, I bet.

Buffy was about to ask Harmony if she knew Jonathan very well when Stephanie and David Hahn strolled up the stairs.

Oh my God.

She had no idea where they had gotten their outfits—as far as she knew, Sluts R Us was closed at night—but they had gone shopping somewhere. Stephanie was wearing a black denim miniskirt that would surely get her sent home and a black baby tee decorated with a large pair of red rhinestone lips. And David . . .

He hadn't shaved his head, exactly, but call what was left mere stubble. His jeans were tight and he had on a white wifebeater beneath an unbuttoned clinging black silk shirt that outlined his scrawny rib cage. And was that a lip ring poking through his upper lip?

On a TV show they would be walking in slow motion as they sashayed up the stairs—someone should clue David in that hot guys did not move their hips like that when they walked—and preening as heads turned in their direction. But the heads that were turning were not heads of admiration and lust; they were heads that were cracking up at the two of them.

But neither Hahn seemed to notice.

Then they were swallowed up by the crush of morning at school, and Buffy was left to blink in their wake, rendered speechless by what she had seen.

"So, Buffy?" Harmony prodded. She had been focused on her list, and so had missed the grand entrance. "Do you think we should sell just any kind of shoes, or only fashionable ones? Boots included?"

"Um." Buffy turned her attention back to Harmony and tried to care anymore. "Definitely boots." Harmony began to write that down. "No, wait. A shoe sale at school, I don't know."

"It would put us on the map," Harmony assured her.

We're already on the map, Buffy thought. *We have more deaths per graduating class than any other high school in California.*

Then Cordelia's voice rose above the dull roar. *"Excuse me? Who gave you permission to ask me to move?"*

Both Buffy and Harmony turned to see what was happening.

At the top of the stairs Cordelia and Stephanie Hahn were

facing off. Stephanie, who was taller than Cordelia, was at that moment raising her chin and looking down her nose with derision at the one and only girl at Sunnydale High School to hold dual black belts in popular and mean. They were glaring at each other at twenty paces, and other students, sensing a girl fight, were beginning to form a ring around them. Not that Cordelia Chase would ever stoop to physical blows. Why exert yourself when you had a tongue like a complete Ginsu kitchen knife collection plus the blade sharpener *and* the shrimp deveiner?

"Just admit it, Cordelia," Stephanie said, thrusting out her left hip. "You're pissed off because *I* am the school's hottest hottie, and everything about you is so very over."

There was scattered applause around the ring of onlookers, which ended as soon as Cordelia scrutinized the crowd to see who was doing it.

"Oh my God," Harmony said, covering her mouth with her hand. "Has that girl lost her mind?"

"Sounds right," Buffy murmured.

"If you know what's good for you, you'll apologize right now," Cordelia said. "If you don't"—she narrowed her eyes— "you'll be so very, very sorry."

"I *am* sorry," Stephanie said. Cordelia visibly relaxed. "Sorry that anyone has to look at you first thing in the morning."

The crowd gasped. Cordelia's answering look could have set off a car alarm.

"Buffy, who *is* that?" Harmony demanded.

But before Buffy had a chance to answer, Harmony was fighting her way up the stairs through the crowd. Not to come to Cordelia's defense, it appeared. Just to get a better view.

No one gave ground as Buffy tried to follow Harmony up the increasingly populated steps. There was blood in the water, and the sharks wanted a taste.

Rather than add to the chaos, Buffy left the stairway and jogged up the grassy hill beside it—only to take note of something even more distressing than the impending smackdown between Cordelia and Stephanie:

On the other side of the main building, Glenn Wilcox and Mark Morel, two of the defensive linemen for the Sunnydale Razorbacks, were whaling the tar out of David Hahn. Correction: Glenn was holding him by the arms while Mark was whaling the tar out of him. Gut-punching him, in fact.

"Not the face!" David yelled.

"Stop it!" Buffy cried.

"Hit him harder, Mark," Glenn urged him.

Mark obliged with another punch, and David's knees buckled as he gasped, "Don't touch my face."

"*I'll* touch your face," Glenn said, letting go of one of David's arms and wheeling him around. He showed him his fist. "I'll show it to you after I've ripped it off your head. Who the *hell* do you think you are, loser?"

He was just about to smash in David's mouth when Buffy wedged herself between David and him, grabbing Glenn's fist and using it to force him backward.

Mark started pointing and laughing, and Glenn got that furious, astounded look bullies got when Buffy interrupted their reindeer games. She had humiliated a bully not only in front of a fellow bully, but also in front of his target, which meant that Glenn Wilcox was now her enemy for life.

What with her habit of defending the weak from jerks like these two, it was getting to be a pretty big club.

"What, is he your boyfriend, *freak*?" Glenn asked, trying to cut her down to size by humiliating her in return. "The only loser you can get?"

"Just leave him alone," Buffy said. She grabbed David by the forearm. "Come on. Let's get out of here."

"No way," Mark said, taking a quick step in front of her to block her exit. "He's ours. He came on to our girlfriends and he's going to pay."

"You're just jealous," David said, sneering over Buffy's head at Mark. "Because your chicks think I'm hotter than you are."

Could you be any more self-destructive? Buffy thought.

She said to Mark, "Let me get him out of here. You can see that something's wrong with him."

"Yeah. He's alive," Mark said, shaking his head. "That's what's wrong with him. And he's going to be very sorry about that."

"Sorry is good," she said. "How about if he apologizes?" She blinked at David and tugged on his shirt.

"Hey, watch the outfit," he admonished her.

Oh my God. You are so whacked. Buffy turned back to Mark. "See? *Seriously* wrong." *Because no one on earth should be seen in that outfit, much less defend its right to exist.*

As an answer, Mark made a fist and slammed it into his open palm.

"Listen," Buffy said, "I really don't want to hurt you."

He snorted and looked her up and down, the big sneer on his face instantly changing into the huge sneer on his face.

Then he took a swing at David, over her head, so technically, not at her—*give him points for chivalry, not*—and Buffy blocked him by raising her arm to block, then extending her arm in a downward arc, using the force of Mark's punch to throw him off balance. It worked: He fell on his butt.

Mark yelled something at Buffy that was not appropriate for family viewing. Then he lunged forward, grabbing for her.

She drew her leg up to a modified stork position and was just about to connect with his chin—

—when Principal Snyder stomped around the corner, froze, and shouted, "Summers! When they told me there was a fight, I should have known."

Without missing a beat, he walked up to David, glared at him, and added, "Visitors are required to check in at the office, and we are a zero-tolerance campus. No weapons, no drugs, and no motorcycle gangs." Obviously he didn't recognize David. Or maybe he had never noticed him before. In their normal state the Hahns were overlookable to the max.

David tentatively pressed his fingertips over his cheekbones. "Are there any bruises?" he asked anxiously.

"As if," Mark said. "Nice going, hiding behind a girl."

"I had to protect my face," David said. "It's my passport out of here."

"Are you on drugs?" Snyder demanded.

"That guy was hitting on our girlfriends," Mark said.

"Is that true? Were you harassing our coeds?" Snyder asked David. Then, frowning at him, "Are you even a student here?"

"I'm a sophomore," David said. "And I wasn't bothering their girlfriends. I was only asking them out."

"And they started beating him up," Buffy interjected. "Those two, not the girlfriends."

"The only hitting I saw was you," Snyder told her.

"You . . . didn't," she argued.

Snyder grinned. "I think I smell an expulsion in the air. Possibly two—one for brawling and one for sexual harassment. What a wonderful way to end a long, exhausting week of school."

He was practically rubbing his hands. "Do you have parents?" he asked David. "Because they should be called."

Buffy wasn't finished. "*They* were the brawlers. He was the . . . brawlee."

Snyder crossed his arms over his chest. "Well, you're the expert on violence on campus, *and*, may I add, these are two of the finest first-string ballplayers we have. Because of them, we may actually have a shot at the championship this year—if nobody on the football team dies before the end of the season. So you can see that I have every reason in the world to believe you when you accuse them of something that could get them benched." His voice dripped sarcasm.

"What?" Mark said anxiously.

"Relax, brain trust, he's on our side," Glenn told him.

"Yes. I am. And in case *you* have trouble following me, Miss Summers, follow me. To my office. *Now.*"

She held out her hands. "But . . ." Dropped them, because really, what was the point? "Fine."

He cricked his finger at David. "We're walking."

"But I look all right. Right?" David asked Buffy anxiously.

You look like you've lost your mind.

"Sure," she said, "you look great."

"You want me," he said. His voice dripped lounge lizard.

Buffy couldn't help the dull flush that traveled up her neck and fanned across her face. She also couldn't help the fact that as soon as her mother heard about this—and Snyder would make sure she did—there would be no mother-daughter shopping trip to the mall. Joyce would ground her faster than one could say "single moms overcompensate."

As she and David trailed after Snyder, Mark and Glenn burst into fresh, rollicking laughter.

"See you, gorgeous!" Glenn yelled. "You too, Summers!"

"Oh my God, things are seriously weird," Buffy said as she sailed through the double doors of Slayer Central—i.e., the school library—as soon as the after-school detention bell rang and she was set free.

Willow was already seated at the study table, a two-foot-tall stack of big, dusty, leather-bound tomes beside her. She had on a standard-issue Willow ensemble—jumper, tights, and running shoes—and her straight red hair hung loosely over her shoulders.

Xander had been pacing, and he stopped when he saw Buffy; he was wearing cords and an oversized plaid shirt topping a dark blue T-shirt. His dark bangs hung in his eyes; he raked them back a little self-consciously and said, "Hey, Buffy."

"Ah. Good." A beat. "You're late." Giles bustled out of his office with a cup of tea and another big thick book, his personal version of Brit nirvana. In tweed, of course. No vest. After all, it was southern California, where the teachers could wear casual clothes like regular people. Except for Giles, who still dressed like Sherlock Holmes.

"That's always good," Buffy ventured, confused. "Being late."

Giles said, "Did you encounter some difficulty getting here on time?"

"No, she's been right here all along, only we didn't notice it," Xander supplied, giving Giles a quick grin.

Giles sighed and sipped his tea, waiting for Buffy's response.

"I did," Buffy told Giles. "Encounter some difficulty.

There was a fight this morning. Two football players attacked David Hahn. Who is a sophomore."

"Who has a twin sister named Stephanie Hahn," Willow supplied, eyes wide as she earnestly nodded. "Who Cordelia has declared war on. Actually, that should be 'whom,'" she said thoughtfully.

"I saw the beginning of that fight, but I also saw what led to it. Last night."

"Oh?" Giles took a sip of his tea.

"I was patrolling last night," Buffy began. "Looking for the Rising."

Giles raised his teacup. "Which has been found. It's a carnival. Angel came by and told me," Giles said. "At the Lucky Pint."

"He was everywhere last night," Buffy muttered. "How come *I* never saw him?" She moved on. "Okay, evil carnival. And?"

"Angel's informant didn't give us much. Neither of his informants, actually. Seems he saved a soldier in an alley who had also heard about the Rising. He called me about it later."

"So you saw him *and* spoke to him on the phone," Buffy said. Humph.

Giles took another sip of tea. "Which reminds me. Willow, can you see if you can find out anything about possible covert governmental activities here in Sunnydale? Perhaps in the Marine Corps?"

Willow pondered that. "Well, sometimes even asking sends up a red flag, you know? I'll probably hit a jillion firewalls. I should probably use a computer in the lab so it'll be harder to trace the search to me."

"Governmental activities?" Buffy asked. "You mean, like making the enemy go crazy by playing the calliope?"

"The army I was in would so do that," Xander informed her. He had become a soldier last Halloween, when a sorcerer named Ethan Rayne had rented the gang enchanted costumes.

"So now we're worrying about the government," Buffy said.

"Not necessarily," Giles said. "Please, continue, Buffy. What did *you* discover?"

"Well, I was in Blessed Memories, near the du Lac tomb, and the twins came screaming past me," Buffy said. "Half a dozen vampires were chasing them. So I went after them."

"Of course," Giles said approvingly.

"And were the Hahns totally into themselves at that time? Maybe trying to date the vampires?" Xander asked.

Buffy pondered. "Hard to say. They were so busy screaming and running for their lives."

Xander nodded. "I've been on dates like that. Several, in fact."

"I think the vampires were only in it for the usual vampire thing," Buffy said.

"Only in it for the necking. I've been on dates like that, too." Xander's voice had an unusual edge to it.

"Go on, please," Giles said, sounding a little weary.

She told the whole story, including the "boo" part in the

forest and the entire adventure in the fun house, complete with the wicked-scary clown.

"Brrr," Xander said, shuddering.

"I double that," Willow said.

"And this Professor Caligari . . . ," Giles said, then set down his tea as Buffy fished the passes out of her purse and held them out to him.

"He was weird, Giles. Woo-woo weird," Buffy assured him. "And Stephanie was flirting with him." Buffy closed her eyes and shook her head at the grossness of that. "She couldn't stop staring at herself in the mirrors. She kept talking about how beautiful she was."

Xander snorted. At the stereo glares from Buffy and Willow, he said, "Sorry. All women are beautiful."

"Then this morning, she picked that fight," Buffy said, ignoring Xander. "She told Cordelia that she was the new school hottie and Cordelia was over."

Willow's eyes got huge. "You're kidding! I missed all that?" She caught herself and lowered her voice, sounding more serious. "I mean, I missed all that. Oh my God, no wonder Cordelia's declared war on her."

"I dunno," Xander said. "That's a little overly, don't you think?" He held out both hands as if he were weighing things. "Why not just laugh in that snotty, spoiled rich-girl way she has and flounce off, making Stephanie feel like a worm beneath her stiletto heel?"

"It was actually kind of a compliment for her to bother

being mean to Stephanie," Willow countered. "It does take some effort."

"Guys, hello, we *are* talking about Cordelia, right?" Buffy asked pointedly. "Missing a chance like that to slaughter someone in public? I don't think so."

Willow shrugged. "All I'm saying is, it's obvious that Cordelia is light-years more gorgeous. I mean, right, Xander?"

Xander flushed and rocked back in his chair. "Hah, I guess. If you're into superficial prom queens with bad breath who make people feel like punctured worms."

"Back to the Rising," Buffy said.

"Yes." Giles activated, picking up a big, dusty book and kind of waving it at her. "I've been researching carnivals. Specifically, Caligari's Traveling Carnival."

"That would be the one," Buffy said. "What'd you find?" She took a seat beside Willow. Willow smiled faintly and turned her attention back to Giles.

"Nothing."

"Well, then it's certainly worth mentioning," Buffy drawled.

Giles scratched his forehead with his thumb. "But that's not to say there isn't anything. Merely that we haven't found it yet." He waved a hand at the leaning tower of knowledge. "We have quite a few books to peruse."

"And also to look through," Xander added.

"What did Angel find last night?" Buffy asked. *Since he didn't find me?*

"The carnival was locked up tight. There was a gate across

the entrance that you ran through. He hopped the fence and looked around, but found nothing out of the ordinary before it was getting close to dawn and he had to leave. Then he phoned me."

"Did Angel find my missing vampire?"

"He didn't mention it. However, as you know, he can be quite laconic."

"He can?" Buffy asked, having had no idea there were going to be hard words in the conversation.

"Taciturn," Giles explained.

I gotta read more.

"Right," she said brightly.

As Willow took a dusty book off the stack and passed it to Buffy, she said, "My father used to talk about running away to join the circus."

"As have I," Giles muttered.

Buffy raised a brow as she traced the picture of a demon on the front cover of the book. It seemed to her that a lot of people talked about running away to join the circus. It was the universal Anywhere But Here destination.

"I would rather be electrocuted," Xander said. As the others stared at him, he said, "What? Clowns."

"The clowns were wicked scary," Buffy agreed, shivering all over again.

"But they weren't real," Willow ventured. "Were they?"

"I don't know. They seemed to be following me in the fun house. And there was that moment in the forest."

"Computerized robots?" Xander asked. "Like in *The Terminator*?"

"Or like Ted, that robot my mom was dating?" Buffy added.

"Or demonic minions of some sort," Giles said. He set down the book he was holding and pondered the large stack beside Willow. He picked up the first, muttered to himself, and set it down. He went through about half the stack.

"Ah, perhaps this one," he said, hefting a book bound in black. He began flipping through thick pages covered with large, heavily decorated lettering.

"This is a diary from the Rhine Valley in the mid-1500s," Giles announced. "Look here."

He pointed at a page. "Did your Professor Caligari look like this?"

She looked down at a tall, thin man wearing an eye patch and a robe with a hood.

"Two eyes," she said. "The resemblance isn't so much. But it's just a drawing."

"A woodcut, actually," Giles said. "This is reputed to be Hans Von Der Sieben. Hans of the Seven. Seven what, I have no idea. He held some kind of occult gatherings for noblemen. No peasants allowed. No one spoke of what happened there, on pain of death."

"I'm guessing they weren't quilting bees," Xander ventured.

Giles continued. "This diary was written by a Germanic

princeling named Jakob Wilhelm, who claimed to have witnessed one of the gatherings. It was he who made the woodcut. I vaguely recalled it as you began to describe your Professor Caligari."

"Not my professor," Buffy protested. "I flunked out of fun house."

"What does Jakob Wilhelm say?" Willow asked.

"About Hans of the Shriners?" Xander riffed.

Giles said, "I'll translate as I go. 'What transpired at the gathering was a terrible abomination. I pray God I may forget the rending of souls from their bodies. It was unspeakable.'"

Giles stopped reading.

"And . . . ?" Buffy prodded.

Giles shook his head. "He says nothing more."

"He unspeaks," Xander said.

"Nonspeaks," Buffy shot back.

They both smiled at Giles, whose head was bent over the book as he studied the page.

"There are no more entries after this one. I researched Jakob Wilhelm. As far as I can ascertain, he disappeared right after having written it and was never heard from again."

"So unspeakable that he didn't speak of it," Xander said.

"Or was prevented," Giles replied.

"Gulp," Willow murmured.

Giles whapped the book shut, making Buffy jump. Dust powdered the air. "However, so many of these old texts are gross exaggerations. People twisted the truth to obtain an end result. For example, during the Spanish Inquisition, several noble families were accused of heresy so that the church could take their lands."

"Maybe we could get someone to accuse Snyder of heresy so they could seize the school," Xander said.

"We'll have to continue researching. However, I suggest we go to the carnival," Giles said, setting the book down. There was more dust. He brushed it off his jacket lapel without even looking. "As a group. We stick close together, and see what we can find out."

"I'm probably being grounded tonight," Buffy informed him, "for the same reason that I was late."

Giles thought a moment. "Perhaps I can help with that. Give your mother a call and explain that Principal Snyder misrepresented what occurred."

"And you can tell her that he lied about it," Xander added helpfully.

"My mom told me she'd be in a meeting until five," Buffy said. "Something about a bank loan. She said not to call her unless it was an emergency."

"Very well. We'll wait until five," Giles said.

Buffy sat next to Willow, who smiled and scooted her chair over. Across the table Xander drummed his fingers and hunkered forward. "Okay. Gimme some books. I'm in."

Buffy was impressed. Xander was not big on the research, but he always did his share. Even though she had turned down his invitation to go to the Spring Fling together, he had her back. A better friend was never born . . . unless her name was Willow.

At five on the dot, Giles made the call. Buffy's mom was amazed, as always, at how much Sunnydale High looked out for its students. She liked Principal Snyder a lot less since "that gang on PCP" (i.e., Spike and his lackeys) had ruined Parent-Teacher Night, so it was easy for her to believe that the rodent-eyed jerk had totally busted Buffy for something she didn't do. She asked to speak to Buffy on the phone. Joyce told her thoughtful child that their shopping trip was still a go, scheduled for Saturday morning, and Buffy could hang with her friends this evening.

Much joy.

Plus . . .

Giles got a second call.

"Angel's going to meet us at the carnival," he announced as he set the phone in its cradle. "At the Tunnel of Love."

Buffy beamed with happiness. Her guy, carnival. It was almost like she was a normal girl.

CHAPTER FOUR

E lsewhere, in Sunnydale . . .
    In the lavish hotel suite he currently occupied under
the name C. Haos, the tall, dark-haired sorcerer smiled
rather unpleasantly at the even taller, darker warlock he had
just defeated in a game referred to in America as "twenty-
one." Sunnydale was quite the hot spot for gambling. The
humans gambled. The demons gambled. One assumed that
was because gambling was a vice, and vices were little bits of
evil. The Hellmouth's vibrations drew and increased evil of all
sorts. The forces of darkness loved Sunnydale.
    Witness the newest arrival. Who would have expected
it? What a treat, the actual carnival of Professor Copernicus

Caligari, legendary in the history of planetary and dimensional evil.

"Malfaiteur, old . . . man, you know how it goes," the sorcerer said as he gathered up the playing cards. "I won. And to the victor go the spoils. So, until I release you, you're bound to me."

Le Malfaiteur scowled. His black eyes narrowed and he clenched his teeth together hard. "You 'ave cheated," he said in a French accent. "There's no way you could 'ave gotten that last hand."

"The twenty-one with the ace and the queen of hearts?" Mr. Haos asked, snapping his fingers. The very card materialized between his fingers, and he grinned as he flicked it toward Le Malfaiteur. "Because you had hidden the queen underneath your chair?"

Le Malfaiteur's purplish eyelids flickered, but he remained silent.

"So it's true," Haos gloated. "You *did* cheat. You French, you never played fair. It's because you're lazy. Your entire nation is a testament to the perils of laziness. You once ruled vast colonies. Now they've all gone their merry ways, and you've become a nation of dressmakers."

Le Malfaiteur twisted his mouth in an ugly smile. "As you are English, I could point out that the sun 'as set on your empire as well. But it does you no good to insult my native land," he informed his foe. "I 'ave no loyalty to France. My only loyalty is to the black arts."

As Haos applauded, the queen of hearts vanished, to reappear as dozens of copies on the table. Gleefully, he made a show of scratching his chin as he regarded his vanquished opponent. "Nevertheless, you did cheat. Let me see. What shall I do with you? Darling," he said over his shoulder, "do you have any ideas?"

Modeling the floor-length Italian leather coat C. Haos had just given her, Claire Nierman glided forward like a vampire—although she was all-too-deliciously human—and put her arms around his neck. She leaned over him in a tantalizing mist of perfume, brushing her lips across his cheek.

"Whatever you do to him, do it fast," she said. "You're due at the carnival."

Her lover tilted his head so that her lips could slide to his earlobe. "Thank you for that reminder, darling," he said. "You're always so careful of me."

"I wish you wouldn't go there alone," she whispered in his ear. "That place frightens me. It's dangerous."

"It is indeed," he said. "You're quite right. I oughtn't go there alone." He grinned across the table at his defeated opponent. "And I won't."

With a wave of his hands, he began to recite a very powerful spell.

Le Malfaiteur recognized it at once. "*Attends!*" he protested, scooting back his chair and jumping to his feet with feral sleekness. "I am a fellow sorcerer! You cannot debase me so! You cannot do this to me!"

"Oh yes, I can," his enemy informed him. "And I will."

He continued to chant.

The transformation took place.

"All right," the victor said cheerfully. "We're off, then."
He rose from his chair. "I suppose I ought to chain him up."

"Y-yes," Claire whispered in a strangled voice, backing
away from what C. Haos had wrought. "Good idea."

"Now, about this attraction," Giles said as they putted along in
the Gilesmobile at about two inches per hour. Buffy wondered
if he would ever buy a grown-up car. She kind of doubted it.
He loved this bucket of bolts.

But who cared? She was moments away from seeing
Angel.

Or maybe hours, at the rate they were going. . . .

"Buffy," Giles said, looking across at her. "I was discussing the attraction."

"Um, I know he's a vampire," she began, feeling guilty.
Clearly, she had not been paying attention to something he
thought was important. "But y'know, he has a soul, and—"

"Whatever are you talking about?" he asked, blinking
at her.

"'Attraction' being another term for 'ride,'" Willow said
loudly—and nick-of-timey—from the backseat. "A *ride* such
as the Tunnel of Love."

"Oh." Buffy closed her eyes and leaned back against the
seat. "Right."

"Angel said that he noticed people acting strangely after they'd been on the . . . ride. They're highly charged, sexually, that is, to the extent that they're, ah, extremely inappropriate," Giles continued.

"Well, it *is* called the Tunnel of Love," Xander said, sitting next to Willow. "People ride it so they can make out and stuff. Some people get tired of closets . . . of closeness in other places."

"Yes, well, I daresay *we* will all keep a level head at this carnival tonight," Giles said.

"On guard we shall be," Xander said. "Like sentries." He flashed a snappy military salute.

"Hey. Listen," Buffy said. She cracked open her window.

It was the calliope.

The tune was jaunty, but beneath it was a coldness that ran down Buffy's spine.

"Angel heard it as well, when we were at the Lucky Pint," Giles said.

"Calliope music, the new music of the bar set," Xander said. "It's got a certain zest."

It was like putting makeup on a corpse before a funeral. Like someone smiling at you with a knife hidden behind their back . . .

"It's wiggy," Buffy said.

"Ya think?" Xander asked. "What's not to like, Buff?"

"*I* don't like it either," Willow said. "It makes my skin crawl."

"Indeed," Giles said slowly. "Mine as well. But not yours, Xander?"

"Well, it may be creepy to some, but actually, it summons images of tasty treats such as peanuts, popcorn, and Cracker Jack, thus making me hungry."

"Everything makes you hungry," Willow teased him.

"Except food." Xander leaned forward and said to Buffy, "You said they had hot dogs on a stick?"

"We probably shouldn't eat anything there," Giles reminded him.

"Then we should have stopped at the Doublemeat Palace for dinner," he retorted. "I'm starving."

"Xander, it's not even dinnertime," Willow said. "I *told* you to eat more mystery surprise at lunch."

"Yeah, well, I was too busy gawking at all the drama," he said. "Plus, mystery surprise . . ." He trailed off. "Even *I* have standards when it comes to my federally funded school lunch program."

Buffy thought to ask about the drama—part of the fun of detention was being forced to eat lunch with the other prisoners, so she had spent most of her time fending off David Hahn—but she was too lost in the anticipation of what lay ahead in her immediate future:

I am meeting Angel in the Tunnel of Love.

Then they were there. The section of the clearing in front of the carnival had been transformed into a grassy parking lot.

"Hey, that's Carl Palmer, Mariann Palmer's brother,"

Willow said, pointing to a guy sliding a piece of paper beneath the windshield wiper of a nearby Volvo station wagon. "I saw him coming out of the copy store yesterday. He had just gotten another batch of missing-person flyers. You know, for Mariann." She leaned forward. "Didn't you say you staked her last night?"

Buffy sighed, watching Carl as Giles rolled down his window and handed a parking attendant some money. There were dark circles under Carl's eyes. He looked like an old man, not a kid one year younger than Buffy.

"Yeah," she said softly. "God, I wish I could tell him to stop looking for her."

"I know," Giles murmured, pausing a moment to watch Carl too. Then he convinced the car to move forward toward an empty space. "But you do understand why you can't, yes?" His voice was kind, gentle.

"I do." Occupational hazard, keeping uncomfortable secrets like this one.

"I wonder what it would be like, to wonder your entire life what happened to someone you care about," Willow said. "I so don't envy him."

"Agreed. He is to be pitied," Giles murmured, turning off the engine.

Because I didn't save her, Buffy thought. *I failed. So many times, I don't get it done. . . .*

Giles turned to her. "Are you all right?"

She pressed her lips into a little smile and bobbed her

head. "I'm good," she said, but her voice was scratchy. She cleared her throat and reached for the door handle.

They joined the masses of Sunnydale citizens moving toward the entrance.

"So far, typical carnival," Xander said, "not that we usually have carnivals in Sunnydale. Except for our own lame school carnival."

"It's fun," Willow protested. "I always win a cake at the cakewalk."

"And I don't. So where's the fun?" Xander argued, smiling to show he was goofing with her.

"Hurry, hurry, hurry, step right up!" cried a man dressed like Uncle Sam in a blue jacket and yards-long red satin pants covering a pair of stilts. He stood in the center of the entrance gate, and he looked a little bit like Professor Caligari.

"Come see the wonders of Professor Caligari's Traveling Carnival! The Chamber of Horrors! The freak show! The fortune-teller! One price for all the attractions! A bargain at twice the price!"

Two ticket booths were backed up against the sides of the entrance gate. Giles handed the ticket-taker four of the free passes Caligari had given Buffy.

Securing a map of the grounds, Giles studied it as they walked beneath the entrance arch. Unlike Buffy's first visit, the carnival was now wall-to-wall people. The smells of popcorn and hot dogs mingled with body odor, perfume, piney evergreens, and sawdust, which had been strewn everywhere.

"I smell nachos," Xander said dreamily.

"We need to go to the left to reach the Tunnel of Love," Giles said.

"Yikes, nightmare merry-go-round at three o'clock," Xander announced.

They all stopped to stare.

The central core of the merry-go-round was an elaborate automated diorama. Men dressed in drooping hats, puffy shirts, and colored tights rode horses whose backs were covered with fancy blankets. Some of the men wore leather gloves decorated with tassels. Large black birds topped with brown leather hoods perched on the gloves.

Other men, less richly dressed, stood beside the riders, banging drums attached to leather belts and clashing cymbals strapped to their hands.

As the carousel began to rotate, more calliope music could be heard.

"What is that, a happy funeral march?" Willow asked.

"Check out the animals," Xander added. "Maybe this thing is the freak show."

On the rotating platform of the carousel, eager kids and indulgent parents rode brightly painted dragons, unicorns, and what looked like a hippopotamus with a fish tail.

Giles nodded to himself. "These are all figures from medieval folklore. That's a gryphon. Over there, a hippocampus. That would fit with the Hans Von Der Sieben time period. The scene in the middle is a great hunt. The lord of the manor would gather all his friends. Those drummers are called threshers. They would frighten the wildlife out of their hiding places so the hunters could slaughter them."

"Hey, check out that moon," Xander said as he pointed toward the carousel's ceiling. "It's so clean I can see myself in it."

Above the hunting scene a silvery sphere hung from a cord covered with silver stars. The carousel's patrons were reflected in it as they rode past. Though in real life the parents and kids were laughing and smiling, their reflections appeared to be screaming as the images elongated.

Buffy stared at the mirror ball and frowned to herself. Her spider sense was tingling. The images reminded her of something, but she couldn't remember what. Something she had seen in another mirror. Something she had dreamed. . . .

A woman in a down vest and a pair of jeans laughed and waved at someone on the carousel. She wasn't riding the merry-go-round; she was standing in front of it, watching other people having a good time.

Buffy knew how that worked.

The people on the merry-go-round were so lucky. Look at that kid; he was maybe three, had no cares in the world. He had no idea that when the sun went down, the world changed. He was free of the knowledge that she carried: Every night might be her last. It made it hard to get out of bed some days.

Maybe she'd just ride the carousel for a while; round and round she goes, where she'll stop nobody knows. Just around and around, relaxing, taking a load off.

As she took a step, the music changed. She could name that tune: *"A-hunting we will go, a-hunting we will go!"*

"Buffy?" Giles called.

The Slayer blinked and looked around. The others had moved on ahead. About twenty feet away Willow was peering at the map and Xander was tucking in his shirt and smoothing back his hair—decidedly un-Xander-like behavior.

With an impatient expression, Giles gestured for Buffy to catch up.

Buffy gave the carousel one more glance, then hurried to rejoin the others.

"We agreed to stick together," Giles reminded her.

"Like glue," Buffy promised.

"Or a half-melted candy cane stuck to a couch cushion," Xander offered; then, off everyone's looks, "What? I can't come up with analogies?"

"Not gross ones," Buffy said.

"Gross? Candy canes are sweet and nutritious," Xander argued. "Even when fuzzy."

Eww, yet speaking of sweet:

There he was: tall, dark, and Angel, standing beside a wooden heart-shaped sign on a post that said TUNNEL OF LOVE THIS WAY. A painted cupid had nocked an arrow in his bow, pointing it to the left.

Buffy's boyfriend was wearing his long black coat. She felt her stomach go up and down just like the carousel horses as she and the others walked toward him.

"Good evening," Giles said.

Angel nodded at him, and at Willow and Xander. Then he said, "Buffy."

Just hearing her name on his lips made her evening, but she forced herself to stay cool and composed.

"Oh my God, Xander, it's the drama!" Willow cried.

A young couple sauntered toward them from the direction of the ride. They were clinging to each other as if they had just survived the sinking of the *Titanic*, and they were kissing so hard that Buffy was afraid one of them would, like, deflate.

They shuffled past Buffy and Company, still locked in eternal make-out.

"Okay, I'm on board. That is weird," Xander announced. "The ride's possessed."

"I missed the drama," Buffy said, looking from Willow and Xander to the couple and back again. "What's going on?"

Willow pointed at the pair as they smooched on into oblivion. "That's Melody Nierman and Chris Holt," she said, probably for Giles's benefit. "Today at lunch she told her whole table that she found out he's on antidepressants. She made fun of him for it. Called him a 'psycho looney.'"

"How perfectly hideous," Giles said.

Buffy's cheeks burned. She wondered if they knew that

Cordelia had once used that trademark term to refer to *her*.

Willow continued, "He left the cafeteria humiliated."

"Perhaps they had a change of heart," Giles said. "As happens in your age group. Quite often, I might add."

"Yeah, some people are into drama like that," Xander ventured. "The making-up smoochies make it worth it for them. 'Cause sometimes those smoochies are *hot*."

"Passion," Angel said. "It's what drives some people." He cocked his head. "You said her name is Melody Nierman? Her cousin Claire was the marine I told you about."

Giles took that in. "Possible covert government operation," he mused.

"Hi, Buffy! Hi, um, her friends!" It was Harmony, she of the blood-drive fund-raiser. Bursting through the crowd, she skipped over to the gang with all her French-manicured nails curled around the biceps of none other than Marc Greenfield, who had been dating Ellen Hubermann ever since freshman year. "Guess what! We're a thing!"

Marc nuzzled her temple. Harmony reached up on tiptoe and kissed his chin.

"Let's go back through again," Marc stage-whispered.

"Okay!" Harmony giggled at the others and said, "Catch ya later!" She and Marc hung a U-turn and trotted off together like they were in a road-show production of *The Wizard of Oz*.

"What the *hell* was that all about?" said a sharp voice behind Buffy. It was none other than Cordelia. She was exquisitely dressed in a black cashmere sweater, dark pants, boots, and a black-and-white-checked jacket. Her hair was pulled back, and Buffy hated to admit it, but she looked very pretty.

Cordelia's perfectly sculpted brows lowered as she narrowed her eyes. "I can't believe Harmony was actually speaking to you guys in *public*. And what is she thinking, stealing such a B-list guy?"

"Hey, Cordelia," Xander said. "How nice of you to greet us all."

She rolled her eyes and exhaled loudly. "Oh, please. I see you, you see me. What are you people doing here?" She lowered her voice and said conspiratorially, "Did some evil vampires sneak in without paying?"

"Cordelia, please, keep your voice down," Giles admonished her. "As we've discussed, there are certain secrets . . ."

"Yes, sorry." She pressed her hand to her forehead. "I'm just so *shocked* to see those two together." She whipped out her cell phone. "I have to call everyone I know."

"I definitely think we should investigate," Buffy said to Angel. "Don't you?"

"Where are you going? What *are* you investigating?" Cordelia asked Xander. "Yes, hi, Emily! I have dish! Call me back!"

"The Tunnel of Luuuv," Xander replied with a silky tone.

Cordelia's hand was poised over the keypad of her cell phone. "I didn't know that was even a real ride. I thought it was just some made-up thing for those stupid sixties beach movies."

"Actually, not," Giles said. "Made up. Although they are from a gentler era."

"Yeah, the *Psycho Beach Party* years," Xander put in.

"Everyone who rides it comes out smooching," Buffy explained.

"That's just terrible," Cordelia deadpanned. She punched in a number. "Samantha! You will never guess!"

Giles ignored them. "I'm reconsidering our plan," he announced. "If the Tunnel of Love adversely affects the judgment of those who ride it, perhaps we should attempt an alternate course of action."

"Oh, what could it hurt," Xander said. "Especially if you go with someone you know you would never be tempted to kiss."

"There's a thought," Giles mused. Buffy could practically see the gears in his brain whirling as they all resumed walking.

"Maybe you should ride with Giles," Willow said to Xander.

"You want me to be seen riding in the Tunnel of Love with a male librarian," Xander said flatly.

"Or Xander could ride with me," Cordelia said. "Because there's no way I would ever be interested in a *loser* like him."

"There's a plan. Because also no way would I ever be interested in a *vapid gold digger* like her," Xander shot back.

Buffy was very impressed that he knew the word "vapid."

Unfazed and unimpressed, Cordelia snorted. "As if."

"I can ride with you, Buffy," Willow said.

"Wil-low," Buffy muttered through clenched teeth. Willow raised her eyebrows. Buffy cleared her throat and jerked her head the merest inch in the direction of Angel.

"But what if you-know-who gets, like, *too* smoochie?" Willow whispered. "And he goes all, 'Grr'?"

"I'm the Slayer. I'll handle it," Buffy whispered back.

Giles shook his head. "But you two are on record as being attracted to each other. You're hardly good candidates to resist possible enchantment."

"Ah, but we're Slayer and vampire," Buffy replied. "We can fight the unknown better than any of you if it attacks us, say, with fists or a claw hammer." She tried not to look too eager.

"All right, then," said Giles. "I must say this goes against my better judgment, but as in other matters, I—"

"Yay," Buffy said.

Giles gave her a look. "Willow and I will serve as the control group, as it were. We'll sit out the ride. At least we will be safe and unaffected."

"Good idea," Willow murmured. "Sitting it out."

"I'm only doing this for the good of humanity," Cordelia said.

"I'm willing to bet that's what you always say," Xander shot back.

"Well, here we are." Giles put his hands on his hips as they came in sight of the potentially evil Tunnel of Love.

Laughing and teasing, guys and girls Buffy's age waited their turn to climb up onto a platform and then sit in a scuffed white fiberglass rectangle—call them actual boats only if you were feeling generous—with a triangular orange beak and beady, raised eyes extending from the front.

The procession of swan boats drifted in shallow water toward a dark gray fiberglass cave that was maybe fifteen feet high. A section on the right side of the cave had worn away, revealing some tar paper and a two-by-four. Fog billowed from inside the cave, enveloping each boat as it entered.

"Where's the exit?" Willow asked, her gaze traveling from the line of waiting riders to the boats disappearing inside. Empty boats drifted past a tattooed man in a red T-shirt at the control panel, but there were no people getting out of them.

"The ride must end on the opposite side of the tunnel," Angel said. "I'm with Giles. I've got a bad feeling about this. I'm not sure any of us should ride it."

"Look," Buffy said, walking over to Angel. "We're here to see what's going on. How are we going to do that if we don't, you know, *do* things? I vote for riding the ride. Let's just all make a pledge that no one deliriously hooks up tonight. Deal?"

Everyone nodded.

"Come on, dork. Get in line," Cordelia grumped at

Xander, grabbing his sweater sleeve and edging behind Angel and Buffy as they joined the queue.

It was a bit of a wait, but Buffy and Angel finally reached their swan. Buffy climbed in first, sitting on a very uncomfortable wooden seat with an inch-thick layer of vinyl padding, which suddenly became more comfortable once Angel's hip brushed hers.

"Well, this is cozy," Buffy said. She was pretty jazzed.

"Am I crowding you?" Angel asked with a sexy smile.

"What do you think?" she answered coyly, while her heart treated her rib cage like a mosh pit.

She looked over her shoulder at Xander and Cordelia. They were arguing. What about, Buffy had no clue. Buffy was sorry that Willow wasn't going to be in the swan with Xander. Maybe one day Xander would finally wake up and smell the hottie.

"Here we go," Angel said as the boat began to move.

They drifted toward the cavern entrance, fog wafting toward them. It was scented, and it smelled like bathroom deodorizer. Okay, not quite as romantic as she had hoped, but darkness, boyfriend . . . what was not to love?

Angel put his arm around her shoulders and rockets blasted off inside her stomach. She leaned her head on his shoulder and closed her eyes, feeling the joy.

"Let's go this way," Giles said to Willow as he began to move through the crowds. "We'll wait for them at the exit."

She nodded, feeling dejected and rejected. Xander and

Cordelia Chase were in the Tunnel of Love together. It seemed so weird. And also wrong.

But to be honest, she was also a little relieved. If there was something to the theory that the Tunnel magickally made people get together, she didn't want Xander to finally finish that end-of-summer-beginning-of-fall kiss that that stupid vampire had interrupted, just because he was under a spell.

"You coming, Willow?" Giles asked her.

"Yes," she said softly. "Of course."

Inside the Tunnel of Love, Angel could hear Buffy's heartbeat picking up speed as he put his arm around her shoulders. Accompanied by syrupy elevator music, their boat bobbed along the mist-laden waters past cardboard displays of bordering roses and hearts.

A male figure dressed in dusty Renaissance clothing came within sight. He was stretching out his arms to a girl in an equally dusty dark blue gown about five feet above him on a plywood balcony painted to look like stone. The figures might be wax, or plaster, but they weren't very lifelike.

Buffy giggled. "This is pretty dorky," she said. "But it's fun."

The boat drifted past the figures. The next display was on Buffy's side of the boat. It portrayed a beautiful Egyptian princess holding a snake against her chest.

"Cleopatra," Angel filled in. "Her lover, Marc Antony, was killed in battle, so she killed herself."

"Huh," Buffy said, her heartbeat picking up. "That's pretty extreme, you know?"

"Dying for love, yes, that's extreme," Angel replied, nuzzling her cheek. "Also, not very practical."

"Ooh, that's kind of pretty," she said, pointing upward.

Angel followed her line of sight. About ten feet above them, garlands of silk roses hung from the ceiling. Gold-painted cherubs and spangly hearts were twined into the garland, and a large ruby heart hung from the center. By the way it sparkled, he assumed it was made of glass. Light moved and drifted inside it. . . . There was something about it . . .

He felt dizzy for a moment. Something silvery shimmered in his line of vision. He tried to blink or turn his head but he . . .

"She's the Slayer. She wants you," a voice whispered seductively inside his head. *"Can you imagine what that would be like? All that strength, that stamina, possibly matching your own?"*

His arm around her tightened. He felt her warmth. Her heartbeat quickened. The rhythm of her blood roared in his ears.

"You're so beautiful tonight," he said huskily.

Her eyes widened. "Thank you." Her lips were moist, her eyes shiny.

"She wants you," said the voice. *"Listen to her heartbeat."*

Lub-dub, take-her, lub-dub, take-her . . .

He turned to her, cupping her chin with his fingertips. Yes, of course she wanted him.

His lips met hers in a long, soulful kiss. There had been other kisses, of course, but none like this. It was as if all Angel's senses were heightened: touch, smell, sound . . . and taste. He had not been able to taste the pungent bitterness of his black and tan, but he tasted Buffy. And she was sweet.

"Oh, Angel," she breathed, putting her arms around him and drawing him closer. Her strength excited him. "This is nice."

He kissed her again. And again. And again.

"Yes," said the voice inside his head. *"Go for it."*

"Whoa," she said, catching her breath and laughing a little. "Maybe we should slow down, you know?" She smoothed back her hair. "Are you feeling extra . . . um, are you . . . ?"

"I'm just me," he assured her. "Me with you."

Her beautiful blond hair. He caught it up, smelling it, closing his eyes as fresh desire washed over him. He inhaled her scent.

"God, you smell so good," he said.

"Vanilla," she said. "New."

"It's great." He sniffed her neck. Smelled the blood. He caught up her hand in his and kissed her fingertips.

"Wow," she murmured. Her heartbeat was faster. He could hear it so clearly.

"Buffy, I can't get over how beautiful you are."

She was blushy. It was so adorable.

"You're sure you're not, like, enchanted, are you?" she asked.

"You know how I feel about you," he said, smiling.

She put her arms around him. "That's nice," she said.

So innocent. So lovely. So alive.

One swan boat back, Cordelia stared up at the pretty rose garlands accented with the big red glass heart. Its bloodred glow reminded Cordelia of flames. Flames reminded her of passion. Passion reminded her of the names of perfume. Perfume reminded her of shopping. And shopping made her hot.

"Cordy," Xander protested. "Um, hello, we're not in a closet?"

"Shut up," she said, kissing him so that he would.

He kissed her in kind—who would have ever guessed that Xander Harris was a good kisser, truly the best she had ever had? His lips were warm and he didn't smell bad, and he put his hand on the back of her neck and it was better than all the closet groping they had shared.

Then Xander murmured, "You said you didn't want anyone to see us together."

"Well, it's dark," she said reasonably.

"Does this mean we're *seeing* each other?" he panted, breathless after another kiss.

"Whatever," she whispered. Kiss, kiss, kiss-kiss-kiss—

Wait.

"No," she informed him. "It does *not* mean we're seeing each other."

A beat, and then Xander said, "Fine."

They each scooted to the opposite side of their swan boat.

And didn't speak for the rest of the long, boring, long, lame ride of boring lameness.

CHAPTER FIVE

All done.

Carl Palmer hoped no one would complain about the missing-person flyers with which he had blanketed the windshields in the carnival parking lot. After all, he was searching for his sister, not trying to sucker people into joining the Sunnydale Athletic Club.

"You there!" said a low, gravelly voice. "What are you doing?"

Carl whirled around.

About ten feet away, a tall, thin man with a mane of white hair stood with his arms folded across his chest. He was wearing some kind of long robe and a little fez. His face was long, his features sharp. And his dark eyes blazed with anger.

"I . . ." Carl held out his stack of flyers. He had at least a hundred left. "My sister's missing."

The man unfolded his arms and gestured for Carl to approach. His fingers were skeletal, his nails like claws. He was a very creepy old guy.

Swallowing, Carl handed him a flyer. The guy smelled . . . kind of moldy. It was gross.

"Mariann Palmer," the man read aloud. He cocked his head. "Haven't seen her." He looked at Carl. "I see the resemblance."

Carl didn't know what to say to that.

"It must be difficult for you," the man said. "Her disappearance."

Carl nodded. "Very," he replied.

The man folded the flyer and put it in the pocket of his robe. Then he swept his arm to the right, gesturing toward the carnival. "Have you been to my playground yet?" At Carl's look of surprise, he said, "I'm Professor Copernicus Caligari. I own this little traveling entertainment."

"Oh." Carl shook his head. "Not really in the mood, you know? No offense."

"Why don't you go on in," the man said kindly. "Take your mind off your troubles for a while. Have a little fun. Indulge yourself."

"No, I . . ." Carl sighed heavily and ran his hand through

his hair. "We're a little low on money right now. My mom hired a private detective, but she's been staying home from work. My dad lives in Texas, so . . ."

"Oh, this is too much for such young shoulders," Professor Caligari said kindly. "Here."

He fished in the same pocket and brought out a small rectangle. "This is a free pass. Go on in. I insist." He pulled back his lips in a smile, revealing scraggly brown teeth. His eyes in the moonlight seemed to be gleaming. Carl was still freaked.

And yet . . . the calliope music sounded so happy. The rides were lit up against the sky. He smelled popcorn and hot dogs.

"Go on in," Professor Caligari said again.

"Okay," Carl replied, ducking his head. "Thanks."

"The pleasure is all mine," the man said.

The man gestured for Carl to run along. Carl did so, scooting around him. Professor Caligari was nice, but he still smelled weird.

Carl hurried through the entrance arches, waving his thanks over his shoulder, mostly to get away from Caligari. There was so much noise and life. He actually did feel a little better, a little more lighthearted.

He wandered around for a few minutes, until he saw a large blinking disk that spelled out MIDWAY in lightbulbs. He ambled beneath it, to discover that he had entered the fun zone: Rows of wooden stalls beckoned with flashing strobes, colorful graphics, and men and women in red T-shirts just like his, wearing head mics and shouting, *"Come win a prize, four throws for a dollar, everyone a winner, go home happy!"*

The closest stall was maybe twelve feet on a side, painted black and decorated with bloodred dollar signs. Carl's fellow Sunnydalians surrounded it. He saw some of the superpopular kids from school, tossing coins at an enormous tower of glass bowls, dishes, shot glasses, and vases. Everything gleamed and shined. He figured out the game—if you threw a coin inside one of the objects, you got to keep it.

Cool.

Easy.

He immediately focused on little purple-tinted glass baskets with frosted handles.

Mom would like one of those, he thought. His mother hadn't had a moment of pleasure since Mariann had gone missing. Maybe a little present would cheer her up.

He fished a bill out of his wallet. It was a twenty. He had just cashed his paycheck from his part-time job at the library.

I'll just get a dollar's worth.

The girl working the booth ticked her glance his way. He was startled for a moment. Her skin was dead white. Her lips, bloodred. Then he realized she was a Goth. She was wearing a black hooded sweatshirt unzipped to reveal a red Caligari T-shirt, and a canvas apron around her waist, over black pants. He bet her hair was a deep, shiny black, but her hood obscured it.

As she came toward him, a wind ruffled his hair, and for a

moment he smelled something foul in the air, like a backed-up toilet. He grimaced, looking for the source.

Then she approached, and all he smelled was strong, heady perfume.

She smiled, raising her dark, painted-on eyebrows, and said, "Try your luck?"

"Yeah, okay. Can you make me some change?" he asked her, showing her the twenty.

She took his twenty. "Two rolls of quarters okay? It's a quarter a throw."

"I just want a dollar in quarters," he said. "The rest in bills."

She made a little face. Her eyes were very dark. He couldn't see any color in the irises. And there was that *smell* again. It was awful. He looked around, then back at her. *She* smelled great.

"Sorry, I don't have any paper money," she told him. "Bills get instantly dropped in the safe. All I carry are rolls of quarters. I'll give you two rolls and you can just save what you don't use."

They made the exchange. She pushed his twenty into a metal box with a slot in the top.

The glassware glittered and shimmered almost as if it were magical—like fairy gold, pirate treasure. It was so bright it just about blinded him. He became aware of a silver flash just beyond the range of his peripheral vision. The space between his eyelids and his forehead ached for a second. He felt dizzy. Then it passed.

Stress, he guessed. *Ever since Mariann ran away, I've been maxed out on stress.*

He hefted a quarter in his palm, judging the distance, the trajectory. If he didn't get the basket, he'd get the shot glass sitting next to it for sure. The shot glass was kind of cool, black with a red seven on it. He might like that for himself.

He lowered his arm, took a breath, and held it. Then he tossed the quarter into the air. He watched it catch the garish neon lights—purple, pink, green—before it landed between the shot glass and the basket, on a section of black wood.

"Oh, too bad." The girl stuck out her lower lip in sympathy. "Want to buy another roll?"

What?

He looked down at his hands. They were empty. The two rolls of quarters were nowhere to be seen.

"I . . . I played them *all?*" he asked. He didn't remember that. He didn't remember anything past the first quarter.

She gave him a quizzical look. "You feeling okay?"

"Sure." Whatever.

"You almost had it that one time. I never saw anyone get that close and not actually win."

He fished another twenty out and handed it to her. "I'd like two more rolls of quarters."

They made the transaction. He took a quarter and flipped it with his thumb into the air—*heads, you win, tails, you win*—

"Man, that one was even closer," she said, theatrically wincing in a gesture of sympathy. "Want some more?"

He blinked. Felt in his pockets. No quarters. None. No more bills, either.

He fumbled through all his pockets again, doing a visible sweep of the ground, of the top of the black wood barrier. Nothing.

"I—I'm out of money," he told her.

She shrugged. "Better luck next time."

"But . . ." He frowned. "I can't be."

"Well, you are." She raised her brows.

"That's impossible." He rooted around in his pockets one more time. "How much did I give you?"

She paused, mentally totting it up. Then she looked at him and said, "Eighty bucks."

He couldn't believe it. "How long have I been here?"

She shrugged. "Long enough to lose eighty bucks."

He stared at the glass baskets. "I have to have one of those baskets. For my mom. I *have* to."

"I thought you said something about going home and getting some more money," she said, hooking her thumbs into the waistband of her canvas apron. The silver stud in her eyebrow sported a tiny little seven. He hadn't noticed that before.

"I don't have any cash at home," he said.

"You said you would go home and steal whatever you can find out of your mother's purse," she replied.

He felt another strange wave of vertigo. A voice inside his head said, *"More than anything in this world, you want a basket. You will do anything for a basket. A basket will make you rich. You need one. You will die without one."*

"Her purse," the girl repeated.

"Oh, that's right. I did," he replied, nodding eagerly.

"And you said that if she caught you, you'd beat her head in." She reached into her apron and handed him a big black flashlight. "With this."

"Yes." He took it from her. Hefted it. It could pack quite a wallop. "*Now* I remember."

"Good."

"Miss?" someone called to her. It was Principal Snyder, rolling his eyes and crossing his arms over his chest. "When you're finished *flirting* . . ."

"Be right there," she sang out. She turned back to Carl. His stomach growled and she giggled. "Maybe you should get something to eat. Our hot dogs are to die for. Old family recipe."

"I'd like to, but I have to hurry," he said. His stomach rumbled louder.

She laughed. He hadn't noticed before how shiny and white her teeth were—like little pearls.

"You sound like you're awfully hungry."

"I am," he admitted.

Her smile grew. "So are we."

"Well?" Giles asked Xander as the six of them regrouped at the exit of the Tunnel of Love.

"Nothing," Xander said emphatically. "I am lust free."
And no lie there.

Much.

"Me too. Very lust free," Cordelia snapped.

"Wasn't it even fun?" Willow asked.

"Completely lame," Xander told his red-haired buddy.
"You are so lucky you didn't go on it."

"No unusual feelings?" Giles prompted.

"I feel less than nothing for this loser," Cordelia said. "The
thought of kissing Xander? Bleah."

"So the Tunnel of Love did not affect you?" Giles asked
Cordelia.

"It was a bunch of wax statues of famous lovers through
history, like Julio and Cleopatra or whatever," Cordelia said.
She counted off on her fingers. "Hokey statues, bubbles, fog,
and it smelled like those little trees people hang in their cars."

"I think it was supposed to be perfume," Angel said, moving toward Buffy. She smiled up at him.

"Well, Angel's the one with the good nose," Xander said.
"Oh, wait. That would be for telling blood in live things apart
from blood in dead things."

"It definitely had a Motel Six bouquet," Cordelia insisted,
perhaps missing the point that Xander was trying to make:
Buffy's boyfriend was not normal. "Not that I have ever been
to a Motel Six in my entire life."

"Yep, just bad statues," Buffy said. "And as a place to
make out, slightly less comfortable than the couch in my

hou . . . than one would expect teenagers to put up with," she finished. "If a teenager was going to make out in a ride with room deodorizer and the statues that have already been mentioned."

Ooh, quick save. Xander silently congratulated her.

Giles was parsing the data. "So, it's your opinion that those rather . . . love-struck pairs we observed previously were simply enjoying their dates?"

"I guess," Xander said. "*We* sure didn't go all romance novel, did we, Cordelia?"

"Yuck."

Buffy smoothed her hair. She was all blushy and rosy. Kissage had obviously occurred, but from what Xander could tell, the sanctity of family hour appeared to have remained intact.

"Then how on earth can we explain Harmony's terrible lapse?" Cordelia murmured, stricken, as she pulled out her cell phone again. "Where was I?"

"Samantha," Willow said.

"Right!" She pressed a key.

"*I* still haven't ridden it," Willow said, raising her eyebrows.

"We're forgetting the Hahn twins," Buffy pointed out. "They went all lookie-loo once they got inside the mirror maze."

"Maybe only certain rides are cursed," Willow suggested.

"Like 'It's a Small World' at Disneyland," Xander agreed. "Everyone knows that thing is the work of the devil."

"Maybe the Hahns were already enchanted or whatever *before* they got into the fun house," Cordelia pointed out. "Maybe they thought they were hot-looking, like, the day before. It's hard to check your appearance when you're running for your life. Believe me, I've tried. But when they had a spare moment . . ." She held out her hands as if to say, *See where I'm going with this?*

Buffy looked at Giles. "Okay, point taken. We don't know if any of the rides are evil. Maybe there's something else lurking around here and *it's* evil. It could be a monster, or a demon that lives inside the fun house."

"Or the prices they charge for admission," Giles grumped. "And parking on top of it."

"Don't you have a Watcher's expense account?" Cordelia asked Giles.

"Hardly." Giles looked affronted.

"Not even a dry-cleaning allowance?" she pushed. "Because I've been meaning to talk to you about that. If I'm going to be running around with you people—well, there's all this *goo* and dirt and stuff. I had no idea demons had green blood, and that it stained!"

"Well, we got in for free, so that's not too bad," Buffy said. She came to a decision. "I think we should split up. We can cover more ground that way."

Xander held up a finger. "Maybe not so much, Buffy. That's the Camp Crystal Lake approach, and that usually results in a machete to the forehead."

"True," Buffy said thoughtfully.

Giles adjusted his glasses. "I beg your pardon?"

"Camp Crystal Lake? Jason? Hockey mask?" Xander prompted. Giles continued to stare at him as if he were speaking Swahili. "Giles, how can you be so up on all things wiggy and not know about this stuff?"

Willow stepped up to the plate. "You see, in slasher movies, when people go off in different directions to search for the killer, that's when they get the ax. Literally." She tapped the crown of her head. She smiled pleasantly at Cordelia. "Brain comes out with Spray 'n Wash."

"Oh my God," Cordelia said, looking ill.

"However, playing devil's advocate here," Xander cut in. "If we observe the *Scooby-Doo* mystery-solving method, we note that all the creepiest things happen to the group when they're together."

"And you do call yourselves the Scoobies," Cordelia put in, cocking her head. "And Xander is kind of like a big, weird, goofy dog."

"All's I'm saying is, either approach has its time-honored pluses and minuses," Xander said. "Splitting up, or hanging together."

"Yeah, because we could die either way," Willow finished helpfully.

"Exactly my point," Xander concluded. They smiled and nodded at each other.

"I still say we should split up," Buffy said. "We can each

do one thing and then meet back in, like, half an hour with a report."

"Oh my God," Cordelia blurted, staring at her. "You had a good idea."

"Still," Giles said. "It may be dangerous."

"Good ideas often are," Xander riffed. "They can lead to political upheaval and . . ."—his gaze wandered to an extremely, uh, woman wiggling her hips past him—". . . the invention of Spandex."

He caught himself. "Buffy's right. We should explore in ones and twos. Hey, we're not the Slayerettes for the T-shirts."

"There are T-shirts?" Willow asked, sounding sad.

"The T-shirts are a metaphor," Cordelia informed her. She narrowed her eyes. "Right?"

"Right. You haven't missed out, Cordelia. There is nothing to get that you don't have," Xander replied.

"*That's* for sure," she said.

"We'll split up, then," Giles said.

"With you there," Xander bit off.

"Me too," Cordelia shot back. "Splitting up forever."

"What are you going to investigate?" Giles asked Buffy.

"Maybe we should go back through the Tunnel of Love," Angel said.

Buffy looked interested. Then she gave her head a little shake. "I'm thinking the Ferris wheel," she said. "We'll be able to see a lot from up there."

"Good thinking." Giles looked at Willow. "What about you?"

"I think I'll go to the fortune-teller's tent," she said.

"I'll go to the freak show," Cordelia volunteered. "Since I've had a lot of experience hanging around freaks."

"Very well." Giles looked to Xander.

"Carousel," he decided. "I'll whirl around in lazy circles and take in my surroundings."

"Gee, that's just like your life," Cordelia sniped.

"Then I'll investigate the Chamber of Horrors," Giles said, "since I've already had so much experience with that."

"A Watcher's existence," Willow murmured sympathetically.

"I was thinking of having to live here, in southern California," Giles informed her.

"Good." Buffy beamed at Angel. "We have a plan. Let's go."

"Gone," Angel said. He laced his fingers through Buffy's.

"Remember, we'll regroup in thirty minutes," Giles said.

"We will," Buffy promised.

"Half an hour," Giles said.

"Aye, aye, captain," Xander replied.

They turned their backs and scooted off.

The carousel.

Xander found a cozy little bench on the carousel behind a trio of angry-looking black stallions with red flames painted on their faces and hooves. His bench was decorated to look like a chariot, and not only could you sit down in it, but you could plop down lengthwise, rest your head, and prop your feet up like you were in a hammock.

Round and round and round I go, when I'll get up, no one knows, Xander thought, settling in.

Feeling very relaxed, he watched the first load of riders trot to their creatures of choice and climb on. Funky dolphin things, unicorns, weird metamorph-style combo creatures.

I might be more impressed if I hadn't already seen a lot of this in real life.

The music started, and the drums banged and the cymbals clanged as everyone went up and down, up and down, like on slow-motion pogo sticks.

He wished he could tell Carl Palmer about his sister. Or at least stake the vamp that had chomped her and changed her into one of the living undead. That was pretty much Buffy's job, but he wished he could do more than he did.

He kept a sharp lookout—with one eye open—all the while inhaling the multilayered, tantalizing scents of nacho cheese, chocolate, and hot dogs. All was laced with the sweet odor of hydrolyzed vegetable oil.

Churros, he thought, with the love he had always thought he would reserve for a woman. *Ooh, I'll bet they have kettle corn, too. Giles said we shouldn't eat anything, but hey, other people are doing the munch thing, and they're not keeling over and dying.*

The little boy on the black stallion in front of Xander's chariot was licking an ice-cream cone, and he was just fine.

Xander shifted his weight, watching the silvery moon-ball glow as the cymbals clanged and the drums crashed and thundered.

Around and around and around. Xander watched and listened, and yawned.

Nothing's happening. This is boring. Also nice. I move around too much, as a rule. Except for all the TV watching. And dozing off in class. But there's the walking, and the skateboarding, and the dancing . . . no wonder I'm so tired.

He opened his eyes, realizing that he had dozed off. The carousel had stopped, and the little ice-cream-cone boy was gone.

He looked up at the bright mirror-moon. The silver glanced and darted across his field of vision, and for a moment, he felt a little dizzy. Probably from hunger.

"You deserve something tasty and sweet. Something delicious to fill your stomach. It's so empty. You're aching with hunger, aren't you?"

Xander's stomach growled.

A little redheaded girl about *Teletubbies* age and her equally redheaded mother were visible. Mom and Mini-Mom were each snacking on an enormous chocolate chip cookie, the tantalizing disks so large that the little girl's resembled a Frisbee in her grasp. The cookies were loaded with chocolate chips and . . . merciful Zeus, were those M&M's as well? Chocolate chips *and* M&M's? Did it get any better than that?

Xander's mouth watered.

The mom handed her cookie to her daughter as she picked her up to set her on the fierce-looking ebony steed. Xander scrutinized the two cookies now in the little girl's possession.

It *did* get better. There were chunks of white chocolate too. Three kinds of chocolate in one delectable cookie.

His stomach growled.

As the little girl settled on her horsie's wooden back, both cookies slipped from her grasp and tumbled to the wooden floor. They broke into large, crumbly chunks. The M&M's poked out from the crumbs like jewels in buried treasure.

Xander thought briefly about reaching out and scooping up a handful.

"All gone, Mommy," the little girl said mournfully.

"That's okay, Boo-boo," the woman soothed. "We'll get some more."

"Yeah, for five bucks each," Xander said under his breath.

The woman heard him. She looked at him and said, "Oh, no, they're free tonight."

Xander blinked. "What?"

She pointed. "They're right over there."

Xander followed her line of vision.

And shuddered.

Sure enough, there were heaps and heaps of cookies on two red trays. The trays were labeled FREE!

Each tray held by two hands.

Each pair of hands belonging to a clown—a fully made-up, dressed-up, wicked-scary clown, grinning and bowing as people grabbed themselves a little bit of heaven.

Xander wasn't at all sure that he could make himself walk up close enough to one of those guys to snag a cookie no matter how hungry he was. Those big weird grins, those blank eyes of doom . . . nope.

He stayed safely prone.

"They're giving away little bags of toffee, too," the woman added. "And kettle corn."

Xander sat up. "*And* kettle corn?"

CHAPTER SIX

The crush inside the Chamber of Horrors was so oppressive that Giles wondered why the tacky wax figures didn't melt. He was hot, and hemmed in on all sides by noisy boys with terrible body odor. There were so many of them that Giles couldn't have left if he wanted to.

And he very much did want to.

The Chamber of Horrors was a series of tableaux, each a ghastly display of the sort of things one expected to find in a Chamber of Horrors—a poor fellow being stretched on the rack by hooded priests of the Spanish Inquisition; a statue of Jack the Ripper and one of his prostitute victims. Everything very crudely done—badly proportioned bodies, amateurishly arranged displays of skulls and bats. Compared to Madame Tussauds, the legendary wax museum back in London, it was farcical. Had he paid a separate entrance fee, he would have demanded it back.

As it is, all I've lost is—he checked his watch—*fifteen minutes of my life.*

He sighed as he was pushed by the crowd along to the next dreary scene. Ah, the French Revolution, of course. A scaffold, and upon it, a guillotine. An unmoving body was posed kneeling in position, with its head thrust through the restraining wooden-stocks portion of the execution device.

From a speaker a voice crackled, "No! I'm innocent!" It was a terrible French accent.

"Guilty!" another voice shouted.

The blade slid down two guy wires and lopped off the head. A wax stump of a neck was revealed. It was painted red. The head tumbled into a basket.

"Dude, this is so lame," said the pale, foul-smelling boy closest to Giles.

His friend, a shorter, tanner, but no-less-foul-smelling boy, yawned and said, "We are totally wasting our time."

Giles had to agree.

All twenty or so of the onlookers moved on. Giles exhaled and snaked his left hand up his side, to dab his forehead with the paper napkin he'd found in his pocket.

Ahead, something glittered, catching his eye. Giles

wearily craned his neck over the heads of the two boys, wondering what less-than-stellar monument lay in store.

"Vampires, cool," the pale boy announced.

It was a scene from *Dracula*. Van Helsing, the vampire hunter, was holding a mirror pointed at a fanged man who was shielding himself from a wooden cross, held by a man in a cowboy hat. Ah, in the original novel that would be Quincy Morris, the Texan.

From the chest of the Quincy Morris statue, a man's voice twanged, "Stake him, professor!"

The vampire hissed. His reflection could not be seen in the mirror. It was probably not a mirror at all, but something sprayed with nonreflective silver paint.

"Lame," another boy opined.

Or the angle of the mirror was deliberately off. The trick worked either way. The trick, because . . . Giles felt a wave of vertigo. Something flashed silver.

It's so hot in here, he thought. *I think I'm going to faint.*

It was so hot that summer, that summer of black magicks and free love and chicks who wanted to be with powerful young sorcerers. Rupert Giles and Ethan Rayne cut such a swath! The black arts belonged to them.

"We're going to rule the night," Ethan told him.

It was midsummer, a powerful time in the lunar year. They were drunk on Guinness and potions and magicks. "We have done the impossible, Ripper-Rupert. That makes us mighty."

"We are the champions," Giles sang. But deep beneath his euphoria, he seethed. Double, double, toil and trouble, his anger was rising to the top.

This is not my life, he thought through the haze. *This is not for me.*

I am a Watcher.

His grandmother, also a Watcher, had written him a terrible letter, a death sentence, and he had received it in the post that morning:

Rupert,

I know this is so hard for you, but you must accept your destiny. The Watchers Council have asked me repeatedly what they are to do about you. I tell them to be patient. You're young. But I fear you, my boy. I sense that you're playing with fire. There may be a girl who will need you, and you cannot fail her. I'm old, Rupert, and I . . . I suppose that I must tell you, dear, that I don't anticipate being here much longer. Before I depart this world, I need to know that you have joined the good fight. Come home.

Your devoted
Gran

God, how he hated her in that moment. Hated her and all she stood for: that damnable Watchers Council, relic of a bygone age, when the only person who could go up against the forces of evil was some young chit. He and

Ethan had proven that wrong a hundred times. Called up viler evil than those old Watchers could imagine, then shot it back down. Raised demons, and destroyed them. The world didn't need a Slayer. It needed more men like Ethan, and him.

I won't do it. I won't go back, he thought. Fury rose inside him like a Roman candle.

Shocked out of his reverie by a blast of cold water, Giles opened his eyes. He was seated on the floor of the Chamber of Horrors with his back against the wall. Two of the several boys were bent over him, and the freckle-faced one was pouring a sports bottle on his head.

"Stop that!" Giles cried.

"You okay, dude?" the boy asked Giles as he obeyed him. He cradled the water bottle against his chest. "Are you, like, having a heart attack or something?"

"Dude, he didn't have a heart attack," the older boy snapped. He looked anxiously at Giles. "Did you?"

Giles touched his forehead. "It must have been the heat. No, that's all right. I'm fine."

"Do you want us to get help?" the older boy said.

"No, thank you. That's not necessary." Calling attention to himself was the last thing he needed. Carefully, he got to his feet. His surroundings swirled.

"You look bad," the freckle-faced boy informed him. "Maybe you should just wait a minute."

Giles felt a sudden rush of anger. He said through his teeth, *"Damn your eyes, I am leaving."*

Goggle-eyed, both boys took a step away from him. "Whoa. No problem," the older boy assured him.

Giles was shocked. *What the devil is wrong with me?* He wanted to apologize to them both, but he didn't trust himself to speak. Because he was very afraid he might give voice to the words that were flashing through his mind:

Dare to question me, will you? I ought to bash your heads in.

Silently, he inclined his head.

And hurried out of the Chamber of Horrors as fast as he could possibly go.

He stood in the rush and glitter, listening to the chatter and the noise and the calliope. Looked up, and saw the Uncle Sam person on stilts.

Looked around . . . at the smiling faces.

And the clown, staring right at him from a little platform across the breezeway. It was holding a seltzer bottle, which it pantomimed spraying at him.

Yes, someone ought to cool me off a trifle more, he thought. *I am out of sorts. I am . . .*

The calliope played. The clown dipped a low bow and began to dance in a circle. Then it pulled three glass balls from its sleeves and began to juggle them with remarkable skill.

Giles watched, his practiced eye following the path of the third ball as the fellow went through the motions. The glass

caught the colored lights of the fair—red, blue, pink, green—
or perhaps the balls themselves were tinted. They seemed to
retain their hues against the white of the clown's gloves.

The clown looked at Giles with its silly, happy face. Giles
found himself smiling back.

Then he glanced down at his watch and thought, *Oh,
damn! I'm late!*

He was furious with himself.

The kissing was great. It was wonderful.

But they hadn't ridden the Ferris wheel yet, and . . .

"Angel, we're late!" Buffy said, glancing at the large illuminated clock face on a pedestal behind him. "We have to go!"

"But you're so beautiful tonight," he said, covering her
face with kisses. It was beyond nice. It was the best.

But they were *so late*.

"Okay." Angel kissed her again.

They stumbled out of their secret hideaway, Buffy walking backward as Angel bent down and kissed her, kissed her,
kissed her. She smacked into something—one of those cutout
figures you can stick your face in and then take a picture with.

This one was a clown. The back of her head filled the hole
for the face.

"Buffy," he murmured, "why can't we just get out of here?"

Someone shouted. "Get a room!"

"We have to stop," she said. She put her hands against his
chest and pushed him gently away.

"God, I love it when you do that," he moaned.

I think we've taken it to the next level, Buffy thought. It was not an unwelcome move. However.

"Smoochies later," she promised. "Work now."

"You drive a hard bargain," Angel breathed.

The sign read WELCOME TO MADAME LAZABRA'S.

Willow stepped through a black curtain and into the darkly lit tent. Glow-in-the-dark objects were suspended in the air—a green drill-team baton, a yellow skull, and a purplish letter with the words FROM BEYOND in red where the address should be.

Exotic scents of the Arabian Nights wafted on the night air. Bells tinkled. A gong sounded, vibrating through Willow's feet.

Across the room the black curtain divided in two as a tall, dark-haired guy about Willow's age emerged from between two black hangings. As he did so, the suspended objects raised up about two feet in the air. She saw now that they were attached to a rod and pulley.

The guy had on a white shirt and an embroidered black vest, and tight black leather pants and black boots that came up to his knees. A red-and-black sash was tied around his waist.

On his cheek . . . was that a birthmark?

He silently stared at Willow.

"Vaclav!" a woman's voice shouted.

"Welcome to the tent of the Gypsy fortune-teller," the guy said in a loud, showy voice. He sounded like the Count on *Sesame Street*. "Madame Lazabra knows all, sees all."

He gestured for Willow to come with him beyond the curtain.

She followed.

Inside were two overstuffed black chairs and a circular brass table. A petite, olive-skinned woman sat in the chair opposite Willow; she was very beautiful, maybe twenty-five, and she wore a dark scarf with scarlet markings that looked like claw marks. Her two enormous hoop earrings caught the light from a black candle burning on top of what Willow hoped was a prop human skull.

Willow noted the rings on the woman's fingers, including her thumbs; some had two or three. Most of them were silver; one had a little skull on the front. Another was a large seven studded in rubies.

The backs of her hands were tattooed with swirly henna designs, and her hands were cupped around something as if she were warming them.

As Willow glanced down, the woman slid her hands away, revealing a crystal ball.

It gleamed, throwing off white light.

It was . . . beautiful.

"Madame Lazabra knows the wishes of your heart," the woman said in the same horror movie whahaha accent. "You have occult gifts. Your red hair promises that. But 'occult' means 'hidden.' Others overlook you. They don't see you as you are."

That'd be nice if that were true, Willow thought. *But I have a feeling I'm just plain old regular me.*

"Sit down. I will show you."

A black cat perched on the back of the chair, looking curiously at Willow with its golden almond eyes.

"Look," the woman invited, gesturing to her crystal ball.

Willow looked.

And she saw:

She saw . . .

Oh, God, inside the crystal ball . . .

Her lids drooped. She heard a buzzing in her ears, and something silvery sort of grew inside her mind, expanding outward, firing neurons and setting up new pathways.

It felt like she was getting *different.*

And different was good.

The interior of the crystal ball blazed with a fiery scarlet. The scarlet became pink, and then silver. It was a mirror. And the face of an elderly man smiled straight at her. His hair was long and white, and his nose and chin were very sharp. He said to her, *"No wonder you're so envious."*

His smile was gentle. *"You are being completely overlooked, aren't you? It's hard to be so young, and so aware of your limitations."*

Yes, she thought, although she couldn't speak. *Oh yes, I'm so glad someone understands. . . .*

Then the ball swirled again; the red fire returned and Willow saw faces, stretched and pulled out of shape.

"Oh!" Sounding surprised, the woman draped a black velvet cloth over the crystal ball as if to hide it from Willow. "That's enough."

Willow's lids drooped again. She saw silver again; the neurons fired like cannons.

Drifting, moving, shifting . . .

She woke herself up with a snore.

"Oh, wow," she murmured, licking her lips. "Did I just fall asleep?"

She opened her eyes to see a tarot reading spread before her. Madame Lazabra sat across from her, holding a glass of water.

"Are you all right?" she asked.

Willow frowned. "Am I . . . ?"

"I went to get you some water and you dozed off." She wrinkled her nose. "It's stuffy in here, isn't it?"

"It's . . ." Willow nodded. "*Very* stuffy."

"I need to tell the management." She shook her head. "The last place we were, it was even warmer than this." She chuckled. "So, what do you think?" She gestured to the cards. "Look at them, each in turn. Each in turn."

The woman's voice was soothing. Calming.

"I . . ." Willow scanned the layout. She didn't remember . . . wait, now it was coming. Now she remembered sitting down, and having a reading.

She had asked about Xander, and the tarot had delivered bad news. She remembered it all now. He was in love with another.

That would be Buffy, obviously.

"I can help you with this problem," Madame Lazabra said.

"Thank you," Willow murmured. Then she inhaled sharply and said, "What time is it?"

"Vaclav!" Madame Lazabra cried, clapping her hands.

The young man who had led Willow in reappeared, holding an ebony clock.

Yikes! She was nearly half an hour late for the rendezvous.

"I'm so sorry. Thank you so much. Is there a charge?" Willow asked anxiously.

Madame Lazabra waved her hand.

"Payment will be made," she assured Willow. Then her mouth practically split open, her smile was so wide. "Soon."

Giles was pissed off.

"The thing of it is, you're all late," he admonished Buffy and her friends. And Cordy, who, of course, was not friends with any of them.

"You were late too," Cordy said. She was *so* not taking his crap. "I saw you walking up at the same time as me."

Giles opened and closed his mouth like a fish. His eyes practically spun. God, what was his deal?

"Okay, look," Xander said. He burped, and a shot of bad breath misted in Cordy's air space. "Sorry."

"Oh my God, you are disgusting," Cordy said. She waved a hand in front of her face to make it go away. "What have you been eating?"

"Eating? Did you eat anything? I specifically told you not to." Giles wiped his forehead. He was all sweaty. He reminded Cordy of some mangy creature about to chew off its own foot.

"I didn't eat anything," Xander assured him. "The only food I could get near was being served by clowns."

"And?" Giles prompted.

"Clowns?" Xander said again.

While Giles was busy scowling at Xander, Angel bent down and kissed Buffy on the earlobe. Flushing, Buffy gently batted him away.

Just then, Willow trudged up, and Giles's wrath was directed at the mousy little Slayerette. Tonight she was screaming street urchin even more than usual, because instead of her usual humble, self-effacing attitude, she looked completely and totally defeated.

"You are very, very late," Giles flung at her. "Where have you been?"

"I'm sorry," Willow said. "I lost track of time." Willow was her usual kick-me self. "I wouldn't have been so late if . . . if I had had a beautiful, expensive watch like Cordelia's," she said.

Surprised, Cordy glanced down at the one-of-a-kind watch her father had purchased for her in Gstaad. She didn't even realize Willow paid the slightest bit of attention to accessorizing.

Because it sure didn't show in the way she dressed.

"This thing? Please," Cordy said, adding silently, *Touch it and die.*

"Well, we're all here now," Xander said. "No machetes in our foreheads either."

"All right, then let's debrief. Everyone, check in," Giles said impatiently. "Did anything unusual happen to any of you? Cordelia, how was the freak show?"

"Freak . . . *oh.* I didn't go," she confessed, so very much wishing she had just lied.

Giles blinked at her as if she had just told him she bought off the rack.

"Okay," she rushed on, holding out her hands. "I was headed for it, but I had to go down the midway to get to it. And there were all these games with prizes. These adorable purple baskets made out of glass, and teddy bears dressed like Elvis and . . . I didn't win any of them!"

Giles said calmly, "You played games."

"Yes. Okay, I said I was sorry!"

"No. You didn't." Giles crossed his arms over his chest.

"Well, I meant to!"

"Giles," Buffy said. "It's no big, okay? Right?" she persisted.

Wow, Buffy is defending me, Cordelia thought. *Maybe I'm in bigger trouble than I know.*

Giles jabbed a finger at Cordy like it was a butcher knife and he was a serial killer. "You specifically said you would go to the freak show! And you didn't, and now we don't know a thing about it!"

"It's okay," Cordy pleaded. "We can still go to the freak show. It's still there. It's not like it's, um, any big deal."

"That's right," Xander jumped in. "Like Buffy said. No big."

"Yeah," Cordy said. "No big."

"No big?" Giles asked icily. "Lives are at stake! In fact, *I* have sacrificed my entire life, and for what? Selfish girls like you who don't do what they're told!"

"Hey, hold on," Cordy said. Now *she* was pissed. "I am *not* one of . . . of you guys, and I know you people have saved my life a few times, but that does not mean you can tell me what to do!"

His eyes bugged out. His face went purple. For a second, Cordy thought he might be having a heart attack.

"Giles, hey, dude," Xander began. "May I use the word 'overly' here? Because—"

"You stay out of this!" Giles shouted at him.

"Giles," Buffy said. "Are you feeling all right?"

"I'm fine," he said. He looked at Cordelia.

"Okay. I'm sorry, okay?" Cordy said, trying to put an end to the discussion. If it could be called a discussion. She was all whiny. She hated whiny, but he was freaking her out. "It's on my list. Freak show."

That seemed to satisfy him. But Cordy wasn't sure it satisfied her. She hadn't signed on for this ghostbusting stuff the way Buffy, Xander, and Willow had. She was still her own person.

"Angel? Buffy? Ferris wheel?" Was Giles actually snapping his fingers at them? God, if she were Buffy, she'd just break them right off and shove them up his—

"Ferris wheel." Buffy cleared her throat. "It . . . the line was so long . . ."

"Long line," Angel chimed in, wrapping his arm around her waist. He was all white-knight protector, and it was a good look for him.

"But we *wanted* to," Buffy said, snuggling up. "We were just worried w-we wouldn't be able to get back to the group in time."

Angel nodded.

"As it was, we were still a little late, because the carnival is so crowded and . . . and we wanted to be *polite*."

"Indeed," Giles sniffed.

"Yes!" Buffy said. "Because I was totally listening to you, Giles, and doing what you told me. So we just did a recon, patrolled around," she finished. "But we didn't see anything weird."

"Nothing," Angel said.

"Nor I," Giles said, sounding exasperated. "Willow?"

The redhead took a breath. "I did go to the fortune-teller. Her name is Madame Lazabra, and she's actually very young. But it was really warm and stuffy, and when she went to get me some water, I dozed off."

"Ah, *I* fell asleep on the merry-go-round," Xander blurted. "Just a little."

Giles hesitated. Then he said, as if it were some horrible sin, "I got a bit faint in the Chamber of Horrors."

Cordelia raised her chin. "Well, I spent, like, a million dollars with nothing to show for it, but other than that, I stayed on my feet the whole time."

"There's a first," Xander said.

"We need to check this out further. Together. No more splitting up." He nodded at Willow. "We'll go to the fortune-teller first. It's closest."

"But why?" Buffy asked. "We already checked out that stuff."

"And have reached no conclusions," he said, quite crankily. "For once, just listen to me and do as I say." He looked at Willow. "Well?"

Even more dejected and rejected, Willow led the way. She supposed he had a point, going back to investigate together. But she had a feeling that if she had suggested it, it wouldn't have happened.

People listen to Giles, she thought. *Even when he's irritable. Me? Not so much. And I'm almost always pleasant.*

"She's in there," she said, pointing at the open tent flap.

Giles led the parade inside.

The area they entered was empty. Giles walked up to the suspended Day-Glo objects and the black curtain. A lettered sign had been attached to the curtain. MADAME LAZABRA HAS

CLOSED HER TENT FOR THE EVENING. PLEASE COME ANOTHER DAY.

Angel looked back at the entrance. "There's no one else around."

"Well, let's take a peek behind the curtain," Buffy suggested. "Look around for a demon or something else fun to kill."

"Your cup of blood is always half full," Xander said. "I like that in a Slayer."

There was a noise on the other side of the curtain. They all looked at one another.

"No," Giles whispered. "Let's leave well enough alone for the time being."

They trooped back outside.

"Let's go on to the carousel," Giles said.

Buffy thought about mentioning what a time-waster this all was, but she didn't want Giles to bite her head off. What was his deal? Gee.

Xander showed them his spot on the carousel. Giles sat on the chariot bench while Willow, Xander, and Cordelia stood beside the black stallions. Angel hoisted Buffy up onto the unicorn; she felt a little silly but it was still fun as the carousel began to rotate and her unicorn went up and down. Angel was glowing. It was like they were really on a date, all happy, with no death or dismemberment anywhere near them.

"Anyone feel anything?" Giles asked them as the carousel slowed to a stop.

Xander burped and covered his mouth. "Well, I'm not feeling so great. And yet, I'm really hungry."

"God, all you think about is your stomach," Cordelia said.

"Currently, yeah," Xander returned.

"Ferris wheel?" Buffy asked.

"Not fond of heights," Cordelia said.

"We haven't gone to the freak show," Willow ventured, looking at the others.

"We could play some games," Cordelia put in. "The games are fun. They have great prizes."

"You said you lost a ton of money in the midway," Willow argued.

"Are we on Court TV?" Cordelia snapped.

"I just . . ." Willow looked confused. She took a deep breath.

"The freak show it is," Giles announced. "Come. No dallying."

"Not liking freak shows," Willow murmured. "Too freaky."

You're not wrong, Buffy thought as she tried to swallow around the lump in her throat.

The group was standing with about fifteen other people in a room painted completely black. Everyone was walking slowly past a row of things in bottles of formaldehyde. Two-headed piglets, a calf with six feet . . . they were basically just accidents of nature. But some of them looked human, and they upset the Slayer.

And I thought I could handle just about anything gross, she thought. Even the word—"gross"—seemed harsh.

"This is appalling," Giles murmured, echoing her thought. She felt close to him in that moment, and a little sorry for all the times she had kept him out of her world.

No, wait. That's part of growing up. But I'm not about growing up, so much. I'm about surviving to fight another day.

"I'll bet they don't have stuff like this in England," Xander ventured. He was green.

"On the contrary, we do, very much," Giles said. "The British fascination with the macabre is well documented. But that makes it no less appalling."

Suddenly calliope music poured from hidden speakers. Strobe lights flashed all over the room, then began to spin. To Buffy's far right, a curtain rose, revealing a small stage hung with red drapes. The silhouette of a tall, caped figure rose from beneath the floor.

"Good evening," said a familiar voice.

A harsh blue light clicked on, revealing Professor Copernicus Caligari.

"Welcome to the House of Freaks!" he cried.

"Not to be confused with the House of Blues!" Xander said sotto voce.

Buffy tugged on Giles's jacket and stood on tiptoe. "Giles, that's him," she whispered loudly in his ear.

Giles nodded to let her know he'd heard.

"Come with me now, to the world of mutations, aliens,

things from another world. Curiosities, monstrosities!"

Thunder rumbled through the speakers, followed by the sound of lightning. Then the calliope music began again—slow, mournful, dirgelike. A few people applauded and a guy in a letter jacket howled like a wolf. The pretty blonde with him giggled.

From another alcove a dark-skinned man in a leather vest, leather pants, and boots appeared with a torch in his right fist. He opened his mouth, leaned his head back, and moved the torch over his lips, then spewed forth a blast of flame.

Willow and Xander moved closer to Buffy and flanked her. Cordelia muttered, "This is so stupid," but her voice was a little wavery.

Professor Caligari waved his hand to the right. "Follow my assistant, if you dare!"

From beneath a red light a hunchbacked figure limped from the shadows. It—he—was dressed like Quasimodo in the Disney movie, and his face . . .

Are those scars, or fresh wounds? Buffy thought. It was hard to tell in the bad light. But his features were a ruin, crisscrossed with deep purple lines and red welts. The only part of his face that wasn't hideous was one eye. The other was covered with an eye patch.

Beside Buffy, Willow caught her breath. Buffy shot her a glance as Willow looked away. Her redheaded buddy was so gentle. It took a toll on Willow to see the things being Buffy's friend made visible.

The assistant raised a hand and brought it down, an awkward gesture that meant "follow me."

He led the laughing, uneasy crowd into a dark tunnel, past a row of little partitioned rooms that reminded Buffy of prison cells. The occupants were separated from the patrons by a wall of glass, and Buffy was glad. Because she needed some distance from what she was seeing.

There was a man whose body ended at his waist and a woman with a full beard and a very hairy back. Also, a guy who was double-jointed and could turn himself into a human pretzel. And a girl who turned into a leopard.

"It's done with mirrors, at least in her case," Giles explained.

Some of the freaks looked very sad. Others, as if they were bored. Maybe daydreaming of Anywhere But Here. Anyone but who they were.

There was a "pinhead," which was a man with a normal-sized body but a very tiny head, and a guy with the beginnings of a third arm growing out of his chest. He looked straight at Buffy and winked.

Buffy pushed against Angel's chest, and he held her, kissing the crown of her head. Then her temple, then her cheek.

Glad of the comfort, she squeezed his hand.

It got worse. It got very gross.

Then, just when Buffy didn't think she could handle any more, the bad went away. The assistant led them into a room called Fairyland. Half a dozen little people—of the human variety—were dressed in ballerina tutus and caps made to look like flower petals. Holding cheap plastic light-up wands, they swooped around the room on wires. Music box music tinkled in the air.

Seven more little men were dressed like the Seven Dwarfs, and they were kneeling before a glass coffin with their heads bowed. Inside the coffin lay the figure of a young girl with brown hair, her arms crossed over her chest. Her face was ashen; her lips, blue.

Buffy knew her dead people, and the woman looked real. As in, real dead.

She looked at Angel, who shook his head and whispered, "Heartbeat."

Buffy gave her one last appraising look before she walked from the room with the others.

"Well, that was disgusting," Xander said as they trooped through the exit and rejoined the crowds. "Especially that last part."

"That was the good part," Willow argued. "Fairies."

"You are a twisted woman," Xander told her. "Those people were dwarfs, Willow. Where does a carnival find twelve dwarfs?"

"Little people," Willow corrected him.

Xander said, "Okay. Sorry. Meanwhile, who thinks Snow White was dead?"

"She wasn't dead. She had a heartbeat," Angel said.

"We should pay close attention to what Angel has to say

on this subject, because he's had a lot of experience *creating* dead bodies," Xander continued.

Angel did not smile.

"Okay, but she looked awful," Cordelia said. "She needed more blush, at least."

Buffy stopped listening as her senses jogged up to high alert. She knew they weren't alone. Not alone, alone, of course, since they were surrounded by people. But alone in the sense of they weren't the only people interested in the conversation they were having.

Without missing a beat, Buffy whirled around and ran back through the exit. She saw someone in the shadows creeping away. No problem for the Slayer, who put on a burst of speed and threw her arms like a lasso around—

"Principal Snyder!" she cried, instantly releasing him.

"Summers, what are you doing?" he demanded, straightening his tie.

"Oh. I thought . . . um . . ."

"No thinking," Principal Snyder snapped. "Thinking is bad."

He grabbed her arm and marched her through the exit, where Giles and the others all looked extremely busted as Snyder stopped and glared at them.

"What are you people doing here together?" he demanded.

"We're . . . on a field trip," Giles replied, then fell silent.

Willow stepped into the breach. "For the research," she finished helpfully. "Did you know that in the Middle Ages, people watched morality plays, um . . ." She looked back at Giles.

"To learn about being good, moral people," Giles concluded. "We're looking for cross-references in symbols and icons to show the continuity from those days to these . . . days of learning about morality."

"Fascinating," Principal Snyder said, in a voice that added, *so not*. "This is what happens with budget cuts."

"And you're here for . . . ?" Giles added. "The fun?"

"I'm here because in the last three days truancy has gone up sixty-eight percent, and I know this carnival is to blame."

Giles looked puzzled as he pushed up his glasses. "But how can that be, seeing as the carnival just arrived?"

Snyder scowled at Giles. "What do you mean? They've been here since last Friday."

There was a beat as everyone took that in.

"No," Cordy said, glancing at the others. "Tonight is opening night."

"Are you on something?" Snyder challenged her.

Giles waded in. "I think what Cordelia is trying to say is that this is the first time any of us has been to the carnival. So she's surprised by the truancy rate."

"No," Cordelia said again, and Xander grunted through clenched teeth, *"Cor-de . . . lia."*

Willow jumped in. "She's not surprised by the truancy rate," she told their rat-headed principal, "um, because we have discovered during our research that most traveling . . .

shows . . . promote truancy and job absenteeism." She stared wide-eyed at Giles, who nodded, urging her to go on. She took a breath. "And it gets worse over time. It's called the Running-Away-to-Join-the-Circus Effect."

She nodded emphatically.

Everyone else nodded too.

Except Snyder.

"You honestly believe that," Snyder said, looking at each of them in turn. They all nodded some more.

"Then I'm going to declare this whole place off-limits to students. Any student caught on these grounds will be personally expelled by me."

"That's a good policy," Giles agreed. "I'm entirely in accord."

Good thinking, Giles. Buffy silently congratulated him. If banning the carnival could keep kids away—

"I'm not sure you can enforce that," Cordelia said. She looked at the others as they made silent pleas for her to shut up. *"What?"*

No one said a word, just kept looking strained.

"No carnival on school days, then," Principal Snyder amended. "I'm sure I can enforce *that*." He looked pleased with himself. "So enjoy the carnival tonight. Tomorrow, it's forbidden territory."

"You got it," Xander assured him. "After tonight, we shun the carnival."

Then Buffy heard someone else shuffling away just behind

her. She looked at Giles, who was looking at Principal Snyder, and said loudly, "Oh, gee, I think I heard"—she searched for a name—"Jonathan. The other member of our research . . . club. We lost track of him," she explained to the principal. "And so, I must go and find him."

She dashed back into the freak show. It was dimly lit, and a large crowd was coming through, but she thought she saw the heel of a leather shoe disappear around the next corner. It resembled the shoes their Quasimodo guide had worn.

"Coming through!" she cried, but there were too many people. Unless she wanted to create a disturbance, there was no way she could plow through fast enough to catch up with the owner of the shoe.

Frustrated, she turned back and rejoined the group out in the breezeway. Except for Principal Snyder, they were all there, looking bewildered. Except for Giles. Giles was jazzed.

"Find anyone?" Willow asked.

"Thinking maybe our freak show tour guide," Buffy replied.

"I thought for a minute that he might be the guy in the fortune-teller tent," Willow said. "But he was all ewww."

Buffy said to Giles, "Why are you smiling?"

"Because something wicked this way has come," he said. On her look, he elaborated, "Principal Snyder thought this carnival has been here nearly a week. But it opened just tonight as far as we're concerned."

"Yeah, so he doesn't get out much," Buffy said.

"Because, for starters, who would let him out?" Xander asked.

"We can ask people when they think the carnival came to Sunnydale too," Willow suggested.

"Excellent thinking," Giles told her.

She smiled, looking pathetically grateful.

The informal survey got a mix of answers ranging from two weeks ago to one week ago, to tonight.

"And it's weird that it opened on a Wednesday," Willow said. "Don't things open on Friday nights? The beginning of the weekend?"

"Boys and girls, I'd say we have Rising liftoff," Xander said and then burped. "I have to go. I'm not feeling so well."

"The carnival's due to close soon," Giles said, checking his watch.

"You have a nice watch too," Willow murmured. "Because you have a job."

Giles apparently didn't hear her. He said, "Willow, tomorrow I want you to research anything unusual in the last two weeks—if, as Principal Snyder has insisted, the truancy rate has gone up, and also if there have been any unusual occurrences."

"I'll check the usual places," she told him. "School records, police reports, internal memos."

"Very good."

"I'm thinking Angel and I really should go check out the

Alibi," Buffy said. Angel sidled up to her again and laced his fingers through hers.

A sudden crescendo of calliope music blanketed their conversation. The notes were hollow and cold. The tune sent icewater fingers up Buffy's spine, and she actually felt her heart skip a beat. Cordelia touched her chest as if she were having the same reaction, and Willow wrapped her arms around herself.

"Look," Willow said, pointing.

A spotlight beamed a blue-white circle at the topmost car of the Ferris wheel. A figure in black rose from the seat and spread its arms wide. The figure was wearing a black cape. Long white hair flowed over its shoulders.

"Ladies and gentlemen!" cried a voice Buffy knew. It was Professor Caligari again. By the reverb, she assumed there were loudspeakers scattered throughout the carnival grounds.

"I am Professor Copernicus Caligari!" The figure in the Ferris-wheel chair bowed from the waist. "Thank you so much for coming. The carnival is now closed for the evening. Please come again tomorrow!"

The crowd around them hooted and cheered.

Cordelia muttered, "Talk about your freaks."

Willow said to Buffy, "Do you think he looks like the guy in the woodcut?"

"I don't know. The woodcut is pretty basic," Buffy replied.

"Maybe the one we saw in the freak show was a robot," Cordelia ventured. "Or someone dressed up like him."

As Buffy stared up at him, something passed in front of

her eyes. It was like light glinting off something metallic, or a camera flash. She shielded her gaze by raising her arm across her face.

And then it was gone.

She glanced at Angel, who raised his brows and said, "What?"

"Did you just see . . . ," she began, and then she couldn't remember what had just happened.

She thought a minute.

"Yes?" he prodded.

"Nothing." Nothing had happened. "I just felt funny for a minute. I'm okay now."

"Then let's go to the Alibi," he said.

"You got it." Buffy smiled at him. To Giles, "We'll walk with you guys to the exit."

They joined the lazy stampede. Buffy searched the faces of those around her. A couple was arguing. A boy in a stroller was crying. Nothing too out of the ordinary there, when you considered the noise level, the amount of people, and the expense of food and souvenirs. People even argued and cried at Disneyland.

Of course, I kept my cool all night, even with Angel here, she thought proudly. *I'm the Slayer. I know how to maintain.*

"Wonder if Willy will be in a talkative mood," Angel said.

"If he isn't, I'll kick his ass until he is," she told him. "I'll kick all their asses." She flexed her biceps. "I'm in great shape."

He laced his fingers through hers and smiled hungrily.

Beside her, Xander slowed and covered his mouth. "It's getting worse."

"Well, if you're going to vomit, for God's sake, do it here," Giles said loudly. "And not in my car."

"Giles, that—that's *mean*," Willow said, rushing to Xander's defense.

"Yeah," Cordelia said. "Cold much?"

Saying nothing, Giles stomped toward the exit.

"God, Giles," Buffy said slowly to his retreating back. She frowned. Then she said to Cordelia, "Maybe you should take Xander home. My Watcher has PMS."

"Buffy," Willow murmured.

"What?" Buffy tossed her hair. "Does he think he can treat my friends that way?"

"I guess he does," Xander said weakly.

"Well, he can't," she finished. "I won't put up with it." She raised her chin. "I don't know why I have to have him around, anyway. I don't need a babysitter."

"Woof. You go, girl," Xander said.

"Are you okay?" Angel asked her.

She blinked. "Never better."

"Because you seem . . . like you need a good kiss." He smiled at her and held out his arm.

Smiling back at him, Buffy scooted into his embrace and trailed her fingers down his arm, putting her hand in the back pocket of his pants.

Meanwhile, Cordelia looked hard at Xander. "What is wrong with you? *Are* you going to vomit?"

"I don't know," Xander said, gasping.

"Do you need some water?" Willow asked.

Xander shook his head.

Giles huffed all the way to the parking lot, muttering to himself. Buffy scooted up a little so she could hear what he was saying.

". . . lazy girl. *Kendra*, on the other hand, listened to me, performed her duties admirably. But Buffy . . . she just goes on about it however she pleases. *God*, she's driving me mad . . ."

Buffy froze. Her breath caught.

"Buffy, he doesn't mean it," Willow murmured, drawing close to her friend.

"Who cares?" Buffy shot back, glaring at the back of Giles's head. "Who the hell does he think he is? He has no idea what it's like to be me. Where does he get off judging me?"

"Buffy, um, not so loud," Willow said.

Buffy snickered. "Really, Willow, what could he do to me? Nothing. What is he? Nothing."

She sauntered off with Angel in tow.

Forking off from the others, Xander and Cordy walked through the parking lot toward her car. As he opened the passenger-side door, she caught it and said, "Don't throw up, okay? These seats are leather and *oooh* . . ."

"Gee, Florence Nightingale, I'm loving your concern.

Maybe you should just tape my mouth shut," he said irritably.

"Oooh," she said again. She walked on steady feet toward the candy-apple-red classic Porsche 911 in the parking lot. It gleamed like the heart in the Tunnel of Love. It was beautiful. So beautiful.

Silver flashed before her eyes; it was probably the chrome detailing . . .

"You need beautiful things. There's just not enough to satisfy you, but you have to try," said a voice inside Cordelia's head.

She was dizzy from wanting the Porsche. It was hard to stand there and stare at it without owning it.

"God, I would *kill* for a car like that," she breathed.

"I'll just bet you would," Xander said drily.

"Yeah," she said, balling her fists. She smiled to herself. "I would."

CHAPTER SEVEN

Tears streamed down Stephanie Hahn's cheeks as she ran for all she was worth. Something was wrong; something was terribly wrong. . . .

"Steph, will you slow down?" David demanded as they burst out of the forest, just a few feet north of the graveyard. "I am breaking into a sweat!"

"Oh my God, I totally ruined my life," she groaned. "How could I say those things to Cordelia Chase? What was I thinking?"

"That you're hotter than she is? Because you are," her twin insisted, coming up beside her. "What is your rush?"

"It's ten," she said. "It closes at ten."

She heard it then, the reedy, sweet call of the calliope, playing up and down her backbone, running along her forehead. Soothing, beckoning, promising . . .

It will be all right if I can get there in time. It was so stupid that we had to go to that stupid chess club meeting. Something is wrong, but it will be okay if I can get back to the carnival. It will be okay.

He said I was beautiful. He told me I was the fairest in the land . . .

. . . the man in the mirror. If he can tell me that again, I'll be all right.

She didn't know why, but she did know it was true. Down to her bones, she knew that the carnival would make it all right.

And not just the carnival. . . .

She put on a burst of speed, as she had last night when those . . . gang members were chasing them. That girl from school had saved them. It was all a mishmash now. She couldn't remember most of it.

I was pretty. But I'm not anymore!

She was in an agony, and it hurt down to her soul. She *used* to be pretty, but her face had melted into what she saw in the mirror now. Hour by hour, she had watched her beauty fade. It had made her shake. Made her sick.

Until she had realized what to do: Come back to the carnival, and it would be all right. It was like a voice whispering: *"Just come back. Come back. You are lovely."*

She dashed through the carnival parking lot, winding her way around the cars, hot tears in her eyes as she mentally willed the calliope to *keep playing, please, keep playing. . . .*

Against the black velvet sky the Ferris wheel was still lit up. Across the arch the words PROFESSOR CALIGARI'S TRAVELING CARNIVAL swam before Stephanie's eyes.

In front of the arch, one, two, three . . . seven clowns were lined up, shaking the hands of people leaving the carnival. One was squeezing a bike horn. Two were waltzing to the calliope music.

One, dressed all in green, spotted Stephanie and flung both arms up in the air, waving excitedly at her. He began to jump up and down, gesturing for her to hurry, hurry!

The other clowns saw her too. She started crying again; she wasn't sure why, but she raced toward them, her own arms open, crying, "Help me!"

David ran up behind her; then they were both enveloped by the clowns, the dear, wonderful clowns, who hustled them through the crowds—*make way for the Hahns!*—the one in green putting his arm around Stephanie as they dashed onto the carnival grounds.

Uncle Sam, the man on stilts, looked down at them and waved. He said, "Back for a recharge, eh?" Then he laughed jovially and walked on, shouting into a mic, "Closing time, folks! Come back tomorrow! We're here until the full moon!"

Past the merry-go-round and the Octopus and the Tilt-A-Whirl, through the game corridor and around the tents, the calliope music rose and swelled and Stephanie thought her heart would burst from her chest, she was running so hard.

And the clowns gamboled and capered with her into the fun house!

Her pulse was pounding in her ears, almost, but not quite, drowning out the calliope, the dear, wonderful calliope.

And then . . . the clowns were gone.

She and David were in the mirror maze alone.

And they were standing side by side, staring into a mirrored panel together.

Stephanie swayed as a wave of dizziness swept over her. A silver blur obscured her vision—just for a moment, a couple of musical notes—and then she stared at herself and whispered, "Oh, God, I am so beautiful."

David licked his lips. "We both are. We're even hotter than I remembered. Stephanie, we are *incredible*."

They put their arms around each other's waists, touching heads, gazing into the mirror.

A voice whispered: *"Mirror, mirror, on the wall, whose souls are the fairest of them all?"*

"Ours," Stephanie said, reaching forward to touch her image.

Her hand slipped through the surface . . . and then long, skeletal fingers grabbed her on the sides of her face and yanked her forward.

A bicycle horn blatted.

Outside, the carousel started up, drumming and clashing.

David shouted and held on to Stephanie, but she was pulled through the mirror, pulled . . . and he with her.

One scream, just one . . .

And the fun house plunged into blackness as maniacal laughter echoed through the twists and turns.

In the freak show Fairyland the eyes of the girl in the glass coffin flew open. They were completely black.

She pounded her fists on the top and sides of the glass. She kicked.

Vaclav, the Gypsy's helper as well as the assistant in the Quasimodo costume, watched from the curtains, his fists clenched so tightly that blood dribbled from his palms.

Light flashed all around the girl in the glass coffin.

Opening the coffin lid, he reached out a hand to the girl. She blinked as if she had never seen a hand in her life.

Vaclav sobbed once, hard, as his heart broke. The coffin hadn't worked. She was still ruined. And Vaclav knew whose fault it was.

He hated Professor Caligari.

Hated him with a vengeance.

As the carnival devoured the successfully tempted, Professor Caligari leaped off the Ferris wheel and soared through the air. Like a bat on the wing, he glided through the night wind, laughing as he landed on the shoulders of the Seven: his faithful jesters, Messrs. Vanity, Envy, Greed, Lust, Gluttony,

Anger, and Sloth. The clowns capered and pranced.

"Have you been playing, Tricksters?" Professor Caligari asked the merry clowns with their painted-on faces and whirligig wigs.

In answer, they carried him to a shiny black dais before his wagon. As one, they fell to their knees, stretched out their arms, and buried their faces in the sawdust, salaaming the Great One.

Through the Employees Only gate the carnies poured in from the carnival grounds. Another day done. A few more souls absorbed. They would gather momentum. It was almost time. And then . . .

Shrouded in darkness, some of Professor Caligari's loyal followers shambled out of their human skins, gathering them up and wadding them into rolls like sleeping bags. Tentacles popped free, faces caved in. Some rolled, some slithered. Some burrowed.

Others, who actually were human but in many cases centuries old, kicked back with cigarettes and popped open beer cans. The fire-eater from the freak show lit a fire.

The carousel creatures detached from their poles, stretching their backs and rolling their heads after long hours of being ridden by humans. The skeletal woman who rode the chariot materialized and took up the reins. Her phantom baby suckled at her desiccated ribs.

Madame Lazabra and Vaclav joined the gathering. Madame Lazabra carried a black velvet box studded with jewels. Vaclav was wearing a pair of jeans and a dark gray sweatshirt. He wore an earring in his left ear and tenderly held the hand of a beautiful young girl, who stumbled forward like a hypnotized maiden in an old-fashioned horror movie.

Her name was Sandra Morehouse, and she had hung herself last night while Professor Caligari was busy with their intrusive guests. His hold on her had wobbled after she had suddenly remembered that a month ago she had shot a man dead because he wouldn't give her his wallet. Apparently that moment of clarity brought remorse so great that she had tried to end her life. A few hours in the magickal glass coffin in Fairyland had restored her—physically, at least.

Returned as well to his control, she would never again remember what she'd done. Of course, she would also never remember her own name, either.

One had to make trade-offs.

Still, it was a pity. Professor Caligari had thought she might make a fine wife for Vaclav, the Gypsy boy who had joined his retinue in 1856. Without his frightening makeup appliances, Vaclav appeared now as he had when he had joined the carnival, tempted by his lust for the fortune-teller. He had been strong and young, and so, rather than allow the soulcatchers to absorb his soul, Caligari had put him to work.

The secret to keeping him youthful and strong, of course, was annual stays inside the glass coffin. The magickal prism healed diseases and rejuvenated old bones and hearts. Caligari had created it himself after torturing a Middle Eastern mystic for the secret. All the humans took turns lying in it.

That counted him out, of course.

With a special smile for Vaclav, who he knew must be disappointed that Sandra's mind was now gone, Professor Caligari spread out his arms in welcome. His long, thin face flickered in the glow from the fire as the monsters, demons, and human monsters gave him their full attention.

"It's happening," he announced. "Order in Sunnydale is breaking down. Murders and robberies are going up. The souls of the weakest are ripe for the plucking. In fact, as I speak"—he cocked his head—"two more are joining our traveling company."

As Professor Caligari gazed into the faces of those who served him, he thought back through the many guises they had worn—as ancient Romans, Druids, witch finders, necromancers, dance-hall girls, snake charmers, contortionists—and the many places they had visited: the Folies Bergère in Paris, the Las Vegas strip, Renn faires, and county fairs. They had lured the unsuspecting with vaudeville revues, belly dances, magic shows, bear baitings, and witch burnings.

"It's souls I'm after," Professor Caligari reminded everyone. "And a few warm bodies to join our ranks. It takes a lot of manpower to run an operation like this."

He gestured to the new recruit, Carl Palmer. Carl smiled dumbly at him and gave him a thumbs-up. Professor Caligari knew that if the young man's mind were not so clouded, he, Caligari, might have another suicide on his hands. At the urging of Tessa, the girl who ran the coin toss, Carl had murdered his mother for the eight dollars in her purse. Not even enough for another roll of quarters.

But Carl didn't mind anymore. Caligari had seen to that.

"As you know, Sunnydale is a special place. It's on the Hellmouth. That means that the mystical energies here are more powerful than other locations in this dimension. Many of the souls we take here will be very, very special."

He took on the tone and rhythm of an itinerant preacher of the Old West, or a man who traveled the plains in his magick wagon and dispensed potions and told fortunes.

"Friends, our business is the collecting of souls. It is our legal tender. It is our life's blood."

To the ignited background music of the carousel, he remembered those traveling days, days of steam locomotives, Comanches, and desperadoes. It had been harder to capture souls back then. There were fewer people, and they lived farther apart. In the pressure cooker of modern life, people cracked faster too. Folks back then were more suspicious. Also more fragile. A lot of them died before their souls could be collected.

"Humans," the professor said derisively. "They are weak, fragmented, and unclean. They're easily tempted, easily caught in the web of my soulcatchers."

The clowns juggled their spheres higher and higher into the air.

"Mirror, mirror, on the wall, I am filled with lust, anger,

vanity, greed, gluttony, sloth, and envy," Professor Caligari intoned, in his special, hypnotic voice. *"And when I see it reflected back to me, I seize it!"*

The crowd laughed.

"Others . . . need a little coaxing." He grinned at his worshipful followers.

"Scare them. Throw them off balance. Kill some, if you wish. But drive them to me. To survive no matter what the cost is their greatest temptation. Humans are so afraid of death that they will barter their own souls to avoid it. And so . . . I want you to stir it up here in Sunnydale. Terrify the inhabitants. Threaten them. Make storms and craziness. Whip them into a frenzy. They'll find that only here do they feel safe. There's something about the carnival . . ."

He snapped his fingers, and at once the carnie clearing wobbled and blurred, and became . . . the keep of a castle.

A church.

A cave.

"Something about being here that makes them feel safe," he concluded. "But, of course, Professor Copernicus Caligari's Traveling Carnival is the most dangerous place in Sunnydale for anyone with a soul."

"And it's about to become a lot more dangerous," came a voice from inside Professor Caligari's wagon.

The owner of the voice stepped from the shadows. Tall, dark-haired, and blue-eyed, an old "friend" of Sunnydale, and of Rupert Giles, the Watcher of the reigning Slayer: Mr. C. Haos.

Also known as Ethan Rayne.

Beside him, a huge puddle of blackness drooped its head, growling at the assembled masses.

"Heel, Malfaiteur," Ethan said to the Rottweiler, yanking at the wickedly spiked chain around its neck. Then to Professor Caligari, "Thank you, Professor. I'm absolutely delighted to be working with you. It's such an honor. I want to let you know that I will do all I can to help you with the downfall of Sunnydale. It holds such a special place in my heart."

Buffy rammed her fist into the vampire's face again. It was a bloody pulp.

Just like the faces of the three other vampires she had beaten . . . before she dusted them.

"You guys think you can hold out on *me*?" she demanded. "The Slayer?"

"N . . . no," the vampire managed. It was a mess. Fairly new, and not a good fighter.

No challenge here.

She grabbed it by the arms and executed a mind-bendingly vicious knee strike to its groin.

The vampire howled.

"Remember this moment. No, wait. In about five minutes, you won't be remembering anything. Because you'll be a big pile of dust."

She reached out her hand. Angel handed her the stake,

running his hand up and down her arm as she got ready for the death blow.

"You have one more chance," she said, showing the vamp the business end of the weapon. "Talk to me about the Rising."

The vampire shook its head. "I just got here," it insisted. "Came to town last night!"

She positioned the stake against its chest. "One more push and you fit in an ashtray," she said.

"I don't kno—"

Dusted!

The vampire exploded.

"God, it excites me to watch you fight," Angel said, kissing her all crazy.

Crazy, crazy, crazy.

Then Angel hissed. He had vamped. He looked up at the sky and pulled Buffy into the alley beside Willy's demon-hangout bar.

"It's getting light out," she realized. "You have to go." She pressed herself against him. "Now."

"We have time." He kissed her again. "Come on, we have time."

Every part of her yearned to say yes. But she also knew it was too risky. In a few minutes Angel would be in grave danger from the sunlight. Willy couldn't be trusted to keep him safe, and Buffy had to make an appearance at . . .

. . . *home,* she thought. *Oh my God, I am so in trouble.*

"Oh my God," she said aloud.

"Is there a problem, ma'am?" came a voice from the other end of the alley. Woman, Southern twang.

Footsteps walked toward her and Angel.

"Hi," Buffy said to the red-haired woman standing behind Angel. "Can I help you?"

Angel turned. "Claire," he said.

The woman smiled. "Oh, hey. Evenin'. Fancy runnin' into you in another dark alley."

Buffy looked from the woman to Angel and back again. Her lip curved. Did this chick actually think Angel was interested in her?

"Let's go," she said, grabbing his hand.

Buffy and Angel reached her home and she climbed through the upstairs window. Angel stayed below, moving under a purple sky to reach his apartment. Buffy quickly changed into boxers and a baby tee, with no idea if her mother had waited up or what.

She crept downstairs and found her mom in the kitchen, asleep with her head on the table. Her big business checkbook was open. Buffy picked up a piece of paper and inspected it. It was the art gallery's utility bill. It was overdue.

Another bill was for three months of the services of a security company. Unpaid.

A collection notice for shipping.

And she was going to take me shopping, Buffy thought. Something in her went *pfffffttt* like a balloon. She had been all into herself, all swaggering around and flaunting how cool she was . . . and okay, Slayer. But also daughter.

She ran her fingers through her mother's hair. Joyce Summers bolted awake, then smiled when she saw her daughter.

"I . . . oh, I fell asleep. I thought . . ." She sat up slowly. "When did you get in?"

"I've been upstairs," Buffy hedged. "I didn't realize you were in here."

"Oh. Did you have a nice time? Did you get your homework done?"

The traditional Mom questions. Buffy felt like the worst of daughters, sneaking around and partying while her mom was worrying and scared.

Buffy offered her hand. "Let's go upstairs."

"All right, honey." Joyce glanced down at the field of papers. "I'll clean this up—"

"In the morning," Buffy urged.

She put her arm around her mother's shoulders and slowly they went upstairs together.

They kissed each other good night on the cheek and then Buffy brushed her teeth and climbed in bed.

If I'm so great, why can't I help my mom? she thought. *I was so arrogant tonight. Snotty to Giles . . . but what was his deal? He was so mean. Oh my God, he dissed me so badly.*

She turned over. Her lips were sore from all the kissage. So nice. Angel was so romantic lately . . . their relationship was moving to a higher level, that was for sure. She had never dreamed a guy could kiss the way he did, be so focused on her. It was almost humbling. But not quite.

If we keep this up . . . we'll seize the moment. I'm only sixteen.

But I'm the Slayer.

She began to drift. As the metal flashed in the night . . . silver . . .

Now Buffy's car on the Ferris wheel swung jauntily at the very top, and all of Sunnydale lay at her feet.

"You are the queen of all you survey," said the voice. *"No one else has power like you. You are unique."*

"I'm the Chosen One," Buffy said aloud. "Me. The Slayer. Tag, I'm It."

"Super strength, super healing abilities. It must be difficult to pretend all the time. To be forced to conceal your magnificence."

"It's kind of a drag," she admitted. "Especially when I get in trouble for it. School, friends, being the Slayer . . . it's hard to juggle it all."

"It doesn't have to be," said the voice. *"I can change all that for you. You can shine like the shooting star you are meant to be."*

And then the Slayer was staring into something shiny. Her face stared back at her. She gazed into her own eyes.

"You were meant for greater things," the voice insisted. *"To take pride in your nature, not to hide it like something to be ashamed of."*

"Oh, I'm proud."

"They don't understand you. They don't really help you. When it comes down to the wire, you always have to handle it yourself, don't you?"

"They're sweet; they try."

"But you are the Slayer."

"It's a burden," she admitted. "But they do help—"

"No. They get in the way. They slow you down. You're only being nice. You would do much better without them."

Buffy's face looked back at her. It was kind of glowing.

"Look at you. You have a halo, like a saint. You're a god. You're above them. Don't expect too much out of them. That is so cruel."

"I never thought of it that way," Buffy confessed.

"You need to leave them behind. Handle things yourself. Alone."

"Alone," the Slayer whispered, to the sweet cadence of the calliope as it now drifted through her open window.

Because she was not on the Ferris wheel. She was in her bed.

And someone was gazing at her through a frame of curlicues and shining stones; a face, a horrible face, stretching and shifting and glaring and staring. And behind him, David and Stephanie Hahn, strapped down, things with knives moving toward their faces. . . .

Buffy groaned and turned over in her sleep.

• • •

Thursday, after school.

Xander had been sick all day, and got to stay home. Cordelia had given him a lift over to Giles's, where they were gathering. Buffy had walked over, but Willow had yet to show.

And there were kittens.

One was gray and white, and one was black, and they weighed as much as a handful of feathers.

"And their names are?" Buffy asked as she nuzzled the black one with her cheek. Xander was lying listlessly on Giles's couch, examining an assortment of little aluminum pouches of cat food. Cordelia was off in a corner, explaining for perhaps the two-dozenth time that she was allergic to cats. Every once in a while she would sneeze very daintily, and someone would think to mutter, "Bless you."

"Names? I don't know yet," Giles said, with a faint hint of pink in his cheeks.

Buffy was glad things were back to better between them. She figured he didn't know that she had overheard . . . what she had overheard. Maybe he'd just been letting off steam. He was under a lot of pressure. After all, he *was* kind of old, and out of his element.

"How about Barnum and Bailey?" Cordelia suggested. "Since we're on a circus theme."

"Carnival," Xander corrected her. "Theme. Not a cruise."

"What*ever*."

"Speaking of the carnival, any new thoughts on what's going on?" Buffy asked.

Giles took a pouch of Little Friskies from Xander and tore it open. "Not so far. I was up half the night with the kittens. They make quite a lot of noise." He picked up their already brimming dish from beside the couch and started to carry both it and the pouch into the kitchen. "They seem to have no interest in food."

Xander moaned. "I think I have rabies."

"Has either of them bitten you?" Giles asked, alarmed.

Cordelia sneezed.

"Bless you," Buffy said.

"No, but I'm, like, foaming at the mouth," Xander said, licking his lips. "I live in Phlegm Town."

"Yuck. Thank you for sharing," Cordelia said. Then she stared harder at Xander. "Is that a piece of cat food stuck to your cheek? Oh my God, Xander! Have you been scarfing their food?"

Before Xander could answer, he was saved by a sharp knock on Giles's front door.

"That's probably Willow," Giles said. "Here." He handed the dish and the bowl to Buffy, and crossed to the door.

As Buffy gazed down at it and then over to Xander, Giles opened the door and took a step back as Willow sailed in.

"Guys," Willow said. She was out of breath. "Carl and Mariann Palmer's mom is dead and Principal Snyder is missing!"

"What?" Xander sat up. "That's such great news! Not the mom part," he amended. "That is *horrible* news." He frowned. "How did she die?"

Willow pantomimed hitting something. "Looks like a robbery. In her own house. Carl's fingerprints are all over a flashlight that was lying next to her."

"Good Lord." Giles pushed up his glasses and scratched his forehead. "Are you saying that Carl Palmer killed his own mother?"

"That, or the electricity went out," Xander said.

"Or he was trying to defend her," Buffy pointed out.

"How can you rob your own parents?" Willow asked.

"Ask Cordelia. She's stealing years from hers," Xander said.

"Her purse was open and her wallet was empty," Willow said. "Which doesn't make sense, if Carl did it."

"Yeah, it does, if you're, like, a drug addict or something," Cordelia argued.

"But he *has* money. He has a job," Willow said. "At the library. Or, he did."

"Is he in custody?" Giles asked.

Willow shook her head. "No. He's missing too."

"Oh, God," Cordelia said, covering her mouth. "Maybe Carl killed Principal Snyder!"

"We can hope," Xander muttered, then added, "Just kidding." Then added, "Not." Then added, "Of course I'm kidding."

"Well, Principal Snyder was last seen at the carnival," Willow said. "And guess what?"

"So was Carl Palmer," Giles ventured.

Her face fell. "You guessed."

"Principal Snyder was going to ban kids from going to the carnival on school days," Buffy said. "And I *swear* that Quasimodo guy was spying on us."

The little gray kitten attacked Giles's shoe. It mewed and batted at the laces. Giles exhaled impatiently.

"Also? Listen to this," Willow said mysteriously. "There is no record of there actually being a carnival in Sunnydale. No news articles, no permits, nothing. It just . . . appeared."

"Out of nowhere, into the here," Giles mused.

"Also? In the last week the crime rate has shot up. There's been a thirty-six percent increase in robberies, murders, and vandalism."

"I thought I noticed more graffiti in the graveyards," Buffy said as she cuddled the naughty kitten.

"Did you notice any extra graves?" Xander asked.

"Can't say I did," Buffy replied. The kitten batted at her hair, and she laughed.

"Well, we ought to investigate," Giles said. "Go back to the carnival and see what we can find out."

"I can't go," Xander said apologetically. "I can barely move."

"And unfortunately I have cheerleading practice." Cordelia sneezed. "Oh, hey, what a nice letter opener." She picked up a shiny blade thingy off the bookcase and inspected it, eyes wide with interest. "There's writing on it. 'Ta-mir-o—'"

"Please, put that down immediately," Giles snapped. "It's

not a letter opener. It's a sacrificial knife used in the summoning of Astorrith, who is a very powerful demon. If you continue saying those words and simultaneously cut yourself, you might very well summon him."

"Oh, sorry," Cordelia said in a little voice, replacing the knife on the shelf. "You shouldn't just leave things like that lying around in the open. What if it fell into the wrong hands?"

"I don't know, Giles. Until you get these little guys housebroken, you might consider some AstroTurf," Xander said, wrinkling his nose.

"Damn. Did one of them do his business on my rug?"

Xander shook his head, gathering up the fabric of his corduroy pants with a grimace. "No. One of them did *her* business on my pants."

Giles balled his fists. "Those little beasts. They're damned infuriating!"

"Jeez, maybe you shouldn't have pets," Cordelia muttered.

"Okay, that was fun. Going to the carnival," Buffy announced, handing her kitten to Willow. "See you later."

"Very well, you and I will go on ahead." Giles turned to Willow. "Meantime, you check and see if you can glean more information about Mrs. Palmer's death and Principal Snyder's disappearance."

"Oh." Willow looked forlorn as she stroked the kitten's back. It was curled up in her hand like a Tribble on classic *Star Trek*. "I can't go too?"

"You'd do better doing your hacking thing," he said.

Willow took a breath. "But . . ."

Giles scowled at her. "Do you want to help or not?"

Willow looked crushed. The kitten mewed, as if echoing her sentiments exactly.

"Giles," Xander said. "Will's always been a big helper."

The phone rang. With a huff, Giles rushed off to take it in the kitchen. "Yes?" he yelled.

"God, what is his deal?" Cordelia asked. "He's so cranky."

"The Watcher gig is a lot of pressure," Buffy suggested, leaning over and giving the kitten a kiss on its small, soft head. "It's hard to keep up with a Slayer. Especially me."

The kitten started licking the end of Willow's chin. "Well, at least *you* love me," she murmured.

As if on cue, the cat scrabbled out of Willow's arms and darted under the couch.

"That's cats. Love you and leave you," Xander said. "Oh, say, weren't you a cat for Halloween, Cordelia?"

"Yes, and how lucky for me that I will never love you," she snapped.

Giles bustled back into the room. "Buffy, that was Willy. Two vampires are down at the Alibi, discussing the carnival. I want you to go down there right now and see what you can find out."

Buffy waved her hands back and forth as if she were a traffic cop telling him to put on his brakes. "Giles, I went there last night, remember? By the time I get to the Alibi, those vamps will be long gone. It'll be a total waste of time."

"I disagree." He narrowed his eyes at her.

"Well, congratulations." She folded her arms across her chest.

"Aren't you Miss Thing today," Cordelia said. "And every day," she added under her breath.

"Well, yeah, actually, I am." Buffy squared her shoulders and gave her hair a toss. "The one girl in all my generation, remember?"

"Buffy," Willow said quietly.

"The one girl who is supposed to listen to her Watcher, remember?" Giles said. His voice was deadly quiet.

"Well, I *would* listen to you if what you were telling me to do made any sense."

"Buffy," Willow said again, a little more loudly.

Giles took off his glasses. Xander sat up slowly, staring hard at Buffy as if he couldn't believe what he was hearing.

The tension in the room was rising toward the boiling point.

Giles said, "I beg your pardon?"

"You heard me." The Slayer put her hands on her hips and raised her chin. "Or maybe you didn't. So I'll say it again. Read my lips. I'm going to the carnival."

"What is wrong with you?" Willow asked her. She looked at Giles. "Something's wrong with her."

"I'm fine, Will. Trust me on this one," Buffy said. "But something is wrong with Giles." She tilted her head. "Because he is way off if he thinks he can tell me what to do."

"He's, um, supposed to tell you what to do," Willow ventured. She slid a glance toward Giles. "Aren't you? I mean, I thought that was what the Watcher was for."

"To guide the Slayer," Xander put in.

"Yeah, guide me, not treat me like his German sheepdog or whatever," Buffy flung at him.

"That would be a German shepherd," Cordelia said. "My aunt raises them."

"No one cares," Buffy informed her. She ticked her attention back to Giles. "Now, I'm going to the carnival. Do you want to try to stop me?"

"How dare you," Giles bit off. His eyes were slits. "I have turned my entire life upside down to be your Watcher."

"Never asked you to," Buffy said, staring him down.

"Hey, you are way out of line," Xander said.

"This just in," Buffy said to Xander. "What you think doesn't matter."

She headed for the door. Giles took a step toward it, blocking her way.

He said, "If you leave—"

"If you don't get out of my way, I will move you," she said.

They faced each other. Giles took a deep breath and let it out. Then he stepped aside, glaring at her.

"You're right. I can't stop you," he said.

She gave him a sour smile. "You're right."

She swept out of the room, opening the front door, walking through it, and slamming it in Giles's face.

As if on cue, both of Giles's kittens began to mew.

"Oh my God, Giles," Willow said.

"Lock up after yourselves," Giles snapped, staring after the Slayer. "And for God's sake, find a way to shut those things up."

CHAPTER EIGHT

G iles blinked.

He was back in the Chamber of Horrors, staring at the false mirror in the Dracula tableau.

But he had had no intention of revisiting the Chamber of Horrors. His plan had been to investigate the games area, because both Carl Palmer and Principal Snyder had been seen there last.

He had not run into Buffy. *I ought to thrash her,* he thought. Only that was absurd, of course. Take on the Slayer? Not bloody likely.

Still, his blood was up. He balled his fists as the crowds snaked past the ridiculous scenes of mayhem and violence—

he'd show them violence, ultraviolence, in fact—and it was only by clenching his jaw that he didn't rail against the girl behind him, who kept snapping her gum. A well-placed palm strike to her jaw, and he could shove her bovine face in.

He found the mirror and stared into it. Waves of dizziness washed over him. Then more anger flooded him, overtaking him.

"Let me out of here," he said, pushing the girl aside.

She stumbled and shouted, "Hey, watch it!" One look from him, and she swallowed hard and looked down.

He pushed, shoved, and got the hell out of there just as someone said, "Call security!"

"Idiots."

He stomped across the grounds, ready to mow down anyone who crossed his path, then out into the parking lot to retrieve his Citroën.

Someone had parked a Toyota Corolla so close that he couldn't get the driver's-side door open.

"Damn it!" he yelled. He pulled back his leg to kick the Corolla as hard as he could, when he suddenly remembered the black flashlight he had in the pocket of his jacket.

He didn't remember how it had gotten there, but no matter.

It would smash the taillight just fine.

The car alarm began to whoop.

He smashed the other taillight for good measure.

Then he climbed into his car on the passenger side and

scooted over behind the wheel, dropping the flashlight to the floor.

Hands clenched around the wheel, he scowled as he drove.

He had given up everything he cared about to become a Watcher. And for what? An ignorant, rude, arrogant American teenager.

I could just . . .

He stared into the rearview mirror. Saw his face. Saw something silver.

He smiled like a damned man.

Yes, he could.

"Wow, sorry, you were really close that time," the white-faced girl in the black hood said to Cordelia. "Want another roll of quarters?"

"What?" Cordelia blinked and looked around. "I'm . . . I'm . . . I was supposed to be going to cheerleading practice." She looked around. It was dark out. When had it gotten dark?

What was that *smell*?

"Well, you ended up here," the girl informed her.

"And I still didn't win?" Cordelia asked her.

The girl shook her head.

"But I don't remember. I . . ." Cordelia fished inside her purse. She had left her home this morning with a hundred dollars. It was time to make another payment to Haley Schricker, the private coach the cheerleading squad had hired.

It was *gone*.

"I spent it all here?" she shrieked. "This is crazy! Is this a dream?"

The girl just looked at her as if she didn't have the slightest idea in the world what Cordelia was talking about.

"It's because I hang out with those people," Cordelia muttered. "Oh, I hate those guys. Something has happened and no one knows it and . . ."

She felt dizzy; saw a blur of silver. She swayed and held on to the wooden post at the corner of the booth.

"I just have to have one of those purple glass baskets," she finished desperately. "I *need* one." She opened her purse and rooted around inside it some more.

"You could go home and get some more money," the girl suggested.

"Yes." Cordelia brightened. "Of course."

The girl leaned forward. "If you hurry, you'll have plenty of time when you get back to win *two* baskets."

"Oh my God," Cordelia said dreamily.

"Do you need a flashlight?" the girl asked. "We have lots of them. They make great bludgeoning tools." She reached in her apron and pulled out a long black flashlight. She extended her arm, offering it to Cordelia.

"No, I'm good," Cordelia told her.

The girl gave the flashlight a friendly little shake. "Because you might want to kill someone, to get that money."

"Oh. You're right. I might." Cordelia held her hand out for the flashlight. "Thanks."

The girl handed her the flashlight. "You might see some-thing you want on the drive home. You might have to break a window, or hit someone really hard."

Cordelia wrinkled her nose. "You're so clever."

The girl extended her arms. "That's why I make the big bucks."

Cordelia stashed the flashlight in her purse.

She gave it a pat and said, "You don't think you could just give me one of those baskets now, do you? I could pay you for it later."

"You *will* pay for it later," the girl assured her. At Cordelia's perplexed expression, she said, "After you win it." She leaned forward and said conspiratorially, "You know, you have poten-tial. If I put a good word in for you, Professor Caligari might hire you. Let you work with me. Would you like that?"

Cordy was thrilled. "Do you make a lot of money?" she asked her.

"I am rewarded," the girl replied. "I've worked for Profes-sor Caligari for practically ever, and I've never regretted it for a minute."

"It sounds tempting," Cordelia said, raising her brows.

"It's meant to," the girl said.

They chuckled together.

"Well, you should leave now," the girl said. "It's nearly eight and we close at ten on the dot. Midnight on the week-ends."

"That's only two hours," Cordelia wailed, turning to leave.

She hesitated, staring down at the baskets. "I really have to have a basket." She gazed at the entire revolving display. "I have to have all of it. Just for me. Everything."

The girl gave her an appraising look. "You're very greedy. That's good."

"Does that mean I *can* have it all?"

The girl smiled. "Of course. If you hurry back in time."

"I will."

Cordelia gave her bag a pat and dashed away.

Then she hurried out off the grounds, got in her car, and peeled out of the parking lot. She raced onto the road to head for home.

All of it was going to be hers. Everything. And while she was at it, maybe she'd snag that knife of Giles's, too. He obviously didn't care very much about it, to leave it lying around like that.

She had to go down Main Street, home of Yasumi Pearl, one of her favorite stores in all of Sunnydale. She slowed, attracted to the beautifully displayed necklaces, bracelets, and earrings. She had been hinting for six months that she wanted the triple-strand choker for her birthday.

But have they bought it? No. How do I know? Because the store only ordered one. And it's still in the window. Right there.

Only, not. Because it was closing time and the clerk, a woman with platinum blond hair wrapped in a chignon, was in the process of taking the triple-strand choker off its field of black velvet at that very exact moment.

Cordelia pulled to the curb, letting the engine idle as she watched.

I want that choker.

The clerk turned away from the window. She was probably carrying the necklace to a safe.

I deserve that choker.

She felt dizzy again. Something bright sliced across her eyelids and she jerked back her head.

She stared.

About a quarter of a block past her car, a streetlight was beaming down on a figure. She squinted. It was one of the clowns from the carnival.

It stared back at her. Then it showed her three glass balls in its gloved hands, and tossed them one, two, three into the air. It began to juggle them, tossing them up, catching them, weaving a comet trail of light as Cordelia watched, her lips parted, her eyes unblinking.

I should have what I want. And I want . . . everything, she thought.

Without moving her head, Cordelia opened the bag and felt inside for the flashlight. There it was.

She laid it across her lap. The clown swayed as it juggled; she could almost hear music as it danced. Calliope music, drifting on the wind.

She got out of the car.

Holding the flashlight down by her side, she shut the door and walked purposefully toward the jewelry store entrance. She put her hand around the knob. It was locked.

So not a problem.

She invented a limp and hobbled to the section of the window where the clerk stood with the choker in her hands. Making a sad face, she gestured to the door.

Closed, the clerk mouthed.

Cordelia could tell she recognized her. She should. She was in Yasumi, like, three times a week, lusting after that choker. It was one of the most expensive items in the store, and that was saying a lot because, hey, matched saltwater pearls the size of marbles were very rare.

And very wonderful.

The calliope music caressed her ears.

With an apologetic smile, she pantomimed having to pee.

The clerk debated.

Cordelia pressed her hands together: *Please?*

The woman relented, walking to the front door *with the choker in her left hand.*

Cordelia tried very hard not to let out a whoop of sheer delight.

She glanced around.

The clown had vanished.

The woman opened the door. She was wearing a black sweater and black pants, and she had on a single teardrop black pearl pendant and matching earrings. Cordelia had to restrain herself from tearing them right off her.

"Thanks," Cordelia said brightly.

"Hi. It's Cordelia, isn't it?"

"Uh-huh." Cordelia gestured to the necklace with her right hand as she hid her flashlight behind her back using her left. "Wow, great timing. I was just about to break your window to steal that."

The woman laughed. "You have such excellent taste," she said. "The bathroom's in the back. I'll show you."

"Thanks," Cordelia said again.

The woman led the way. Cordelia followed. The clerk pulled a ring of keys out of her pants pocket and inserted one of the keys into a door with a placard that said EMPLOYEES ONLY.

"Here we go," the woman said as she pushed the door open.

"Yes," Cordelia said. "Here we go."

She transferred the flashlight to her right hand, raised it over her head, and brought it down hard on the back of the clerk's head. The woman grunted and crumpled to the floor.

Cordelia fell to her knees beside the woman and eased the choker from her limp grasp. Nice sweater. She thought about taking it, but she was in too big a hurry. She put the choker in the pocket of her pants.

She grabbed the clerk by the wrists and dragged her into the bathroom. It was functional and nothing more; you'd think a store that charged the prices Yasumi did would have something a little nicer.

There was a skylight of frosted glass; in the moonlight Cordelia caught sight of a roll of silver duct tape on a white wood shelf above the toilet.

She picked it up. There was a box cutter, too. How handy. She retrieved them, then bent down and wound the tape around the woman's head, completely covering her mouth. Then Cordy wrapped her wrists together, and then her ankles.

She remembered from all those cop shows that she should wipe for prints and keep the evidence.

Then she grabbed up her flashlight and wrapped her sweater around the bathroom doorknob, making sure the door locked after her.

As she began to cross the showroom, she glanced at the assortment of black velvet boxes laid on the counter. The clerk had been putting everything away.

I'll need earrings to go with this, Cordelia thought as she stopped in front of a mirror on the counter to put the choker on. Boxes were piled up all around it. *And rings. And pins. I'll take it all!*

There were footsteps behind her. Catching her breath, she glanced into the mirror. She saw nothing.

Oh my God, is it a vampire?

The footsteps drew closer.

And something growled.

Just before it sprang.

It was nearly eight fifteen at night, and they were making progress.

Willow looked up from the Hans Von Der Sieben website and said to Ms. Calendar, "Here's something. His name was actually Caligarius. He was called 'Hans of the Seven' because it was said that he lured people into his cult with 'pleasures of the flesh.' But in reality he was snaring their souls by getting them to give in to temptation."

"Let me see that," Ms. Calendar said.

The two were sitting in the computer lab, each at a Mac. The smart, beautiful dark-haired woman was dressed in one of the long, earth-tone skirts she favored, plus a silky chocolate-brown sweater. And boots. She had such good clothes.

Because of the job, and the money, and of being grown-up and smart.

After the weirdness at Giles's condo, Willow had not gone home as Giles had told her to. She was terribly shaken by what had happened. Buffy and Giles had practically come to blows. If Willow and the others hadn't been there, she wasn't sure if the situation between Slayer and Watcher might have escalated.

So Willow had walked to the school—Giles lived close by—to see if Ms. Calendar was there. Luckily, she was.

Willow had told her everything—including the fact that she was beginning to suspect that all of them were under a spell.

"I just don't know what my spell is," she said. "I'm so clueless. But I figured *you* would be able to figure it out."

"That's sweet, Willow," Ms. Calendar said kindly. "But you're not clueless. You're very bright."

I'm a nerd, Willow thought. *I would give anything to be like you.*

"Temptation. That's interesting," Ms. Calendar said, coming around Willow's chair to lean over her shoulder.

Willow scrolled down the list, reading aloud. "'The temptations were seven in number: Lust, Envy, Vanity, Greed, Sloth, Anger, and Gluttony.'"

Ms. Calendar nodded, scanning silently as Willow read aloud. "Hmm, mine's gotta be lust," she murmured, then cleared her throat. "Have the others been exhibiting these traits?"

"Well, with Cordelia, it's hard to say because vanity . . . oh, wait." She thought hard. "The Hahn twins went into the fun house and they couldn't stop staring at themselves. That's what Buffy said, and then they thought they were hot."

"Vanity," Ms. Calendar confirmed.

"And Giles keeps losing his temper," Willow continued.

"He does?" she asked. Willow nodded.

"Anger," Ms. Calendar said. "What about Xander?"

"Oh my God, of course! Gluttony." She made a face. "He kept burping and I think he ate some cat food."

Ms. Calendar wrinkled her perfectly shaped nose. "So, that's two for vanity—Cordelia and those twins—and anger, for Rupert."

"Angel's been far more, um, physically affectionate in public," Willow added.

"That would be lust as well." Ms. Calendar tapped the screen. "So that leaves sloth, greed, and envy."

"Mrs. Palmer was robbed for the money in her purse,"

Willow said. "Oh my God, could it be that Carl got infected by greed?"

"It seems possible."

Ms. Calendar even smelled good. Willow flared. Why did Ms. Calendar get everything? And she got nothing?

"What about Buffy?"

"I think anger, too," Willow said. She clenched her jaw. After all her work, Ms. Calendar was going to put the pieces of the puzzle together. She'd solve it and everyone would think she was a genius as usual, and she was not.

I hate her, Willow thought fiercely. She was staring at the face of Hans Von Der Sieben as her fingers clenched like claws. *She has everything, everything, and I—I just—*

"Giles took this other teacher to the carnival," she said. "Really pretty. Very smart. Well employed."

Ms. Calendar's lips parted. "Oh."

"Yeah. I think he really likes her," Willow said savagely. *That'll take her down a notch.*

Ms. Calendar swallowed. She glanced over at the list of temptations. "You know, these are also known as the Seven Deadly Sins," she said slowly. "One doesn't just yield to them, one commits them."

She smiled gently at Willow. "Yours must be envy." She put a hand on Willow's shoulder. "I think you are under a spell."

Willow was startled. "How—how do you know?"

"Because you are the kindest girl I know," Ms. Calendar

said. "You would never intentionally hurt someone. Especially not someone you care about. And you care about me."

Tears welled in Willow's eyes. "But I—I . . . what do you care if I try to hurt you? I'm *nothing*."

"Let me sit down," Ms. Calendar said, putting her hand on Willow's shoulder. "We have a lot of work to do."

The kittens scattered as Giles slammed his front door shut. Sweat rolled down his forehead as he got a bottle of Scotch from the kitchen cabinet and poured himself a drink. His hands were shaking.

He threw it back, drank another.

There was a black book lying open on his table. It was the grimoire he and Ethan had used to summon the demon Eyghon. They had paid a pretty penny for it, and he had carefully packed it away when he'd moved to Sunnydale.

When did I put it there? he wondered. *Has someone been in here?*

He looked around and decided he didn't really care.

He carried the bottle with him, drinking from it as he began to turn the thick vellum pages.

He couldn't raise Eyghon again. The demon inside Angel had killed it. But there were other dark gods he could call. And he would, just to show Buffy who was boss. Take her down a notch. Make her more malleable, compliant.

"Kill her."

"Yes," he hissed. The letters swam before his eyes as fresh

rage overtook him. Why not? She had ruined his life. All that was precious, all that was dear, she sullied it.

He pressed the bottle to his lips and guzzled down the alcohol.

He heard a sound outside his window. Was that a bicycle horn?

As if in fright—or perhaps to be playful—one of the kittens scampered toward him and leaped on top of his shoe.

"Get off me," he said between clenched teeth. *"Or I will kill you, too."*

Everywhere Buffy went, there she was. And that was so very.

Loved the carnival. Loved herself. And why not? What was not to love?

She saw her face in a dozen mirrors as she rode the Octopus and the Tilt-A-Whirl. Another dozen in the totally lame Chamber of Horrors.

Lucky thing I'm so hot, she thought as she strutted down the midway.

Sensing her power, the other fairgoers glanced at her and hurriedly ducked out of her way. *Make way, make way, Slayer coming through!* No one protested when she cut in line to go on a ride. When she reached her hand into a little kid's popcorn bag, he whimpered and ran away, letting her keep it.

Mmm, wow, best popcorn I ever had!

She sauntered up to a game booth. People were throwing

coins onto plates and into cute little baskets made of glass. No one was winning anything.

"I'll show you how it's done," Buffy said to a tall guy wearing a UC Sunnydale sweatshirt. She grabbed a quarter out of his hand.

"Hey!" he said.

She ignored him, zeroed in on a purple glass basket, and flipped the coin into the air.

It turned end over end, catching the light, and then it landed with a satisfying *clink* inside the basket.

The white-faced girl working the stall jerked up her head. She looked from the basket to Buffy to the basket again, and the look of complete and utter shock on her face made Buffy laugh aloud.

"What?" she called to the girl. "Haven't you ever seen anyone win a prize before?"

"You . . ." The girl swiveled her head to the left and the right, as if she was looking for someone to tell her what to do next.

"That's mine," Buffy said, pointing to the basket. "And I want it *now*."

"Technically, it's mine," the guy said, his gaze riveted on the basket. "Since you used my quarter."

The girl hadn't moved. So Buffy hopped the counter and sauntered toward the display. Now the girl looked even more freaked.

"Security," she called, but her voice was barely a whisper.

"I'll just take this," Buffy announced. She bent over and plucked the purple glass basket from the tower of prizes. She smiled at the girl. "You're freaking out because no one's supposed to win, right? Because the game is rigged."

She tossed the basket in the air and caught it. She saw that she had the attention of the other players and hopped onto the wooden barrier.

"They're cheating you, people! And you're just too stupid to see it!"

She threw back her head and laughed at them all as she jumped to the ground. Sawdust flew.

She said to Quarter Guy, *"Mine."* Waved it under his nose. "Want to fight for it?"

He took a step away from her.

"You're smarter than you look," she said. "Guess this is your lucky day after all."

With a harsh laugh, she sauntered off. People made way for her. It was her due.

She reached the end of the line for the Ferris wheel and snickered. Slayers didn't wait in lines. She started to walk around it, planning to cut, when she heard her mother calling her name.

"Buffy?" Joyce *was* standing in line, about six people from the end. That wasn't good enough for the mother of the Slayer.

"Hey," Buffy said offhandedly.

"Hi, honey, I didn't expect to see you here," Joyce went on. "Of course, I don't see much of you these days."

"You've been busy," Buffy said generously. She took her mother's hand. "If you want to ride, you really don't need to wait," she said. "We can just go to the head of the line."

Joyce drew back, firmly planted in line. "Buffy, we need to wait our turn just like everyone else." She cocked her head, a quizzical expression on her face. "Are you feeling all right?"

Buffy shrugged. "Never better."

"Good," Joyce Summers said slowly, still giving Buffy the once-over.

Move along, Mom. Nothing to see here. Nothing going on.

"This place is fun," Joyce continued. "I was sitting at home working on the bills . . . just some paperwork," she amended. "And I heard the calliope music, and I thought about when you were a little girl. We took you to the circus." She looped Buffy's hair behind her ear. "We took you everywhere." Her voice grew wistful. "There was more money then. I didn't know how good I had it."

She cleared her throat. "Anyway, I decided to come to the carnival." She wrinkled her nose and added conspiratorially, "I had my palm read in the fortune-teller's tent."

That piqued Buffy's interest. As she rearranged her hair from around her ear, she asked, "What was your fortune?"

Joyce laughed softly. "Oh, the usual false optimism they dish out at things like that. Fame, fortune, love." She made a face. "I must have a sign on my forehead that says 'Needs encouragement.' I envy people who can make themselves believe in horoscopes and crystal balls."

"Well, some people think they're real," Buffy ventured. "The horoscopes and crystal balls."

"That's what I mean. I guess I'm just too grounded in the real world to believe in the occult." Buffy could hear the strain in her voice. "It would be so nice not to be so well-informed."

"We can make our own luck," Buffy insisted. "Or at least, *I* can."

"That's my girl," Joyce said warmly.

The line moved quickly—lucky thing, or Buffy would have been tempted to persuade Joyce to change her mind about cutting—and soon they were in one of the little swinging cars, which were painted black. They looked like black coffins, to Buffy's way of thinking. But then, her mind ran to things like coffins. And falling to her death from the top of the Ferris wheel.

"Ours is number seven," Buffy told her mom as they zoomed backward on the exterior of the massive wheel. Chilly night wind blew in their hair.

"How lucky," Joyce teased, sitting back.

Drunk, in a full fury, Giles had stripped down to his pants. He was bare-chested and barefoot, and he meant business.

Teach her a lesson. Make her sorry. Make them all sorry. Make them pay.

He was sweating and dizzy, and so drunk he could barely think straight. But he knew what to do.

Surrounded by candles, Giles swayed in the center of

the pentagram he had drawn on his carpet with melted wax and blood. He had retraced the pentagram on his chest, with a knife. The letters of the profane name of Astorrith formed from the cuts, and threw glowing black light against the walls of his condo.

Shadows moved over the ancient maps and framed photographs of home, hissing and whispering. The minions of Astorrith had been awakened.

Blood dripped from Giles's hands; he had performed the sacrifices and uttered The Names That Must Not Be Spoken, thrice, thrice, thrice.

"Baal! Cthulhu! Jezebel! Wake your brother Astorrith! Bid him come! I command thee!"

Lightning flashed across the front window, blacked out in part by a shape—a figure wearing a small pointed hat. Giles figured it was a minion, stepping through the veil. A sign that his spell was working.

That meant that the dark god would come to him directly. The time was at hand.

He raised his arms and threw back his head.

"Astorrith, Dark One! Lord of Revenge and Retribution! I have been wronged and I have suffered! I have been insulted and humiliated! See the slights heaped upon thy acolyte and wreak havoc on my enemies! Vanquish all who plague me!"

He bent down—it was a long, shaky road—and plucked up the Blade of Astorrith in his right hand and his grimoire in the other. He began to read.

"*Ta-mir-o,*" he began. "*Dark God of Shadows and Tumult, I summon thee! From the depths of confusion and tumult, rise up! Bring the Wild Ones with you and smite my blood enemy, Buffy Anne Summers! Wreak havoc on her land! Fill her days with storms and monsters!*

"*It is Buffy the Vampire Slayer of whom I speak! Bring doom upon her! Make her long for her own death! Destroy all that makes her smile!*"

He sliced the air with the blade. The veil of reality was diced into chunks, like jagged pieces of a jigsaw puzzle. The edges of the world inside his condo began to bleed, and the first chunk slammed against the floor two yards away from Giles's bare feet.

The floor buckled beneath the oppressive weight. Giles stayed inside the pentagram, riding it like a surfboard as one half of the floor splintered, while the other rippled and broke apart.

The walls cracked like frozen glass dropped into boiling water.

The plumbing burst. Water geysered upward.

The stairs pulled away from the loft. The ceiling bowed downward.

"*Torment her!*" Giles yelled, dropping to his knees.

"Isn't this a lovely view?" Joyce asked Buffy as they dangled at the top of the Ferris wheel.

All of Sunnydale was spread below them. Buffy felt a

fierce rush of pride. All those lights, those toy-looking houses, those antlike people. She protected them all, night after night. How many would have died by now, if not for her?

"It's like Paris," Joyce said dreamily. "There's a Ferris wheel near the Eiffel Tower."

"You've been to Paris?" Buffy asked, surprised. She hadn't known that.

Joyce leaned Buffy's head against her shoulder and stroked her hair, the way she had done when Buffy was a little girl.

"No, but I would like to. I wonder if I'll ever get to. But you . . . you have your whole life ahead of you, Buffy. You're so young." She sighed. "I envy you."

"Well, about that," Buffy said. "I've decided to move out."

Joyce's hand stopped in midstroke. "What?"

"Yeah. Listen, I'm . . . really strong and I can . . . ah, become a boxer. Or something like that. Get back into my skating." She smiled at her mother. "I'm ready to live on my own."

Joyce lowered her chin and peered up through her lashes— mom face, the face of dawning suspicion. "When you woke me up in the kitchen, did you look at my papers?"

"Your bills," Buffy confirmed. "Yes, I did. Without me around—"

"Oh, Buffy." Joyce put her arms around her daughter and held her closer. "You are so wonderful. But I'll take care of you, sweetie. You don't need to worry."

"Mom, I'm not worried." Buffy's words were muffled against her mother's shoulder.

"I'm so proud of you," Joyce continued.

Well, of course you are, the Slayer thought smugly. *Isn't everybody?*

"You're such a dear." She jerked. "Did someone just take our picture? Oh, I feel a little dizzy."

"Are you all right, Mom?" Buffy asked, turning her head to look at her.

"Yes. I'm fine. I'm just so . . . relaxed." She leaned her head back. "It's nice to just sit and do nothing." She chuckled. "I feel so lazy."

That was when the wind began to blow.

Xander began to blow.

He was sick, sick to death, and that was before he had eaten the candied apple and the four hot dogs.

He didn't remember how he'd dragged himself to the carnival. Last thing he could remember, Giles had dropped him off at the lovely Harris estate, where his parents were "watching TV," which was what they called drinking and arguing.

Retreating from the combat zone, he had hunkered down in the basement, hurling, and figured he would have to skip tonight's further exciting adventures at the carnival.

But he was back, and sicker than sick, staggering down the midway.

And clowns were following him.

An entire pack of them, in your typical clown garb with your typical clown accessories—a horn with a big rubber ball on the business end, a spray bottle, and a terrifying air of menace.

He didn't like those guys.

Why did I eat that apple? Giles told us not to eat anything here. I couldn't stop myself. It . . . called my name. And I think I mean that literally.

And he remembered now that the night before, he *had* eaten some cookies. About seven of them. He couldn't stop.

I didn't ever remember eating them. And the cat food . . . and all the Cheez Doodles I had stashed in my nightstand . . . and the stale Oreos I found in my backpack. . . . I have eaten so much crap in the last twenty-four hours and I can't stop myself. I want more.

He doubled over, clutching his stomach.

Overhead, thunder rumbled. A wind began to blow.

"Buffy," he whispered. "Someone. Help."

He looked back.

One, two, three, four clowns. They strolled toward him with their frozen, terrifying smiles and their flappy feet and their big, gloved hands.

And everything in him told him to keep the hell away from them.

But he was fading. He could hardly walk.

The wind picked up.

Okay, still in the mood for love . . . so where is she?

Angel paced around the gravestones and headstones, the

monuments and the tombs of Blessed Memories, listening to the calliope as fierce wind whipped at his coat. With a shriek, it snatched the note he was carrying and skipped it away like a stone on a river. The note was from Buffy, on girlie paper decorated with cows; he had found it taped to his door and all it had said was "Meet me near du Lac. B." He recognized her girlish handwriting, the *B* finished with a little swirl.

But Buffy was nowhere to be seen. Maybe he had misunderstood. He had figured this rendezvous was to continue where they had left off—though of course, he would have preferred it to be continued in his apartment. Or someplace equally nice and cozy.

Of course, the Slayer got detained on business more often than not.

The haunting notes of the calliope whispered on the wind. Sweet and tantalizing . . . like Buffy.

What was I thinking, denying myself the pleasure of being with her?

It was great to feel lusty and vigorous. He felt like a man again, not a shadow. Not someone set apart—a vampire, yet more than a vampire. And yet, not just a man, either.

The things I can do for her, with her. . . .

Whoever said that the blood was the life, was wrong. It was the flesh.

Maybe she's at the carnival.

He turned around and began walking in the direction of

the calliope's sound. Giles's condo was nearby. Maybe he'd stop in, see if he had seen Buffy.

Then something changed.

The wind howled, hard; it picked up and became a gale, ripping leaves right off the trees. Yanking branches and flinging them into the air.

Dirt and pebbles pelted Angel as he lowered his head and walked into the wind. It was a full-on storm such as he had never seen in southern California unless . . .

Unless something is very wrong.

His coat streamed behind him like wings as he pushed forward. The gale force pushed back at him.

Then from out of the maelstrom, something padded toward him. He smelled it rather than heard it—it reeked of the sulfurs of hell, and of death and decomposition.

It smelled of evil.

And it had no heartbeat.

Squinting, Angel ducked behind a headstone and braced himself to meet it.

CHAPTER NINE

Cordelia's head was throbbing.

She moaned.

Or tried to.

As she slowly came to, she realized that there was tape across her mouth. And her hands were tied behind her back.

The moon had moved, but enough light still streamed through the skylight of the jewelry store bathroom for her to realize the horrible truth: Someone had attacked her, tied her up, and dragged her in there, placing her next to the clerk she herself had attacked, tied up, and dragged in there.

She pushed her chin against her chest, trying to feel the choker around her neck.

Nada.

I've been robbed, she thought, panicking. *Someone took my choker!*

Ignoring for the time being that she had also stolen the choker, Cordelia zoomed into high anxiety. Her cat allergy made her nose stuffy, and it was very hard to breathe.

Oh my God, what if they took my watch, too?

She blinked and stared hard at the salesclerk. The woman's head was bent to the side, revealing her pearl earring.

She calmed down a little.

At least I can still have the earrings, she consoled herself. *Maybe she's still got on her pendant, too.*

Then she frowned as she listened hard to what sounded like a terrible wailing, or shrieking, or . . .

It's wind, she realized. *Are we having, like, a tornado?*

Angel peered above the shield of the headstone.

A pack of things crab-walked toward him, scrabbling over the tree roots, headstones, bushes. They flowed like mercury, then snapped back into six compact forms that resembled mastiff-size dogs. Their bodies were covered with dozens of bloodshot eyes surrounded by fangs that blinked and snapped.

Demonic minions.

Then, of all things, two clowns appeared, whooping and dancing in their mufti attire. One carried a seltzer bottle, which it aimed at one of the minions. The creature shrieked, leaping straight up into the air, and erupted into flames.

The clowns doubled over with laughter. Sniggering, the one with the bottle aimed it at another minion, but its aim went wild and the spray hit a tree. The bark ignited.

The other clown danced a little jig, and then the two slammed their huge bottoms together.

They hadn't noticed Angel. Taking advantage of their distraction, he clambered on top of the du Lac crypt and flattened himself against the roof. Below him, a minion sniffed eagerly, homing in on a new and different scent.

The pack moved on, and the clowns with it.

That was close, Angel thought.

Then the roof of the crypt began to rumble, a subsonic vibration Angel felt through his whole body. The trees trembled, shaking off leaves that the wind whisked away.

He looked down the hill as the shaking grew worse. There. In the vicinity of Giles's condo complex, a shadowy figure emerged from the building and rose into the sky like someone hunched over, then straightening up. A massive, dark tube shape, it towered maybe fifty feet into the air. The head was elongated and covered with horns. Its long neck sat on shoulders that were hooked, and its arms were covered with talons. The rest of the body was snakelike, with tentacles undulating from its long, cylindrical body.

Calliope music and battering winds combined with screams of terror from the humans below as the creature swayed above them.

One of the tentacles unfurled and snapped downward, like the tongue of a frog. When it snapped back,
a struggling human being was caught in its grip. The
tentacle brought the writhing victim toward the mouth,
which opened wide to reveal a huge bonfire and smoking,
charred teeth.

The human was tossed in.

The mouth closed.

Smoke emanated from the horns on its head.

It's Astorrith, Angel realized. He had never seen the
demon before, but Darla, his sire, had. She had described him
as a tentacled creature wearing a horned hood . . . fearful to
behold, impossible to defeat.

"If you ever see him, Angelus, you must run," she had told
him, as together they dined on a fat Spanish grandee. "Never
go up against him. It would be insane. And fatal."

Another tentacle reached down. As it moved, the sky
around it . . . cracked. Pieces of the ebony sky flared, and then
became darker still. It was the weirdest thing Angel had ever
seen; he had read about black holes and wondered if that was
what the dark places were.

Whipsaw fast, the tentacle wrapped around another human
and hoisted it into the air.

He could hear Darla whispering, *"Don't do it."*

Never one to listen, Angel leaped off the tomb and ran
toward the creature as fast as he could.

• • •

As the Ferris wheel spun crazily in the windstorm, Buffy held on to her mother and stared wide-eyed at the monster looming above Sunnydale. It had appeared out of nowhere, along with the wind. And it was killing people.

What is that thing?

Then the wheel zoomed downward; the ground flew up to meet them, and Buffy curled herself protectively around Joyce.

"Brace yourself!" she cried to her mother.

Joyce screamed and clung to her. Then their car zinged back up and around. Buffy anchored herself with one hand wrapped around the metal restraining bar across their laps as she held on tightly to her mom.

They reached the top again and began to bullet back down. As they sailed down, Buffy looked over the side of the car.

"Oh my God, Xander is down there!"

He was lying flat on his back on the ground next to Buffy and Angel's make-out bushes. The girl from the coin toss was bending over him, and four clowns bent over to grab his arms and legs.

It was Slayer time. But what to do? Abandon her mother on the Ferris wheel or let the clowns get Xander?

Mom, Xander, Mom, Xander.

But there was no choice, really, and Xander would understand. Plus, maybe the clowns were going to help him.

And if you believe that, you deserve no new suede boots, she told herself.

She kept hold of Joyce as the Ferris wheel jittered and scraped, not yet free of its moorings but threatening to be. The vibration set her teeth on edge.

All she could think of to do was wait until their car came unbolted, and then wrap herself around her mother like a human escape pod and eject from the car.

That might kill us both, she thought, but she wasn't sure what else to do.

She got ready, and said, "Mom, listen. Here's the plan. When I say go, get ready to jump."

"What?" Joyce cried.

"Yes, on the count of one. Two. Thr—"

But at the last possible moment—the double *e*'s—Buffy spotted a red-painted hand brake beside the girders of the supporting base. It was about two feet long and clearly marked: PULL IN CASE OF EMERGENCY. An arrow pointed in the same direction the wheel was spinning.

Just as they were about to swoop past it, Buffy reached out and grabbed it, preparing herself to lose an arm as she yanked the brake hard . . .

. . . and ripped the brake free.

"Bad design," she muttered, scowling at the red handle in her grip.

But it got the job done: The brake mechanism had engaged, and there was a noticeable drag on the wheel's momentum. It was stopping. Buffy felt confident she could climb down instead of jumping.

And so could her mother.

"Mom," she said, prying Joyce off her.

Her mom's eyes were as big as, well, Ferris wheels.

"Oh my God, Buffy, are you all right?"

"Of course I am." Buffy was mildly piqued. "After all, I'm . . . who I am." She had to remember that her secret was still a secret. "Mom, we need to get down. We're only about twenty feet above the ground." She pointed over the side of the Ferris wheel. "Can you climb that?"

"I . . . I think so," Joyce said.

"Good. Let's go."

Buffy raised one leg out of the car and put her foot firmly on the thick metal supports that extended from the wheel. The wheel groaned. The car swung wildly.

As she reached for her mother's hand, she glanced down at Xander. He was on his back, flailing his arms and legs like a tipped-over insect, trying to fight off the clowns. But he wasn't going to win.

"Mom," she said. "You need to keep climbing. Do it slowly. I have to go help Xander."

"Buffy!" her mother cried, her eyes widening with fright as she half-stood in the rocking car. Then she took another deep breath and nodded. "I'm okay. Go."

It was quicker to cling to the support and move hand over hand, so the Slayer did so. Once her feet found purchase on the elaborate structure of the wheel proper, she worked her way in toward the center, and then shimmied down until she found another support. It was like playing a life-size version of Chutes and Ladders.

Then she dropped the rest of the way. The wind nearly picked her off her feet; she stood with her face into it to keep her hair out of her face as she gazed up at her mother. Joyce was methodically inching toward the superstructure by the trail Buffy had blazed.

Satisfied that her mother was safe . . . or rather, safe enough, at least for the moment, Buffy ran to rescue Xander.

"It's her!" the white-faced girl shouted as Buffy raced for them.

Alerted, the clowns straightened and assumed battle stance.

Pow! Buffy's foot connected with the chin of Clown number one, the dude with the Rasta braids, and it staggered away from Xander.

A well-aimed punch to Clown number two's jaw, and he was out of commission too.

The other two backed away.

Then the Goth girl attacked, fingers forming claws, and Buffy smashed her fist into her face and . . . *whoa* . . . her skin split apart, revealing purple, leathery stuff beneath.

Demon, Buffy translated.

A huge roar rent the air and a tentacle slammed down on top of the demon girl, crushing her.

Bigger demon, Buffy thought as she threw herself out of the way.

The retreating clowns scattered into the wild, panicking crowds.

"Xander," she said, falling to her knees beside him. "Are you okay?"

"That's a negative," he gasped as she raised his head. His eyes were puffy and half-shut. His face was sheened with sweat. "Buffy, I'm so sick."

"It'll be okay. I'll make it all better," she promised him.

She hoisted Xander over her shoulder firefighter-style. Last time she had done this, she was in the fun zone with the Hahns. So not having fun now, either.

The Ferris wheel creaked and groaned but did not move. Most of the people in the remaining cars were following Joyce's example and shimmying down the superstructure. Buffy watched a moment longer, her gaze traveling to see if anyone was badly hurt, or somehow incapable of getting down under their own steam. So far so good.

But there were three guys who were just sitting crammed together in one little car, smiling kind of like they weren't all there. They weren't lifting a finger to save themselves.

"Hey!" Buffy shouted, gesticulating wildly with her left hand as she held on to Xander with the other. "Move it *now*!"

The one in the middle—a guy wearing a UC Sunnydale baseball cap—laughed and waved at her. The other two sat rocking back and forth.

"Hey!" she cried. "You're in danger!"

The one who waved seemed to sort of jerk. He looked around, then down, then shook the guy to his right. He activated too. Then number three got with the program.

"Climb down!" Buffy bellowed.

She didn't know if they could hear her, but they did start evacuation procedures.

Weirdos.

Buffy didn't have time to wonder what was wrong with them; her mom had maneuvered her way about ninety percent of the way down when she let go.

"Mom!" Buffy screamed, as her mother plummeted—

—right into the make-out bushes, which cushioned her fall.

Still carrying Xander, Buffy ran to her. Joyce was lying flat on her back on a crisscross of leafy branches; she pushed herself off the canopy of bushes and Buffy spotted her gymnastics-style, with a firm arm absorbing some of her momentum as she landed on the ground.

"Mom, are you okay?" Buffy demanded.

"Buffy, are *you* all right?" Joyce replied, which was a mom's way of saying yes. She looked at her daughter carrying Xander, who was not small, and said, "You must be having an adrenaline rush." She looked around. "We need to get out of here."

"With you on that," Buffy told her, checking to make sure she had a good grip on Xander as mother and daughter took off.

"There she is!" someone shouted.

Buffy glanced over her shoulder to see . . .

. . . *What the heck?*

Several of the freaks from the freak show were barreling after her. Also, a pack of demons that bore no resemblance to humans—gelatinous mounds—and a leathery, lizardlike thing. They all came after the Summers women as they ran toward the exit. Weirdest thing, though: The regular inhabitants of Sunnydale—the fairgoers—were running toward *them*, *not* toward the exit. Faces rigid with terror, fleeing from the enormous tentacled demon, they were flooding the carnival as if they were drowning and it was their only lifeboat.

"People! No!" Buffy shouted, whirling around in a circle. She jabbed fingers at the bad guys closing in in hot pursuit. "Wicked evil that way too! Come with me!"

No one listened. No one seemed to care demons and monsters were alive and among them.

Buffy grabbed her mother's hand as they made for the exit.

"We're almost there," Buffy assured her. "You're safe with me, Mom. Right, Xander?"

There was no answer.

"Xander?" Buffy tried again.

"Oh my God," her mother panted as she loped beside the Slayer. "Buffy, I think Xander's *dead*."

Running, Angel could see the bright lights of the Ferris wheel as antlike people climbed down from it. Though it appeared that they were all going to be okay, the scene reminded him of the sinking *Titanic*, how the lights had blazed, then winked out in succession as they hit the frigid water.

He balled his fists and clenched his jaw. If Buffy was at the carnival . . .

Angel was about to enter the other side of the forest when a figure rocketed out of the shadows. He saw Angel and headed right for him.

He was a young guy, about eighteen, dressed in dark cargo pants and a loosely knitted sweater that reminded Angel of chain mail. Angel couldn't place him, but there was something about him that was familiar.

He was carrying something against his chest, and moonlight refracted off of it.

A hundred feet above them both, the demon Astorrith roared. Flames shot from its mouth. And on the ground, the guy put on an impressive burst of speed as he ran straight toward Angel.

Angel met him halfway. He slammed against Angel's chest with something hard, and for a moment Angel thought he had been staked.

Then the guy collapsed, leaving a glass sphere in Angel's grasp.

It looked like a crystal ball.

From the ground the guy shot out a hand and yelled, "Sanctuary!"

• • •

Ethan Rayne tried very hard to at least appear contrite as Professor Caligari paced the floor in front of his fantastically infernal calliope. He kept his calm and jerked on the chain of his "pet," Le Malfaiteur, who was growling.

The entire wagon was rocking back and forth in the rough, wild wind, and Ethan half-expected it to rise up into the sky like Dorothy's house in *The Wizard of Oz*.

"I said to terrorize Sunnydale, not destroy it!" the good professor sputtered.

Ethan had to bite his cheek to keep from laughing.

"I assure you, I didn't do this," he told the man . . . if man he was. Ethan sincerely doubted that Caligari had ever been human.

True, Ethan hadn't done it. However, he *had* instructed one of Caligari's clowns to place Ripper's grimoire out where he would find it.

He had also investigated the break-in at the jewelry store a few short blocks away because he recognized a certain car parked at the curb from his Halloween escapade here in Sunnydale.

As he'd strolled over, Le Malfaiteur had gotten loose and nearly killed that adorable girl, Cordelia Chase. While subduing the enchanted warlock, Ethan had realized she'd been about to rob the store because she was under the influence of the carnival.

He still didn't know why he had knocked her out and tied her up after he stopped Le Malfaiteur from mauling her to death. Obviously to give her a cover story that would exonerate her from her attempted robbery. But why? Because she was an attractive bird? What had caused him such an impetuous moment of Good Samaritanism, if he could be so bold as to coin a phrase?

Ethan was nothing if not bold. But one could never accuse him of being a Good Samaritan.

Then maybe I did it to mix it up, he thought. *After all, I did leave her there to potentially die. Tied up and helpless, with an enormous demon stomping about the place. . . . And I left a note for Angel to look for Buffy in a graveyard. Keep the lad busy and out of the way . . .*

He felt better about his predilection for evil. He would hate to think that he was getting soft in his old age—especially where friends of the Slayer were concerned.

Professor Caligari, of course, was completely unaware of Ethan's internal monologue. He was stomping about . . . and was that *smoke* rising from his skin?

"Sunnydale is running amok!" Professor Caligari raved.

Then let's break out the cigarettes, Ethan thought, watching a curl of smoke lift from the man's scalp. But he said mildly, "At the risk of sounding accusatory, you weren't terribly specific about what degree of terror and mayhem you wanted. Or what sort, either."

"On the streets, friend. The clowns marauding, causing mischief, that sort of thing," Professor Caligari said, tapping his forehead with his finger, as if to indicate that Ethan was remarkably thick.

And as he bellowed and gesticulated, the strangest thing happened: The dead center of the calliope began to glow with a faint green, pulsating light. Ethan watched it out of the corner of his eye because he wasn't certain Caligari was aware that Ethan could see it.

It beat like a heart. Surreptitiously Ethan laid his hand over his own heart, to see if the rhythms matched. They didn't. The one in the calliope was much, much slower.

"Do you at least know who—or what—that demon is?" Professor Caligari demanded. Ethan figured that any second now, Caligari's minions would be pounding on the door and demanding to be let in.

Ah, there they were now. Sounded as if they had a battering ram.

Caligari swore in a language Ethan didn't know and threw open the door.

A clown burst inside, carrying a young white-faced girl, whose human skin actually covered just the left half of her face. The other flat ovoid eye was smoking.

Fascinating.

"Tessa!" Professor Caligari cried. "That thing killed her!" He burst into a rage, stomping, whirling around. Little flares of flames flickered over his face and scalp.

Le Malfaiteur rose and stretched.

Ethan gestured. "Can't you put her in that glass coffin thingy?"

"It's only for humans," Caligari said, his voice laden with

sorrow. "She's been with me for centuries. Damn it."

The clown tenderly picked up Tessa and went back outside. Pushed by the wind, the door smacked back open. An uprooted oleander bush tumbled past. It was followed by several vampires.

And I was told they couldn't fly, Ethan thought merrily, wondering what precisely they were doing there.

Pulling on Le Malfaiteur's chain, he crossed to the space and peered out.

"I'll go see what I can do about the demon," he said. "But that means my price will go up."

The professor narrowed his eyes. "You *did* do this," he said. "You're shaking me down!"

He's smarter than he looks, Ethan thought, for of course that had been his plan. One of several Ethan had set in motion. The clowns weren't the only ones who could juggle several things at once.

"You wound me, Professor Caligari," he said mournfully. "Come, Malfaiteur."

Sorcerer and enchanted warlock stepped into the storm.

"Where are you going?" Professor Caligari shouted after the pair.

To see a man about a demon, Ethan thought.

Angel stood in front of the refugee from the carnival. His name was Vaclav, and he was trembling with terror. Apparently the sight of Astorrith and the death of his girlfriend had pushed him over the edge. He told Angel that he'd been the one to eavesdrop on the Scoobies at the freak-show exit, and he had been searching for them ever since. But when Astorrith had approached, he had run as far away from the carnival as he could, with no thought of where he was going.

"It was destiny that brought me to you," he told Angel, in a thick Eastern European accent.

Angel wasn't so sure.

Now the two surveyed the wreckage that had once been Giles's condo complex. Fires raged; a hydrant shot water straight into the air. A woman with blood in her blond hair lurched toward them, waving her arms. Dogs barked.

Angel headed for Giles's condo.

On the second story of what had been the Watcher's home, a purple-haired clown was dancing in the firelight. It was rooting through a pile of notebooks—the Watcher journals, Angel realized.

Getting information on the Slayer?

Embers dervished around the clown, igniting its clothing until the wind extinguished it again. It looked as though it were dressed in old-fashioned flash paper, the kind Victorian magicians used to make dramatic mini-explosions during their tricks.

"Please, we must run," Vaclav begged. "I have Madame Lazabra's crystal ball. I stole it. If they find it on me, my punishment will be hideous."

Angel patted his coat pocket. "*I* have her crystal ball," he reminded him. "And they *won't* find it on me."

As if on cue, the clown stopped dancing and stared down at the pair. Then it opened its mouth, threw back its head, and let out an ungodly shriek.

"No," Vaclav moaned, whipping Angel around.

Five more clowns faced them, spreading out. Then one flickered out of sight. It reappeared. Then another.

Then the one that had stood on the second story of the condo tapped Angel on the shoulder and said, "Boo!"

Angel didn't hesitate. He went into heavy action mode, hitting and kicking, leaping, smashing. He fanned in a circle and took on all comers, while Vaclav raced away, shrieking, without trying to help.

The clowns ringed around Angel, tiptoeing, prancing, giggling, and laughing. One raised a seltzer bottle and aimed it at Angel's face; he shielded his eyes with his hands. Acid hit his palms and he grunted from the searing pain as the skin dissolved.

Ignoring his wounds, he rushed forward toward his attacker, catching it by surprise. He kept running, knocking it over, and took off after Vaclav.

Down the block around the corner and across—

—*Giles?*

The half-naked, soot-drenched librarian was staggering across the street, waving a Scotch bottle at the cars squealing their brakes to avoid hitting him. He was carrying a large book, which the wind kept trying to yank away from him.

Angel easily caught up with him, pushing him out of the way of an oncoming car and to the curb. Giles fell into the gutter on his knees. He reeked of alcohol.

"Astorrith," Giles slurred, "wrath upon my enemies."

"*You* summoned Astorrith?" Angel asked incredulously.

Giles's eyelids fluttered. "Spoiled girl."

Angel pulled him to his feet. "Come on," he said. "We have to find Buffy."

Giles wagged his head from side to side. "*Kill* Buffy." He narrowed his eyes. "Angel," he slurred. "Kill you, too."

With the clumsiness of a drunk, he tried to hit Angel with his bottle. He missed, and his book tumbled from his grasp.

Angel caught it. It was a grimoire. With his free hand, he grabbed the bottle from Giles and threw it down. It crashed against the sidewalk.

"Come on," he ordered Giles.

"Not going wiz you," Giles informed him petulantly.

"Yes. You are." Angel made a fist and hit Giles squarely on the jaw.

As he anticipated, Giles's knees buckled. Angel hoisted Giles over his shoulders and took off.

Angel found Vaclav two blocks away, flagging down an olive green truck. "USMC" was painted in black on the passenger-side door. United States Marine Corps.

And none other than Claire Nierman was driving.

Angel raced toward the truck. Vaclav looked over his

shoulder, and he brightened when he saw Angel.

"Oh my God!" Claire cried. "This is so crazy!"

"Yeah. It is," Angel replied.

"I'm sorry I deserted you," Vaclav said.

"It's okay," Angel told him. He looked back expectantly at Claire. "We need to get out of here," Angel told her.

"Of course," she said. She ticked an uneasy gaze toward Vaclav and Giles. "Who are these guys?"

Angel regarded Vaclav. "I'm not sure about him, but this one's a friend."

"I am seeking sanctuary. I . . . I know things," Vaclav said. He looked anxiously at Angel as though he were begging him not to say anything to betray him.

Angel said, "Hold on." He carried Giles around to the truck bed and carefully laid him down. Giles had cut sigils and signs into his own chest. Was he drunk *and* possessed?

Angel lingered a moment, then hurried back to the passenger door while Vaclav waited for him. Angel nodded at him, then at Claire, and said, "Get inside."

"Perhaps I should ride in the back with . . . that man," Vaclav said.

"I'm not sure about his condition," Angel said. "Better stay in here with us."

Claire frowned. "I thought you said he was a friend."

Angel nodded. "He is."

When he said nothing further, Claire shrugged and said to Vaclav, "Come in and scoot over. Make room."

There were only two seats, so Vaclav wedged himself between them, half-squatting and half-kneeling, as Angel got in and slammed the door.

Claire peeled out.

"What the hell is going on?" she said.

"End of days," Angel tried, "or something close." He tried to think of where to go. Buffy's?

Vaclav said, "Please, I beg of you. Get us as far away from here as you can." He glanced at the book on Angel's lap. "A grimoire? Are you a sorcerer?"

Angel didn't reply.

"I'll take you three to headquarters," Claire suggested. "We've got a detail going out after that thing. My boss has some special weapons." She looked excited. "Real experimental stuff."

Wait a minute, Angel thought. *She said she was here on R&R.*

And she's not freaked out enough, considering what's going on. . . . And people in the armed services don't refer to their commanding officers as their "bosses."

"Headquarters," Angel said nonchalantly. "Do you mean the Armory?"

"No," she said, after a beat. "I mean, yes."

Claire took her right hand off the wheel and reached down to her left side. She came back up with a wicked-looking pistol and pressed it against Vaclav's temple.

"Let me guess," Angel said. "You're not with the military."

"No, sir." She smiled grimly at him. Then to Vaclav, "We

saw you give the crystal ball to Angel," she continued. "You hand it over, Angel, or I'll blow his brains out."

She knows who I am. That whole vampire attack in the alley was a setup.

"She's with the professor," Vaclav said, panicking.

"No, I'm not. Give it to me, Angel," Claire said firmly.

"Please," Vaclav rasped. Angel could smell the fear on him, hear his fluttering heartbeat.

"Okay," Angel said.

He reached in his pocket and pulled out the crystal ball. He held it up where she could see it.

Claire's pupils dilated. She smiled.

Angel threw it at her. Not as hard as he could—there was no sense in killing her—but it clocked her. As she slumped forward, Angel pushed her against the side of the cab. Then he grabbed the wheel and steered while Vaclav bent over and retrieved the crystal ball from the floor.

"I can't believe you did that!"

Angel glanced from the road to the ball. It was intact. Inside, dozens of faces writhed and stretched—some of whom he recognized—the principal of Buffy's school, the waitress at the Lucky Pint. They were all in terrible agony.

Angel knew what was going on: They had been trapped in a hell dimension, where they were being tortured. The ball was a window to their suffering.

The truck swerved to the left as a blast of wind buffeted it. Angel tried to straighten it out.

"Look out!" Vaclav shouted.

The wind hit it from the other direction. The truck jumped onto a curb and roared up the grassy knoll directly in front of Buffy's school.

His right hand on the wheel, Angel knocked Claire's foot off the gas pedal. Then he pushed down on the brake pedal.

The truck lurched to a stop and slid back down the hill.

Lights were on in the school's main building. Angel hoped that meant someone was there.

The wind blew hard against the driver's-side door as Angel forced it open. He grabbed the unconscious Claire to keep her from falling out.

Vaclav clutched the crystal ball and the grimoire.

Angel carried Claire over one shoulder, then laid her down on the dewy grass while he collected Giles. The wind slapped his face and clawed at his coat.

In the back of the truck Buffy's Watcher was coming to, raising himself up on his elbows and groaning. The sound was lost in the wind, but Angel could hear it.

"Giles, can you walk?" Angel asked him.

"How dare you!" Giles sputtered, his head lolling. "You kidnapped me!"

Angel picked Giles up by his shoulders and put him on his feet. Giles could barely stand.

Then Angel flung Claire over his shoulder and half-dragged, half-carried Giles toward the front door, where Vaclav stood diffidently by.

Vaclav said, "Is this sanctuary?"

"For no one else but you," Angel said, "to hear Buffy tell it."

He pushed on the door—it whipped open hard, propelled by the wind—and pulled Vaclav inside.

"Angel!" It was Willow, followed close behind by Ms. Calendar.

"Rupert!" she cried.

"Damn you," Giles bit off. "All of you."

Ms. Calendar drew back. Then she said, "He must be under the influence of an anger spell. Like you said, Willow."

"Where's Buffy?" Willow said anxiously. "And Xander and . . ." She gestured to Vaclav. "Hey, that's the guy from the fortune-teller's."

"I am Vaclav," he said. "I seek sanctuary."

"You can have it, if you help us," Angel said.

"Who's that woman?" Ms. Calendar asked Angel.

"Claire Nierman. Working for someone," he replied. "She said she was military, but she's not."

Ms. Calendar paled. "If the military ever heard about the Slayer, then . . ."

She trailed off as Angel gazed at her. "You have the most beautiful voice," he said. "You're incredible. Has anyone told you what pretty hair you have?"

"Lust spell, definitely," Ms. Calendar murmured.

"And your eyes . . . they're like doe eyes." Angel was mesmerized.

"Yes, well, gaze on them quickly. Astorrith will rip them from their sockets," Giles proclaimed.

"Oh my God, Giles," Willow blurted. "That's awful!"

"They're bewitched," Vaclav told Willow. "It's the carnival. My master tempts mortals to weakness, and then he tears their souls from them! He destroyed the woman I love!"

"We were right," Ms. Calendar said, nodding at Willow. She said to Vaclav, "It's okay. We've created a spell that restores victims to their original states."

"Yes," Willow said. "I'm no longer envious." She flushed. "Well, no longer acting on my envy. It's good and suppressed."

"We'll do the same for you and Giles," Ms. Calendar told Angel. "Let's get to it, shall we?"

"I'm sorry about your woman," Willow told Vaclav as they began to walk. "Maybe we can help with that, too."

"I'm not going anywhere with you lot," Giles proclaimed, crossing his arms over his chest.

"I stole this," Vaclav said, holding out the crystal ball.

"An Orb of Thesulah?" Ms. Calendar asked, growing pale.

Angel had no idea what she was talking about. He didn't care. Her mouth was incredible.

"It's the Gypsy's crystal ball," Willow filled in. She turned to Vaclav. "Tell us what to do with it."

"I will," he promised her.

"That's my grimoire!" Giles said, lurching at Vaclav. "You stole my book!"

Ms. Calendar seized it from Vaclav. "Then come and get it," she said, turning and hurrying down the hall to the computer lab.

Like an angry two-year-old, the drunken Giles followed.

CHAPTER TEN

Joyce looked at Buffy in the rearview mirror. "We need to get some help."

They had found Joyce's SUV in the carnival parking lot. Her purse long gone, Buffy's mom retrieved the extra key she kept in the magnetized box in the wheel well, and they were off.

"Mom, no one can protect you like I can," Buffy assured her. "I can handle this."

Joyce glanced from Xander to her daughter and back again.

"Buffy, if he's not already dead, then he is dying. We have to get him to the medical center. He needs immediate attention."

"No, Mom," Buffy insisted. "They won't be able to help him."

"How do you know?" Joyce's voice was shrill. She was scared. "You're a sixteen-year-old girl, not a medical doctor."

"Mom, just drive," Buffy snapped. "I know what I'm doing. I . . ." She trailed off.

The huge demon creature stood dead ahead.

An enormous tentacle rose up into the air, curling and undulating, then whipped downward, aiming at the vehicle.

"Back up!" Buffy yelled. *"Now!"*

Joyce obeyed. Their vehicle screamed backward one hundred, two hundred, three hundred feet. But the thing rolled toward them, tentacles flapping, curving up into the sky, then coming down hard, smashing trees, crushing a bus stop.

"Okay, stop!" Buffy ordered.

Joyce looked at her daughter. *"Stop?"*

Buffy nodded. "Yeah. I'm going to take that loser down."

Joyce's mouth fell open. "Buffy, you can't possibly do anything to that—that monster! You're just a girl!"

Buffy looked at her coolly. "Oh, Mom, I *so* am not."

She reached for the door handle.

Cordelia thought she heard movement beside her. A shifting. A rustling.

"Dear heart?" a man called from the doorway of the jewelry store bathroom. Something told Cordelia to keep her eyes closed and pretend to be unconscious.

"Miss Chase, is it not? I'm wondering if you've seen my old friend Ripper. It seems his condo is gone."

Oh my God, it's that Ethan Rayne guy, Cordelia thought. *No one else would call Giles "Ripper." And Ethan Rayne is completely evil.*

Is he the guy who knocked me out and tied me up? Why would he do that? Is he that into pearls?

Then she heard the same growl she had heard just before everything went black. Adrenaline flushed through her and she began to panic.

Stay calm. Stay . . .

He bent over her. She could feel his shadow move across her.

"It's all right. I know you're awake," he said. "You may as well open your eyes."

She debated.

"Come on," he urged her.

She opened them.

"Oh!" He smiled down at her. "I didn't think you were awake. But nice to see you, all the same."

Damn it!

He reached a hand toward her mouth. "Now, if I tear this off, will you scream?"

She shook her head.

"Because if you scream, I shall be very cross with you. And you don't want to see me cross, do you?"

She shook her head again.

"Very well, then."

He gathered up a corner between his thumb and forefinger, and pulled.

Yow! It hurt!

She screamed.

Still filthy but much calmer, Giles sat at Jenny Calendar's desk with a cold pack against the lump on his forehead while she set down a fizzy glass of Alka-Seltzer beside his grimoire. He was bare-chested, and he had redrawn the symbols he had inflicted upon himself for the summoning of Astorrith with blood she had fetched from the science lab. Angel informed them both that it was pig's blood, which, to Jenny's way of thinking, was too much information.

Himself again, Giles was preparing to send Astorrith back into his—its—own dimension.

"And the spell you used is called a Weakening Spell, you say." Rupert's voice was calm. His horrible fury had dissipated.

Jenny was very relieved by the change in him. He had been like a man possessed; she knew of what she spoke. She hoped never again to see Rupert act like he had today.

"Yes," she told him. "Willow and I prepared it."

"I was her guinea pig," Willow confirmed shyly, looking up from her job of drawing the pentagram on the floor.

Jenny could tell that the spell had worked on Angel, too. He'd said nothing about his lusty behavior, but it was obvious he was embarrassed.

Claire Nierman was still unconscious. They had yet to learn who her real superiors were. But Rupert had advanced the theory that she was working with Ethan. Vaclav had told them about Ethan's alliance with Professor Caligari, which had surprised Giles not in the least. Nor Jenny. Leave it to Ethan Rayne to work so many angles that they collided with one another.

Jenny hated him. He was once responsible for her own demonic possession. She was not a violent person, but she did believe in justice. And if she ever had the chance to deal some justice in Ethan Rayne's direction . . .

"I'm ready," Giles said. He drank down his Alka-Seltzer and rose, bringing the grimoire with him. He had to clear his head before beginning the ritual to send Astorrith out of their dimension.

Vaclav moved from the student desk where he'd been sitting and flanked Jenny as she stood outside one of the points on the pentagram. Willow got up from the floor and stood on her other side.

Rupert cleared his throat, walked to the center of the five-pointed star. He opened his grimoire and began.

"Baal! Cthulhu! Jezebel! I call upon thee!"

"Will this work?" Vaclav whispered to Jenny.

She nodded. "I hope so."

He hesitated, and then he said, "Pardon me, but are you by chance of Gypsy blood?"

She blinked. Swallowed. Ticked her glance toward Willow and Angel, to see if either of them had heard.

"No," she said firmly.

"Ah. My mistake." Vaclav turned his attention to the ritual. Rupert was shouting.

"Minions of Astorrith! I summon thee!"

"Buffy, get back in this car!" Joyce shrieked at her daughter through the open driver's-side window of her SUV. Had Buffy lost her mind?

Seemingly oblivious to the horrible danger, Buffy was swaggering—that was the only word for it—toward the creature that had nearly smashed in the top of the SUV more than once.

The monster zeroed in on her child like a huge cat spying a mouse. Bizarre, horrible noises emanated from it.

Standing in the whipping wind, girl and nightmare regarded each other.

Joyce was so terrified she could barely think. Somehow she managed to put the car in drive and drove it forward, toward Buffy. It was a miracle; she was so numb she couldn't feel her foot on the gas pedal.

Buffy flung wide her arms. "You want me?" she cried. "Come and get me!"

The monster squealed again as it began to bend forward, tentacles flapping. From the center of its head, its mouth opened, revealing a raging fire.

"Buffy!" Joyce screamed. She pushed back the door latch and prepared to leap out.

Except that she couldn't. The wind was blowing directly against the car. It pushed hard; the SUV rocked; it began to tip on two wheels. The wind threw her out of her seat. As she lay sprawled on her side, she hit the button on Buffy's armrest to close the windows.

The monster lurched forward, its tentacles undulating. It flapped two of the tentacles toward her daughter, who moved into a prizefighter's stance.

Joyce sat back up and laid on the horn.

Buffy waved her off as if to say, *Don't bother. I can handle it.*

Sobbing, Joyce floored it, burning rubber, zero to sixty in—

The monster's tentacles were smoking. Its mouth was boiling flame. And all of that came crashing down on her baby, who didn't move a muscle as it rushed toward her.

She screamed again as Buffy was engulfed and—

—the creature vanished.

Vanished.

And the wind died with it.

Joyce braked, flung herself out of the car, and ran to Buffy, who lowered her arms, straightened her knees, turned, and strutted toward her.

As Joyce threw her arms around her and began to sob, Buffy said proudly, "See? Piece of cake."

"I didn't mean to scream," Cordelia told Ethan as they sat with their backs against the door to the bathroom. His bizarre dog-thing, Manufacturer, really liked her. It was laying its creepy head on her thighs, and she was letting it, because Cordelia Chase had a plan. Her hands were taped together, yes, but she could still move her fingers. While she was pretending to pet the dog, she began slipping her fingers into her front pants pocket . . .

. . . where the box cutter was located.

"It was like getting a free lip wax," she continued, "but still . . ."

She wondered if he realized that she had managed to gather up the dog's chain, too. And that Manufacturer couldn't raise his head from her thighs even if he wanted to.

"Hush," he said, cocking his head. "Listen."

"What?" Pet, pet, pet, inch, inch, inch.

"*Listen.* The wind is gone."

But there was something else:

The calliope. She heard its eerie . . . no, scratch that . . . its beautiful, haunting melody.

It was calling to her.

She said to Ethan, "I have to get back there. All my prizes are waiting for me. I can give her pearls for rolls of quarters."

He regarded her with a quirky grin.

"Well, I've never been one to turn a hostage away," he said.

Astorrith was gone, sent back to the dimension from whence it came. Giles quickly washed all trace of acarna from his body, found a light gray Sunnydale High T-shirt in the lost-and-found, and rejoined the others in Jenny's computer lab. Jenny herself was studying the crystal ball of Madame Lazabra.

Giles wondered if she would forgive him for this one.

Willow was standing at a whiteboard. She had made some headings in blue marker:

> *CALIGARIUS.*
> *ETHAN RAYNE.*
> *VACLAV/SANDRA.*
> *SPELLS.*
> *SOULCATCHERS.*
> *HELL DIMENSION.*
> *BUFFY?*
> *XANDER?*
> *CORDELIA?*
> *CLAIRE/MILITARY?*

When Willow saw Giles, she smiled hopefully at him. They were all looking to him for answers, even Angel, who stood silent and apart from the others. Giles just hoped he could provide some. His head hurt and he was deeply worried about Buffy, but he had to focus.

Walking to the whiteboard, he took the dry-erase marker from Willow. Everyone settled in for a strategy session; he, in turn, looked at Vaclav.

"Tell us everything you know," Giles said. "Leave anything out, and we will deny you sanctuary. Are we clear?"

"Yes," Vaclav said anxiously.

Willow raised her hand. "First of all, our friend Xander Harris has been really sick ever since he went to the carnival."

"Does he like to eat?" Vaclav asked. "My master may have tempted him with food. Gluttony. The Tricksters often poison it." He looked down, ashamed. "They enjoy inflicting harm on others. It's what nourishes them."

"I . . . He said he didn't eat anything," Willow said. "But we've all been under these terrible spells."

"If he has been poisoned, what can be done to make him well?" Giles asked intently.

"He is human, yes?" Vaclav asked.

Willow blinked. "Yes."

"Then he must be put in the glass coffin in the freak show," Vaclav said. "It is ancient, as are many of us. Well, I'm just two centuries. The coffin is what keeps us all alive. Heals us, if we are injured."

"So that's why that woman was in the coffin?" Willow asked. "To make her stay young?"

"Or to heal her?" Giles asked quietly.

Vaclav's lower lip trembled. "She was brought back from near death. But not completely."

"What do you mean?" Giles said, tapping the end of the marker against his finger.

There was a long pause. Then Vaclav said hoarsely, "Her mind was gone. It happens. They can still be useful." His chest heaved and the stillness in the room stretched into what Giles surmised was a moment of silence to acknowledge the girl's suffering. And Vaclav's own.

He loves her, Giles realized. And if that was why Vaclav had decided to betray Caligari, Giles was glad of his suffering. No, that was wrong. Glad that he had a reason to help.

Then Vaclav cleared his throat and said, "For most of us, it works. It will probably work on your friend."

"Probably?" Willow looked from Vaclav to Giles and wondered if he had the ability to explain that probability away.

"What keeps your master alive?" Ms. Calendar asked.

"Souls," Vaclav replied. "He collects them. You can see them in the crystal ball. He preys upon your weakness, and then once he rips your soul from you, you go there. To be tormented." He shivered. "You cannot let him capture me! He'll send me there!"

"We'll do everything in our power to keep you safe," Giles said.

"How are we going to get Xander into the glass coffin?" Willow fretted.

"We'll have to find him first," Giles said gently.

Angel pushed away from the wall. He still thought it was awfully convenient that Vaclav had "just happened" to run into him.

"I'll do that. I'll look for him and Buffy. And Cordelia." Angel gestured with his head to the unconscious Claire Nierman. "I'll take her truck."

Giles nodded. "Yes. Good idea. Willow will tell you how

to perform the Weakening Spell. Perhaps it will cure Xander's sickness as well."

Quickly, Willow gathered up the ingredients for the spell—several kinds of herbs, a white candle, and a handful of the half-dozen talismans Ms. Calendar had created from a book she had found in Giles's vast collection in the library. They looked like tiny people made out of cloth. She put everything in a plastic grocery store bag.

Meanwhile, Ms. Calendar typed out the ritual and printed it for Angel. She went over it with him, making sure he understood every word. Angel folded the paper and put it in the grocery bag.

After she was done, Ms. Calendar hesitated. "Maybe one of us should go with you. What if . . . what if something happened to you and they took *your* soul?"

Angel hadn't stopped to consider that. Take away his soul, and he was a monster.

But there was no time for that now.

"You're all needed here," he insisted.

Then he left.

He went outside, got in the truck, and drove away. He'd go to Buffy's first. Maybe she had—

Calliope music.

Angel unrolled his window.

Sweet and beckoning, tempting, whispering, insinuating. *"Come to me and I will give you pleasures. Your greatest weakness will be your greatest delight.*

"Come to me."

Angel's scalp prickled. He could almost taste the music. It played inside him. Inside his bones and his mind and his unbeating heart.

"*Come to me.*"

And then he saw them, emptying out of late-night bars and convenience stores, houses, and apartments: the citizens of Sunnydale, in long pants and jackets, bathrobes and slippers, shuffling down the dark streets. They reminded him of zombies.

"*Come.*"

Oompapa.

"*Come now.*"

Deedle-deedle-dee.

"*Step right up and feed me your soul.*"

Angel shook his head to clear it.

"*Come.*"

He got the paper out of the grocery bag and read it aloud to himself. He pinched the herbs between his fingers. He used the cigarette lighter to light the white candle's wick, and let it burn until he felt more centered.

The calliope's tune was no longer a siren song.

But it would be for anyone else who hadn't yet been on the receiving end of the Weakening Spell. For them, it would be a sweet call . . . to their doom.

Angel floored it. Buffy would likely be headed for the carnival, just like everyone else.

He hung a left onto Main Street. The sidewalks were

crammed with people trudging past the Sun Cinema and the Espresso Pump. Neon signs painted their slack faces with bright pink and lime green.

He cruised past the alley where just two nights ago, he had first run into Claire Nierman. Things happened fast in a dangerous world.

He drove carefully. The wind had caused a lot of damage. Tree limbs had smashed car hoods. Trash cans, benches, and newspaper containers were tipped over. The crowds walked over them, around them, as the calliope beckoned them with whispered promises, delicious temptations.

The Seven Deadly Sins.

From the corner just beyond Yasumi jewelry store, someone waved at him.

It was Ethan Rayne. Cordelia was with him. Also, a strange black dog.

Then Ethan froze, turned, and ran; it was a quick and easy thing for Angel to stop, leap out of the truck in hot pursuit, tackle Ethan, and throw him to the ground.

The dog-creature began to growl and show its teeth.

"Hullo. It's Angel," Ethan managed, huffing as Angel turned him over on his back. "Fancy meeting you in the center of mayhem and destruction."

"I could say the same," Angel replied.

"Angel!" Cordelia cried, sounding far happier to see him. "You have wheels!"

"Where's Buffy? What's going on?" Angel demanded.

"Haven't the slightest," Ethan said.

Angel shot out his arm, grabbed the animal by the neck, and vamped. "Tell me *now*."

"You wouldn't dare bite Le Malfaiteur," Ethan said. Then, sighing, "I thought you were Claire. You're driving her truck."

"Angel, we have to get to the carnival right away," Cordelia said. "All my stuff is there! My glass basket! It's all mine! She's promised them to me."

So Cordelia's weakness was greed. He was surprised. He had expected it to be vanity.

"We'll go," Angel told her. He said to Ethan, "You're going to help me stop this."

"Not bloody likely," Ethan said, smirking.

"I'll kill you if you don't," Angel threatened. "And your big dog, too."

"Oh," Ethan said, startled. "In that case . . . kill my dog." He chuckled. "You know I'm nothing if not practical, Angel. While I would love to trust that your highly developed sense of morality would kick in before you made my heart stop, I'll help you."

Grimly satisfied, Angel kept hold of him and the dog as they walked to the truck. He said, "Cordelia, there's a plastic grocery bag on the seat. Get it."

"No, we have to go to the carnival *now*," she insisted.

"If you get it for me, I'll take you there."

"Okay," she said, hurrying to retrieve it for him.

"Got it," she reported, showing it to him.

Making sure the keys were not in the ignition, he threw Ethan and his dog into the cab.

Cordelia handed him the bag. Angel took out the herbs, the talismans, and the page of instructions. He laid everything on the hood of the car and quickly performed the ritual, down to lighting the candle again with some matches he found in the street beside his right front tire.

"Oh," Cordelia said, rubbing her hands over her face. "Angel. Oh my God. I—I'm better." Her eyes grew enormous. "I knocked out the Yasumi salesclerk. Oh my God!"

"It's okay," Angel said.

"It is *not*!" she cried. "They'll never let me shop in there again!"

"We've all been under a spell." Maybe she was still under it, if the foremost thing on her mind was the future of her relationship with a jewelry store. On the other hand, she *was* Cordelia.

"Buffy, too," she told him. "She's been under a spell."

"Of lust?" he asked, wondering just how obvious the two of them had been. When they'd been bewitched, it hadn't mattered.

"Lust?" she echoed, sounding confused. "Buffy?"

He tried another tack. "What's she been like? Angry? Greedy?"

Cordelia shook her head. "She has been totally stuck-up. Well, she's always stuck-up, but she's been arguing with Giles, telling him to leave her alone because she can do everything herself. Miss Thing to the max!"

Angel listened hard, running down the list of the Seven Deadly Sins: Lust, Envy, Anger, Sloth, Gluttony, Vanity, and Greed. Which was Buffy's?

"Pride," he said slowly, answering his own question. "Vanity is another word for pride. Buffy's proud."

"Well, if you want to call it that. I would say 'stubborn' or maybe even 'stupid,' but whatever it is, she nearly took Giles out for telling her what to do."

"That's not good," Angel muttered.

"Hel-*lo*? Haven't I been saying that?" Cordelia raised her eyebrows and pursed her lips.

"She might not listen if I try to do the spell," Angel continued, parsing out what to do.

"And that would be *so* new for her, the rascal," Cordelia grumped. "Are *you* listening to *me*?"

From inside the truck, Ethan Rayne laid on the horn; Cordelia screamed and hopped into Angel's arms.

"Oh, I'm just so overstressed," she murmured. "I'll probably break out. This is all Buffy's fault."

Easing Cordelia down, Angel glared at Ethan through the side window. Wide-eyed, Ethan jabbed a finger straight ahead through the windshield.

As a flood of vampires and demons raced toward them.

"I feel like dancing," Joyce announced as she and Buffy skipped the parking lot and drove straight up to the entrance of the carnival. They got out of the car and walked onto the enchanted ground of the carnival.

Joyce sighed and smiled pensively. Then she yawned. "The music is so beautiful. Oh, I want to just sit and listen to this music forever. I never want to move another muscle as long as I live."

Buffy was barely listening. The voice inside her head was the one worth listening to.

"Slayer, this is your kingdom. Come to me. Come and receive the crown you so richly deserve."

"I am," Buffy said.

A large, shimmery rectangle appeared directly in front of her. It was silver, gleaming. A mirror, or a door?

"Come," the voice urged her.

Buffy stepped forward, into the rectangle. She was bathed in silver light. Her skin gleamed as if it were metallic.

I am so beautiful, she thought.

"Yes, you are," a voice replied. It was Professor Caligari, with his white hair and his long face and his extremely yucky hands.

He was sitting on an ivory—bone?—bench in front of a pipe organ made of bones. Skulls, both human and demon, grinned at her. Spinal columns rose to the ceiling of a dark room.

Not a pipe organ. A calliope.

A noise behind her startled her. She turned.

There were seven clowns, each dressed differently. She

had seen some or all of them before. One wore a little pointed hat; another had Rasta braids. A third, purple hair.

As she gazed at each in turn, it began to wipe off its makeup with a piece of cloth—a red bandanna for one, a lacy handkerchief for the more elegant one in the pointed hat. Yet as they swiped at the bright white, red, and blue, she couldn't see their faces. She wasn't sure they had any.

Next came their costumes. Beneath them, they wore black robes decorated with random red sevens. Their hands were hidden inside their sleeves, and their hoods hid their faces.

And now Buffy stood in the center as they encircled her, the dark room blurring into a silver horizon.

"I told you that there are exceptional souls to be savored here in Sunnydale," Professor Caligari said to the seven men. He extended his hand toward Buffy. "This is a Slayer. The reigning Slayer. Can you imagine what her soul will taste like?"

"Wait a sec," Buffy said.

Then Professor Caligari began to play the calliope. The notes danced over her skin, whispering at her, making her forget what she was going to say. Oddly, that didn't bother her.

The men began to move, swaying, dancing. Buffy joined them, stepping in a smaller circle inside their larger one. All her cares and fears evaporated. There was nothing she could not handle, here inside the protective ring of music and

magicks. The men, the calliope music, the world were silvery
and beautiful.

> *"Mirror, mirror, on the wall,*
> *Who's the strongest of them all?*
> *Who's brave and true?*
> *Who's the queen of the carnival?*
> *You, Buffy Summers, you."*

Then she saw herself on the cliff again, as she had long
ago in a dream . . . or had it really happened? Watching the
leapers through the bonfires. Druids, on Samhain.

She smelled the wood smoke, and the burns . . .

. . . the burning of the witches as the eager villagers
screamed for their deaths . . .

. . . the lions roaring in the Colosseum as the hapless
Christians flung themselves against the barred exits . . .

. . . Professor Copernicus Caligari, Doctor Emeritus,
surrounded by glass jars labeled MEDICINALS as he stood
in front of his black wagon, thumbs hooked around the
lapels of his goin'-to-meetin' suit. He had a handlebar
mustache and thick sideburns; his hair was short and he
had a bit of a paunch from all the dinners widows in cal-
ico fixed for him as he made his way across the prairies
and the badlands.

"Step right up, folks, step right up! We've got it all! Wild
West show! Indians! A trained bear! And a mermaid!"

The crowd pressed forward eagerly.

"Forget your troubles! Forget the drought! Sit a spell and partake of our marvelous entertainments!"

Then her vision shifted back, and the seven men in robes surrounded the Slayer as Professor Caligari played his calliope.

She wore a crown of roses and a white dress, and she was perfectly, wonderfully unique.

"You are the one girl in all your generation," Professor Caligari reminded her as the calliope music slid across her skin like a lover's caress.

The seven men bowed low.

"Let me introduce you, Slayer, to Greed, Lust, Anger, Sloth, Gluttony, Envy, and, of course, your favorite: Pride."

The men straightened. They were dressed as clowns again—

—Buffy blinked—

—who pulled spheres of glass from their colorful sleeves and began to juggle them.

"*Round and round and round she goes,*" the calliope sang. Up, down, around, up and down . . .

". . . *like your life, your oddly mixed life of boredom and death-defying adventures that does not do justice to the specialness of you. But we here, we understand.*"

The glass spheres glittered and twinkled. The calliope played.

And Buffy stood radiant and alone, chin raised.

Proud.

The clowns winked in and out of existence, grinning and

flirting. She grinned back, reaching for the glass spheres. But they appeared and disappeared like soap bubbles.

Then they were the men in deep-hooded cloaks again; seven ringed around her. They pulled their hands from their sleeves and she saw hooks and barbs and talons, but no fingers—

She froze.

"No, it's all right," said Professor Caligari. Only that wasn't his name. It wasn't even Hans Von Der Sieben. It was Caligarius. She knew that now. And these were his first acolytes, the men who made the sacrifices of their souls that gave him his first taste of power. They were ancient beings, devoid of souls, or pity, or any bit of goodness.

"These are not for you," Caligarius assured her. "You will reign beside me, lovely queen. All you must do is vanquish our enemies. They have never respected you, never admired you. That must anger you."

Buffy was terribly confused. Because she *was* angry. Very angry. Furious. But . . .

"They will come, and they will try to stop us. You can't let that happen."

"Of course not," she said slowly. "But what did you say about my soul?" She couldn't remember.

His features softened. "Don't worry about that. I would never harm you. Why should I harm you?" Caligarius asked softly.

The calliope played on. Only it wasn't a calliope anymore; it was flutes and drums . . . the clashing of cymbals as the hunters searched the forests and hills not for rabbits or deer, but for human sacrifices . . .

This is wrong, she thought.

"Shh," Caligarius whispered. *"It's all right."*

The silvery notes enfolded her, soothed her, eased her back into the good place she had found.

Where she was special.

"Yes."

"Wait," she said, fighting against it, fighting . . . why was she fighting?

Because I am a fighter. That's what I am.

Because something here was not right.

Buffy blinked at the silver door.

But it wasn't a door. She was standing in the mirror maze, staring at herself in one of the panels. Alone. Her reflection stared back at her.

"Mom?" she called.

The calliope music played.

"A-hunting we will go, a-hunting we will go . . .

"Come to me. Be with me. Your pride will be your greatest pleasure. And you should be proud. You are one of a kind. The only one in all your generation."

"Come to you," Buffy said, reaching out a hand toward the mirror.

Something reached back.

And grabbed hold.

Hard.

• • •

"Oh my God, Angel!" Cordelia cried as demons and vampires swarmed over the people in the streets. It was like a monster stampede, and as they approached, the sleepwalking people woke up and started screaming and trying to get away.

Two demons with corkscrew horns roared and leaped on their closest prey; a shambling corpse in a grave cloth bit into the shoulder of a man in an Emeril sweatshirt and a pair of sweatpants. A couple of trolls grabbed the shins of a heavy-set woman in a flannel nightgown. A pack of Sunkist-orange, slithery snake-things with enormous rows of teeth sprang at two teenage boys in Sunnydale High School letter jackets.

It was a madhouse!

Angel opened the cab and yanked Ethan Rayne out. He flung Cordelia inside, tossing in the sack of stuff he had used in his magick spell on her. He slammed the door hard behind her.

As she grabbed the sack, she fell on top of Ethan's dog-thing. It stank like matches being lighted. And it growled!

With a shriek she turned back to the door.

Mere feet beyond it, three vampires and something purple and gooey were dragging Angel off. And Ethan Rayne was cheering them on—until a pack of trolls and two big gray blobs converged on him.

"Angel!" she cried, cracking open the window just the teeniest little unsafe bit.

"Get to the carnival!" he yelled over his shoulder as he

whomped the purple gooey thing with a totally solid round-house kick. "Follow the directions for the ritual!"

"Keys!" she cried, batting at the window. Then something clinked; she looked inside the grocery bag and found them. She jammed them into the ignition and started the motor as a vampire in a black leather jacket flung itself onto the hood of the truck.

She screamed, shifting into reverse as fast as she could. She was crying and shaking. Monsters were coming. Monsters were everywhere!

All glowing eyes and big, sharp fangs, the vampire was clinging to the windshield and grinning at her in anticipation. Ha! She hit the brakes.

The vampire's face rammed into the windshield, which held. Then it ricocheted off the hood. Another one leaped at the truck. Some kind of round, glowing thing rolled up beside her door and started flinging itself against it.

Cordelia backed up as fast as she could go, gaze ticking from the glowing thing to the crowds of demons and monsters to the zombie-people and back again.

"Carnival, carnival," she said, forcing herself to stay calm. After all, she was good at maintaining, even when the pressure was intense. Look at how well she handled the terrible burden of her popularity.

"I'll get to the carnival. I'll follow the directions on the paper." She stuck her hand in the sack. "Oh my *God*, where's the paper? It's not here! The paper's not here!"

Her fingers brushed the folded edge. "Oh, wait, here it is. All I have to do is follow the directions. I can do that."

"And ah will 'elp you," Ethan Rayne's dog-thing told her in a French accent.

Cordelia started shrieking.

CHAPTER ELEVEN

Xander heard the voice of an angel.

"Xander, Xander, oh my God, he's dead! Look at how pasty he looks. Well, he always looks pasty. You can carry him, right?"

Or rather, the voice of Cordelia.

He tried to open his eyes. Every part of him was nauseated. He was so sick. He couldn't imagine being sicker. He wanted to die. Really. In case anyone was listening.

There was a lot of jostling.

"Your spell is working, right? No one can see us? They don't know we're here?"

"It should 'old." It was a guy's voice, deep and French.

No one Xander knew. He didn't care, except for the knee-jerk jealousy. He hated the jostling. The jostling was evil. If it didn't quit, he'd . . . he'd . . .

Calliope music.

Yes. Gentle and beckoning and reassuring and . . . food.

He was soothed. And hungry.

"Okay, Xander, listen, um, if you aren't dead, I'm doing a spell on you, with the help of this warlock named Le Malfaiteur. That's right, right?"

"Oui," said the guyful voice.

"Anyway, he is really *hot*, I mean, ha, he was Ethan Rayne's imprisoned dog, only he got free of the spell while Ethan was distracted fighting for his life from all those demons and vampires and things and so now he's helping me. He wasn't even attacking me in the store, just trying to warn me about Ethan! You got that?"

Xander had not a clue, but it didn't matter. The music filled him.

He was so hungry for more.

"Okay, I'm ready. I've got the herbs and everything. Wait! Le Malfaiteur, do you have any matches? Oh, that's so *amazing*! What do your other fingers do?

"Xander? Can you hear me? It's called a Weakening Spell. It should help you. If you're not dead. Hey, Le Malfaiteur, can you move it along? Maybe they can't see us, but I can see them. And Xander may be on the brink . . ." She let out a little sob.

The calliope whispered to Xander. It sang. It said, *"Eat of the fruit of good and evil. Eat more. Consume. Devour. You are ravenous."*

The music crept into his gut. Xander floated on the notes, listening to the crescendo. He drifted and dozed.

"'. . . and so I demand his unbinding!'" Cordelia recited.

Xander heard the rustling of a paper near his ear. "Okay, I hope that helped." Fingers snapping. "Hello? Hello, do you hear me?"

He couldn't open his eyes, but he knew he was lying on a very hard surface. It was very cold.

"You're sure the wards will hold?" Cordelia asked.

"For now. I can't make any guarantees."

"Okay, listen. We're going into the freak show, but no one else will be able to go in. They'll think it's locked. Except maybe if the bad guys are snooping around, they might figure out that it's bewitched."

"My wards are very strong," the guy said, sounding a bit offended. "And we have the amulets your sorcerer made for you."

"My . . . oh! Giles! He's not a sorcerer!"

"If you say so, *ma belle*."

"Okay, you're creeping me out."

"It would be best to hurry," the guy prodded.

"Okay, all right. Xander, we're putting you in something that will help you get well. It's that glass coffin in the freak show, but don't freak out. It'll heal you. I hope. Angel said so.

That girl we saw in it? They were using it to heal her. That didn't go perfect, but it was better than nothing. Anyway, don't be scared. We're going to close the lid now. We don't know if we're supposed to, but here goes nothing!"

Whump!

Knock-knock-knock.

"Xander? *Xander?* Oh my God, he's not breathing!"

"They're overrunning the town," Willow announced as she looked up from her screen. She had hacked into the dispatcher's computer system at the Sunnydale Police Department. They're saying 'gangs,' but you know that's what they always say."

"Vampires and demons everywhere," Ms. Calendar murmured as she moved to the window and peered through the venetian blinds at the night. "According to those dispatches, it's worse than when the Master tried to open the Hellmouth. And we have hours until it's light. They're sure to come here."

"My master . . . tried to open the Hellmouth?" Vaclav asked in a frightened, hushed voice.

"Different master," Willow explained. "But same Hellmouth. Which, well, we're pretty much sitting on top of it." She made a little face. "Sorry."

"We prevailed that time," Giles reminded them. "And we'll prevail again."

Ms. Calendar moved from the window and picked up the crystal ball. "Rupert," she said, "there are more people in here.

In the hell dimension. I recognize some of my students. Larry. And there's Chris Vardeman."

"Damn. One assumes they're being absorbed via Caligari's dread machinery," Giles said. He crossed to Vaclav. "Explain it to me again."

"The professor has soulcatchers on the grounds," Vaclav said. "They hypnotize you, make your temptations rise to the surface."

Giles nodded. "Those would be the clowns. With their juggling balls."

"No. But they help the process." He shook his head impatiently. "The Tricksters are his minions. From the First Days. The soulcatchers all have shiny surfaces." He pointed to the crystal ball. "The word escapes me. Mirrors, only more focused. Normal ones make rainbows. But these make a . . . rainbow of the vices. The Seven Deadly Sins."

"A rainbow. You mean a spectrum," Giles considered.

"Yes," he said in his Bela Lugosi voice.

"Prisms," Willow offered.

Vaclav looked excited. "Yes, that's the word. They are prisms. They focus your weakness, and then you are lost in it. In lust, or greed . . . and we lure you in. We promise you what you want most."

"But why set out my grimoire for me to find?" Giles asked. "Why tempt me to summon a horrible demon that can just as easily destroy the carnival itself?"

Vaclav shook his head. "That I cannot tell you. It makes no sense to me, either."

"Ethan Rayne," Jenny Calendar said coldly. "He loves chaos. Worships it. He wouldn't pass up a chance like this to pump up the volume."

Giles exhaled. "When I get my hands on him . . ."

"The soulcatchers," Willow said, keeping the grown-ups on task. "Shiny surfaces. Prisms that focus our bad impulses. What and where are they?"

"I'd be willing to guess that one of them is located inside the Chamber of Horrors," Giles said. "In the vampire scene." He looked at Vaclav. "Yes?"

Vaclav hesitated, fingers kneading the edge of his sweater. "I don't know where they are."

"What about the moon ball on the carousel?" Willow said.

"Perhaps," Vaclav said, lowering his gaze.

Willow pushed back from her computer. "We should go to the carnival now and see what we can find."

"First we should try to figure this out," Giles asserted.

"But the others don't know about the . . . soulcatchers," Willow argued. "We need to help them."

"You can't help them now," said Claire Nierman as she awkwardly sat up, her hands bound behind her back. "It's too late."

Everyone turned. Giles walked toward her, squatting down beside her. "Why do you say that?"

She looked away. "I only have to give you my name, rank, and serial number."

"We know you're not with the Marine Corps," Giles said

with deadly calm. "You're with Ethan Rayne, aren't you?" he said. "He's been working both sides of this, just like Jenny said."

At the name, Claire's eyes flickered, and Willow knew that Giles was right. Maybe she was even Ethan's lover.

"And you probably know who I am. I'm Ethan's old mate Ripper. And I'm willing to bet he told you why I was called that."

Claire frowned and bit her lower lip.

"So tell me," Giles suggested. "Why do you say that it's too late to help them?"

A little bit of her fear faded with her bravado. "Tonight's the Rising. Caligari's strength is at its peak. He'll take out everyone in Sunnydale before this night is over."

"Tonight?" Giles stared at her. "But the Rising was two nights ago."

"You had it wrong, honey," she said disparagingly. "You got fed misinformation. It's now."

"Well, I don't see why you're smiling about it," Willow piped up, protectively crossing her arms over her chest. "I mean, you're here with us and not Ethan."

"He'll find me. He'll come for me," she said, crossing her legs at the ankles as she got more comfortable.

"Oh my God, look!" Ms. Calendar shouted. She nearly dropped the crystal ball; then as she caught it, she thrust it toward Giles and Willow.

Willow ran over and peered into it.

Her blood turned to ice. Her face was a flash fire.

Xander's face swirled in the glass.

Mottled, bruised, and screaming.

Angel was no quitter, but two hundred and forty years of living made a man realistic.

Even if that man was a vampire with a soul.

Far be it for him to say that Sunnydale was beyond redemption, but it wasn't looking good.

Everything in him wanted to abandon this fight and get himself to the carnival, where he might be able to do something that would tip the odds toward a better outcome than this one. If Buffy was there, she was probably in trouble. Unless Cordelia had been able to cast the Weakening Spell on her, she would still be in thrall to Caligari's magicks.

Up to his neck in assailants—at last count, three lizard-green Shrieker demons, a Lindwurm, and an albino poison-spitter—he was worried about Cordelia's chances of getting to the carnival, much less casting a spell on a prideful, bewitched Slayer. He wondered what she had done about the dog.

He raced down an alley with his attackers in close pursuit. Ethan Rayne had disappeared from his radar. If he wasn't dead, then he had probably headed for the city limits. That was Ethan's way—wreak havoc and leave.

He got around a corner and leaned against the brick exterior, regrouping as he waited for the mob that was after him to arrive. It was nice to have a second to rest. But it would be two seconds at most. He knew that.

He pushed away, preparing for a fight.

As a clutch of ax-wielding ogres dropped down from the roof above him.

The merry-go-round of the damned:

The threshers in the center of the carousel diorama finished beating Xander with their drumsticks and their cymbals. The falcons soared back onto the gauntlets of the hunters, their prey dangling from their claws and beaks: half-eaten hot dogs; pieces of popcorn; chocolate chip cookies soggy with soda; cold, congealed onion rings; and kettle corn mixed with gum.

Carnival carrion.

Holding Xander down, the men in gauntlets force-fed it to him as he choked, struggled, and gagged. They laughed. They sang, *"A-hunting we will go!"*

They laughed harder when he vomited.

They fed him more.

In his terrible new world the hunters and their threshers were real people. Xander was trying to figure out how many there were. He thought maybe eight. He was so sick it was hard to pay attention.

Then one of the sadists carried him back onto the carousel floor and plopped him on his fiery black carousel horse. *"Behold the wages of the sin of gluttony!"* he bellowed, and he rechained Xander's wrists to the pommel on the saddle. The horse reared, chuffing smoke and fire. Its hide sizzled, and Xander gasped.

He could no longer scream.

Then the now-familiar sizzling erupted deep inside his chest and head, and he shuddered as the golden carousel pole rose. He knew the rhythm now: up when it sucked the life out of him, down for a moment of release. In tune with his heartbeat.

Each time it went up, the carousel rotated one increment. Of what kind of measurement, he had no idea.

He was not alone. Hundreds, if not thousands, of tortured people sat on creatures all around him, beside him, behind him, and in front of him. The carousel was a vast machine, and the bruised and beaten people on the carousel animals were like galley slaves, only instead of sitting at long oars and rowing, they were powering the rising movements of the poles.

And each time the poles went up, a calliope note sounded. Their energy was making the calliope play.

In this dimension or the other one or both, Xander had no idea.

"Food, glorious food!" the calliope played. And God help him, Xander was hungry.

Then two of the hunters were unchaining him again; he moaned because he knew what was coming.

They held him down and force-fed him again.

Then he was on his horse, his insides crackling, and the carousel rotated again.

He was losing consciousness when he heard a familiar voice.

"You people are in so much trouble. I have friends in high places, you know, and once they hear about this, you are going to have more than the school board to answer to!"

It was Principal Snyder, one creature ahead of him. The man sat astride a half-horse, half-fish creature. Xander stared at his bald head, drinking in the sound of his voice over the discordant notes of the calliope. How bad was Xander's world, that he was happy to see him?

"Hey," Xander called to him. "Principal Snyder."

Snyder looked over his shoulder with a horribly bruised face and two black eyes. His lip was split.

"Harris!" He glared at him. "I should have known you were behind all this."

Xander huffed. "Do I *look* like I'm behind all this?"

Then the person riding beside Xander turned to him. Despite the bruises on his face, he looked vaguely familiar. He was a guy from school. Xander suddenly realized that he was surrounded by Sunnydale High students.

Whoa, gluttony was big in the California public school system.

The guy said, "Why are you different from us?"

"Different?" Xander asked.

"Yeah. Look at me."

Xander really looked. The guy was kind of half there, like a ghost, or a hologram. Xander could see the black stallion he rode right through him. And it looked like a regular carousel horse, not a frothing nightmare.

Xander hadn't noticed that before. He was too busy getting tortured or something.

"Look at yourself," the guy said.

Xander was nearly solid. Still a little blurry, but not like the other guy.

"How did you get here?" the guy asked him. "What ride were you on?"

"Ride?" Xander considered. "I wasn't on a ride. I was sick, and I got put in something. I think it was a coffin."

The guy said, "Well, I was riding this carousel. Only it wasn't like this."

"So was I," said the girl on the other side of Xander. Her face was black-and-blue.

He realized he was beginning to see them more clearly. He was able to think, where before he had just plodded along.

Something was happening to him. Something that he thought might be good.

I'm getting better.

He yanked on the chain tied around his wrist.

It broke with a *clank.*

In the center of the carousel one of the falcons on an outstretched arm jingled its bells and cocked its head. The hunter who held it frowned and swept his gaze out at the riders.

Xander swallowed hard.

The hunter moved back into position in a jerky, automaton motion. His face grew hard, and he looked like a statue.

I think that's good.

Xander freed his other hand, grabbing the chain so it wouldn't make a sound. As the girl and the guy watched in astonished silence, he reached across and pulled the girl's left hand free of her chain. Her right was still tethered.

"Try it yourself," Xander whispered.

She tried, but nothing happened. Same with the guy.

Xander leaned over and wrenched the guy's right hand free. Then the guy's left.

Others saw and moved their hands, straining against their chains. But they were held in place.

"How did you do that?" Snyder hissed, struggling against his own chains. Xander tried not to take satisfaction in that. It had to have something to do with the coffin, or the spells Cordelia had been talking about. Now he wished he'd been able to pay better attention.

"There was something about a warlock," Xander told him in a low voice.

"Warlock? Are you insane?" Synder shot back. Xander waited to see if it occurred to Snyder that believing in warlocks was, at the moment, nowhere near the craziest aspect of their existence.

"Not so loud," Xander cautioned him.

"Are you telling me what to do?" Snyder asked. His blood-shot eyes were so huge Xander half-expected them to fall out of his head. "You are a student!"

"Shut up," Xander told him.

"What?"

Ignoring Snyder, Xander broke the chain around the girl's right wrist, and she covered her mouth with both hands as if to keep herself from crying out. Xander motioned for her to put them down. There was no telling when an evil-statue-guy might notice.

"Oh, God, can you get us out of here?" the guy to Xander's right whispered excitedly.

Then their attention was taken up when the threshers banged their drums and crashed their cymbals. The noise rang in Xander's ears, until louder screams masked it. Something—someone?—appeared in the diorama. It was another Sunnydale High School student, a beefy guy in a letter jacket who, yeah, could very well have gluttony issues. He was on his hands and knees, looking around as he screamed, and Xander didn't blame him because it was extremely terrifying simply watching the figures in the diorama as they lost their robotlike stiffness and began whaling on the guy with their drumsticks and cymbals.

"What's going on? Who *are* you people?" the guy was shrieking.

"Behold the wages of the sin of gluttony!" one of the hunters proclaimed, lifting the hood from the falcon on his arm.

"Oh my God! Someone help me!" the guy screamed. "Please!"

Xander hated not being able to help, but he did the next best thing he could: He took advantage of the distraction to slither off the black stallion and creep to the trio of riders ahead of him. He yanked hard on the chain of the guy beside Principal Snyder. The chains broke immediately.

"Me next, me!" Snyder demanded.

"Shut up," Xander said again, and he got to work.

"You can't just leave me here," Claire said to Giles from the door of the computer lab.

Willow's forehead wrinkled. Giles commiserated; the police dispatches indicated that the riots were heading this way. It was quite possible they would overrun the school. At least they had untied her hands. That would give her a better chance at survival. But not much of one.

"She was going to shoot me," Vaclav reminded Giles. "Angel stopped her."

"Don't be silly," she said quickly. "I was just pretending. I would never hurt anyone."

"I'm sorry," Giles said. "Lock the door behind us."

Then they raced down the hall and into the library, where Giles began grabbing holy water and stakes while Jenny Calendar threw together some protective amulets.

Willow said, "What should I do? Tell me what to do!"

And then the phone rang.

Startled, they all glanced at it, and then Willow raced to grab it.

"Hello?" she said, and then, "Cordelia!"

"I'll take it," Giles said, dashing across the library. "Yes, Cordelia?"

"Giles," she whispered, the signal fuzzy and faint. "We need you. You have to come now. Le Malfaiteur knows what to do and you have to come and Xander's messed up and . . . oh my God!"

"Stay calm," he urged her.

"Hel-*lo*?" she blurted. "I am in the middle of total evil here!"

"Yes. Who is Le Malfaiteur?"

"He's this warlock. He is, like, French or African or something, and Ethan Rayne cursed him because he cheated in cards, hold on, he says he only cheated because . . . *Listen, we don't care why you cheated!* Where was I?"

"The warlock."

"Yes! He used this invisible spell on us to get Xander into the coffin, only now I think Xander is dying."

"We believe he's in another dimension," Giles said.

"Really." There was a beat. "Well, that's good! They don't think Xander is dying," she said away from the phone.

"Okay, listen, I have all this stuff to tell you," she continued.

"I, as well," Giles said. "Are you—"

"Me first," Cordelia cut in. "This phone wasn't even worth stealing. It is a piece of junk! It weighs a ton and the signal sucks and *oh my God, I am being greedy! The Weakening Spell is wearing off!*"

"No, no, it's not. You're always greedy, remember? You're fine. Stay with me, Cordelia," Giles urged. "Have you seen Buffy?"

Ms. Calendar and Willow listened as they finished putting together the supplies. Vaclav chimed in on Giles's side of the conversation, and Willow started putting the puzzle pieces together. It was as Vaclav had told them: The carnival used magickal prisms to find people's weak spots. Then Vaclav broke down and spilled. He had been too afraid to tell them everything, but now that Cordelia and the French warlock were on the grounds, he obviously felt more confident about sharing.

There were seven prisms, each attuned to one of the Seven Deadly Sins. Bewitched by the mirror ball on the carousel, Xander's gluttony had gotten the better of him. The crystal ball was the focal point for envy.

Willow wondered what she, Willow, might have done if she had more fully succumbed to her envy. She was deeply ashamed that she had tried to hurt Ms. Calendar's feelings, even if the computer teacher understood and forgave her.

What might Angel have done if he got too lusty?

Giles's anger had raised a demon that had nearly destroyed Sunnydale.

Vaclav said that next the carnival sucked the souls right out of people. But where did the people go?

"But what are we to do with the prisms?" Giles asked Vaclav. "Yes, hold on, Cordelia. Vaclav is going to explain things to us."

Vaclav hesitated again, and Willow was about to encourage him to speak up when he exhaled and said, "I'm not sure.

I do know that they are somehow connected to the calliope. There have been times when one of them would be damaged, and the calliope would sound . . . sour."

"So maybe what we should do is find them and destroy them," Willow suggested.

Vaclav considered. "When the calliope sounded wrong, Professor Caligari would touch his chest. The way a person does when there is something wrong with his heart."

"So you're saying his heart is connected in some way to these prisms?" Jenny asked. She looked at Giles. "There's a lot of literature online about symbolic magicks. These prisms could represent the chambers of his heart. If the chambers are completely destroyed, his heart will fail."

"Are you hearing this, Cordelia?" Giles asked.

"So . . . we find and destroy the prisms," Willow ventured again.

"The thing is," Jenny cut in, "in cases like these, you usually have to inflict a lot of damage very quickly or the being can stop you. It's a little complicated, but . . . "

Giles took up the threat. "What you're saying is, if we don't destroy all the prisms . . . wait." He nodded. "Yes, Cordelia. I'm listening."

Everyone was quiet. Then Giles said, "Oh, of course. Why didn't I think of that? Thank you, Le Malfaiteur."

After a few more minutes, Giles said, "Yes, good, all right, we'll try to meet you at the freak show. Yes, Jenny has a cell phone."

Ms. Calendar nodded.

"Yes, it's a lovely cell phone. Very good," Giles went on. "No, I don't think you'd be allowed to keep it once this is all over."

Giles hung up and faced the others.

"We have a plan," he said. "I'll explain it on the way."

He, Ms. Calendar, Willow, and Vaclav took off, racing through the student lounge to the faculty parking lot. Jenny unlocked her car and everyone slid in, Giles in the front seat with her, Willow and Vaclav in the back.

Willow stared into the crystal ball, watching Xander's face. He was still beaten, but he was looking around at something they couldn't see, and talking, although they couldn't hear him.

I wonder if he's where the people go when their souls are stolen, Willow thought anxiously. She was so scared to go back to the carnival. Scared it would happen to her. But she would go to hell and back to save Xander. Or Giles. Or even Cordelia.

And especially Buffy. Where is she?

Jenny peeled out like a teenage boy and they headed for the carnival.

Demons and people were racing all over the streets. Buildings blazed. Smoke choked the moon and screams pierced Willow's eardrums.

"Can you summon Godzilla?" Willow asked Giles.

A man spotted them and waved both his arms as he ran toward them, calling for help.

"Drive on," Giles said quietly. "Get around them."

Not needing to go to hell to help, Willow thought. *Hell has come to us.*

"This is what my master brings," Vaclav yelled. "This chaos and mayhem. And then the people come to us like lambs to the slaughter. We devour their souls." He buried his face in his hands.

"It's not your fault," Willow said, patting his shoulder. "Um, not that much, anyway."

Vaclav dropped his hands into his lap. "I was his collaborator for two centuries. And then, when Sandra's mind was taken . . . only then did I rebel."

"But you did rebel," Willow said. "You're trying to help us stop him now. That's good."

"But my soul . . . he'll take my soul," Vaclav said.

"Only if he defeats us," Willow said.

They shared a look.

"He'll take my soul," Vaclav said brokenly.

"Right, then," Giles said. "On that triumphant note of optimism, let's go through our plan one last time."

Willow listened carefully.

"Le Malfaiteur has corroborated Vaclav's opinion that the prisms, the calliope, and Caligarius are connected. We need to collect all the prisms and put them together so that they're touching," Giles said. "Once that is done, then we perform a Tobaic Ritual of Destruction. It's a very ancient rite said to have been used against a number of the last pure demons who walked the Earth before humankind banished them."

"So, we think he's that kind of demon, a . . . tobacco demon?" Willow asked.

"It's a sort of all-purpose destruction ritual," Ms. Calendar said. "It works in a lot of cases." She nodded at Giles. "That's a very elegant solution."

"Thank you," Giles said.

"A lot of cases, but not all?" Vaclav asked worriedly.

"There is a chance it won't work," Giles said. "In which case, we may simply try to smash the prisms."

"Then why not try smashing them first, in the rides?" Vaclav demanded.

"Because they're prisms," Giles began patiently, but Ms. Calendar turned around from the front seat and said, "Believe me, we want him stopped as much as you do. Rupert's right. The method that has the best chance of working is to gather them together first."

Vaclav nodded, still looking pretty worried.

And then . . .

"Wow," Willow whispered.

The calliope played over the landscape, and the people who had survived the gauntlet of monsters had become hypnotized again . . . or zombified, or whatever one wanted to call it.

Although it was three in the morning by Giles's watch, the carnival was in full swing. The Ferris wheel was com-

pletely restored, and shone brightly. The other attractions—
rides—sparkled and whirled. The carousel creatures bobbed
up and down.

From Giles's distant vantage point, he could see riders,
and people pouring into the entrance like cows placidly walking into the slaughterhouse.

Jenny stopped short of the parking lot, which was full of
cars. People had driven here in a fog, gotten out, and were
trudging slowly toward the carnival.

As the group got out of Jenny's car, Giles said, "Everyone,
do you have the wards I made for you?"

They were protective amulets he had cobbled together from
things Jenny and he had on hand, guided by Le Malfaiteur's
instructions over the library phone.

They all nodded. Then he said, "Jenny, your phone?"

She took it out of a bag clanking with weapons and supplies and handed it to him. He fished into his pocket for the
number of the phone that Cordelia had "appropriated" from a
person or persons unknown, and dialed the number.

It was answered on the first ring. It was Le Malfaiteur.
He said, "*Alors*, Monsieur Giles. You are ready?"

Giles said, "Yes," and gestured to the others to crowd in.

As they did so, the warlock invoked the magick spell that
would cloak them in invisibility.

They faded from sight, and then Giles was staring at
trees, and streets, and other people shuffling past them.

Quietly the four crept toward the carnival.

• • •

"Okay, now what?" Cordelia whispered to Le Malfaiteur as she peered at Xander through the top of the coffin. He didn't look any better.

"I don't know why the coffin's not working," Le Malfaiteur said beside her. Since they were both invisible, she couldn't see him. But she hadn't lied on the phone: He was tall, dark, and probably twenty-four; he had worn perfectly tailored gray wool pants and a navy blue silk shirt. And a thin silver chain, and a matching, tiny hoop in his left ear. Stylish, but with a little bit of flair.

The warlock went on. "Maybe he had to be part of Caligari's evil family or something. Maybe there was a spell to perform first. Ah don't know."

"You don't know? We stuck him in there and you don't know?"

"Shh. Someone's coming."

Cordelia held her breath. Along with utilizing the wards, they had put up a closed sign in front of the freak show entrance, but some people just didn't pay any attention or assume that rules and regulations applied to them personally.

She looked fearfully, waiting, watching. And seeing no one.

Hey, seeing no one!

"You guys?" she whispered.

"Yes. We're here," Giles replied.

• • •

In the mirror maze Buffy yanked back through the mirror, equally hard.

And whatever had hold of her, released her at once.

"Okay, then," she said.

Then she saw the reflections of the seven robed men.

She whirled around.

They were nowhere to be seen.

And the fun house went dark.

"I am getting really tired of this place," the Slayer muttered.

"Okay, you know your jobs," Giles said. They were standing around Xander's coffin. Or so Giles hoped. They were still invisible. "Each of us has a prism to collect. I'll go to the Chamber of Horrors and get the mirror."

"I will get the one in the Tunnel of Love," Vaclav said. "That's lust. Lust is what brought me under Caligari's thrall."

"Lust can be cool," Cordelia said. She cleared her throat. "I'll get the purple basket in the coin toss."

"The mirror ball in the carousel," Ms. Calendar said. "I'll get that since lust . . . is taken. That's gluttony, right? Seriously, I'm on a diet every other week."

"You would never guess that," Willow murmured. "The crystal ball is the sixth, for envy. And we already have that."

"So you're going to the fun house," Giles reminded her. "To get the mirror in the maze."

"For vanity, right."

"That leaves sloth, for me," Le Malfaiteur said.

"Yes," Vaclav said. "It's on the Ferris wheel. There is a little mirror at the top. Not all people notice it. Only those for whom sloth might be tempting."

"All you did was cheat at cards," Cordelia said.

"Ah, but when one is a warlock, it is so tempting to use magicks instead of stirring oneself to perform physical labor."

"Oh, I'll bet your performance is just . . ." Cordelia trailed off. "How much longer will the invisibility spell last?"

"It's hard to say," Le Malfaiteur confessed. "This is a magickal field. I can sense it growing stronger and stronger. Soon it will negate my magick. Your talismans will only prolong it a little while."

"Then we need to hurry," Willow said anxiously. "Okay, once we've taken the prisms, we bring them back here."

"If you can," Giles replied. "Otherwise smash them where they are."

Buffy ran through the dark, feet flying, Slayer senses fully ratcheted past stun to kill. She remembered the twists and turns of the maze before she got to them, ducked down, around, zooming for all she was worth.

Then it was time to get the heck out of there.

No problem, she thought, racing down a corridor as the crazy laughter followed her.

Except there was a problem:

The floor gave way and Buffy tumbled down, down, down, like Alice in the rabbit hole.

She landed on her feet and whirled around. She was in a pit about two stories high and a football field wide. It was carved out of the earth. She could smell the mud, and something else—the distinct odors of evil: sulfur, ash, smoke, and the stench of death. The ground vibrated rhythmically; steam rose from vents in the ground and the sides of the pit. A strange red glow revealed Caligarius; he was standing approximately a hundred feet away from her.

Only, he wasn't Caligarius any longer.

He was a wicked-tall demon, maybe not as tall as that other guy who had appeared with the wind, but far more terrifying. He was a brilliant red, with horns on his head, and he looked exactly like the sort of bad guy to be tempting people with sins.

Brrrr.

He reached down and plucked Buffy up as if she were featherlight and raised her to his face, which was, like, ten feet across.

His laugh rumbled and echoed like a genie laugh in a cartoon.

Wind whipped at her hair. And she heard the calliope music.

It was coming from his chest.

"Slayer," he said, in deep reverb. "I am humbled by your greatness. I have tried numerous times to defeat you."

"Well, you get an F in defeatation," she said. "Don't feel bad. French is the subject that stumps me."

As he laughed again, she ticked her eyes left, right, trying to come up with a strategy. She didn't have enough clues. But she was willing to bet what she smelled was the Hellmouth, and Big Demon Guy was using its energy. Power user, power source.

Except she didn't think she could shut the Hellmouth down.

"This town has been so good for me," he said as if he were reading her mind. "It's so evil here. The Hellmouth has nourished us. The souls here are so ripe."

"That's because we put ourselves in paper bags and sit on the counter for a couple of days."

More reverb laughter. "I like you. I don't want to kill you."

She wrinkled her nose. "Gee, I wish I could say the same. But my mom taught me never to lie." *And speaking of my mom, where is she?*

She wanted to scan her surroundings some more, but as the veteran of many fights against many demons, she knew she'd better stay focused on her adversary.

"All these people will feed me soon enough," he said. "And I'll grow stronger, and I'll move on to the next town. And the next." His eyes narrowed. "I understand there's another Hellmouth in Cleveland."

"I'll stop you," Buffy promised him.

"I've been stopped before," he replied easily.

"I will end you."

"So proud." He smiled, revealing more fangs than one demon decently ought to have. "You're one of the proudest human beings I've ever met. You like to go it alone, don't you?"

I have to go it alone, Buffy thought. *I'm the Slayer.*

But even as she thought the words, she knew that they weren't true. She had friends.

"I'm like you," she said. "I'm so proud it's sinful."

"Your soul will be nectar on my tongue," he said.

And then he picked her up, dangled her above his mouth, and tossed her in.

Yes! Vaclav exulted as he traced the mesmerized gazes of the people in the swan boats at the large, ruby heart above his head. They began to activate, as if someone had thrown a switch, falling into each other's arms and kissing.

I'll climb up the balcony, he thought, *and . . .*

. . . and then he saw Sandra, sitting in a boat by herself. She was staring at the heart. And she was *smiling*. There was life in her eyes again.

"Sandra?" he whispered, hurrying toward her.

She opened her mouth and extended her hand.

"There he is!" she screamed.

Faces tightened. The shuffling crowd staring at Van Helsing's mirror began to grumble about pushing, about it being too hot, about how lame the Chamber of Horrors was.

When the mirror disappeared, they began to howl with disapproval.

And the rooms filled up with a strange, purplish glow. It cast them in silhouette.

The jig's certain to be up now, if it wasn't already, Giles thought as he slipped the mirror under his arm and raced out of the tent.

On the revolving floor of the carousel, Jenny looked from the chariot bench to the mirror ball. She had taken gymnastics in high school, but she doubted she'd be able to vault to so great a height. And if she fell . . .

Then she studied the three black stallions in front of the bench. If she climbed the pole and shimmied over . . .

Yes. A much better solution.

The Ferris wheel turned slowly as Le Malfaiteur, still invisible, watched for a chance to sneak onto one of the carriages.

But none of the passengers wanted to get off. Too tired, they said. Too relaxed.

Too lazy, Le Malfaiteur thought.

The people in line began to grumble.

Then he thought he heard a scream, thin and strangled, from the topmost carriage.

When it came back down, no one was sitting in it.

They 'ave been taken, he thought.

He felt his magickal field shift. As he had explained to the others, the power of the carnival was increasing.

He considered what he was doing. Perhaps it was too complicated. The girl—Cordelia—was beautiful, and she was attracted to him. She had inadvertently freed him by reciting her Weakening Spell while Ethan Rayne was distracted. But she loved the boy who lay in the coffin, whether she knew it or not. So it was doubtful that she would willingly step into the embrace of Le Malfaiteur. And he was tired of seducing women with magicks.

These people were not wealthy. They would offer him no financial reward if he helped them further.

And if Professor Caligari's minions caught him, he was certain to be sorry.

He wasn't sure why he should bother.

He looked up at the top of the wheel. It was a long way up.

A lot of effort.

Buffy was suffocating. She lay on the floor of the room where she'd seen the calliope while the clowns pranced around her, doubled over with hooting laughter.

Caligarius turned and smiled at her from over his shoulder as he put his hands on the calliope keyboard. He played a dirgelike funeral march she had heard before, then stopped and shook his head.

"'Pavane for a Dead Princess' is far more appropriate," he said.

He played on as Buffy clutched her neck, fighting for air.

Then the calliope notes went sour, and faint, and she figured she was dying.

But the clowns stopped laughing and looked at Caligarius. He frowned and squinted, staring hard at Buffy; then he cleared his throat and resumed.

The calliope screeched. The sound was fainter still.

"What are you doing?" he blurted.

And although Buffy knew that what she was doing was nothing, she smiled.

That flustered him. He rose from the calliope and advanced on her, his image doubling and blurring. Buffy was on the verge of passing out and trying hard not to show it. Something was going wrong, and Caligarius was freaking out. From her point of view, that could only be good.

The room flickered.

Two of the clowns disappeared.

Then the side of the room vanished.

The clowns came back. The side of the room reappeared, but a part of the ceiling winked out. There was blackness above it, and twinkling stars.

"What's going on?" he said, grabbing her arm.

Big mistake. Maybe this was an illusion, maybe she was really in the demon's stomach, but it seemed to hurt Caligarius when she grabbed his throat and squeezed as hard as she could.

He gagged and tried to pull away.

But Buffy held on.

• • •

The evil carousel of doom flickered. Lights on, lights off, lights on again. Drums banging, drums . . . silent. The hunters were people . . . they were animated figures. The fiery steeds rose up.

Froze.

Descended.

Xander traded glances with the girl beside him. They both looked at the guy on the other black horse. He swallowed hard and nodded at them. They had a plan: When Xander gave the word, they would flank him as they broke the chains of as many riders as they could. Then they would fight their jailers. Xander didn't have much of a plan past that, but at least it was better than waiting for another round of torture.

The guy licked his lips and said to Xander, "Your call, man."

The carousel slowed down. Principal Snyder looked over his shoulder and said, "If I'm not the first person you free, you are having detention for the rest of eternity."

Maybe he's just plain nuts, Xander thought. *That would explain a lot.*

"Okay, this is it," Xander announced. To the girl, "Get ready. On my count."

But before he could even say "one," the carousel went completely dark. His horse bucked, and then it stiffened.

Cheers and screams mingled in the darkness.

"Three!" he shouted.

The carousel vanished, and he tumbled to the ground.

He began to run.

Le Malfaiteur shifted his weight and yawned.

I'm being affected, he realized. *I just don't have the energy for this. We have the perfect word in French: ennui.*

This is not my battle. I wish them well, all of them.

He ambled away from the Ferris wheel, preparing to leave. He had no idea where Ethan and his little girlfriend had gone. He didn't care, as long as their paths never crossed. Revenge was too much work to even ponder.

He looked down and saw that he could see the vague outline of his hand. His spell of invisibility was wearing off.

He hurried his pace. It was easier to leave quickly than it would be to fight his way out of the carnival.

"Adieu," he said, thinking of Cordelia. He kissed his fingers and blew her a kiss.

Xander landed in the midway, or what passed for it in hell, the food stalls and games all lit up. But there was no one playing. There were no customers. Except two: Carl Palmer was flinging coins at stacks and stacks of glassware. He was chained to the booth, and he had been severely beaten.

And was that . . . *Cordelia*?

Xander ducked around a concession stand to stare at her. He caught his reflection in the shiny surface of a glass platter, and he was stunned. He looked worse than Carl.

Then everything flickered, as it had on the carousel.

Cordelia cried out and Xander ran to her, throwing his arms around her; they passed through her but she turned around and screamed, "Xander!"

"Cordelia!" He lunged for her again.

Missed again.

"It's a prism!" She darted forward and grabbed a purple basket made of glass.

Then she disappeared. And like the carousel, the midway went dark.

"Cordy!" Xander shouted. "Carl!"

"Who's that?" Carl shouted back through the darkness. "Where are you?"

Xander ran to his voice.

Willow stood in front of the fun house, which was glowing with a silvery light. She did not want to go inside. But she mustered up her courage and took one step in; then another, twisting and turning in the metallic glow.

I hope I'm not being exposed to radiation, she thought anxiously.

She thought she felt someone behind her. She cried out and whirled around.

Above her head, a skull wearing a pirate hat shouted, "Arr!" Laughter echoed down the corridor.

Willow stumbled left, right; she got twisted around more times than she could count.

She was trembling from head to toe. She was so scared that tears began streaming down her face.

But she kept on going.

Buffy told us the layout, pretty much. Shouldn't I be coming to the mirror maze soon?

As she turned another corner, she caught her breath.

A clown statue smiled from the end of the corridor.

She raised a hand, wondering if it could see her. Waved back and forth to see if it reacted. It didn't move, didn't blink.

Didn't try to kill her.

Maybe I'm still invisible. If I could find the mirrors, I'd know.

She crept forward.

The clown remained motionless.

She tiptoed along the left wall, trying to keep as much distance between herself and the clown as possible.

She dodged around it.

And around the next corner, she reached her destination: the mirror maze.

Willow stared in amazement. Every single mirror was smashed. Every one.

Is this really bad, or kind of bad? she wondered. *Or was Giles wrong?* She didn't know what to do now. He had said for each of them to bring the prism back if they could.

She went past panel after panel, shattered into pieces that were strewn across the floor.

Where they had stood, silvery rectangles glowed and

vibrated, and she heard faint shouting emanating from them. It sounded like human voices, like a big, intense, angry crowd.

Is it the souls being tortured in the hell dimension?

She tried to make herself call Xander's name. But her throat was dry as dust.

Then she looked down and saw a blur of her hand.

The spell is losing power, she thought. *I'd better get back to the others.*

Sparing one more look at the glowing rectangles, she gathered up as many fragments of the mirrors as she could and made her way back out of the fun house.

"Anyone here?" Giles asked as he carried the mirror into the freak show and laid it beside the crystal ball, alongside Xander's coffin, as had been agreed. Once he let go of it, it was visible again.

Then he saw his hands, and his shoes. He was visible again.

At that moment Willow ran into the room with large jagged pieces of mirror in her hands. He saw her clearly.

"Giles, oh my God!" she cried. "I went into the maze and all the mirrors were broken!"

"Let me help you," he said. "You're about to cut yourself." He rushed to her and carefully took the shards, putting them beside the crystal ball. What happened?"

"I don't know."

"Did you notice anyone about? Did you see Buffy?"

She shook her head. "No. A clown, but it didn't move. Maybe it broke the mirrors."

"Perhaps Buffy broke them."

"I don't know," she said. "The entire fun house was glowing, Giles. Everything was silver. And on the way here, I saw the carousel. It was glowing all yellow!"

"The Chamber of Horrors was bathed in a sort of black light," Giles said. "Perhaps when we remove the prisms, their absence causes some kind of refraction of light." He looked down at the fragments. "I don't know what this means. But we'll proceed on our course and see where it leads, yes?"

"Yes," Willow murmured. She felt somehow responsible for the broken mirror, although she'd done nothing to cause it. She was becoming more afraid. Things weren't going as planned.

We've always pulled it off before, she reminded herself. *But Buffy's the Slayer because some other girl didn't pull it off.*

Buffy won't fail. But we might.

At that moment the room they stood in seemed to . . . flicker. Fairyland lost its distinct edges; then it returned.

"What's happening?" Willow asked, moving in a circle.

"I don't know. Perhaps more of the same effect." Giles examined the mirror he had brought, experimentally shining it against the walls.

There were footsteps, light and quick.

It was Ms. Calendar, also fully materialized, carrying the

mirror ball. "Rupert, the carousel is giving off this golden light! And the Tunnel of Love is shimmering with some kind of scarlet energy."

"Then perhaps Vaclav managed to steal the red heart," Giles said. "Did you see him?"

"No," Ms. Calendar replied, looking worried.

"I hope nothing happened to him," Willow murmured.

The freak show winked out again, longer this time.

"What's that?" Ms. Calendar cried, her dark eyes flashing. "What's happening?"

"I think the carnival is beginning to break apart," Giles told them.

"That's great!" Willow said. "Right?"

"Yes, if it happens fast enough, and if it's a complete job," Giles replied. "However, they'll certainly trace the source here. We have to think about leaving."

"What about the destruction spell?" Willow asked. "Should we do it now?"

Giles considered. "Perhaps we can wait a little while longer for Cordelia and Le Malfaiteur. But if they don't show soon, it might be prudent to go ahead and try to do as much damage as we can."

"We're missing two prisms," Willow said. "All the mirrors in the fun house were broken, which was probably a good thing. I'm not sure I would have been able to break the glass."

"Buffy didn't mention anything about that when she told

us about the fun house." Giles picked up a shard. "I wonder if she did this."

"Or someone or some*thing* else," Ms. Calendar ventured.

"Gulp," Willow said.

Ms. Calendar nodded. "Yes. Bringing the pieces of the mirror was good, Willow." She took a breath. "I have the printout of the incantation," she said, reaching in the pocket of her skirt and unfolding it.

"We'll start arranging the objects in a circle." Giles gestured for Willow to help him.

They were almost finished making the circle when Cordelia rushed in. The purple basket was cradled in her arms. "It was so weird! I got, like, stuck, and I thought I saw Xander, but . . . I'm so confused. I think I was hypnotized again and *ooh*, this basket is pretty." She held it in her outstretched hands, smiling with a dazed expression on her face.

"Put it down in our circle," Giles told her. "It's tempting you."

She groaned.

"Cordelia."

She set it next to the mirror.

"All right. I guess this is it," Ms. Calendar said.

"Help me!" It was Vaclav. "Help!"

He came barreling toward them with the ruby heart against his chest. In close pursuit, horned demons and humans raced after him. The girl who had been in the coffin was one of them, a bright smile stretched across her face, although her eyes were vacant and unfocused.

"We need to erect a barrier!" Ms. Calendar spread her arms and began to chant. Giles recognized the structure, if not the precise vocabulary, of a Sumerian warding spell. He joined in, striving to reinforce it as best he could.

The warding spell worked. The horde of attackers smashed into the invisible barrier Giles and Ms. Calendar had erected. Their monstrous faces contorted with rage; they balled their fists, claws, and talons and pummeled at the perimeter, roaring with fury.

"Run out the back! We'll try to hold them!" Giles said to Willow, standing with his legs wide apart and extending his arms. *"Ta-mir-o! Baal! Cthulhu! Jezebel!"*

"Not him again!" Cordelia protested.

"You don't have the blade!" Ms. Calendar reminded him.

"Yes, I do," Giles said, yanking it out of his pocket.

"Don't call that Astorrith guy," Cordelia begged him. "He'll take out half of Sunnydale."

"Cordelia's right, Rupert," Ms. Calendar said. "It won't help."

Giles thought a moment, then nodded his agreement; Ms. Calendar turned to Willow and said, "All right, then. Let's proceed with the spell of destruction as fast as we can. Willow, you need to help us with this, good?"

"Okay." Willow licked her lips and took a deep breath as

she looked anxiously at the horde of monsters pushing at the barrier. "I'm ready."

"We only have six prisms!" Vaclav protested.

"We can't wait any longer," Giles replied. "Jenny, please, begin."

Ms. Calendar took a slow, cleansing breath. Then she began to speak in a low, authoritative voice, *"In the name of the Goddess of Destruction, I order the beating heart of this demon to shatter!"*

She went on, and Vaclav held his breath as the young red-haired Willow joined in when Ms. Calendar invited her. Also Mr. Giles.

"These chambers must sunder! Hear me, Dark Lady, and break his heart, break it, make it shatter!"

Vaclav's mouth filled with bile as he pressed his fists against his mouth to keep from screaming.

"Nothing's happening!" Cordelia cried.

The five looked at one another. Vaclav saw frustration on their faces. Also despair. And terror, and he knew they were mirrored on his own face.

But he also saw a fine resolve settle over them. They were noble people, these friends of Angel's. He could not be one of them—he had done too much evil—but he could help them.

"So . . . we need all of them, right?" Cordelia said shrilly. "The prisms? And we're missing the Ferris wheel one?"

Just then, the barrier they had created . . . wobbled. Vaclav had no other word for it. It was weakening. He knew why.

"The magicks are building," he told them. "It is the Rising. The power of my master is at its zenith tonight! The dark forces gather. We are lost!"

"Great," Cordelia bit off. "So let's get the hell out of here."

"I'm afraid we may no longer have that choice," Giles said as he and Ms. Calendar moved toward the barrier. "Let's try to keep it going," he told her. "For as long as we can."

She nodded.

"If we can't leave, then someone needs to get the prism and bring it back here," Willow said.

Vaclav raised his hand. "Me. I'll do it." He was moved by their courage; he had been a part of evil for so long, he hadn't thought there was any good left inside him. His love for Sandra and his admiration of these people—and Angel— had brought it forth. "I will do it," Vaclav vowed, laying his hand over his heart. "Or die trying."

Giles hesitated.

Cordelia huffed. "*You* can't go," Cordelia said to Giles. "You have to stay here and help with the ward. Same with Ms. Calendar. And Willow is your, like, magickal backup, plus, *please*, she'd get, like, two feet before they slaughtered her. And *I* have a fear of heights. So. He's our only hope." She smiled grimly at him. "Since my guy bailed."

"We don't know that," Willow said. "He might have been killed." She looked stricken. "I mean, he might be delayed."

"I can do it," Vaclav insisted. "They haven't come through the back way. If I go now, I might be able to get out."

"Go then," Giles said softly. "And thank you."

Vaclav inclined his head. "I will not fail."

Then he raced out the exit.

Ms. Calendar looked over her shoulder at Willow. "Willow, help me erect another ward at the exit. I'll teach you the words." She looked at her earnestly. "Can you do that?"

Willow swallowed hard. "Um, yes, yes, I can."

Buffy kept squeezing Caligarius around the neck as the room flickered and shifted and changed and rearranged—from room to enormous, viscous internal body parts to room again. And as she squeezed, Caligarius grew; he was becoming the demon once more. She couldn't let that happen; she didn't understand what exactly was going on, but she knew she had to kill him as he was or . . .

He shrank back down. Fighting to pull her off him, his gaze ticked anxiously from her to the calliope behind him.

To the calliope behind him.

She looked.

The center of it was glowing a brilliant emerald green. It was pulsing rhythmically.

Green steam was shooting from the pipes.

No, not steam . . . green demon blood.

It's his heart, she thought.

But it didn't matter. She had no more oxygen; she was beginning to faint. She wouldn't be able to do anything about it.

She was going to fail.

And he knew it. An evil, triumphant smile spread across his face. His eyes glittered.

"What now, proud one?" he taunted her.

Now I'm going to die, Buffy the Vampire Slayer thought, beginning to let go. *Mom, I'm so sorry. Willow, Xander, Giles . . .*

Vaclav flew like the wind blowing across the steppes of his native Bulgaria. The carnival had disintegrated into pandemonium; the patrons had awakened from the mesmerizing effect of the soulcatchers and the calliope. Now they were screaming hysterically and running in panic from Caligari's minions. Vampires had joined the fray.

Vaclav had to stop the carnage, end this here, now. He had lost Sandra—she was still one of *them*—but he could save Angel's friends.

He ran so fast he almost fell over his own feet. The carousel was glowing; the Tunnel of Love as well. Mr. Giles was right; when the prisms were taken, the rides that concealed them glowed with color.

Since the Ferris wheel did not throw off any unusual hue, he could assume that Le Malfaiteur had failed in his duty.

There was no longer a line of people waiting to get on, and no attendants overseeing the ride. All the carriages were empty, and still the wheel turned.

With a mad dash, he hopped into a carriage as the wheel swooped downward. As it arced back up into the air, someone cried, "Vaclav!"

Terrified, he looked back down at the ground. It was Madame Lazabra, surrounded by the freaks of the freak show. He had wondered where they had been. All he knew was that somehow Le Malfaiteur had been detained. Vaclav had dared to hope that that meant he had destroyed them.

Otto, the man with three legs, was aiming a crossbow at him while the twelve dwarfs of Fairyland raced to the Ferris wheel ramp and piled into the next approaching carriage.

Their carriage was three below his; as he looked down on them, they shook their fists at him. Six of them scrabbled out of the carriage and began to climb up the superstructure. They moved much more quickly than Vaclav would have thought them able.

From the ground Otto let a crossbow bolt fly.

It hurtled through the air, and missed.

But the next one might not.

He crouched inside the carriage, gazing fearfully over the edge at the ground below as he was swept aloft. The members of Caligari's dread family were massing. Beyond, he saw domes of ethereal color surrounding some of the other rides—the Tunnel of Love, the fun house, the Chamber of Horrors, the carousel.

Demons and humans were beginning to climb into other carriages in pursuit of him, he knew; others crowded around the console at the base, pushing buttons, then pulling on the emergency brake.

With a terrible groan, the Ferris wheel slowed, then ground to a halt.

They will get me, he thought sickly. *They will stop me.* Then he saw a flash of movement on the superstructure of the wheel itself. He squinted, seeing nothing . . . or was there a hand gripping a metal strut?

Then he heard a voice.

"What the 'ell, *merde!*" the voice shouted. "Vaclav?"

It was the voice that had cast the spell of invisibility over them on the cell phone. It was Le Malfaiteur.

"How do you know me?" Vaclav shouted back.

"I was Ethan Rayne's dog. I saw you at the encampment."

The hand flickered back into Vaclav's range of vision, and then the man's head.

"I can see you!" Vaclav told him.

Le Malfaiteur intoned the words of the invisibility spell; then he vanished.

"Where have you been?" Vaclav said. "They waited and waited!"

"I was . . . I'm 'elping now," he said. "I thought of Cordelia, so lovely. Too pretty to die." He chuckled. "Ethan and I both have an eye for the ladies."

"Well, she may be dead by now!" Vaclav told him. "You have to get the prism. They need it to complete their spell!"

He heard shouting, voices getting louder. One of his "friends," Max, who was wearing his true visage—he was a purple chitenous demon with clawlike legs—was scrambling toward them like a man-sized crab; he was being followed by Bettina, the Lindwurm, who was inching up the metal girders. Heading for him.

He added, "You need to stay invisible. If they see you, they'll go after you."

"I can't 'old it very long," Le Malfaiteur said. "The magickal field is too strong."

"Hurry!" Vaclav implored him.

Le Malfaiteur did not reply. Vaclav waited, then called out, "Where are you?"

And then he realized that he shouldn't talk to him any longer. Their enemies—once his only family!—were getting closer. He could see their eyes, which seemed so foreign to him now.

"Vaclav, damn you, what are you doing?" Max shouted at him.

Vaclav took a breath. He ticked a glance where he had last seen Le Malfaiteur. He could see the barest outline of his body. He had moved an astonishing distance; of course, he was a warlock!

But he was becoming more solid.

I have to do something, Vaclav thought.

He looked at Max, and at all the others. At the glowing domes surrounding the rides. He thought of the centuries he had traveled with the carnival; he could hear the chuffing of the horses and the jingling of the bells on the Gypsy's wagon.

Maybe it's not too late. Maybe they will take me back, he thought desperately. *I'm so terrified.*

But he knew what Caligari would do to him. He would take his mind and make him like Sandra, and that new one, Carl.

He peered over at Le Malfaiteur. He was almost there. But he was nearly fully visible.

He stood in the carriage. "What we're doing is evil!" he shouted at Max. At Bettina, whose underbelly was beginning to glow as she moved into position to shoot her heat at him, wrapping herself around a girder. "The carnival must be stopped!"

"*You* must be stopped!" Max shouted back.

Yes, Vaclav thought, shaking with fear. They were focusing on him.

Rushing at him.

Getting ready to kill him.

"You are dying, Slayer," Caligarius crowed as the world grew dimmer around Buffy. She couldn't breathe. She wasn't sure her lungs were even working anymore.

Things were flickering around them, and she could tell he was freaking out.

But he was still standing, and she was not.

"You are dying," he said again, maybe to rub it in. "And Sunnydale will die with you. Even better, it will go to hell. And it will be your fault."

My fault?

Those were fighting words.

My fault?

Better than any magick spell on earth, they galvanized her.

Blindly she pushed past him, flinging herself at the calliope. She reached out both her hands and grabbed at it.

If this is his heart, I'm going to squeeze the life out of it.

It was not pretty, but death rarely was.

Vaclav's self-sacrifice had bought Le Malfaiteur the time he needed to get to the prism. It was a simple little mirror secured to a metal rod, and angled such that as one passed, one might take a glance into it . . . and feel so incredibly lazy.

He chuckled and reached out a hand. He still didn't know why he had bothered to come back. On the one hand, he had nursed a niggling little fear that perhaps if Caligari won the day, Ethan would return to claim a reward. Ethan Rayne on his own was a formidable foe, but allied with one such as this . . . Ethan might do more than turn him into an animal next time their paths crossed.

Was it self-preservation, then? Or . . . was it because of that pretty *jeune fille*, Cordelia? Hard to say. At any rate, *bien*, here he was, like some ridiculous musketeer in a novel by Dumas.

But he plucked the prism like a ripe piece of fruit—a tempting apple, perhaps—and recast his invisibility spell.

They were still tearing Vaclav's body to shreds.

Requiescat in pace.

• • •

In the freak show, the monsters slammed against the wards that Giles, Ms. Calendar, and Willow had erected and strengthened numerous times.

"The barriers are weakening," Giles said.

Oh my God, Cordelia thought, *we're gonna die!*

And then, like some kind of hero, Le Malfaiteur appeared beside her. *Poof!* Just like that! He was holding a small mirror in his hand, and Cordelia cried, "Wow, am I glad to see you!"

"And I you," he said, laughing as he grabbed her around the waist and gave her the best, juiciest kiss. It was an earth-shaking, mind-blowing—

"Ritual," she said breathlessly. "Now."

"Now," Giles agreed.

While Le Malfaiteur strengthened the wards, Cordelia placed the mirror with the other prisms. Then Giles, Ms. Calendar, Willow, and Le Malfaiteur spread out their hands.

"By the dark Goddess of Destruction, by the power of entropy, we call upon the ending! The ruination! Break this heart!"

Willow was crying, afraid of the strange, shadowy sensation that was pouring through her as they chanted; and she was grieving for Vaclav. Le Malfaiteur had told them of his sacrifice.

But they had to press on. They had to try to destroy this thing, now—

"Make the heart of the demon end, make it stop!"

"We call upon the Goddess, the Dark Lady, stop it now!"

"Oh my God, something is happening!" Willow screamed.

Blinding white light filled the room.

The carnival was strangling. Withering.

And though Caligari knew it, he was not willing to go down without a fight; he reappeared as his huge, demonic self, clutching his heart as Buffy, trapped inside it, did all the damage she possibly could.

"I would have made you my queen," he thundered.

She didn't know how she could hear him. How she could understand the words he spoke. She was blind from lack of oxygen. She couldn't feel. She could only . . . slay.

So she ripped and clawed and tore. She swam in green demon blood, drowned in it, as his heart began to pound too fast, too hard, trapping her, pulling her inside the chambers and flinging her from one side to another.

I'm dying, she thought. *But so is he.*

"I will not die. The souls will feed me," he gasped. "They will feed me and I will rise again! I always have. And I will now!"

The carnival glowed with lights, refracting and shimmering against the black velvet night. Seven attractions blazed with light—the six that had housed prisms, and the freak show—and then they all became white, crystalline, and pure.

In the fun house, figures burst out of the glowing rectangles: Carl Palmer, the Hahn twins, Principal Snyder and the carousel riders; and leading the charge—Xander Lavelle Harris.

They were the souls Caligari had trapped and fed on for millennia. Following Xander, they flooded the fun house as the lights flashed and the laughter echoed down the corridors for the last time—thousands of shimmering ovals poured out after them, having no form other than light.

But having an agenda nevertheless: escape.

"No!" Caligari shouted. "No, stop them! Stop *him*!"

Then he fell to the earth in an enormous, ground-shaking collapse.

Buffy yanked and pulled her way out of his chest cavity, swimming in foul demon blood as it gushed out of the exit wound she created.

She panted, sucking in breath after breath. Her lungs felt seared; her mind began to clear.

She turned and stared at the demon. He was beginning to disintegrate already.

She slipped and slid on the viscous liquid as she cried, "Mom! Where are you?"

The carnival shifted and shimmered, a kaleidoscope of the disguises it had worn: burlesque houses and opium dens and the Grand Guignol of France; public executions and cockfights and medieval jousts. Witch burnings and Druid festivals; raves and concerts and gladiatorial combats.

Images crisscrossed one another as they winked in and out of existence, as the people in the images lost definition, some to decay into skeletons, others to dissolve into light.

And then Caligari's body came apart in huge, decaying chunks. Maggots wriggled in the flesh. It quickly liquefied and sank into the ground in rivulets, soaking the earth with its foulness.

Buffy staggered backward, covering her mouth. The need to inhale was stronger than her revulsion, but she hated drawing the terrible stench into her body.

From out of the ground a black mist rose on geysers of steam. It was pure, distilled evil. It was the heart of darkness.

It was what was left of Caligari, and if she could have flung herself into the air to destroy it, she would have.

The steam and the foulness formed the shape of a horned death's head, which hovered high into the air and glared down at Buffy.

"It is the Rising," it told her. "It is not too late to join me. We can start anew."

She realized it was trying to appeal to her pride. She was amazed.

"No, you can lose, *loser*," Buffy said, heaving with exhaustion. "You can end."

It glared down at her one more time. Then it began to dissipate, fading out against the starry, moonlit sky.

Buffy staggered forward, calling for her mother.

The freak show was gone. Giles, Ms. Calendar, Cordelia, and Willow stared in wonderment at one another. They were standing in the clearing by Blessed Memories Cemetery.

Then they looked down at Xander, who was lying on the grass at Cordelia's feet, bathed in moonlight and in the strange lights filling the sky.

He opened his eyes.

And Willow and Cordelia both burst into tears.

"Buffy!"

Joyce Summers ran to her daughter in the dark clearing in the forest.

They embraced, hard. Buffy closed her eyes, wincing because she was covering her mother with demon blood.

Only she wasn't.

There was no demon blood.

Buffy looked around. All trace of the carnival was gone. No rides, no lights, no people, no demons.

She listened.

No calliope.

She looked toward Sunnydale. There was a hazy glow of flames on the horizon.

There was still work to be done, then.

"What's going on?" Joyce asked, bewildered.

"It's all right, Mom," Buffy said.

The two held each other.

Then Xander, Cordelia, Giles, and Ms. Calendar ran toward them.

She looked at Giles.

"Where's Angel?" she asked.

• • •

It's not a bad way to go, Angel thought, as he beheaded another Shrieker with a sword he had taken from an orc. He was covered with green demon blood, and plenty of wounds of his own.

But I would have liked to say good-bye to Buffy.

The ground shook and he thought, *What now?*

He wasn't ready for what he saw: a glowing swarm of oval lights, rising into the sky and arcing across the face of the moon like a phalanx of comets. Darting and shimmering. Dancing and rejoicing.

Souls. Liberated.

Buffy did it.

Angel did something he very rarely did: He smiled.

Around him, his attackers stopped and stared. A trio of albino poisoners spat venom on the sidewalk; as it sizzled, they slunk away, casting anxious glances over their shoulders at Angel, who let them go.

Weapons dropped. Vampires darted back into the shadows.

The fight was over.

There might be some mop-up, but the good guys had won.

She did it, Angel thought again.

But did she survive it?

His answer walked out of the smoke, slowly at first; then, as Buffy Summers the Vampire Slayer saw him, she ran to him. She whispered, "Angel," and put her arms around him.

And his soul soared.

EPILOGUE

It was really over. Giles, Ms. Calendar, and Le Malfaiteur had cast runes, searched for portents. The carnival was gone. The nightmare, ended.

"It's so weird how no one, like, notices," Cordelia said as she admired her new choker. And her pendant. And her earrings. "I mean, saltwater pearls this big are so *rare.*"

The Yasumi company had richly rewarded Cordelia for foiling a robbery and saving the life of the salesclerk, whom Cordelia had gone back to and untied. She had her picture in the paper, which caused her no end of grief because she had a scratch on her cheek. Giles told her to wear it proudly because it was a symbol of her bravery in battle.

"Oh, *please*," she had sneered.

"It is remarkable," Giles said of the oblivious after-state of the little town still swimming in denial. "I think we are able to remember what happened because of the magicks we used."

"Or we're just lucky that way," Buffy said with a sigh.

He, Buffy, Willow, Cordelia, Xander, and Ms. Calendar were standing in the clearing where the carnival had stood. It was gone now, all trace . . . and all memory of it. Not a single person beyond their small company had any recollection that Professor Copernicus Caligari's Traveling Carnival had come to town. As there had never been any permits or articles about it in the paper, there was no proof that it had ever been there.

No one remembered the crazed swath of destruction caused by Astorrith. Giles's condo was said to have burned down because of a gas leak. While it was being rebuilt, he was staying at a nearby hotel, and Ms. Calendar was helping him shop for new clothes and kitchen things.

Buffy thought he looked great in his new Dockers and loose-fitting sweater. But it was obvious he felt like he wasn't decently clothed. He kept tugging at everything and muttering under his breath.

But of the carnival of souls: All anyone remembered was a terrible storm, and some deaths. One of them had been the bludgeoning of Anita Palmer, Carl and Mariann Palmer's mother.

Carl was in custody for the homicide, and under suspicion for his sister's disappearance.

Giles had promised Buffy he would try to help him get out of it. But she wasn't sure Carl wanted out. He didn't recall why he had killed his mother, but he knew that he had.

She felt so sorry for him.

If I can explain it to him, I will, she decided.

Joyce Summers's memory was also blank. Which made things ever so much easier for the Slayer.

Witness the brand-new kick dress she was wearing!

As for Vaclav . . . they didn't know exactly what had happened to him, but they were glad he had helped. They had a moment of silence for him. And then they moved on, just as Sunnydale had.

As for the chaos . . . no one remembered much of that, either. The dead were buried with reasonable explanations for their passing. Car accidents, mostly. There really weren't very many deaths—by Sunnydale standards.

Life was back to normal . . . by Sunnydale standards as well.

"Well, we'd better go to school," Buffy said to the others.

Giles drove them back. They trooped into the auditorium where they had once died a thousand deaths in a talent show. Giles, almost literally.

They found seats and settled in. Jenny Calendar sat next to Giles, and they smiled at each other.

The Hahns were there too, in amazingly nerdy sweaters

with moose faces on them. They sat beside each other in the center of an otherwise empty row, the outcasts they had always been . . . or nearly always.

Principal Snyder came out to a mixed chorus of boos and cheers. Like the others, his face was undamaged. Well, except for its natural appearance.

"How can he not remember that I saved his immortal soul?" Xander kvetched. "That is so unfair."

Snyder held out his hands for silence. The students all settled down.

"I'm happy to announce the results of our student council fund-raising survey," he relayed, with an expression that was anything but happy. He actually looked like he was chewing glass.

"We're going to have a blood drive." He huffed. Then he threw down the clipboard. "This is idiotic. We'll have a carnival, just like all the other schools."

"This is so inappropriate," Cordelia said. "He has no clue." Then she brightened. "Ooh, carnival! I'll be the queen!"

Buffy exchanged weary glances with the others.

Willow said quietly, "You know, even with the lust spell, Angel was never attracted to Cordelia."

Buffy blushed. "Wow. That's true."

"Score one for Dead Guy," Xander said grumpily.

"Participation will be mandatory," Snyder went on.

It always is, Buffy thought.

She whispered to Willow, "Anywhere But Here."

Willow thought. "Tuscany, John Cusack, riding mopeds."

"Good," Buffy complimented her.

"Your turn," Willow said.

Buffy cocked her head. "Graveyard, Angel, smoochies."

Willow frowned slightly. "That's not Anywhere But Here, Buffy. That's *here*."

Buffy smiled. "Yeah. It is."

ONE THING OR YOUR MOTHER

FOR PATRICIA A. BEYER
AND HER MOTHER,
JEWELL PELLEGRINO

MY WATCHERS

Patricia and Fred. Their sons, Matthew and Paul. Matthew's wife, Beth. Vivian. Her mother, Ollie. Her daughters, Debra and Donna. Their spouses and children, Bill, Michael, Justin, Chris, and Derek. Madeline and Bob. Their daughters, Elizabeth and Katherine. Anna. Heather. Samantha. Her husband, Sean. Their children, and my godchildren, Katey, Maggie, and Jack. Allan and Candy. Their daughters Christiana and Carolina. Fred and Marianne. Their son, Freddie. Tony. Vanessa. Cappiello. Tara. Art. Brett and Jenn. Jolene. John. Maura. Patrick. Emily. Cara.

To you, these names may not mean anything. To me, they mean the whole world. They are my family, my friends, the people who made me who I am, and who, one way or another, made this project possible.

Special thanks to Katherine for the title. To Heather, for always helping me find my way when I'm lost. To Emily, for the opportunity. To Cara, for her careful editing. And to my mother, Patricia, and my grandmother, Jewell, for being nothing at all like the villain of this piece. I, too, know how lucky I am.

Joss Whedon is a genius. His work inspired mine, long before I had the chance to write about Buffy Summers. I am also indebted to the writers of *Buffy the Vampire Slayer*, and to the actors who brought their characters to such dazzling life.

Finally, David. He teaches me daily that there is nothing love cannot accomplish. Whatever I am, whatever I might achieve, it means nothing without his constant patience, understanding, support, and selfless devotion.

Thanks, guys.

CHAPTER ONE

Three to one wouldn't normally be considered the best odds to take in a fight. Of course, the math changed a bit if the "one" in question happened to be Buffy Summers. Technically, she was the Vampire Slayer. But the fine print of her unwritten contract with the powers that be didn't distinguish between vampires, demons, witches, ghosts, or any other purveyor of paranormal power that happened to make its way to Sunnydale, California, Buffy's home, and one of only a few cities on the planet whose claim to fame was being situated on a Hellmouth. Sunnydale's tourist brochures would never highlight this particular piece of trivia, because Buffy and a few of her closest friends were among the handful of folks who even knew what a

Hellmouth was, let alone that its proximity to the quaint Southern California town made it a magnet for all things evil.

"Tell me the truth," Buffy said as she landed a solid kick to the chest of one of her assailants that sent him crashing into a really lovely marble headstone. "You got that jacket at David Lee Roth's yard sale, didn't you?"

The vampire on the receiving end of her barb was too busy trying to pull himself up to find a witty retort. Buffy briefly considered pulling her favorite stake out of her jacket pocket and finishing him right then and there with a quick lunge and thrust. Unfortunately his buddies, whom she had already dubbed Tweedle-Dumb and Tweedle-Dumber, were regrouping to lurch at her from opposite flanks. Not to mention the fact that part of her, a tiny, secret part that she rarely gave this much rein, was thoroughly enjoying pounding these three losers to a pulp. The adrenaline coursing through her veins—and pushing her enhanced strength and fighting skills to their limits—had already worked her up into a satisfying righteous rage. Though the three punching bags she was currently working weren't really the source of her anger, she decided that for now she could settle for making them suffer a little for Angel's betrayal and his perverse sense of revenge before sending them off to their dusty and final oblivion.

"Come on, guys," Buffy taunted, backing up a little to keep Dumb and Dumber in her peripheral sightlines. "I get that you're new to this whole 'creature of the night' gig, but I know you can do better than this."

Dumb decided to feint to his right, a move he telegraphed as clearly as if he'd written Buffy a memo beforehand, complete with a color-coded diagram of their fight. As she shifted her weight to counter, Dumber charged Buffy's back, throwing his whole weight into his attempt to knock her to the ground before baring his fangs and going in for a good long gulp of Slayer blood.

That was certainly the plan, anyway.

Unfortunately for Dumber, it took more than what had probably been in life the frame of a slight accountant to knock Buffy off her feet. Instead, she took his weight and used his own momentum to send him flipping over her back, feetfirst, into Dumb, who had unintentionally lined himself up perfectly to receive the full force of his accomplice's misguided efforts. Had this particular move been attempted by the Van Halen wannabe, it might have been a different story. He had a good fifty pounds on his buddies, and as strong as Buffy was, her petite frame was hardly invincible. Lucky for Buffy, strength wasn't everything in these nightly death matches. Speed and skill counted for much more than brute force, as she had learned again and again in the years that she'd been slaying vampires.

As Dumb and Dumber were busy untangling themselves from each other, poor David Lee Wrong had finally come to his senses and regained his feet. Instead of jumping back into the fight, he seemed to be seriously considering the better part of valor, also known as making a run for it.

Oh, no, you don't, Buffy thought as he turned to find his escape route. Without pause, Buffy grabbed her trusty stake and sent it flying through the air, straight through his back and into his heart. Though she couldn't see the expression on his face, she did hear a faint "Bummer, dude," as what had begun as dust quickly turned once again to dust, exploding into a million tiny fragments with a satisfying *whoosh*.

Unfortunately, the sense of minute accomplishment that usually followed the death of a vampire did nothing to assuage Buffy's anger. She turned back to the idiot twins who remained, fully prepared to finish the fight, hoping against hope that in the process some of the feelings she'd been struggling to wrestle into submission would find release.

For the moment, both Dumb and Dumber were staring in disbelief at the untimely defeat of their compatriot.

"Sorry, guys," Buffy said in the world-weary tone she often adopted when confronting newly risen vampires. "I know you haven't had time to read the handbook or attend any of the meetings, but here's how this works. Whoever makes the rules decided a long time ago that if vampires like you were going to treat this planet like an all-you-can-eat buffet, there would be at least one girl in every generation—that would be me— born with the strength and skill to balance the scales a little bit." Taking the bull by the horns, Buffy rushed the two vampires and, grabbing Dumber firmly by the lapels of his rayon-blend suit jacket, lifted him off his feet and tossed him atop Dumb before continuing.

"So, much as I regret raining on your parade," she said, punctuating her remarks with a swift kick to Dumber's side, which sent him rolling off Dumb, "it's my sacred duty to see to it that stupid"—another kick—"ugly"—a good stomp—"bloodsucking losers like you"—a final kick to Dumber's backside—"never have a chance to hide from the light of day."

Neither of her remaining foes was putting up much pretense of a fight any longer, and though Buffy hated to see this come to an end, she knew it was long past time. Grasping an overhanging branch, she pulled it from its resident tree and snapped it in half. With less ceremony than she would have liked, she thrust the first half through Dumber's back. As he exploded into dust, she turned on Dumb, who had risen to his knees.

"That sucks," he said weakly, already sensing the inevitable.

"Tell me about it," Buffy replied, finishing him off with the second half of the branch.

Buffy's rage ebbed ever so slightly as she placed her hands on her knees and caught her breath in the lonely cemetery.

It did suck.

It sucked more and harder than anyone in the world could possibly imagine.

The battle had been good. But that was little comfort. The battle she needed to fight right now was with her former boyfriend, Angel, the man who had taught her both the meaning of love, and the definition of tragedy.

She should have known it would never work. Truth be told, she had known. He was a vampire, and she was a Slayer. It was classic "Do not enter" territory.

Angel.

A vampire, yes. But not just any vampire. As foul and demented a demon as had ever walked the earth, he had once delighted in the infliction of exquisite pain on anyone unfortunate enough to cross his path. It was ultimately a camp of Gypsies who had found a way to make him pay by giving him back the one thing that could make him truly regret his violent ways: his soul. By the time he had first met Buffy he'd had over a hundred years to wrestle with that soul and come to terms with the only choices before him. He could remain in the shadows of the world eking out a meager existence, or he could re-enter the fight on the side of the good and somehow try to redeem himself. He had made the harder choice. But with Buffy by his side, redemption had slowly begun to seem possible. Long before they had admitted their love to each other, he had proved time and again that he would always be there for her, protecting the Slayer when he needed to, supporting her whenever he could, and always fighting beside her through the worst the world could throw at her.

So in what universe was it fair that actually loving Buffy was the thing that destroyed him? The curse that restored his soul came with a little-known caveat: If he ever knew real happiness, the soul that was meant to torment him would be taken from him. He had known happiness, and Buffy had known it with him, ever so briefly. And now Angel was gone. Worse than dead. A demon now wore his face, and since his transformation a few weeks ago he had done everything in his power to taunt, terrify, and torture the girl who had risked everything to love him.

It was like a bad dream that just wasn't ending.

Every time Angel had confronted Buffy since that fateful night when her world had changed forever, she had come closer to accepting the unacceptable. Angel was dead, and she was going to have to find it within herself to kill the monster that now roamed Sunnydale in his guise. And she had almost reconciled herself to that fact. Until a few days ago, when two frustrated ghosts, James and Grace, who had shared their own star-crossed affair over fifty years ago, had possessed Buffy and Angel in an attempt to resolve their own issues.

Buffy could have done without the bad drama that was their last moments on earth. But she couldn't deny, even now, the unutterable joy that had washed through her when Angel had pulled her into his arms, talking only of love and forgiveness, and sealed that bond with the deepest and most passionate kiss they had ever shared. How much of what she had felt had truly belonged to James and Grace, Buffy would never know. What she did know was that feeling Angel's love again, even briefly, had made it harder than ever to accept the fact that what she'd once had was now gone forever, and for her and Angel there would be no fairy-tale reconciliation.

Taking a quick scan of the rest of the cemetery, Buffy

decided that she'd probably seen all the action this particular location had to offer for the evening. She still had hours of homework waiting for her before she was going to be able to get some sleep. Finals were only a few weeks away and despite her best efforts, her classroom performance had been seriously subpar this semester. With a sigh, Buffy turned away from the neat rows of headstones and trudged toward the cemetery exit.

She had to admit that the last few nights her patrols had been particularly fruitful. She'd bagged more than a dozen newly risen vampires. In the days past, this would have been cause for pride, if not a small celebration. Now the victory seemed strangely hollow. Buffy had decided a long time ago that there needed to be something, not much, but a little something more to her life than being the Slayer. She wanted a place she could call her own, a tiny garden inside of her that she could quietly tend and fiercely protect from the rest of her life. She'd found that and more in loving Angel. But now, Angelus had made it perfectly clear that he was taking special care in his plans to crush the heart and spirit of the Slayer before he took her life. Passing through the cemetery gates, her footsteps directed toward home, Buffy wondered idly if the recent increase in numbers of undead rising from their graves meant that Angelus was considering a new tactic: raising his own personal army to help him take on Buffy.

No, she thought wearily. *This is definitely a job he's going to want to finish himself.*

It seemed strange on this otherwise serene spring night that her thoughts were so chilling and bleak. In fact, it was more than strange. It was unfair. Mature as Buffy had become in the last few years, when the weight of the world was placed firmly on her shoulders, there was still a small petulant part of her that from time to time would cry out from the depths, *It's not fair!* Grace had forgiven James for killing both of them when she tried to deny their love. There wasn't a jury in the world that would convict Buffy when the day finally came for her to take Angel's life. But the question of forgiveness plagued her. Was she going to have to forgive Angel before she killed him in order to find some sense of peace? Did she even have the power to forgive him? Or, more importantly, herself?

It wasn't fair.

But in the life of the Slayer, that's just the way it was.

Unlike Buffy, Sunnydale High School freshman Josh Grodin had already finished his weekend homework. This was a good thing, since the last few hours sitting cross-legged on the floor in a circle of his own blood chanting by candlelight had left him exhausted, sweaty, and in no mood to think about algebra.

Josh was raising a demon.

At least, that's what he hoped he was doing. It had taken him the better part of six months of hoarding his paper route money to afford the beetle dung, newt eyes, iddlywilde root, and various other strange components the spell required. Had he been forced to also purchase a spell book from the quaint little magic supply shop he'd found on one of Sunnydale's seedier downtown streets, he'd have been a junior before he would have had a chance to make this work, but thankfully, the book in question had been found in the school library tucked between two reference books he'd been seeking about twentieth-century American poetry.

He hadn't bothered to check the book out. A handwritten notation inside the front cover and the absence of a date stamp tab in the back indicated that this book was the personal property of the school's quaint British librarian, Mr. Giles. Beggars couldn't be choosers, and though Josh thought of himself as a good, respectable kid, he had quickly thrust the spell book into his backpack the moment he'd found it, only realizing later that this time last year he would never have thought of stealing from the school, or the librarian, let alone had the guts to attempt it.

But then, everything had been different a year ago. Josh had been a good student with a few close friends, and was a promising forward on the all-city soccer team. His father had been holding down a full-time job as a plumber's assistant, and his mother had been alive.

Three months after Josh's mother had been diagnosed with cancer, she'd gone from the solid place on which his life was centered to a pale shadow of her former self. Alone in his room he had sobbed nightly for what seemed like distant delirious months as his mother teetered on the brink between life and death. At the time, he had believed that was as close to hell as he would ever come in this world, but once she was gone, he had been shocked and sickened to learn that hell had many circles and his mother's death had only granted him access to the first and most mundane.

His father, Robert, had taken his wife's death even harder than Josh had. What had been in his mother's lifetime a slightly annoying tendency to toss back a few too many beers once in a while with his fellow plumbers had become a daily ritual. It began with the top being popped from the first of at least a case of beer, followed by several bottles of harder stuff that usually left his father in a self-induced comatose state by the wee hours of the night. From this, he would awake mid-morning in time to make a quick trip to the nearest liquor store and begin the process again by early afternoon.

Disheartening as the beginning of the process was to watch, and disgusting as the end was to witness each night, the problem was the middle, the hours when Josh usually returned from school or practice to find his father alert and belligerent, waiting on the living room sofa to pick a fight.

At first, Josh had tried to understand and be patient. Even when the abuse had escalated from verbal torments to the occasional shove or slap, Josh had reminded himself that his father had to be feeling as bad as he did. Surely, this would pass. But as the weeks turned into months, Josh had slowly come to accept the reality that his mother wasn't the only parent he had lost. The monster that now padded around the house in his father's old pajamas bore no resemblance to the man who had raised him.

Josh was alone and defenseless. He had no idea where to turn. Even the school nurse didn't question him when he told her he'd broken his arm in a skateboarding accident or received that huge black eye from an errant soccer ball. He needed help, and the answer to his prayers had come in the form of a dusty old book and an ancient incantation that would wake the spirit of a demon known as Hector, who, the spell promised, would be bound to protect the one who raised him until the end of time.

Josh didn't think it would take that long for his dad to get the message. A few rounds with Hector would surely be enough to make him understand that using his son for a punching bag was no longer an option. Maybe his father would just leave. Josh didn't like to think much about what would come after that. He vaguely imagined himself surviving through the next few years on cereal and TV dinners. But whatever it was, it couldn't possibly be worse than the life he was living right now. Hector would come and save him, and the rest he'd figure out later.

The problem was he'd been chanting the incantation over and over for the better part of five hours, and so far, no Hector.

Josh considered reaching out of the circle to grab the book, which was resting open on his bed only a few feet away, but he worried that breaking the plane of the circle, something the book clearly instructed him not to do once the ritual had begun, might mean he'd have to start again from the beginning, and he didn't think he had that in him. He was also afraid that the blood he had procured by opening a vein in his arm and that had dried some time ago might no longer have the potency required to call the demon.

Resigning himself to continue, he began the chant again, hoping he wasn't making too much of a mess of the words. He thought they might be Latin, but most he could barely pronounce. Then he heard it.

"Josh?"

A guttural growl from down the hall, followed by the sound of kitchen cabinets being slammed open and shut.

"Damn it, Josh!"

Louder.

Next would come the footsteps pounding their way down the hall. Then the incoherent shouting that was meant to communicate the rage his father felt at having already finished his day's supply of whatever had been cheapest when he made his morning pilgrimage to the mini-mart.

"Where are you?"

Maybe he'd get lucky tonight. Maybe his father would forget that it was Sunday and Josh was home. Maybe his father would trip over his own feet on his way down the hall and pass out for a few more hours somewhere between the kitchen and Josh's bedroom.

Willing himself to remain calm and hold on to some of these happier thoughts, Josh began the incantation again. He could hear his voice rising in fear and panic, but he didn't care. Truth was, the only thing that could save him this night was probably Hector. If he didn't show up soon, all bets would be off.

Suddenly something in the room changed. Josh couldn't be sure it wasn't his imagination, but it seemed that the temperature had dropped severely. The next thing he knew, the black pillar candle he held in his hands and all of the other candles surrounding the circle simultaneously blew out. As a twinge of excitement coursed through his veins, a small speck of bright light appeared at eye level and began to flutter before him. The light grew brighter, then, with a crack, the entire house seemed to shake on its foundation. It was like an earthquake that only lasted a fraction of a second.

In the cold darkness, Josh heard a voice, and it was not at all the voice his imagination had already assigned to Hector.

"Joshua," the voice said, low, but almost sweet, "are you there, dear?"

The bedroom's overhead light flicked on, and Josh turned immediately to face the doorway, where a small, white-haired woman in a pink floral dress with a lace collar and very sensible shoes stood with her hand on the light switch.

"There you are, dear," she said kindly. "Do get up, and let's find a rag to wash that floor. Bloodstains in hardwood can be very difficult to remove, especially when they've had time to set."

Josh had expected to be frightened when Hector appeared.

The sight of this woman, whoever she was, did little to instill terror, though her presence and knowledge of whence she must have come did keep Josh riveted to the floor, despite her benign and almost grandmotherly demeanor.

"What are you waiting for?" she asked a little more sternly.

"Who are you?" Josh finally found voice to say.

"I'm Paulina, dearest. But you can call me Polly. All my friends do," she replied.

"I thought, that is, I don't mean to be rude," Josh continued, choosing his words very carefully. "It's just, I was trying to reach Hector," he finished.

"Oh, Hector got out of the protector business years ago. I think he spends most of his time now in that lovely dimension where everything is made of shrimp. Or perhaps it's the one where there is no shrimp. It can be hard to keep track, you know."

"B-but . . . ," Josh stammered, unsure how to begin, let alone end the sentence that was forming on his lips. "How can you . . ." The question trailed off.

"Protect you?" Polly replied, her face breaking into a wide and kind of disturbing smile. "You let me worry about that, Josh. And you worry about cleaning up this mess, all right?"

Josh rose from the floor. He couldn't say exactly why, but something in Polly's firm and commanding nature told him that while she might not be the most frightening demon on the block, it probably wouldn't be wise to cross her. The rags and disinfectant he would need to clean the floor were in the kitchen, and he paused before he reached the door, concerned that he would encounter his father between here and there. Polly had busied herself testing the surfaces of his bookcase and footboard for dust as he crossed the room, humming softly under her breath.

"And don't worry about your father," Polly said suddenly, as if she'd been reading his thoughts. "He won't trouble us again."

"What did you do?" Josh asked, suddenly extremely nervous.

"What you wanted," she replied.

Josh shivered involuntarily.

Swallowing his fear, he said simply, "Oh, okay. Thanks."

"You're welcome," Polly said sweetly. "And when you get back, we'll talk about what you're going to do for me."

Josh couldn't be sure why, but something in her tone and words filled him with cold dread. As he opened the door and quickly scanned the hallway, seeing no sign of his father, he silently wished that Hector had been the one to answer his call. His picture in the spell book had been terrifying to behold, but instinctively Josh knew that he would rather have faced a hundred Hectors than one Polly.

Drusilla couldn't sleep. She'd had a very full evening. Hunting in Sunnydale had a particular charm that even months after her arrival had yet to pale. Or perhaps it was just hunting with Angelus again. She had always felt a special bond with him. Of course that was natural between a vampire and her sire. But what she shared with Angelus was something more. He rarely, if ever, hunted merely for the sake of feeding. Had that been the case, any random passerby would have sufficed. Angelus had managed to elevate a simple biological need into poetry. And the past few nights had been particularly gratifying in that regard.

Poor Angelus had been violated. His body had been invaded by love, and he was determined to purge himself of every last shred of love's painful and disgusting thrall. She would have thought the toddler they had managed to snatch from its weary mother at the bus depot the very night he'd been possessed would have more than satiated his visceral need to bathe in evil. But each night since then he'd continued to ratchet up both the forcefulness and the foulness of his desires. Dru had found herself struggling to keep up, which was absolutely thrilling.

But that wasn't the source of her restlessness. She was troubled by a secret wish she had yet to put into words. Perhaps if she were to share her desires with Angelus, or her longtime lover, Spike, they might subside, but somehow she knew that neither of them, much as they adored her, would have any patience for the scandalous thoughts that refused to give her a moment's peace.

Drusilla had been toying with the idea for weeks now, ever since she, Angelus, and Spike had moved from the factory to the abandoned mansion on the outskirts of Sunnydale that they now called home. The mansion had needed work when they first arrived, most of which they had already accomplished. Though they spent much of their time in the spacious den, whose most impressive feature was a vast fireplace, or bathing in the moonlight that fell into the first-floor courtyard, the main floor's master bedroom, which they had transformed with deep red velvet curtains and a massive four-poster eighteenth-century bed, had become Dru's favorite room in the house.

Only a few days after they had arrived, however, she had made her way through the second floor of the east wing.

Three large bedrooms took up most of the space, but at the end of the hall, Dru had discovered a playroom. She could smell the remnants of many happy hours spent here by the children for whom the room had been built. It left her faintly nauseated. But at the same time, there was a tangible thrill to it.

Her first thought upon entering the brightly colored room was to wonder if its former occupants had had any sense of how lucky they were to have had such a room at their disposal, or how she would have treasured the opportunity to enter the room while the children played and descend upon each of them, one at a time, filling their tiny souls with terror before they succumbed to the darkness that would be her final gift to them.

But the thought that halted her in her tracks, and kept her awake these many nights hence, had come second. She found herself wondering why, in all the years she had spent roaming the world, it had never occurred to her. Since her new life as a vampire had begun, she had known all manner of vampires and demons. She had ruthlessly treasured every moment spent playing vile games and making new conquests with her beloved Spike and Angelus. They belonged to one another in a way that no living person could ever comprehend and with a dark depth that was both rich and satisfying. But neither Spike nor Angelus actually needed Drusilla; not the way the children for whom this playroom had been built had needed their parents or their siblings. Drusilla had been desired in life and adored in death. But had she ever been needed?

There was only one answer before her. It both tantalized and terrified her. Something buried deep within her was actually vaguely repulsed by the thought, which in and of itself made it worth exploring more deeply.

In her secret, no longer beating heart of hearts, Drusilla had decided she wanted someone to love and need her in a way that neither Spike nor Angelus could ever imagine.

Drusilla wanted a child of her own.

CHAPTER TWO

Buffy was a firm believer in the two-and-a-half-day weekend. In fact, she wouldn't have found any strong moral objection to a three-, four-, or five-day weekend, come to think of it. If she ever ruled the world, that would certainly be one of the first agenda items she would propose. In the meantime, she was almost as pleased as most of her fellow students that they'd been given Monday morning off and would start this short school week on Monday afternoon. It was a blessing, and such little gifts from the universe were rare enough in the life of the Vampire Slayer. It wasn't world peace, but she'd take what she could get.

Why the teachers of Sunnydale would be required to

have an in-service day so close to the end of a school year, Buffy couldn't imagine. Perhaps it had something to do with the extremely paranormal makeover the school had received the previous week when the ghosts who possessed Buffy and Angel had been running rampant. It was possible that mysterious locker monsters, staircase landings that turned to quicksand, and plagues of wasps hadn't been as easy to recover from as the more tame adventures of the school's past—for instance, possessed students who ate their principal for lunch.

Sometimes Buffy was grateful that she had been given the power to fight the world's demons. But more often than not, as she passed small groups of students relaxing on the school's sun-drenched front lawn before fourth period trading reviews of the movies they'd seen that weekend, Buffy wished that she were as blissfully ignorant as most of her peers. She vaguely remembered what it was like to live in a world that made sense, a world where the monsters under your bed at night were vanquished by nothing more than a reassuring parent's smile and a glass of warm milk, a world where a girl was more concerned about which color nail polish was "in" this spring than how to get demon blood out of a favorite tank top.

Unfortunately, being the Chosen One was a one-way deal. No one had considered whether or not Buffy *wanted* the job when she was called to be the Slayer. And strangely, knowing all she now did, even she could not say for certain whether or not she would have embraced her calling or refused it, had the "Chosen" part included any input from the "choose-ee."

At the very least, she had to be grateful that she wasn't the only student at Sunnydale High who was painfully aware that things that went bump in the night were real and usually kind of smelly. Spotting Willow Rosenberg, a petite redhead curled into a corner of the student lounge sofa, head buried in a book as usual, Buffy quickly darted through the early morning hallway traffic and grabbed the open seat next to her best friend.

"Is that how those book thingies work?" Buffy asked as she tossed her own pile of texts onto the table before her. "You have to open them to get the prize?"

"Oh, hey, Buffy," Willow replied without lifting her gaze.

Gently rebuked, Buffy considered her friend. Willow was easily one of the smartest people she'd ever met. And usually she managed very well not to flaunt her intellectual superiority in the faces of those less fortunate, including Buffy. In fact, her truly sweet and generous nature had been one of the first things that had drawn Buffy to seek out Willow's friendship— that and Buffy's need to not fail out of Sunnydale High within a few days of her arrival on campus. Although Buffy could not have known it at the time, the nerdlike surface that had caused so many to overlook Willow for so long had merely been the delicate facade that shrouded the strongest heart and most courageous spirit Buffy had ever encountered. Despite Willow's sensitivities, including frog fear, Buffy was more grateful than she could ever express that Willow had chosen to stand beside her in her fiercest battles, lending incredible moral support along with enviable research skills to the Slayer's missions.

It was therefore vaguely unsettling that Willow seemed to be leaning toward the mopes this early in the day. Buffy decided to move on to a topic toward which even grumpy Willow would warm.

"How was the in-service this morning? Have your fellow faculty members shared with you the power to give detentions yet?" Buffy asked.

"What? Oh, sure," Willow replied, still not really giving her full attention to Buffy.

"All right, Will, what gives?" Buffy replied a bit more tersely. "It's the beginning of a school day. Granted, it's a short day, but usually that's cause for joy in the land of Willow."

"I'm sorry," Willow replied, closing her book and gracing Buffy with a faint smile.

Suddenly, Buffy regretted her choice of topic. True, Willow seemed to be enjoying her new position as temporary teacher in the computer science lab. But Willow had only accepted the job upon the untimely death of the regular teacher, Jenny Calendar. Ms. Calendar had been more than a teacher. She'd been warming the heart of Buffy's Watcher, Mr. Giles, and was a Gypsy spy sent by her people to watch over Angel. It had taken Buffy some serious in-the-moment maturing to make some sort of peace with Ms. Calendar once she learned that she wasn't just hanging out with Giles and occasionally helping Buffy solve whatever crisis was at hand out of the goodness of her heart. But nothing Ms. Calendar had done had warranted the brutality with which Angelus had snapped her neck, and even weeks later, the loss was still fresh among all who had known her, particularly Willow and Giles.

"No, Willow," Buffy began. "My bad. It's not anything to joke about."

"No. 'A' for effort, really," Willow replied. "It's just, I didn't get to go to the in-service."

"What happened?"

"It's nothing," Willow said hesitantly.

"Will, that's not your 'nothing' face. That's your 'something' face. Actually, it's your 'this is really something and I don't think I want Buffy to know about it' face."

"It's no biggie," Willow replied. "Mom was doing a little spring cleaning on Sunday and found that crucifix we nailed to my wall when we were doing the spell to uninvite Angel."

"Oh," Buffy said, absolutely certain that there was no way this story ended well.

"So there was talking and a little crying and a call to Rabbi 911," Willow continued.

"How bad is it?" Buffy asked.

"They're thinking about sending me to a kibbutz this summer, but I think I can get out of it. Maybe Giles knows a spell," Willow suggested, brightening just a bit.

"I'm sorry, Will," Buffy said quickly. "It's my fault."

"No, it absolutely is not," Willow said defiantly. "I was the one who invited Angel into my room in the first place."

"You had no reason not to at the time," Buffy interjected.

"And you had no reason to think any of the rest of it would happen either," Willow insisted. "I didn't want to tell you because you already have enough to worry about. It's nothing, really," she finished, doing her best to smile. "And you're right. It's just the beginning of another fun-filled week at Sunnydale High. How bad could it be?"

"You're not seriously asking that question?" Buffy replied.

"No, I guess not," Willow said thoughtfully.

Their musings were interrupted by the sound of Principal Snyder shouting at the top of his lungs, "Who did it? Who thinks this blatant display of disrespect is amusing?"

The friends turned in unison to see the troll of a man who had been terrorizing Sunnydale High since last spring marching down the main hallway, stopping at every cluster of students he encountered to check hands and bags and to hand out detentions at the slightest smirks in his direction.

"Sounds like someone hasn't had his coffee yet." Buffy smiled. It was impossible for her not to hate the man who had gone out of his way since they'd first met to remind Buffy that she was a delinquent and that he would relish the chance to expel her given the slightest provocation.

"Oh, how cute," Willow said, offering the first genuine smile Buffy had seen from her all day and pointing in Snyder's general direction.

"Did you just use the word 'cute' in reference to Snyder?" Buffy asked in disbelief, following her friend's gaze. It only took a moment to see what was wrong with the picture before her. The principal was wearing only one shoe. His left foot was clad in a baby pink argyle sock. Given Willow's eclectic fashion sense, Buffy no longer had any difficulty understanding her friend's reaction.

"Fun as this is to watch, I should really check in with Giles before fourth period," Buffy said, collecting her books and rising from the couch.

"Is anything wrong?" Willow asked with sudden seriousness. "How was your weekend, by the way?"

"Oh, you know," Buffy replied as both moved gingerly toward the main hall, careful to avoid Snyder's scrutiny. "I hung out at the mall, took in a few movies, got a manicure, and Mom sprung for this really cute bag I've had my eye on."

"Really?" Willow asked in obvious disbelief.

"Sure," Buffy replied, "in the *Fantasy Island* version of my life. In reality, our undead friends were out in full force, and I broke the last two nails I had dusting some newbie named Brower. He wasn't all that strong, but he was fast."

"Oh," Willow said sadly. "Conrad Brower?"

"I think so," Buffy replied, trying to remember the full name on the headstone.

"He was my ophthalmologist," Willow said.

"You don't even wear glasses. Why do you need an ophthalmologist?"

"You can't neglect the health of your eyes," Willow replied.

"Everyone should have their eyes examined at least once a year. And he gave out these yummy butterscotch lollipops with each exam."

They had almost reached the library, Willow continuing to opine about the dearth of really good butterscotch, when Giles emerged from the double doors that separated his haven from the rest of the school. A vision in tweed, Giles was Buffy's Watcher, appointed by a council in England to train and mentor the Slayer.

"Ah, good morning, Buffy, Willow," Giles said cordially.

"Hi, Giles," Willow said cheerfully.

"I'm so glad to have run into you before class," Giles continued.

"Cut to the chase, Giles," Buffy replied warily. "Who's trying to destroy the world this week?"

"Oh, no one, actually," Giles said evenly.

"Really?" Buffy asked, a faint note of hope creeping into her voice.

"Yes," Giles continued. "All is quiet on the Hellmouth. At least, for the moment."

"That's what I like to hear," Buffy said. "Maybe I'll actually make it to a few classes today."

"Indeed," Giles replied. "Though there was one rather disturbing disappearance reported in the weekend papers."

"I knew it was too good to last," Buffy countered.

"It's probably not demon-related, though of course one never knows," Giles went on. "An eight-year-old girl, Callie

McKay, was reported missing from the park. Her parents are quite beside themselves with worry."

"And upsetting as that is," Buffy retorted, "unless she was kidnapped by a demon, it's not my responsibility, right? I mean, the Sunnydale police force does get to solve a crime once in a while, don't they?"

"Of course, such as they are," Giles replied.

"Good," Buffy finished. "Now, if you'll excuse me, I have a chemistry quiz to fail."

As Willow was required to be home immediately after school that day, and Xander, Buffy's other best friend, was doing his best to make her want to take her own life by openly reveling in his new relationship with their frenemy Cordelia, Buffy actually arrived home from school rather early for a change. She was first shocked, then dismayed, when she popped into the kitchen to make a quick snack and found her mother seated at the counter, her face etched with worry and her foot shaking up and down expectantly.

"Hey, Mom," Buffy said cautiously, wondering why at-will invisibility wasn't one of her Slayer powers. Joyce Summers ran a local art gallery, and there were very few things that would bring the concerned small-business owner home before dinnertime. "Shouldn't you be gallery girl, or art girl, right now?" Buffy asked, opening the fridge.

"I should," Joyce replied. "Instead, I had a daughter."

Uh-oh, Buffy thought.

"Principal Snyder called me at work today," Joyce said ponderously.

"I didn't steal his shoe," Buffy said quickly.

"What?" Joyce asked.

"Never mind," Buffy replied. "What did he want?"

"He wanted to make sure I was aware that your finals are coming up."

"Has there been a rash of calendar thefts?" Buffy asked. "School ends in, like, three weeks. Who doesn't know that finals are coming up?"

"He also wanted to make sure that I was aware that you are currently barely scraping up passing grades in history and English lit, and are actually failing chemistry. Apparently, unless you perform at a level that he is fairly certain is unattainable for you, you will not be spending your senior year at Sunnydale High. You'll be repeating your junior year at another school."

This was hardly a new theme in the Summers house. Buffy's grades had never been the best, but they had certainly been good enough to avoid parental scrutiny—until she had been called to slay vampires. The cold, hard reality was that saving the world often cut into valuable study time, and though Buffy did her best at school, in the last couple of years her best had become seriously underwhelming in the grade department. Since Joyce was unaware of her daughter's status as the Chosen One, Buffy couldn't actually make her understand that the fact that she attended school at all was cause for celebration. Sighing deeply, Buffy put on her bravest face and said, "Not to worry, Mom. Willow and I are on the study wagon. My chemistry exam is more than half of my final grade, and I'm already doing practice essays for English."

Shaking her head, Joyce replied, "You and Willow do nothing but 'study.' All hours of the day and night you are always at the library or with Willow, supposedly studying."

This was as far from the truth as it was possible to get, but Buffy was unfortunately unable to share with Joyce the reality that "study time" had become the convenient parental code word for fighting vampires and demons. Any time spent in the school library was either about honing her slaying skills with Giles or reading up in some dusty tome about whoever or whatever had just rolled into town determined to permanently remove the sun from Sunnydale. Buffy rued the fact that she would never be tested on the history of ancient vampires, the mating habits of giant praying mantises, or the hatching cycles of Bezor demons. Those exams Buffy had aced, though they would never appear on her transcript or help her GPA.

As Buffy reveled in the unfairness of it all, Joyce continued: "Principal Snyder tells me you've been placed in a special category of academic probation."

"Principal Snyder hates me," Buffy said truthfully.

"Be that as it may, your record has been brought before the school board, and they've recommended a special tutor for you."

"But, Mom!" Buffy whined.

"You'll meet with him four times a week until finals," Joyce finished, giving no ground for argument.

"Starting when?" Buffy asked, clearly dismayed.

"Tonight," Joyce replied firmly.

Buffy had already planned a night at the Bronze, followed by a sweep of two of the local cemeteries for the evening's festivities, but it was clear from her mother's face that her foot was firmly in the down position. One of the things that made Buffy's life bearable was her mother's seemingly endless capacity to make allowances for the strange things that surrounded her daughter without asking too many questions. The parenting manuals that had occupied most of Joyce's bookshelves since her daughter had been expelled from her previous high school for burning down the school gymnasium (it had been filled with vampires at the time) all told her that teenagers needed space as well as understanding, and Joyce had given Buffy more than enough of both. But Buffy knew that her mother could only be pushed so far. Deciding that "dutiful daughter" was the card to play here, Buffy acquiesced, saying only, "Tonight. Perfect. Thanks, Mom."

Two hours and several desperate but fruitless phone calls to Willow, Xander, and Giles later, Buffy heard the doorbell ring and with a heavy heart and leaden feet made her way to the staircase landing to meet her doom.

She was totally unprepared for the sight of her tutor, a boy who couldn't have been more than twenty, with casually disheveled brown hair and truly striking green eyes.

"Good evening, Ms. Summers," he said, politely shaking her mother's hand as he entered the front hall. "I'm Todd Harter. I'm here to work with Buffy."

"It's nice to meet you, Todd," Joyce was saying calmly as Buffy found herself wondering who in the world had just sucked all the oxygen out of the room.

She couldn't remember the last time she had had such a visceral reaction to the cuteness of a boy. Actually, she could. It had taken place a year and a half earlier, the night Angel had walked into her life with his brooding good looks, cryptic warnings, and his first gift to her, a silver crucifix she now had a hard time wearing without regret.

Thankfully, the minute she connected the feeling she was currently experiencing with Angel, it lost some of its potency. There had never been a love that had come with a higher price tag than hers and Angel's, and Buffy had decided weeks ago that the words "Never Again" were going to be etched on her tombstone.

It was just hard to keep that in mind as Todd walked calmly up the stairs and, reaching out his hand with a genuine and perfect smile, said, "I sure hope you're Buffy."

Spike was debating a night on the town with his beloved Dru—*Where the hell is she, by the way?*—when the front door of the mansion was thrown open and Angelus swept in, unceremoniously dropped a frail-looking man at Spike's wheels, and said casually, "I thought you might like some leftovers for dinner."

Cringing at the overwhelming rankness wafting from the body of the man lying prostrate before him, Spike swallowed the nauseating bile that had started to boil within him almost every time Angelus spoke and quipped, "What, the streets of Sunnyhell were all out of anemics tonight?"

"Buggers can't be choosers," Angelus tossed over his shoulder as he disappeared into the mansion's courtyard.

Spike knew full well that Angelus's apparent largesse was nothing more than a backhanded reminder that Spike hadn't been at full strength for months. He had been severely injured in a church fire during one of many perfect plans the Slayer had turned to crap. A ceremony meant to kill the old soul-filled Angel and cure Drusilla of her illness had ended in flames and near death. Difficult as it was to believe, he and Angelus were now at even more deeply entrenched cross-purposes than when Angel was doing time as the Slayer's lap-dog. Back in the days when Angelus, Darla, Spike, and Dru had cut a fearsome and bloody swath through most of Europe and Asia, Spike would never have guessed that a friendship such as theirs, forged in blood, could have come to this. But Angelus had changed. Or maybe Spike had. Either way, his old friend was now a wanker of the worst sort, and Spike only longed to be rid of him.

Still, dinner was dinner. Nudging the still form at his feet with the tip of his boot, Spike rolled the man over and was rewarded by a hefty stench of sweat and Thunderbird for his trouble. *Not if you were the last meal on legs,* Spike decided, realizing that Angelus hadn't fed off the vagrant either, probably for the same reasons that had turned Spike's stomach. Whatever blood was left in the man was so poisoned by years of deprivation and a diet of cheap wine that Spike would have tasted it for weeks. At this point, he wasn't even sure if setting the man on fire right then and there would be enough to get the stench out of the carpet.

These bleak thoughts were quickly dispelled by a gentle sound coming from the direction of the front door.

"The stars and the moon, the dark and the gloom," Drusilla was singing softly as she made her way up the front walk. Though Spike didn't like to think of Dru and Angelus hunting together—*Hell, I don't like to think of the two of them watching the telly together*—at least the light of his life was finally home. Spike allowed his mind to drift to thoughts of the painful and satisfying games they would play once they had retired to the master bedroom at sunrise.

His joyful anticipation was only heightened when Spike caught his first glimpse of his beloved, her long black fur-trimmed coat barely concealing the bloodred gown that he'd found for her on their last visit to Paris, its plunging neckline gloriously accentuating the perfection of her pure white skin. As if that vision were not enough to set his flesh tingling, Dru was gently guiding a beautiful young girl with golden curls, clad in a frilly pink jumper, toward him, holding one of the child's hands with the tips of her perfectly manicured nails.

"Now, this is more like it, pet," Spike cooed lovingly. "To what do I owe this incredible generosity? I know the young are your favorite. Did you actually save this little bit for me?"

"Patience, love," Dru replied, bending to whisper in the child's ear.

Savoring the anticipation of the delectable morsel to come, Spike wheeled himself a bit closer, stopping in horror only when the little girl's face suddenly transformed into that of a vampire.

"Callie," Dru whispered softly, "say hello to your new daddy, Spike."

"Oh, sodding hell," Spike sputtered.

CHAPTER THREE

Monday's soccer practice had not gone well for Josh. He didn't know if he was more distracted or exhausted, and the extra mile Coach Bradley had demanded he run at the end of the afternoon had done nothing to improve the situation. As much as he dreaded returning home, by nightfall he had little choice.

Making his way through the backyard to his kitchen door, Josh slowed his steps, lost for a moment in the pleasant memory of a spring afternoon he'd spent picking grapefruit from his mother's favorite tree that dominated much of the yard. Somewhere in his distant past were gentle days when his mother had lifted him in her arms and allowed him to choose a fruit, tickling him as the sweet, tangy pink grapefruit juice ran down his chin. Tonight he could see that the tree was one of the few things in the backyard that hadn't died, though it was well past time to trim it back, and fruits in varying stages of decomposition littered the ground beneath it.

Josh turned again toward the back door, and as he did so, something assaulted his senses, threatening to drive him even further into his past. It wasn't the tree, or the yard. Instead, it was a smell that wafted through the open kitchen window, a rich aroma that set his stomach rumbling.

Somewhere, just beyond the door he so feared to open, was a home-cooked dinner.

Alert and anxious, Josh entered the kitchen and his eyes confirmed what his nose suspected. The small Formica table was set for two, and steaming dishes of mashed potatoes and mixed vegetables sat beside a freshly roasted chicken, still on the bone and ready for carving.

Without thought, Josh dropped his backpack and jammed his finger into the potatoes for a taste, but before he could bring that finger to his lips, a shrill "Joshua, what do you think you're doing?" met his ears, and he instinctively pulled both his hands behind his back and turned to face Polly, who was busy removing a tray of freshly baked dinner rolls from the oven.

"I—I'm sorry," he stammered.

"Sorry doesn't cream the corn," Polly replied sharply. "You will wash your filthy hands and face and put those foul-smelling clothes in the laundry room before you enjoy so much as a crumb from this table. Do you understand?" she finished.

"Yes, ma'am," Josh replied automatically, before adding apologetically, "everything smells great."

"Of course it does, dear." Polly smiled warmly. "Now move!"

Josh found himself hurrying to do her bidding, unable to believe his good fortune. Hector might have been his first choice in a protector, but he doubted the mammoth demon would have known his way around a kitchen, or a vacuum cleaner, he mentally added, realizing as he made his way down the hall that the house was the cleanest it had been in over a year. His room smelled of fresh pine and lemon. The starched and ironed pillowcases atop his perfectly made bed and the ordered arrangement of his books and soccer trophies on his desk all testified to the fact that Polly had made herself more than useful during the day. He rejoiced inwardly at the knowledge that when he presented himself at her table—*funny how the entire house now seems to belong to her*—he would do so with something to offer her by way of thanks.

It hadn't been easy. In fact, it had been terrifying, but that very afternoon at school Josh had managed to accomplish the only thing Polly had asked of him in return for her protection.

Josh had stolen Principal Snyder's shoe.

He would never have been able to manage it without specific instructions from Polly the night before as to how exactly he might accomplish this minor miracle. It had depended upon two things. The first was the existence of a small faculty bathroom just down the hall from the principal's office that Snyder had immediately designated for his exclusive use once he had joined the administration of Sunnydale High. Though few faculty members seemed to genuinely like the principal, ever fewer seemed willing to risk his displeasure on any given day, so the rest of the faculty had given up this small privilege without too many complaints. The second was an odd personal habit of Snyder's. Apparently, whenever the principal retired to his private domain and entered the bathroom's only stall, he removed his shoes and placed them on the floor in front of him before he sat down. This, Polly had assured him, he had done ever since he was a little boy.

Josh's heart had been in his throat as he had silently entered the bathroom that afternoon, a good forty-five minutes before the bell was to ring. But just as Polly had said, he had seen Principal Snyder's polished black dress shoes poking out from the stall door, and he was out of the bathroom, shoe in bag, and well down the hall before he had heard the first shriek of alarm from the principal echoing behind him.

Now that the deed had been accomplished, and fortified by the prospect of the most delicious meal he'd had in a year as a reward, Josh re-entered the kitchen a few minutes later with a spring in his step and the slightly ripe dress shoe in his hand.

Polly turned immediately to face him upon his return,

and he reveled at the glimmer of satisfaction in her eyes as he approached her, holding the shoe before him like a holy relic.

"Oh, my dear, dear boy," Polly cooed warmly. "Well done."

"You're welcome," Josh replied as she quickly plucked the shoe from his hands and clutched it to her heart, regarding it with almost the same affection a mother would have for a newborn child.

"Do sit down and eat something," Polly said absently, still cradling the shoe.

"Thank you, ma'am," Josh answered, and immediately sat and began to pile his plate with as much fresh food as it would hold.

The first bite of potatoes had barely touched his tongue when a wave of nausea tightened his gut. As Polly took her place beside him, setting the shoe in her lap, she seemed to notice his attempt to force down the food.

"Is everything all right, dear?" she asked with genuine concern.

"Oh, yes," Josh replied as best he could, though he hesitated to fill another forkful.

The potatoes tasted so foul, he could barely swallow them. He didn't know if they had been rank before she had cooked them, or if she had mashed them with sour milk. In any event, they were inedible. He turned his attention to the chicken, hoping for something better. Though his appetite had gone with the first of the potatoes, in his limited experience there was little harm that could be done to a freshly roasted chicken.

Like the potatoes, however, the first bite of chicken was also to be his last.

"Eat up, dear," Polly was saying as she filled her own plate. "You're a growing boy, and you need your nutrition."

The meat assaulted his taste buds with a riot of decay and rot that he could only associate with a cat that had once died in his backyard. It had been found several days too late to do anything about the smell but wait it out.

"Is there a problem, dear?" Polly asked sweetly as Josh instinctively spat the chicken back onto his plate and dropped his fork.

"No, ma'am," Josh replied feebly. "I guess I'm just not as hungry as I thought."

"I spent the entire afternoon preparing this meal, Joshua," Polly began sternly, "and you will finish every bite of it before you leave this table."

Josh looked at the plate, then at Polly, and took a moment to evaluate where the greater threat lay.

Unfortunately, he chose wrong.

"I have a history paper to write," he said as he began to rise from the table.

"What did you say, young man?" Polly asked, standing as well and suddenly taking on a more menacing appearance than he would ever have thought possible in floral cotton and lace.

"I—I . . . ," Josh started to stammer.

"Boys."

Polly spat the word as if it tasted as bad to her as the chicken had tasted to Josh.

"Just like my Cecil," she began. "You're all the same: ungrateful and selfish. You don't understand a mother's love, and you have no respect for the time and energy it takes to care for pathetic little wretches like you," Polly continued.

Josh stepped back from the table and found his back against the kitchen wall. His hand started to move of its own accord down the length of the wall until it found the knob to the basement door. As Polly continued her rant, flecks of spittle flying from her lips along with insults, Josh threw open the door and, as quickly as he could, rushed down the basement steps.

Polly followed him to the doorway, the pitch of her voice rising until her words became unintelligible shrieks, and Josh quickly realized he had all but cornered himself. As he searched for a defensible position, he noted for the first time in the shadows cast by the basement's single overhanging bulb a hand reaching out to him from the far corner, nearest what had been his father's workbench.

"Dad?" Josh whispered.

As Polly began to descend the steps, Joshua reached for the hand only to find that it was ice cold to his touch, and much lighter than it should have been. This made immediate sense when he tugged on the hand, only to find that while it was still connected to his father's forearm, the rest of his father was no longer attached to it.

"What did you do?" Joshua screamed, turning on Polly, who now stood, arms crossed, at the base of the stairs.

"I did what you asked," Polly replied evenly. "Your father will never hurt you again."

"I . . . I . . ." But Josh couldn't finish the thought. Much as he had hated his father, much as his father had made his life a living hell over the past year, Josh was completely unprepared for his dismemberment. Josh no longer knew what exactly he had wanted when he had summoned Polly. All he knew for sure was that he hadn't wanted *this.*

Mustering all the courage that remained in him, Josh turned to Polly and shouted, "And I stole that shoe for you! We're even. Now get out!"

Polly seemed to have collected herself. She only smiled slightly at his words.

"I will, dear," she said simply, "just as soon as I've finished cleaning up this mess."

"What mess?" Josh asked. "This house has never been so clean."

"The mess you make by your presence, my boy," Polly replied.

The next thing Josh knew, the hand that still held his father's cold, dead arm felt as if it were on fire. It was almost a pleasant release as the fire subsided, despite the fact that his hand had been pulled from its place on his arm and fell to the floor, alongside his father's arm, with a *splat.*

The rest of his joints were tingling and beginning to burn

when Josh realized just how big a mistake he had made. The last thought he had before the darkness took him was simply, *I'm so sorry,* but he died long before he knew for whom exactly that apology had been meant.

Buffy entered the library Tuesday morning before the start of classes to find Giles standing over Xander, who was seated at the central research table intently studying what appeared to be an ancient manuscript of some kind. Cordelia stood by, anxiously tapping her foot in a manner that suggested in no uncertain terms she would rather be anywhere but there.

"So is there any way to reach this dimension?" Xander asked seriously.

"It would be most unwise," was Giles's characteristic response.

"But if that's where all my extra socks are—oh, hey, Buffy." Xander interrupted himself, his eyes brightening at the sight of the Slayer.

"Geez, Xander," Cordelia interjected wearily, "if the sock demons—"

"Gnomes," Giles couldn't help but correct her.

"Whatever," Cordelia continued. "If these guys love your socks so much, I say let it go. That's why somebody out there created Target."

"We're talking about a crime against humanity," Xander argued back. "To take one sock at a time, leaving a man with dozens of mismatched pairs—that's just evil."

"Do I need to be here for this?" Buffy asked, stifling a yawn.

Giles busied himself rebinding the manuscript as he answered, "Not at all. Xander was just curious about this rather common phenomenon of seeming to misplace one sock each time one does a load of laundry, and I was attempting to explain—"

"Yeah, we got it," Cordelia interrupted, checking her watch. "Xander has angered the sock gods. Can we go now?"

"Gnomes," Giles added weakly.

"You could show a little compassion," Xander rebuked her. "We don't all have access to your daddy's credit cards, you know."

The very thought of her purchasing power brought a faint smile to Cordelia's lips.

"How was your patrol last night, Buffy?" Giles asked in an obvious effort to change the subject.

"I think he's trying to kill me," she replied, settling for a moment in an open chair and again placing her hand over her mouth to cover a larger yawn.

"Who?" Giles asked, instantly alert. "A demon? A vampire?"

"Angel?" Cordelia added. "'Cause we all knew that."

"My tutor," Buffy replied pointedly. Though she had always known it would be inappropriate to use her powers as the Slayer to harm a human being, there were days—and this was one of them—when she honestly wondered if Cordelia really met that requirement.

"Ah, I see," Giles said thoughtfully. "Terribly demanding, is he?"

"Did you know that King George the Third of England, the guy who was supposedly running your country during the American Revolution, was actually insane?" Buffy asked.

"In fact, I did," Giles replied.

"Or that by the time World War One broke out, most of the monarchs of the various countries that went to war were actually related to one another?"

"Yes, I'm sure I read that somewhere too," Giles continued evenly.

"Well, now I do too," Buffy replied, "along with about fifty other useless facts that I'm going to need to discuss on my world history final, and will be quizzed on tonight, right after I finish my practice essay on the use of metaphor in 'Ode on a Grecian Vase.'"

"Urn," Giles corrected her.

"I thought it was a vase," Buffy said.

"It is, it—never mind. While I'm pleased to see that you're making progress in your studies, I must caution you that this is no time to neglect your slaying duties."

"Like there's any way I don't know that?" Buffy said sharply. Before Giles could retort, she added more gently, "I'm sorry. I'm just really tired. I didn't sleep very well last night, and until finals are done, I have my regular homework, plus lots and lots of extra homework."

"Can't Willow be of some assistance?" Giles asked.

"Unless Willow can somehow take my finals and hers at the same time, I'd say no," Buffy replied, then added, "I promise I'll patrol tonight, right after my study session."

"And after that, you should join us at the Bronze," Xander suggested. "Dingoes are playing tonight. Should be happening."

"Yes, well, whatever your plans, do make sure—," Giles began.

"I will. Chosen One. Destiny. Got it," Buffy cut him off, collecting her books and joining Xander and Cordelia as they made their way to the doors. "Why do they say there's no rest for the wicked? Boy, did they get that one wrong."

She didn't need to turn around to know that Giles was looking after her, both concerned and resigned. The truth was, he knew that being the Slayer and a high school junior was no picnic, but there was little he could do at such times to ease her burdens.

As Buffy, Xander, and Cordelia merged into the early morning hallway traffic, Xander picked up on his earlier theme.

"So how about it, Buffy? Up for a little fun tonight?"

"I don't think so, Xander," she replied. "I really have to hit the books tonight. Come to think of it, if hitting them was all I had to do—"

"What's up with him?" Cordelia interrupted.

Buffy and Xander followed her gaze and found she was watching Principal Snyder walk serenely past them, seemingly oblivious to the students around him and the many opportunities for detentions in his wake.

"He looks almost . . ."

"Happy?" Xander finished for Cordelia.

"He probably just saw my score on that chemistry quiz yesterday," Buffy said sadly.

"Oh, what's the big deal," Cordelia said frankly, obviously trying to raise Buffy's spirits in her own special way. "I mean, it's not like you're ever going to need chemistry."

"I will if I want to graduate," Buffy replied.

"Assuming you live that long," Cordelia added.

"Cordelia—," Buffy began.

"That's my girl," Xander said firmly, placing himself between Cordelia and the Slayer, "always trying to find the silver lining."

"I'm just saying . . . ," Cordelia trailed off as he grasped her by the elbow and steered her away from Buffy's frowning face.

"Catch you later, Buffy. And think about tonight. Should be fun!" Xander babbled before saying more quietly to Cordelia, "Sweetie, how many times do we have to talk about quiet, inside thoughts?"

For the moment, Buffy decided to let it go. Truth was, Cordelia had a point. And much as she hated to admit it, she'd often wondered herself how important it was to be a good student, given the life expectancy of the average Slayer.

• • •

"So, basically, they get all tweaked just because they weren't into queens?"

Ah, Buffy.

Angelus couldn't help but adore the way her mind worked. In fact, the subject had occupied most of his waking and sleeping hours for the better part of the past several weeks. This evening, as he perched outside her bedroom window observing her study session and her new tutor, Angelus fought the temptation to swoop inside and literally drink it in. Of course, that would have been impossible, given the fact that he no longer had an invitation to enter Buffy's home, though Angelus doubted that minor obstacle would stop him for long. After a moment he forced himself to focus again on Buffy's conversation.

"No. They liked queens. They usually came with kings as kind of a matched set. But they didn't like the idea that the queen would actually inherit the kingdom."

Then there was *Todd.*

Angelus didn't know Todd. He didn't get the impression that Buffy knew him very well either. But, clearly—and this was the troubling part, or the happy accident, depending on how he chose to look at it—Buffy seemed to like Todd, or at least respect him.

The tutor was still speaking. "Despite the fact that Henry the First specifically stated before his death that his only surviving child, his daughter, Matilda, should succeed him, the nobility of what was really a very young Britain at the time had never been ruled by a woman, and most of them were terribly disconcerted by the idea."

"So this Stephen guy, even though, he's, like, her cousin, and also swore to protect her, turns on her the minute her father dies?" Buffy asked.

"Basically, yeah," Todd answered.

"Typical," Buffy said, rolling her eyes.

And there's the smile.

Angelus had been watching Buffy's study session and her new study partner since sundown. And *Todd*, as that little smile seemed to confirm, was just beginning to realize that there was definitely a whole lot more to the petite blonde with the dusky hazel eyes and the short attention span than one might assume at first glance.

"Why typical?" Todd asked.

"Men in general," Buffy replied curtly.

"I see," Todd said thoughtfully.

That's right, big guy, she's been hurt. Recently. And it's going to take more than that crooked smile and a big brain to make her forget it. In fact . . . she's never going to forget it, if I have anything to say about it.

"So men aren't your favorite subject these days?" Todd asked just innocently enough.

To her credit, Buffy caught the faint whiff of flirtation immediately.

That's my girl.

But then she turned to Todd, and instead of taking the

perfect opportunity he had given her to wax rhapsodic about men and their inconstancy, she softened a bit and said, "Not all men, I guess."

"Well, that's good to hear," Todd replied with a bigger smile. "I mean, I can't speak for all men, but for me . . . I guess . . . well, I haven't had a lot of time for . . ."

"What?" Buffy asked, seeming genuinely interested.

Angelus didn't like where this was starting to go one bit.

"It's just, I work pretty hard. Always have. You know . . . I'm trying to put myself through college, but money's pretty tight, so I've got a couple of part-time jobs."

"You mean you're not spending your evenings tutoring the less intellectually inclined just out of the goodness of your heart?" Buffy teased.

"No, I mean, I like tutoring . . . ," Todd began.

"It's okay," Buffy chuckled. "I can relate."

"You work part-time too?" Todd asked.

"Not exactly," Buffy replied a little evasively. "I guess the 'never having enough time' part just sounds familiar."

"Oh." Todd nodded. "You're probably pretty busy at school," he suggested. "And I bet you're really popular."

Buffy laughed dismissively. "Then you'd lose."

"Now you're teasing me."

"Nope. I mean, I have friends, good friends, but being popular takes the kind of effort I don't usually have to spare," Buffy said.

"So what do you like to do that takes up so much time?" Todd asked with serious interest.

Angelus watched as Buffy considered her response. Anyone who didn't know her as well as he did would not have questioned the sweet mask of innocence that she'd worn through their entire exchange. On the surface, everything about Buffy definitely suggested what Todd was seeing. She was beautiful, funny, and terribly charming. She had "cheerleader" and "homecoming queen" written all over her. And before she'd been called to slay vampires, that, and the mall, had been the sum total of her existence. But now that beguiling sweetness was tempered by a wealth of experiences, both dark and powerful, at which Todd could never guess. And the reality was, for a man to truly know Buffy, he had to get past the candy shell and dig for the gooey center. That was where the truly good stuff was, and that was the part of her that Angelus was determined to destroy before he allowed himself the exquisite pleasure of killing her.

"You know, it's getting pretty late," Buffy said, clearly ready to change the subject, "and we still haven't talked about my English essay."

That was more like it. She obviously liked Todd. But she was nowhere near letting him get close to that inner sanctum she guarded so carefully. Trust was a huge issue with Buffy, and Angelus sensed that, despite the fact that Buffy seemed flattered by Todd's attentions, it was going to take more than a little flirting to break down the walls she had built around her heart.

Good girl, Angelus thought as he dropped silently from the roof onto Buffy's front yard and caught the faint scent of infant from a few houses down. He toyed with the idea of getting himself an invitation into that house, but sweet as newborn blood was, there wasn't usually enough there to do more than whet his appetite.

Maybe he should wait for Todd. Buffy had miles to go before she slept that night, and it sounded like their session was about to come to an end. The tutor would undoubtedly be heading out the front door in minutes. But then, how much more delicious would it be to wait for Buffy to actually develop a serious liking for Todd before Angelus sucked the life out of him? Today, Todd was a harmless flirtation. Given enough time, he could become someone Buffy would be truly sad to see die.

In his hundred-plus years of existence as a demon, Angelus had definitely learned patience. And when it came to Buffy, there was nothing worth having that wasn't worth waiting for.

Todd could wait.

For now.

CHAPTER FOUR

Buffy didn't want to think about Todd's dimples. She didn't want to think about how smart he was, or how normal he was, or what a nice change of pace it would be to spend time with a boy who didn't even know vampires were real, let alone how plentiful they were in this neck of the woods. She also didn't want to think about how much better she seemed to feel when Todd was around. Buffy's self-esteem had been one of Angel's many casualties of late, and it did her more good than she realized to feel another boy's attraction, especially such a cute boy's.

Mostly she didn't want to think about a civil war that had erupted in England almost a thousand years ago.

Her head was so full of all the things she didn't want

to think about that as she sat poised over her world history textbook, highlighter in hand, she found all of those things coalescing into a vaguely blurry ball that buzzed and hummed until she was faintly aware that her eyes no longer wanted to stay open.

Patrol.

When that word came darting through the haze, Buffy found herself fully awake.

She also found that she was really, really cold.

Her room was exactly what it should be. The desk lamp glowed brightly, and the sky outside her open window, *hence the cold,* was still pretty dark.

What was I supposed to be doing? she found herself wondering.

Her textbook lay open before her, but a quick glance at the clock by her bed told her that almost the full night had somehow elapsed since she had asked Todd to leave so she could finish her assignments on her own. Of course this had been a flimsy excuse to get him out the door so she could do a little patrolling before going to bed.

Crap.

Now fully awake, and still too cold, Buffy rose and started to shut her bedroom window before accepting the fact that she would never hear the end of it from Giles for two nights in a row of zero slaying and that the window was as good a way as any to leave the house in the wee hours of the morning.

Grabbing her heavy leather jacket and a few spare stakes

from the trunk in her closet, Buffy did a quick hallway check to confirm that Joyce was snoring softly in the next bedroom before she shimmied out her window and landed with a soft thud on her front lawn.

She honestly didn't know what was wrong with her. Though her sense of time was not as finely honed as your average vampire's, Buffy had often found that her internal clock was subconsciously sensitive to the passage of time. Many a night, walking these same streets with Angel, she had found herself growing anxious as part of her felt the approach of dawn, knowing this would require them to separate.

Stop thinking about Angel and concentrate, Buffy demanded of herself.

Despite the fact that her body had apparently forced a full night of sleep upon her, and the reality that she had lost valuable study and slaying time in the process, Buffy still had at least an hour before dawn and remained cautiously optimistic that something that shouldn't be was still probably lurking the streets of Sunnydale.

She decided to cut through the playground of a nearby park en route to the cemetery nearest the high school when she pulled herself up short before jumping a chain-link fence. In the faint moonlight she could barely make out the form of a young girl, and she could hear the metallic whine of one of the playground's swings.

This couldn't be more wrong, Buffy thought immediately as a tiny bit of adrenaline pushed her into a hyper-conscious state. There was no rational explanation she could conceive of that would include a little girl on a swing set just before dawn. A memory forced itself into her consciousness: Giles . . . yesterday . . . and something about a little girl who was missing. Buffy didn't like to let herself hope, but she quickened her steps as she approached the girl, and was gratified to see that as she did, the girl looked up and met Buffy's gaze shyly.

Immediately conscious that she should try to keep the little girl at ease, Buffy stopped a few paces short of the swing and knelt so as to address the girl at roughly eye level. "Hi, there," she said gently.

"Hi," the girl replied.

"My name's Buffy," the Slayer said. "What's yours?"

"Callie," the girl said with a faint smile as she pushed herself off from the ground a bit to start the swing going again.

Buffy cursed herself for not having paid more attention to Giles but thought that the name did sound vaguely familiar. Hopeful that she was on the right track, Buffy rose and took the swing next to Callie's before she continued.

"It's kind of late . . . or kind of early, to be playing, isn't it?" Buffy asked. "Do your parents know you're here?"

The girl shrugged and continued to swing.

"You know, the swings were always my favorite too. But I hate to think that someone might be out there missing you right now. Why don't you let me walk you home?" Buffy suggested.

"I'm hungry," was Callie's defiant response.

"Okay," Buffy said, rising and extending her hand to Callie. "Come to think of it, I'm pretty hungry too. Maybe we could find a little something on the way back to your house."

"Do you like to eat people?" Callie asked sweetly. "Because I don't."

The transformation was instantaneous. One moment, blond ringlets had framed chubby cheeks and a perky little heart-shaped mouth, and the next, the girl's forehead protruded and the blue of her eyes was lost to a feral yellowish glow as the child-vampire's fangs extended themselves from her gruesome mouth.

Buffy was poised for action, a stake in her hand, before her mind even registered what was happening. She put a couple of feet between them and waited for a lunge, but Callie remained seated on the swing looking up at Buffy, almost sadly.

Buffy knew what she had to do. This was the easy part of the job. Find demon. Kill demon. Unless the demon had a soul, or had once been her boyfriend, it was rarely more complicated than that.

But she couldn't. This was a child.

No, it isn't, another voice within her reasoned.

Time and again she and Giles had discussed the reality that, once a human was turned into a vampire, the human was gone. The vampire that remained might remember the details and relationships of the previous life, but the body was all demon. There was nothing to be saved, no hope for the victim. This child had already been killed by a vampire. The fact that something newborn and evil now wore her face meant nothing. Callie was already dead.

Callie seemed to sense Buffy's reluctance. For the first time since they'd met, she smiled broadly.

"What's wrong, Buffy?" Callie asked.

"Nothing," Buffy replied less forcefully than she would have liked.

"Then come and get me," Callie shouted, and sprang up.

Buffy instinctively jumped back to avoid the attack. She actually hit the ground butt first before she realized that Callie was now running off in the opposite direction.

She considered giving chase. Vampires were faster than humans, but so was Buffy. Even now she might still catch her. But something kept her rooted to the ground.

Buffy had never before faced a vampire who was a child. Now there was something else in the world she didn't know if she had the strength to kill.

She needed to talk to Giles.

Though she didn't think Giles would be awake for another few hours, she knew he'd forgive the wake-up call, under the circumstances. Retracing her steps back toward her home, Buffy was running so quickly, she narrowly avoided smashing full-force into a pedestrian she encountered just a few blocks from Ravello Drive.

Though it seemed a bit early for a jog, Buffy had almost put it from her mind as she offered a quick apology, until she realized that the "jogger" wasn't so much jogging away from her as lumbering casually along as if he didn't have a care in the world.

Then it hit her.

"Principal Snyder?" Buffy said in disbelief.

The balding pate and unfortunately large ears were unmistakable, as was the civil servant's budget suit. For reasons that defied understanding, Buffy's principal was roaming the streets of Sunnydale before dawn like a sleep-walker.

Uh-oh.

Maybe Callie wasn't the only new vampire in town. But though she wouldn't have hesitated to strike down a vampire Snyder—in fact, she would have taken great pleasure in it—she knew in her gut that Snyder was still very much alive.

And limping?

Snyder walked on, favoring his left foot, oblivious of Buffy. Homing in on the principal's feet, she realized with alarm that he was barefoot, and leaving a distinct trail behind him.

Buffy couldn't smell blood, but she certainly knew it when she saw it. Kneeling at the closest part of the trail, Buffy satis-fied herself that Principal Snyder's left foot was bleeding—rather copiously, from the looks of things.

It was too much. Something was seriously wrong with this picture, but between Callie and the reality of a new school day dawning on the horizon, Buffy decided that rather than confront the principal here and now, she needed a shower, a change of clothes, and a telephone . . . probably not in that order.

Well done, Rupert, Giles thought as he rose from the insufferable wooden chair before his small office desk in the school library, cursing the stiffness in his back and wondering how he had managed to fall asleep there rather than in his perfectly comfortable bed at home. Truth be told, he couldn't remember.

It wasn't that sleeping in the library was such a rare occurrence. During many of Buffy's more complicated trials of the last few years he had burned more than his fair share of the midnight oil in this very spot. He even kept a few clean dress shirts and a toothbrush at the library for such occasions. But as there was nothing particularly apocalyptic on his schedule for the week, he found it odd that he'd lost track of time over a well-worn edition of Tomberlin's *Demons of Eighteenth-Century Europe* and had dropped off for more than eight hours while seated at his desk.

An urgent call from Buffy had awakened him here, just short of six a.m. As he debated between boiling a kettle or firing up the coffeemaker in the faculty lounge, he realized that from the tone of Buffy's voice he had only minutes before she would come bursting into the library, so he opted to settle for a quick round of morning ablutions in the nearest restroom, followed by a fresh shirt.

By the time he'd returned to the library, Buffy was already

waiting for him, seriously studying a number of large reference books he'd left on the main table.

"Good morning, Buffy," he greeted her.

"There you are," she shot back. How she could be peeved this early in the morning escaped him, but he had no doubt she would illuminate her problem as best she could with little prodding on his part.

"The little girl, the one you mentioned yesterday," Buffy began.

"Callie McKay?" Giles offered.

"I thought so," Buffy said, shaking her head.

"What happened?" Giles asked. "Did you find her?"

"I think so. Do you still have the paper?"

Giles hurried to his office, retrieved Monday's paper from the trash can, and had opened it to the article about Callie's disappearance before he realized Buffy was right on his heels. He handed her the article, but the serious disappointment on her face as she studied the picture told him all he needed to know about Callie's fate.

"I'm sorry, Buffy," he offered gently. "I suppose we should alert her parents as to her . . . whereabouts. Where exactly did you find her?"

"At the park, swinging," Buffy replied angrily.

Giles was suddenly confused. He'd assumed Buffy had intended to confirm the identity of a body she'd found, but if the child was still alive . . .

"She wasn't—?" he began.

"Oh, she's dead," Buffy replied quickly. "In fact, she's undead."

"But . . ." Giles truly didn't know where to begin. "Are you certain?" he asked.

"She transformed right in front of me, Giles," Buffy countered. "How much more certain do I need to be?"

"It's just—"

"What?" Buffy demanded.

"W-well . . . , " he stammered, "it's just that most vampires instinctively shy away from siring children as young as Callie."

"Then somebody's tossed out the rule book," Buffy replied, then added, "No prizes guessing who."

With all the questions running through Giles's head at the moment, it took him a few seconds to catch her meaning. "Angelus?" he said.

"Sure." She shrugged. "You said he's big with the psychological warfare. I have to hand it to him. He did catch me off guard this time."

For the first time since she'd called, Giles regretted not making some coffee. He didn't feel particularly well rested from his night sleeping upright, and it was already promising to be a spectacularly long day.

"Then I take it you found it difficult to—"

"Stake her?" Buffy finished for him.

"Yes."

"I didn't."

"What?" Giles said with genuine concern. "Didn't stake her, or didn't find it difficult?" he clarified, wondering who was responsible for teaching America's youth proper grammar, and wishing them all great bodily harm.

"She ran off before I had a chance."

Giles considered Buffy carefully. He had a hard time believing that Buffy couldn't have fairly easily dealt with one vampire, particularly an immature vampire.

Buffy looked into Giles's eyes, the battle between anger and sadness clearly raging. He instantly pitied her the encounter and the difficulty of the choice she'd faced that night. He had to remind himself again that much as she'd grown since he'd become her Watcher, she was still, in so many ways, just a girl.

"Buffy, you must understand that Callie is already dead. Her appearance may be startling, but she is still a demon and, unfortunately, must be destroyed," Giles said as compassionately as possible.

"I know," Buffy answered glumly. "But it was so strange."

"I can well imagine," Giles replied.

"She said she didn't like to eat people," Buffy offered. "Is that even possible?"

Giles paused before answering. "To be honest, Buffy, there is very little known about child-vampires. As I said, most vampires are extremely reluctant to turn children. Though they do gain the expected strength and stamina of an adult vampire, children do not mature instantly when they are turned. Though they couldn't be called innocent," he continued, choosing his words carefully, "they do tend to retain the willfulness and impulsiveness of their former age. They are difficult to manage and, frankly, usually more trouble than they are worth—at least from the point of view of a potential sire."

"I hesitated, Giles," Buffy said simply. "I knew what I had to do, but I just couldn't bring myself to do it."

"It's perfectly understandable," Giles said, placing a comforting hand on Buffy's shoulder. "You were taken by surprise. But I must tell you, I have a hard time believing that Angelus would trouble himself to do this, despite your quite natural misgivings. I understand that dealing with Angelus is your primary focus of late. But any number of vampires could have been responsible for this. Frankly, it strikes me as the act of either a very young, or a very unstable, demon."

"Either way, I guess I know what I have to do," Buffy said softly.

She turned away and started toward the doors. Giles struggled to find words to either comfort or inspire her, but he hadn't settled on any when she turned and said, "By the way, have you noticed anything odd about Principal Snyder the past few days?"

Giles had often suffered serious mental whiplash at the myriad twists and turns of his Slayer's mind, but this caught him entirely unprepared. "I beg your pardon?"

"After I saw Callie, I almost ran into Snyder. He was out

for an early morning walk. But it was like he didn't even see me. And his foot was bleeding."

Though Giles found this puzzling, his focus on Callie and her effect on Buffy made him quick to dismiss it.

"Well, I'll make it a point to speak to him later, if you like, but I'm certain it's nothing to worry yourself about."

"Right," Buffy said.

"Your priority must be to find Callie," he reiterated.

"Got it." She nodded, then added, "Thanks for coming in early. I'm sorry I woke you."

"Never a problem," Giles said cordially as she disappeared into the hallway. "Have a good morning," he offered much too late.

"Wait . . . he was doing what?" Xander asked, pausing before he bit into a fried fish stick.

"He was walking down the street, just before dawn, and leaving a trail of fresh blood behind him," Buffy replied as she toyed with her fruit salad.

"What kind of socks was he wearing?" Willow asked.

"Can we not start with the socks again?" Cordelia pleaded, stifling a yawn.

"Guys, you're missing the point," Buffy said briskly. The entire gang had gathered in the cafeteria for lunch: Xander and Cordelia, Willow and Oz, and Buffy and her salad. Normally the sight of her friends and their respective romantic interests didn't trouble Buffy, but lately she had started to feel too much like a third, or in this case, fifth, wheel. Xander's passion for Cordelia had been difficult to accept in its early days, but over time, Buffy had come to terms with it. Willow's newer romance with the sweet but taciturn Oz, who'd only recently discovered he was a were-wolf, was truly a source of happiness for Buffy. Still, there was something in the new couple's cuteness and playfulness that brought Buffy's loneliness into sharper focus than she could ever say. Most days it simply brought vivid images of all she'd lost in Angel to the forefront of her mind. On afternoons like this one, when she was both troubled by her slaying duties and insufficiently rested, it almost made her crabby.

"Am I the only one here who thinks that's just too weird?" Buffy continued as diplomatically as she could.

"I'd give it an 'odd,' but I'd like to withhold 'weird' until we get a judge's ruling on the socks," Oz said simply.

"No, I'm with Buffy on this one," Willow decided. "Only because Snyder didn't say anything mean to her."

"Thanks, Will," Buffy replied.

"So you're thinking demon, Buffy?" Xander asked.

"I don't know," she retorted sharply. "Giles didn't seem to think it was that big a deal."

"Then what are you worried about? If Mr. I'm-All-Smart-and-British doesn't care, I say let it go," Cordelia offered, clearly exasperated that Xander was, once again, paying more attention to Buffy than to her. "So the little twerp exercises. So he does it first thing in the morning. If you ask me, it's the most normal thing Snyder's ever done."

"Were your ears in the upright and open position when I mentioned the blood?" Buffy snapped.

"Maybe he cut himself shaving," Willow offered.

"How many men do you know who shave their toes?" Buffy asked.

"Well . . . ," Oz began.

But before he could continue, the attention of everyone at the table was drawn to the cafeteria line, where Larry, a likable enough jock who had recently and inadvertently revealed to Xander that he was gay, and Jonathan, a sweet, rather quiet junior who always seemed to find himself in the line of fire, were screaming at each other at the top of their lungs.

"I called dibs on the red Jell-O, man!" Larry shouted, shoving Jonathan into a gaggle of freshman girls who were trying to pay for their lunch at the counter.

Jonathan recovered quickly and shouted back, "What are you, five? There are no dibs in the lunch line! It's first come, first served."

The next few moments were a blur. Larry grabbed Jonathan by his shirt, and a few of Larry's football buddies who were behind him in line piled on as Jonathan started swinging for dear life. Without thinking, Buffy jumped into the fray, dodging punches, and, with no small effort on her part, succeeded in pulling the entire Sunnydale High School offensive line off of Jonathan, who ended up on his back and covered in red Jell-O.

When everyone had settled for a moment, Buffy grabbed Larry and demanded, "What's the problem?"

"I don't know," Larry replied lamely. "I just wanted my Jell-O."

Buffy's anger downshifted to concern. Larry wasn't the brightest bulb in the package, but he was also no longer the overcompensating school bully she'd first come to know. He seemed as confused as she was by his actions. He shook his head and looked about, almost as if he were just now realizing where he was and what he was doing.

"Step away from the lunch line," Buffy said both calmly and commandingly, handing Larry his very own bowl of Jell-O and turning him toward the cashier.

"Right. Sorry," Larry said, then added, "I guess I'm just really tired. I don't think I slept last night. Maybe it's low blood sugar."

Buffy turned her attention to Jonathan and, as she helped him to his feet, suddenly realized that everyone in the cafeteria was now looking at her. *One of these days I'm going to remember to think before I act,* she chided herself. She didn't necessarily mind being the center of attention, but this really wasn't the kind of attention she enjoyed. Still, she was gratified to see that Larry and his buddies were moving slowly away from the lunch line.

"Thanks, Buffy," Jonathan said quietly.

"What got into you?" she asked him. "In what bizarro universe was that a fight you were going to win?"

"It pissed me off," Jonathan replied. "This is supposed to be high school. No one has seriously called dibs on anything since the fifth grade."

"Okay, but next time, you might want to think before you take on the entire football team over the last of the red Jell-O," Buffy said. "There's something to be said for picking your battles, you know?"

"I know. I'm just so tired of those guys picking on me. Really tired."

As he spoke, Jonathan stifled a yawn, and Buffy saw his eyes start to glaze over with weariness. All the energy seemed to drain from his face as he turned to find a lunch table.

That's weird, Buffy thought. One minute, they're at each other's throats, and the next . . . well, it wasn't a chorus of "Kumbaya," but it was pretty darn close. Her musings were interrupted by Cordelia, who, along with the others, had gathered her things from the lunch table and was heading for the door.

"Gee, Buffy, if this whole Slayer thing doesn't work out, you clearly have a brilliant future as a hall monitor," Cordelia said, grabbing Xander by the sleeve and dragging him into the hall.

"Stuff it, Cordelia," Willow snapped.

Cordelia feigned deafness to Willow's jab, but Buffy turned to her friend, concerned.

"Are you okay, Will?" she asked.

Willow thought about it for a second longer than it usually would have taken.

"Yeah, I don't know."

"I mean, I know you're still the acting president of the I-Hate-Cordelia Club, but that was a little harsh, don't you think?"

"I can't help it," Willow said defensively. "She just makes me cranky."

It seemed clear to Buffy that everyone had taken their edgy pills this morning. To lighten the mood she waited for a "Later, guys" from Oz as he headed upstairs to his next class, and lowering her voice to a conspiratorial level, she asked Willow, "So, last night . . . any good Oz dreams?"

Willow blushed instantly, but then seriously considered the question. "No," she finally replied remorsefully. "I don't remember any of my dreams from last night."

"Well, fear not," Buffy said, placing a playful arm over Willow's shoulder, "there's always tonight."

As they made their way through the hall, Buffy was stopped in her tracks by the sight of Principal Snyder standing outside the chemistry lab holding a freshman boy, whose name Buffy couldn't recall, by the ear.

"Sleeping in class, young man? Maybe on somebody else's campus," he said in his typical I-have-all-the-power tone.

Willow, Xander, and Cordelia immediately dodged into the nearest classroom to avoid Snyder. But Buffy paused, toying with the right way to ask the principal what the hell he'd been doing that morning, when he caught sight of her and, still holding the boy's ear, remarked with a snide smile, "Ah, Miss Summers, how goes the tutoring?"

It might have been a record. In less than a second Buffy had gone from actually worrying a little about the man to wishing she could have just a few minutes alone with him in a dark alley to teach him the meaning of power.

"It's going great, Principal Snyder," she replied, raising her chin in a small act of defiance.

"I hope so, for your sake." He smiled. "As I understand it, the tutor the school board recommended for you is the most demanding in the business. Not that I think it will do much good," he added with a deep sigh of satisfaction.

"He's great," Buffy replied, as if she wouldn't have wanted it any other way. "Really very helpful."

"Aren't you late for class?" Snyder asked, oblivious to the fact that he was still holding the freshman's ear and said freshman was writhing in considerable agony beneath his fingers.

"Nope. I have study hall this period," Buffy replied with a smile. "I'm library bound to complete some of my extra assignments."

"Well, what are you waiting for?" Snyder sneered. "Go."

Buffy did as he suggested. Only when she reached the library did it occur to her that Snyder was wearing the same suit today she'd seen him in earlier that morning, a light blue polyester blend, but he'd matched it with a pair of white wingtips that, apart from being out of season, were totally wrong for daytime.

Maybe his foot is still hurting, Buffy mused. She knew it was wrong to enjoy that thought, but she just couldn't help herself.

Buffy was a Slayer. Not a saint.

CHAPTER FIVE

Angelus was having the most delectable vision. Buffy was bound and gagged at his feet. Her friends Xander, Willow, and Giles were already eviscerated, their respective guts pouring from their bellies and spilling out onto the blood-soaked ground. Todd was kneeling before him, a picture of smarmy tutorial terror pleading for his life, when Angelus was startled out of his reverie by the sound of breaking glass. It only took a second to discern the direction from whence it had come: Drusilla's sitting room.

He flirted with the idea of leaving Dru and Spike to whatever they were doing, settling himself down to continue revising Todd's last moments of life, when a second shattering of glass and muffled raised voices met his ears.

What the hell?

He hurried down the main hall toward the master suite. Before he could enter, Callie flew past him screeching, pausing only to kick him hard in the shin before darting into the living room and jumping onto the couch, holding one of Dru's many precious china dolls above her head and shrieking, "You are not the boss of me!" at the top of her little lungs.

Dru was right behind her, alight with rage.

"Put her down, Callie," Dru demanded. "She sings beautiful songs to Mummy. Bring her to me at once!"

But that was all Callie needed to hear. The moment Dru made it clear that the doll meant something to her, Callie brought her arms down, thrusting the porcelain doll to the floor, where its face shattered when it met the hard stone.

"No!" Dru cried out, as if physically struck by the loss. She rushed to the floor and began gently picking up the pieces in a vain attempt to reassemble them.

"Welcome to the village of the damned," Spike offered drolly as he rolled himself into the entryway, holding Dru's beloved pet dog, Sunshine, on his lap.

Callie continued to rampage through the room, tearing into pillows, knocking over tables, and upending anything that wasn't nailed down.

"Oh, I don't think so," Angelus retorted sharply. In a few quick steps he was across the room, and, grabbing Callie securely by the shoulders, he bent to say firmly, "Callie, it's not nice to destroy Mommy's things. Now play nice and say you're sorry."

"Make me!" Callie screamed back, struggling in Angelus's grasp and punctuating her disdain by attempting to bite his hand.

"Gladly," Angelus replied. His patience didn't extend to spoiled brats, and in a flash he had dragged Callie to the heavily curtained French doors that separated the living room from the main courtyard and opened them just enough to show Callie the bright patch of afternoon sun that still fell onto a corner of the patio.

"Sounds like someone needs a time-out," Angelus said as he threw open the doors with one hand and, with the other, tossed Callie unceremoniously toward the sunlight. As she struggled to regain her feet, Angelus noticed approvingly that one of her hands had tumbled into the light. It singed only slightly in a sweetly scented, smoky vapor before she pulled it back and retreated into the late afternoon shadows, hissing at him between cries of "Owie!"

Content for the moment, Angelus turned on Drusilla. "Look, honey, I know how much you love your pets," he began.

"Oh, Angelus, you mustn't kill her," Dru pleaded.

"There's still plenty of shade out there for now. How else do you expect her to learn her lessons?" Angelus asked.

Dru nodded, turned mournfully to Spike, and began to sob. Angelus looked to Spike, who dumped Dru's little dog onto the floor, only increasing the intensity of her sobs.

"It seems Callie was a bit peckish and decided to have Mr. Sunshine here as her afternoon snack," Spike explained with just a hint of malicious glee.

"She stayed out all night, Angelus," Dru cried despondently, "but didn't eat a thing. I don't know what to do with her," she finally said mournfully. "She doesn't seem to love me at all."

"I told you when you brought her into this house that Callie was your responsibility, Dru," Angelus said menacingly. "I know you wanted a playmate, but if you can't control her . . ."

"Were you born at night or last night?" Spike shot back. "You don't control a child, particularly a child-vampire. You stay the hell out of their way."

"I just wanted . . ." But Dru was again overcome by her anguish.

Angelus knelt beside Dru, placing a comforting arm around her shoulder. "There, there," he said gently. "She'll come around."

But instead of accepting Angelus's kindness, Dru rose quickly to her feet and said, "I can't do this alone. Callie needs her mummy and her daddies. She doesn't know how to hunt properly."

"Hunting isn't something you learn. It's instinct," Angelus retorted.

"She needs time," Dru countered.

"That may be, love," Spike interjected, "but I don't think the furniture can take it."

"Then what do you suggest?" Dru asked sharply, glaring at both Angelus and Spike in turn. "She's starving. She has to eat. You should go and find her someone so she's not tempted to snack between meals."

"I don't have time for this," Angelus replied.

"Right, you're too busy not killing the Slayer," Spike said.

Angelus answered him with a simmering glare before adding, "If she won't hunt for herself, send Mr. Meals-on-Wheels for take-out. I have better things to do." And with that, he stormed from the room.

Once Angelus was out of earshot, Spike turned to Dru and said softly, "Why don't you let me have a go, pet?" Dru nodded forlornly, and Spike wheeled himself over to the doors and let himself onto the patio where Callie knelt in a shaded corner. Keeping well out of the light, Spike made his way to her, stopping a few feet short, but giving her no room to run far.

"I see we have a problem playing well with others," he said simply. "Lucky for you, I can relate."

Callie looked up at him, her fight clearly spent for the moment.

"A little birdie told me you don't think you want to eat people," he said gently. "Do you like people?" he asked. "Are you afraid to hurt them? Is that the problem?"

Callie shrugged. "It's just . . . wrong," she said finally.

"Wrong?" Spike asked.

"Like telling a lie, or cheating on a test in school," Callie clarified.

"I see." Spike nodded. "And you know, I agree. Standards, codes of conduct, aren't necessarily bad things. It's true, most vampires don't care who they eat, but if it's something you feel strongly about, I think we can work with it." He paused, watching her closely and pleased to see that she was hanging on his every word. "Let me ask you this, pet. Are all people good? Does everyone care as much as you do about telling the truth or earning their grades?"

Callie seemed to seriously consider the question.

Spike continued to lead her on. "I mean, aren't there people you know who used to be mean to you, or upset you?"

Callie's bright eyes met Spike's. "Michael," she said softly.

"Michael?" Spike asked. "And what did Michael do to you?"

"He teased me on the playground," Callie said. "He never let me on the swings."

"Sounds to me like Michael needs to learn a lesson or two, doesn't it," Spike said gently.

For the first time since they'd met, Callie actually smiled at Spike, and for reasons that he couldn't place, it felt almost . . . good.

"I could definitely eat Michael," she said. "But how do I find him? At night, he'll be at home, and I don't know where he lives."

"You let me worry about that, little one," Spike said, reaching out a hand to help Callie up. After a moment, she took it and clambered up onto his lap.

"Is there anyone else you can think of?" Spike asked.

"Tony!" Callie smiled, clapping her little hands.

Spike wheeled the two of them back into the living room as Callie whispered to him her stories of Tony, and Adam, and a number of other boys and girls who in very short order were going to seriously regret not having been nicer to Callie when she was alive.

Dru stood near the fireplace, watching them anxiously as they entered. With a slight wink to Dru, which was rewarded by one of her most vicious smiles, Spike encouraged Callie to tell him more about the children she disliked. Twenty minutes later, a much happier Callie had fallen into a deep slumber, curled up on his lap.

"My Spikey has a way with children," Dru cooed lovingly.

Spike accepted the compliment, along with the subtle satisfaction of having succeeded in doing that which pleased Dru and alienated Angelus. If he could drive Callie between them, it would be well worth the effort. Besides, against all laws of nature, he found he was truly beginning to like the child. Maybe it was the fierceness of her passions. Or maybe it was the way she had looked at him earlier when she'd first glimpsed the ease with which pain could be transformed into evil. Either way, this was turning out to be a much better day than he'd reckoned when he'd first found Callie feeding on

Sunshine not an hour earlier. After so many months of neglect and frustration, Spike had found someone who might come to love him almost as much as Drusilla did, but who, more than that, could offer him something Drusilla hadn't in months.

Callie might just *need* him.

Buffy's day had taken a definite upturn following lunch. She'd actually joined in on a class discussion on Keats, receiving a series of surprised compliments from her English teacher, Mrs. Massey, and felt she'd done extremely well on a world history pop quiz. Though she wasn't going to be winning an academic decathlon anytime soon, Buffy had to admit that the extra study time with Todd was already paying off. By the time she got home, she was actually looking forward to seeing him, and found that he was already waiting for her in her bedroom.

To her surprise, Todd seemed startled by her. He rose abruptly from the seat by her dresser, quickly slamming shut one of the drawers and smiling as if he were trying to hide something. "Oh, hi, Buffy," he said quickly.

"You're early," she replied warily. A small knot formed in her stomach as she realized that the drawer he had just been snooping in was one of her emergency drawers, containing a few crucifixes and some holy water. Not hard to explain if you were contemplating entering a convent, but a little out of the ordinary for your average high school junior.

Buffy considered trying to come up with an excuse for the

drawer's contents, but opted against it. He had no business going through her personal things, and if it weren't for her mother, the school board, and the fact that she was actually learning something, she might have physically thrown him from her house right then and there.

Todd seemed to sense the tension in her silence and said, "I don't know about you, but I'm pretty thirsty. How about I get us a couple of sodas before we start?"

"Sure," Buffy answered, still on guard.

A few minutes later he was back, two tall glasses in hand, and Buffy did her best to shake the ick factor. It was probably nothing. Just curiosity. And if Todd wanted to know more about her, maybe that was a good thing. At least it hadn't been her underwear drawer.

Still, as they tackled her chemistry chapters, her mind refused to stay on topic.

"It's official," she declared a few hours later. "Organic molecules suck."

"Oh, go easy on the poor molecules," Todd teased. "They don't mean to be so complicated."

"There is no way any future version of me is going to use chemistry," Buffy replied, refusing to give in to Todd's charms.

"You don't know that," he replied.

"Oh, but I do."

"Things change all the time, Buffy. None of us can see the future. You know how it is. One minute you think you have it all figured out, and the next, out of the blue, something totally unexpected happens."

Todd's eyes caught Buffy's. There was something almost hopeful in them. But it was quickly clouded over by doubt.

"I mean, who knows?" Todd continued. "Give chemistry a chance and you might just see more than math and particles. There's mystery in chemistry too."

"I usually like a good mystery," Buffy found herself saying before she could help herself.

Todd smiled.

Buffy returned the smile, and for a moment, that tiny withering garden in Buffy's secret heart saw a few fresh sprigs of green pushing themselves up through the earth. She found herself turning away, trying to push the hope that had started to rise back into its box before someone got hurt.

Because, in her experience, someone always got hurt— and it was usually Buffy.

Her gaze fell on her open bedroom window. Across the street, her neighbor Mr. Hall was watering his front yard.

"It's getting a little chilly, isn't it?" Todd said, more to break the silence than anything.

"Oh, my bad," Buffy replied quickly. Crossing to the window she placed her hands firmly on the frame to shut it when the sight of Principal Snyder walking casually past Mr. Hall caught her attention. He walked in the same measured gait that was both odd and troubling, and he was still wearing his white wingtips.

Her Slayer senses tingling, Buffy searched for a reasonable excuse to end her tutoring session a little early. She was surprised to find that, for once, the truth would make a compelling case.

"You know," she said, smiling apologetically, "I think organic molecules have turned my brain to mush. On top of that, I feel like I didn't sleep at all last night. Would you mind if we waited until Saturday to get back to history?"

Todd nodded, his disappointment obvious, but he covered nicely, saying, "No problem. I'm actually a little tired myself. We'll do the quizzes on chapters twenty through twenty-two first thing Saturday afternoon, deal?"

"Absolutely," Buffy agreed.

Buffy watched Todd make his way down her front walkway and was pleased to see that his road home led in the opposite direction from Snyder. As her mother would be working late tonight on inventory, Buffy quickly scrawled a note to her indicating that she was headed for the library, before exiting through the back door and cutting through a few neighbors' yards to catch up with the principal, not far from where she'd found him that morning.

Her hunch had been accurate. She found the principal crossing the first main intersection east of Ravello Drive, and with practiced ease had no difficulty keeping him in sight for the next six blocks as he walked slowly toward the southeast section of Sunnydale. Doing some quick mental geography, Buffy decided he was heading for Arborville, a development built in the early 1940s that had been a lovely neighborhood in its day. Unfortunately, its day had come and gone, and now most of the houses in that area withered under the neglect of the retirees who no longer had the resources or the inclination to keep them properly maintained.

Snyder walked slowly, as if he were out for an afternoon stroll through the park. When he came to a four-way intersection at Oak Street, he turned south. Unfortunately, a driver turning left into Snyder's path probably didn't even see him in the early evening gloom.

Within seconds, Buffy threw herself into the car's path, knocking Snyder out of the way as the car screeched, then swerved to avoid the pedestrians, and ended up plowing into one of dozens of stately oak trees that lined the thoroughfare, giving it its name.

Buffy's first thought was for the principal. He picked himself up off the ground, without bothering to wipe the gravel from his hands or knees, and continued on his walk as if nothing had happened.

Definitely a ten on the weird-o-meter, Buffy decided. But before she could continue after him, she realized that the horn of the car that had hit the tree was blaring incessantly and traffic had slowed as other commuters tried to make their way around the accident.

Buffy's concern momentarily got the better of her curiosity. She approached the car and saw that the driver was crumpled over the steering wheel, his head resting on the horn. Buffy quickly opened the driver's door and asked, "Hey, are you all right?"

The driver didn't respond. Given that the car's collision with the tree had been fairly low impact, and there was no blood or even a scratch on the driver's face, Buffy wondered how the driver could have been knocked unconscious by the accident. She gently lifted the driver's head from the horn and set him upright in his seat. To her amazement, she heard a series of soft snores. The man wasn't injured. He had simply fallen asleep at the wheel.

"Hey, miss!" A voice interrupted Buffy's thoughts. Turning, she saw that another driver had pulled to the side of the road. "Everything okay?"

"Can you call 911?" Buffy asked—*or maybe the sandman,* she thought—and with a nod, the Good Samaritan was on his cell phone, alerting the police.

"An ambulance is on its way," the driver called back. In the confusion, it finally dawned on Buffy that she had lost sight of the principal. Hurrying back to the last corner where she'd seen him, she searched the increasing darkness for any sign of him but was quickly disappointed.

He probably couldn't have gone far. Once she heard the sounds of the approaching ambulance, satisfied that the driver was in good hands, Buffy took off down the street. Within a few minutes she had doubled back to the nearest main intersection and followed the opposite direction, until she was nearing Sunnydale's quaint main street, a series of storefronts and coffee shops flanked on one end by the old movie theater.

Her gut told her that now she would probably never find the principal, and she had almost decided to simply cut her losses and sweep back through a few parks in search of Callie when she saw a familiar figure talking animatedly into a pay phone that bordered the town's central square.

It was Todd. Though his voice was low, his body language told her loud and clear that he was arguing with someone on the other end of the line.

Buffy considered just approaching him, but almost as quickly decided that she didn't have a good excuse to be out walking the streets at night when she had ended their session so early. She closed the distance between them, finally pausing behind a nearby tree. Her stealth was rewarded, though her conscience pained her a bit. Just a few hours ago she had been frustrated with Todd for snooping around in her things, and here she was actually spying on him.

"No!" Todd said vehemently into the phone. After a pause: "I know what we agreed, but I'm saying I can't do it. I won't do it!" he finished forcefully.

Buffy had to admit, it was intriguing; maybe not crosses and holy water intriguing, but definitely oddly interesting. This was not the gentle, sweet, and concerned boy she'd spent so much time with over the last few days. This Todd struggled to keep his voice down, clearly conscious that he was in a public place from the furtive glances he threw all around him as he talked. Furthermore, he was obviously angry. He seemed almost like a cornered animal, lashing out. A quick pang in her stomach told Buffy that suddenly Todd was more than a cute boy—now he was a cute boy with a secret, and though most of the secrets Buffy had unearthed in recent months hadn't been cuddly kittens, they *had* been worth knowing.

"There's more to him than meets the eye, wouldn't you say, sweetheart?" a familiar voice said behind Buffy.

Instantly her hand was searching her coat pockets for a stake, and the blood pumping through her veins had turned to ice.

"I'm sure I don't know what you're talking about," Buffy said stiffly as she turned to face Angelus.

He stood a few yards away, his arms crossed as he leaned against another tree, his expression one of smug pleasure that Buffy had only recently come to know and hate.

Her senses divided between keeping an eye on Angelus and protecting the unaware Todd, Buffy forced herself to keep one ear on the conversation going on behind her as she stepped gingerly toward Angelus's striking range and was rewarded seconds later by the sound of "Just tell him what I said," followed by the receiver slamming into the phone hook and Todd's steps hurrying obliviously up the street.

"Sure you do, Buffy," Angelus answered. "I get the distinct impression that *Todd*"—he drew out the vowel sound in a jeer that made Buffy want to pummel him—"has the hots for his new student."

"*How do you—,*" Buffy started to ask, but stopped herself quickly, unwilling to allow him to see any surprise that he was keeping on top of every new development in her life. Of course he knew who Todd was. That was his style, even before he'd turned evil. Instead, she forced herself to smile, as if she were delighted by Todd's potential attraction, and replied, "Well, he wouldn't be the first, would he?"

Angelus's pose lost some of its nonchalance. Buffy wouldn't permit herself to imagine that Angelus was threatened by her interest in Todd. That would have been flattering. But sick and twisted as it was, that's exactly what seemed to emanate from Angelus as he stepped toward her.

"Careful, Buffy," Angelus warned.

"Oh, now I'm scared," Buffy taunted right back. "If I remember right, you used to kill first, ask questions . . . never. You want me dead. What's the holdup?"

"Sometimes I like to play with my food," Angelus replied charmlessly.

They were now both poised for battle. Ten kinds of tension cracked between them like a whip.

"Jealous much?" Buffy asked sweetly.

Angelus threw back his head and laughed, but there was no joy in it.

"Get over yourself," he replied.

"You first," she tempted, then dropped her right shoulder as if she was about to turn away and, as he instinctively moved in, rewarded him with a quick spin-kick that landed squarely midshoulder and sent him reeling to his left.

Once the battle was on, all thoughts melted away. There was nothing in the world but this moment, this fight. There were plenty of demons that Buffy could fight these days with half a night's sleep and one hand tied behind her back. Angelus wasn't one of them.

The past few times they'd met like this, Buffy had developed the distinct impression that Angelus was toying with her. He parried her punches and kicks with a graceful ease, never inflicting too much damage when he went on the assault. She pressed hard, taking each advantage that came her way, forcing Angelus farther from the main street, leading him into the more densely wooded park.

Once they'd found a little privacy, Buffy intensified her attack. A solid punch to his head sent him reeling back, and she followed it with a roundhouse kick that knocked him to the ground. In any other fight, this would have been the moment to go for the kill, but Buffy stepped back, not from fear or hesitation but simply because she knew Angelus and how he fought. He was trying to lure her into a position that would reverse their momentum. He wasn't seriously damaged by anything she had inflicted so far, and he wasn't tired. But if she hadn't fought by his side a hundred times before this, she would never have suspected it.

He rose from the ground with a smile on his face. "That all you got, gorgeous?"

"Oh, I'm just getting warmed up," she replied, catching her breath.

Angelus's retort was a direct charge that threw Buffy to the ground on her back. He tried to pin her down, but she carried his weight forward, throwing him off, and scurried in the opposite direction as he recovered.

"Looks like someone's learning some new moves," Angelus taunted. "Is your little hot Toddy teaching you more than history? Almost makes me sorry I was your first. I might have actually enjoyed myself if you'd known a little something about men instead of making me do all the work."

There were two interesting pieces of information in this last remark for Buffy. The first was that Angelus knew at least some of the specifics of her study sessions with Todd, which would indicate that he was watching her more closely than she was aware. The second was that even though he was hiding it in an insult, he really didn't like the idea of anyone being closer to her than he was.

Of course those two thoughts would only rise to Buffy's conscious mind several hours later when she was replaying the fight in her head and dissecting it, free from the emotional intensity of the immediate conflict. All she heard at that moment were the words "sorry I was your first."

She'd told herself a thousand times that the things Angelus said to hurt her had nothing to do with what Angel might really have thought about their first and last night together. But every time Angelus pricked her with this particular barb, Buffy immediately wanted to claw at his eyes, pound his face into a bloody pulp, and refuse to let up until he was a mangled, miserable, tortured shadow of his former self.

But even this short time to grieve had taught her something else. Angelus wasn't the only one who knew how to play dirty in a fight.

So instead of lashing out with her fists, she rose calmly from her crouch and, squaring her shoulders, said simply, "What Todd and I do in my bedroom is none of your concern. He's taught me things that a cold, lifeless stiff like you never could. He's not one to waste his time whoring and gambling and drinking himself into oblivion like you did back in the day; he's worked hard to earn what's his. He pleases me, Angel, on a level you never could."

For a moment, there was silence. Angelus seemed to pale a little more in the moonlight, but that could have been a trick of the darkness. Only when he leaped forward, throwing her to the ground and pinning her hands above her head, did Buffy feel a tiny surge of delight in knowing that she had actually managed to hurt him.

He lowered his face to hers, giving her a moment to fear the fury she saw in his eyes even as the Slayer inside her sought a maneuver that would throw him off of her.

"Never forget this," Angelus hissed. "There is nothing you can love in this world that I cannot take away from you."

"No, Angel," she replied, "there is nothing in this world that you can keep me from loving—not anymore."

Angelus's grip around her wrists tightened. But she no

longer worried about having pushed him too far. Finally, he was the one who was knocked off balance by her. The power of this knowledge was intoxicating.

She was about to embrace the advantage and throw him off her, setting up for the kill, when he bent his face closer, his lips almost touching hers.

"Finally," he said softly.

Finally what? A part of her mind that she refused to give voice to demanded.

But he answered her unspoken question when he continued, "You're almost worth killing."

"And you're almost a bad memory," she replied, thrusting her knee into his back.

But her knee met empty air. In a flash, Angelus was gone and Buffy rolled over onto the ground, winded and weak. She waited for the sobs to come, rising from the depths of her wounded heart and pouring out onto the dry earth.

They didn't.

Instead, a cold chill made her shudder as she realized that, great as her victory this night was, it had come at a price that would probably cost Todd his life.

CHAPTER SIX

There was no easy way for Buffy to tell Todd everything he needed to know about the danger in which she had unintentionally placed him. She knew that somewhere out there a Slayer handbook existed. Kendra had told her about it shortly after they'd met and Giles had confirmed its existence though admitted he'd never shown it to her because he hadn't felt it would do much good. As she toyed with the telephone in her bedroom, Buffy wondered if "Uncomfortable Conversations with Cute Boys Who Might Want to Date You" was a chapter she'd find there.

If she ever learned that it was, she was going to kill Giles for not sharing, but she seriously doubted the words "Cute

Boys" even appeared in the handbook, unless they were followed by the words "are usually eaten alive by . . ."

She did the best she could. At least Todd hadn't answered the phone when she called, so she managed an almost intelligible message, including the high points of the jealous ex-boyfriend who had learned that Todd was tutoring Buffy, and not inviting any strangers into his home if he could help it. Truth was, if Angel wanted Todd dead, there was little short of guarding him twenty-four hours a day she could do to protect him, and somehow she knew Giles would never go for that idea. At any rate, she was pretty sure that Todd wasn't going to be looking at her with that sweet, mysterious kind of hope in his eyes anymore once he heard her message. Maybe it was for the best. Besides, what was with that angry phone call near the park?

Then again, who died and made me center of the universe? Buffy thought as she changed into her pajamas. Odds were, whatever Todd was so upset about had nothing at all to do with her.

Contrary to her usual routine, Buffy's head hit the pillow within minutes of hanging up the phone. It was as if her pre-bedtime ritual of an hour of anxious love-life ruminations had never existed. The next things Buffy was conscious of were the sun sweeping through her bedroom window and her alarm blaring in her ear. Unfortunately, she still felt as though she'd been up all night.

As she entered the kitchen, she realized with alarm that

she wasn't the only one in her house this morning who was sleep-challenged. Joyce stood before the stovetop, a griddle of burning pancakes before her. Even the rancid smoke rising to her nose wasn't enough to wake her. Buffy's mom was literally asleep on her feet.

"Mom!" Buffy shouted, startling Joyce into a conscious state as she grabbed the griddle and moved it off the stove and into the sink.

"Where am I?" Joyce muttered.

"Trying to set the kitchen on fire," Buffy said, running water over the griddle and forcing the burnt pancakes down the garbage disposal. "And while I appreciate the effort, haven't we discussed avoiding heavy machinery until you've had your coffee?"

"I'm sorry, honey," Joyce replied, moving gingerly toward the coffeepot and pouring herself a large cup. "I don't think I slept a wink last night."

"Are you still doing inventory?" Buffy asked.

"Am I? No, we finished yesterday afternoon," Joyce replied. "I guess I'm overtired."

"Stress will do that to you," Buffy said, then added, "Maybe you should take the day off and get some rest."

"Don't be ridiculous," Joyce snapped. "Haven't you come across the definition of the word 'responsibility' in any of your tutoring sessions?"

"Easy, Mom. It was just a suggestion," Buffy replied, a little wounded by Joyce's tone.

"I know, Buffy. I'm sorry," Joyce said sincerely. "I don't know what's wrong with me this morning."

"Hopefully nothing that a bowl of cornflakes won't cure," Buffy replied, pouring cereal for them.

"I think your faith in the power of corn might be misplaced, but I guess it's worth a try." Joyce smiled. "At least they don't have to be cooked."

Fifteen minutes later, Buffy was on her way out the door to join her mother in the car when the phone rang. "Hello?" she answered briskly.

"Hey, Buffy, it's Todd," came a slightly husky morning voice through the receiver.

Damn.

"Hi, Todd," Buffy said, attempting to sound as cheerful as possible. It wasn't that she didn't want to hear from him. She just wasn't looking forward to hearing him tell her that he didn't tutor crazy people and ending their relationship right then and there.

"I got your message," he began.

Here we go.

"Okay," she replied.

"It was . . ."

Insane?

"Really sweet of you to worry about me," he finished.

Buffy heaved an audible sigh of relief.

"It's probably nothing," she lied. "I just . . . I've had problems in the past—"

"Oh, you don't have to explain," he interjected. "I was just wondering . . ."

"Yes?"

"Well, we're only supposed to do four sessions a week, but I thought you might want to get together tonight."

"Oh." Buffy smiled in genuine surprise.

"Or, if you're not up for it, maybe we could just get some coffee, or something. . . ."

Joyce lay on the horn from the driveway, and Buffy jumped.

"I'd really like that," Buffy said honestly. "Thing is, I'm not sure what the rest of my day is going to be like yet. Can I call you later?"

"Sure," he replied, Buffy's spirits rising even more at the faint disappointment she was sure she heard in his voice.

"Great," she said. "Talk to you soon."

"Can't wait."

Willow didn't know what was wrong with her. Ms. Hegel was giving a perfectly fascinating lecture on the symbolism of dreams, and she'd been keeping her dream journal for weeks in preparation for this section of her life sciences course, excluding, of course, her favorite recurring dream that featured her and Oz swimming in the inflatable backyard pool Xander had popped when he and Willow were seven. Sometimes she was naked in the dream, though Oz was always fully clothed, and usually wearing mittens. Still, she didn't think that particular dream was any of Ms. Hegel's business, so she hadn't felt too bad about leaving it out. The only other omission in the journal was for the past few days and that hadn't been intentional. Willow simply didn't remember having any dreams since Monday, and she didn't think she'd be graded down for that since she already had two full spiral notebooks completed on the assignment.

The problem was, she couldn't concentrate. Though Ms. Hegel seemed less perky than usual, Willow didn't think that was the issue. Xander sat next to her, his head resting in his right hand, eyes closed, and a small pool of drool collecting on his desktop. Behind him, Cordelia's head kept nodding forward only to snap back up every thirty seconds or so.

Two rows back, it sounded like Susan Walker and Ellie Thompson were training for a synchronized-snoring competition. In fact, everyone in class was either asleep or on the verge, and Willow herself felt like she could easily have nodded off without any effort at all. Ms. Hegel droned on, seemingly oblivious, which was also most unusual.

No matter what she did, Willow couldn't force herself to concentrate. Stifling a yawn, she opened her textbook to the section Ms. Hegel was covering, determined to read along, when she paused over the section immediately preceding that on dream symbolism, entitled "Sleep Disorders."

Five minutes later, Willow had excused herself from class and was headed for the library. She had been tempted to wake Xander, but he looked so cute when he was asleep. And he would have insisted on bringing Cordelia, which was never a plus, as far as Willow was concerned.

When she arrived, she was pleased to see that Buffy was already there, talking with Giles.

"No, Giles," Buffy was saying. "A ballpoint pen. Jeff was convinced Steven stole it and two seconds later, they were at each other's throats. Just like Larry and the Jell-O yesterday. I'm telling you, all is not as quiet on the Hellmouth as you promised a few days ago. Either everyone here ate some serious cranky puffs for breakfast, or something more demon-y than usual is getting on everyone's last nerve."

"As I said, Buffy," Giles said wearily, "the end of the year is a very stressful period for the students and the faculty. No one gets much sleep until finals are over—"

"Try *any* sleep," Willow interrupted.

"I beg your pardon," Giles said.

"Hey, Will," Buffy added. "What do you mean, 'any sleep'?"

"We're studying dreams in my science class today. Well, me and Ms. Hegel are. Everyone else is in dreamland . . . or lack of dreamland."

"In something resembling English, please, Willow," Giles said.

Willow opened her textbook to the "Sleep Disorders" section as patiently as she could. She noted that Giles's eyes were bloodshot as he took a moment to clean his glasses and look over the text.

"There are five stages of sleep," Willow began. "Alpha state is the first and lightest."

"Willow, am I going to be tested on this material, or is there an abridged version of this theory somewhere?" Buffy interjected.

"Okay," Willow said, cutting to the chase, "the sleep stages where we actually get our rest occur around REM, the fifth and most important stage of sleep. It's called REM because there's rapid eye movement along with increased respiration and deep muscle paralysis at the same time. You move through all the stages of sleep several times a night, but if you never reach REM sleep, you're not really sleeping deeply enough."

"So you think no one is getting enough REM sleep?" Buffy said. "But how do you know?"

"What did you dream about last night, Buffy?"

Buffy paused. "Nothing. I mean, I don't remember."

"Giles?" Willow asked.

"Well . . . nor do I," he admitted.

"REM sleep is also when you dream. When you are deprived of REM sleep long enough, even after just a few days, there are serious side effects."

"Do they by any chance include sleepwalking?" Buffy asked, immediately beginning to connect the Principal Snyder dots.

"They do." Willow nodded. "They also include lapses in concentration, increased anxiety and irritability, and fatigue."

"Then it is your belief that the vast majority of the student body is having their sleep disturbed?" Giles asked.

"It makes sense," Buffy said. "I remember going to sleep every night this week, but I don't remember dreaming at all and, to be honest, I feel like I could nap for a week right now." Turning to Willow, she asked, "Is Snyder causing this? Because I wouldn't mind punishing him for a change."

Willow shook her head. "I don't think so. It seems more like he's a victim, like the rest of us."

"Well, can't have everything," Buffy said in obvious disappointment.

"We have to figure out what it is," Willow continued. "Giles, are there any references to demons that could cause this sort of thing?"

Giles shook his head. "Off the top of my head, I'd have to say no. What you're suggesting is very specific and sounds more like a spell than demonic intervention."

"Do you mind if I take a look?" Willow asked.

"Of course not." Giles nodded.

"I'll help," Buffy said. "Chemistry class was canceled this afternoon. Mr. Olsen didn't show up *or* call in, so no one thought to get a substitute."

"Actually, Buffy, there's something else we need to discuss."

"What?" Buffy asked, alarmed.

In response, Giles placed the morning paper in front of her and opened it to an article about an attack on a second-grade

T-ball team that had taken place the night before. Buffy stared in shock at a picture of a mother holding the body of her son, eight-year-old Michael Holmes, and sobbing amid the chaos of several ambulances and police cars in the parking lot of a local park.

"Are there Cliff's Notes?" Buffy asked, noting that the article covered the entire page and was continued in another section of the paper.

"Two young boys, Michael Holmes and Adam Neilson, were attacked last night after a practice session. The coach who was supposed to be looking after them until their parents arrived apparently left to help a disabled man who was having difficulty crossing the street. A parent leaving the parking lot described the man as having light blond hair and using a wheelchair. She also indicated that she thought he might have had a British accent."

"Spike," Buffy said grimly.

"I think it's also worth noting that both boys were classmates of Callie McKay's," Giles added somberly. "I take it you didn't come across either Spike or Callie while you were patrolling last night?"

"No," Buffy replied. "I had my hands full keeping Angel in check."

"I've got it!" Willow announced from the other side of the table. "A Siberian Sleeping Sloth."

"Only able to survive in the remotest regions of northern Russia," Giles answered briskly.

"I'm sorry, Giles," Buffy said sadly. "I'll find her tonight. I promise."

"If Spike has taken her under his wing, there's no telling—"

"I know," Buffy interrupted, "though he doesn't strike me as the father-knows-best type."

"I agree," Giles replied. "In your encounter with Angelus, did you confront him about Callie?"

"No," Buffy confessed. "He's been spying on me, and my new tutor. I think Todd made Angel's most-wanted list last night. I honestly forgot all about Callie."

Giles shook his head in obvious disapproval.

"Really, really sorry," Buffy added. "I promise I'll find them tonight. Maybe I could get a jump on it this afternoon."

"Good." Giles nodded.

"What about a Somnambulatory Shudder-moth?" Willow piped up. "Or a Helvorkian Sleep Shaker?"

"The first is mythological, and the second has been extinct for five hundred years," Giles replied.

"In the meantime . . . ?" Buffy asked.

"I'll help Willow," Giles agreed.

The most difficult part of Buffy's assignment for the afternoon was zeroing in on a place to start looking. Since the factory where Spike, Drusilla, and Angelus stayed had been destroyed in a fire, she had no idea where she might find the unholy trio and their new Cabbage Patch Killer. She was loading up her backpack at her locker and contemplating playing "Kick the

Crap out of the Demon" with Willy the Snitch for a lead when she caught sight of the principal leaving his office for the day. He passed her in the hall with a faraway smile on his face and not even a glance of insult in her direction. Buffy noted that he was no longer wearing the white wingtips with the blue suit. Instead, the principal was actually wearing a pair of faded red sneakers. Buffy did a little quick math in her head, trying to account for the array of natural disasters that would have to have occurred for Principal Snyder to be caught dead wearing those shoes in public, never mind leaving campus before the school day was over.

A whole lot of nothing came to mind, and as there was plenty of time until sundown, Buffy decided that she could easily keep her promise to Giles and still satisfy her raging curiosity about Snyder. The man had changed more than his footwear in the last few days, and Buffy wanted to know why.

Maybe Willow's wrong and this is *his fault,* she thought with an inward smile.

Buffy followed Snyder off campus and into the streets of Sunnydale at a safe distance and within twenty minutes was, once again, on the road to Arborville.

Snyder managed to avoid any close calls reminiscent of the night before as he trundled along, and a few times Buffy got close enough that she could have sworn she heard him humming softly under his breath while he walked. The sun was starting to fall toward the horizon, and Buffy was beginning to worry that she might have to let the principal go and start searching for Callie, when he turned down a street lined with houses buried deep within the old suburban district.

Come on, come on, Buffy pleaded silently. This was as off the beaten path as it was possible to get. She scanned the street as she walked. Many of the houses lining the street looked deserted, and those that weren't were still several gallons of paint shy of presentable. Apart from the loud barking of a really cranky-sounding dog and the rattling of a chain-link fence, she didn't sense any potential dangers unless you counted the serious lack of curb appeal.

Finally, Snyder reached a house at the end of the street and turned up the front walk.

Hallelujah, Buffy rejoiced inwardly. Only when she turned up the path herself did it dawn on her that she might have spent the last hour and a half accomplishing nothing but determining Snyder's home address. As she contemplated the overgrown front yard, the peeling paint, and the rotting boards overhanging the front porch, she was surprised to find herself thinking, *If this is all he has to come home to each night, no wonder he's such a miserable excuse for a human being.*

Snyder had reached the front door. Buffy ducked behind a dead jacaranda tree and waited for him to let himself in.

He did.

Just not the old-fashioned way.

CHAPTER SEVEN

S nyder didn't bother with the doorbell or knocker. In fact, he didn't bother with the doorknob. Instead, he stepped into what should have been a solid wood door and was quickly enveloped in a burst of blinding white light.

When Buffy's vision had cleared, the porch was empty.

I knew it! Buffy thought, thrilled to finally have some proof that her instincts about the principal had been right. She couldn't wait to tell Giles and Willow she told them so.

But at that point it dawned on her that now that she'd learned part of the truth, she was duty bound to figure out the rest. With a sigh, she hurried up to the porch and, pausing only for a second, walked into the front door. "Ow!" Buffy said aloud.

All she received for her trouble was a solid thwack on the head.

Stepping back, Buffy reached for the door. Running her hand over the worn surface, she decided it felt real enough.

But she knew what she'd seen. This was definitely not just a door. Normal doors didn't go all Lite-Brite when one person entered and then turn solid again. She considered knocking, or simply breaking it down, then thought better of it. With all that Snyder had against her, she didn't need to add stalking to the list, and stealth could be fun in small doses.

Searching the rest of the porch, she saw two windows on either side of the door. Both had been boarded up for years, if the cracked paint and rusty nails were any indication.

Buffy quickly pried one of the heavy planks from the window nearest the door and peered into the darkness. All she could make out was a faded, dusty, cobweb-covered sofa placed before a low table, also shrouded in webs. There was no sign that any human being, or Snyder, had inhabited the house in years.

A few more boards and a broken window later, Buffy climbed into the living room and allowed her eyes to adjust.

It was worse than staking out a cemetery. At least there you had the outdoors, the moonlight, and some really spectacular engraving work to look at. To see the faded, moth-eaten tablecloth and dusty plastic fruit arrangement centered perfectly on the dining table opposite the living room gave Buffy a whole new kind of creeps. Someone had lived here.

Someone had made this a home. Someone had cross-stitched a "Home Sweet Home" pillow for the center of the sofa, and that someone had obviously died, leaving no one to care for their earthly possessions. It was sad.

It was also empty.

Buffy cautiously made her way through each room of the main floor, disturbing nothing bigger than a family of mice that had taken up residence in the kitchen cabinets. She was faintly surprised to find that, once inside, she could open the front door with a sturdy pull and step easily out onto the porch and back into the house without fanfare.

The second story was much like the first, a few bedrooms and a small bathroom with a tub guarded by a dusty plastic duck. Only one of the rooms gave Buffy pause. It was a boy's bedroom, if the blue sailboat wallpaper and matching bedspread were any indication. The closet and dresser still held clothing sized for a child of ten or twelve, but apart from a well-worn stuffed snake, none of the toys or games you would expect to find, nothing personal to the boy who had lived here, remained. Atop the dresser, however, was a small square patch directly in the center. The patch was unusual because it was the only surface in the entire house Buffy had seen that wasn't covered in at least an inch of dust.

Something was here, Buffy decided. *Something that was removed pretty recently.*

With her thumbs and forefingers, Buffy was able to measure and commit to memory the rough size of the dustless square, and with only that much information, she left the house to its solitude and slow decay. She considered waiting to see if Snyder would leave the house the same way he'd entered, but it was almost nightfall and the logic of the last few mornings suggested that the next time he would be roaming the streets would be just before dawn.

Buffy knew she needed to set out in search of Callie, but now armed with proof that Snyder was perhaps trafficking with the demon world, which might be grounds for his termination—either from his job at the high school or more permanently—Buffy decided to check in on Willow first, to see if she'd made any progress with her research.

"Good evening, Mrs. Rosenberg," Buffy said politely when Willow's auburn-haired mother opened her front door twenty minutes later. Buffy had considered first searching for her friend at the school library, but reminded herself that Willow was still under a strict curfew and had probably returned home shortly after she'd set off after Snyder, undoubtedly with piles of take-home reading in her backpack.

"Oh, hello, Bunny," Mrs. Rosenberg replied absent-mindedly. Though it was hardly bedtime, Willow's mom was already wearing a fluffy cotton bathrobe, and her demeanor was that of someone who had been awakened from a sound sleep in the middle of the night.

"I just stopped by to pick up some history notes from Willow," Buffy said.

"All right"—Mrs. Rosenberg nodded—"but keep it brief."
She stepped back to allow Buffy to enter.

"Brief is my middle name," Buffy said, and smiled as
she headed upstairs, certain that from now on, Willow's
mom would probably refer to her as Bunny Brief Summers.
Mrs. Rosenberg, like Joyce, had a superhuman ability to
rationalize and ignore the myriad strange things that had
surrounded her daughter once she had become friends with
Buffy. What never ceased to amaze Buffy and Willow were
the odd and random facts that managed to stick, as well as
those their mothers chose to care about. If, for example,
Mrs. Rosenberg were ever to find out that Willow was now
dating Oz, Buffy was pretty sure that the problem wouldn't
be that he was both older than Willow and a werewolf; the
difficulty Mrs. Rosenberg would have to overcome was the
fact that he was in a band.

She found Willow in her room, seated on her full-size
bed, surrounded by dozens of well-worn books. One of them
was open in her lap, and though her head was bent forward
as if she were reading it, Willow's soft, regular breathing told
Buffy that her friend had dozed off. Looking past this adorable
scene, Buffy felt a quick pull in her stomach as she noted that
Willow's aquarium was still empty. A few weeks earlier Angel
had sent the Slayer a warning in the form of killing Willow's
fish. The only upside was that they were relatively new fish
for Willow, and she hadn't even had a chance to name them
before they had met their untimely end.

Knowing how exhausted Willow must be, Buffy almost hesitated to wake her. Unfortunately, she had no choice.

"Will?" Buffy said softly, gently nudging her friend.

In response, Willow's head snapped up with a snort.

"Oh, Buffy . . . what am I . . . I have to get home . . . ," she stammered.

"You *are* home, Willow," Buffy replied gently. "And I need your help."

Willow blinked her eyes rapidly and rolled her neck back until it clicked. She then put the kibosh on a huge yawn and, rubbing her eyes, said, "Did you find Callie?"

"Not yet," Buffy said, shaking her head. "I caught Snyder leaving campus early and decided to follow him."

Even tired Willow was intrigued. "You mean the principal was playing hooky?"

Buffy gave her the broad strokes of her trip to Arborville, and by the time she was done, Willow had already relocated to her computer and was pulling up any information she could find about the house in question.

Struggling between yawns, Willow did a quick search of the county tax files and a number of other databases that Buffy was certain weren't accessible to the public at large but thankfully were no match for Willow's hacking skills.

"Well . . . the house is in Snyder's name," she finally said.

"What does that mean?" Buffy asked. "It can't be his house. You know what a neat freak he is. The smell alone would give him hives."

"It's not his primary residence, at least according to the tax records," Willow continued. "He lives in a condo near the bluff. But he inherited this house fifteen years ago when his mother died. There are no records indicating that it was ever listed for sale after that."

"It's definitely a fixer-upper," Buffy said.

"I'm pretty sure it was the house he grew up in, though," Willow added. "It was originally purchased in the fifties by Thomas Snyder, but he died not long after that, when Snyder was seven or eight, and it went to Snyder's mom, Paulina."

"So when do you think they installed the trick door?" Buffy asked.

Willow turned to her friend with a wince. "I don't think there's a permit you can pull for that kind of thing. Oh, wait . . ." Willow rose quickly and tossed a few of her reference books aside until she found what she was seeking.

"Don't tell me Giles has a book about demon home contractors," Buffy said.

"No . . . gateways," Willow replied, flipping pages. "They're barriers between our dimension and other dimensions."

"And I'm guessing that some of those gateways have demons behind them," Buffy said.

"Gateways are extremely rare," Willow continued. "Usually they're not static, and most often you have to be a demon to use them."

"Haven't I been saying for over a year that Snyder has to

be a demon?" Buffy interrupted. "Between the attitude and the fashion sense . . . he's not fooling anyone. The man is evil."

"I know"—Willow nodded—"but before you slay him, we need to make sure that he's not being drawn to another dimension against his will."

"That would be less fun for me," Buffy acknowledged.

"Yes, but it's also possible," Willow said pointedly.

"So how do I use one of these gateways?" Buffy asked. "The thing wouldn't light up for me no matter what I did, and I have a bump on my head to prove it."

Willow did a little quick reading and finally arrived at a verdict. "Oh, gross," she said.

"What?" Buffy demanded.

Willow showed Buffy the text in question and read aloud: " 'To gain access, a human must be either expected or invited. In the absence of an invitation, the blood of one who is invited may suffice to pass the barrier.' "

For the first time since they had started to piece the puzzle together, Buffy smiled.

"So I need to get some of Snyder's blood? And it's for a good cause?"

"Yes," Willow said, "but, Buffy . . ."

"I know." Buffy rolled her eyes. "I don't get to kill him unless I can prove beyond a shadow of a doubt that he's not just annoying but that he's really taken out a time-share with Satan. Still . . . this could be fun."

Willow closed the book and tossed it back on her bed.

"Are you going back there now, or are you going to look for Callie?" she asked.

"I don't imagine I'll have any luck tracking Snyder down until morning, so I'm Buffy the Vampire Hunter for now," she replied, then considered her friend's slumped shoulders and paler-than-normal complexion. "Why don't you get some sleep . . . or as much sleep as you can," she offered. "Have you had any luck with your theory on Sunnydale's sleeping sickness yet?"

Willow shook her head. "No. But I have to keep looking. This can't go on. Are you as tired as I am?"

Buffy thought about it for a minute. She had to admit that she was exhausted. But she'd been to the land of no sleep many times before and so far she didn't seem much worse for wear. *I guess that's just the luck of the Slayer,* she mused, though if she'd had her pick at the superpower store, this gift would have come well behind a number that she didn't possess, including the ability to force her mother to give her a car, or at least allow her to get a driver's license. Still, not wanting to rub it in, she replied, "Yeah. I could sleep for a month. But I'm not going to until we sort this out."

Willow nodded. "I think I'll make myself some coffee," she decided.

"Seriously, Will," Buffy started to protest.

"No. My mind is made up. See my tired but determined face? Anyway, if I'm right, closing my eyes won't do any good."

"Okay." Buffy nodded. "Thanks for this, and I'll see you in the morning."

"Bright-eyed and bushy-tailed," Willow added. "Or maybe dark-circle-eyed and straggly-tailed."

"Either way." Buffy smiled and gave her friend a quick hug before heading back downstairs.

On her way out, Buffy passed Mrs. Rosenberg asleep in front of the evening news.

I hope Willow's wrong about this, she thought as she let herself out the front door. Thing was, Willow was usually right, and if she was, the demon who was denying all of Sunnydale their sleepytime was going to move right to the top of Buffy's crap list. She honestly couldn't help thinking that the dice would come up Snyder.

Giles was accustomed to working all hours of the day and night. Obviously, so were the pair of detectives who summoned him to a quaint suburban home several miles west of the school after ten o'clock in the evening. Unfortunately, they needed no introduction. The first was a middle-aged man named Stein, who shook Giles's hand limply and offered a weak "Thanks for coming on such short notice." Giles vaguely remembered meeting Stein at the school a few months earlier, when the police had been investigating Buffy's assault on a man named Ted Buchanan. Though Buffy was never charged in the case, and Ted had turned out to be a homicidal robot, Giles still remembered darkly those few days when Buffy was devastated by the thought that she had harmed a human being.

Stein's partner in the current investigation was the clearly overworked Detective Winslow, an African-American woman Giles had already had the pleasure of meeting when his past came back to haunt and try to kill him in the form of a demon called Eyghon.

On the one hand, Giles hated the idea that he was so well known among Sunnydale's law enforcement community. Rule one of being a Watcher was to keep a low profile. Rule two: See rule one. On the other hand, Giles had often wondered how oblivious those who were entrusted with securing the safety of a town situated on a Hellmouth could be to the supernatural phenomena that surrounded them. He had no proof, but his instincts told him that someone, somewhere had to know more than what was reported in the papers. It was much too convenient that vampire attacks were almost always described as "kids on PCP." It smacked of a cover-up that had to go higher than the flatfoots who worked Sunnydale's streets. Just how high, however, Giles did not know.

Giles had been at home when the call came. Though he wasn't convinced that Willow's theory about the strange sleeping sickness was on target, he had to admit that he was exhausted, and he had planned to make an early evening of it when he was roused by the late-night jangling of his phone. He'd rushed to answer it, assuming it would be Buffy, and was taken aback when Detective Stein advised him that they had found evidence of a crime that they believed Giles might be able to illuminate for them.

Twenty minutes later he was standing in the middle of a full-blown investigation. The house was surrounded by yellow police tape, and several portable lights had been brought in to aid the detectives who were searching the front and back yards for clues.

Giles's concern intensified when he noted the coroner's van pulled discreetly up between the police cars that lined the street in front of the house.

"We need you to take a look at this for us," Stein said simply as he ushered Giles through the foyer. Most of the activity seemed to be centered around the kitchen and an open doorway that probably led to the home's basement. Officers wearing protective clothing moved silently past the remains of a dinner table set for two, pausing occasionally to dust for fingerprints.

Stein led Giles, with Winslow trailing behind, away from the kitchen and down a dark hallway toward a bedroom. He paused outside the second doorway on the left and gestured for Giles to enter ahead of him.

Giles did so, still completely at a loss to understand what possible connection he might have to what appeared to be the room of a normal teenage boy. Giles quickly recognized many of the textbooks lined neatly on a small desk as those of a freshman year student. A number of various-size soccer trophies were arranged neatly on a shelf above the desk. The only odd thing, as far as Giles could tell, was the incredible neatness around him. Even he hadn't been this fastidious as a child.

A book bag hung on the back of the desk chair, and what Giles presumed were its contents had been neatly laid out on the perfectly made bed. As Winslow rather obviously studied Giles's face for any spark of recognition or interest, Stein moved past Giles to the bed and, with gloved hands, picked up a medium-size, well-worn leather book and offered it to Giles to examine.

"Does this look familiar to you?" Stein asked warily.

It did.

It was a copy from his private collection of Marc Leon's *Raising Demons*, a spell book valued more for its detailed illustrations than the efficacy of its spells.

"There's a dedication inside the front cover," Winslow said, motioning to Stein to open the book. Stein complied and read, "'To Rupert Giles, best of luck with this one, signed Quentin Travers.'"

The book had been something of a joke between Giles and the man who now ran the Watchers Council. In younger days, both had been tested several times in the use of rather complicated spells that might serve in their work as Watchers. Quentin, who had never demonstrated Giles's skill with magicks, had been challenging Giles's abilities, certain that Leon's formulas were outdated at best.

Giles hadn't seen the book in months, but of course that

meant nothing. Though he kept most of his private collection locked in the library's cage or in his office, the intensity of the research required of him in the last two years had made keeping track of such minor works less of a priority than he would have liked. Still, he couldn't imagine how it had ended up at this house.

"Mr. Giles?" Winslow interrupted his musings.

"Yes? Sorry," Giles said quickly. "The book is mine, as you've no doubt already surmised."

"A little light reading?" Winslow asked.

"It was actually what you might call a 'gag' gift," Giles said honestly.

"A gift from you to Joshua Grodin?" Stein asked.

"I'm sorry," Giles replied. "I don't know anyone by that name. It was a gift to me. I've never lent it to anyone."

"Joshua was a student at Sunnydale High," Winslow offered.

"Was?" Giles asked, though in his gut he already knew the answer.

"His body and that of his father, Robert, were found this evening in the basement," Winslow continued. "They were obviously the victims of a brutal and vicious attack."

"Hell, they were practically ripped limb from limb," Stein said, and shuddered.

Given the potential results of a successful demon raising, Giles didn't have a hard time imagining the condition in which the bodies must have been found, though he did have difficulty believing that a novice could have successfully used

Leon's book to raise anything resembling a demon. It was probable, however, that performing a ritual on the Hellmouth, even an inefficient one, had an exponentially better chance of success than if it were done in another location.

"I see," Giles said. "I'm terribly sorry to hear that." Turning his attention back to Stein, he asked, "May I?"

Stein nodded and handed the book to Giles. He leafed through it for a moment, noting that a page had been turned down in a chapter devoted to Protection demons. Giles didn't necessarily want to know more, but duty demanded that he gather as much information as possible, for Buffy's sake. It was now highly likely that a new threat had arisen, and that Buffy would be the one to face it.

"Do you have any idea how that book came to be in Joshua's possession?" Winslow asked pointedly.

Giles shook his head. "I don't," he answered. "It's possible he meant to borrow it from the library and simply forgot to check it out."

"An interesting choice for a school library," Stein said.

"As I said, Detective, this was from my personal collection and might have inadvertently been mixed in with the rest of the stacks. Teenagers, as you know, have both active and vivid imaginations. Who knows why a boy Joshua's age might have found this book interesting. I'm afraid it's also possible that the book was mixed in with some other legitimate research materials and Joshua might not even have been aware it was in his possession," Giles finished.

Of course he was lying. The question was, did Stein or Winslow have the good sense to see that he was lying?

Both detectives studied him carefully as he made his best poker face. Their scrutiny was interrupted moments later by a male voice calling to Detective Stein from down the hall.

Giles followed Stein and Winslow back toward the living room, where they were met by a flushed-faced young man in uniform who had obviously spent the last few hours digging through the area's garbage cans. He had collected in a small evidence box an assortment of items that included partially burnt candles, dried herbs and roots, and several rags that were covered in a dark red substance that was obviously blood.

Though Giles couldn't be sure what the detectives would make of this find, it clarified for him at least some of what had happened in this house. Someone, most likely Joshua, had in fact attempted to raise a demon. It was also quite possible that he had succeeded. Giles studied the house for telltale signs of recent demon activity, really nothing more complicated than obvious signs of destruction. Demons called to this plane from alternate dimensions usually didn't adjust immediately to their new surroundings. The wreckage should have been intense.

It wasn't. Apart from the book and the description of the basement, there was nothing to suggest that anything demonic had ever been in this house.

Giles was troubled. He asked quietly if there was anything further the detectives required from him, and though they requested that he make himself available for further questioning should the need arise, and promised to return the book to him as soon as possible, they had nothing further for him at the moment.

Though Giles wanted nothing more than to return home and get a few hours of much-needed rest, he, like Buffy, knew that his responsibilities must come first. Instead of heading for his house, he left the Grodin home and returned to the school library. Pulling a few choice weapons from his storage cage and keeping them handy, he locked himself in his office and set to work, doing his best to find out what kind of new hell Joshua Grodin had just released on Sunnydale.

Todd couldn't believe what he was seeing. Buffy had taken him completely by surprise. Sure, she was gorgeous, and she was disarmingly easy to talk to. Usually a girl had to be more than easy on the eyes and reasonably witty to get his attention, though. He didn't like to be a brain racist, but the only girls he'd ever seriously fallen for had all been sharper than he was, *and that was saying something*. Buffy's brain trust, on the other hand, seemed seriously underfunded at first blush, but there was something there. It was hard to put his finger on, but it was in the neighborhood of a word Todd had never before applied to a girl under twenty.

Wisdom.

She obstinately kept her mind free of the facts and tools that made academic achievement possible, but there was something else taking up that brain space, a level of experience, perhaps, that belied her age. She seemed older than she was, as if she had lived more, if that was possible, than any other high school junior could or should have. It wasn't the information contained in her mind that was so alarmingly delightful; it was the way her mind worked, how she seemed to take personally the fact that a good man had betrayed his cousin to steal a kingdom, or how a turn of phrase from a Victorian poet could make her eyes well up once the metaphor had been explained. Her reaction to this newfound knowledge seemed to indicate that she was linking it to secrets locked deep within her, secrets she couldn't possibly have had a chance to learn at the age of seventeen.

She was a complete enigma to him. She was utterly intriguing. He'd found himself flirting with her before he could help himself, and even after only a few nights in her company had begun to imagine many more, once they were free of the burden of her final exams.

So what was his mystery woman doing trading punches with two men with bad skin, wearing strangely formal attire for a spring evening in the middle of a public playground?

Todd had actually stopped by Buffy's house fifteen minutes earlier. She hadn't returned his call from the morning, and he was half hoping that this lapse hadn't been intentional and that he'd find her there, appropriately apologetic and happy to see him and ready to spend a few hours with him studying or talking. But her bedroom light had been off when he'd turned up the front walk, and her mother's car wasn't in the driveway. He had started walking over to the Bronze to see if she was with her friends, and only paused at the unmistakable sounds of violence from the other side of the wall that separated Rosewood Park from its street entrance.

Todd didn't plan on getting involved. He was a good citizen, but he didn't need to be a hero. He wasn't above a quick 911 call, though, and had turned through the side gate to see if that was in order.

A few yards from the thick of the fight, a young woman, probably not much older than Buffy, lay on the ground. Meanwhile, his student kicked, punched, dodged, and took blows that he was sure would have knocked him unconscious several times over. He debated making his presence known and seeing if he could lend a hand, but Buffy seemed to have things more than under control. For a few moments he lost sight of them as they moved behind a jungle gym. The next thing he knew, the sounds of punching and bone crunching ceased and Buffy emerged winded and alone.

She rushed quickly to the side of the other young girl and helped her to her feet. Todd ducked behind a tree as the two girls made their way to the gate and out of sight.

Shaken, confused, and, he had to admit it, a little turned on, Todd rose to his feet and decided to cross to the main gate to make his exit so as to avoid any possibility of running into Buffy.

He needed to think, and possibly, a drink.

He'd read Buffy's academic file before accepting his

assignment. He knew she had a history of delinquent behavior, but once they'd met, he'd found it impossible to square the profile with the person. Now he was unhappy to find that everything he'd heard and read about Buffy was probably true.

Buffy thought she'd seen everything. But tonight had been a first. When she'd crossed through Rosewood Park, hoping to catch a glimpse of Callie or Spike, she hadn't been terribly surprised to see two vampires. The thing that had topped the charts was the fact that the vampires had already found a victim, a girl Buffy vaguely recognized from the volleyball team, and instead of feeding off her like run-of-the-mill bloodsuckers would, they were actually doing a Thunderdome Death Match with each other over who had seen the girl first.

After confirming that the girl was just injured, and far from dead, Buffy had thrown herself into the fray. She had actually had a difficult time keeping the vampires away from each other and focused on her. She hadn't seen either of the two soon-to-be-dusteds around, but she got the distinct impression that they weren't new to the whole suck-squad routine. This made it even harder to understand why they were wasting their time fighting each other over something they could have easily shared.

And then it struck her.

Just like Larry and Jonathan in the school cafeteria.

It was a scary thought. Buffy paused before her closet door as she tossed her now bloodstained white tank blouse into the "Do Not Show Mom" pile, realizing that it was altogether possible that whatever was screwing with the sleep patterns of the living population of Sunnydale might be affecting that of its undead residents as well.

Come to think of it, Slayer strength aside, Buffy had to acknowledge that she hadn't been at her sharpest in the evening's battle. She'd managed, of course, but she'd telegraphed too many punches and kicks, giving the vamps too much time to dodge or recover.

Once the fight was done, and Valerie the volleyball queen had been safely seen to her front door, Buffy had quickly decided that Callie and Spike would have to keep for another night. She hadn't even bothered with preparing speeches for Giles as she'd made her way back home. She'd walked in a daze, only certain of the fact that she intended to be up before dawn and back in Arborville to see what happened when whatever demon dimension had sucked Snyder in spat him back out again.

She really needed to get some rest. And she had a sinking feeling that tonight, once again, that wasn't going to happen. She set her alarm for an hour before sunrise and lay down to grab less than four hours of not too deep sleep.

The next thing she knew, it was morning. Her alarm had been going off for over two hours without waking her, and she had not only missed Snyder, but was about to be late for school.

CHAPTER EIGHT

O nly once Buffy was hurrying up the steps that led to the school's main entrance did she mentally slap herself upside the head, thinking, *Todd.* She was supposed to call him yesterday and she'd been so out of it when she got home that she hadn't even bothered to check her messages. Worst-case scenario, she was scheduled to see him the next afternoon, but she didn't want to waste the "I think he likes me" vibes she was already getting from him by flaking this early in the potential relationship. She also wanted to make sure that Angel hadn't killed him, or worse, turned him, but she wouldn't have a chance to do that until after school. The good news was, if he wasn't dead yet, there was little chance he would be before sundown.

Buoyed by these hopes, she rushed through the main doors just as the second and final morning bell was shrilling through the halls.

The deserted halls.

The only sign she got that she hadn't shown up at school on a Saturday by mistake was running into Jonathan, who still stood at his locker despite the fact that classes had just begun. Unlike Buffy, however, Jonathan didn't seem to be troubled by his tardiness. He wasn't rushing.

No, he's not moving, Buffy realized.

Opening his locker a little wider, she saw his closed eyes and slack-jawed mouth and realized he was, like Joyce the previous morning, asleep on his feet.

She gently nudged him and received no response.

"Jonathan?" she said, and again louder, "Jonathan?"

Nothing.

She was contemplating a good solid slap to wake him when a bone-chilling scream echoed through the otherwise empty hall. She quickly turned to see Cordelia running toward the girls' restroom a few yards down shrieking and scratching at her arms and neck.

Buffy hurried into the bathroom after her and found her at the sink, splashing water all over her arms and shouting, "Get them off me! Get them off!"

"Cordelia," Buffy said, grabbing her and checking her

arms for good measure. Buffy wasn't a doctor but they looked like normal, healthy bare arms, apart from the welts starting to rise where Cordelia had already scratched herself deeply enough to leave marks.

"Get them off!" Cordelia screamed louder.

"Get *what* off?" Buffy said, matching her tone and holding Cordelia's arms down to keep her from further harming herself.

For a second, Cordelia's eyes finally focused on Buffy, and she was surprised to see a flash of relief in them. She knew that she and Cordy were never going to be BFF, but there was something gratifying in knowing that her mere presence could calm Cordelia down.

"Oh, Buffy," she said, dazed. "Spiders . . ."

But as the words trailed off, Cordelia abruptly lost consciousness and fell to the floor.

Okay, this is ridiculous, Buffy decided.

She was tempted to pick her up and carry her to her next stop, the library, but quickly decided that, in this case, it wouldn't do Cordelia any permanent damage to stay where she was until Buffy figured out what was going on and how to kill it.

Moments later she rushed into the library, calling out, "Giles!" but the only response came from Willow, who was seated at the main table surrounded by stacks of books four feet high in every direction.

"Buffy . . . finally," Willow said weakly.

Concern trumped curiosity at the sight of her friend, bleary eyed and struggling to remain conscious.

Buffy hurried to the table, grabbed Willow by the shoulders, and examined her condition. Her breath was shallow and ragged. She was paler than usual, and she struggled with every blink to keep her dry and bloodshot eyes open.

"Willow, what is it?" Buffy demanded.

"Can't fall asleep . . . ," Willow said.

"Okay," Buffy said in her most reasonable voice. "Why not?"

"Won't wake up," Willow said, pushing Buffy aside and, staggering behind the library counter, downed a few gulps of the remains of what had to be at least a day-old cup of coffee.

The good news was this seemed to fortify her a bit, for the moment. Buffy could only pray that the coffee in question had at least once belonged to Giles, because anything else was too yick to contemplate.

"I think I figured it out," Willow said more firmly as she rejoined Buffy at the table.

"You have my undivided attention," Buffy replied.

"It's a spell," Willow began. "And it's caused by a demon."

"This, I can work with," Buffy replied. "Just point me in the right direction and I'll kill the rest."

"The sleep deprivation is only the first part," Willow said. "None of us has really slept in days."

"Right." Buffy nodded. "I've already seen the trailer to this movie."

"Instead, we're experiencing what's called 'the sleep of living death.'"

"Wait a minute," Buffy said. "Where have I heard of that before?"

"It's like a trance," Willow continued. "Everyone affected loses consciousness, like when you sleep, but you're not really sleeping."

"So the demon in question is putting everyone in a trance so it can swoop down and, what? Eat our brains? Steal our socks? What does the demon want?" Buffy asked.

"I don't think it's meant for everyone," Willow said, pulling out one of her reference books and handing it to Buffy. "I found this legend about a town in France that fell asleep for a hundred years."

"*The Ice Capades!*" Buffy said with enthusiasm.

"Huh?" Willow had to ask.

"They did a really cool version of 'Sleeping Beauty on Ice' a few years ago. My dad and I went."

"Huh?" Willow repeated.

"That's the story where I heard about the sleep of living death thingy. Doesn't the spell put the whole kingdom to sleep for, like, a hundred years?"

"Buffy!" Willow said as sharply as she could through the grogginess.

"Right, sorry," Buffy said, chagrined. "Focusing now."

"This story predates any of the known sources for 'Sleeping Beauty' or any other fairy tale by hundreds of years. In fact, it's very likely that this story might have been the inspiration for the tale that was eventually made famous by the Brothers Grimm. I've always thought their stories, though well told, were incredibly derivative, and just because they got all the credit—"

"Um, Willow?" Buffy interrupted. "Stay on target."

"Oh, sorry," Willow said, shaking her head to clear it. "The legend is about a farmer who angered a demon."

"How?" Buffy asked.

"He had pledged his best cow in return for a good yield on his crops, and when the time came, he never paid up."

"It's almost hard to believe no one ever made an animated film about that one," Buffy said.

"So the demon cast a spell over the whole town, only it wasn't about the villagers. It was designed to put the farmer into a highly suggestive trance-state so that each night, the demon could draw the farmer into his dimension, where he was tortured mercilessly until sunrise."

"Wait, let me guess," Buffy interjected. "He brought the farmer to his dimension through a gateway?"

"Yes." Willow nodded. "This happened night after night, for more than a week. The farmer didn't have any memory of what happened to him in the demon dimension. The problem was what happened to the rest of the town. The first part, we already know: People got agitated, then really cranky, and eventually they started trying to sleep at inappropriate times of the day because their bodies were literally shutting down. If you try to go long enough without sleep, eventually your body will make you sleep, or worse."

"So where's the 'worse'?" Buffy asked. "I thought sleep is what we all need right now."

"Yeah, but the villagers who fell asleep while under the spell didn't just sleep. They fell into the sleep of living death, from which no one could wake them," Willow replied.

"Until when?" Buffy asked.

"Until forever," Willow said.

"Okay," Buffy said thoughtfully, "so what about the prince and the dragon and the happily ever after part of the story?"

Even exhausted Willow had the presence of mind to roll her eyes at this one. "Buffy, how many times do we have to talk about fairy tales and propaganda?" she asked pointedly.

"Okay, so if you're right, the farmer in our scenario is Principal Snyder. I get some of his blood, I use it to go through the gateway. I find the demon and I kill it. That will stop the spell, right?" Buffy asked.

"No, the gateway is actually the key," Willow replied. "The spell emanates from the demon dimension that is linked to ours via the gateway. . . ." She trailed off.

It was clear that, despite the restorative powers of day-old caffeine, Willow was once again starting to fade.

"Willow?" Buffy said with genuine concern.

"Sorry. As long as the gateway exists, the spell will still bleed out into Sunnydale. It will remain open until that which was stolen is returned," Willow continued, reading a passage from her text as she pointed it out to Buffy.

"You lost me," Buffy said. "What was stolen?"

"I don't know," Willow said, frustrated. "In the legend, the demon stole something of the farmer's and used it to open the gateway in the first place. The only way to break the spell is to close the gateway, and the only way to do that is to find what the demon took from Snyder and bring it back with you."

Suddenly Buffy remembered the small dust-free patch on the dresser she'd found in the house.

"I think I might know what we're looking for," Buffy said. "Or at least its shape and size. I have to go back to the house. How long before everyone falls into this sleeping-death thing?" she asked.

"It depends," Willow replied. "If you were pretty well rested before it started, that would buy you some time. But . . ."

"From the looks of things around here, time has already started to run out," Buffy finished for her. "Have you discussed any of this with Giles?" was her next question.

Willow shook her head. "I haven't seen him this morning. I came in pretty early, once I found the legend at home. I wanted to cross-check it with the other sources . . . ," she said, struggling to keep her eyes open.

Buffy quickly scanned the library for any sign of Giles. The door to his office was locked, but that wasn't unusual when he wasn't present. Opting for the most efficient solution, she turned the knob hard, breaking the lock, and pushed open the door, where she was immediately met with the sight of Giles, collapsed on the office floor, holding a crossbow at his chest pointed directly at the door.

Buffy knelt beside him and deftly extricated his fingers from the crossbow, then shook Giles a few times in a vain effort to wake him. Even after a good sharp slap across the face, for which she was sure he would forgive her—*he's certainly endured worse during our many training sessions*—Giles could not be roused. Now more frightened than anything, Buffy returned to the main table, where Willow sat dazed but still fighting to stay awake.

"Willow," Buffy said sharply, "I don't care what you have to do, you keep those peepers open."

"I'm trying," she said weakly, her head drooping forward.

"Willow!" Buffy said more firmly.

Willow's head snapped up, but at that moment their attention was drawn to the library door, which was thrown open by an incoherent, pajama-clad Xander.

"She's after me! Stop her!" he cried out in alarm, rushing to Buffy and cowering behind her.

Buffy immediately moved to check the door, but the hallway outside the library remained deserted. When she turned back, Xander had hidden himself under the table and seemed to be trying to barricade himself in with stacks of books, fortified by chairs.

"Xander!" Buffy demanded. "Stop with the building blocks and tell me what happened."

"All I did was grab a piece of toast," Xander insisted, the fear in his voice rising to a fever pitch. "It's toast. Not a federal crime. Why would she make the toast if she didn't want me to eat it?"

Buffy exchanged a worried glance with Willow, who seemed to have perked up a bit at Xander's entrance.

"Xander, I don't understand," Buffy said, her exasperation rising.

"I grabbed the toast, and suddenly she was going after my fingers with the butcher knife," Xander replied with what would have been an appropriate amount of terror in a five-year-old girl.

"Who?" Buffy asked.

"Mommy!" Xander shouted. He paused, searching his memory for a moment, then added, "At least, it was my mommy at first."

"Xander, I don't understand," Buffy said, beginning to pull some of the books away from the barricade to get closer to her friend and hopefully calm him a bit.

"It was Mom, and then it wasn't," he said, as if he were just as confused as Buffy. "It was my mom, and then it was a pig. A little pig. A pig that spoke English. It was angry with me because it said I had eaten it, but I never ate a pig. Well, there was that one time, but that wasn't really me, was it? Buffy, you have to kill that pig!"

Buffy turned to Willow, who was shaking her head.

"He's delirious," she said, answering Buffy's unspoken

question. "He's hallucinating, taking stuff from his subconscious and confusing it with reality. It comes with the no sleeping."

"With a side of paranoia, I'm assuming," Buffy added.

Buffy didn't need a psychology course to understand the symbolism. A year earlier, Xander had briefly been possessed by a hyena demon, along with a pack of other students, and one of their most disgusting acts had been eating Sunnydale High's first and only living mascot alive.

Then she remembered Cordelia and the bathroom and the imaginary spiders. She also remembered how quickly Cordelia had collapsed after doing battle with her spiders.

"Xander," Buffy said in her most conciliatory tone, "don't worry about the pig. The pig can't get you here. You're safe."

Unfortunately, Xander had already lost consciousness behind the walls of his makeshift fort.

"Xander, wake up!" Buffy shouted.

He didn't respond. Like Giles, he was now one of the sleeping dead.

Buffy's heart started to race. Most of the really scary stuff she did as the Slayer she did alone, but that didn't mean she wasn't both fortified and secured by the presence of her friends and their constant support. One by one, she was losing those she held most dear. Part of her demanded that she suck it up and get moving, while another part, the part that was still grieving the loss of Angel, demanded that she give in to her own fear and curl up in a tiny ball next to Xander until the danger had passed.

The problem was, the danger would never pass if she didn't pull herself together and go out and kick the danger's ass.

Forcing her fear and abandonment issues aside, she turned again to Willow, who was still seated at the table, but with her head tipped back and snoring softly.

Oh, and I was so close to not panicking, Buffy thought.

This ends now, she decided. She knew she would ultimately accept the loss of her first love. But strong as she was, she didn't think there would ever be a time or place when she could also resign herself to the loss of Willow, Xander, or Giles.

It was time to do what she did best.

It was time to be the Slayer.

CHAPTER NINE

*F*irst things first, Buffy thought as she squared her shoulders and walked briskly toward the library doors.

I need to find Snyder.

Buffy had no doubt he was the target of the demon, as he was the only person who seemed to be able to enter the gateway at will. She tried to imagine what in the world the demon would have stolen to draw him there. The legend didn't seem to indicate that it needed to be anything particularly meaningful to the victim, but Buffy firmly believed that whatever had once rested alone on the top of the chest of drawers in that little boy's bedroom had been a most prized possession. Given its size, it could have been a packet of Chiclets, or maybe more like a Rubik's Cube. Of course, they didn't have Rubik's Cubes a hundred years ago, or whenever it was that the principal had actually been a child. That fad had only started a few years before Buffy's birth, never mind the fact that Buffy seriously doubted that Snyder would ever have been able to solve the thing on his own.

Whatever it was would be found in the demon dimension on the other side of the gateway. She'd never actually been to a demon dimension, but in her imagination, anything brought over from her world would probably clash with the fires and chains and severed body parts and would hopefully be pretty easy to spot.

Buffy wanted to find Snyder immediately and force him through the gateway. The sooner the spell was broken, the sooner things would return to the abnormal state she had come to think of fondly as normal. She started with his office. Though most of the school was deserted, she allowed herself a fleeting hope that something might go her way and she'd find him there, but no luck. The office was empty.

Though she usually preferred to leave the Nancy Drew–ing to Giles and Willow, she did spend a few minutes looking around. She'd always hated this office, mainly because every time she'd ever been there, she'd been on the receiving end of Snyder's witless ranting. She wasn't surprised at all to find that her file was on top of his desk in a wire basket he'd marked "Beyond Hope," along with the files of several other students Buffy only knew by reputation as destined to spend the better part of their adult lives as guests of the state's penal institutions. She wasn't sure if the red and silver star stickers that Snyder had placed on her file next to her name were a good sign, but she seriously doubted it.

His desk was filled with your basic office supplies, though they were meticulously organized. It was in the rear of one of the lower file drawers where she found something that definitely gave her pause. Tossed behind a series of file folders were several days' worth of white bandages soaked generously with dried blood.

Oh, yuck.

Buffy didn't know if the blood she was going to need to go through the gateway had to be fresh, but just in case, she tucked a snippet of bandages into her pocket and immediately refused to think further about how thoroughly disgusting it was to have them anywhere near her.

The only other interesting discovery was a heavy stain on the carpet beneath Snyder's desk. A guy who arranged the pencils in his drawer by sharpness and length wasn't one to tolerate an obvious stain. Buffy had seen enough blood, dried and otherwise, to guess pretty quickly that here was more Snyder blood. The important thing to note was that it was fairly recent.

Obviously whatever games the demon is playing with Snyder each night must include some serious pain for him to be bleeding all over the carpet each day, Buffy thought without too much concern for the principal.

Buffy wished she had made note of the condo Snyder owned that Willow had identified as his permanent residence. Odds were, he was probably collapsed there, like most of the rest of Sunnydale by now. But given the demon's interest in him, Buffy doubted that this would be enough to stop him from keeping his evening date with the gateway.

With hours before he would make his appearance in Arborville, Buffy decided that between now and then she would do well to stock up on a few supplies from her weapons locker at home. Only now did it dawn on her that nothing Willow had told her gave her any clue about the demon she would be facing soon enough or how best to kill it.

I'll probably just use whatever's handy, she decided, wondering for the first time what demonic torture devices would look like. She had just started training with a really cool mace, a long silver shaft with a head of pointed spikes, and decided that that, plus several stakes and a small ax, would be the best accessories to complete her ensemble for the evening. She hurried back to collect the mace from Giles's personal weapons storage cage and then turned her steps toward Ravello Drive, where she'd find the rest of her things.

Walking the streets of Sunnydale midmorning, Buffy found her spirits sinking as she got a visceral feel for the impact of the sleep spell. Every business she passed was either empty or closed. The only cars she saw were parked, and a few contained drivers who might have tried to set off for work that morning but had finally succumbed to exhaustion and were now passed out in their seats. There was no traffic, not even the faint roar of engines a few streets away. It was the feeling Buffy usually associated with walking these same streets in the middle of the night, but the bright sunlight was jarring and dissonant.

As she turned off the main street and passed another car, still running with the driver collapsed over the armrest into the passenger's seat, she realized that she was going to have to end this thing well before nightfall, or as soon after as possible. If, as she suspected from her fight the night before, Sunnydale's undead population was also affected by the spell, the townspeople were safe for the time being. But if last night had just been a case of two vampires too stupid to live, then come sundown, the town might as well hang a sign saying "Smorgasbord" at the city's entrance. All of these defenseless people would be a vampire's Suck-a-palooza, and Buffy shuddered at the thought.

Nearing her home, she noticed that the suburban streets shooting off from the town's main thoroughfares were a little more clogged with early-morning traffic. Of course, the traffic wasn't moving. A few people had left their cars and collapsed on the sidewalks. In the distance Buffy clearly heard a man screaming at the top of his lungs. She started to run toward the source of the shouting, but the minute the man caught sight of Buffy, he started to run in the other direction, still screaming something about "killer kumquats." Buffy decided he was, like the others, probably hallucinating and only moments away from dropping.

Hurrying up her front walk, Buffy noted that her mother's SUV was still in the driveway. Rushing inside, she called out, "Mom!" but received no answer. She finally found Joyce curled up on the bathroom floor, still holding her toothbrush and with a few dribbles of toothpaste caked on her mouth. Though she knew it was probably useless, she tried to wake her mother. Her pulse once again doing the mambo, she lifted Joyce carefully and took her back into her bedroom, arranged her on the bed as comfortably as possible, and wiped her hands and face with a wet washcloth. Her mother looked peaceful enough as she slept, but Buffy couldn't shake the overwhelming desire to try to force her mother to wake up.

Strange to be the handsome prince who gets to slay the dragon and wake the princess with a kiss in this scenario, she thought. *Just once, I wouldn't mind being the rescued.*

With a deep sigh, Buffy hurried to her room, grabbed the last few things she needed, and set out for the Snyder house.

All she could do until he arrived was wait.

Buffy hated waiting.

"For God's sake, either kiss her or kill her," Spike said aloud to the television screen, frustrated that, once again, the producers of *Sunset Beach* seemed determined to draw out the "will they or won't they?" question for Annie and Gregory until he was well past caring. He knew the chaps who wrote this twaddle were just doing their job, but seriously, if these two didn't start shagging soon so that Olivia could come in and find them and—*wishful thinking*—cut them both into tiny pieces for their betrayal, he was going to have to find a new daytime drama.

There was little else to do when the sun was up. Spike didn't think of himself as high maintenance. He didn't need much sleep, and though he was definitely much wearier than usual this morning, he rarely turned in for a little rest until his programs were over. Give him Drusilla, a few hours of telly, and a little fresh blood each day and he was a happy man.

Though he had to admit that little Callie was also quickly becoming something that he wasn't sure he wanted to live without. He cast a quick glance in her direction and satisfied himself that she was still humming softly to herself on the sofa as she whittled the hours away.

Thankfully, feeding time was no longer an issue. Once Callie'd had her first taste of human blood, she'd been a new girl. He would forever treasure the look on that snotty little Michael's face when Callie had jumped him from behind and sunk her little fangs into his neck. That had been passion. She'd sucked him well past dry and, turning to Spike, her face aglow and Michael's fresh blood still dripping from her lips, had screamed, "More, Daddy!"

Adam had come next. Only the sounds of approaching sirens had stopped Spike from turning her loose on the entire team and their coaching staff. What the hell was T-ball supposed to be, anyway? There simply wasn't a sport that Americans couldn't find a way to muck up.

He and his little pet would be hunting again tonight. *After I've caught a quick nap,* Spike decided. Callie had set her sights on a young girl named Amanda who had once teased her for weeks at a time for having the audacity to wear little pink bows at the ends of her braids, and this was a sin for which Amanda must pay dearly.

He was grateful that Callie had yet to ask him any questions about the birds and vampire bees. It didn't seem to have occurred to her yet to wonder where vampires came from, or to want to sire any herself. Frankly, he preferred it this way. He didn't really want to share Callie right now with anyone but Drusilla, who had expressed more than once her delight in the changes Spike was bringing about in their child. Callie had even taken to spending the occasional few minutes with her mummy, playing nicely with her dolls. They were becoming something resembling a happy family, just the three of them, and thankfully, Angelus seemed too preoccupied with Buffy and someone called Todd to bother them much.

In fact, if all went as well as Spike hoped this evening, it was altogether possible that none of them would be troubled by Angelus at all in the near future.

It hadn't totally been Spike's doing. Though Callie didn't seem concerned with understanding the birth of a new vampire, they had discussed at some length those things, including a pair of Slayers named Buffy and Kendra, that could hurt or kill a vampire. Until Spike was certain that Callie was either strong enough to hold her own in a fight or cunning enough to know when to run, he was going to make sure that she and the Slayer from hell never crossed paths. But once Callie had learned that vampires were killable, she had begun to ask many leading questions about their housemate, Angelus.

Callie didn't like Angelus. The "time-out" had been a huge mistake, and Callie had apparently decided then and there that the world wouldn't miss Angelus much. So, with Spike's permission, she wondered if she might not be allowed to kill him.

Normally, Spike would have resisted. He knew full well that demons often killed other demons, but once a bond had been forged between them like the one that bound Spike to Drusilla and Dru to Angelus, killing out of spite was simply not done. *Unless I am absolutely certain I can get away with it.*

Spike wasn't going to be starting an "I Love Angelus" fan club any time soon either. Though he wasn't planning to deal the death blow himself—*there'd be ten kinds of hell to pay with Dru*—he didn't see the harm in staying out of Callie's way.

"What do you think, Spikey?" Callie asked sweetly, holding up the little stake she'd been carving for hours.

Spike tested the pointy end himself and managed to prick his finger with it. "Very nice work, pet," he replied with a smile.

"Can I do it now? Please, please, please?" she asked.

Spike hadn't seen Dru or Angelus since last sundown. For all he knew, they were hiding out in the sewers after a long night of hunting.

I guess it wouldn't hurt to look, though, he decided.

"Climb on up, then." Spike nodded, and Callie crawled onto his lap.

As they rolled down the main hall toward Angelus's suite of rooms, Callie hummed contentedly to herself.

"What's that you're singing, love?" Spike asked softly.

"One of these things is not like the others," Callie sang softly in his ear. *"One of these things just doesn't belong. Can you tell me which one is not like the others, before I have time to finish . . ."*

"That would be Angelus," Spike whispered back, wondering again why he was so bloody tired this morning.

Callie rewarded him with a bright smile. "Daddy Spike always knows," she said happily.

That he does, love. That he does.

Any vague doubts he might have been nursing were silenced when they finally found Angelus. He wasn't in his room, or the dining hall, or anywhere else in the living areas. Spike had almost despaired of their chances, when a bleak thought had stuck in his gut, a thought too troubling to dismiss.

He wouldn't, Spike told himself.

But then, this was Angelus. That phrase almost never applied to him.

They'd found Angelus, just as Spike had feared, in Drusilla's bed. Had he been alone, Spike might have killed him then and there just for being so cheeky.

But he wasn't.

Angelus lay on his side, curled up beside Spike's beloved Dru, both of them sleeping deeply. And the worst part: Dru was smiling in her sleep.

Spike swallowed his rage.

"Go ahead, then, little bit," he whispered to Callie. Part of him wanted this moment for himself. He'd been looking forward to a good knock-down, drag-out with the bastard since Angelus first joined them, once again soul-free just after Drusilla had reassembled the Judge. But this had been Callie's plan, and part of him wanted to see her succeed. It was a gift he was giving her, a new side of the powers that lived within her that she would only now begin to explore in all their glory. Once Angelus was out of the way, he, Dru, and Callie would kick the dust of Sunnydale from their feet and go elsewhere—Europe, South America, anywhere but here.

And then, what games we'll play, he thought with a smile.

Callie gave Spike a quick pat on his head.

"Stay here, Daddy," she said. Then she crawled off his lap and, with slow, delicate motions, began to make her way in between Angelus and Dru.

Spike saw her clear the space and noted with relief that neither Angelus nor Dru even stirred. Callie turned back to smile at Spike, then raised her pale little hand, holding the business end of her stake pointed directly at Angelus's heart.

That was the last thing Spike saw as the blackness took him.

• • •

Buffy felt like she'd been waiting forever. In fact, it had only been a few hours. As the afternoon sun had started to wind its way down in the sky, she'd found slivers of shade beneath the branches of the jacaranda tree near the edge of the front porch. She was grateful she'd thought to bring a few diet sodas with her for her little stakeout. Though she was far from dropping in her tracks, she was certainly feeling the burn of the past several sleepless nights, and sitting around waiting was almost as much fun as watching Giles reorganize his ancient reference book collection.

As the sun dipped toward the horizon, casting longer shadows down the row of dilapidated houses, Buffy started to worry that perhaps Snyder, like the others, had succumbed to "the sleep of living death" and might not show up. She'd toyed with the idea of using the bandages in her pocket to try to enter the gateway on her own, but even if she found the demon and killed it, she didn't relish the idea of searching an entire other dimension for the object that would close the gateway and break the spell. For all she knew, the demon had parents, or babies, or groupies, and once she crossed over, she could be lost there for days, years, or even the rest of her life if something went really wrong. At least she knew that Snyder could find his way out, and though some of the potential scenarios she had imagined that afternoon included his untimely death *at the hands of the demon, of course*, she both hoped and feared that once the big nasty had been disposed of, Snyder would be able to lead her back to the gateway.

If the sun set completely, she would have no choice. With or without the principal, she was going in. She rose to stretch and started to pace the length of the front yard, changing her mind with every minute that passed about just how long she would wait for Snyder to show.

Finally, a few minutes after six, by her watch, a loping shadow approached. With the sun behind him the figure was shrouded in darkness, but the outline, from the balding head and unmistakable ears, as well as the definite limp, told her that, finally, her quarry had arrived.

As expected, Snyder took no notice of Buffy. He walked in a daze, a faint smile playing across his lips. Tonight, along with his uniform suit, he was wearing a pair of open-toed sandals. Buffy took a moment to imagine Snyder in the shorts and probably Hawaiian-print shirt he might have bought these sandals for, and couldn't help shaking her head. She doubted the man knew the meaning of relaxation, let alone how one might go about getting some. She also noted that the toes of his left foot were covered in blood-soaked bandages. He was leaving a fresh trail behind him with every step.

Without a glance in Buffy's direction, Snyder walked straight up the front path and disappeared in a flash of light through the front door. She followed his steps to the porch and, for good measure, removed the fouled bandages from her pocket and dabbed them in the blood Snyder had left as he passed the spot. Taking a deep breath and clasping her weapons bag firmly in her right hand, she walked again toward the front door and, instead of meeting any resistance, suddenly found herself surrounded by a burning white light.

The next sight that met her eyes wasn't at all what she had expected.

CHAPTER TEN

Buffy thought she'd had time to prepare herself. She'd imagined the dimension where Snyder would be tortured nightly, and frankly, she was hoping for something grim. The best mental picture she'd been able to concoct had been something akin to the basement beneath the University of California–Sunnydale fraternity house where she and Cordelia had bonded several months earlier while chained to the stone walls in preparation for being fed to a giant snake named Mikida. Add a little fire and brimstone, or maybe a river of blood, and the picture would be complete.

She hadn't been prepared to cross into her very first

demon dimension and find herself in the entryway to a house that looked like it was sold to the Snyders by June and Ward Cleaver.

It was, in fact, the exact house she had searched the evening before, minus the dust and cobwebs and the stench that reminded her of her grandmother's closet. To her left was the living room. The sofa looked like it had been shrink-wrapped, but upon closer examination, Buffy realized that the cushions were simply slip-covered with plastic. The same "Home Sweet Home" pillow whose sad abandon she had lingered over before looked positively perky, giving the otherwise bland room a splash of festive color.

Buffy could have eaten off of the coffee table, the surface was so clean. In fact, every piece of furniture had been dusted and polished to within an inch of its life. Though the wood paneling that ran the length of the far wall only vaguely resembled real wood, it glowed with a warm sheen that only hours of elbow grease and a rag could have produced.

The front window that Buffy had unceremoniously broken the first time she had entered the house was intact, and framed with slightly yellowed lace curtains that had certainly once been white. The faded color was not a product of neglect. The curtains actually looked freshly ironed. It was their age that betrayed them.

To the right of the entryway, Buffy saw the dining room table, still adorned with its arrangement of fake apples, bananas, and grapes, still covered by a freshly pressed peach

linen cloth, minus the moth holes. Taking better inventory of
the dining room, Buffy noted an antique china cabinet that
housed a complete collection, up through the mid-1960s, of
presidents of the United States dinner plates. Each was boldly
etched with the name and years of service, along with a truly
frightening portrait of Herbert Hoover, Theodore Roosevelt,
and Grover Cleveland, among all the others.

A swinging door separated the dining room from the
kitchen, at least if the savory smells of a home-cooked dinner that set Buffy's stomach rumbling were any indication.
Listening closely, Buffy was almost sure that she heard a faint
and pleasant humming coming from the other side.

Buffy returned to the entry hall and saw Snyder reach the
landing at the top of the staircase and turn to his left, toward
what Buffy knew was the little boy's room she'd searched
before. To her surprise, there was a definite spring in his step.
At the very least, he no longer appeared to be limping.

Torn between facing whatever was in the kitchen and
making sure she had a chance to find the all-important stolen
object, Buffy opted to follow Snyder. As quietly as possible,
she crossed the hall and tiptoed up the stairs.

A few steps down the upstairs hall, Buffy noted a swash
of light spilling out from the first bedroom. Cautiously, she
crept toward it. Though the door was slightly ajar, Buffy had
to push it open another few inches to really get a good look at
the room.

Snyder stood with his back to Buffy near the open closet.

He was removing his sandals and lining them up neatly with what appeared to be several other pairs of fully-grown-man-size shoes. Flabbergasted, Buffy realized that Snyder's toes were no longer covered in bloody bandages. In fact, his bare feet looked positively healthy as he wriggled his toes in the deep beige pile carpet.

Buffy did a quick check of the carpet in the hall and stairs and satisfied herself that Snyder was no longer leaving a trail of blood behind him. Whatever damage was done to him in this place didn't seem to affect him until he re-entered the real world. Willow had seemed so sure about the being tortured part, but apart from the 1950s suburban nightmare decor, Buffy could see little that would cause anyone, least of all Snyder, any pain here.

Taking a deep breath, Buffy opened the bedroom door wide enough to enter. She fervently hoped that, just as before, Snyder would take no notice of her, and at first he did just that. The principal sat cross-legged on his bed, one arm wrapped around the stuffed snake that was now restored to its full glory in a plush pattern of orange and yellow diamonds, absent-mindedly stroking it with one hand while the other nimbly turned the pages of a comic book resting in his lap.

Buffy turned immediately toward the dresser, whose surface she could only see once she'd entered, and with a triumphant smile saw that standing in its center was a small trophy. A golden bee rested atop a small wooden base, almost certainly the exact size of the dust square she'd committed to memory.

Buffy moved closer and peered in to read the inscription on the plaque attached to the trophy's base: "Cecil Snyder, 5th place, Arborville Elementary School Spelling Bee."

She honestly didn't know what was more shocking, the idea that this little trophy might be so prized by her principal that he would have displayed it so prominently, or that his first name was Cecil.

Suddenly, Cecil's face was next to hers. "That Bobby Matthews thought he was so tough, but I sure showed him, didn't I?" he said, the exuberance on his face a clear indication that Bobby, whoever he was, hadn't cracked the top five in the spelling bee.

"You sure did?" Buffy replied, unsure how to proceed.

Cecil smiled warmly at her as he gently picked up the trophy, blew on it to create some condensation, then rubbed it vigorously with his shirtsleeve. Once he was satisfied with the faint gleam of the fake bronze leaf, he restored it to its place of honor, nudging it slightly a few times to make sure its position was perfect.

"So . . . um . . . ," Buffy began, wondering when he was going to demand to know what she was doing in his bedroom and begin to describe in detail the many ways he was now going to expel her.

His next question came out of the blue, even more so than the last comment, if that was possible.

"Do you like comic books?" he asked sweetly.

Okay, am I on "Demon Candid Camera?" Buffy thought.

She was starting to wonder if all of this—the gateway, the house that looked like a set from *Leave It to Beaver*, and, most of all, "Cecil"—was some kind of demon practical joke.

Maybe demons don't have cable and this is what they do for fun.

Cecil was waiting expectantly for an answer. When she didn't respond right away, he dashed over to his bed and lifted the mattress from the box spring to reveal dozens of comics, most of which looked like they'd been read and reread many times.

"I've got *Denizens of the Dead*, *I Was a Teenage Zombie*, *The Creature Within*—only volumes three through seven, though. Once the creature gets his heart back and starts going all lovey-dovey with Miss Constance, I think the story really goes downhill, don't you? Oh, and I also have the very first edition of *The Ascendant*—have you heard of that one yet? It's pretty new."

Buffy's head started to spin. She hated this man. He had never once been anything less than horrible to her. He'd taken every bit of power entrusted in him by the school board and wielded it toward his own perverse little ends. Human or not, he *was* evil. What began to dawn on her through the haze was the fact that he hadn't always been the man she knew. Once, many, many years ago, he had been little Snyder. He had been Cecil, in a bedroom with sailboat wallpaper, and with a best friend who was a stuffed snake.

Once, Snyder had been a child.

And apparently, once wasn't enough.

To all intents and purposes, the man who had terrorized every moment of her school life for the past year, starting with his insistence that she, Willow, and Xander humiliate themselves at the school talent show, and including the Parent-Teacher Night for which he'd made her create posters and refreshments so that he could corner Joyce and share with her his conviction that Buffy belonged in a juvenile detention facility rather than on his campus, had vanished. He stood before her barefoot, but still wearing his brown pin-striped suit and black clip-on tie, every last inch an adult, but with the mentality of a ten-year-old boy.

Take a moment and marvel at the incongruity.

Okay. Marveling done.

Cecil was still waiting for an answer. Buffy moved closer to the bed and took a good look at his comic book collection. In one sense, it wasn't disappointing. Apparently, even as a small child his tastes had leaned toward the dark side. Image after image of hell-demons mutilating humans, brain-eating zombies, and something that looked vaguely like a half-man, half-giant spider assaulted her eyes. That had to be a sign of something, right?

Maybe it would be more disturbing if he spent his time reading Pat the Bunny, Buffy had to admit.

"Um . . . Cecil," Buffy said hesitantly.

"If you don't like comic books, that's cool," Cecil said, closing the mattress lid on his treasure trove. "A lot of girls I know aren't into them."

"You know a lot of girls?" Buffy couldn't help but ask.

"Oh, sure." Cecil shrugged, obviously trying to play it down. "There's Marsha, who has had a crush on me since third grade. And Susan. I'm gunning for her this year."

"Gunning?" Buffy asked, half hoping he didn't mean what she feared he meant.

"Yeah," Cecil said, nodding toward his trophy. "She took fourth place in the spelling bee last year, but this time it's going to be different. I mean, anybody can spell 'abacus,' right?"

"Not in my experience," Buffy replied.

"Sure they can," Cecil said, punching her playfully on the arm. "Abacus. A-b-a-c-u-s. Abacus," he demonstrated. "Want me to use it in a sentence?"

"Please don't," Buffy answered quickly. There was something so . . . she hated to think it, but . . . so *needy* about young Cecil.

"She took fourth in the final round on 'abacus' after I got knocked out by 'awl.'"

"You don't know how to spell 'all'?" Buffy found herself asking in spite of herself.

"Not *'all,'*" Cecil corrected her, "*'awl.'*"

"Oh," Buffy replied, as if that had cleared it all up for her. As she and Todd had discussed more than once this past week, synonyms had never been her strong suit.

"Still, Bobby cracked like a cheap piggy bank," Cecil went on. "Want to know how I beat him?"

"Okay," Buffy said, absolutely certain that she didn't.

"It was just the six of us. Only five get trophies, so I knew I had to get rid of one of them. Rachel was a lock. Principal Dumbhead Donovan just gave her 'totalitarian' because he likes her. Her mom gives him and all the other teachers cookies at Christmastime. It's bribery, but what are you going to do? Sun and Ashley are the smartest girls in the whole school. They have the entire *Oxford English Dictionary* memorized. There's no way you're going to beat them. Which left Bobby and Susan. Now, I know Susan hates spiders, but I hadn't thought far ahead enough to bring a few spiders in my pocket to shake her. Won't make that mistake again this year, that's for sure. But Bobby . . . he's a sweater. Can't handle the pressure. So just before he goes up for his final-round word, I lean over and whisper in his ear, 'Did you see that?'"

"What?" Buffy asked, jumping to look over her shoulder.

"No, that's what I said to him: 'Did you see that?'" Cecil said, continuing his story.

"Oh, right."

"Then I pointed to the front row where Margaret Johnson was staring up at him. He's had the hots for Margaret since kindergarten. He'd kill for her. But she's always liked Chad. So then I say, 'Margaret just waved at you.' And he says, 'No, she didn't.' And *then* I said, 'Yeah, she did. Better not screw it up now, Bobby.' Then I patted him on the back, like I was his friend, you know . . . like I wanted him to do well, when all I know for sure is that he probably can't spell his name anymore if he thinks Margaret might actually like him. And sure enough, his word is 'circumstance,' and he choked . . . choked . . . choked so hard. . . ."

Cecil slapped his thigh and almost doubled over with laughter. "'Circumstance,'" he began in what Buffy could only assume was an imitation of poor Bobby Matthews. "'C-e-r,'" Cecil continued, now starting to suffocate on his glee. "Ding. That was the end of Bobby. You know, it was almost too easy."

"Sounds like it." Buffy nodded.

"Just like when Spiderhead took on the Green Onion. Green Onion's all talking tough and, boom! Spiderhead slashes him right across the throat. Took his head clean off. Want to see?" Cecil said, grabbing the comic book still lying open on his bed.

"That's okay, Cecil," Buffy interrupted, then asked, "Um . . . is anyone else here right now? I mean . . . is your dad home?"

Cecil's face clouded over momentarily. "He's dead," he said simply.

"Oh," Buffy replied immediately. "I'm so sorry."

"Mom said it was a hunting accident, but he'd never gone hunting before that one time and I'm pretty sure a quail can't do that much damage," Cecil said. "Maybe killer quail from the fifth dimension, but I don't—"

"Is your mom home?" Buffy interrupted.

"Sure," Cecil replied, brightening instantly. "Oh . . . it's meat loaf night. Want to stay for meat loaf? My mom makes the best meat loaf in the whole wide world."

"That would be great," Buffy lied.

Cecil inhaled deeply.

"Mmmmm," he almost moaned with delight. "She added lots of extra garlic tonight, I can smell it. Just the way I like it."

"Sounds yummy." Buffy nodded in a manner she hoped was convincing.

"Are your shoes dirty?" Cecil asked, suddenly concerned.

"I don't . . . I don't really think so," Buffy replied, automatically checking the soles of her sneakers.

"My mom won't stand for a dirt trail," Cecil warned. "She works too hard to put up with that kind of nonsense. Maybe you'd better leave your shoes up here with mine. That way, she won't even ask." At this, Cecil crossed to his closet and slid one of the doors open so that Buffy could clearly see six pairs of adult-Snyder's shoes lined up like good soldiers.

Wait a minute.

There were actually five and a half pairs, Buffy mentally corrected herself. At the far end, right next to the white wing-tips, was a single black dress shoe, one of the shoes, if memory served, that Snyder usually wore to school.

"Oh, I'll risk it," Buffy replied.

Suddenly, as Cecil shut the closet door, a singsongy nasal voice shrilled through the air.

"Oh, Cecil . . . time for dinner."

Cecil's face went slack.

"Cecil?" Buffy said. When he didn't respond, she waved a hand in front of his face. "Cecil . . . are you in there?"

Without a word, Cecil walked through the doorway and down the hall toward the stairs.

Buffy glanced around the room once more to make certain there was nothing else about retro demon dimensions she might need to know. There wasn't. Kneeling, she opened her weapons bag and fished around for the ax. She'd so wanted to try the mace, but this wasn't practice time. Killing demons usually meant beheading, and that was best accomplished with a really sharp slicer. Besides, she had no idea what she'd find when she entered that kitchen.

Buffy rose and took a deep breath to calm herself. The house had been creepy enough. Having what had passed for a civilized discussion with her principal was almost more than her brain could wrap itself around, even if it was a younger version of him.

Okay, she thought.

Time to meet Mommy Dearest.

CHAPTER ELEVEN

Buffy made her way gingerly down the staircase and passed through the entry hall, pausing behind the short wall that separated the entry from the dining room. From the sound of clinking dishes still coming from the kitchen, it seemed that both Cecil and his mother had not entered the dining room yet, but Buffy poked her head quickly into the room, just to check. As she'd suspected, it was empty, though there were now two presidential place settings laid out neatly on the table, along with cloth napkins, shiny flatware, and a pitcher of water, already sweating with condensation.

Buffy didn't know exactly why she was so hesitant to face whatever was waiting for her behind that swinging door. Clearly, Cecil wasn't going to be any kind of threat to her. Apart from the unsettling possibility that he might ask her to join him for a sleepover, she didn't think there was much he could throw at her in his condition that she couldn't handle.

His mother—well, that was definitely going to be a different story, whether or not she was the demon Buffy'd come through the gateway to kill.

Mothers, whether they were human or demon, shared a willingness to defend their offspring that was particularly dangerous. No matter how often they had butted heads over the years, Buffy had never doubted for a moment that Joyce would willingly have thrown herself in front of a bus for her daughter. Add to that protectiveness demon strength and speed, and you had yourself an enemy that Buffy could not relish facing.

Still, her friends and her own mother were counting on her right now. If she did nothing, or worse, if she failed, Sunnydale would remain under the sleeping spell forever, and those she loved most would never awake. Not an acceptable option.

Shored up by the mental picture of Joyce collapsed on her bathroom floor, Buffy took a deep breath and a firm grip on her ax, and approached the swinging door.

She paused momentarily as the sound of what had to be Cecil's mother's voice grated through the cracks.

"What did you say, young man?"

"I already washed them," Cecil replied evasively.

"Really? You think I can't smell the filth on them?"

The next sound Buffy heard was a muffled *smack, smack,* the sound of an open hand impacting a meaty rear end. A faint *"Ow"* from Cecil confirmed that he'd been on the receiving end. This was followed by water pouring into the kitchen sink and another yelp of pain from Snyder, suggesting that the water was scalding hot, and the whoosh of hands being scrubbed.

"Don't forget to pry that filth from under your nails, young man," the harsh nasal drone added.

"I'm trying, I'm trying," Cecil whined.

"Don't try. Do it."

Buffy felt her ire rising a bit as the scrubbing continued. It was unsettling to hear pain in the voice of a child. Despite his appearance, Cecil was, at least in this place, powerless, and Buffy felt the unusual need to protect him.

Finally, the water was turned off. Buffy pulled back behind the wall and listened as someone entered the dining room and placed several heavy plates on the table. Her stomach started to rumble again at the smell. She couldn't remember the last time she'd had a hot meal. The diet sodas she'd nursed throughout the day didn't count as nourishment. She knew this wasn't the time or the place to indulge in dinner, but she also knew that she was stronger on a full stomach.

The swinging door swished again, and Buffy risked another glance into the dining room. It was, again, empty, but there were now serving plates filled with steaming meat loaf, potatoes, and vegetables in the table's center.

Buffy decided to risk it. She darted toward the table, retrieved a slice of the meat loaf, and took a quick bite.

In an instant, she understood why, despite appearances, this was a demon dimension. Though all the food looked and smelled amazing, it was the foulest thing Buffy had ever put in her mouth. Buffy didn't honestly know what maggots tasted like, but she knew the taste she had imagined whenever she'd seen them crawling over rotting flesh. Suddenly, she needed desperately to vomit, but she took several deep breaths, calming herself, and finally, the wave of nausea passed.

As she collected herself in the entryway, Cecil emerged from the kitchen and took his place at the table. Though he didn't take note of her, Buffy quickly darted across the hall and planted herself behind the corresponding archway that separated the living room from the entryway. From this vantage point she could face the dining room and, by poking her head around the short wall, easily see into the room, but she doubted that whoever or whatever eventually took the place at the head of the table could see her without almost completely turning around.

Her patience was rewarded a moment later as she caught her first glimpse of poor Cecil's mother.

She was not at all what Buffy had imagined, but then, considering the meat loaf, she decided instantly that in this realm, appearances were bound to be deceiving.

Buffy searched her memory for the name of Snyder's mother. She came up with nothing but *P* names—Patricia,

Pamela, Penelope—but none of them sounded right. Finally she settled for Mrs. Snyder.

The woman was a vision of a sweet grandmother in pink flowers and lace. Her white hair was neatly trimmed in a straight bob, and her face was etched with deep lines. The flesh of her neck sagged beneath a generous drooping chin, and her hands, which moved deftly about the table as she served herself and Cecil, were veined and covered with age spots. Only her voice betrayed the mettle beneath the deceptively sweet appearance.

Once both of them were served, Mrs. Snyder removed a crisp white apron from around her waist and disappeared briefly into the kitchen to discard it. When she returned, Buffy noted that her shoes were of the orthopedic variety, completing the picture of dowdy, plain, and neat with just a hint of Laura Ashley style.

"How was your day at school?" Mrs. Snyder asked politely as she and her son began to dig in to the meal she had placed before them.

Cecil took a generous bite of the meat loaf, and Buffy watched his face for any sign that he would find the dish as disgusting as she had. To her surprise, he ate like a man at his last meal. Her gorge rose as she saw him stuff one forkful after another into his mouth and chew and swallow with great satisfaction.

Buffy thought she'd begun to understand where the torture promised in this dimension might be coming from, but apart from Mrs. Snyder's somewhat overbearing and demanding nature, and perhaps her quickness of temper, Cecil seemed quite happy to be under her care.

"It was great, Mom," Cecil finally answered after a couple of bites.

"Close your mouth, Cecil, until you've swallowed your food. Haven't I taught you better manners than that?"

Cecil did as he was told, then went on proudly, "I got a B-plus on my fractions quiz."

"A B is a B, with or without the plus, young man," Mrs. Snyder answered sharply. "And it certainly isn't an A."

Buffy saw young Cecil's face fall a bit, but he went on gamely. "And I got an A-minus on today's spelling quiz."

"An A-minus?" Mrs. Snyder asked.

Cecil nodded with a satisfied smile.

"It should have been an A-plus," she said dismissively.

"But, you just—," Cecil began.

"I hope you don't think that with grades like that you're going to get anywhere in this life, young man," Mrs. Snyder continued. "An A-minus is not an A-plus, and you will be an A-plus student or you will end up digging ditches like your pathetic excuse for a father. How do you expect to do better than a measly fifth place in this year's spelling bee if you don't even know how to prepare for a test when you're given the words in advance? I am so disappointed in you, Cecil."

"I only missed the bonus words," Cecil tried to defend himself.

"You're weak, Cecil," Mrs. Snyder went on. "You should be ten chapters ahead of everyone else in that class. You're better than all of them, but you refuse to apply yourself. By the time I was your age, I had already been promoted two grade levels above my peers. Your stupidity is unacceptable. You will work harder if I have to stand over you with a belt every minute of the day until your grades improve."

Cecil seemed to have lost his appetite. Buffy could easily understand why. Joyce would have rewarded Buffy warmly for academic performance such as Cecil's. She always wanted Buffy to excel, but never chastised her daughter unless she thought Buffy wasn't doing her personal best. That had always been Joyce's only expectation of Buffy, and to this day, Buffy knew in her heart she had lived up to it, even if her current grades made that hard for Joyce to see.

"You haven't finished your dinner," Mrs. Snyder said with a hint of menace when she noted the same look Buffy had seen on Cecil's face.

"I'm full," Cecil said softly.

Buffy couldn't help the ache that started to pound in her heart at his obvious disappointment. She knew he must have been thinking of his treasured fifth-place spelling bee trophy. She also thought she had begun to understand why he would have gone to such lengths to get it.

"You are an ungrateful worm," Mrs. Snyder replied. "I slaved over that stove for hours today to make your favorite dinner, and this is how you repay my generosity? You will finish every last crumb of food on that plate and you will do it with a smile on your face or so help me this will be the last meal I will ever prepare for you."

Wow.

Finally, Buffy saw clearly the monster she was about to face.

As best as Buffy could tell, Cecil was a pleasant enough child, despite his taste in comic books, and he obviously strove daily to please his mother in everything he did. But there never was nor would there ever be any way of pleasing this woman. People like Mrs. Snyder weren't interested in accomplishment. They were only interested in power.

Buffy had been given a crash course in power once she'd become the Slayer. She'd already learned it was a difficult gift, one she tried to wield with respect and as much humility as she could muster. But Mrs. Snyder didn't understand power. She obviously had needs that little Cecil could never fill, but she would ride him mercilessly in an attempt to force him to do so. She didn't care about Cecil's grades or his dirty hands. She fed off of the power she had over him. She beat him with it, running him down to make herself feel better and to ensure her place of dominance.

It was sick.

And it had undoubtedly made Principal Snyder the man he was.

Buffy had come here imagining all kinds of physical abuse that Snyder might be suffering. Instead, she realized, his punishment at his mother's hands was infinitely more subtle and cruel. By transforming Snyder back into a child and forcing him to submit to her will, the evil demon was ripping apart his heart and tearing at his spirit, just as she had undoubtedly done every day of his young life.

Buffy understood emotional torture. She'd endured it for months at Angelus's hands.

She'd heard more than enough.

Buffy raised the ax that rested in her hand and stepped into the entryway so that both Cecil and Mrs. Snyder could see her clearly. "Hey," she said sharply. "Why don't you pick on someone your own size?"

Mrs. Snyder's face turned quickly. Her mouth hardened into a sneer, and her eyes glinted. "Who are you?" she demanded. "You were not invited to this place and you certainly don't belong here."

"Hi!" Cecil said, smiling at Buffy. "Mom, this is my friend. Can she stay for dinner?"

"Your friend?" Mrs. Snyder said incredulously. "You don't have any friends."

"But, she . . ." Cecil trailed off.

"With the people skills you've taught him, that's almost hard to believe, isn't it?" Buffy interjected.

Mrs. Snyder rose from her seat at the table and moved to face Buffy squarely. "Who are you?" she asked again.

"I'm the Slayer," Buffy said simply. "And you're done. I don't know where you came from and I don't really care.

'Cause you're not going back there, either. In fact, I don't think there's a hell hot enough for momsters like you."

"Then you've never seen hell," Mrs. Snyder replied. "But I'll gladly fix that."

Buffy felt her hands start to tingle.

Then she felt the pain as the muscles in her arms and legs began to burn and pull.

Without thought she sent the ax in her hand spinning toward Mrs. Snyder. It embedded itself firmly in her chest with a satisfying *thwump*, and Buffy instantly felt the pain subside.

"Mommy!" Cecil cried out, rising from the table.

"Stay out of this, Cecil!" both Buffy and Mrs. Snyder shouted in unison.

Cecil replied by rushing to a corner of the dining room, where he cowered in terror, whimpering.

"Probably not a good idea to waste your only weapon so quickly," Mrs. Snyder sneered, pulling the ax from her chest and splintering its handle in her grip. Looking up, Buffy watched as the face of the sweet, beneficent grandmother began to fade. Mrs. Snyder didn't seem bothered by the boils and harsh red welts erupting all over it, spewing pus and yellowish bile. Buffy had to admit, however, that it made what had to come next a little easier. Finally the monster she was fighting looked the part.

"You might want to see a dermatologist about that," Buffy said.

In an instant she closed the space between them and jabbed a quick kick combination into Mrs. Snyder's chest. The demon fell back, crashing into her chair and breaking it to pieces before she hit the floor.

But she was on her feet again, almost before Buffy could recover her balance. Shrieking, she flew at Buffy, her arms outstretched, and grabbed the Slayer by the throat.

Buffy replied with a knuckle punch to the demon's neck. It shocked Mrs. Snyder enough to loosen her grip. Buffy threw both arms up between the demon's, spinning quickly to disengage herself. She completed the turn, crouching low and extending her right leg, and succeeded in taking Mrs. Snyder off her feet.

Once she was down, Buffy landed on top of her and began to pummel her ooze-caked face.

But Mrs. Snyder wasn't going to be finished off that easily. She squirmed for a moment, then, catching one of Buffy's punches in her meaty palm, grabbed Buffy firmly by the waist with her other hand and threw her over her head, sending Buffy flipping through the air and into the china cabinet. Buffy was caught for a moment in a rain of glass shards and splintered wood, but she quickly pulled herself up and, rounding the dining table, caught her breath with the table between them. Mrs. Snyder rose from the ground and began to slowly circle the table toward Buffy.

"Is that all you've got, girl?" Mrs. Snyder demanded.

"Nope. Not even close," Buffy replied.

With that, Buffy leaped up on the table and, grabbing the chandelier above her head, swung herself back for a little momentum before pitching herself feetfirst into the demon.

Mrs. Snyder was thrown back clean through the dining room wall and into the entryway.

She recovered her feet quickly and waited for Buffy to follow. The Slayer did so, landing a series of punishing jabs to her face and torso. Mrs. Snyder answered with a right hook of her own that pushed Buffy back toward the front door.

"You will leave this place!" the demon shouted. "You are not welcome here."

"Oh, don't kid yourself, lady," Buffy replied. "No one is welcome here."

"This is my home!" the demon shouted between punches.

"This isn't a home," Buffy replied with a jump kick that uppercut Mrs. Snyder's jaw. "It's hell."

The insult struck Mrs. Snyder more heavily than any of Buffy's blows.

"You're just a child," Mrs. Snyder replied, sucking wind. "You couldn't possibly understand a mother's love."

"I understand that you don't love your child even a little," Buffy retorted, taking the advantage and knocking the demon to the floor, where she skidded back toward the staircase.

"Cecil is my whole world." Mrs. Snyder shuddered. Buffy couldn't be sure, but she thought that the demon might be on the verge of tears. "I gave him everything I had to give. I even sacrificed the love of his good-for-nothing father so that Cecil wouldn't be tainted by his bad example."

Buffy paused.

I guess Cecil wasn't wrong about that quail-hunting trip.

Mrs. Snyder pulled herself up and actually seated herself on the bottom stair as she continued. "All I ever wanted was his love."

"I don't believe that for a minute," Buffy replied.

"He was such a timid child."

"Gee, with you as a mother, I can't imagine why," Buffy snapped back.

"As long as he was mine, I could protect him. Push him to do better. Make him see that this world has no place in it for the weak."

"And fun as this little trip down rationalization lane is," Buffy retorted, "could you get up so I can kick your ass some more?"

"He betrayed me," Mrs. Snyder whimpered weakly. Reaching into her pocket, she removed a crumpled piece of parchment, rough around the edges, and tossed it toward Buffy.

Equal parts wary and intrigued, Buffy picked it up and opened it. It was written in a script Buffy didn't recognize, heavy black strokes and curls in an ancient and no doubt evil language. The only words that Buffy could clearly read were midway through the third paragraph: "Paulina Christina Snyder."

Paulina! That's it, Buffy thought, remembering Willow's research.

"You know, my demon-translating skills are kind of rusty," Buffy finally said, tossing the paper back to Paulina.

"He sold me to the demons!" Paulina shrieked with pain and rage. "My own son paid in his flesh and blood to have me banished to a demon dimension!"

Buffy did a little quick math in her head and realized that if Paulina was speaking the truth—and Buffy didn't doubt she was—then Cecil would have made this pact with the forces of darkness well into his adult years.

Paulina had wound herself up into a full rant.

"I gave him my entire life. But that wasn't enough for him. He lived with me for years, even after he'd finished college, and I never said a word. If he was happy here, I was happy to have him."

Maybe we all need to look again at the definition of "happy," Buffy thought.

"And what he gave me in return was an eternal existence in a place . . . I can't begin to describe. No one understands how to make a bed or clean himself properly. They've never even heard of detergent. And the food . . ."

"Picked up a few tips there, did you?" Buffy asked.

Paulina replied with a glare.

"All I wanted was to have my life back to the way it was before Cecil made that terrible mistake. I know if he'd really understood what he was doing, he would never have traded my life so cheaply. I had a little boy who loved me. I just wanted him back here at home, where I could love him and teach him and know that he was mine again. Is that so wrong?"

Buffy couldn't even begin to count the number of wrongs around her. All that she knew for sure was that Paulina Snyder had most certainly reaped what she had sown.

"Look," Buffy said, "I'm not your judge or your jury. The demon dust you use to bring your son back to you every night through that gateway is seeping out into my world and putting everyone to sleep. You want to go back to whatever snake pit you crawled out of, make it quick and don't ever let me see that incredibly ugly face of yours again. Otherwise, it's fight to the death time."

Paulina didn't even take a second to consider Buffy's more than generous offer. Leaping up off the step, she flew at Buffy, punching her hard in the chest and sending her flying back into the dining room.

All right, Buffy thought. *Option two, it is.*

They could trade blows like this indefinitely. Buffy needed to finish this, and for that, she needed a weapon. Her ax lay in pieces on the floor across the room. Though the blade was still intact, it was too far for her to reach with Paulina bearing down on her again. Turning to her left, she found her answer.

The face of President John F. Kennedy.

The image smiled up at her in all of his youthful, charismatic charm. With only a hint of regret, Buffy grabbed the plate, snapped it in half to give herself a sharp edge, and brought it swinging wide across her body as Paulina swooped down upon her. Putting all of her strength into the sweep, Buffy felt the impact of the clean, sharp porcelain blade as it met Paulina's neck, severing her head in one motion.

Paulina's headless body fell across Buffy's. She quickly pulled herself out from beneath it and clambered to her feet, standing to catch her breath amid the wreckage of the room and the lingering odor of garlic-infused meat loaf that would forever turn her stomach from this point forward.

The first part of her mission accomplished, Buffy started to hurry upstairs to retrieve the trophy and get out when she was stopped in her tracks by the sounds of Cecil whimpering behind her. He still sat in the corner of the dining room, rocking back and forth, his legs pulled to his chest protectively.

"Did you . . . did you see that?" he stammered.

"I had a pretty good seat," she replied.

"Her . . . *face*," he finally forced out.

"Yeah, well, that's what happens when they run out of moisturizer in hell," Buffy said simply.

"No one else has ever seen it," Cecil said, looking up at Buffy in something close to awe. "My friends all think she's so sweet, at least the ones she lets me have over. They don't think much of her cooking, but I guess they just can't handle the spice. Otherwise, though, they think she's a perfect mother. I tried once to tell them about that face, how she changes so quickly when I make her mad, but no one ever believed me."

Buffy paused for a moment, then crossed to Cecil and held a hand out to him. He took it and allowed her to help him to his feet.

"I believe you, Cecil," Buffy said, surprised at the warmth in her voice. "Now let's get out of here."

Buffy turned to head upstairs, and Cecil was immediately right on her heels. "You're not going to leave me, are you?"

"Nope." Buffy shook her head reassuringly. "I just have to get something. I'll be right back."

Moments later, Buffy was back downstairs with the trophy in her hands. Cecil's face lit up when he saw it.

"Oh, please," he pleaded, "can I have it?"

"Sure," Buffy said. "It's yours, after all." Passing it to him, she took his free hand and together they walked through the gateway and onto the porch.

To Buffy's surprise, it was nearing dawn in Sunnydale. But it was a silent dawn, the same oppressive silence that had hung over Sunnydale the entire day Buffy had waited for Snyder to return to the house for the last time.

Cecil stood on the porch beside her, somewhat disoriented. "What am I doing here?" he asked.

Buffy turned quickly to face him. It wasn't what he said that betrayed him, it was his tone that gave everything away.

"Miss Summers?" Principal Snyder asked incredulously.

There was now no doubt in her mind that little Cecil Snyder was once again buried in the adult Snyder's subconscious, and the man she was facing was going to want an explanation.

She didn't know where to begin.

Fortunately, she was spared the need to say anything as

Snyder realized he was holding something in his hand. His confused concern gave way to something resembling faint delight as he considered the trophy.

"You know, it's the damnedest thing," he said. "I woke up the other day in my mother's old house, and there it was, just like I remembered it, on my old dresser. I must have been carrying it around with me since then, I just don't remember. . . ." He trailed off.

"My guess is, there will be a lot of that going on," Buffy suggested.

"Where are my shoes?" was Snyder's next question. "Do you know that's the fifth pair of shoes I've misplaced this week?"

Suddenly, Snyder doubled over in pain. At first it seemed that he had been gut-punched, and Buffy instantly went on alert. Invisible demons were rare, but certainly not unheard of, in her experience. Seconds later, however, the source of Snyder's pain became clear. Dropping the trophy, Snyder fell to the porch, both hands grasping his bare left foot. As Buffy watched in fascinated horror, his left pinkie toe was ripped from its rightful place on his foot and disappeared in a magickal twinkle of light.

"Owwwww!" Snyder shrieked in pain as blood began to pour from the small gaping wound.

Mystery solved, Buffy thought. *No wonder he's been wearing bloody bandages everywhere he went this week. He must have lost that toe each morning. . . . Oh, wait a minute.*

"Don't tell me," Buffy said, growing queasy at the very idea. "The price you paid in flesh and blood to have your mother banished to a demon dimension was your toe?" she asked in disbelief.

Snyder was in too much pain to answer. He clambered onto all fours, trying to rise up on his remaining good foot.

Buffy started to help him, when another thought occurred to her, a thought that made the oppressive silence around her a little more understandable.

Turning back to the door, Buffy braced herself, then re-entered the house. Sure enough, the gateway was still active and she found herself in the destroyed entryway. Paulina's headless body remained on the floor of the dining room.

It wasn't the trophy at all, Buffy thought. Whatever the demon had stolen was still somewhere in this house, and Buffy was going to have to find it to close the gateway and end the spell.

"That's the fifth pair of shoes I've misplaced this week," Snyder had said.

Buffy took the stairs two at a time on her way back to Cecil's room. Hurrying to the closet, she glanced at the five pairs neatly lined on the closet floor and the single black dress shoe that had no mate.

"Poetic, I guess, from Paulina's point of view," Buffy said aloud. Then she grabbed the single shoe and hurried back downstairs and through the front door again.

This time, there was no mistaking her success. Once Buffy had gained the porch, she turned to see the bright light of the gateway swirling behind her as it started to fade. Finally, as the glowing circle grew smaller and smaller, collapsing in on itself, there was an earth-shaking bang, and Buffy found herself staring only at the normal front door.

As if in answer to her unspoken *that had to have worked* thought, Buffy was suddenly aware of the faint chirping of birds and the distant barking of a dog.

Good morning, Sunnydale, Buffy thought with a smile.

She had started down the front walk when she realized she was alone. Snyder was gone, though a fresh trail of his blood told Buffy he was limping his way home.

Happy to have avoided any further conversation with the man she could now go back to genuinely disliking, Buffy turned in the opposite direction, grateful that, at last, this much of her work was done and now, like everyone else, she might get a little rest before it was time to face whatever was coming next.

CHAPTER TWELVE

Joyce awakened to find herself in bed and, strangely, in her bathrobe. She couldn't remember much of the night before, but she thought she'd checked Buffy's empty room, realized she was still at the library putting in some extra study hours, *which hopefully will pay off,* and just barely made it into her pajamas before she'd fallen exhausted into bed. She also thought she remembered waking and brushing her teeth, but she decided that must have been one of those early-morning dreams where you thought you were getting up and getting dressed to start your day, maybe even were on the way to work, before your alarm started blaring to remind you that you had yet to accomplish any of those things.

It was disorienting and vaguely unsettling, but Joyce tried to shake it off, along with the nagging sense that she could really use another few hours of sleep.

Still, it was clearly the beginning of a beautiful day, and Joyce decided it was best to make a good start of it. Crossing to her bedroom door, she called out, "Buffy?" Though it wouldn't have been the first time Buffy had stayed out all night, Joyce wasn't going to be pleased if her daughter had chosen to spend the evening gallivanting around with her friends rather than getting her rest this close to finals.

"Buffy?" she called again, louder.

Her fears were allayed when she heard from the kitchen below a familiar voice reply, "Mom?"

Joyce barely made it to the staircase landing when Buffy rushed up and threw herself into her mother's arms, hugging her so tightly, Joyce felt her spine popping.

"Good morning, honey," Joyce said warmly once Buffy had released her and she found she could take a full, refreshing breath.

"You're okay," Buffy said with obvious relief, looking her mother up and down in a manner that suggested Buffy was seriously worried that Joyce might have started dating again.

Joyce examined Buffy more closely. Her ponytail was askew, and telltale wisps of hair surrounding her face gave the impression of a good hairdo gone bad. Her denim jacket had a new tear in the right sleeve, and her jeans sported fresh stains that Joyce wanted to believe were dirt or grass but which gave the uncomfortable impression of something stickier.

"Are you just getting home?" Joyce asked, dismayed.

"It was kind of a long night," Buffy replied a little evasively.

"Well, you can tell me all about it on the way to school," Joyce said gamely. She knew Buffy had taken her worries about her studies to heart, and Todd's reports to Joyce about Buffy's progress had been promising. Rather than emphasize an understandable lapse, Joyce decided to accentuate the positive and hope for the best. Buffy was a good girl, if a peculiar one, and Joyce knew better than anyone that Buffy was harder on herself than any other critic, including her mother.

"Um, Mom," Buffy said, "it's actually Saturday."

"What?" Joyce asked. She was certain it was Friday.

"Trust me," Buffy said.

Joyce marched back up the stairs behind Buffy and turned on the morning news in her bedroom. Sure enough, she was greeted by the weekend anchors. As she struggled to remember what had happened to Friday, Buffy surprised her by wrapping an arm around her waist.

Joyce responded automatically, draping her own arm over Buffy's shoulder and giving her a firm snuggle.

"Someone's affectionate this morning," she said, smiling.

"I just really love you, Mom," Buffy said simply.

"I love you, too, sweetie," Joyce said, trying to keep the

surprise out of her voice. Buffy was sweet, but it had been some time since she'd willingly sought the comfort of her mother's arms. "Are you okay?" she found herself asking.

"Sure," Buffy replied. "I think I'm just appreciating you more than usual right now," she finished.

Oh, God, Joyce thought, and placed the palm of her hand to Buffy's forehead.

"What?" Buffy asked.

"Either you're running a temperature, or you want something," Joyce replied firmly.

Please tell me you didn't burn down the school gymnasium again, Joyce mentally added to the list of things that might be wrong.

"A girl can't just love her mother?" Buffy asked a little defensively.

"A girl can—she just usually doesn't express it this way unless she's brought home a bad test score or found a really cute dress at the mall," Joyce replied.

"Well, this morning, the answer is neither," Buffy said, smiling. "But sometimes I forget how lucky I am to have you as my mom."

"Okay," Joyce said, still at a loss to see where this might be leading.

"You really are something," Buffy finished.

"Where do you think you get it from?" Joyce asked, smiling.

Buffy rewarded her with another squeeze and then started for her room.

"Don't you have another study session this afternoon?" Joyce asked Buffy's back.

Buffy's shoulders slumped visibly. "Oh, that's right."

"How about some pancakes for breakfast?" Joyce asked. "Get the morning started with some good brain food."

"Since when are pancakes brain food?" Buffy asked.

"Since I didn't make it to the store this week and we're out of eggs and cereal," Joyce answered.

"Sounds perfect," Buffy replied. "Just *after* you've had your coffee, okay?"

Joyce smiled in reply. As her daughter headed toward her bedroom, she sighed, deeply touched by Buffy's uncharacteristic expression of love and happy to take it as a small blessing. She honestly didn't know if she would ever truly understand the little girl she'd brought into the world, but on mornings like this, it hardly mattered.

Buffy was the littlest bit grateful for her evening spent with the Snyders. Though Joyce certainly had her moments, on her worst day she wasn't in the same ballpark, let alone county, as Paulina Snyder. Buffy rarely thought of herself as lucky these days, but the glimpse she'd had into her principal's childhood had been a visceral reminder that there were many people in the world who had it much worse, even if you counted the fact that Buffy had been called to a sacred duty she often wished had been passed to someone else.

As soon as she reached her bedroom she put in a quick call

to the library. She spoke to Giles for a few minutes, receiving confirmation that he, Willow, Xander, and Cordelia had all awakened that morning a little worse for wear, but certainly in good form. Though he attempted to quiz Buffy on the night's events and her encounter with Paulina, Buffy desperately needed a shower and breakfast before Todd showed up, so she deferred his questions to Willow and promised a full debriefing session on Monday morning before class. When Giles asked if she'd had any opportunity to locate Callie, Buffy admitted that she'd seen the whole sleeping spell as the higher priority, and he heartily concurred but insisted that she patrol that evening in search of the young vampire.

Buffy agreed, then called Willow's house to confirm that her best friend had made it home after waking up in the library with Xander and Giles. Willow also wanted a blow-by-blow description of the demon dimension, and given the amount of effort Willow had put into resolving the crisis, Buffy felt honor-bound to satisfy at least some of her curiosity before thanking her profusely and jumping into the shower.

Joyce made good on her pancake threat, and nourished by the delicious and filling breakfast, Buffy decided to forgo her much-needed nap and complete a few of Todd's assignments instead. She was actually feeling quite proud of herself a few hours later when Todd knocked on her bedroom door and she could honestly say she was prepared to work with him.

Todd entered Buffy's room with two tall Styrofoam cups of cold soda already in hand.

"So you're a full-service tutor?" Buffy asked playfully, hoping he would forgive the lack of returned phone calls over the past few days.

His sincere smile and flirty "Let's sit down and define some of those terms" in response put the Slayer immediately at ease.

They were interrupted briefly by Joyce, who poked her head into Buffy's room to announce that she was going to run by the gallery for the afternoon and ask if she could bring home pizza for dinner for all of them. Appropriately embarrassed, Buffy suggested that Todd probably had better things to do, but he seemed to warm to the idea and, with a grateful smile, accepted Joyce's kind offer.

"You've got a great mom," Todd said, once Joyce had left them to work.

"I really do." Buffy nodded, then wondered momentarily if actually liking one's mom would lose her any cool points with Todd. To change the subject, she asked how Todd had been the past few days, apologizing somewhere in the middle for not calling him back sooner.

"Oh, it's no problem," Todd replied quickly. "I actually slept in most of the day yesterday. I don't know what happened. I hope I'm not catching that flu bug that's been going around," he added.

"I'm sure it's nothing a few hours of English history won't cure," Buffy teased as she took a hearty sip of the soda Todd had placed beside her.

"Well, I'm game," Todd replied, searching Buffy's face for something she truly hoped was a sign that she was seriously falling in like with him.

"By the way," Todd continued as he pulled a few reference books out of his backpack, "I haven't seen any sign of the boyfriend you were so worried about."

Buffy felt the tension in her neck and shoulders begin to relax at his words. "I'm glad to hear that," she responded honestly. "He tends to be a night person," she added, hoping to keep Todd on his guard.

Quite suddenly, that sense of relaxation spread down her arms and legs.

Maybe that nap would have been a better idea after all, Buffy thought, worrying that she had finally pushed herself too far.

"Buffy?" Todd asked with genuine concern.

The next thing she knew, Buffy could barely keep her eyes open.

"Buffy?" Todd asked again.

Buffy took a deep breath and tried to reach again for her soda, hoping the caffeine might rejuvenate her somewhat. She fumbled clumsily for the cup and ended up knocking it over onto her desk. Though her instinct told her to jump up and out of the way, she felt positively glued to her chair. To her surprise, Todd also remained where he was, studying her carefully.

"Don't . . . know . . . wha- . . . wrong," Buffy tried to say, but her voice and eyes were beginning to fail her.

The last thing she thought she heard as her world started to spin toward oblivion was Todd saying softly, "I'm so sorry, Buffy."

What the bloody hell?

Someone was screaming, someone with a high-pitched piercing wail that Spike could not immediately identify. As the shrieking continued behind him, followed by the distinct sound of the slamming of doors, Spike came fully awake and found himself seated in his wheelchair in Dru's bedroom before the empty four-poster bed.

What was I just doing? Spike wondered. The alarm tightening his gut told him that it was probably important, but clearly not important enough to have stayed awake for.

"Oh, no, you don't, you little brat!" came clearly to Spike's ears.

Angelus.

But Angelus was supposed to be dead.

In a flash, Spike suddenly remembered his last conscious thoughts. Angelus had been sleeping with his beloved Dru, and Callie had carved a small stake that had a date with Angelus's heart.

Spike's unease grew perceptibly as he realized that the stake intended for Angelus now rested with its pointy side embedded deeply in the fabric of his wheelchair, directly between his legs.

"Well, that's rude," Spike muttered aloud before tossing

the stake aside and wheeling himself quickly toward the living room.

Once he'd arrived, the story of the last few minutes was painfully clear to him. Angelus and Drusilla stood by the closed French doors. Beyond them, cowering in the few remaining shadows of the patio, which was about to be drenched by full exposure to the morning sun, was Callie, screaming, positively begging to be rescued.

Callie saw Spike before the others did. She started to reach out for him with both arms, calling, "Please, Daddy!" and was rewarded for her efforts by hitting a patch of sun and singeing her arms. She pulled them back instantly but soon cried out for him again.

Spike instinctively moved closer, the whole time figuring the distance to the doors as well as the number of seconds remaining in Callie's afterlife if he didn't do something.

"Don't even think about it, Roller-boy," Angelus said, turning on Spike sharply.

"Oh, I was just moving in for a better view," Spike quipped, hoping his feigned nonchalance would keep Angelus off his guard.

"Callie was a bad, bad girl," Dru offered. "She tried to hurt Angelus."

"I see," Spike said calmly. "While that's most regrettable, don't you think the little bit has learned her lesson?" he asked.

"She's about to," Angelus said menacingly.

He was baiting Spike, and though sorely tempted, Spike refused to rise to it for the moment.

"You know, love," Spike said, turning toward Dru, "she's only a child. *Your* child," he added with emphasis. "Don't you think she deserves a chance to at least explain herself? I mean, Angelus threatened to kill her not two days ago. Maybe she's just . . . acting out?"

"She doesn't love me, Spike," Dru said sadly. "I tried to make her love me, but she won't."

"In fact, the only one in this house she seems to listen to is you, Spike," Angelus added. "Makes me wonder whose idea it was to crawl into my bed with a stake this morning."

"Oh, don't waste your time, mate," Spike replied. "If I wanted you dead, you'd already be a footnote in history."

Angelus growled, baring his fangs at Spike.

"Now, boys," Drusilla interrupted, "play nice. Callie has come between us all. I think Angelus is right. Things were better before she was here."

Spike didn't know what angered him more, Drusilla or Angelus. Drusilla was insane. He'd always known that and, to a degree, that fact mitigated most of her actions. It was, after all, a good insane, one he'd found incredibly twisted and tempting over the years. But Angelus was playing Dru, pretending to be threatened by Callie because he already knew that Spike had taken a liking to the little girl.

Damn his soulless body to hell.

Spike had options here. His strength had already started to

return weeks ago, and for reasons even he was at a loss to delve into too deeply, he had chosen to keep that piece of information from both Angelus and Dru. Still, he was more than capable of rising from his chair and rushing to Callie's rescue, but that would have betrayed his secret. Put simply, Spike had serious "trust" issues with Angelus, and he couldn't afford to squander the only advantage he had over him. Dru, he somehow knew, would completely understand and forgive the little deception, should she ever learn of it. In fact, she would probably find it charming. The question was, was Callie worth it?

Spike's heart surprised him for the first time in a long time by saying yes.

Callie continued to cry out to him, her screams growing louder as the sun encroached millimeter by millimeter upon her little corner of life.

Callie was a child, but she was also a good student. Given time and patience, she would become every bit as fierce a companion as Drusilla had been to him. She had already learned to silence what little remained of her conscience, and Spike had delighted in watching her take her first steps into the world of her new vampire existence. It was rewarding in a way he had never before experienced to watch her abandon her old ideas and spark to newer, darker dreams.

Strange as it might seem, Spike had to admit that since Angelus had returned to his and Drusilla's world, Spike had lost something of his love. Dru's attention had been divided at first, but lately, Angelus had been the one she had turned to in most of her needs, and he had gloried in satisfying her, all the while pretending to defer to Spike's intimacy with Dru but clearly only waiting to take Dru from Spike forever.

But Callie was his. She had no love or patience for Angelus and only a little for Dru. Much as Dru said she had wanted this child, the moment Callie had become difficult, Dru had lost interest where Spike had found a project he could literally and figuratively sink his teeth into. Hunting and killing had become new to him, as he experienced them through Callie's eyes, and her uncomplicated love for Spike had soothed the part of his heart so carelessly bruised by Drusilla.

But, were he to defend Callie now, he would be taking sides against Dru and Angelus. Where he had once hoped Callie might be the wedge that would drive Dru and Angelus apart, this would only strengthen their alliance, and Spike might as well pack his bags then and there. Angelus, he could handle. Angelus and Dru united . . . that was a horse of a completely different color.

"It makes no difference to me, love," Spike said, moving closer to Dru and, with pretended carelessness, fondling her hand gently.

Dru shivered appreciatively.

"As long as you're sure that's what you want," Spike added smoothly. "Just last night Callie was telling me what good games you'd been playing at the schoolyard and how much she wanted to find you a new puppy."

"Really?" Dru's face lit up.

Spike shrugged. "But if you think death is an appropriate punishment for teasing Angelus a little, well, you are her mother, so it's entirely up to you."

Dru looked to Spike and then Angelus.

"Spikey . . . please!" Callie pleaded through the door, and Spike's head started to pound with fear.

"Perhaps she has learned her lesson, Angelus," Dru said softly.

"Let me make this easy for you, Dru," Angelus replied. "It's her or me. I'm not going to watch my back in my own home."

Dru sighed, resigned.

"Maybe it's for the best," she said.

That was it. Spike had lost. He could still clutch a small victory and spare Callie's life, but it would cost him Drusilla. Angelus would make certain of it.

"As I said, love," Spike replied, "it's your choice."

But the time for choosing was past. Callie's words dissolved into shrieks as the sun finally caught up with her and her tiny body erupted in flames before dissolving into dust.

"I don't know about you, but I'm starving," Angelus said, turning to Drusilla. "I was thinking we might hit the sewers before sundown."

"Sounds lovely," Dru said with a smile. "Care to join us, my darling Spike?"

Spike hesitated to reply. Inside, he was burning, as the

image of Callie's death throes etched itself into his memory, adding to the long list of things for which one day he would make Angelus pay.

"That's all right, dearest," Spike finally answered. "I'll just catch up on my programs and find a snack later, a little closer to home."

"Whatever," Angelus said, taking Dru around the waist, pulling her away from Spike. "Maybe we'll bring you back a little dessert."

"Oh, don't put yourself out, mate," Spike replied. "I was never one for sloppy seconds."

Though Spike had appeared to be a vision of complacency over the next half hour as he cooled his rage with a bottle of whiskey and suffered the unbearable torture of pretending to enjoy a golf tournament on television, he was only counting the minutes until Dru and Angelus set off to hunt. He had already decided that he would spend the evening tracking their every move. He'd lost Callie, but he wasn't about to lose Dru as well. He'd keep both eyes on Angelus from this point forward. Soon enough, he'd find a way to separate them forever. Angelus would screw up. Overconfidence such as his always came with a price. Spike just wanted to make sure he had a front-row seat when the bill finally came due.

CHAPTER THIRTEEN

When Buffy awoke, her head pounding, limbs heavy with fatigue, and mind still shrouded in a hazy mist, the first thing she was conscious of was the fact that she was lying on her bed. The room was dark, though not quite pitch-black. If she'd had to guess, she would have called it dusk outside.

She tried to sit up, but an anvil seemed to be sitting atop her shoulders. The best she could manage initially was to rise up on her elbows and scan her bedroom.

What the hell happened? kept running through her mind like a song that was stuck and stubbornly refused to go away.

A sharp gut-punch of memory brought her more fully

to her senses when she made out the figure of Todd standing in the shadows near her bedroom window. His arms were
crossed, but he leaned against the wall in what looked like
relative comfort.

"Buffy?" he said. There was hope in his voice. But there
was also something else: sadness, maybe . . . tinged with a bit
of fear.

"What the hell happened?" Buffy finally said, giving voice
to the most coherent thought in her head.

Todd didn't answer her directly at first.

"My guess is that you're still a little hazy from the tran-
quilizers I put in your soda. I didn't ask, but I think they're
commonly used on elephants. The man who sent them to me
swore you wouldn't be hurt by them, just weakened."

Todd was right. Buffy was still hazy. But she was also
growing more and more alert each second. She had no idea
now who or what Todd really was, so to lull him further into a
false sense of security, she remained where she was and intentionally paused longer than necessary between her words,
hoping Todd would still assume she was not a serious threat
to him.

"You gave me . . . elephant . . . pills?" she asked. "Why?"

His answer struck Buffy directly in the gut more forcefully than a perfectly timed punch.

"I was hired to kill you," Todd said simply.

The haze in Buffy's mind vanished completely. Though
Todd still stood across the room from her, he straightened

his posture and moved into the only light available, cast by Buffy's desk lamp. She still couldn't see his face clearly, but she recognized the relaxed demeanor of a foe who honestly believed he was in charge of the situation.

Well, you're just King Wrong from Wrongville, Buffy thought as every muscle in her body tensed and she struggled to resist the urge to fly across the small space that separated them and pin him to the floor before pounding the answer out of him she now required.

"You change your mind, or do you get paid by the hour?" Buffy asked wryly.

Todd took a hesitant step closer to the bed.

"I can't do it, Buffy," he said, almost desperately.

You sure as hell can't now, Buffy thought.

Buffy pulled herself up to a sitting position, taking much more time than she needed, and noted that Todd quickly stepped back again. His nerves were definitely starting to show.

"Okay." She sighed. "Why don't you start somewhere closer to the beginning?"

Todd nodded, then started to pace slowly as he spoke.

"A man contacted me. He offered me a full ride to UC–Sunnydale and any graduate program in the country in exchange for my cooperation. He knew you were on the list for special tutoring and he said he could make sure I was assigned to you." Todd paused, swallowing hard before he went on. "He said you were a killer, a vicious killer."

"He" wasn't necessarily wrong.

"He said you were a danger to Sunnydale, but that you'd never be prosecuted for your crimes. He sent me your record and frankly, it wasn't hard to believe him. Vandalism, arson, assault—it's all there in black and white."

"Weren't you the one who told me that history was written by the victors, so it's not always a good idea to believe everything you read?" Buffy asked.

"I was," Todd agreed, "and I didn't, especially after we met. It just didn't seem possible. But, then . . ." He trailed off.

"Who was he? Who hired you?" Buffy asked softly.

"He never gave me a name."

We'll see about that.

"Okay, then what?" Buffy demanded, more sternly than she'd intended.

"I saw you at the park night before last. You were fighting two grown men. I couldn't see everything, but I saw you fight. You were stronger than they were. And you were the only one who walked away from that fight," Todd said, obviously struggling with his own confusion.

"I'd already tried to tell him I couldn't do it," he went on. "But after I saw that, I decided I had to. I came here today so certain of what I had to do. But once you were asleep, I just couldn't."

"Why not?" Buffy asked, going for alluring and pretty sure she already knew the answer.

"I didn't expect to like you so much, Buffy," he said sadly.

Buffy figured those were pretty much the high points of

Todd's story and she wasn't in the mood to coax anything further from him.

In the space of a breath she was off the bed and a startled Todd was pinned against the wall, Buffy's arm pressing firmly on his chest and his options now severely limited.

"Why don't you just ask me what you've been wanting to ask me all day, Todd?" she said firmly. "This has nothing to do with liking me. This is about satisfying your curiosity, isn't it?" she demanded. "Ask me, Todd."

Todd had broken out in a cold sweat the moment he was pinned. It was clear that he now realized he had misjudged Buffy in more ways than one, and struggled to find the answer that would satisfy her. As it happened, it was also the only true question he'd had from the moment they met.

"Who . . . what are you?" he stammered.

Buffy smiled.

"I'm the thing the darkness fears," she replied.

Forcing her arm harder into Todd's chest, she asked, "Who hired you?"

"I told you, I don't know," he said, clearly distressed.

"I heard what you said," Buffy replied. "I just don't believe you."

"I swear to God," Todd insisted. "The guy never used his name. He just promised half the payment up front, and when I contacted the registrar's office, they confirmed that my school account had been paid up through next year."

"I saw you on the phone, Todd," Buffy said simply. "I

heard you talking to someone. You at least have a phone number, don't you?"

Todd shook his head. "That call was prearranged. I just had to wait by the phone at a certain time, I swear."

Buffy searched his terrified face. He was scared, but he was also telling the truth. Abruptly, she lowered her arm and stepped back. For a moment, Todd looked like exactly what he was: a condemned man who had just been offered a last-second reprieve.

"You have no idea how lucky you are," she said as he caught his breath. "See, everything you think you know about me is true . . . from a certain point of view. You don't deserve the truth, Todd, not after the way you've lied to me and put my life in danger, but I will tell you this much: I do fight. I fight evil. The man or whatever the hell hired you undoubtedly fights too, just for the wrong team. You did the right thing here today. And my guess is, you're going to pay for it with your life. Oh, I'm not going to hurt you," she went on in response to the genuine terror that flashed across his face. "That's not my job. Times like this, I wish it was, but it isn't. I'm going to leave you to him, and believe me when I tell you, men like that don't tolerate mistakes."

Todd considered her carefully. He must have seen more clearly than ever before how complicated the young woman standing before him was. Buffy felt his regret, but it didn't console her one bit.

"I'm so sorry, Buffy," Todd said honestly.

"Yeah, I heard that the first time you said it," Buffy tossed back. "Now get out."

Todd did as he was told, without bothering to collect his bag or books.

Torn between rage and confusion, Buffy listened for the slamming front door, then watched from her bedroom window as he hurried down her front walk.

Once she was satisfied he was gone, she turned from the window and threw herself back down on her bed.

If I had a nickel for every guy who ever fell in love with me and then tried to kill me . . . , she thought sadly.

You'd have a dime, a more rational voice inside her head offered. *Twenty cents at the most.*

After leaving Drusilla to her fun in the alley behind the movie theater, Angelus had hurried to Buffy's house just after sundown. Though he couldn't help but feel he'd lost some momentum over the past few days, he sincerely hoped that Buffy and Todd hadn't. After mulling over his options, he'd decided the most elegant approach was usually a simple one. He didn't honestly believe that Buffy was nearly as close to Todd as she'd suggested, but there was an easy enough way to find out. The next time Buffy and Todd met, Angelus intended to be there, and assuming the time was ripe, he would slowly torture Todd before Buffy's eyes.

At least, that had been the plan. And, initially, it had looked promising.

When Angelus arrived at Buffy's window, he'd seen Buffy sitting up in her bed talking with Todd. Their voices had been pitched too low for him to make out all of their conversation, but he certainly caught the significant points of interest.

Turned out there really was more to Todd than met the eye. Angelus had seen Buffy's determination and strength. He'd smelled Todd's fear. And he'd witnessed the sadness written plainly on Buffy's face once Todd was gone. It wasn't exactly the epic despair he'd hoped to create that night, but it would do.

Thing was, it was also the slightest bit irritating. Todd's death now wouldn't hurt Buffy nearly as much as Angelus had hoped. She might even be expecting it, though not necessarily at Angelus's hands. And if Todd had any sense, he'd be on his way right now to have some eyes installed in the back of his head. But Buffy was Angelus's special project. He struggled with the disquieting sense that someone had invaded his territory.

At least the solution was uncomplicated.

One moment, Todd was hurrying down Ravello Drive toward the center of town, and the next, he'd been plucked from the sidewalk by the back of his shirt collar and deposited on the ground pinned down by Angelus's foot in his gut.

"You hurt Buffy," Angelus said menacingly.

He saw something like recognition along with the terror in Todd's eyes and could only assume that Buffy had mentioned something about him to Todd.

Good to know my reputation is still intact, he mused.

"I . . . I . . . don't . . ." Todd was trying to find words.

"Shhh," Angelus hissed softly as he lifted Todd from the ground and held him firmly by the throat. "No one gets to do that but me," he whispered.

Bringing Todd's neck to his lips, Angelus sank his teeth into the traumatized tutor and within moments had sucked every last drop of life from him.

"Is that the nasty teacher man?" a dulcet voice sung in his ear as he was reveling in the intense pleasure of a fresh kill.

Angelus dropped Todd to the sidewalk and turned to face Drusilla, noting that her own mouth was still wet with the blood of her most recent feeding.

"It was," Angelus replied with satisfaction.

"But where's Buffy?" Dru asked. "I thought you wanted her to see this."

"Slight change of plans, dearest," Angelus said, drawing Dru close with one arm and firmly pressing her lithe frame into his.

"That's my Angelus," Dru cooed. "One never knows what he'll do next."

"You always know," Angelus said suggestively, and punctuated the remark by planting a firm kiss on Dru's mouth. He tingled with pleasure as she licked the last of Todd from his lips.

"Promise me . . . ," she whispered as they pulled apart.

"Anything," Angelus replied.

"Promise me that in the days to come, the whole world will bleed."

"That's definitely the idea," he assured her.

Dru clapped her hands in delight, then draped her arm across Angelus's shoulders as they strolled up the street.

"The stars and the moon," she sang softly.

"So tell me, my sweet," Angelus interrupted her. "Who would you like for dessert?"

Spike stepped into the light of a streetlamp just outside Buffy's house and watched as Angelus and Dru meandered, oblivious to his presence. Though he believed he should have been feeling something like simmering rage at the sight, he found the experience strangely cold. What he had just witnessed was what he had always imagined when Dru and Angelus set out into the night together. Confirmation of his fears did nothing but steel his resolve.

The more unexpected part of the experience was the detachment that washed over him as he watched Dru snuggle into Angelus's arms.

After a moment, he dropped his gaze to Todd's body. He couldn't manage to feel anything at all. It had nothing to do with his timeless love for Drusilla. That feeling lived in a part of his heart to which no one else would ever be granted access, and it wasn't going anywhere anytime soon. But something else had clicked into place, and Spike examined it from a palpable distance.

It definitely had something to do with Callie. Forced to hide the genuine regret he felt at her death, he'd simply done his best to refuse to let those feelings surface within him. Those feelings were best left alone. They drove a person to do incredibly insane things; things almost as insane as most of Angelus's actions of late.

So what's his excuse? he wondered.

Angelus was allowing his obsession with the Slayer to blind him to a very obvious reality.

He's not hurting her at all. He's just pissing her the hell off. And a pissed-off Slayer is one thing none of us needs right now.

Suddenly, something else was quite clear to Spike. It was just a thought. But it was an incredibly intriguing thought.

Spike had made his fair share of enemies over the years. It came with being the big bad. And the Slayer had, for more than a year now, definitely been near the top of his list of those who would undoubtedly be better off dead.

Funny thing about enemies, though, and the company they keep. The only thing Spike hated more than the Slayer right now was Angelus. And Angelus was undoubtedly the thing that the Slayer hated most of all.

Ergo . . .

The enemy of my enemy might just be my friend.

Spike allowed the thought to wind its way through his mind, a faint flicker of delight growing brighter as it coursed through him.

That flicker was only extinguished when the Slayer knocked him to the ground and began her assault to his face with her fists.

Buffy had grown restless, sitting in her bedroom, thinking about Todd, and imagining what might have been if just once, a cute boy with a quick wit and a sparkling personality turned out to be no more than that.

The only surefire way Buffy knew to deal with the regret was to stop dealing with it. And the best way to do that was to focus her attention on something else. Something she could do something about with a stake or a crossbow.

She had already planned to find Callie that evening. Though her mother would be home soon with pizza for three, Buffy soon found herself scratching out a quick note expressing her sincere desire for leftovers, and heading out into the darkness to do the one job she knew she did well.

And then she'd seen Spike.

Standing over Todd's very dead body.

It's amazing how the universe works, Buffy thought as she tackled him from behind. It had taken Todd from her, even before Spike had made a meal out of him, but it had also given her exactly what she needed in order to find Callie . . . the only person in town besides Buffy who had definitely seen her in the past few days.

It probably wasn't a fair trade, especially from Todd's point of view, but she'd take it.

Buffy had fought Spike several times in the past. He was incredibly strong and equally quick, but that wasn't what made him so dangerous. Though it was always tempting to dismiss the bad Billy Idol wannabe fashion sense, Spike was easily the most tenacious vampire she'd ever faced. The guy just didn't know the meaning of the word "quit," and he seemed to truly enjoy pain, both the giving and the receiving.

So she had a hard time understanding what the hell his problem was at the moment. He'd just made a fresh kill. He should have been brimming over with fight. But instead of tossing her off and laying into her with all his might, he was dodging her punches without throwing any of his own.

Come to think of it, this is the first time I've seen him out of his wheelchair, Buffy realized. *Maybe he's not quite up to strength.*

Finally, Buffy's curiosity got the better of her. She didn't stop punching, but she did ask, "Is it me, or is your heart just not in this?"

"If you'd just stop for a minute, I might answer that," Spike replied between blows.

In a quick motion, Buffy grabbed Spike by his collar and rolled to her right. She then picked him up and forced him off balance, tossing him into a nearby tree. She pulled back, expecting a charge, but Spike surprised her again by slowly rising to his feet and holding up his hands in the universal sign of "I surrender."

"Okay," Buffy said, "you want to play nice. Tell me one thing. Where can I find Callie McKay?"

"She's dead," Spike said with obvious, and what seemed like genuine, regret.

Buffy didn't want to believe him, but she couldn't help herself. She did.

"Angelus killed her," Spike went on with a hint of anger.

Buffy was stunned. On the one hand, she was definitely relieved. She hadn't honestly been looking forward to solving this problem, but she'd known what she had to do and was prepared to do it. On the other hand, *why should this bother someone like Spike?*

"Did Angelus sire her in the first place?" Buffy demanded.

"No, that was Drusilla," Spike replied. "She wanted a new toy and then got bored when it didn't dance to her tune."

Buffy could hardly believe what she was hearing.

"Callie was a good kid." Spike shrugged. "But she didn't fancy Angelus, and he, being the bigger and badder of the two, made quick work of her."

"Boy, you guys are really something," Buffy said.

"You don't know the half of it, pet," Spike replied almost cordially. "Oh, and P.S., he's also the one who killed your little friend there. Not that I mind taking credit for a good kill, but that was Angelus's doing."

The nonchalance with which Spike tossed this out galled Buffy. After Todd's confession, she wouldn't have put good money on him surviving the week. Whoever had hired him to kill the Slayer must have been playing in the big leagues of evil. The fact that Angel had gotten to him first was really just a matter of being in the right place at the right time. She couldn't help but wonder, however, why he hadn't made more of a show of it for her benefit.

Maybe he knew the truth about Todd before I did and he was just clearing his own way, she decided.

Either way, this was no time to get too wound up in the mystery. She was, after all, still facing the only vampire she'd ever confronted who had actually killed a Slayer. Two, if memory served.

"So what's your story?" Buffy asked. "You just out for a walk?"

"Honestly, I've been thinking," Spike surprised her by saying.

"Not your strong suit, Spike," Buffy replied.

"Hear me out," he said. "I know you want to off Angelus, but up until now, you've played right into his hands. You want to beat him, you have to stop playing defense. Take the bloody fight to him."

"And you're telling me this why?" Buffy asked.

"I don't know. I'm a puzzle, aren't I?" Then Spike almost smiled, shook his head, and took off running down the street.

Buffy found herself strangely reluctant to follow, so stunned was she by both the message and the messenger. It only took her a moment to come to a shocking revelation.

He's right.

She hated to admit it, but he was. For weeks she and

Giles and the rest of her friends had driven themselves crazy researching Angelus's past and trying to foresee his next move. She knew their final confrontation was just around the corner, and she'd busied herself preparing to face him whenever and however he eventually chose to come after her. In fact, the only one of them who had taken any kind of offensive action against Angel had been Giles, and only when he was in a blind rage over the death of Jenny Calendar. Though Buffy had chastised Giles for rushing in, he had succeeded in destroying the factory that Angel, Dru, and Spike had called home. Only Giles had scored anything resembling a point in their favor recently.

So what the hell was she waiting for?

The deaths of Callie and Todd would trouble Buffy's dreams in the coming days. But infinitely more troubling would be Spike's advice. It would force her to ask again and again the question she'd been avoiding and to see clearly the answer she'd only thought she had come to accept.

Buffy had been waiting. Subconsciously. Unintentionally. Whatever. She'd been biding her time, telling herself that she was preparing for the coming battle, but in reality, she had been waiting for some kind of miracle that would make the nightmare end and bring Angel back to her.

But Angel wasn't coming back. The time for hopes and dreams had passed.

Buffy now knew what she had to do.

She would only lose sleep now wondering why Spike had been the one to make her see it.

CHAPTER FOURTEEN

Monday morning, about half an hour before class was to begin, Buffy and Willow were on their way to the library to check in with Giles. Everyone including the Slayer had done much catching up on lost sleep over the weekend and as best Buffy could tell, things were back to as normal as they ever got on the Hellmouth.

"I'm really sorry to hear about Todd," Willow said once she'd gotten the whole sordid story from Buffy.

"Which part?" Buffy asked.

"I guess the 'he was really trying to kill you' part," Willow decided, "though I'm also not happy that Angel killed him." After a moment, she added, "You don't think Angel . . . you know . . ."

"Turned him?" Buffy finished the sentence for her. "The funeral was yesterday," Buffy replied. "I didn't attend, but I did spend some time there last night making sure Todd wasn't just *mostly* dead."

"Well, that was almost thoughtful of Angel," Willow suggested.

"No brownie points on this one, Will," Buffy said decisively. "Angel is evil. And he's going to go the way of all evil that is unfortunate enough to cross the Sunnydale city line."

"What did your mom say about Todd?" Willow asked, as much to derail the Angel conversation as anything.

"I told her he wouldn't be coming back. She wasn't pleased about it until I told her it was because he'd developed sort of a crush on me and I didn't think that was appropriate in a student-tutor relationship," Buffy replied.

"Well, it was sort of true," Willow said.

"It was as much of the truth as she needs to know," Buffy agreed. "I think she was actually a little impressed that I showed so much emotional maturity, given the circumstances. She said that as long as my grades stay up through finals, she won't insist on hiring another tutor anytime soon."

Willow paused thoughtfully. "You know you've got a great mom, don't you?"

"I do." Buffy nodded.

"Come to think of it, I wouldn't mind trading," Willow added.

"Is Mrs. Rosenberg still restriction-happy?" Buffy asked.

"She's mellowed a bit. No more afternoon curfew. But

she's still looking into that kibbutz," Willow said with disappointment.

"Don't worry," Buffy said reassuringly. "There's always a chance the world will end before you have to go."

"Very true." Willow nodded. "Or maybe she'll just conveniently forget. It wouldn't be the first time."

"Good morning, Buffy, Willow," Giles said cheerfully as they entered the library. Xander and Cordelia were there as well, seated side by side on top of the main table, clearly awaiting the arrival of the Slayer.

"So, Buffy," Xander said enthusiastically, "you saved the world . . . again. What are you going to do now?"

"I'm going to see how I did on my latest chem quiz, and turn in a truly spectacular essay on Victorian poetry," Buffy replied without missing a beat.

"I must say, Buffy, you really did a wonderful job this past week," Giles said.

"Thanks," Buffy replied. "A few more like this and I should make employee of the month in no time."

"Yes, we'll see about getting you a plaque," Giles joked.

"Or a good set of steak knives," Xander suggested. "Or maybe just a really good set of stakes. You know, not the everyday stakes, but the kind you only bring out on special occasions."

As everyone had spent their waking weekend hours trading telephone accounts of Buffy's adventures with the principal as well as the secret agenda of her tutor, there was little else to discuss at this point, and the group seemed pleased to default to attempts at witty banter.

"I do have a question for you, Buffy," Giles interjected.

"Shoot, Coach."

Giles accepted her retort as gracefully as possible before asking, "Did you happen to know a freshman by the name of Joshua Grodin?"

Buffy thought before replying. "Doesn't ring any bells."

"I have him in my fourth-period computer lab," Willow offered. "Why?"

"He's dead," Giles said seriously.

"Oh no." Willow sighed. "He was a really good student. Kind of quiet. I think his mom died last year."

"Yes, well, his body and that of his father were found dismembered in their basement last week. Apparently the neighbors started to complain about the smell. The police contacted me because they found this book among his things," Giles went on, passing the old, leather-bound tome to Buffy for her perusal.

"*Raising Demons?*" Buffy asked as she read the title.

"It's from my private collection," Giles said somberly.

"He keeps it right next to his first edition of *Demon Recipes: One Hundred Ways to Eat Entrails*," Xander offered.

"Did Joshua steal it?" Buffy asked Giles.

"He must have." Giles nodded. "And he appears to have paid quite a high price for it."

"So that's how Paulina got into Sunnydale?" Willow asked.

"It's hard to know for sure," Giles replied. "None of the

spells in the book relate specifically to her, but she was a relatively new demon and might have been able to answer Joshua's call. At any rate, it's highly likely that the two events were connected."

"Well, I think we can all learn a valuable lesson from this," Cordelia interjected.

"What's that?" Buffy asked.

"Raising demons is bad," she said, as if it weren't already obvious.

"And they say kids aren't learning anything in school these days," Xander quipped. "It's not all about test scores, you know."

Buffy wanted to let it go, but she had come to the library that morning with a purpose, and taking Giles aside, she asked quietly, "Have you had a chance to find out anything about the person or persons who might have hired Todd?"

Giles shook his head. "It's hardly the first assassination attempt, Buffy, nor is it likely to be the last. Though for a demon to hire a human, it's just . . ."

"What?" Buffy asked.

"Pedestrian," Giles replied. "Normally any self-respecting demon would look to the Order of Tiracca, or the Benevolent Brotherhood of Malpasa . . ."

"The Benevolent Brotherhood . . . isn't that kind of false advertising?"

"At any rate, Buffy, you must remain on guard," Giles warned her.

"I am. And I will. But I think we should talk more later about Angel."

"Why is that? You said yourself you don't think he was responsible for hiring Todd."

"I think we might want to consider some new tactics," Buffy countered. She hadn't gone into detail yet with Giles about her encounter with Spike, apart from reporting his news about Callie. But she hadn't been able to stop thinking about it either. "It might be time to start playing offense instead of defense," she added.

"It's definitely worth considering." Giles nodded. "See you after classes?"

"Where else would I be?" Buffy asked, then added, "Isn't that depressing?"

"Hey, Buffy," Xander interrupted from across the room, "tell me again about the toe."

"The toe?" Giles asked. "Do I want to know?"

"Xander, we've been over this," Willow said, obviously not warming to the topic.

"No, I mean, did it just disappear, or was there actual ripping involved?" Xander wanted to know.

"There was ripping." Buffy nodded. "And then there was lots of blood."

"It *is* actually kind of fascinating that Principal Snyder regrew that toe every night when he entered the demon dimension," Willow said.

"Paulina said she wanted her son back just the way he was

when he was a little boy," Buffy reminded them. "I guess that included toes."

"I wonder what's worse," Willow said, "losing that toe every morning when he left the gateway, or living with the idea that he sold it in the first place to get rid of his mother?"

"Personally, I want to know who in the demon world is so toe-happy that they'd accept Snyder's littlest piggie as payment in full for turning someone into a demon," Xander added.

"Did anyone see the game this weekend?" Cordelia interrupted, apropos of nothing.

"What game?" Xander asked.

"I don't know. It was the weekend. Somebody must have played somebody else at something. I'm just done with all this talk about ripping and toes," Cordelia replied.

Xander jumped off the table and helped Cordelia to her feet as well. "And that's our cue, ladies and gentleman. Time for another fun-filled day at Sunnydale High."

"See you guys at lunch?" Buffy asked as they made their way into the hall.

"Absolutely," Xander replied. "Fish sticks all around, on me."

Willow and Buffy exchanged a smile at Xander's generosity as they passed the principal's office and the group went their separate ways toward their respective classes. Though Snyder's office was unoccupied, Buffy did pause long enough to note through the office door window that the spelling bee trophy that had been retrieved from Paulina's home now sat on one corner of Snyder's bookshelf. It wasn't exactly a place of honor reminiscent of the dresser top, but it would also never be out of Snyder's eye line when he was seated at his desk, Buffy realized, surprised by the twinge of sadness that welled up inside her at the sight.

In all of the telling and retelling of the story of her encounter to her friends and her Watcher, Buffy had found herself leaving out the details about the spelling bee and the trophy. She didn't know why. It wasn't embarrassing for her in any way. She just felt strange about it. It was like seeing somebody's report card or test score by mistake. Snyder and his love for that trophy, despite the tactics he had used in order to acquire it, was somehow too private for casual conversation. It was like she'd seen him naked, and that was a memory she was determined to bury as soon as humanly possible.

Still, as she passed him a few doors down in the hall berating a freshman girl publicly for the length of her miniskirt and the height of her shoe heels, Buffy found the unpleasant memory easier to bear.

It takes a monster to make a monster, Buffy thought as she passed him, pleased that he hadn't even bothered to glance in her direction.

"Isn't that right, Cecil," she said just soft enough that he might not have heard it.

Buffy would never know if he had, but she would often wonder. The moment the words left her mouth, Snyder stopped his harangue in midsentence, looked quickly around the hall, and, with a huff, hurried back toward his office.

Buffy smiled to herself as she saw the immediate relief on the young student's face at her sudden reprieve. Being the Slayer was a huge responsibility. But from time to time, it also came with unexpected rewards.

EPILOGUE

Monday was Mayor Richard Wilkins's favorite day of the week. And Monday morning was the best time of his favorite day. The offices of city hall positively buzzed with activity and energy. His staff reported for work, well rested from their weekend, optimistic and ready to face the week's challenges. It was truly the time when all seemed most possible.

This particular Monday was especially gratifying, as many of his staff members had been out of the office sick toward the end of the previous week. The Mayor himself had only worked a half day on Thursday before heading home with what felt like a bad case of the flu and remaining in bed until Saturday morning. But the Mayor was pleased to see that everyone was attacking their work on this beautiful Monday morning with both gusto and verve.

There was a knock on his office door so slight that he almost missed it what with closing and refolding the comics section of the morning newspaper.

That Allan, always so cautious, the Mayor thought to himself. He had often wondered whether or not that was really a good thing. Deference and respect were important. But so was confidence. He made a mental note to recommend Allan for an upcoming Dale Carnegie Leadership Seminar. It would do the young man good.

"Come in," Mayor Wilkins said pleasantly. Allan entered the office carrying a number of file folders, undoubtedly for the Mayor's review. He looked as if whatever he had eaten for breakfast that morning had not agreed with him.

"Good morning, sir," Allan said quietly. It was like he knew he had to say it but at the same time wished he could express the sentiment and not be in the same room with his boss.

"Good morning," the Mayor replied with a smile. "I'm no psychic, Allan, but I don't think I need to be one to see those dark stormclouds hanging over your head this morning."

The Mayor rose from the chair behind his desk and caught the brief flinch Allan made before retreating as casually as he could back toward the office door, still clutching his file folders.

Undeterred, the Mayor continued the short walk around to the front of his desk, where he then perched himself and crossed his arms.

"I know. It's no fun taking your medicine, but best to just swallow it down and move on. What's the bad news, Allan?" he asked evenly. "What could possibly spoil such a beautiful spring day?"

Allan swallowed hard. "Sir, it's Todd Harter."

The Mayor's eyes darted to Allan's. He held his assistant's gaze for a moment, just long enough to be certain that the rest of that sentence was not going to have a happy ending.

"Go on," the Mayor said gamely.

"He . . . he . . . he's dead, sir," Allan finally finished. The Mayor sat for a moment as Allan studied his face, no doubt anticipating the disappointment with which the Mayor would greet this news.

The Mayor rose from his desk, paced a few times to and fro before it, then paused to say, "Well, that's a darn shame."

Allan's relief was so obvious, the Mayor almost thought he might burst into song right then and there.

Come to think of it, there are ways to make that happen, the Mayor mused. *Could be fun for a while.*

"Cause of death?" the Mayor asked, getting back on track.

"Um, severe"—Allan paused, searching for the right word—"anemia," he replied.

"I see," the Mayor said sadly, then added, "He was such a bright young man, and with a promising future ahead of him."

"I have assembled a list of other potential candidates for the position, sir," Allan added quickly. He then approached the Mayor, holding out his precious file folders.

The Mayor nodded appreciatively. "Leave them on the desk. I'll review them later this afternoon," he said. He was pleased to note that Allan had labeled the folders "Candidate 1," "Candidate 2," etc., rather than "Potential Slayer Assassins," and for that he was grateful. Discretion was a difficult quality to come by in assistants at Allan's level, and the young man was proving that he possessed that in abundance.

"Anything else?" the Mayor asked as Allan turned toward the door.

"Not at the moment, sir," Allan replied.

"Very good."

Allan had almost made it out when the Mayor added, "Oh, Allan?"

The young man turned back, as if he knew he had escaped too easily. "Yes, sir?"

"Did I hear that one of our local vampires decided to turn a child last week?"

"Uh, I believe so, yes." Allan nodded.

"Am I wrong, or is that just not done?" the Mayor asked.

"It is . . . unusual, sir," Allan replied, choosing his words extremely carefully.

"Check into it for me, will you?" the Mayor asked pleasantly. "Can't have the demon population running completely amok on my watch, can we?"

"No, sir."

"Excellent." The Mayor nodded. "Carry on."

"Thank you, sir," Allan said, then hurried from the office, closing the door quietly behind him.

Once he was alone again, the Mayor stood for a moment before his desk, considering the file folders. Though he was certain that Allan had assembled a strong list for him, he doubted that the right person combined with the right opportunity was anywhere among them. Slayers were both a blessing and a curse, in the Mayor's experience. On the one hand, they did keep the vampire population under something resembling control. That was good for the city and, therefore, good for city hall. On the other hand, they were a powerful force for good. The Mayor didn't mind that, in theory. But as he had carefully laid out his time line for the next twelve months, it had occurred to him that things would be considerably less complicated for him if Sunnydale's Slayer were to meet her end well before next May, and the next Slayer to be activated come from a place very far from Southern California.

It was a nice thought. Long-range strategic planning was one of the Mayor's strong suits, after all. But it was doubtful that he was going to find another human being with Todd's advantages, the ability to get close to the Slayer for a plausible reason and then betray her when she was at her weakest. If memory served, the Slayer's eighteenth birthday would be coming up in a few months and her Cruciamentum, her rite of passage trial of strength, might provide another such opportunity, but whatever the Mayor chose to do, he would have to play it very carefully. Above all, he must remain as far from suspicion as it was possible to get until the last hundred days before his Ascension.

And who knew? Maybe Buffy Summers would find a way to get herself killed well before then with or without his interference. Slayers weren't known for their longevity. It was an unfortunate occupational hazard. At least the second Slayer, Kendra, who had only come to the Mayor's attention a few weeks earlier, lived very far from Sunnydale. With a little luck, they might never cross paths.

Despite Allan's efforts, the Mayor decided that the files he'd brought him that morning were best kept out of sight. He collected them and crossed to the wall opposite his desk, which was hung with some of the many commendations and certificates he'd received over his many years of public service in Sunnydale. Reaching for a recessed button in the wall, he opened a hidden compartment that displayed memorabilia and commendations of a very different order, though also a memorial of sorts to the many services he had provided to the city in his several hundred years as a resident.

A number of personal files were kept in this cabinet, along with an impressive display of ceremonial swords, daggers, a few potions too dangerous to leave out, and the odd ancient artifact. One such artifact caught his attention as he placed the file folders in a secret drawer: a shrunken head, a power source for the demon Vrachtung, which was adorned with a necklace of human toes. Vrachtung was one of the Mayor's oldest acquaintances, and a heck of a card player.

The Mayor took a moment to look closely at the string of toes and decided that his eyes were not playing tricks on him. The fourth toe from the right end, a toe that hung just below Vrachtung's tiny Adam's apple, had withered and blackened sometime in the last few days.

Who was that?

The Mayor searched his mind and finally found the memory he was seeking.

"Polly Snyder," he said softly to himself.

Such a nice lady. And a promising demon. I wonder what happened to her.

The Mayor considered contacting Vrachtung to find out, but decided it could keep until the next biannual conclave. The withered toe told him that poor Polly was no longer living, dead, or undead. In time, that toe would fall from Vrachtung's necklace and disappear completely.

Poor dear, the Mayor thought. *I wonder if Cecil knows?*

Though Cecil Snyder had first placed himself in the Mayor's power years earlier with this initial transaction, he had proved over the years to be a faithful lackey. The Mayor no longer worried that his only hold over Snyder had been the knowledge of that old contract. Once he'd pulled the strings necessary to get him appointed as principal of Sunnydale High, he knew that Snyder would always be his to command.

The Mayor made a quick mental note to send a brief condolence card to Cecil, then closed his secret cabinet and returned to his desk.

He had a very busy year ahead of him.

BLOODED

TO TOM.
I'M SORRY THERE ARE NO MONKEYS.
—C. G.

TO THE MEMORY OF MY FATHER,
KENNETH PAUL JONES, AND THE HAPPY
MEMORIES OF OUR YEARS IN JAPAN.
—N. H.

The authors would like to thank: our agents, Lori Perkins and Howard Morhaim, and Howard's assistant, Lindsay Sagnette; also, our editor at Archway/Minstrel, Lisa Clancy, and her assistant, Elizabeth Shiflett. Our gratitude to Caroline Kallas, Joss Whedon, and the entire cast and crew of *Buffy*. Thanks to our patient and supportive spouses, Connie and Wayne, and to our children, Nicholas and Daniel Golden, and Belle Holder, who remind us daily what it's all about.

PROLOGUE

The front row of the old Majestic Theatre was filled with corpses. Glassy-eyed, their throats ripped out, the dead had the best seats in the house.

But the final curtain had yet to fall, and as far as Buffy Summers was concerned, until it did, there was no telling how the show would end.

Time for a little improv, she thought.

She'd have been way more confident about the whole scene if not for the fact that she was without a clue as to what the hairy, loudmouthed, badly-in-need-of-Weight-Watchers vampire—who called himself King Lear, of all things—had done with Xander and Cordelia.

A single spotlight shone down from the balcony on the heavy red velvet curtain that hung across the stage. The Majestic was ancient, but still beautiful despite its state of disrepair. Kind of like Mrs. Paolillo, who had subbed as Buffy's English teacher for three days the week before. Dust spun in the beam of the spot, and the rest of the theater was dark.

Amazingly, the Majestic had existed as a venue for musicals and stage plays until two or three years earlier and had never been transformed into a movie theater.

"I . . . well, I do suppose you realize that this is a trap?" Giles whispered behind her.

Buffy rolled her eyes. "Come on, Giles, give me some credit," she said, sighing. "I may not like being the Chosen One, but I've been Little Miss Vampire Slayer long enough to know when I'm being set up."

"Yes, um, quite right then," Giles mumbled. "It's only that . . ."

"Only that there are four majorly ravenous bloodsuckers in the balcony above our heads?" Buffy whispered.

"That would be it, yes," Giles replied. "Remind me again why I persist in joining you on these excursions. You do seem fully capable of handling them on your own."

Buffy reached into her Slayer's bag and handed Giles a large wooden crucifix and a long, tapered stake.

"One hundred people surveyed, top five answers on the board," Buffy quipped. "Number one answer: Giles has no social life!"

Despite the tension that filled the darkened aisles of the theater, Buffy had a half smile on her face as she turned to look at Giles. He sputtered, cocking his head the way he did when he wanted to look as though he were majorly offended. Rupert Giles was her mentor. As her Watcher, he was responsible for the Slayer's training and general well-being. As her friend, he had to put up with all kinds of teasing. Starting with the fact that he was Sunnydale's high school librarian—so totally the honey-magnet occupation of all time—as well as a bit of a stiff.

But Giles was her uptight Englishman, and Buffy wasn't about to let anything happen to him. Which meant that in about two seconds she was going to have to knock him on his woolen-clad behind yet again.

"Giles, down!" Buffy snapped.

Her smile disappeared as the Slayer went into action. She was all business as she stepped forward, bumped Giles with a hip to send him stumbling into a row of wood-and-metal folding seats, and held a sharpened stake above her head.

It was rainin' vampires.

The first one came down on her stake. He weighed close to two hundred pounds, and she started to buckle under his falling corpse. She'd planned to fall, roll, spring up again. But she didn't need to bother. The second the stake pierced his heart, the vamp exploded in a shower of ashes. Two others came down at the same time, and one of them tagged her arm, grabbing the fabric of her blouse as he landed. A button popped at her neck and her sleeve tore.

"Ooh!" she grunted. "You are not my friend."

Buffy launched a kick at the vampire's jaw that snapped its head back hard. She followed with a roundhouse kick at its solar plexus. The other one came at her from the side, and she ducked and used the vamp's own momentum to send him flying into the seats. The one who had ripped her blouse came after her again, snarling.

Buffy snarled back. She blocked his attack and drove the stake up through the vampire's ribs and into its heart.

"That was silk," she snapped, and turned her back on him even before he turned to dust.

A few rows up the aisle, Giles cracked his heavy cross across the head of the vampire Buffy had thrown into the seats. As she watched, her mentor staked the vamp in fine style for a guy who was fortysomething going on seventysomething and, well, not the Slayer. Still, Giles knew his stuff. Knew enough to teach Buffy more than the average red-blooded American high school girl ever needed to know about fighting vampires, demons, and the forces of darkness.

But, hey, who wanted to be average, anyway?

Well, actually, Buffy did. But they'd been over that so many times.

"You seem a bit rusty, Buffy," Giles said, straightening his tie. "Which leads me to wonder if I've been too lenient of late."

"Am I the only one who's noticed you're still breathing?" Buffy asked.

"Hmm?" Giles said, focusing on Buffy again. He did have a tendency to get distracted. "Of course not. And I do thank you for that, very much indeed. It's simply that I'm concerned that against a more powerful vampire, your technique might require—"

"Giles," Buffy said.

He prattled on. "—a bit more of a—"

"Giles!" Buffy shouted.

She ran for him, but too late. Another vampire had leaped out from the balcony above them and fallen on him. Buffy felt her adrenaline surge as she considered the horrible idea that something awful might actually happen to somebody close to her. It had happened before.

Fortunately, Giles was quicker on the uptake than his absentmindedness seemed to indicate. He fell under the weight of the vampire, but even as Buffy reached for the bloodsucker, the vampire did that extremely rewarding dust-detonation thing. Giles had managed to turn the broken end of his large wooden crucifix up, and the vampire had impaled himself on it.

"You did remember that I said there were four of them up there, didn't you?" Buffy asked as she helped Giles to his feet.

"Hmm? Oh, yes," Giles replied as he wiped the dead-again ash from his glasses. "Just a bit distracted is all."

"Maybe you should work on your technique," Buffy said.

"Yes, well, you do have a point," he conceded. "But perhaps we should concentrate on finding Xander and Cordelia before this Lear fellow decides they've outlived their useful-ness as bait," Giles replied.

Buffy grimaced, eyebrows knitted. She was plenty focused; nothing was more important than getting Xander and Cordy out of there safely. That's why she and Giles had split up from Willow and Angel to begin with. But she was nervous and angry, and sarcasm helped her with both feelings.

"Haven't you ever heard of whistling in the dark?" she asked.

With a sudden, metallic whoosh, the curtains began to draw open. Buffy and Giles moved quickly down the aisle toward the stage. The Slayer was careful not to pay too much attention to the not-so-grateful dead in the first row, right in front of the orchestra pit. She'd seen more corpses than a serial killer, but it never got any easier.

"Why am I always the life of the party?" she whispered to herself, and grimaced at her silent answer. *Because I'm always the only one still alive!*

There was a second curtain at the back of the stage. Buffy figured the layout of the Majestic was a lot more complicated than the auditorium at Sunnydale High, where they'd held their talentless show. But even that stage had four or five cur-tains. It looked like they were going to have to go onstage, maybe take the spotlight, even, if they wanted to find out what Lear had done with Xander and Cordelia.

On the other hand, it wasn't as if the huge bad dude didn't know they were there. Which gave her an idea.

"What are you waiting for, Lear?" she shouted. "The audience is here!"

Giles stared at her like she was, well, her, and Buffy had to admit that though she enjoyed taunting pompous vampires who looked like Santa's evil twin, doing so when said obese, bloodsucking actor-guy was holding some of your friends hostage was generally a not so specially good idea. But she'd figured with an ego like Lear's . . .

"'Attend the Lords of France and Burgundy!'" came the deep bass voice of Lear. The vampire strutted onto the stage in full Shakespearean costume.

Buffy might have laughed if not for the lives that hung in the balance. Instead, she looked at Giles for some kind of understanding. After all, the only Shakespeare she knew was that rock-and-roll Romeo flick with Leo and Claire Danes. Well, that, and the one Mel Gibson did. Her mom had insisted on renting that one. Not bad. "Lear's first line in *King Lear*," Giles whispered to her.

Buffy watched Giles for a moment as he muttered to himself as though he were trying to remember song lyrics. On the stage, Lear walked into the spotlight, staring out at the "audience" but not even glancing down at Buffy and Giles.

"'I shall, my liege!'" Giles shouted suddenly, making Buffy jump. Onstage, Lear smiled.

"'Meantime'"—Lear smiled smugly, so pleased with himself he was practically drooling—"we shall express our darker purpose.'"

At that cue, the second curtain began to draw apart behind the corpulent vampire, and Buffy couldn't stop the gasp that escaped her lips as she saw Xander and Cordy. They were both gagged, and locked into a wooden contraption that snapped down over their wrists and necks, leaving them completely helpless. Maybe it had been a stage prop, once upon a time. But right now, it was all too real.

The worst part was, they were awake. Buffy could see their eyes, and though both of them had seen a lot since the Slayer had come into their lives, she could tell that they were terrified.

"Oh, my," Giles murmured.

"'Is man no more than this? Consider him well,'" Lear roared madly.

A chill ran through Buffy. She'd thought Lear was just a cruel moron. But that was wishful thinking. The only thing worse, in her opinion, than a fat, slobbering, undead, blood-sucking show-off was one who was also completely out of his head, a few bricks shy of a mausoleum.

She saw rustling behind Xander and Cordelia, where the backstage curtains hung. There were other vampires there, she knew—others who followed Lear. But she didn't know how many.

A quick glance at Xander's face, at the fear in Cordelia's eyes, and Buffy realized it didn't matter how many. But what could she do? How could she get to Lear before he could get to the rack Xander and Cordy were trapped in?

Suddenly, Giles began to applaud.

• • •

Willow followed Angel up the stairs that led to stage left. They had discovered a tunnel that ran under the stage from one side to another, which would allow actors to move from side to side without disturbing the stage crew. She'd been certain they'd find some vampires in it, but, so sad, no joy.

Not that there was any shortage of vampires. From stage right they'd seen at least six of them, lurking behind various curtains and offstage in the wings, working pulleys to open curtains and move props.

Willow shivered. She hated vampires. Well, present company excluded, of course, despite the fact that Angel had tried to kill her once. Well, tried to kill them all. But that hadn't really been Angel, that . . . made her head hurt to think about.

Angel glanced back at her as if he could read her mind, and she offered him a helpless, why-me smile. Frankly, she didn't know why he'd agreed to let her tag along. She didn't have a clue why Buffy even wanted her around when it came to stuff like this. Giles knew his stuff, and he was the Watcher, after all. Xander at least could fight. Angel was Buffy's boyfriend, and there was that whole thing about him being a vampire—but the only good vampire they'd ever heard of.

Not to say Willow hadn't held her own before, for at least seven or eight seconds. She had. And she wanted to be there, in a kind of Three Musketeers solidarity thing kind of way.

But once the research was done, she'd already served her purpose in the little cadre of Friends of Buffy that Xander affectionately referred to as the Scooby Gang.

Willow, sad as she was to admit it, was Velma. The brainy but relatively useless one. And she hated being Velma.

She sighed as she followed Angel into the rows of curtains that hung in the wings at stage left. Willow had a stake, but that was more for protection than offense.

There was a thump ahead of her, and the curtains swayed. Angel peered around them, his serious, soulful eyes—and wasn't that ironic, soulful?—making her feel a little safer. He motioned for her to follow.

Clawed hands grabbed him around the throat and drove him hard to the floor. The vampire on Angel's back was leaning forward, trying to rip out Angel's throat, when Willow moved in to stake it. She didn't see the willowy blond vamp girl coming at her until the last second, and then she got the stake up just in time to have it knocked from her hands. The vampire girl reached for Willow, but she ducked, pulling the curtains between herself and her attacker.

That bought her three whole seconds. Then the vampire girl was there again, smiling at her—until the one who'd attacked Angel body-slammed her to the ground. Only when Willow saw Angel going after them did she realize what had happened.

No second-string vampire was going to take Angel out of the game.

Willow shook herself. *Sports analogies,* she thought. *I must be in shock.*

Angel made short work of the two vampires. But there were at least two others, possibly three, making their way across the stage behind the backstage curtain. Onstage, things had gotten way tense. Buffy had to do something, or Lear was going to kill Xander and Cordelia.

Willow and Xander had been best friends since forever. She just couldn't let that happen. She looked down at a pile of old, dusty props. Flagpoles, broomsticks, wooden swords, chairs, a wooden cart . . . a three-foot metal crucifix.

With two quick strides, she bent to pick up a wooden sword and threw it to Angel.

"Help Buffy," she said.

Angel looked at her, frowned, glanced at the curtains moving as the vampires came across the stage—obviously too terrified of upsetting their master to disturb his performance— and then he ran out on the stage, holding the wooden sword in front of him as though he knew how to use it. Which, given the fact that he grew up in the eighteenth century, Willow figured he probably did.

Willow picked up the huge metal crucifix. She was Jewish, of course, but she figured that, hey, whatever worked. It was heavy, but the weight felt good in her hands. She tried to make herself feel tough, tried to look mean. Tried to be more like Buffy.

• • •

It all happened quickly for Buffy. One second, Giles was applauding, and Lear had a supremely pompous, pleased grin on his face. He was playing them like a total media harlot, and their job was to adore him. Giles's applause had him so slaphappy, Lear actually stepped forward and executed a deep bow.

Idiot.

Buffy took three strides, put her foot on the armrest of a front-row chair, and did an aerial somersault to land behind the obese vampire on the stage. She'd put herself between her friends and death.

That was where she belonged.

That was why she was the Slayer.

"No curtain call for you, Urkel," she sneered. "I may not know Shakespeare, but I'm pretty sure this is not his proudest moment."

Unfortunately, Lear was faster than he looked. He batted the stake from Buffy's hand, grabbed her by the throat, and lifted her high off the stage, fury burning in his eyes.

"Everybody's a critic," he growled.

Buffy grabbed his wrist and kicked him hard in the face, and Lear dropped her, howling in pain and humiliation. She scrambled to her feet, trying to stay between Xander and Cordelia and the raging vampire. Problem was, she had no stake.

"Buffy!"

Angel's voice. Behind her.

Lear dove for her, Buffy sidestepped, brought a knee up into his ample belly, and spun around behind him. She chanced a look up. Angel had smashed Xander and Cordelia free, and they were already moving to help Willow hold off the three other vamps who'd come from backstage. Then she saw what Angel held in his hands. A long wooden sword. He threw it to her just as Lear barreled at her again, all pretense at sanity gone. Buffy had to jump to grab the sword's hilt in the air. When she came down, she dropped to her knees and turned the point of the sword straight for Lear's oncoming girth.

The sword slid into him, and Lear staggered, a step forward, a step backward. She hadn't pierced his heart, at least not completely.

"Giles!" Buffy shouted. "Stake!"

"'Fortune, good night,'" Lear croaked. "'Smile once more. Turn thy wheel.'"

The vampire collapsed forward onto the stage, wrenching the sword upward in his chest. He burst into a huge cloud of ash, a spray of dust that flittered to the stage and then was still.

In the front row, Giles tsk-tsked. "King Lear," he said. "King of melodrama is more like it. Had to overplay it, right to the end."

"Oh, wonderful," Xander said with his usual sarcasm. "I hope I gave my performance just the right note of terror for you, Giles."

"Okay," Buffy interrupted. "Enough with the dramatic metaphors, now. It's getting a little tired."

"So am I," Willow agreed. "Good thing it's not a school night." Cordelia and Xander exchanged a glance.

"Think the Bronze is still open?" Cordelia asked.

"Perchance," Xander replied, feigning a bad Shakespearean accent. "Prithee escort me, thou fairest maiden."

"Whatever that means!" Cordelia snapped. She rolled her eyes and strutted up the aisle and out the door. Xander followed.

"You're welcome!" Buffy called.

"Come on," Angel said, sidling up next to her and putting his arm around her waist. "I'll walk you home. The streets of Sunnydale aren't safe after dark."

Twenty minutes later, Willow was almost home. Giles had offered her a ride, but she'd sort of half-lied and told him she had a way home. Which was true. Walking was a way.

She wanted to walk and think and come down off the adrenaline rush of playing Slayerette, which was, like, one of the Slayer's backup singers. Or whatever.

It was intense and cool and all of those things. It was also necessary. Since Willow knew that Sunnydale was built on top of the mouth of Hell—which made it kind of a hot spot for things that went bump in the night—she kind of felt like she had to do something about it. Like Spider-Man always said, "with great power comes great responsibility."

And Willow knew better than anyone that knowledge was power.

At the end of the day—or night, as it were—Willow didn't really mind being backup. She could sometimes be effective backup, like tonight. Which was fine. At least she wasn't the Slayer. Willow couldn't even imagine the pressure of being the Chosen One, whose job it was to save the world from the forces of darkness.

If the pressure of being the Slayer wasn't enough, there was that whole staying-alive thing, too. Trying not to get as dead as the guys you were killing. Who were already dead. Or undead. So staying alive was sort of important.

"I need sleep," Willow said to herself.

Which was when powerful hands grabbed her from behind and swung her sideways into the brick side of Mona Lisa's Pizza. With a gasp, she whirled around, facing her attackers. They were two guys, their faces shadowed. Both were tall and muscular, one in a jeans jacket, the other wearing a dark blue sweatshirt.

Attack, she told herself, but she just stared at them helplessly. She couldn't even make herself scream. She was frozen on the spot and she just stared at them.

With a low, mean laugh, the one in the jeans jacket took a step toward her. It was then that Willow collected her wits and started to run.

"Oh, no, you don't!" he said.

Thick arms trapped her and drove her to the pavement.

Willow's head hit the ground too hard, and her wrist was trapped beneath her.

She felt something in her wrist give way, just before the darkness claimed her.

CHAPTER ONE

Monday morning. The words alone were enough to send tremors of fear shuddering through even the most stalwart of students. And the adults thought they had it hard!

Still, despite the awful Mondayness of it all, it was a gorgeous morning. Birdsong filled the air. The scent of flowers floated in from a nearby garden. The sun shone brightly down, sparkling on the windows of Sunnydale High. It was almost enough to make you forget you lived on the Hellmouth.

Almost, but not quite.

Fortunately for them, most of Sunnydale High's students didn't know they lived on the Hellmouth. In blissful ignorance, they went on wasting their lives—a full-time job for a teenager, especially if you wanted to be really good at it. Kids were boarding down the sidewalks—which was illegal even if skateboarding had never been, was not now, and would never be a crime—and palavering about their weekends and their homework and doing all those fun teen-things that most high school students got to do on a much more regular basis than the Chosen One.

As for that Chosen One, Buffy was quaking with fear. A little. As much as the Slayer ever quaked. But it wasn't vampires or demons that had her sweating the day ahead. Uh-uh. This was *much* worse.

Math test. Today. No studying. Bad equation. And it wasn't like she could show up with a note from the vampire community. "Please excuse Buffy from her test today. She was busy out on Slayer patrol last night, keeping the world safe from dead folks." Yeah, that'd go over big.

No. She was doomed.

"And how would *you* like *your* stake?" she grumbled.

"Buffaleeta!" Xander cried, screaming up beside her on his board. He braked and hopped off, then brought his foot down onto the front and flipped it into his grasp in exactly the same way Buffy stomped crossbows into battle position. Despite her math tremors, Buffy grinned. Her buds had most definitely picked up a few tricks from watching her. Which was good, given the fact that being her friend put them in danger on a regular basis.

"Heya," she said. "Where's Willow?"

He inclined his head, arched an eyebrow. "Fine, and you?"

"My bad." She made a little I'm-sorry face. "It's just that you two usually show up on school days as a matched set."

"Joined at the hip, like Siamese twins. That's me and Will. Sadly, I had an errand to run this morning, thus causing my solo-ness."

"An errand?" she pressed, intrigued. Who did errands before sunrise? Besides vampire minions, that is? "Like what, Boy Wonder? You had to drop your bat cape off at the cleaners?"

"That would be my Robin cape." He looked at her sternly and wagged his finger at her. "Tsk-tsk, Slayer. How are you going to get invited to all the cool parties if you can't keep your pop culture minutiae straight?

"Actually," Xander drawled, "the blame for my lateness rests firmly on the shapely shoulders of the conniving Catwoman!"

"Not Catwoman?" Buffy gasped. "That cheap hussy!" She arched an eyebrow as he had done. "We done with the Batman shtick now?"

He pointed slightly to the left of the swarm, at that familiar figure with the trendoid clothes, accent on upscale, and every single brunette hair exactly where it had been ordered to be.

"And speaking of cheap hussies," he said, "there's mine."

Cordelia Chase turned, registered their approach, and launched herself in their direction. It was clear she had something that she considered important to discuss.

"Now my morning is complete," Buffy said, sighing. "A Xander spouting nonsense, a math test, and a chance to be insulted by the why-are-you-dating-her-again girl, all in one day. How can one simple girl have so much?"

As Cordelia drew near, Buffy saw the concern on the girl's face and rolled her eyes. "It's probably my fault that she broke a nail or something."

"It's just that crazy life you lead," Xander drawled.

"I need to talk to you guys!" Cordelia said hurriedly, glancing around, obviously hoping she wouldn't be spotted talking to them by any of her friends.

"Cordy," Xander greeted her brightly, "what's the haps? Crush any young male egos yet today?"

"No." She grimaced at him.

"Well, no need to fear, the day is young," he said cheerily.

Cordelia rolled her eyes. "Whatever." She turned to Buffy. "Listen, I just want to know if there are any bizarre events planned for next weekend—you know, like if it's Curse of the Rat-People Night or anything. I have plans next Saturday, and I do not want them ruined just because some monster who's been trying to kill the Slayer for a thousand million years decides that would be the perfect night to rise from its grave."

"Yeah, Buffy, break out your Calendar of Dreadful Events,

just make sure that night is clear for Ms. Chase, would you?" Xander snorted, and glanced at Cordelia. "Do you think Buffy plans these things?"

Cordelia squinted at Buffy with intense irritation. "You know, when you first came to Sunnydale, I tried to bring you into the elite circle. But no, you had to hang with the losers. Don't you ever wonder what might have been?"

It amazed Buffy that after all this time, Cordelia still had the ability to hurt her feelings. But she did have that power, and she also had the skill. Because yes, Buffy did wonder what it would have been like to be popular at her new school. She missed having lots of friends and getting invited to the good parties and all the same things she had started missing once she found out back in LA that she was the Slayer. It was an occupational hazard, and not one any seventeen-year-old girl would cheer about.

But she knew Cordelia was specifically referring to the fact that Buffy had dared to be nice to Willow when Cordelia had, frankly, treated her like dirt, publicly humiliating her and bullying her. By being friendly to Willow and asking her for homework help, Buffy had sealed her own fate as an outcast. As for that other "loser," Xander, he came with the package, since he and Willow had been best friends since preschool.

And if achieving popularity would have required dissing them in the least, then Buffy wasn't missing a thing.

"Is it me, or did someone erase your short-term memory?"

Buffy asked her. "Specifically, all that stuff about you dating one of those losers?"

"Hello!" Xander protested. "Isn't there a kinder word?"

Cordelia glared at him. "No."

"Once you regain your soul, you'll find you regret harsh words such as these," Xander shot at Cordelia.

Cordelia looked startled, and then she clenched her teeth and narrowed her eyes at Xander. "Ha-ha. You are so completely anti-hilarious."

"But I'm a great kisser," he said, raising his chin and smiling proudly.

After a moment's pause, Cordy smiled. "I'll let you know when you've hit 'great' status."

"And you'd know," Xander said pleasantly. "You've tried them all."

Cordelia huffed and stalked away.

"Oh great *sensei*, tell me how you did that," Buffy pleaded as they watched her disappear back into the throngs. "So I can do it too."

Xander made a show of stretching and putting his hands behind his head. "It's all in the timing, Ms. Summers. She lunges, you parry." He grinned. "And then you thrust."

"Do not even go there," Buffy said, and shook her head as they began walking again. "It's best I don't hear any more. I still don't understand what this thing is between the two of you. Somehow you get through the chinks in her armor."

"Or the cracks in her makeup. Did you notice that she had on just too much foundation? You're right; it does make her look like a cheap hussy. You should talk to her about it, Buffy."

She chuckled slyly. "Maybe. The right place, the right time . . ."

"She'd stew for at least two classes," he assured her. "Better yet, ask Giles to do it. She'll really go nuts."

Buffy smiled, but halfheartedly. She hadn't failed to notice that Xander had riffed on her own life while he was teasing Cordelia. His crack about Cordelia's regaining her soul had obviously been about Angel and the horrible guilt he had suffered after regaining his own soul.

Xander's wit could be just plain silly, but it could also be cutting at times. Especially with Angel. Of all of them, Xander reserved his hardest comments for Buffy's undead boyfriend. Actually had the guts to call him Dead Boy, even though Angel despised the name. In fact, Xander called him that specifically *because* Angel hated it so much. Xander was jealous of Angel, no question about it. But Buffy knew that when the mouth of Hell coughed up something nasty, Xander would risk his own life for any of them, including Angel, despite all they'd suffered at Angel's hands.

Buffy's wandering mind was halted when she spotted Willow sitting on the bench where the three of them often met.

"Well, if it isn't our willowy Willow," Buffy said, and pointed.

Willow was wearing a baggy coat thrown over her

shoulders and, as usual, she was bent over a book. She used to read science books, computer guides, that kind of thing. However, since meeting Buffy, her reading material tended toward dusty, heavy, leathery encyclopedia-sized doorstops about demons and monsters. Either that or she was surfing pagan websites. With the death of Jenny Calendar, Willow had struggled to do even more than her fair share. And her fair share was often a lot more than anybody else's.

It's too bad Willow isn't the Chosen One, Buffy thought; she did a heck of a lot more research on the wonderful world of slayage than the actual Slayer. Imagine, a girl who could kick monster butt while reciting all the legal vampire holidays from memory. Giles would love it.

Too bad nobody had a choice about who was the Slayer, who was the Watcher, or who chose the wardrobe for Seven of Nine on *Star Trek: Voyager.* Poor thing had to be in serious pain.

"Will, hey," Xander called, waving. "I called you yesterday for a 911 rescue attempt on my biology report, but you never picked up the pho . . ." Xander trailed off, and he touched Buffy's hand.

Buffy's lips parted. She rushed to Willow and dropped down beside her. "Willow, what happened?"

Willow's face was mottled and bruised. Her left cheek was crisscrossed with deep scratches.

And her left hand was in a cast.

Buffy's mind raced back to their night at the theater. Willow had been fine when they'd split up.

"Willow?" Xander sat on her other side. "God. Did you have an accident?"

Willow tried to smile, but it made her mouth hurt. She thought about trying to make a joke, but nothing about this was funny. So she told them the truth.

"I got mugged."

"By vampires?" Xander cried. He grabbed at Buffy's Slayer's bag. "Quick. Give me something sharp, Buff."

"Nothing supernatural," Willow assured them. "I was walking home alone."

"Didn't Giles give you a ride?" Buffy interrupted.

"Oh, well, I kind of wanted to be alone. I had some thinking to do," she added sadly.

"You could have been alone in your bedroom," Xander chided her. "And you can think there, too."

Willow swallowed hard. She didn't know why she was so embarrassed for them to see her injuries, but she was. Her first impulse after the attack had been to call them both, but something had made her put down the phone.

"Who was it?" Buffy demanded, her thinking apparently running along the same lines as Xander's: It was payback time.

"I don't know," she replied meekly, and half-protested as Xander closed her demonology book and set it on his own lap. "I was just walking along and these two guys—regular ones, I think, not vampires or demons—jumped me. They took my watch and twenty bucks."

She glanced at Xander and felt a rush of sadness. "I'm

sorry, Xander. It was the Tweety Bird one you gave me for my birthday."

"Darn. And that promo's over at Burger King."

Tentatively he examined her cheek, cupping her chin very gently. "Oh, Will . . . ," he began, and she could hear the frustration in his voice. Xander wanted to help, but it was too late for anyone to help.

"Did they break your wrist?" Buffy asked.

Willow shook her head. "It's a bad sprain. From when I fell weird." She realized she was near tears, and fought hard to hide them. "After all these times I've watched you practice falling with Giles, and seen you in action, you'd think I'd know how to do it."

"It's an acquired skill," Buffy said kindly.

"Take up skateboarding. You'll get lots of practice," Xander added, obviously trying to lighten the moment. But he wasn't smiling. His dark eyes were serious and his mouth was set and angry.

"Willow, why didn't you call us? Tell us?" Buffy asked.

Now Willow did smile. She was lucky to have such great friends. Although, of course, in Xander's case, she still wished he was more than a friend. But she'd been wishing for that longer than Buffy had been the Slayer. And, well, there was Oz now.

"It was . . . I don't know," she said. "I felt . . . like not talking."

"I understand," Buffy told her, and Willow figured she

did. After Buffy had been killed by the vampire known as the Master, she had bottled up her feelings for a long time. All her fear and frustration had poured out in a long crying session in Angel's arms.

"Listen, I hate to do this," Buffy said, grimacing, "but it's almost time for class, and I promised to check in with Giles before first period. Will, are you going to be okay?"

"Sure, Buffy," she said in a small voice. "Go on ahead."

Buffy looked unhappy about leaving Willow, which touched Willow deeply. She had never had a friend like Buffy. Buffy was brave, and strong, and no dumb mugger would ever take her down . . .

"Aw, c'mon, Rosenberg," Xander said as a tear trickled down her cheek. He pulled her against his chest, kissed her on the top of her head. "It's okay."

"No. It's not. Because this kind of stuff is going to keep happening to me," Willow said, letting the tears flow as Buffy disappeared into the building. "I'm useless, Xander. A liability. Half the time Buffy has to risk her life to save me, and—"

"—and the other half, she has to save me," Xander finished, trying to get her to meet his eyes.

Willow was miserable. For so long, she had wanted Xander to hold her, and now he was just being nice. Just pitying her. He would never pity Buffy.

"Maybe you should ask her for some fighting tips."

"Huh?" Willow sniffled. "I could never be like Buffy. I

see those vampire guys and I totally freak out. I hate being Velma."

"Come on!" Xander protested. "Velma's the coolest! The smart chick always saves the day—as long as she doesn't lose her glasses. Hey, look, at least you're not Daphne. Now, Daphne was useless."

"So who's Daphne?" Willow asked, allowing herself a small smile at Xander's waxing philosophical about *Scooby-Doo!*

"Please!" Xander snapped. "Cordy, of course. What, you thought *I* was Daphne? See, I figure Angel and Buffy are Shag and Scoob. Giles is Fred."

"So who are you?" Willow asked, shaking her head in confusion.

"Me?" Xander asked. Then his eyes dropped and a deep sadness came over his face. "I'm afraid I'm not even first-string, Will. To my everlasting shame, I'm . . ."

He took a deep breath.

"I'm Scrappy-Doo."

Willow started to smile, just a little, but it felt good. Then Xander stood, held up his right fist, and shouted, "Puppy Power!" and Willow laughed so hard that the pain of her injuries came back full force. A few more tears slipped down her cheek, from a combination of amusement and discomfort.

"Ah, Will . . . ," Xander murmured.

"Hey, hi," a voice said.

Hastily Willow dried her tears and looked up. It was her

boyfriend, Oz. His band, Dingoes Ate My Baby, played a lot down at the Bronze. He also happened to be a werewolf.

Willow saw the concern in Oz's eyes, and it cheered her up a bit.

"What happened to you?" he blurted.

"I fell," Willow said quickly, mentally begging Xander not to contradict her. She was embarrassed about not having been able to defend herself. Actually, not even trying to defend herself. But the Scooby Gang knew about that part. "I was doing a chore—a chore of housework—I was painting the house—which is a chore—and I fell off the ladder."

"Whoa. Bummer," Oz replied, nodding sagely. "Painting the house, though. That's impressive." He took her backpack from beside her feet. "C'mon. The bell's going to ring. I'll carry your stuff for you."

"Okay." A bit unsteady, she stood up. She looked uncertainly at Xander, who was smiling faintly like a big brother, nodding his approval. Even though she really liked Oz, part of her still wished Xander would get jealous. Maybe he even was jealous, in a way. But only because they were so close, Willow knew. Not because Xander felt anything . . . anything romantic for her. Not like he did for Buffy.

But Oz didn't lust after Buffy. Nope. He seemed to like Willow just fine. And he was pretty cute. . . .

The three of them entered the school and started down the hall.

• • •

"Oh my God, Willow, what happened?" Cordelia piped. She was flanked by two of her Cordette wannabes, who stood just so, smirked just so, and were just . . . not. It was kind of sad, really, to want to be someone else so badly, or so Xander thought. Of course, there had been many moments in his life when he had wanted to be someone else: someone suave, someone rich . . . someone with a car.

Also, someone Buffy would seriously adore. As long as he didn't have to be Angel. 'Cause, y'know, being dead had to kinda suck. No pun.

"Good morning, Mistress Cordelia," Xander intoned, extra politely, as if they had not spent an hour this morning being more than polite to each other. It was their shtick around the Cordettes, not being a cute couple, so that she wouldn't lose her hard-won status as a stuck-up snob.

He looked hard at Cordelia, trying to ESP her a message: *Don't you dare be mean to Willow.*

"Did you fall off your trike, or is this just some tiresome bid for sympathy?" Cordelia asked, gesturing to Willow's face and arm.

"Don't," Xander said, and Cordelia looked mildly shocked.

"Or were you trying to use a new mask, and . . ." She frowned at Xander. "What?"

"I know your species culls the weak and aged," Xander said, "but they obviously don't have any rules about the thick-as-a-brick. Willow's off-limits today, Brunhilde."

"Well, I was just, I . . ." Cordelia clamped her mouth shut.

"You were just on your way to the library with us," Xander said meaningfully, "to check the calendar for special gatherings of the crazed and possessed."

"Are you speaking English?" one of the Cordettes asked, sneering.

"It doesn't matter," Xander told her. "I'm talking Cordy's language. Am I not?"

Cordelia gave her hair a toss. Clearly, she had recovered from the momentary shock of someone pushing her off her venom-powered steamroller. "It doesn't matter. I don't have time for your weirdness. The buses are leaving for the museum in five minutes."

Xander thought a moment. "Oh, the field trip!" In all the worry over Willow, he had completely forgotten about their break for freedom. "What a sweet surprise on a Monday morning!"

"Especially for Buffy," Willow concurred, cheering a little. "If we pay extra specially close attention to the exhibits, so we're late getting back, then Miss Hannigan will have to postpone the math test."

"Oh, good heavens, I see what you mean," Giles said to Buffy as they approached Xander, Willow, and Cordelia. "Poor Willow."

"You were supposed to give her a ride home," Buffy snapped at him.

"Oh dear." He was stricken. Giles was good at big-time guilt. Maybe it was a British thing. "She was so insistent about other arrangements . . ."

"Being insistent never does *me* any good around you," Buffy huffed.

"So, Giles, Buffy. Field trip," Xander said as they approached.

"That's right!" Buffy clapped her hands. "I'm saved." She thought a minute. "Am I saved? How long is this field trip?"

"I think it will be long enough," Xander said with a wink.

"Yes. Quite. There will be a lot to see, from what I've read of the exhibit catalog," Giles said, and gestured for them to keep moving.

"You can buy the exhibits?" Cordelia asked.

"On your mark. Get set," Xander said.

"No. The catalog merely describes the exhibits. I've been anticipating this for months, actually. It's a traveling exhibition about the art and culture of ancient Japan." Giles smiled excitedly. "Such a rich and varied history."

"History." Buffy grimaced. "Oh, joy."

"I believe you'll find it a nice change of pace," Giles insisted. "For all of you."

"Yeah, uh-huh. Reading little plaques about a bunch of old stuff." Buffy yawned. "Wake me up when it's over."

"I just had a thought," Xander said. "Wait, where'd it . . . ah, there it is! Seems to me that a museum of that size would have a large number of closets."

"God, you never stop, do you?" Cordelia sighed.

"Me an' that bunny," Xander agreed.

They all started for the exit, where the bus was waiting.

"So," Cordelia said to Xander. "Lots of closets?"

CHAPTER TWO

The museum was one of the things Sunnydale's mayor always crowed about, one of the things he claimed made Sunnydale more than just another Southern California paradise.

However, none of the truly unique things about a town whose original Spanish settlers called Boca del Infierno—the Hellmouth—seemed to make it into the tourist brochures the Chamber of Commerce kept putting out.

Yet, somehow, even with a decent museum and a picturesque downtown that looked like something Spielberg stole from Frank Capra, tourists managed to bypass Sunnydale for the most part. *Lucky them,* Buffy thought. She and her mom hadn't just visited . . . they'd moved here!

The exception to the tourist rule seemed to be when an upscale exhibit came to the Sunnydale Museum of Art and Culture, or the Sunnydale Drama Society put on a decent play. There were art galleries—like her mother's—and an annual Renaissance Faire and a whole host of other things for aging baby boomers to do. But for teens, the ultimate consumers? Nada.

Or at least so close to nada that it didn't matter. The Bronze could get boring if you went there every night. At least, Buffy thought so. But when you'd lived in LA, it was hard to imagine having to cross into the next town just to go to a movie made this year. Sunnydale was no LA. It wasn't even LA's little sister.

As the bus pulled into the museum's parking lot, Buffy sighed and let her head rest against the window.

"Suddenly, I'd rather be slaying," she muttered to herself.

And that was saying something.

"Hey, hey!" Xander said. "What's this I see?"

Buffy glanced up at that familiar, goofy grin, and couldn't help but smile in return. Xander had turned around in his seat and was looking down on Buffy and Willow, waving a finger in their faces like a stern parent.

"I don't recall giving permission for glum faces today," Xander chided. "Okay, so the museum is not the coolest place to be visiting on a Monday morning. Okay, so on our last merry outing to these hallowed halls of pots and pans, we ran into a particularly attractive and exotic young lady who had a . . . all right, I confess, she had a thing for me." He smiled modestly and touched his chest. "And turned out to be an ancient Incan mummy, and sure, I was way too young for her," he added.

Xander tilted his head to one side and leaned over the back of his seat so his face was only a foot away from Willow and Buffy. His smile was manic, impossibly wide.

"But think of the hideous alternative to this trip." His eyes flicked toward Buffy. "Maaaaath teeeeest!" he moaned in a ghostly voice.

"Mr. Harris!" a voice snapped from the front of the bus. "Do you mind?"

"Ah," Xander sighed, an apologetic expression on his face. "The Professor has spoken. I must behave. Or die trying." He spun and sat down in his seat.

Buffy looked at Willow and grinned. "Mr. Harris!" she mimicked.

Willow covered her mouth to hide her smile. Buffy was relieved. Will had been on a major blues trip all morning. Not that she could be blamed. The extreme number of muggings in this burg was another aspect of Sunnydale that never got much press.

"Did a little research for ya last night," Willow said under her breath.

"The über-scholar," Buffy replied.

They were riffing on Mr. Morse, the teacher who'd yelled at Xander. Buffy's usual history teacher was out on medical leave. Nobody knew exactly what was wrong with her, but of course all the really good gossip ran toward the loony bin angle. For the past several weeks, they'd had to put up with Mr. Morse instead.

He was a little, bespectacled guy with a comb-over that did more to accent his increasing baldness than disguise it. Mr. Morse obviously thought that most of his students were morons, and didn't do much to hide his opinion. He began each history class session by plopping a huge stack of books on his desk and announcing, "I did a little research for ya last night" as if it had been a major favor and weren't they so totally fortunate to have him for a teacher.

Uh-huh.

On the other hand, Xander was right. The alternative to the museum caper was even nastier than said caper. Miss Hannigan might be nicer, but Buffy would take a Carnival Cruise with Mr. Morse if it meant missing a math test.

Okay, well, maybe not. But the museum wasn't half bad in comparison.

The bus screeched to a stop, and Buffy followed Willow as they filed off. She glanced up and saw Giles, who gave her the patented Giles earnest nod as he helped Morse shepherd the wayward students toward the museum's entrance. As Buffy and Willow passed, Giles put a protective hand on Willow's shoulder. Buffy felt a sudden rush of affection for the proper British librarian. For her Watcher.

Buffy rarely gave him credit for all he'd done for her. Mostly, in fact, she gave him grief. But Giles had taught her a great deal, enough to keep her alive—most nights. Buffy smiled at him. She wouldn't want anyone else in her corner when it came down to the last round.

She only wished it didn't come down to the last round quite so often.

"Y'know, this place is actually pretty cool," Buffy admitted, glancing around as they walked through the museum. She scanned the ancient artifacts and weaponry from cultures throughout history and across the world as they passed from one exhibit to the next. "I just don't know how they manage to get all this stuff. I mean, the zoo has a few hyenas, and one saggy old grizzly, and that's about it. But this place is almost as good as the one we used to go field-tripping to back in LA."

"Yeah," Xander agreed, "Sunnydale is just like LA. Without the celebrities, the movie studios, the chic eateries, the attitude, the incredibly gorgeous females . . ."

Willow and Buffy glared at him.

". . . who are so completely unreal. Plastic. Horrible creatures, really," he said quickly.

"Are you brain-dead, as if I have to ask?" Cordelia chimed in as she caught up with them. "LA rocks."

"Ah, speak of the mannequin, and she appears," Xander snapped.

Buffy shook her head. Ever since Xander and Cordy had started sneaking off to grope together in the shadows, she'd been expecting them to act all couply. But they were just as vicious with each other as ever. Maybe more so, at times. Ah, love.

"Actually," Willow said softly, "we're pretty fortunate to have such an excellent museum. This place is world-class. Sometimes we get exhibits on tour that don't even stop in LA."

"See, now that's what *I* don't get," Buffy replied. "I'm asking, why? What's so special about Sunnydale?"

"*You're* asking *us*?" Cordelia said, staring at her in disbelief.

"Definitely the nightlife," Xander volunteered.

Buffy just gave him the Jack Nicholson eyebrow, and he shot back with puppy-dog eyes and an I-can't-help-it shrug.

"Which nightlife are you talking about?" Willow asked, and glanced knowingly at Cordelia.

"Oh, please!" Cordy sneered. "Can't you people just cold shower for thirty seconds?"

"Yeah," Xander said, making a show of siding with Cordelia. "You people are so smut-oriented. *I* was referring to the ever-popular, much-anticipated Curse of the Rat-People Night. Wasn't that what you were referring to, Cor? The specialness of this very special little town?"

Cordelia seethed in silence.

"Seriously, Willow," Xander continued, "why does Sunnydale rate?"

"The best and most common of reasons," Willow replied. "Money. The museum's endowment is huge. Apparently, a lot of rich people come from Sunnydale, and even the ones who leave are generous enough."

"And no doubt sold their souls for those generous riches," Xander said. "Like those frat boys who almost fed Buffy and Cordelia to their worm-monster god-guy last year."

He smiled brightly at Buffy. "Just think, there are probably several more secret organizations you'll have to bust up to save all the town's virgins—and other people—from certain death."

"Let's hope not." Buffy sighed, then noticed that Cordelia's cheeks were turning pink.

"And we move on," Xander suggested.

They passed into the visiting exhibition hall, which was a labyrinth of rooms filled with art and artifacts from ancient Japan. Almost immediately, Buffy became fascinated, despite her earlier grumbling. The culture of ancient Japan was so different from Western culture of the period, and even more so from the Western world of modern times.

In the second room, they came upon Giles examining what appeared to be a tiny plastic garden.

"Ah, there you all are," he said, as though he'd been desperately searching for them. "Isn't this a marvelous exhibit?"

"Maybe not the word I would have picked, but it's pretty cool, yeah," Buffy admitted, joining him in craning over a miniature curved bridge and tiny evergreen trees. What is it?"

"Hmm?" Giles hmmed, then glanced back down at the

tiny garden. "Oh, right. Quite impressive, actually. It seems that Sunnydale was, at one time or another, the sister city of Kobe, Japan."

"Wait, isn't that where they had that big earthquake?" Xander asked.

"Indeed."

"Wow, that's a weird coincidence," Willow said. "I mean, with us having *our* earthquake and all."

"My thinking precisely. That parallel is what has captivated me," Giles explained, pushing up his glasses in his Giles-is-thinking way. "You see, I'm not entirely certain it was a coincidence."

"I don't get it. And I really don't get what this has to do with your big Chia Pet there," Buffy said, already glancing around at other exhibits in the room.

"This is a friendship garden," Giles said impatiently. "The people of Kobe planted and groomed a real Japanese garden here in Sunnydale, recreating one just like it in their city. Apparently, after the earthquake in Sunnydale, the garden was abandoned and all of its vegetation simply withered and died. Quite unnaturally, in fact. It seems that local authorities went so far as to bring in botanical specialists, but no one could explain it."

"So this happened right after the Hellmouth opened under Sunnydale," Xander said. "And your thinking is what, vegetarian vampires?"

"Well, it's merely conjecture, of course . . ."

"Giles, your conjecturing is a little like the oracle at Delphi. Spit it out," Buffy said.

They all stared at her.

"What?" Buffy asked. "Come on, Willow is my history tutor! I do know some things."

From across the room, a whiny voice said, "I heard that, Summers. Let's hope you know enough to pass this semester."

Buffy gave Mr. Morse a purposely fake smile and batted her eyelashes at him, hoping he got the sarcasm in her reaction and suddenly terrified that he'd miss it. Pip-squeak would probably think she was flirting with him.

She sighed and glanced at Giles. "You were saying?"

"Well, it does strike me as odd that the garden died in the wake of the earthquake, and that Sunnydale's sister city had an earthquake not long afterward."

"Wait, you think that the Hellmouth somehow caused an earthquake halfway around the world by, I don't know, infecting another city through some friendship garden?" Xander asked incredulously.

"Well," Giles said stodgily, "when you put it that way, it does sound a bit dodgy, but it does still seem an odd confluence of events, wouldn't you say?"

"Is this going to lead up to me having to kill something?" Buffy asked.

"No," Giles replied with an odd look. "I can't say as much." He murmured, "For certain."

Buffy grinned happily. "Then, oh yeah, Giles. Definitely

super-odd, the um, conflue-thing. Can we see what else is here now? Mr. Morse threatened to test us on this field trip, and I can't afford to miss a thing."

"By all means, do," Giles said, obviously a little disappointed that his theory hadn't interested them more. But he got over it quickly and was soon lost among the artifacts once more.

They'd lost Cordelia early on, but soon Buffy, Willow, and Xander also drifted apart, each gravitating toward different displays, different rooms in the maze of the exhibit. From time to time they'd cross paths and share information.

Xander quickly became interested in displays about samurai and the art depicting their legends. There were reproductions of traditional samurai garb and information about the privileged life they led.

"Man, these guys had it good," Xander said when they met up.

"Yeah, sweet life," Buffy replied. "Someone gave 'em trouble, they could just hack them to ribbons and nobody would ask a single question. I'm Kermit with envy."

Xander looked at her. "Buff, they were slaying humans, y'know. It wasn't the same thing."

She shook her head. "That's even more unfair. I'm always worried about getting in trouble, and I'm not even killing anyone who's still alive."

Cordelia appeared suddenly, spotted them, and came buzzing across the room.

"Okay," she said, "this is so completely disgusting. Did you know that married women in ancient Japan plucked their eyebrows, and I mean, all of them?"

Buffy and Xander stared at her.

"But wait," Cordelia said importantly. "There's more."

"Promise?" Xander asked.

Cordelia gave him a backhand to the shoulder and directed her attention at Buffy. "Okay, Summers, I know you're not exactly House of Style, but listen to this: They painted their faces white, and their teeth black!"

Buffy winced. "That really is disgusting."

Cordelia sniffed at Xander triumphantly.

"Y'know," he said, "I can see it now, Cordy. You on the runways of Paris, bringing back the fashions of ancient Japan. A whole new trend, and a devastating blow to toothpaste manufacturers everywhere."

She narrowed her eyes and drawled, "Why do I even bother with you?" As usual, Cordy left in a huff.

"What about you, Miss Summers?" Xander asked. "What's caught your particularly fanciful fancy?"

Buffy grinned shyly. "What do you think, Xander?"

Xander stroked his chin, pretending to consider. "The weapons, but of course."

"But of course," she replied.

Willow had kind of hoped Oz would be on the field trip, but after she'd wandered around for a while, she gave up hope of seeing him. She didn't really want to talk about what had happened to her, but that was one of the coolest things about Oz. He always seemed to know when to just be quiet.

Her friends had done their best to cheer her up, and it had worked a little. But not much more than a little. Willow was still at a loss to understand what exactly had happened to her, and why. But she understood how it had happened all too well. She only wished the others could understand too.

Xander had been her best friend almost her whole life, and he might be sympathetic, but he'd never really get it. After all, he was a guy. Sure, he wasn't Schwarzenegger, but he wasn't scrawny, either. He just wasn't as vulnerable; guys weren't.

And then there was Buffy—who could kick Xander's ass and not even be able to call it exercise. How could she ever possibly understand what it felt like to feel powerless?

"Hey, Will."

Willow turned and saw Buffy standing next to her. She hadn't even noticed, and it occurred to her again how cool it was to be the Slayer. The bad guys wouldn't even know Buffy was coming until she took them down.

"Hey," Willow said, and sighed.

"See anything interesting?" Buffy asked, too cheery.

"Well," Willow said, and realized that she had, indeed, seen something interesting. Something that would take her mind off what a weakling she was for an entire minute.

"Actually, yeah," she replied. "I really liked the display on Kabuki theater and Noh plays."

"Color me purple, but I didn't even notice them," Buffy admitted. "And you know they'll be on any test, them being so historical and all. Where are they?"

"Let me show you," Willow said.

They walked into the next room together, and Willow told her what she'd learned about the ancient forms of entertainment, and pointed out the masks that she thought were especially cool or nasty-looking.

"What about you?" Willow asked. "Did you see anything cool?"

Buffy's eyes brightened, and she dragged Willow back through the labyrinth and into a huge room filled with ancient Japanese weaponry.

"Yeah," Willow said, nodding. "I figured you'd like it in here."

"Some of these weapons aren't like anything I've ever seen," Buffy admitted. "And the way the Japanese made their swords, folding the metal over and over, hundreds of times. The craftsmanship was incredible."

Willow's eyes were drawn to one sword in particular. Hung on the wall, it was a huge, crudely fashioned thing that looked like it would be more use beating someone to death than running them through. It didn't have the elegance of the traditional Japanese warrior's set of gently curving long and short swords.

"What's that?" she asked, pointing to the huge blade.

"Isn't that amazing?" Buffy asked. "Nothing like a *katana* or *wakizashi*."

Willow smiled slightly and thought about how easy it was for Buffy to learn when she was interested in the subject. She stepped over to the huge sword and began to read aloud from the plaque affixed to the wall beneath it.

"'This form of sword, called a *ken*, is actually of Chinese origin, and was used in Japan in the eighth century, before the more familiar *daisho*, or sword pair, of the ancient Japanese warrior was developed. This example, recently discovered in the Chugoku mountain range, has proved to date back even further, and is one of a kind,'" Willow read, only half aloud. "Wow," she added.

"Read the rest," Buffy urged. "You'll love all the mythology stuff."

Willow did, but *silently* this time.

"'Upon the sword's discovery, locals began to claim it to be the *shin-ken*, or real sword, of the god Sanno, a Japanese mythological figure also known as the King of the Mountain, and usually considered to have made his home on Mount Hiei, near Kyoto and Kobe, Japan.

"'According to this legend, which some of the older farmers in the region believe to this day, the Mountain King was responsible for protecting Japan from invasion by foreign supernatural forces, an obvious reference to the tense relations between Japan and China at that time. This theory is supported by the myth surrounding Sanno's greatest battle, in which he apparently vanquished a Chinese vampire named Chirayoju, who had wanted to eat the Emperor of Japan, and thus destroy the nation. According to legend, neither Sanno nor Chirayoju survived the battle.'"

Willow was stunned. "So, wait, you think this Sanno guy was the Slayer?" she asked.

Buffy blinked. "No. Big male-type person with a huge sword who lived on top of a mountain and let the spookables come to him? It's only a legend, Will. I just thought it was kind of cool."

"Yeah," Willow agreed. She looked at the sword again. "It's different from other vampire legends we've heard about. Or, y'know, met."

But Willow was thinking that it was also interesting because of Sanno. Not the Slayer. Just a big guy with a big sword. Taking care of business. For a moment, she thought about what she could do if she worked out a little. Worked out, and maybe had a big sword, too.

"Y'know," she said idly, not really paying attention to what she was saying, "with all the tutoring I've helped you out with, I was thinking maybe you could tutor me a little."

"Huh?" Buffy said, confused. "What subject could I possibly tutor you in, Willow? You're our Brainy Smurf."

Willow reached out with her uninjured hand toward the sword, touched the cool surface of the metal. Cool, yes, but with some weird heat to it as well. Like it was burning inside.

"Self-defense," she whispered.

Buffy sort of smiled and frowned at the same time.

"You do pretty well, Will," she said.

Willow held up her injured hand, wrapped in its small cast. Her smile was pained.

"No," she replied. "I don't. I've been lucky up to now. I don't want to be a liability, Buffy. I don't want you to have to protect me all the time."

Buffy touched the cast on Willow's hand. "Will," she said, "it's not your fault those guys jumped you. And, trust me, there have been plenty of times when I would've been toast for sure if it hadn't been for you. So I'm better with pointy objects. So what?"

"I'd just feel better if I could defend myself," Willow said meekly, and turned to look at the huge blade on the wall again. "I'd love to be able to use something like this. Nobody would mess with me if I had a big sword in my hands."

"Especially if you were strong enough to lift it off the ground," Buffy said, trying gamely to lighten the moment, to cheer Willow up.

And failing.

Willow brushed her fingers over the blade and up to the cloth covering the hilt of the sword. Beneath the crisscross pattern was a trio of metal disks that looked like they were made of bronze or something similar. There was some kind of weird inscription on them, and Willow tried to get a better—

One of the disks fell out.

"Whoops," Willow said, trying to catch it.

A long drop to the floor, where it clanged like a fallen coin. Blushing, Willow bent to pick it up, and quickly tried to slide it back where it had come from. Her fingers found the blade instead.

"Will, I don't know if you should . . . ," Buffy started.

Too late.

Willow hissed and pulled her hand back. There was blood on the index finger. She'd somehow slipped and cut her finger. The sword was so sharp it had only stung, but the cut looked kind of deep.

"That's gotta hurt!" Xander said as he stepped up behind them.

Willow spun on him in alarm, as if he were going to attack her.

"Back off!" she snapped.

"Whoa," Xander said, eyes blinking his surprise. "What'd I do?"

Willow shook her head as she sucked at her cut finger, hoping she wouldn't need stitches.

"Nothing," she said. "Sorry, just edgy after Saturday, I guess. Let's get out of here."

"Sounds good," Buffy said happily. "I guess we've stayed long enough for me to miss my math test."

"Goody for you," Willow said crankily.

Buffy looked taken aback, but suddenly, Willow didn't much care. She didn't feel well and she just wanted to get home and crawl under the covers. And Buffy's cheeriness, even if it was for her benefit, wasn't really cheering her up at all.

It wasn't until the bus pulled into the parking lot at Sunnydale High that Willow realized she'd stuck that weird metal disk into her pocket. And as soon as she realized it, she promptly forgot again.

Willow went home sick just before fifth period.

CHAPTER THREE

By the time the bus pulled back into the school parking lot, Willow was feeling a bit nauseous.

"You look really pale," Xander told her.

She waited for the requisite crack about vampirism, or ghostliness, or her usual less-than-bronze pallor, but it didn't come. Xander wasn't teasing her, just concerned. That was when Willow realized that she'd better go home.

Even Mr. Morse was nice to her.

"Really, Willow, it's all right," the history teacher said, nodding too much as he almost pushed her toward Giles in the parking lot. "I'll tell Principal Snyder that you were ill. Go home and get some rest. You don't want to miss my pop quiz tomorrow, do you?"

A joke, Willow thought, beginning to feel disoriented. Mr. Morse had made a joke. To make her feel better.

And, of course, it only made her feel worse.

Willow felt like she was seeing everything in a weird, out-of-focus hyper-reality. Almost like a VR game, but with snippets of her real life. Xander looked at her, all brotherly, and told her to get some rest and that he'd call to check up on her when school was out. Buffy promised to tell Oz she'd gone home sick. Cordelia made a face and asked if Willow was going to throw up on her.

Giles drove her home. She didn't remember talking to him much. He made game attempts at small talk for a bit before giving up. In the end, he walked her to the door, where her mom made a big fuss as Willow had known she would, thanked Giles, and hustled her upstairs.

Willow fell into bed at one o'clock in the afternoon and didn't wake up until it was time for school Tuesday morning.

She slept like the dead.

"Hello, zombie alert!" Xander quipped as Willow walked through the library doors the next afternoon when classes had ended.

She smiled. Her first smile since the day before, and it felt good.

"I know I don't look my best," she said, "but I feel a lot better. Much. Much better."

"I'm glad," Xander replied, and smiled. "I was worried

when you didn't call back last night. Your mom didn't want to wake you up, so I stayed up all night, tossing and turning with my concern for your well-being."

Willow raised an eyebrow. "You didn't even last until the news, did you?"

"Not even the ten o'clock," Xander admitted. "Which doesn't mean I wasn't worried! I'm just glad you're feeling better."

She was pleased. "Yeah. Feeling better is good. I don't know what was wrong with me yesterday. I just . . . I don't know, I totally lost it there for a bit. I've never felt like that before. I mean, I've talked to people who have had migraine headaches, and it sort of reminded me of some of the things they said. Except for the part where your head aches. Mine didn't."

"That's good," Xander said encouragingly.

"I'm just happy to be human again," she went on.

"Human is even better," Xander agreed.

"So where is everyone?" Willow asked, looking around. "I've barely seen Buffy all day."

"Oh, apparently she killed something else last night. Broke a centuries-old curse or something. Par for the course. The danger's over, but it seems that Giles is still excitedly inter-rogating her off somewhere. I'm actually just waiting for—"

"You ready?"

Willow and Xander turned to see Cordelia standing in the open library door looking as impatient as always. Willow still didn't get it, but she wasn't about to interfere.

"Hey, Cord," Willow said.

"Hi, Willow," Cordelia replied. "Feel better?"

"Kind of tired, actually," Willow said. "If I didn't know I'd been practically comatose for seventeen hours last night, I'd say I pulled an all-night study session." She glanced at Xander. "I'm much better, however."

"All-night study session?" Cordelia asked, frowning. "You're such a party animal, girl."

Then Xander was pushing Cordelia out the door. Cordy waved to her, and Willow offered a halfhearted smile in return. After they were gone, she sat for a moment in silence, then walked over to the library computer that Giles always had her working on.

She spent a lot of time on her computer at home, and even more here at school, doing research, but also checking out blogs and message boards, meeting new people and surfing for information that might help Buffy and Giles. Too much time, she often thought. She had friends online, but she was never certain if they were *real* friends. If they were who and what they claimed. It was a lesson she'd learned painfully once before, and ever since, Willow had been less inclined to look into the Web world for a social life.

The real world was no picnic, but it was real. And she had friends who cared about her. Watched out for her. So, she wasn't a warrior princess, that much was clear. But she knew enough to know that there were things she was good at, things she could do that the others couldn't. For starters, of all the kids in school, she'd been asked to substitute teach Ms. Calendar's computer course after the teacher had been . . . had been murdered.

Willow Rosenberg might not be able to do backflips or roundhouse kicks, or even punch really hard. But she was a sorceress when it came to the Internet. Online, she had power. She was confident. And when she'd woken up that morning, she'd known just what she was going to do: She was going to find her attackers. Or, at least, she was going to try. It was what she knew how to do. Then she would feel as though she had fought back in some small way.

And that was what haunted her still. She hadn't fought back.

Willow began her search. The local papers, local and state police databases, crime reports from nearby towns. It was going to take a while, but Willow knew that if she was ever going to get over this feeling of helplessness, of horrible vulnerability, she had to do something.

Half an hour later, the library doors opened, but Willow didn't even look up as Buffy and Giles came in.

"Think carefully, Buffy," Giles was saying. "How many different demonic voices did you hear coming from inside the Monsignor?"

"Y'know, Giles, I wasn't really counting," Buffy replied, obviously tired of the subject. "I was just trying to stay alive. And I thought we'd already established that only one demon could ever exist inside a body at a time."

"Yes, well, the Monsignor is—or rather, was—the exception that proved the rule. It seems a sixteenth-century Italian noblewoman, a de' Medici, I believe, had her magician place a horrible enchantment on the Monsignor that acted as some sort of magnet for demons, attracting any of them within the city of Florence to occupy the poor man's body. Naturally, the strain killed him, and he became a vampire. But the—shall we say—overpopulation of his body also drove the Monsignor quite mad prior to his unfortunate demise, and transformed the demons inside him into gibbering idiots."

Willow looked up at last, intrigued by the conversation.

"This was the trouble you had last night?" she asked Buffy.

Buffy nodded. "Complete looney tunes. But Giles thinks he was a celebrity or something."

Willow watched as Giles's face went from surprise to wounded pride in milliseconds.

"Not at all." He sniffed. "I merely found it fascinating that the Hellmouth continues to attract creatures that have been widely considered little more than myths for centuries. I have read the Watcher journal that stated outright that the Monsignor was nothing but a legend."

"He might as well be, now," Buffy said.

"Quite right," Giles said happily. "You freed him from his curse."

Willow had the impression that he couldn't wait to write down Buffy's latest exploit in his own journal. But the conversation was over, and the two of them moved on to more important things.

Sparring.

While Willow continued her search, Giles put Buffy through the hell she called "Slayer practice": weapons and martial arts training that more often than not left poor Giles with large welts and bruises he would be hard-pressed to explain if he had a love life. That's why Jenny Calendar had made the perfect girlfriend for him. She knew. Of course, her knowing had also gotten her killed.

Willow kept thinking about Ms. Calendar now. Thinking that maybe if she had known what Buffy knew, if she had had that training, maybe she would still be alive. Maybe she would have been able to escape Angelus, or hold him off until help arrived.

As she went through the motions of her search, this thought filled Willow's mind more and more, and she paid less and less attention to what she was doing. Finally, she gave up altogether and turned to watch as Buffy launched kick after kick at a heavily padded Giles. Her fists and feet flew, then landed hard, each blow connecting with a confidence that Willow didn't think she could ever feel.

Willow wasn't a fool. She knew that Buffy was capable of things that other girls simply were not. But she also knew that she would benefit from a bit more than the basic self-defense she already knew.

When Buffy and Giles started to fight with long wooden poles called bo-sticks, Willow watched with wide eyes.

Finally, Buffy noticed her.

"Giles, could we take a break for a bit?" Buffy asked sweetly.

For his part, Giles seemed more than relieved to have a few minutes to rest between getting his pride as bruised as his body. He slipped out of his pads and disappeared. Off to the men's room or the stacks—Willow wasn't sure which because she honestly wasn't paying all that much attention.

As soon as he was gone, Buffy strolled over, cocked her head slightly, and raised her eyebrows, studying Willow.

"So, are you going to tell me what's on your mind, or are you going to force me to relive the nightmare game of charades that my mother made me play constantly as a child?"

Willow smiled. "I was just watching you," she said. "I wish I could fight like that."

Buffy chewed her lip a moment, then seemed to nod to herself, as though nobody else was watching or would notice.

"This is getting serious," she said. She pulled up a chair and sat down next to Willow at the computer. "This mugging is really haunting you, isn't it?"

Willow looked away, shrugged a little. She gestured toward the computer screen. "I've been kind of trying to track them down. See if there's been a bunch of attacks like this lately or if anyone has been arrested."

"So what did you find?" Buffy asked hopefully.

"Lots of attacks," Willow reported. "Unfortunately, most

of them sound more like vampires than bullies robbing kids for milk money."

Willow heard the bitterness in her own voice, but she couldn't help it. And when Buffy reached out for her hand to comfort her, she couldn't help but draw back as if she'd been burned. She wanted help, not pity.

"Willow, there wasn't anything you could have done," Buffy said. "It wasn't your fault, and it has nothing to do with being strong. If you had tried to fight them, you might have been hurt worse."

Willow felt hot tears start to fill her eyes, and she gritted her teeth, determined not to let those tears fall.

"You're missing the point!" she snapped. "There was something I could have done! I could have fought them, but I didn't! Buffy, I just froze up—completely paralyzed with fear. I've been in situations with you where I knew for a fact my life was in danger. In this case, it wasn't even that. They didn't want to kill me, or I'd be dead."

"Will," Buffy began, but Willow shook her head.

"Angel wanted to kill me, once. He would have, too, if not for Ms. Calendar. Yes, I know that wasn't really Angel, but that's not what I'm talking about. He wanted to kill me, but I can still look him in the face. I can talk to him and turn my back on him. I can give him my trust."

Buffy nodded seriously and looked as if she wanted to say something, but Willow couldn't stop herself.

"Maybe that's because of who he is, but I think it's

because of who I am too. Because when it comes to this life, to slaying, it doesn't feel like just me, Willow Rosenberg, against all this horrible stuff. It's *us* against *them*, do you understand?

"But alone in the dark. On that street with nobody around? I froze, Buffy. I didn't even try to fight back. I haven't admitted that to anyone, never mind to myself. That's part of the reason I didn't report it to the police . . ."

"You didn't?" Buffy asked, staring at her.

"Of course not," Willow said. "How was I going to explain where I'd been, where I was coming from, and why I was out without my parents' permission?"

Buffy looked sort of embarrassed. "Will, I'm sorry."

"It isn't your fault, Buffy," Willow replied shakily. "It isn't even my fault, I know that. But I could have prevented it. If I'd been better prepared."

Buffy seemed to be at a total loss for words. For once, she didn't know what to say. *So she isn't perfect after all, is she?* a small voice in Willow's head asked.

"Y'know," Buffy said, "Giles and I are pretty much done now. If you really wanted, I could . . ."

She started to gesture toward the open area of the library, where she and Giles had been training. Willow flinched as if Buffy had slapped her. *Now she offers,* Willow thought bitterly. *Now that I've humiliated myself.*

Confusion spread though her in an instant. Where had all these bitter thoughts toward Buffy come from? She certainly hadn't done anything to deserve them. Nothing except try to be a good friend.

But Willow could not get over the pity she saw on Buffy's face.

"Know what, I think we should try it another time," Willow said. "I'm actually still not feeling completely better from yesterday." She gestured to her arm. "I'm just going to work on this a while longer, and then I'm going to go home."

"You sure?" Buffy asked, looking a little hurt and confused herself.

"I'm sure," Willow replied, and offered a smile that she barely meant at all.

Later, when Buffy had left and Giles was toiling away in silence up in the stacks, Willow returned to her computer. But she abandoned her previous search efforts. This time, she began to search for information about weapons from around the world and their uses. She was a smart girl. She would figure them out for herself.

In fact, just looking at several of them—mostly the swords—she could almost feel their weight in her hands. Feel the heft and hear the whickering of steel through the air as her blade whipped down toward its target. Feel it slice flesh and snap bone.

Willow's eyes rolled back in her head for a moment, and she nearly blacked out. Her lids flickered, and she heard a small voice—maybe the voice of her conscience, maybe another voice entirely—whispering in her head.

Yesssss, it hissed.

Her hands flexed around the hilt of an imaginary blade.

Willow's eyes snapped open.

"Whoa," she said to herself.

She stood shakily and gathered up her things. Maybe she wasn't all better after all, she thought. She certainly wasn't feeling normal.

Normal girls didn't have daydreams about swords. About . . . murder.

CHAPTER FOUR

They are screaming."

The Great Empress Wu bowed low before her own dragon throne, its jade wings outstretched, its pearl eyes gleaming evilly in the glow of oil lamps. Her vast silk robes shimmered across the floor like the Yellow River in a summer sunset. But it was winter now, and near dawn, and deadly cold inside her palace.

On the throne sat Lord Chirayoju, her former Minister of the Interior, who smiled and folded its hands across its chest. Its fingernails were sharp claws. Its teeth were fangs tinged with blood.

It had recently fed.

She herself had brought it the victim, a good man completely undeserving of such a horrible death.

"Tell me, Great Empress, are they screaming in pain or in fear?" it asked, closing its eyes as it anticipated her reply.

"I—I know not."

Its eyes opened. They were completely black. Soulless. The fires that raged within them were all that was left of the ambitious court sorcerer that Chirayoju once had been. That man, who had toiled for years to wrest the secrets of the universe from the gods themselves, had also died a vile death. But his sacrifice had been the necessary price.

That which remained was immortal. It was a savage demon that flew like a falcon over the fields and paddies of China. It was a merciless spirit that compelled fire to scorch the lands of those who dared oppose it and to burn their sons and daughters alive. It was a force above nature, commanding even the wind.

And it was something worse.

Something magnificent.

It opened its mouth wide and showed the Empress Wu its fangs. She shrank back, and it knew she feared it utterly. After all, she had seen it feed. Beautiful maidens with tiny, bound feet, who meekly submitted to their fate like the dainty peonies they were. Fierce warlords in full armor, their swords and lances drawn and slashing as it advanced on them. The soldiers always fought hard to the end. Chirayoju vastly preferred the valiant tigers to the timorous rabbits.

"If you know not if it is pain or fear, let us go together and observe them," Lord Chirayoju said, rising.

The Empress could not suppress her shudder as it stepped down from the jade dragon throne and approached her with its hand outstretched. Together they glided from the throne room to the secret door in the lacquer panel behind the great chair. Before its great change, she had graciously taught it where the pressure plate was located and now it smiled at her as it pointed with one taloned finger at the plate and the door magically opened.

The cave entrance was narrow, and Chirayoju invited the Empress to walk ahead. It saw her terror in the stiffness of her back and the manner in which her shoulders rose as she passed in front of its cold, dead body.

It couldn't help its smile of delight—could barely resist whipping her around and tearing her heart from her chest. But it would be a fleeting joy, and for the moment—perhaps a long moment—it needed her.

She led the way to the first chamber.

With a flick of its hand, Chirayoju illuminated the chill, evil-smelling place. This was the Cavern of Vengeance. The smallest of the three caverns, it reached as high as a dragon's head. From floor to ceiling it was walled with human bones. These were the remains of Chirayoju's most illustrious enemies.

The second chamber was the Cavern of Divination. It was larger, and in it Lord Chirayoju kept the treasures that had once belonged to the piles of bones in the first room. It surveyed with pride the heaps of jade, pearls, and silver—the treasure with which it had bought the Empress's loyalty. Here, too, rested its favorite square cauldrons, where it had performed the human sacrifices that had gained it the knowledge of eternal life—the calling forth of the vampire that had taken the sorcerer's human life. There were also heaps of dragon bones, which it used to foretell the future.

And Chirayoju had foreseen a glorious future indeed.

The screaming echoed from the third chamber, which was so immense Chirayoju could not see the far wall as it and the Empress passed through the entrance carved to resemble a great fanged mouth. The walls and the ceiling were carved into images of sorcery: monstrous tigers, dragons, and human skulls. Vast columns of ornate pillars held up the ceiling.

This was the Chamber of Justice.

Chirayoju had killed over twenty thousand of its enemies in this place. Including the sire who had turned Chirayoju, a sorcerer consort to demons and witches, into Chirayoju the vampire, the demon sorcerer.

Now Chirayoju cocked its head and listened. Agony, terror, despair, horror. The four elements of its being.

The Empress shrank back. It took her elbow and urged her forward.

Below them, in an enormous pit, five hundred men screamed as serpents and starved rats attacked them, biting and clawing, stinging, shredding. Around the perimeter, the

Empress's quaking guards thrust their spears at anyone who attempted to scrabble out of the death trap. Not that they could escape. The walls were straight and high, and by now, very slick with blood.

Chirayoju looked at the bulging eyes of its enemies. These were scholars and scribes, men who had dared write about him. Their scrolls and books had already been burned, along with their families, friends, and anyone they might have told of the dread lord that lived in Empress Wu's mountain fortress.

"It is only pain," it said with disappointment. Then it brightened as it gestured with its right hand. "But now it shall be fear."

Chirayoju swept his hand over the pit. Invisible doors opened in the sides of the pit. With unholy shrieks, legions of vampires rushed from the doors into the whirling mass of human misery. Like the rats, they, too, had been starved for just this occasion.

The blood drove them mad.

As they slaughtered the human prisoners, Chirayoju watched in delight. And some envy.

It, too, was hungry.

But it was also suddenly very tired. That was the sign it had awaited.

With great anticipation, Chirayoju pointed to the ceiling.

"Let us depart, Your Majesty," Chirayoju shouted into the ear of Empress Wu. "It is time."

As they hurried from the Cavern of Justice, Chirayoju made a fist. The roof exploded. Chunks of rock crashed down on vampire and human alike.

The dawning sun poured into the hole.

The screaming vampires burned to dust.

Empress Wu and Chirayoju returned to the throne room. As the ceiling in the third chamber collapsed, the palace shook violently. The alarm was sounded. Earthquake! The Empress's household was in a panic. Gongs rang. Men shouted and ran to their Empress for protection.

"What if some of them survived?" Empress Wu asked Chirayoju in a shaking, awe-filled voice as her courtiers poured into the throne room.

"I shall deal with them," it promised her.

But it lied.

Another night fell. The enraged survivors raced through the palace. The fanged, moldy-faced vampires spared no one in their fury.

As the Empress was thrown to the gold-plated floor of her sleeping chamber, she shouted, "Chirayoju! Help me!"

But by then, Chirayoju had flown halfway across the sea.

Let great China become a graveyard, for all it cared.

Its dragon bones had spoken to it a single word.

Japan.

CHAPTER FIVE

Willow, are you all right?" her mother asked softly as she pushed the door ajar.

Lying in bed with the covers drawn to her neck, Willow kept her back to the doorway and clenched her fists. *Yeah, I'm terrific,* she wanted to shout. *That's why I keep coming home sick.*

Sweat poured down her forehead. She was soaked. The room spun so fast she had to close her eyes or be sick, despite the oddly comforting sight of twilight darkness floating through the venetian blinds and edging across the carpet. With the night would come solace. With the darkness, she would be well again.

It was Thursday, and she'd come home sick from school

again. She'd felt mostly all right on Tuesday and Wednesday, though each night she'd seemed to sleep heavily and without dreams, and still woke up in the morning feeling more tired than when she went to bed. And maybe that's all this was, exhaustion creeping up on her.

Maybe.

But Willow thought, when she allowed herself to really think, that maybe there was more to it than that. That maybe she was going a little bit crazy. There was that voice, after all. The one that didn't sound like her conscience at all, if she was honest with herself.

The one that wanted to hurt people.

And not just in that frustrated way you want to push people out of the way in a crowd. No, she'd thought about it. It wasn't that. And it wasn't the weird urges she knew people sometimes got—like wanting to slug Principal Snyder just to see the look of astonishment on his face. Yes, ladies and gentlemen, even meek little Willow had a streak of the rebel in her. It was just buried very deep.

But this wasn't that. This was much, much worse than that.

"Honey?" Mrs. Rosenberg persisted.

Stop bothering me! she almost screamed. Instead she counted to ten, flexing and balling her fists, taking deep breaths. With tremendous effort she controlled her fury enough to respond, "I'm just real tired, Mom. I think I'll go to sleep." Stupid woman. Wasn't it obvious she was tired? She was in bed, wasn't she?

"Okay. Let me know if you need anything."

"Mom?" Willow called out, suddenly afraid. Something was happening to her. Something very weird.

"Yes, Willow?"

Get out get out get out.

Willow swallowed hard. "Could you shut the door, please?"

"Sure, honey."

And lock it up tight. Because if you don't, I just might jump out of this bed and . . . and . . .

Willow panted as the rage built inside her. She heard the door shut. She clenched her teeth. She balled her fists.

She burst into tears.

And then she laughed.

He was going to die. Of that, Xander was convinced. But sometimes the fulfillment of lust was a higher priority than survival. Witness black widow spiders—and the entire male half of the human race.

"Cordelia? The cliff says stop," he said anxiously, hanging on to the armrest on the passenger side of her car with one hand and the gearshift housing with the other.

"Xander, don't be a backseat driver," Cordelia snapped as she shot toward the stupendous view of Makeout Point. The cars of other, ah, view-seekers were lined up in a row like at the Sunnydale Drive-In. Except that, unlike Cordelia, they had decided to simply admire the night sky and the lights of the town below rather than become one with them.

"Cordy," he pleaded. "I'm so young."

"Do you have any idea how many times I've been up he—" She seemed to realize what she was saying—for Cordy, a truly amazing feat—and switched gears, both in her car and in her brain. The car went faster. "I know what I'm doing."

Xander wondered how many years of his life would fly before his eyes before he flew through the windshield. "I know you're eager to get there and all, but gee, girl, show some self-control."

"Oh, Xander, I don't know why . . . ," she gritted out. His eyes bulged as he realized that she was checking herself out in the rearview mirror instead of watching the bushes and trees that were bearing down on them in a blur. "Why I have sunk so low . . ."

He thought of all the times he had seen movie and TV stars dive out of cars, roll on their shoulders, and leap to their feet. Fire off a couple rounds, save the day. Good thing he wasn't on TV.

"Help!" he shouted, pounding on the window.

"Xander, what is your damage?"

She slammed her foot on the brake and the tires squealed, burning rubber to within inches of the dropoff. Xander closed his eyes and rubbed the back of his neck.

"Some call it whiplash, but others pay a chiropractor fifty bucks."

"Shut up." Cordelia set the emergency brake and turned off the car. "And it's seventy-five, at least where I go." As if they'd simply pulled out of the driveway, she checked her hair and snapped open her purse. As he took slow, deep breaths, she whipped out her lipstick and carefully reapplied it.

"What are you doing?" he asked in amazement.

She regarded him with utter disdain. "Providing you with a marked target," she shot back. "Since you're so blind and timid."

He blinked at her. "Timid? *Moi?*"

She raised her chin. "Show me otherwise, Harris." She pointed to her mouth. "Anything to shut you up."

He smiled and said softly, "Geronimo."

The gray twilight was good.

The black would be better.

As the little body writhed in the bed, the spirit grew in strength and began filling her. Undulating like a serpent, it slithered into her lungs, her heart, her eyes, her brain. It cascaded into her hands. Ah, so soft and small!

It burrowed through the muscles and veins of her legs. Not strong. Not powerful.

Yet.

It moved into her face.

It smiled.

It sat up.

The moon shone on the face of the Chinese vampire sorcerer known as Chirayoju as, for but a moment, it knew itself. Its face stretched long and jade green with mold. Its eyes shifted into the almond shape of its home country. Its fangs grew long, sharp, and deadly.

Its hunger was overwhelming.

And then it was the girl again, her arms around her legs, face buried against her knees, sobbing gently from the pain and the fear.

It spoke to her: *Why fight me? Power is what you desire. Strength. I have them both. I am not greedy. I will share.*

"Mom?" Willow called tremulously.

Call her again and she dies, the vampire spirit promised.

Willow touched her forehead. She was burning up.

She felt like she was on some kind of very bad drug . . . that she had never taken. Drugs. Ever. But she was incredibly disoriented. When she looked around her room, it was as if she had never seen any of it before.

Her fever dreams were nightmares.

Groaning, she groped for her phone. She would call Buffy. Or Xander.

Something in her registered the names. Invaded, as if it were tearing her mind apart in search of something. Memorized the pictures in her mind that were attached to the names.

It knew their secrets.

Frightened, she pulled her hand away from the portable phone and cradled it against her chest. It was the hand on which she had cut a finger, and it throbbed terribly. It felt as if fire were burning deep inside it.

The blackness seeped through the gray, twilight giving way to full dark, and it both calmed and terrified her.

Cordelia came up for air and said, "Whoops, time to go."

Xander's face was covered with Sequin from the MAC makeup collection. He caught his breath and rasped, "Time to go?"

"I have things to do," she said imperiously, shooing him over to the passenger side. She started the car. It purred submissively and then roared to life.

"That's okay. Ego crushed." He smiled to himself. "Lips crushed. Fair Trade Agreement."

She screeched backward. "I hate it when you mutter to yourself. No." She held up a hand. "Actually, I prefer it. When you speak in a tone that I can hear, you scare me." She took a breath. "Most of the time."

"Face it, Cordelia," Xander said, patting her shoulder. "You adore me."

She snorted and put the pedal to the metal.

Xander found many new gods to pray to.

It raised its arms as the moon washed across the girl's face. And then, it knew itself at last in the dark night.

"I am Chirayoju. I am free. I live again."

It walked jerkily across the room, testing the body of the girl named Willow—excellent Chinese name, little Weeping Willow!—and flexed its arms. It had pushed her deep into the thing that she would call her soul, but it could sense her there, sense both her terror and the thrill of the presence of so much power around her. It was her hunger for that power that had allowed it to use her so completely.

It arched its back and grunted. Now and then she fought, but her struggles were puny compared to its strength. Had it not threatened the entire Land of the Rising Sun?

And this land, this strange new land. Without Sanno to stop it, would Chirayoju not be a conqueror once more?

A strange box glowed on a table. Chirayoju walked to it and studied it. *Computer*, came the word, in the tongue of this land. Images flooded into the spirit's mind. *But spirit no longer,* it thought. *Vampire, in living flesh!*

Chirayoju looked at the computer and realized that it did not need to learn these new things; in a sense, it already knew them. Possessing this body and this girl, it was itself and yet something more. As if there could be anything more powerful, more terrifying and wonderful, than the vampire Chirayoju!

It was time to move into this world. Time to begin assuming its rightful place.

It stared down at the flimsy cast covering its newly acquired wrist, and then tore it off. No more pain. No more injury. And the cut on the other hand? The slice in the girl's flesh where she had touched the razor edge of the sword of Sanno? Where her blood had flowed and allowed Chirayoju to take a bit of her life force and free itself? It would heal that as well.

Its host would be perfect, healthy and strong.

It found the knob of the French door to little Weeping Willow's room and pushed it open. A sweet breeze wafted over its face. What joy it was to feel again. To smell the scented flowers—roses? It thought longingly of the jasmine in the gardens of Empress Wu's Chinese palace. Of the beautiful Chinese maidens and strong young warriors who had done its bidding, including baring their necks to its fangs so that it might live. It had abandoned all that to cross the sea to the Land of the Rising Sun, in order to devour their Emperor and reign over his people. Flying across the water on the wings of night, Chirayoju had wept for the grandeur of its homeland—mighty China!—but it had pronounced the sacrifice worthy.

But then Sanno had appeared. King of the Mountain, warrior god.

Sanno had defeated it.

Chirayoju laughed to itself. Sanno was not here. This place was undefended.

Buffy, came the thought of the girl. And Chirayoju listened to the thought.

Nodded.

Smiled.

If this girl, this Buffy, was the only defender of this land of Sunnydale, then Chirayoju would be Emperor very quickly. Perhaps the girl, this . . . Slayer? Perhaps she would be a handmaiden in his new court.

Or fresh entertainment for the new pit he would dig . . .

It stepped across the threshold and was about to shut the door when Mrs. Rosenberg called out anxiously, "Honey?"

"It's okay, Mom," Chirayoju answered. "I just need some air. It's stuffy in here."

"Stay bundled up. You've got a fever, you know."

"Yes, I know."

But the fever was coming down. The possession, which had weakened this body, was now strengthening it. Chirayoju could feel its power growing along with its hunger. It had taken all this time to fully exert control over Weeping Willow's body. Even now, it would have to give up that control at dawn. For now.

But not forever.

As for this night, it must feed, and soon.

It walked, more steadily this time, from the door to the front of the house, and from there to what was known as the street. A car flew by—remarkable creation!—and it knew it would have to have one.

It raised its face to the stars. Their light beamed down on it. A poem came to mind:

Night, absent of soul.
Gardens wither, the earth shakes.
Open, gate of death!

Chirayoju walked down the street, reveling in its freedom. It would walk until sunrise if it wished. It would walk until the feet of this child bled, and it would make the night scream.

Xander gave Cordelia a when-did-you-get-released look of amazement and scratched his head.

"Let me get this straight. You drove over a rock."

"Or something," she agreed.

"Or something. And your tire went flat. And now you want me to get out of the car and change your tire so you can go to do these 'things to do,' which I assume have something to do with a guy who is not me."

She said nothing. She only stared at him. Xander stared back.

Finally Cordelia said, "And your point is?"

"Is the word 'tacky' even in your vocabulary?" he asked her. "Let me spell it for you. N. O. Way."

"Fine." She glared at him. "I'll just do it myself." She spread her fingers as if her nails were still wet and scanned the dashboard. "The jack-thing is in the trunk," she said to herself. "And all I have to do is, um, here!" She brightened and pushed a button. Her emergency flashers began to pulse.

Xander sighed the sigh of the truly victimized and opened his door.

"Thank you!" Cordelia called plaintively after him.

He bent back in to narrow his eyes at her.

"You know, it's nights like these psychos escape from the nuthouse on the hill," he said in a low, scary voice. "So if I don't come back . . . lock your doors and close your eyes. Because the drip, drip, drip you hear will be the blood running out of my neck. And the smack will be my severed head landing on your front end."

"Oh, Xander." She gave him a look. "I don't know how you can even joke about stuff like that, after all the weirdness you and your bizarro pals have put me through."

He batted his lashes at her. "Cordy, my sweet. Lest you forget, you are now one of my bizarro pals."

"As if." She leaned toward him and grabbed the passenger armrest to urge the door shut. "Just go do it, okay? I'll be nice to you or something."

"'Or something' will do just fine." He rubbed his hands together like a mad scientist. "Wa-ha-ha, just fine, my pretty."

She let go of the armrest and threw her head back against her seat. "Oooh."

Xander grinned and shut the door. Then he walked back toward where the jack-thing would be, muttering, "Harris, you are such a schmuck."

The dogs of Sunnydale bayed as Chirayoju glided past their houses. Cats arched their backs and hissed. The moon itself hid behind a veil of clouds. It moved quickly, smelling fresh young blood beating through vibrant hearts. Eagerly it inhaled the aroma. After centuries of imprisonment, it was starving. Not merely for blood, but for what truly sustained it—life. The life essence of living beings.

To begin its reign of terror, though, Chirayoju knew that it would need slaves and acolytes.

And suddenly it knew where to find them. The air sizzled with the presence of other vampires, and it was so delighted its eyes welled with scarlet tears.

It raised its head to gaze at a hill above the town, and small, unmoving shapes upon the hill. They were cars.

Other shapes moved toward them, darting over the landscape like a small band of locusts. They were vampires.

Eagerly, Chirayoju began to lope toward the hill. Up it climbed, now running, though the body was tired. It willed power into the limbs and pushed blood through the heart. This body was young, but at this rate it would wear out quickly.

When that happened, it would have to find another.

Once he had put Cordy's spare tire on, Xander sat glumly in the passenger's seat as she drove down the hill. Cordelia drove past a small blur of a figure on the side of the road and shook her head. "Honestly. Someone is hitching to Makeout Point, can you believe it? Don't they have any idea how dangerous that is?"

"Who? Where?" Xander asked, looking up from sifting through the CDs in Cordelia's glove compartment. He glanced back but saw no one.

Cordelia looked in the rearview mirror. "Am I smeared?"

He pointed desperately. "Cor, look at the road."

"Just tell me if I'm smeared," she demanded, turning toward him.

"No, no, you are a goddess," he begged. "You look perfect." He stared hard at her, doing his best to look entranced by her beauty instead of petrified by her driving. "Honest. Please, please don't kill me."

She rolled her eyes. "Xander, you are *so* superficial."

Her foot was lead.

His life was over.

The wind whipped around Chirayoju as it glided behind the vampire swarm. There were only three of them—apparently, the other dots had been dogs—and they were scattered and unfocused, little more than ravening beasts. So had it been in China, before Chirayoju had left for the Land of the Rising Sun. And then so had it been in Japan. Few of its kind were truly intelligent. Few possessed the ability to truly lead. And none but Chirayoju had mastered the dark arts as a vampire. The demon within the spirit was flush with pride at its achievements.

No, the others were like children to Chirayoju.

Which was to the good. They were easier to control and dominate.

Chirayoju watched as the hunt progressed. Better to call it a massed attack, for a hunt implied direction and working in concert. They swooped down on the cars, yanking open the doors and pulling out the inhabitants. A young girl with short, dark hair shrieked in terror as a female vampire with long, blond hair dragged her out of the car while another vampire, darker and larger, lifted out a boy in a leather jacket and ripped out his throat.

The third vampire, tall and balding, attacked a car farther down, which allowed the couple in nearer vehicles to attempt escape. However, the other two vampires were too fast for them. For a few heartbeats, there was screaming.

And then there were no heartbeats.

At that instant, Chirayoju stood up and spread its arms. Lightning crackled. The wind shrieked.

It boomed, "Know me as your master!"

The other vampires stopped in their tracks.

"What?" the female cried, and began to rush him.

"Stop!" Chirayoju commanded.

At first his words had no effect. Then it was as if the female vampire were little more than a marionette. She was brought up short as if strings held her back, and Chirayoju reached out to her dead mind, to the demon spirit that lived within, and it was the demon that he controlled. The demon that he enslaved. The demon that he forced to its knees.

"Master," the girl whispered.

"Hey, man, what's your deal?" the darker vampire said contemptuously.

Chirayoju turned its gaze on him. Their eyes met, locked. It knew the creature saw a mere girl, and willed him to see the truth behind the mask that was Weeping Willow.

The other vampire's mouth opened as if in pain—or shock.

He knew what it saw, now. The vampire remembered death, of course, the time between the loss of his human soul and his resurrection as a vampire. He did not want to face that horrible void again, nor did he relish the even more nightmarish horrors he was promised as he gazed into Chirayoju's eyes.

Chirayoju stared at each one in turn, pushing its will against theirs. It felt their struggle.

The sky cracked open and rain pelted them. The blood of the victims on the ground mixed with the earth; the mud ran crimson.

Chirayoju singled out the balding vampire and willed him to approach. To kneel. To bare his neck.

"Speak my name," it commanded.

In a steady voice, the vampire answered, "Lord Chirayoju."

The moon hung in the trees above the graveyard, casting Angel in a glow of stark white that accentuated his pale skin. His eyes were dark, and as he looked down at Buffy, he touched her cheek with a tentative gesture. His fingers were cold, but his caress warmed her. Her lips were swollen from his kisses.

"In this light, you look like me," he said softly.

"Like a vampire." Her voice was louder, bolder. "You avoid saying it, like it was a dirty word."

His laugh was short and bitter. "You're the Slayer, Buffy. To you, it is a dirty word."

Buffy cocked her head and gathered up his hand in both of hers. "Angel, for us to move along, we need to move . . .

along." She stood on tiptoe, raising her mouth toward his. "This 'hate me, I'm a vampire' stuff is old territory for us. We've been over the worst terrain we could possibly find. I have the map memorized. It's time to blaze a new trail."

He looked down at her mouth, and she could tell he was struggling not to kiss her again. Her heart pounded. She could tell he heard the faster rhythm.

He whispered, "You know there's more to me than we both realized at first."

"I'll say." She put her hand around his neck and urged him closer. "And if I'm not afraid, why should you be?"

"Maybe because I lo—" He turned his head.

She did too. There was something in the air, something that floated across her and threatened to pull her down, or to put its hand over her mouth and smother her. Something that held hands with death.

"Did you feel that?" she asked. "It was almost like a . . ." She searched for the right words. "Like the air got heavy. Or like a scream in my head." She frowned. "Something's wrong."

Angel nodded slowly. "Something's very wrong."

As one, they looked up toward the night sky and all around. Beneath the gravestones and monuments, the dead stayed buried. Through a sheen of clouds, the moon glowed. An owl hooted directly above their heads. All was peaceful. Yet the presentiment of evil lingered like a fog.

"I think I'm getting better at this Slayer thing," Buffy murmured. "I think something's up. I think I need to go see Giles."

Almost unconsciously, Angel draped a protective arm across Buffy's shoulders. "I think I'll go with you."

Together they hurried toward the graveyard gates.

CHAPTER SIX

As Friday morning began, Willow was elsewhere.

Some voice from the real world echoed down the long, twisted dream corridor to her elsewhere, and the first real spark of awareness hit her. Music, from a long way off.

Country music.

Computer geek she might be, but Willow Rosenberg did not listen to country music. Oh, sure, she thought Shania Twain was cool enough, but that wasn't *you-listen-to-country-music?* country music. No, having country music on your alarm clock was just inviting ridicule. And, truth be told, Willow had never needed to send invitations. Uh-uh. The Willow ridicule party was eternal, and everybody crashed.

Except Buffy, and Xander, and Oz, and other people who were the objects of vast amounts of ridicule.

Alarm clock. Usually meaning you're asleep. Or have been.

Only the warmth of the sun streaming through her bedroom window made Willow realize how cold she was. Cold and aching all over like she'd climbed to the top of Everest for a midnight snack.

Midnight . . . snack. Something weird there. Something she could almost remember.

Then she felt the drool on her chin. Realized she'd been sleeping with her mouth open, even snoring, which wasn't something she did often, as far as her waking self knew.

Willow's face crumpled into an expression of disgust as she wiped her chin, realizing at last that she was, indeed, awake. Awake and exhausted and her eyes were burning like she'd been up all night watching infomercials again. Insomnia could make a person do strange things. But no, she hadn't done anything like that. Couldn't really remember doing anything last night after coming home sick from school. Except that somehow, she had set her alarm for the dulcet twang of the Grand Ole Opry.

Weird. Weird and disgusting, she thought. How could she ever spend the night with a guy if there was even a chance that he'd see her sleeping with her mouth open with drool on her chin? Uh-uh.

She opened her dry, burning eyes, then gasped and

closed them tight as the sun hit her retinas. Willow hissed as a spike of pain shot through her head. She lay a moment, waiting for the pain to pass, assuming it was like the frozen headaches she got when she ate ice cream too fast. But it didn't pass.

In fact, by the time she crawled out of bed and dragged herself to the shower, Willow's headache had only grown worse. It wasn't a pounding ache, the kind where you could feel the blood pumping through your head. It was more like someone had pounded a nail into her skull.

Even after her shower, Willow didn't feel much better. Her mother called to her from downstairs, but the words didn't even register. Nor did she pay any attention to what she was putting on except to note that the clothes were clean.

It was while she was sitting on the edge of her bed tying her shoes that she glanced up at the computer on her desk and saw the little green sprout sticking up from her mouse pad. Willow frowned, a decidedly ill-advised action for someone with a headache so bad that her face hurt.

She stood and walked to her desk. Next to her mouse was a small, crooked bonsai tree, the kind that trendy stores in trendy malls sold to people who couldn't handle the responsibility of a pet to take care of. But this was nothing from a mall. It had long roots still covered with dirt from where it had been torn from the ground.

"Okay, thanks, but it's not my birthday," Willow mumbled uneasily to her empty room.

How the plant had gotten there, of course, was the big question. With the pain in her head discouraging much contemplation—much thought of any kind, really—the only thing she could think of was: maybe Angel?

Running around at night, showing up unannounced at people's windows. That was kind of vampirelike behavior. At least, Angel-like behavior. But she didn't think he would do that, unless it was some big surprise for her or something. And, come to think of it, during that whole Angelus thing that nobody really wanted to talk about, she and Buffy had placed a kind of ward over her room to keep him out.

So not Angel. But when she started to consider other options, the nail in her skull turned into a knitting needle. She massaged her forehead, realized she was going to be late for school—as if anyone would notice after a hellish week like this, when Willow Rosenberg and tardiness seemed as inseparable as PB&J. Still, she'd better show up today. Who knew what she had missed this week? Even the days that she had been there, she couldn't quite remember.

Except for the fact that she'd somehow scored a perfect grade on the pop quiz Mr. Morse gave about their museum visit to the exhibit on the art and culture of ancient Japan. Somehow, through her fugue state, she'd obviously learned something. And if she ever wanted to learn anything again, it was back to school for Willow.

Just before she left, she noticed something beside the uprooted bonsai. It was the disk or coin that had fallen from the hilt of that big sword at the museum on Monday. She'd forgotten to put it back after cutting herself; she'd been too distracted. Then it had made its way into the pocket of her jeans, and later disappeared. Or not, considering that it now sat prominently displayed on top of her computer.

Willow felt a little guilty about it. Maybe she should try to take it back this afternoon? As she reached for it, noting its odd engravings, someone started pounding that knitting needle into her brain with a hammer. Willow forgot all about the coin, turned, and stumbled toward the hallway, feeling suddenly as though she was going to throw up.

Strangely, and with great relief, Willow began to feel better almost immediately. The headache never disappeared entirely, but it receded until it was more of a thumbtack than a nail. It still hurt, but she could live with it. She might even be able to pay attention in class.

As she hurried out the door, her eyes ached from the bright sunlight, and she slipped on a pair of sunglasses she hadn't worn in months. They weren't her style.

Before.

Buffy sat alone at a round table in the cafeteria, math text open in front of her. The Noxzema-filled plastic tubes the school dared to call baked stuffed manicotti sat untouched on her tray.

She had told Giles about the weird sensation she had had in the graveyard. He was intrigued but could find no specific reason for it. Even now, she supposed he was researching to see if Curse of the Rat-People Night was looming—which it probably was.

She saw Oz and gave him a wave. He smiled and moved on like he was hunting—ah, make that searching—for something. Or someone. Buffy hoped that someone was someone she knew. Known as Willow.

"Two plus two equals?" a voice asked behind her.

It barely registered. Xander slid into the chair next to her and began ferociously tearing into his plate of tubes with a zeal that might have given one the impression that he thought it was real food. Buffy spared a glance and a bemused frown for his table manners, then looked back at her book.

"Oh, hi, Xander," Xander said. "Sorry I don't have time to be sociable, but I've done it again. Bad me. I put off studying in favor of more athletic nocturnal activities, and now I'm up crit peek without a shaddle. Again. Oh, woe is me, my tutor Willow has forsaken me."

Buffy still didn't look up.

"See, I can tell you're nervous about the test because instead of your usual choice of beverage, Mango Madness, you've gone with the sixteen-ounce chocolate Quik. Major Buffy comfort food. Y'know, if it was food and not drink. Liquid. Beverage thing."

Buffy still didn't look up, but she did respond. "Eat your lunch, Xander."

"Which means, I guess, that you want me to be quiet so

you can study for the makeup math test you have in, oh, thirty-two minutes?" Xander inquired.

"Eat your lunch, Xander," Buffy said again.

"Hey, no problem. I'm shuttin' up. I'm good at shuttin' up. Nobody's better than the X-Man at shuttin' up."

"Shut up shuttin' up," Buffy drawled in her best Warner Brothers cartoon gangster voice.

Xander grinned broadly. "See. Now, haven't you always wanted to say that?"

"Yes," Buffy replied, finally looking up and fixing him with an amused but frustrated glare. "Thank you so much. One of my life's great wishes, really. You're a prince."

Willow plopped her tray on the table and slid into a chair. "A prince?" she asked. "Somebody kissed a toad and didn't tell me? I'm always the last to know."

Xander and Buffy stared at Willow as she started to dig in to the most terrifying meal the school ever served—and they served it once a week—the perversely named vegetarian meat loaf. But it wasn't her meal choice that had drawn their attention.

"Good God, what happened to you?" Xander asked, bobbing his head toward Willow in that head-bobbing, inquisitive way that he had.

Buffy whacked him on the arm.

"Will, are you okay?" he pressed.

"After a week like this, why wouldn't I be okay?" she snapped. No smile. No sheepish Willowy self-effacing grin.

"Did you get mugged again?" Xander demanded, shifting into the rescuing-the-damsel-in-distress mode that he'd been trying so gamely to perfect. Which explained the tire-changing thing, he decided. He was not Cordelia's schmuck boy after all. He was her knight in shining armor.

Willow finally looked up at them. Or at least, looked up at them through the black lenses of her sunglasses. Which she had on. Inside the caf, like she thought she was Courtney Love or some other demented denizen of the rich and famous lifestyle universe.

"Huh?" she asked. "No. Not even. In fact, my wrist is totally fine. Healed up real fast."

"Not really the concern," Buffy admitted. "It's more, well, cosmetic. Look, I'm pretty sure you don't have a hangover, so what's up with you?"

Cordelia had walked over and pulled up a chair as they were talking, and now she tsk-tsked and tilted her head in her best imitation of a sympathetic friend.

"Willow," she said kindly. "I think what Buffy is trying not to say is that you look like a two-dollar hooker who hasn't made it back to her corner of the alley yet."

Buffy wanted to defend Willow, but for a moment she couldn't. Because Willow really did look that bad. Her hair was a mess, clean but uncombed and wildly tangled. She had on a lime green, very fashionable top and purple sweatpants, an offense that should have brought the Fashion SWAT team down on the school the second Willow walked in.

And just when had she walked in? She certainly hadn't made it in time for first bell. Or even her first class, as far as Buffy knew. And what was up with those sunglasses?

Willow glared at Cordelia, her gaze intense though her eyes were hidden behind the dark glasses.

"How sweet of you to say, Cordelia," Willow snarled. "Particularly coming from you."

"Well, excuse me," Cordy said, flicking her fingers into the air as if she were trying to dry her nail polish. "Aren't we testy. I was just trying to save you from postapocalyptic embarrassment. See, I always told my therapist that trying to be someone's friend was just a waste of precious time better spent on self-improvement."

"Well put," Xander teased. But of course, teasing Cordelia was only fun when she noticed. Which at this moment—sigh, like so many others—she didn't. Or she didn't care, which, since it was Xander, was likely.

"You're right," Willow told her. "You could use some time on self-improvement, Cordelia. Maybe then people would stop mistaking you for Barbie's sister Skipper turned crack-ho."

Buffy smirked. She couldn't help it. She almost burst out laughing, in fact, and probably would have if not for the look on Willow's face. It wasn't the triumph she expected to see there—she had, after all, just trounced Cordy in the insult category—but a look of such contempt that for a moment, Buffy thought Willow was going to hiss up a cat fight.

Instead, Will stood up abruptly enough to knock over her chair, then turned and stormed from the cafeteria, leaving her food and her friends behind.

"Wow," Cordelia said. "What's gotten into her? Sharpen those claws. It's going to be a bumpy ride." She reached for Willow's tray. "Guess she's not going to eat her tofu."

Xander slapped her hand. "Now cut that out!"

Cordy shot him a wounded look, but Buffy barely registered their exchange. She was watching Willow go.

"What is your talk show topic?" Cordelia sneered at Xander.

"Did you look in the mirror and strike yourself blind or something?" Xander snapped at her. "I've known Willow my whole life. She's been my best friend since . . . just since. Something's obviously really bothering her. She was so un-Willowy. It'd be like you wearing the same outfit to school twice."

Cordelia blinked. "You think it's that bad?" she asked worriedly.

"It's that bad," Buffy said, and they gave each other uh-oh looks.

"What do we do?" Xander asked.

"Give her some space, I guess. Try to talk to her, no pressure, and not all together. Ask Giles to talk to her," Buffy said, rattling off the ideas as they came into her head. "I think maybe getting mugged had more of an impact on Willow than we thought."

"Like post-traumatic stress disorder or something?" Cordelia asked.

Buffy cast a sidelong glance at her, faced with the realization once again that Cordy wasn't nearly as thick as she usually seemed. Well, not entirely. Sometimes.

"I'll talk to her," Xander said.

"Yeah," Buffy agreed. "I'll try to get her to open up too."

Cordelia whistled, eyes searching the blank, whitewashed walls for something to look at. Lips puckered, she stopped whistling midnote and rolled her eyes.

"All right!" she said. "I'll try too."

"That's my Cordy," Xander said with pride. "Always thinking about others."

But none of them saw Willow again that day, and Buffy was so caught up in the Math Test from Hell that she didn't even think about trying to talk to her until she was on the way home.

Sometimes Buffy had company when she was on patrol, scouring Sunnydale for something unnatural that she could return to nature. Giles might come along to lecture her on becoming a better Slayer, hang on to her big bag o'tricks, and hand her a stake when she needed one. Other times, when she didn't think it would be too much of a distraction—who was she kidding?—whenever he wanted to come along, Angel prowled the night with her.

Also, there would be big smoochies during Angel-prowling nights, as Xander so quaintly put it on occasion. Very big smoochies.

"I could use a little distraction, right about now," she muttered to herself.

It was quiet, and a little chilly, and Buffy thought it would have been nice to have Angel around, or Giles. For different reasons, of course. She wondered if she ought to bring homework with her sometimes. She could sit under a streetlight and study if it got slow, just sit and wait for something inhuman and vile to attack her. Kind of like sitting in front of Greg "The Octopus" Rucka in bio.

"Deep sigh," Buffy whispered.

She slung her bag over her shoulder and started for home. On the way, she got kind of sidetracked and wandered over to the Bronze. Once she got there, though, she only stood on the curb outside looking at the door. It was possible Angel was there, inside. But if she went in, and he was in there, she wouldn't be in any kind of rush to get home.

Home. That place they named homework after. Where that work intended for home was usually done. And Buffy was way behind.

Tomorrow night, she thought. She'd see Angel tomorrow night.

She spun on her heel, started for home, and then stopped short. A weird feeling very like the graveyard sensation from the night before ran through her, and she turned to peer into the darkness of the alley next to the Bronze.

Three of them, two guys and one very innocent-looking girl with short, dark hair. Buffy was the wariest of her. It was like high school: Sometimes the ones you expected the least of really surprised you. If only her teachers' expectations of her would sink a little more, she'd be the pride of Sunnydale High.

"See, that's what happens to my grades," she said aloud, letting her bag drop to her side. "I have the best of intentions about my homework, but something always comes up."

Their faces were hideous, feral, and they snorted like animals as they stepped out of the alley and began to spread out to surround her. Buffy slid a stake from the bag, then dropped the bag to the sidewalk.

"Hello, procrastination," she said, and smiled.

"And a good evening to you, Slayer," the girl growled. "I hope you've enjoyed it, 'cause it's going to be your last."

"Thanks for caring," Buffy retorted. "You're so sweet."

"Oh, not at all," said the second, a balding-type guy, moving around behind her.

Buffy turned, switching the stake from hand to hand, trying to keep them in her field of vision. They made a semicircle and they moved in unison, creeping right, then left. Very drill team. Very weird.

"We've been waiting for you for hours," said the third, dark-skinned and heavyset. "We'd almost given up hope of killing you tonight."

For a moment, Buffy felt that sensation again, and an additional chill at the realization that they'd been waiting for her. Not out hunting for fresh blood. Just hanging out behind the Bronze, waiting for the Slayer to come by.

Vampires weren't generally known for their patience.

Buffy shook it off, slapped the stake into her right hand, and smiled. "You'd almost given up hope," she said with mock sympathy. "Now here I am, what you've been waiting for, and all I'm going to do is break your hearts."

Her face changed then. A sneer—almost cruel—twisted her mouth.

"Oops, my bad. I meant *stake* your hearts, of course."

Baldy leaped at her, and Buffy acted. She threw her leg out toward him, lifted her left hand to grab him by the shirt front and toss him at the heavyset one on her right.

That was her intention, anyway.

But she never got hold of him. Baldy stopped short, stood up, and simply smiled at her. Buffy knew instantly what had happened. They had set her up. Big Boy was rushing in from her right, and the girlish bloodsucker was already reaching for her hair. Buffy was extended in the wrong direction, off balance.

The girl snagged her hair, hissed, bared her fangs. Big Boy barreled in from the right.

Buffy fell backward and the girl came with her.

"Oh," Buffy said. "A wise guy. Remind me to kill you later."

Big Boy thundered past the spot where she'd been standing and nearly flattened Baldy with his bulk. Buffy threw a foot up into the girl's stomach and tossed her over her head to land in the street. Cars passed by now and again on the cross street, but nothing turned down toward the Bronze.

Fine with her. Nobody reporting back to her mom or the school that they saw her fighting in front of the club on a school night.

The girl was quick, though. Even as Buffy was getting up, she was rushing at Buffy again.

"Well, if you insist," Buffy sighed, and sidestepped, kneed her in the stomach, pulled her up by the hair, and staked her.

She exploded in a blast of ashes. Buffy didn't have time to appreciate her demise, however. She sensed Big Boy and Baldy behind her, and took off into the darkness of the alley.

They gave chase.

Morons.

A battered Chevy was parked in the alley. Buffy jumped onto the hood, then the roof. The two vamps got on either side of the car, and their smiles told her they figured they had her trapped.

"Now we've got you," Big Boy snarled.

"Y'know, I can see where you might have a hard time getting an actual date, but this is taking things a little too far, don't you think?" she asked. "Of course, I've heard the Internet is fertile territory to meet that special someone if you want them to love you just for your brains."

"I'll love you for your heart, Slayer, while it's sliding down my throat in ragged pieces!" Big Boy screamed, and swiped at her legs.

Buffy leaped again, did a somersault, and came down behind him.

"Isn't that an oh-so-lovely image," she said, and staked Big Boy through the back. Harder that way, but if a girl worked at it, the end result was the same.

Poof.

Baldy stared at her across the roof of the Chevy.

"You could run," she suggested.

"I would be killed for my cowardice if I ran," Baldy growled. "In any case, I'm not afraid of you, little girl."

He leaped up onto the roof of the car, where she'd stood only seconds before. Buffy grabbed the Chevy's door handle and pulled. It was unlocked. She opened the door and hopped in, slamming the door just as Baldy shoved a hand in after her. She heard the snap of his arm bone and the howl of pain as he withdrew the arm.

Buffy slammed the door again. But she didn't try getting out the other side. Just sat there behind the wheel. Well, just a little closer to the middle of the car. Baldy shattered the window with his working fist a second later, and then his face appeared in the broken window.

"Boo!" Buffy said, and punched him in the face.

Baldy slid off the roof, scrambled to his feet, and stared at her through the broken window.

"Scared of me now?" she asked.

"Get out of that car!" he roared at her.

Buffy smiled slyly. "No."

Baldy came at her and grabbed for the door handle, and Buffy shoved the stake through the broken window and into his chest.

"You didn't say please," she told him as he exploded into dust.

The adrenaline pumping through Buffy as she made her way home felt good. There was a certain Rocky Balboa–ness about being the Slayer, though Buffy would never confess that exhilaration when she was bitching to Giles about her life.

But that feeling was overshadowed tonight. Completely eclipsed by the dread that was beginning to weigh heavily on her. It was racing around her mind and she had a feeling she wasn't going to be getting much sleep that night.

These vampires weren't that much harder to kill than most of the others she'd taken on. But they were more focused. They'd waited around for her. They'd set her up at the start of that fight, as if they could predict what her first move would be. Actually, they *had* predicted it.

And when she'd told that last one to run, what he'd said in return had creeped her out.

"I would be killed for my cowardice."

Which meant someone had *sent* them after Buffy. Someone organized. Someone she hadn't already killed.

On the night after the night of the graveyard weirdness-thing.

Not good.

CHAPTER SEVEN

S ome called it morning.

After a refreshingly uneventful weekend—relatively uneventful—Buffy let out a vast Monday-morning yawn as she walked into the library and said, "Many vampires. Much homework. Vampires slain. Homework somewhat less than attacked."

She sighed. "So sign me up for remedial you-name-it, call my mom, and explain to her why I'm flunking unflunkable classes, such as PE."

"Hmm?" Giles asked, looking up from one of his oh-so-dusty books. Buffy reflected that so much of her life revolved around dust. Inhaling it during research sessions, and creating it . . . out of dead vampires.

Giles smiled, pushed up his glasses, and closed his book. "Good morning, Buffy. You were saying there was a lot of activity this weekend?"

"Vampy only," she answered, mentally ticking down a list of things that had not happened: homework, the Bronze, big smoochies from Angel.

"Well, yes," he said, as if that were the only kind that mattered. Easy for him to say. He was not flunking being a librarian. Which raised some questions: How did people know if you were doing a good job? Check to see if the books were shelved in correct alphabetical order?

"'Well, yes,'" she repeated. "Only, these vamps were different from the vamps of yore." She perched on the study table and swung her legs, half-admiring her heeled boots, which were new—a product of a Saturday afternoon mother-daughter bonding ritual called "hitting the mall."

"These were organized vamps, like there's another leader in town," she informed her Watcher. "Had some nasties Friday night. Another pair last night. No trouble, but it was kind of freaky."

"Really?" His brow crinkled. With both hands, he set the book down on the table. Dust rose off the cover like fog off the ocean.

"Really." Buffy leaned backward and peered into the stacks, on the lookout for her best friend. "Speaking of demons, Willow was a big no-show all weekend. She didn't show up at the Bronze and hasn't returned my phone calls.

Plus, she isn't in school today. No one's seen her. That spooks me a trifle."

Giles raised an eyebrow. "Spooks you a trifle?"

"Trifle. A little less than *Poltergeist*, a little more than Casper. Trifle."

"Ah," Giles said, then quickly moved on. "What does Willow's tardiness have to do with demons? Did you and she have a quarrel or something?"

"Or nothing. Ever since she got mugged, Willow's been getting funkier by the day." She pursed her lips. "She's actually acting . . . witchier . . . than Cordelia. And you know how pointed *her* hat is." Buffy sat forward and crossed her arms.

"Well, we do all have our bad days," Giles offered, scrutinizing her. "But I should like to hear more about these—"

Buffy frowned impatiently. "She was wearing sunglasses, and they were Gargoyles."

He blinked, clearly not getting it.

"Giles, read the magazines, don't just subscribe. Even geeks have put their Gargoyles away. And as for wearing them indoors, well, that went the way of the sequined glove and Bubbles the Chimp. It's so over even the geeks think it's over."

She reddened. "Not that I'm lumping Willow in with the geeks. Because I would never do that. She's my friend. And that's the point of my babblesomeness. She is not acting like herself."

Giles sighed. "Buffy, please, I beg of you, slow down. For someone who insists she's not a morning person, you bring with you a certain manic exuberance to our preclass chats that I, for one, occasionally find a bit, well, exhausting."

"Well, of course," she said cheerily. "You're old . . . er than me," she amended, at his crestfallen expression.

They both glanced up as Xander strolled in, already talking as he walked through the door.

"Subject: Willow. Not even Oz the new true love werewolf boyfriend has seen her today."

"Subject: Willow," Buffy agreed, rubbing her hands together.

"Buffy, I really think we ought to concentrate on these vampires who targeted you over the weekend," Giles insisted. Before Buffy could protest, he held up a finger. "First. After which we may discuss Willow's change of attitude and declining fashion sense to your heart's content."

"Oh, all right," Buffy said, pouting. "Xander, come." She patted the study table. "Sit."

"I pant like a dog and obey like a doormat." He sat beside her and gave her a friendly bump with his elbow.

"We were going back through some odd occurrences of late," Giles told Xander. "Over the weekend, Buffy met up with some vampires who were very focused, very organized."

Xander nodded knowingly. "All right. Teamster vamps. Filed away. Next item?"

"She was in the graveyard with Angel the night before and felt something weird."

"*Buffy,*" Xander said, scandalized.

"We both had this weird feeling," Buffy said.

"Yeah, I'll just bet you did. It being that weird feeling popularly known as lust." Xander looked angry. "Do you know how dangerous it is to make out when you're on patrol?"

Buffy frowned indignantly, even though she figured her flush was giving her away. "Not making out. We were both hunting."

"Hunting what?" he asked. "For rabies? 'Cause if you keep kissing Dead Boy, you'll probably get it. I warned Willow about the same thing with Oz."

"And I'm sure Willow appreciated it as much as I do," Buffy said, frowning at him.

Xander held up his hand. "Plus, what kind of message are you sending to all those impressionable young vampire girls who might be spying on you two? You know, as the Slayer, you are a role model, whether you like it or not."

"I'll keep that in mind," she drawled, giving him a knowing look. "Next time I find you all over Cordelia."

"We are not talking about *my* strange hobbies," Xander said without a hint of embarrassment. "We're talking about your taste in boyfriends."

Buffy slipped off the table and began to pace. "Meanwhile, Will. I think she was so shaken by the attack that she's putting up walls so she won't get hurt again." She trailed off, thinking of when she had been defeated by the vampire known as the Master. How angry she'd been once she'd been brought back to life. How bitter and mean to all her friends.

How Xander had brought her back to life with CPR.

"At first I thought it would pass, but it's been more than a week now since she was attacked, and she's only getting moodier. Now she's dropped out of real life completely, or something. We have to help her," she finished softly, giving Xander a look as she recalled how many times he had been there for her and Willow both. For everyone.

Xander said quietly, "And we will, Buff."

They smiled at each other.

"Okay, let me figure this out," Cordelia said as she drove Xander over to Willow's house. "Whenever I inform you that we must cut short our perverse and disgusting display of mutual passion or whatever, I am then on a date with another guy. But whenever you call it quits and ask me to drive you to Willow's house, we are checking up on a friend?"

Xander peered through the window on the passenger side and nodded. "I swear, babe, hanging with me has increased your brain power."

"I am not 'babe.' I have never been 'babe' and I will never be 'babe.' Babe is a pig." She stomped on the brake. "And no dumb whiplash cracks, either. And as for my brain power—"

"I have said nothing. I have nothing to say," Xander said, opening the door and rushing to Willow's front door. The porch light was on, but it looked like nobody was home.

He rang the bell. They waited.

"I'm hungry," Cordelia whined.

"I've got a half-eaten candy bar on the floor mat on my side," he said. "Formerly, it was in my hand, but I had to drop it when we careened on two wheels around that last curve. The chewed part is probably covered with carpet fuzz, but what the hey, we all need our fiber."

"That's disgusting," Cordelia said. She leaned past him and knocked hard on the door. "She's not home. Come on. I have two hours until cheerleading practice."

Xander was tempted. Two hours in Cordelia's arms were two hours well spent. He was certain she was dumping an extreme amount of money into lipstick these days, because she was wiping it all over his face with an extravagance matched only by his purchases of Altoids breath mints.

But his concern for Willow was stronger than his practically overwhelming desire for big smoochies, et cetera.

"What's the big?" Cordelia demanded as he stubbornly stayed on the porch. "So she's out."

"You don't get it, do you?" Xander asked. "It's a school night."

"So she's Bronzing with Oz." Cordelia shrugged. "Maybe she's gone shopping with Buffy." She thought that through. "No," she said decisively. "Those two would never actually go shopping for fun. If they put the least amount of effort into it, they'd just have to have better wardrobes."

He stood his ground. "I'm going to wait for her a little while." He put his arm around her and urged her against his chest. "C'mon, Cor, we can make out in your car here just as easily as at the Point. Moon, stars, lips? What do you say?"

She sighed heavily, a martyr to ecstasy. "Come on," she said, and led the way to the car.

Buffy gasped and froze in her tracks. "What's the matter?" Giles asked. "Do you feel that . . . 'oddness' again?"

"Weirdness, Giles. It was a weirdness. And, no," she said slowly. "It was just that . . . well, I think I forgot to change the dryer setting to 'delicate' before I put my clothes in." She groaned. "My new shirt is going to shrink."

"I see. Alas," Giles mumbled dismissively.

"Okay, maybe *you* don't care what *you* look like," Buffy said angrily, "but you are not a seventeen-year-old high school female."

"Quite true, Buffy, quite true," Giles agreed.

Buffy didn't miss his whispered "thank the Lord," but she chose to ignore it.

"You were going to tell me about the research you've been doing, sans Willow?" Buffy prompted.

"Ah, yes," he said, happy to be back in familiar territory. Giles hefted her Slayer's bag and used the stake he was carrying to push up his glasses. "There has been a veritable surplus of recent disappearances."

She nodded, all business now.

"Many of them are teenagers," he said pointedly. "They were known to frequent a well-known area where young people congregate for the purposes of—"

"Makeout Point," Buffy said, nodding. "Get on with it, Giles. I may not have a social life, but I know what one is. So, what, did someone go up there and vampirize a bunch of kids who were swallowing each other's tonsils?"

"It would appear so, yes," Giles said, clearing his throat. "If you are correct about there being a new leader of sorts on the Hellmouth, it may be that he is gathering a group of vampires loyal to him to do his bidding."

"Much joy there," Buffy said. "If I can just get him on my good side, maybe he can force them to do my homework." She waved a hand to stave off the inevitable request from Giles to be more serious. "Or I can ask him to—"

She stirred, alert, gesturing to her Watcher.

A vampire lurked nearby.

Giles raised the stake.

"Wait," Buffy said, smiling.

A vampire, yes. Tall, dark, and not fangy at the moment. But handsome. Very, very handsome.

"Hi, Buffy," Angel said. He bobbed his head at Giles. "Good evening."

"What's the haps?" Buffy asked, trying to sound casual.

"I was out." He shrugged. "I was hoping we could—"

Just then, a ring of vampires fell from above, shrieking as they landed in a circle and surrounded Buffy, Giles, and Angel. At least a dozen of them in full fang face, crouched and waiting. Not rushing. Not crowding.

Not acting like your typical demon-infested, ravening corpses.

Buffy glanced around at the odd mix of vampires. Young and old, of varied races and sexes, they also differed in another way. Some were in funereal clothes, indicating that they had been taken to funeral homes and buried in the ground before reviving to undeath. But others were in street clothes or work clothes. One man wore only a bathrobe and boxers. Those were people who were killed and dragged away and never given a proper burial. Whoever had turned them had simply sat around waiting for them to come back to life.

Whoever had made them was making an army.

"This is not good," she whispered, glancing at a man in black who wore a white collar.

Giles said quietly, "This morning, a priest was reported missing. And an elderly lady wearing a jogging suit."

The priest was going after Angel. The old lady jogger growled menacingly at Giles.

The chubby guy in the bathrobe leered at Buffy. "Prepare yourself, Slayer," the vampire growled. "The master has plans for you. You will make a most powerful slave."

Buffy spun, launched a high kick that took bathrobe boy in the chin and rocked his head back hard . . . but not hard enough to snap his neck, she thought with disappointment.

"Okay, people. *Former* people," Buffy corrected. "Maybe if you tell me what's going on, I'll let you live. Who's this master you're all so hot on? 'Cause I knew one guy who called himself that, but what's left of him is in some kid's sandbox somewhere."

The priest vamp laughed. "Soon you will know. When you bow down at his feet and beg for your life!"

As one, the vampires attacked. The priest, bathrobe boy, and a young girl with multiple nose rings and a stud through her lip all went after Angel. But behind them, things got worse. The next three hulking vamps were dressed in their Sunday best—the suits they were buried in. Young guys, not much older than Buffy when they died, and they looked vaguely familiar. She pushed the almost-recognition away. Maybe they'd played football for Sunnydale High or the parochial school two towns over. Buffy didn't want to know.

Giles was attacked by the lady in the jogging suit and a younger boy who looked no older than fourteen. Even as she fought off the vampire offensive line, Buffy kept an eye on Giles, concerned for his safety as always. But, as always, his skill surprised her. The old jogging lady was dispatched instantly. The boy proved to be a different matter indeed, making passes in the air with his hands and shooting out his legs as he twirled in huge, distracting circles.

Some kind of weird martial art, Buffy figured. Not something she'd seen before, though.

Whump! A fist connected with the side of her face. Not a solid hit, but even a graze of knuckles when the punch had vampiric strength behind it was enough to send her reeling.

"That'll teach me to pay attention," she mumbled to herself, and returned to the battle.

Pierced girl shot a kick up toward Angel's head, but he

blocked her attack, parried, and sent her tumbling across the ground. The priest was right in front of him, and Angel kneed him in the gut, then brought both fists down on the vampire's back, forcing him to the earth as well. The overweight guy in the bathrobe came at him then.

"Throw me a stake!" he shouted to Buffy.

But it was Giles who answered.

The Watcher ducked away from the youthful male vampire trying to gut him and hurried to the Slayer's bag. Half-turning, he was about to throw Angel a nicely carved stake when the boy vampire hurled himself at Giles. Giles's reaction was all instinct—the stake came up just in time, and the boy shrieked and exploded into dust. Though the smallest bit taken aback, Giles didn't miss a beat as he tossed the stake to Angel.

As Angelus, he had been called "the Scourge of Europe." That was a different creature entirely, as far as he was concerned. But still, Angel was fierce in battle. With the stake in his hands, the other vampires didn't stand a chance. In moments, the priest was gone. Next, he took out the bathrobed man by flinging him onto his back and landing on top of him. Straddling him, Angel brought the stake down hard.

Of Angel's assailants, only the pierced girl remained. She sneered at Angel, "When we are gone, there will be more. My honorable lord has returned, and he will conquer this land and grind your bones to dust."

"Returned? From where?" Buffy called out, anxious for information.

"If we all die, you'll never know," the girl said to Angel.

Angel looked at her for a beat, part of him unwilling to stake one so young. Then, as she bared her fangs and rushed him, he reflexively thrust the stake hard into her chest.

"Guess we'll have to take that chance," he said as she exploded into dust.

Buffy saw Angel rush to help her, but she was faring just fine on her own. Already, one of the dead jocks had been dusted. The other two were persistent, and she'd fought them off several times without getting the opening she needed for a staking.

They moved around to trap her between them, and Buffy smiled. That trick hadn't worked the last time she'd been ambushed. It wasn't going to work now, either. They started in toward her. Buffy dropped to her hands, swept her legs around under her body in a move the gymnastics coach would have kissed her for, and took one of the dead jocks down at the knees. The other one was looming over her, but Buffy did a backward handspring and brought both of her boots up into his face.

He grabbed his nose and eyes, staggered backward, and didn't even look at her as the stake slid into his heart. While his buddy exploded in a cloud of ash, the last dead jock started to get to his feet.

He never made it.

"Who's next?" Buffy shouted through the dust cloud, but the handful of remaining vampires broke into a run, fleeing like a pack in the same direction.

Buffy watched them a moment, thinking how odd it was that they should stay together. They were so much more . . . disciplined than vamps she'd seen before.

Panting, Buffy slid into Angel's now empty arms and snagged a quick kiss. Giles approached, stake in hand. The three looked down at the piles of dust their conflict had left on the ground.

Then a chill wind kicked up, lifting the piles and scattering them. It whipped at Buffy's hair and clothes, stinging like buckshot.

"We should get out of here," Giles said, gathering up her slayage equipment and stuffing it into her bag.

Angel took off his jacket and put it around her shoulders. "This is the second jacket of mine you've gotten," he teased her, having to yell over the wind. "Pretty soon I won't have anything to wear."

"That's a nice thought," she shouted back.

A bolt of lightning flashed across Angel's face and landed not five feet from them. Buffy shouted and jumped in surprise.

She turned and stared hard at something odd that had been illuminated by the lightning. The departing vamps were running behind a figure who laughed and capered. Even now, Buffy could see her silhouetted in the moonlight.

"Oh my God," Buffy whispered.

It looked like Willow.

CHAPTER EIGHT

As was his custom, Sanno, the god whom men called King of the Mountain, rose from the dawn clouds surrounding Mount Hiei and walked the earth like a man. Each of his footsteps was like a small earthquake, summoning the faithful to greet him like the sun. For Sanno was a gracious god, benevolent and generous. He gave his people clear mountain springs to drink from, hares and other animals to devour, and wood for their villages and the castle of the local branch of the Fujiwara clan, nestled in the foothills of Mount Hiei. He anticipated their every need, and he provided for them.

So he walked, anticipating a fine morning with those who

loved and revered him in the beauty of his shrine, on the far side of Mount Hiei.

But on this snowy winter morning, no one came.

Frowning in displeasure, he ascended Mount Hiei once more and with his mighty breath blew away the clouds. Then he looked down upon his lands and observed his people, gathered on the opposite side of Mount Hiei, cowering before the entrance to a newly erected temple with a strange, curved roof. Some of the women wept and tore their clothes. Their farmer husbands lay prostrate on the ground, their faces buried in the mud.

To the left of the wailing multitude, the local noble family sat on white tatami mats clothed in their formal kimonos adorned with the Fujiwara clan crest. They sat unmoving, like statues, mute and pale with grief. Sanno knew them well. Husband, wife, and son he saw, but not their beautiful daughter, Gemmyo, named after the empress who had reigned some seventy years before.

Of late Sanno had thought of marrying Gemmyo, for should not gods possess all the happiness that mortals do? She was the loveliest maiden in the environs of his mountain, and the most gentle as well. Additionally, she was skilled in music and song. Many nights, he had made the earth tremble violently while dancing to the lively melodies of her koto.

He descended to earth again and walked into the midst of his worshippers, searching both for signs of Gemmyo and for the cause of all this distress.

At the sight of him, the villagers and nobles exchanged glances among themselves. Eyes red, chins quivering, they parted to make him a path as he advanced toward the entrance of the new, oddly fashioned temple.

Within the structure, beneath a canopy decorated with stars and on a bier of red satin lay his beloved. Gemmyo's eyes were shut as if in repose. She was dressed in a beautiful white kimono decorated with herons. At first glance, one might think that she was asleep, even though her body was stark white. For on occasion, it was not unheard of for women to paint themselves with an ivory sheen.

But at her neck gaped two large wounds, and from these wounds blood had run onto the folds of her gown.

Sanno caught his breath, realizing that she had been foully murdered and by the vilest of demons: a vampire.

His eyes filled with ungovernable rage. The pulse at his neck throbbed with fury. Thunder and lightning crackled and roared across the sky and the clouds quickly gathered. The earth rolled like the back of a dragon disturbed from its slumber.

Sanno whirled on the hapless villagers, who stood in stark terror, and bellowed at them, "Who did this?"

No one spoke.

Sanno stamped his foot against the earth and it cracked.

"Who did this?" he bellowed again.

The villagers remained silent.

Then, as Sanno prepared to shake the earth to pieces beneath their feet, a wizened old man staggered forward.

Though it was cold, he wore no shoes and his coat was made of straw. Sanno recognized him as Genji, a poor farmer whose wife was dead and who had no children to serve him in his old age. He had come often to pray at Sanno's shrine.

The old man feebly raised a hand and said, "Sanno-no-kami, these cowardly villagers are silent because the murderer of Gemmyo has threatened them with death if they name him. But I am very old, and I have prayed often for happiness in my declining years. Now I see that my prayers are answered, for I, and I alone, dare to challenge your enemy. If it means my death to reveal his identity to you, then I shall die happy."

In the clutches of his anger, Sanno reached for his great, ancient sword and said, "Speak then, Genji, and know that if your courage deserts you, I shall kill you myself."

The old man shook his head and bowed low several times. "Please, my gracious lord, do not trouble yourself. I'm glad to speak his name aloud. He is Chirayoju."

At the mention of his name, the other villagers drew back in horror. A few began to weep, others to wail.

"Chirayoju?" Sanno repeated. "I know no *tengu* by that name."

Genji said, "He is a vampire who has flown over the sea from the great land of China. And he is a sorcerer who can set fire to our houses with the merest flick of his wrist. He can fan the flames with the smallest exhalation of his breath. And he has promised to do all this if we tell you who he is. For this reason, all fear his wrath. But I shall burn myself to death willingly before I displease you, great Sanno-sama."

"You foolish old man!" shouted another villager, a young man named Akio. He ran to Genji and struck him down with his fist. "You've doomed our whole village!"

"No. *You* have done so," Sanno replied to the youth.

The Mountain God stomped violently on the earth, forcing Akio to his knees. Then he raised his sword and brought it down on Akio's neck, beheading him.

Sanno stomped until no one could stand. He took the heads of those nearest. Then he whirled around and from his hands shot flames of purification onto the body of Gemmyo, so that she might enter Paradise.

The flames traveled from her body to the canopy of stars, to the rest of the temple in which she lay, to the trees, and to the huts of the villagers. And over the trees and bushes to the garrisoned keep of Gemmyo's Fujiwara clan.

That day, a thousand people died because of Sanno's fury.

No longer was he seen as benevolent or kind. No longer was he worshipped.

He was only feared.

CHAPTER NINE

Panting in the backseat of her car, Cordelia pushed Xander away. "Stop moaning," she ordered, sitting up. She leaned into view of the rearview mirror and fluffed her bangs. "I hate it when you moan."

"Wh—wh—," he panted back.

"Because when you moan," she continued, answering the question he had been unable to ask, "it reminds me that it's you, okay?"

"Reminds you . . . *oh*." Xander scowled at her. "Isn't that lovely? So what you're saying is that when you're with me, you pretend you're with someone else."

When she said nothing, only turned and blinked at him in

that blank, yeah-so? expression of hers, he looked at her in complete disgust.

"Okay, fine. I am outta here," he said. He flailed for the door handle. Cordelia reached around his head, obligingly flicked the handle, pushed open the door, and let him fall half out of the car.

"I am so outta here that I am . . . really outta here." He scooted backward the rest of the way and tumbled to the sidewalk. Standing, he regained his footing, if not his dignity, and slammed the car door shut.

"Fine!" Cordelia scrambled back into the driver's seat and started the car. She peeled out and shot down the street.

"Buckle your seat belt!" Xander bellowed. "You nympho!"

She roared down the street, tires squealing.

Xander stomped to the porch and sat down, pulling his knees beneath his chin. He sighed. Wished he'd brought something to do. Even his homework. Now, there was a novel notion.

He was just about to doze off when he heard light footsteps on the walk. He opened his eyes and sat up.

"Will," he said happily. "I was worried about you."

Willow stood with her legs wide apart and her hands on her hips. "Little boy," she sneered, "you worry for me?"

"Well, sure, Will," he said slowly. "Um, have you been forgetting to eat again? Because I know the computer can be all fun and everything, but you're kind of grouchy and perhaps the blood sugar has plummeted? So—"

BUFFY THE VAMPIRE SLAYER

"Silence!" Willow ordered.

"Willow?" He gave her the Nicholson eyebrow. "Are you trying out for a play or something? Because otherwise, I think this is an act you should drop. You are not exactly making friends and influencing people. We want to help you, if you'll just let us."

Willow's face seemed to change. For a moment she looked very sad and little-girl-lost. He went to her with open arms, fully expecting her to slide into them and finish that cry she'd begun last Monday morning.

"Xander," she said miserably, coming toward him. She was limping. Her hands went up to her head as if she had a monster hangover. Which she would not, she being Willow.

"Xander, something's very wro—"

And then she shouted, "No!"

She flew at him, kicking him in the face before he had time to react. Then she landed on top of him and pushed him back, grabbing his hair and slamming his skull against the porch. She made a fist and rammed it into his face. Hit him again. And again. She pummeled him with both fists as he fought to throw her off.

"Wi . . . Wi . . ." Blood streamed down into his throat. He began to choke on it, until the only sound he could make was a desperate gurgle.

"Ah, the scent of life is upon you," Willow said. She threw back her head and laughed. Then, just as he thought she was going to let him up, she hit him again, very hard.

Fade to black.

Very black.

The familiar squeal of tires. Chirayoju looked up from the boy and listened. The mother of Weeping Willow was about to drive down the street. She would see the form of her daughter crouched over her young friend and she would ask far too many questions.

Chirayoju stood and picked up the body. Hoisting the boy over its head, Chirayoju walked to the side of the porch and unceremoniously dumped him in the bushes. Chirayoju was furious at having been interrupted: The youth was not yet dead. His spirit would be delicious. With its sorcery, Chirayoju fed not on mere blood, but on the essence of life itself.

But not this night.

The car pulled up.

"Honey?" Mrs. Rosenberg said as she got out of the car. "What are you doing here? I thought you had a tutoring session with Buffy."

"It ended early," Chirayoju answered. "I wasn't feeling all that hot and Buffy said she was coming down with something too. Xander gave me a ride," it assured Willow's mother, who was looking concerned.

"I've been kind of nervous ever since you were attacked," the woman admitted.

Yes, ever since your daughter was attacked, you have allowed me to take her over and use her. You will allow me

to kill her. You Western mothers and fathers, with your blind-
ness and self-interest, allowing your children to wander the
streets like orphans. Is it a wonder that they are all so weak
and foolish? That I have pickings here the like of which I
never saw in ancient China and Japan, where the parents
were more careful?

It took every ounce of Chirayoju's strength not to burst
into laughter and crack the woman's spine in two, then drink
the life, the spirit, from her paralyzed and dying body. But it
needed shelter from the coming dawn, and the sanctuary it
had found elsewhere was a distance away. More importantly,
it had become apparent that all the girl's friends were vampire
hunters—and the lovely blond maiden was their leader—and
it saw no point in revealing itself to them at this moment. Or
perhaps at any moment. So when the woman came up to it,
put her hand on the forehead of its host, and said, "You feel
hot. Come on inside, sweetie," it meekly obeyed.

As soon as the door is shut, it promised itself, *she dies.*

Such a puny body could be easily hidden.

"Okay. One more time," Buffy said to Giles. Angel, glancing through a book that featured various incantations against
"vampyres and other creatures most abhorrent," set it down
and listened.

She held out her hand. "Vampires." Held out her other
hand. "Demons." Juggled. "Demonic possession."

"Yes. Quite right," Giles said. He looked proud of Buffy.

Angel knew the feeling. Buffy was the one thing in his life he could point to with unmitigated pride.

Then Buffy made a face and juggled again. "But vampiric possession? Oh, Giles, I don't know."

"How else can one explain what you saw?" Giles asked. He looked to Angel as if for backup. Angel shrugged. He was just about as perplexed as Buffy.

"None of this sounds at all familiar to me," he had to admit, flicking the pages of the book as if the answers lay there. "I've never come across anything like it. As far as I know, vampires can't possess the living."

"However," Giles mused, "one could argue that vampirism is a form of demonic possession. Vampires are basically soul-less human corpses with demons residing within." He had the grace to clear his throat and say, "Present company excepted."

"I'll go along with that," Angel conceded. "But the demons who inhabit vampires can't jump from body to body, or influence another person the way other demons can. There was that vessel thing with the Master, but that was just a vicarious way for him to feed."

"Well, I'm very sorry I didn't pay closer attention to your concerns about Willow," Giles said to Buffy. "Clearly, something quite serious is happening to her and—"

Buffy shifted uneasily. "I don't know what I saw. I thought it looked like Willow, but maybe it wasn't. I only saw it for an instant. Maybe I thought I saw her because I'm so worried about her." She gazed at the phone. "I'd like to call and check on her, but her mother would kill her. And then mine would kill me."

"It's been a very long day . . . and night, for all of us. Perhaps it's best that we wait until the morning," Giles agreed. "I'm certain Willow will be at school, and all will come clear." His half-smile was only half-reassuring.

"Come on, I'll walk you home," Angel said, taking Buffy's hand.

"Okay," she said, with her quick, eager smile that sometimes cut him to the quick.

Once outside the school, Angel took Buffy in his arms and kissed her long and hard. He couldn't believe that of all the mortal girls there were in this world, he had fallen in love with the Slayer. And knowing that she loved him too made his strange and lonely existence more bearable. He was an outcast among vampires, yet still one of them, and sometimes her love was all that sustained him. That, and his vow to rid the earth of his brother and sister abhorrent creatures of the night.

He smiled down at her as she peered up at him with her huge blue eyes. She had no idea what dark thoughts were running through his mind.

She murmured, "Angel, I'm so confused."

"Why?" He trailed his fingers through her hair.

"It's just that . . ." She shrugged and laid her head against his chest. "Well, like with Willow, She's been acting like such a b . . . bad person, bad, and so cranky and all. So then we get attacked by vampires and I decide I see her with them."

"You might have."

"No. In my heart, I know Willow's not possessed. She's just scared. I can't believe I would even think such a thing. But then, it's like my mom and me."

"She thinks you're possessed?" Angel said, amused. He suspected he knew what was coming.

Buffy did not disappoint.

"It seems like half my life, my mom is saying, 'Buffy, this just isn't like you.' Whenever I've done something to disappoint her. But if it wasn't like me, I wouldn't have done it. I couldn't have done it." She tilted her head back and gazed up at him. "Do you know what I mean?"

He let his smile fade so she wouldn't think he was laughing at her, but his heart went out to her. There was nothing he could do to spare her from growing up.

"I think so," he replied.

"Look at Xander and Cordelia," she went on. "Talk about possessed. They can't even explain why they do what they do." She shuddered. "I mean, it's just so weird."

Chuckling, he nodded. Xander and Cordelia had surprised him, too. But when he thought about it, the spark had always been there. The way they bantered, throwing barbs at each other. Hotheaded and passionate, both of them.

Yes, it made sense.

"It was a lot easier when I was your age," he told her. "When people did the unexpected, we said they were possessed and left it at that." He moved his shoulders. "Actually, we didn't leave it at that. We usually burned them at the stake or hanged them. Or, on a good day, we committed them to asylums."

He cupped her chin. "A strong-willed girl like you would have been labeled a witch. We'd definitely have burned you."

"'C'mon, baby, light my fire,'" she quipped, but he could tell he had unnerved her.

He knew that sometimes she forgot how old he was—242 to her 17. It was easy to forget because when he had been turned into a creature of the night, he had been near her age. The decades had not aged his physical appearance at all.

Some of the mortal women he had known through the years had considered that a blessing . . . and begged him to change them at the height of their beauty. That he had not done, once his soul was restored to him. Not one could have fathomed the curse he would have laid upon their shoulders had he done so.

"Your mother sees all that's best in you," Angel told Buffy as he traced the hollow of her cheek. She, too, was a beauty, but like many truly astonishing women, she didn't see it. "Your face is the mirror of her love for you. When she looks at you and sees a flaw, a part of her blames herself for failing you in some way."

He cupped her chin and raised her face toward his. "That's why she's so hard on you, Buffy. Because she loves you so much."

"I'm her mirror?" Buffy asked tentatively. She thought that over. "Her cracked mirror," she snorted.

"No. Clear as glass," he said. "Pure."

She shook her head. "Not me."

"Yes. You."

"But what about you, Angel?" She was changing the subject. He let her. "You don't have a reflection."

"When I look at you, I do."

He kissed her, tentatively at first, then with more passion. She answered back, and he held her tightly. With all his heart, he wanted to be what Buffy wanted him to be. He wanted to be exactly what she needed. But he was a vampire, a half-demon, with a human soul warring against the darkness within every moment of every day.

And he blamed himself fully for the many times he had failed her in the past. If there was any way he could undo what he had done . . .

"Angel," Buffy whispered, "I love you."

"I love you, too, Buffy."

"I want—," she began, but he stilled her voice with a finger across her lips.

"Let me walk you home now," he said gently.

They strolled arm in arm, like a girl and a guy going home from a date.

In Willow's room, Chirayoju got ready for bed and listened to the boy's slowing heartbeat in the bushes outside the house. The youth would very likely be dead before dawn. If not, Chirayoju knew it would have another chance at the boy. Xander. He cared for Weeping Willow, and it would be the death of him.

The vampire sorcerer glided to the high windows and looked out. In the darkness, it could see the silhouettes of its minions, the many vampires it had pressed into its service, as well as those it had caused to be created. Those that had already hunted and were sated for the night had gathered near the home of Weeping Willow, where their master resided, to pay homage to him until the dawn forced them to seek shelter.

Chirayoju had begun to build its army. A small force, true. But growing with each passing night. Or it would have been, if not for the damnable Vampire Slayer. As Chirayoju continued to gain strength, it would need more time to assemble its troops, not as in the days of old when it could command entire villages to rise up as one. But once it had reached its full strength, not even the Slayer would stop it from building a regiment of the dead large enough to enslave all the lands touched by the light of the moon.

A cold breeze whistled through the open window. It thought of the cherry blossoms on the mountains of Japan, and the beautiful trees that had once bloomed in the garden in Sunnydale. Even now, it saw their quivering phantoms, recalling its peace as it had sat among them, plucking from the earth a withered bonsai tree to begin its shrine in the girl's room.

Willow's mother knocked on the door. Chirayoju said, "Yes?"

"Honey, I'm . . . are you all right?"

"I'm fine," Chirayoju snapped. "Just tired."

There was a pause. "You don't seem yourself."

Chirayoju crossed to the mirror on the wall and stared into it. Through the sheer force of its will, the girl's features blurred and its own floated over them like a shimmering green diaphanous mask. It grinned at the fury it saw there. The unconquerable spirit. The vitality and strength of purpose.

"I am myself, Mom," Chirayoju answered. "Who else would I be?"

Willow's mother gave a short, awkward laugh. "I guess that's the question most parents of teenagers ask themselves."

She pushed the door open, came in, and sat on Willow's bed.

"You were so cute and little when you were born," she said wistfully. "I held you for hours, just staring down at you. I couldn't believe how perfect you were. Your hands and feet. Each finger, each toe."

The woman picked up a pillow and held it against her chest. "The first time you had a temper tantrum, I was so shocked. My perfect little baby! But I was proud of you too. You were becoming independent."

She plucked at the corner of the pillow. "As soon as a baby is born, she spends her days learning how to leave her parents' care. First she rolls away, and then she crawls away, and then she walks away."

She sighed. "But I have hope that in the end, when she's all grown up, she'll come back. Not as my little baby, of course." She smiled. "But maybe as my friend."

Chirayoju stared at her. It couldn't believe her utter weakness. Nor that she honestly believed that the parent, who should be idolized and worshipped as a god, could be looked upon with such lack of respect that he—or she—would be treated as a friend.

When it conquered this land, it would ensure that all such thinking was banished.

Even by the dead.

It smiled. "I hope that too, Mom," it said.

She was alive only because as they entered the house, it had realized that if it murdered her, there would be an investigation. Because she was an adult, there would be too many questions. Already, the authorities were looking into some of the deaths it had caused—the holy man, the old lady killed by his minions. But the boy in the bushes was only a boy, and children died in all kinds of tragic and unexplained ways, even in these modern times.

In fact, especially in these modern times of drive-by shootings and incredible violence. And especially in this place, the Hellmouth, where evil flourished and grew.

So it was safe to kill the boy. He was disposable. And unnecessary to the furthering of its ambition.

Willow's mother crossed to it and kissed it softly on her daughter's cheek. It was very sorry that it could not kill her.

Every time Weeping Willow heard her voice, she fought to regain possession of her being. Chirayoju found her struggles distracting and slightly tiring.

With time, it would obliterate her, and she would struggle no longer.

Outside, the boy's heartbeat slowed even further.

Soon, very soon, his struggles would also end.

CHAPTER TEN

Mirror, mirror, on the wall," Buffy said to herself as she checked her visual presentation in the girls' bathroom. Around her, girls milled and talked about guys and clothes. The pleasant aspects of teenage-hood. And the not so pleasant: homework and fights with their parents.

The pleasant stuff she couldn't really relate to. The other stuff, sadly, she knew all too well: Last night her mom had gotten a gander at her latest catch of "below averages." And when she said, "Buffy, is this the way it's always going to be?" Buffy tried to remember Angel's lovely speech about how she was a mirror and her mom loved that mirror, but all it felt like was that she was in for seven years of really hard labor.

A few girls said hi to Buffy but no one really rushed over to get her autograph. She had no other real girl buds except for Willow. She missed Willow—her version of Willow, not the update, Will version 6.66—more than ever.

In fact, she sort of missed the way things had been when she'd first come to Sunnydale—the basic threesome of her, Willow, and Xander: the Three Musketeers, one for all and all for one. Now Willow and Oz were getting together, and Xander and Cordy were doing whatever it was they called it. Their friendships had changed, and that had changed their lives.

On the other hand, she had Angel. As if that weren't weird enough.

But since she was the Slayer, relationships had to take a backseat. Top priority was figuring out who the new top vamp in town was. So far, she'd had no luck beyond being haunted by the idea that the lithe figure she'd seen in the cemetery the night before had been Willow.

She meandered out of the bathroom and was about to have a post-Starbucks, pre-first-period chat with Giles when Cordelia rushed toward her with her cell phone in hand. Buffy raised her brows and waited for whatever bombshell Cordy was about to detonate. Probably about the fact that her hair was "askew," as Willow would put it. It was true: Bad hair day was upon the Slayer. Cordelia's revelation would not be news.

Cordelia stopped short, looked left, right, must have decided none of the Cordettes could possibly witness her speaking to one of the untouchables, and rushed over to Buffy.

"Buffy," she said, taking a breath, "Xander isn't in school today. And neither is Willow."

"Aha," Buffy said slowly. "And you're thinking what? Xander and Willow have eloped to Las Vegas?"

"I'm thinking, Miss Slayer, that I left Xander at Willow's last night because he was all so worried about her, and now they're missing."

Buffy considered. "Given the fact that we live on the Hellmouth, and that Willow has been acting more like you than herself—"

"And that Xander and I have been, ah, meeting for breakfast every morning and he would have called if he had to skip . . . breakfast," Cordelia insisted.

"Have you considered that maybe he's mad at you and just blew you off?" Buffy suggested.

Cordelia rolled her eyes. "Trust me. Xander would not miss one of our . . . breakfast . . . meetings if he had a choice in the matter." She huffed. "C'mon, Buffy, this is *me* we're talking about. I mean, I know I feel like I must have done something horrible in a past life to be so completely unable to control my attractions, but Xander . . . Xander must feel like he's won the lottery. He wouldn't just not show."

Hard as it was for Buffy to admit it, she did see Cordelia's point. Xander was, after all, a guy.

"What did he say when you called him?" Buffy asked, looking down at Cordelia's cell phone.

Cordelia looked as if Buffy had shot her. "When *I* called *him*? Buffy, excuse me, I do not call boys. They call me."

"Except if they're dead," Buffy said, letting her irritation show.

"Ooh." Cordelia whipped open her cell phone and demon-dialed Xander's number.

"I was changing my nail appointment, you know," she said to Buffy, then blinked and nodded at Buffy. "Hello, Mrs. Harris?" she asked sweetly. "This is Cordelia. What? Cordelia *Chase*! Xander must have told you about . . . May I *speak* to Xander? *What?*" She looked stricken. "The police?"

"Oh my God," Buffy whispered. "What? What?"

"Okay. Yes, of course. Yes, of course I do. I will. Good-bye."

Cordelia whipped the phone shut and grabbed Buffy's forearm. She had a surprisingly firm grip.

"Buffy, Xander never came home last night." Her eyes were actually welling with tears. "His family thinks he might have been abducted or murdered or whatever, you know, with all these missing persons lately." She pressed her fingertips against her eyelids and choked back a sob. "And if he's dead, the last thing I told him was to stop moaning."

Buffy took that in but moved on. "What about Willow? Call her house too." Now Buffy was sorry she hadn't gone ahead and phoned last night, no matter how late it had been.

Cordelia handed her the phone. "You. I don't know her number."

Buffy punched it in. Waited. There was no answer. She hit redial, in case someone in the Rosenberg household was on the other line. There was still nothing, not even voice mail. She traded stricken glances with Cordelia.

"Giles," they said in one voice.

They raced to the library. "We'll get him to cover for us," Buffy said. "We can spend all day off campus without getting busted for anything. He's got all these amazing hall passes they never tell us students about, Cordelia. Work furlough thingies or something."

"I always knew this place was just a well-disguised prison," Cordelia muttered. She skidded on the tiled floor. "Of course I had to wear heels today."

Shoulder to shoulder, Buffy and Cordelia pushed open the double doors to find Giles speaking very seriously to Oz and handing him a large canvas sack that clanked as Oz took it. The two guys looked startled, then both relaxed.

"Hi, girls," Oz said. "Just picking up the new and improved Oz-wolf restraint system." He pointed moonward. "It's that time of the month."

"Oh." Buffy nodded. "Werewolf time. Understood. Um." Oz had recently learned that due to a little finger nip from his three-year-old nephew, he turned into a werewolf three nights of every month. Willow understood, which was very nice. In fact, all the Scooby Gang understood. It wasn't his fault, and he never hurt anyone.

Oz peered at her. "Are you okay? Is everything all right?"

"Sure." She smiled and elbowed Cordelia, who lit up like a Christmas tree.

"Everything is super-duper," Cordelia assured him.

"I hope Willow gets over that stomach virus soon," he said, and started to leave.

"Wait," Buffy said urgently, grabbing his arm, then let go of him and cleared her throat. "You spoke to her?"

"Got an e-mail. See ya."

Clank, clank, clank, he was out the door.

"If she's sending e-mail, maybe she's okay," Cordelia said, at the same time that Buffy ran up to Giles and said, "You've got to cover for us. Xander and Willow are missing."

"Yes, yes, of course," he began, a worried expression on his face, "but what—"

"I'll drive," Cordelia said. "I'm the obvious choice."

"Since you have the car, and a license, and y'know, know how . . . I'll go along with that," Buffy said. "Pit stop at my locker for my slayage stuff."

They whirled and left. Behind them Giles called, "Yes, all right. But what's going on?"

"Please don't kill me," Buffy murmured as they shot around the corner and headed down the straightaway toward Willow's house.

"You sound just like Xander," Cordelia said. "Only, I can understand it from him. He's lived in Sunnydale all his life. Home of the five, count them, five, major traffic intersections. But you've lived in LA."

"Just jumpy, I guess," Buffy said. "And more aware that it's possible to die at an early age."

"Here we are."

Cordelia slammed on the brakes just as Buffy, having been warned, rolled herself forward like you do when your 747's going down. Cordelia sighed, irritated, but flew out of the car and chittered toward the walk in her very high heels.

Buffy, in knee-high boots, met her there, then stopped Cordelia from leaping onto the porch.

"We don't know who or what is in there," she whispered. "No one answered the phone."

"Oh, right." Cordelia was wide-eyed, excited and scared at the same time.

"Let's look around first," Buffy said quietly. "I'll go left and you—"

"I'll go left too," Cordelia said firmly.

"All right. Stay behind me."

Buffy hefted her Slayer's bag, making sure she had both a stake and a cross within easy reach. It was the middle of the day, of course, but you never knew what you were going to run into in Sunnydale. She scrutinized the lawn as they tiptoed silently over it, seeing nothing that would cause any alarm.

They came to a cluster of bushes. Buffy parted the nearest one. Nothing. She moved to the next one and crept around it.

On the other side Xander lay, his face mottled and bruised, as still and white as death.

"Oh my God!" Cordelia shrieked.

The front door burst open and Buffy whipped around, stake in hand, ready for a fight.

Instead, she saw Willow's mom in her chenille bathrobe, her eyes ringed as if she hadn't had any sleep.

"Buffy, what's wrong?" she cried.

"Mrs. Rosenberg, go call 911. It's Xander."

"He's dead," Cordelia wailed, throwing herself across Xander's still form. "Oh my God!"

Mrs. Rosenberg started to go toward Xander, but Buffy took her firmly by the arm and led her into the kitchen. She took the portable out of its charger and punched in 911. "Where's Willow?" she asked.

"She took off," Mrs. Rosenberg said anxiously. "I've been hoping and praying for a call, but . . ."

"I called here about half an hour ago," Buffy said.

"Emergency services," the operator said.

"There's been an accident," Buffy announced. "Please send an ambulance." She handed the phone to Willow's mom to give out the particulars of her address. Buffy was so freaked out that she couldn't remember Willow's house number.

Then she flew down the hall and into Willow's room while Mrs. Rosenberg dashed outside to check on Xander.

As Mrs. Rosenberg had said, the room was empty. The bed was unmade, and Willow's stuffed animals lay in clumps on the floor. In twisted, headless clumps, Buffy noticed as she bent and examined one of them, a tiny white unicorn. A pencil had been driven through its chest.

Her hair stood on end. Her face was hot. *Willow, what's happened to you?* she asked silently.

Then the computer announced, "You have mail."

Buffy stood and walked to it. She clicked on Willow's mailbox. It was from Oz.

Hope you feel better. Drink lots of liquids and take a lot of vitamin C, he had written. *P.S. Luv ya.*

So they were still in the puppy phase, not having progressed to the more committed conjugation of the verb, which was, *I love you.*

Next to the computer was a little dried-up bush. Buffy picked it up and examined it. It looked vaguely familiar, but she couldn't place where she'd seen something like it before.

Beside it lay a foreign coin. No. It was the disk Willow had accidentally knocked off the big Japanese sword on the wall. And beside that, a little green flower made of folded paper. Buffy stared at it a moment. Her heart pounding, she unfolded it.

A siren blared outside. Red and blue lights strobed through the venetian blinds. The ambulance had arrived.

Buffy put the disk and the tree in her Slayer's bag. As she moved from the room, she unfolded the note. It read, *I'm sorry.*

"The paramedics are here," Mrs. Rosenberg called. "They'd like to speak to you, Buffy."

Without speaking she nodded and dropped the note into her bag as well. She would show them to Giles.

Walking back down the hall, she stumbled and fell against the wall. She was trembling from head to toe, terrified for her friends. Tears streamed down her face. If she lost them, if she lost any of them because of who and what she was, she would never forgive herself. Ever.

Which is the burden Angel carries, she realized sharply. He had not only lost loved ones, he had killed them himself, and done it with a song in his heart, as he had once told her.

She shivered, pitying him beyond words.

Then she ran to the ambulance, following Xander's gurney. He was strapped to the cot. Blood and liquids dripped into his right arm, and there was an oxygen mask covering his face.

"I'm going with," Cordelia insisted, scrambling into the ambulance.

"Me too," Buffy said.

Cordy sighed. "All right, I'm not leaving my car here, so we'll drive."

This ride in Cordelia's car was significantly different. Not that Cordelia was any more cautious or skilled than before. But this time, Buffy said nothing. She was preoccupied with her fear. Fear that Xander could die, though it now seemed he would be all right with a transfusion and a few days' bed rest. Fear that Willow might already be dead. All of it because she had not focused on finding the vampire that was organizing a new wave of horrors that swept across Sunnydale.

And now seemed to be focused on Buffy and her friends.

But there was another fear building inside Buffy. One that she wanted very much to push away, to ignore. Instead, it started to overwhelm her with its logic. Fear that she *had* seen Willow the night before, in the cemetery, silhouetted in moonlight. And now Willow was gone, and the note she had left behind was an apology. For what? Buffy thought she knew, and her suspicions made her sick and afraid.

Vampiric possession. It had seemed just a theory last night. Now it seemed one of the most horrifying possibilities she had ever encountered.

Despite technological advances that would have made futurists such as H. G. Wells and George Orwell faint with amazement, the world's scientific community hadn't been able to make an international phone line that didn't have that hollow, tinny quality that Giles found so annoying. It had taken him several phone calls to finally track down the phone number he was looking for, and when he finally did, he hesitated to use it.

In Sunnydale, it was just about noontime. But in Tokyo, Japan, it was already five o'clock the following morning. He didn't relish the idea of waking a seventy-three-year-old man at the crack of dawn. But then, he didn't have much choice, and even less time to quibble over social courtesies.

After he'd dialed the number, Giles was pleased to hear it ringing clear on the other end. Hollow and tinny, yes, but at least without that horrible echo that sometimes accompanies international long distance and makes real conversation almost impossible.

There was a click, the sound of the phone being picked up on the other end. *"Mushimushi?"*

"Ohayo gozaimasu," Giles said, in the little Japanese he had learned for this call. *"America kara, Giles desu . . ."*

"Ah, the esteemed Professor Giles," the man replied in perfect English. "This is Kobo. It is an honor to speak with you. Your Japanese is excellent, but if you would be so kind, I would enjoy taking this opportunity to practice my English."

Giles smiled to himself, despite the gravity of the situation. He had never spoken to Kobo before, but he knew the man by reputation. And his response fulfilled Giles's expectations completely. For Giles's Japanese, what little of the language he knew, was horrible. Kobo had offered to speak English not because he wanted practice—he was obviously fluent—but because he wanted to save Giles the embarrassment of speaking Japanese so very badly.

The Japanese culture was so completely different from American culture—or any Western culture, for that matter, including his own—that at times it was difficult for Giles to remember just how different.

The Japanese would never address a subject directly when it could be gotten to by a more circuitous route. And certainly, they would never embarrass someone else, or even allow them to embarrass themselves, for fear of humiliating themselves, or losing face, as they called it.

Kobo was a traditionalist. Giles would have to tread carefully in this conversation in order not to offend the old man. However, he did feel that he possessed a certain advantage in that he was British, more reserved than an American, and, one hoped, less brash and impatient. At least, that was how he had been when he'd arrived in Sunnydale.

But when one spent the majority of one's time in the company not only of Americans, but Southern Californians, and to add to that, Southern Californian adolescents, one could no longer assume that one's cultural reflexes remained intact. After all, even the sarcastic young Xander had referred to him recently as "one happ'nin' dude." And only with a certain amount of irony . . .

"Thank you, *sensei*," he said, using the Japanese word for "teacher," the highest title of honor there was in that language beyond prostrating oneself before the gods and the Emperor. Besides, it was an accurate title: Kobo was a professor at Tokyo University.

"Please forgive me for waking you at this unconscionable hour, but I am in the midst of a rather urgent matter, and I had hoped you might be able to illuminate certain areas where my own records and research are lacking."

There was silence for several moments at the other end. If it hadn't been for the crackle and hiss of the open line, Giles would have thought he's lost the connection. When the Great Teacher spoke at last, his words came as a great surprise.

"I knew your grandmother," the old Japanese man said.

"My . . ."

"She was the greatest Watcher I ever knew," Kobo-*sensei* continued.

"That's very kind of you," Giles said, slightly taken aback. "She spoke very highly of you as well, *sensei*. In fact, she often said that everything that she knew she learned from you."

"Ah, no, it was she who was the teacher, Professor Giles. Your grandmother was already a Watcher when I knew her," Kobo replied. "I would be honored to be of whatever humble assistance I can."

Giles pushed up his glasses and leaned on his elbow as he gestured to the piles of books on his desk, despite knowing the man couldn't see him.

"Well, to be honest, I have had little time to even begin my own research on the matter at hand. At the moment, I'm still attempting to put together a hypothesis from which to begin."

Giles told the retired Watcher all that had happened in Sunnydale thus far, including the behavior of the vampires that had been stalking Buffy, as well as the events at the museum, and Willow's, and now Xander's, disappearance. As he hadn't heard from Buffy since she and Cordelia had left, he had to assume something was going on. Given Buffy's position as Slayer, and their geographic location on the Hellmouth, it was a safe assumption.

"If you know anything about this Sanno deity, it might be helpful," Giles mentioned. "I am a bit confused, however, because I've found no Japanese references to vampires at all in Japanese legend."

"Excuse me, please, Giles-*sensei*. Though I am certain your research was exhaustive, I can only suggest that the texts you consulted were unfortunately incomplete. The truth is that there are few, if any, *Japanese* vampires in Japanese legend," the old man said, his voice crackling over the line. "In our stories, vampires are usually portrayed as Chinese, due to the historical rivalry between our two nations."

"I see," Giles said carefully, not wishing to force the professor to rehash any painful past history of his nation.

"In fact, most of them probably *were* Chinese in antiquity. China was a more advanced nation, where the undead were more likely to be discovered and effectively hunted. Japan must have seemed fertile territory at the time."

"An excellent point," Giles allowed.

"You honor me." The old man cleared his throat. "As for Sanno, if he is the Mountain King from the legends I am familiar with, I know him as *Oyamagui no kami*. I'm sure he has other names. It's an old legend, and not one that is often repeated. Though I do seem to recall . . ."

The old man paused for a moment before continuing. "Excuse me, please, but are the collected Watchers' journals available to you, Professor Giles?"

"Yes, of course." He would be horribly remiss as Buffy's Watcher if he did not have a full set.

"How fortunate. Do you recall Claire Silver?"

Giles searched his memory for several seconds before recognition hit him. "I have examined her journals," he said, "but the last time I did so in depth was years ago."

Silence again on the other end of the line. Giles thought again of the Japanese traditions of honor and face, and wondered if, despite his required compliments, Kobo might be quietly disapproving of Giles's lack of knowledge on this subject. Of the Watchers left alive, Kobo-*sensei* was one of the most respected. The idea that the man might look down on Giles's performance as a Watcher had not actually occurred to him until now, pressed as he was to help Buffy, and now that it had, the tone in the older man's voice was unmistakable, no matter how hard he tried to hide it behind politeness.

"I respectfully suggest, Giles-*sensei*, that a man of your scholarly achievements might find Claire Silver's journals instructive," the old man said. "I seem to recall discussion of the King of the Mountain in them. But the last time I read them was a very long time ago, when I still had a Slayer to watch over. Thus I have allowed the story to slip from memory."

There! Giles thought. That was a barb, for certain. An implication that Giles himself had been lax in his duties by not committing more of the Watchers' journals to memory. He ignored it. The information he required was more important than saving face for himself.

"But Claire Silver was a Watcher in Britain in the nineteenth century," Giles countered. "What has that got to do with ancient Japan?"

"Sadly, I have told you all I can remember, Mr. Giles," Kobo said simply. "I fear that I have wasted your valuable time."

Giles paused before replying. The old Watcher had admitted he didn't know everything. But for Giles not to defend the man, even to himself, would be a direct insult. Kobo might have insulted him, but he had done it indirectly. Even if it was just for appearance' sake, or for the memory of his grandmother, Giles would do what was expected of him.

"Oh, no, *sensei*," Giles insisted, "you have been a great deal of help. Your wisdom and experience are unparalleled and you honor me with your assistance. I thank you. I am certain that this conversation will be of great help. It might even save the life of the current Chosen One, as well as several of her friends."

This time, Giles actually heard Kobo sigh. "Giles-*sensei*," the old Watcher said slowly, as if reluctant to speak. His amiable tone was obviously forced now. "I must applaud your dedication to the Chosen One, for of course I have heard of it. Ah, yet it is most unusual for a Watcher to place the satisfaction of the Slayer, even her well-being, and particularly the well-being of her *friends*, above the mission of the Chosen One. Few Slayers have ever *had* friends. You honor her by your loyalty to her many needs, even those that may seem frivolous to an old Japanese man."

Giles froze, stared at the phone as if it were the offending object, as if it had insulted him.

"I apologize if such concerns do not meet with your standard for the appropriate behavior of a Watcher," Giles snapped. "And, with all due respect, sir, and as you pointed out, at least the Slayer I am responsible for is still alive."

He hung up, angrier and more confused than ever. For several minutes, he searched the volumes of journals for those of Claire Silver, but he had been in the midst of reorganizing them when this crisis arose.

The phone rang. He glanced at it before picking it up, wondering if it was Kobo, ready for another volley.

"Yes?" he demanded sharply.

"Giles, it's Buffy. We're at the hospital. Xander's been . . . um, he's . . ." She whispered into the phone. "*Attacked*, if you know what I mean."

"I'm on my way," he said, rising from his chair.

"I'm going to look for Willow."

"No. Wait for me, Buffy," he said sternly.

"But—"

"Wait." He hung up and ran out the door, nearly crashing into Principal Snyder.

"So sorry," Giles said in a rush. "Must dash. Sorry."

"Mr. Giles?" Principal Snyder called after him.

"Sorry!" Giles called back.

At the hospital, the nurse was trying to reach Xander's mother on one phone, even as Buffy hung up with Giles on the other. Their conversation was brief and hushed, and when Buffy was through, she felt even worse about things than on her ride over with Cordy. More than anything, she wanted to run out and find Willow, as quickly as possible. But Giles had ordered her to stay put.

Buffy was a strong-willed girl—you had to be when you were the Slayer—and she didn't like taking orders from anyone. But if Giles felt strongly enough about it to try giving an order, the least she could do was follow it.

So she paced in Xander's hospital room with Cordelia, who was sunk tiredly into a chair pulled up to his bedside. She'd cried a little when the doctors were fussing over him, and her makeup was a mess, but not once did she ask Buffy if she looked okay. She only held Xander's hand, half-holding and half-massaging it, as if she could warm him again and take the ghostly pallor from his cheeks.

He had lost a lot of blood, and there were holes in his neck.

Could Willow have actually put them there? Willow, a vampire? Buffy wondered if she would have to . . .

. . . would have to . . .

"No," she said, clenching her teeth. She couldn't be certain what she would do when she found Willow.

But one thing was certain: It would be very much better to find her friend before the sun went down. For the moment, however, she could only pace.

By the time Giles got there, she was frantic. Though stunned by the sight of Xander, he briefed her on his conversation with the Japanese Watcher, and she practically pushed him back out the door.

"Library, Giles," she begged. "We've got questions. You get answers."

"I'm not certain I should go," Giles argued.

Buffy looked at him, then glanced quickly at the others in the room. Cordelia, who sat next to Xander with a worried look on her face. Xander himself, who was still unconscious, although recovering, according to the doctors. He wouldn't be running the hundred for a couple of weeks, but he'd be home sucking down chocolate milk shakes and making his mom do Blockbuster runs within a few days.

Buffy glanced around to make sure Xander's mother—who had stepped out into the hall to speak with the doctor—hadn't returned, and then she looked up at Giles again.

"We need to know what happened to him," Buffy said, staring down at Xander. It was obvious Giles's protective streak was overpowering his sense of logic. Buffy was touched. Her Englishman was the best Watcher a girl could ask for.

"Your job is not to stare at Xander and fret," Buffy insisted. "That Kobo guy told you where to look for the knowledge stuff, and a librarian's gotta do what a librarian's gotta do."

Giles was obviously about to protest when Cordelia said Giles's name. Her voice was so low that at first Giles didn't hear her.

"Giles," Cordelia said again, emphatically. "I'll be here.

I'm not going anywhere, not right now. Whatever happened, I'll call you as soon as Xander's able to talk about it."

Giles pursed his lips. "You don't think it would be better if . . ."

"I can handle it," Cordelia said, only half-looking at him. "I'll find out what happened to Xander. You go back to the library and read Claire What's-her-name's journals." She looked at Buffy with satisfied self-importance. "We all have jobs to do, right, Buffy?"

"And that's my cue to start the hunt for Willow," Buffy said.

"Take my car," Cordelia said generously.

"I don't have a license," Buffy said quickly.

"Yeah, but you can drive it if you have to, right?" Cordelia asked.

"I'm not sure that's the wisest course," Giles began, but Buffy cut him off. Cordelia was right.

"I think I can manage," Buffy said. "Okay, I'm gone."

Then she turned and almost ran from the hospital. It was nearly one o'clock already. Dusk already seemed too close.

Of course, in Sunnydale, the night always came too soon.

CHAPTER ELEVEN

A h, this undefended land! These foolish, weak people!
And, best of all, these demons!

They flocked to Chirayoju, desperate for a leader. *Oni*, who had traveled from China with the Buddhist faithful. The vampiric *kappa*, strange, scaled creatures whose bowl-like heads were filled with magick water. When the water spilled, the *kappa* lost their powers, but not their yen for blood.

Blood that Chirayoju found for them in plentiful supply.

Itself, it had not dined on anything as exquisite as the maiden Gemmyo—although it had sampled at least a hundred humans since it had left Mount Hiei—but its new army of followers had assured it that the Emperor, being holy, would taste the best of all.

And so, with its minions who now numbered in the thousands, Chirayoju descended like a nightmare upon the capital of this Land of the Rising Sun, called by some Heijo and by others Nara.

In the forest its army camped and measured the defenses of the Emperor's palace. Fierce warriors guarded the walls, but within, the court of the Emperor Kammu languished like fat cattle. They were obsessed with the airy cultivation of art and culture and the monotonous veneration of the Lord Buddha. Nunneries and monasteries littered the wooded hills. A statue of Buddha as tall as eight men greeted the sun daily. Chirayoju was contemptuous, considering the Buddha himself a weak, unambitious being who preached the obliteration of ambition as the key to happiness.

While the nobles within the palace walls wrote poems and discussed philosophy, the people outside the walls starved. Taxes were high and crops failed despite the fertile land. They were ripe for unrest and rebellion.

Chirayoju saw much to please it.

So it left behind its fearful minions and walked the nights among the starving peasants, whispering to them of all the things it could give them—treasures, weapons, and warriors—if only they would call it master. They began to listen. They began to believe. Soon, they looked forward to its nightly visits and its tales of how their lives would be, if only they would deliver the Emperor to it.

It began to seem natural for them to hate their supreme lord, who was a god on Earth, and to practice the hacking and slashing of mortal combat with their fishing poles and pitchforks. They began to anticipate the battle with the heavily fortified palace, forgetting that they possessed neither armor nor weapons, and unaware that their general, Chirayoju the Liberator, had promised its second wave of attackers their own blood in exchange for *their* loyalty and aid.

This second wave were the *oni* and the *kappa*.

Who likewise did not know that it had promised its third wave of attackers the delicious and magickal blood of the *oni* and the *kappa* in exchange for *their* loyalty and aid.

This third wave consisted of the vampires it made from the ranks of the *eta*. In the dark of night, alone and in secret, it would fly to the hovels in the filthy quarter of these, the Untouchables of Japan, who butchered animals and tanned their hides into leather and prepared the human dead for burial. Shunned by all except other *eta*, reviled and cursed, they fully embraced the new life Chirayoju offered them. They would willingly die any death Chirayoju ordered in exchange for the power and freedom it gave them.

So, with its three ranks of soldiers ripe for battle, Chirayoju shut itself deep within a cave and on the longest night of winter, cast its dragon bones. It sought the most auspicious moment to strike at the Emperor and devour him.

Not knowing, at the time, that Sanno, the Mountain King, had gathered thousands of followers of his own and stood poised in the foothills for battle. In his left hand he held fire and lightning. In his right, water and wind.

He vowed he would destroy Nara before he allowed Chirayoju to escape him. He would destroy all of Japan, if need be.

His only thought was of vengeance.

But his actions spoke otherwise: He went with a small company of retainers to the gates of the palace and demanded an audience with Kammu. From the guards' behavior, he deduced that word of his deadly temper had not spread as far as Nara, and that he was believed to be the benevolent deity he once had been. For the guards, astonished to see the god in their midst, quickly ran and informed the Emperor of his esteemed guest.

Hasty and elaborate preparations were made, and Sanno was welcomed with pleas by Kammu himself that he excuse the poor banquet and clumsy entertainment laid out in his honor. In fact, of course, the entire evening was most sumptuous. Sanno and his retinue enjoyed the meal and drink, and when he rose to dance after many toasts and protestations of loyalty and friendship, the palace shook to its foundations under the tread of the Mountain King.

Thus was Chirayoju alerted that Sanno had arrived.

The vampire sorcerer called its armies together, and the siege began.

CHAPTER TWELVE

Buffy had no license, but Buffy drove. If you could call it that. Shrubbery suffered. So did curbs. But she managed to avoid getting pulled over.

She was halfway down the block—actually, down the center of the block—when she realized she'd forgotten to tell Giles about the little shrub and the disk and the note. Maybe there was something to that whole take-a-deep-breath-and-think-things-through thing he had going. She'd decided to kill two birds with one stone and meet up with him back at school. It could be that Willow had her wits about her, and it was possible she would go there looking for help from Giles.

It was worth a shot.

Way too short a time later—at least as far as Sunnydale's speed limits were concerned—she pulled into the school's faculty parking lot, tires kicking up sand as she put on the brakes. She was in a rush, or she might have cared a bit more about positioning the car between the lines. Details, details.

Before she ran into the school, she slipped the disk onto the chain she wore around her neck with a large cross dangling from it, then jumped when a jolt shot through her. It could easily have been static electricity, she reasoned, but she took note of it nonetheless.

She made sure she had the little tree and the note from Willow's bedroom, and then she was off.

It was already fifth period, and the halls were empty as she hurried toward the library. She banged open the door, a naive little part of her mind hoping she'd see Willow there, at the computer, doing that hacking thing that she did.

Uh-uh.

"Willow!" she called. "Please, come out, come out, wherever you are!"

"Yes, I'd like to know where Miss Rosenberg is as well," an insinuating voice sneered from behind her. "And the school librarian as well."

Buffy whirled, ready to fight off whatever horrible monster had followed her into the library. But it was worse than that.

It was Principal Snyder.

"Oh, um, good afternoon, Principal Snyder . . . ," she

began to stammer, glancing around, before remembering that Giles would arrive in time to rescue the Slayer in distress.

No joy.

"Don't give me that, Miss Summers," Snyder said, cynical as ever.

She knew Snyder had never liked her, and the feeling was mutual. The guy looked only slightly more human than one of the Ferengi on *Star Trek*. But he was the principal, and after all, he knew Buffy's mom's phone number. By heart.

"Um, give you what, sir?"

"I'm on to you, Summers. On to you and all your delinquent friends. Bad enough you run roughshod over the rules of this school, over the fundamental respect for authority that we all need in order to get along in this world. But then you come in here and holler for your friend as if you were at one of those drug-addled rock-and-roll clubs all of you hoodlums frequent."

"Speaking of which, have you seen Willow? Or, um, Mr. Giles?" Buffy asked, wincing in anticipation of the principal's response.

"Don't interrupt me! There is a thing call decorum, Summers."

Buffy didn't have time for this.

"Y'know, Principal Snyder," she flared, "maybe if you'd asked what I was in such in a hurry for . . ."

"I was just getting to that, Summers. Don't think I haven't noticed that you were off campus. I saw you running up the walk. You know I could suspend you for that alone."

Buffy thought fast.

"Well, actually, sir, Mr. Giles had sent Cordelia Chase and me over to the Sunnydale library to get a book we needed for a research project he's helping us with."

He looked less sure of his self-righteousness. "That's no excuse . . ."

"I'm sure he'll show you our permission slip to leave campus whenever he gets back from . . . wherever he is," she added earnestly, keeping her eyes wide and innocent and terror-free. "And when we left, we both had study hall, so you see, we didn't miss any classes or informational content or, um, knowledge acquiring."

"Don't think I won't check on your story," Snyder grumbled. "And it's fifth period now. You're definitely missing class." He narrowed his eyes at her. "You know, that knowledge-acquiring thing you find so foreign and new? I'd say you're both in for detention all next week, even if your story checks out."

Buffy *really* didn't have time for this.

"Listen, you . . . sir . . . Xander Harris is in the hospital and Willow Rosenberg is missing. Her mother thinks she might have been abducted or something. That's why Cordelia and I were gone so long. Cordelia's at the hospital with Xander right now."

"Why would Cordelia Chase have anything to do with any of you, particularly That Harris Boy?" Snyder remarked, crossing his arms and looking very stern. "You're going to have to do better than that, Miss Summers."

Buffy sighed. Though it was hard for her to call Cordelia a friend, she supposed that it was true. But as much as she brushed it off, it hurt to know that Snyder couldn't even conceive of such a thing. Sure, Cordy tried to maintain her rep as the most popular girl in school by not letting anyone know she hung out with Buffy and company. Which would have really hurt if she thought Cordelia had any idea how insulting that was. But when a child-hating geek like Snyder was dishing on her, Buffy had had enough.

"Y'know what?" she said huffily, "I'm completely powerless to stop you from doing whatever it is you want to do."

She realized it was useless to try to wait for Giles. Useless, too, to even hope to write him a note about Willow's strange little collection. And no way was she leaving Willow's stuff where Snyder could scoop it up and throw it in the trash.

She raised her chin. "So I'm going to go to the bathroom, and then I'm going to my sixth-period bio class."

Buffy spun on her heel, ignoring Snyder's vows to suspend her the next time she pulled a stunt like this. Next time. Those were the operative words. Detention was even okay, since that didn't necessarily mean a call home.

Of course, next time could be awfully soon. Especially since, once inside the bathroom, all she did was pop open the window and slip out. Then she was sprinting across the lawn for Cordelia's car.

There was a ticket stuck under one wiper.

Buffy grimaced.

• • •

Miraculously, the ticket was still there when Buffy pulled up in front of the main branch—in fact, the only branch—of the Sunnydale public library in Cordelia's car, gears grinding. She parked illegally there, too, but she hoped the ticket would keep her from getting another. On the other hand, the only thing that really mattered at the moment was not getting towed. Getting towed would be bad.

No Willow at the library.

Xander had once pointed out, with his usual teasing, that before Willow started to spend so much time hanging out at the school library because of the whole slaying thing, she had spent almost as much time at the public library. Quiet. Surrounded by lots of books and computers. It was just Willow's kind of place.

Not anymore, apparently. Which sent Buffy scrambling madly across town in Cordy's car, burning gas as the afternoon wore on and she checked small specialty bookstores, the place Willow had gone to have her hair tinted, and the weird video store Xander had dragged them to when he'd gotten on his Hong Kong action movie kick.

She phoned the school library to talk to Giles. The phone was busy.

It was busy the next time she tried.

And the next.

By the time she stopped for a breather and fed the Cordy-mobile, it was nearly six. There was one message for her on the message machine at home, but it was only to say that he was back in the library. Yet the phone was still busy. She began to worry that the phone was off the hook. Then she got through, but there was no answer.

Dusk wasn't that far off, so she left off trying to reach Giles and called Willow's mother to find out if there'd been any word. None. Mrs. Rosenberg had been crying.

After Buffy hung up, she had to take a few deep breaths. A sinking feeling was setting in with the sinking sun: This was going to end badly.

Buffy slapped the roof of Cordy's car as she finished pumping the self-serve.

"C'mon, Willow, where are you?" she said aloud. Her only answer was the weird stare she got from a heavyset man gassing up his Lincoln.

The dim light of encroaching dusk filtered into the hospital room where Xander Harris lay, still unconscious from a few nasty raps to the noggin and the fact that his best friend had turned him into a Slurpee. Or at least, that's what somebody was saying about him as Xander started to come around. He thought he remembered the phone ringing, but there wasn't much else in his head except cotton and some kind of liquid that sloshed around in there when he tried to move.

"Not so loud," he croaked.

"Oh God, Aphrodesia, I've gotta go," the voice beside his bed said. "I think he's waking up."

Click. That was the phone going back in its cradle. Really loud. Really, really loud, and Xander didn't like it at all. He winced again. Carefully, he opened his eyes just slightly. Not too bright in there, which was nice. With the way his head hurt, the light might just crack it open.

"Xander?" that same voice said in an excited hush. "Are you . . . okay?"

A face floated down into view above him. He knew that face.

"Daphne?"

With a snarl that was nearly a roar, the face dropped down so that he was eye to eye with it, with the girl . . . with Cordelia.

"And just who is Daphne?" Cordelia demanded.

Xander blinked. "Huh?"

"Daphne!" she snapped. "You just called me Daphne. I've been parked here for hours waiting for you to wake up, completely ruined my makeup crying because I thought something horrible had happened to you, and here you're talking about some girl named Daphne!"

Xander exhaled, frowned, though it hurt his head even worse. "Um, Daphne from Scooby Doo?" he suggested, though he had no idea if that was the truth. He already couldn't remember ever having called her that, at least to her face.

"Uh-huh," Cordelia replied.

With another sigh, Xander slumped back against the bed

and stared at the ceiling. He was in a hospital, that much he knew. But be couldn't quite recall how he'd gotten here. When it came to him, it struck hard, like a blow to the gut, and he struggled to sit up, staring at Cordelia.

"Where's Willow?" he asked urgently. "Or Buffy?"

Cordelia rolled her eyes. She opened her mouth to complain but was interrupted by the arrival of a rather frazzled-looking Giles. In his right hand he clutched a pair of thin, faded books that looked like old diaries.

"Yes, that's what I'd like to know," Giles said, rubbing his eyes beneath his glasses. Xander thought he looked haunted, but as far as he was concerned, Giles always had that kind of distracted thing going on. Sort of a cross between Obi-Wan Kenobi and the Absent-Minded Professor.

"It seems my timing is propitious," Giles said. "Xander, what did happen? Willow is missing, and there have been enough clues and coincidences to lead us to some horrible conclusions. I hope that you can dispel them as erroneous."

Xander blinked. "Whatever you said. But if one of your horrible conclusions is that Willow fanged me . . . yeah, that's the way it looks."

Xander felt sick. Just saying the words gave him a chill. Willow was closer to him than a sister, and the idea that she was now . . . one of *them*, was more than he could bear.

"Actually, we have reason to believe that Willow is not, technically, a vampire. At least, not yet. She was seen in daylight as recently as Monday by her mother, and though she is still among the missing, if we can find her, we might be able to save her from further harm."

"Let's go," Xander said, and sat up painfully.

"Xander, what are you doing?" Cordelia cried.

He winced with pain from the bruises on his head, from the tightening in his chest that told him he probably had a few ribs that were at least cracked, and he reeled from the disorientation that made him feel like he was on a fishing boat instead of dry land. But Xander got up. He put a hand against the wall to steady himself. Felt a draft. Hung his head and smiled at his own abject humiliation.

"And, of course, Xander Harris is wearing a hospital gown, isn't he? The kind that covers about as much as an apron? Yes, of course he is!"

He spun around quickly and slumped against the closet door, frantically searching for the knob.

"Ah, nothing. Nothing to see here," he said. "Or, well, nothing that should be seen . . . that very nothing anyone needs to see at this particular moment."

"When he starts talking about himself in the third person, that's usually a sign that he's embarrassed," Cordelia observed. She looked very proud of herself. "Third person being an English grammar, um, thing, where it's *him*, *her*, and *it*."

Giles began to study his shoes as if they were completely fascinating, and was still doing that when Xander stepped unsteadily from the closet wearing the greatest invention in the history of mankind.

Which would be pants. Pants were very, very good.

Xander started for the door to the room. Whoa. The tide was coming in. He staggered awkwardly and lurched forward.

"Xander, what do you think you're doing?" Giles demanded.

"Wearing pants is what I'm doing. What a man does. Wear pants." Xander stuck out one hand to stop the room from spinning on its axis, reached out the other one, and found himself being steered by Giles back toward the bed. He sat quickly and squinted at the sudden jolt of pain in his head.

Giles cocked his head. "Xander, get back in bed. You're in no shape to be up."

"We've got to find Willow," Xander insisted. "And Buffy. Before she . . . before they end up hurting each other. We've got to do something."

"Xander," Giles said gently. "We've got to do what we're good at."

Suddenly Xander shivered as fresh memories rushed to fill the blanks.

"When she . . . she bit me, she laughed," Xander said, and fought off the burning sensation in his eyes, the urge he felt to cry at the thought of it. She was his best friend, and now this horrible thing had happened to her, and in a way, to him as well. "Willow laughed while she drank my blood."

"Did . . . did you drink her blood as well?" Giles ventured.

Xander frowned. "What am I, pervo boy? I don't think so."

"Okay, I missed something," Cordelia said. "Willow was out during the day, yesterday, right? We've established that.

So now, what are we thinking? She's somehow *possessed* by a vampire? Can that be done?"

"It certainly seems that way," Giles replied.

"One thing's for sure," Xander added. "The person who attacked me last night? Maybe it has Willow's face, but it wasn't Willow. It wasn't even her voice. And it referred to itself as something else. Some weird Japanese name or something."

Giles softly said, "Perhaps it was Chinese."

"Perhaps," Xander said. He went on alert. "So this makes some kind of sense to you?"

Giles sighed. "It's beginning to."

"Look, I read the last panel of the Sunday comics first to save myself the suspense. Could you spill, already?" Cordelia said, her hands flapping the way they always did when she was frustrated.

Giles walked to the window and looked out at the darkening sky.

"I suspect the name you heard was Chirayoju," Giles said. "Do you recall our visit to the museum the other day? Willow cut her finger on an ancient sword that belonged to a Japanese warrior-god called Sanno, the King of the Mountain."

"Riiiight," Xander said, tentatively. Nervously. Less than joyfully.

"Which has exactly what to do with this Cheerios guy?" Cordy asked.

Giles faced them, looking as troubled as Xander had ever seen him. Maybe even more so, if that was possible. They'd all seen some pretty troubling things in the company of the Slayer.

"The text that accompanied that sword told of a legendary battle between Sanno and a Chinese vampire called Chirayoju, which ended with both of their deaths. I had a conversation earlier with a retired Watcher, who directed me to this."

He held up the pair of slim journals he'd had when he came in.

"*The Journal of Claire Silver, Watcher*," Giles explained. "During the first half of the nineteenth century, Miss Silver was instrumental in cataloging the journals of all the Watchers down through the ages. She was quite a scholar."

"Yeah, great, we can read it later," Xander said. "C'mon, we've got to go!"

Giles held up a hand. "We need to arm ourselves, Xander. We can't just run out into the night. Much as we would want to," he added under his breath.

"Actually, much as we have before, and it turned out okay," Xander insisted incredulously.

Giles opened his book. "I'll read to you."

"Just put me to sleep," Xander said. But he started to sway, and much as he wanted to stay upright, he lay back in his hospital bed.

"If it starts with 'once upon a time,' I'm outta here," he grumbled.

"Shh." Cordelia was all ears, and she sat up straight. "*I'm listening.*"

"Very well."

Giles opened one of the books.

Journal of the Watcher, Claire Silver
January 6, 1817

The doctor has just left, taking with him all my hopes for Justine. The poor girl lies senseless upon her pillow, her wounds grievous and many, and there seems nought that I can do.

I must face it, but I cannot: She is dying.

As I look up from my pen to stare at her pale form, I know that somewhere on this vast planet, another Watcher has been alerted, and readies his young lady for her debut (if I may be so macabre) into the terrible world that shall be her secret domain: the world of the Vampire Slayer. As my young miss escapes at last this most unholy and unwholesome life, another soon shall find her existence irrevocably transformed—shall I say what I am thinking, that this new Slayer's life will be ruined?!

All that shall then remain of my dear Justine and her many battles, victories, and this ultimate defeat, will be these words that I write, and her monument in the churchyard.

I cannot bear it. I cannot face the notion that the forces of darkness have beaten us at last, not after all that Justine has suffered and endured.

And I—if I can bear to think for one moment of myself—I shall become what Justine and I have so often scoffed at: a genteel English lady, gowned and ribboned like a useless bisque figurine. I shall fill my days with teas and dances and gossip. I shall pretend I know nothing of weaponry and fighting and beheadings and the proper way to stake a vampire through the heart. All that I have learned in order to serve as Justine's Watcher I shall lay aside. I shall be as useless as a retired governess.

But who comes? For upon the window clinks a pebble. Does someone come to pay his respects? Someone who knows that Justine, the Slayer, lies dying after a vicious attack?

In our society, it has not been possible for Justine to accept suitors, knowing as she does what her life is, and what society requires of young ladies. Imagine explaining to a young man that you must of a night cudgel demons to death, or that the lady posing as your aunt last Tuesday sent a warlock to a fiery death in another dimension!

And yet, of what use have all our efforts been, and to what benefit our sacrifices?

Will this visitor be someone to whom I can utter these thoughts?

The maid knocks now, and waits for my permission to enter. I lay my pen aside, and shall return . . .

I do not know whether to cry in triumph or in fear, but my hands tremble so that I can scarcely put pen to paper. Our visitor was none other than Lord Byron, that infamous poet and ladies' man. He was impeccably, if eccentrically, dressed, wearing a brocade vest of Italian design and affecting some sort of large, floppy hat.

I was much amazed, for he has not been seen in England for five years. I was also much frightened, I must admit, for as I have written before, Justine and I have often wondered if Byron himself is a vampire. So much points to it—his pale complexion, his strange hold over numerous persons, and his extreme passions.

In any case, Justine has never met Byron before, and I only once, at a party Midsummer last, yet here he arrives on what may well be the last night of her life, giving to me certain books as well as fragments of ancient Oriental scrolls! With a strange smile, he told me of his high regard for "our work" and made several veiled references to Justine's "special talents." Thus I may conclude that he knows All, though I cannot swear to it.

But hush! Justine awakes, and requests some water. My girl, my Slayer!

I would give my life would it save her own.

January 7, 1817

Justine has survived the night, and though I am weary, I rejoice to tell her of the marvelous tale I am unfolding! It appears that the legend we have often wondered at may be indeed true. This, namely, being the Legend of the Lost Slayer. As opposed to the tragically usual way of it—a Watcher outliving his Slayer—I have upon occasion come across references to a Slayer who lost her Watcher quite early in her career. We have no idea who the Slayer was, nor what happened to the Watcher, but we have both often wondered at it.

Nearly all the writings contained within this box have been translated into the tongues of Europe, but the whole of it is a jumble, with scattered notes on fragments of paper, passages referring back to various scrolls translated into English by one hand, and others discussed in Italian by another. Additionally, a few are in Latin. Fortunately, these are two languages in which I possess facility. I have had a time putting things to rights, and much of it I have not been able to decipher at all. Some of it is in German, and to translate those items I will have to appeal to a third party. This appears to be a life's work.

The irony of those words is not lost on me. For most marvelous indeed is Justine's weak promise to me to remain on this earth until we solve the mystery. If searching among these writings for the key to the legend keeps her beside me but a single moment, I shall go to my own grave praising Lord Byron's name.

And so, to work . . .

February 1, 1817

What we had not counted on was that Justine, though in a weakened state, is still alive, and therefore remains the only Slayer of her generation. Though she cannot rise from her bed, she alone wears the mantle of the Chosen One against whom the forces of darkness are arrayed.

This has depressed her greatly, for she feels that she is failing in her duty, and at one point today cried out to me, "Oh, Claire, if only I could simply stand aside! Better that I die than leave the world unprotected!"

I encourage her to believe that she shall recover, but the doctor has taken me aside several times and reminded me that on occasion, those who soon will leave us rally briefly so that they may bid farewell. He still holds little hope for her recovery. I find this astonishing, for she does seem much improved.

Tonight I shall go out hunting. Someone must, and she is in no condition for it. In truth, I undertake it only so that she will not fret so. I am for myself, selfishly, much afrighted. I am only a Watcher, though at this moment I would I were more.

February 13, 1817

I feel that we are in a race. As the doctor predicted, Justine has taken a turn for the worse. Her face is ashen and her chest rises and falls as if she is perpetually gasping for breath. And yet, an hour ago, she opened her eyes, smiled like an excited little girl, and asked, through her pitifully cracked lips, "What have you discovered now? Are we still on the trail?"

Either she is being brave for me, or else remains as captivated by the search for the Legend of the Lost Slayer as I. Through a lengthy volume of Chinese lore called **Emperor Taizu's Book,** *we have found this:*

It is true that in the first place, demons owned this world. They lost it in a grand battle with the Emperor, and fight to this day to take it back again.

This is precisely what Watchers and Slayers are taught to believe! Although, of course, we believe that it was not a battle with a Chinese Emperor which caused the forces of darkness to lose their control over the world. But what is significant is that according to our unnamed translator, these words were written in A.D. 971!

February 28, 1817

My girl is dead. In the moment that I saw the light go from her eyes, I clutched the bedpost and cried aloud, "Truly, I knew not it would be this difficult!" For though I have steeled myself for this moment, I was—and remain—unprepared.

They are coming to help me wash and dress her poor body. To the churchyard we shall go on the morrow. I cannot bear this. I am in a state of agony. Whatever shall I do with my days and nights?

The answer lies in the scrolls and parchments. For her last words to me were, "Promise me you'll solve the mystery."

And so I shall.

Oh, Justine!

January 6, 1818

It is a year since Justine's defeat in battle. I am glad to say that her successor found her murderers and dispatched them as a personal favor to me. I went to the churchyard to tell Justine of our side's victory.

At the least, I am not as useless as I had believed I would become. I am someone honored among the Watchers, for I was Justine's Watcher, and she was much admired. And as I continue unraveling the Legend of the Lost Slayer, others have begun sending me pieces of information they have unearthed. In some cases, this includes entire volumes!

To wit, I have just opened a packet from a colleague at the new University in Ghent. It concerns a certain Japanese legend about a god, or goddess, named Sanno. This Sanno was also called the Mountain King, and he or she was the patron deity of Mount Hiei in Japan. Part of the legend concerns a Chinese vampire who vowed to devour the Japanese emperor. Sanno saved the emperor by dispatching the vampire with a magickal sword through the heart.

My colleague writes, "Could this Sanno be your Lost Slayer? I have no idea. If Sanno was female, perhaps she is!

May 18, 1819

How delightful! I have just received a copy of my book, Oriental Magick Spells as Collected by Claire Silver, *a Watcher.*

Privately printed by one of our own, there are five copies now circulating among my fellow Watchers. It is a comfort to me to be of use to my fellows, for though it has been over a year since my Justine left me, I feel the loss of her as deeply as though it were yesterday. I visit her grave daily, telling her of the progress I have made.

Though I have now discerned that Sanno was not the Slayer, as he was male, yet pursuit of that knowledge led me to investigate and record many fascinating and useful Oriental spells, contained now in my very own published work! I will take it to show Justine this afternoon.

Giles looked up from the book. "Damn," he said.

Cordelia blinked. "What?"

"I have the feeling that's the volume we're really after. Her book of spells." He checked the other book he had with him, flipping through the pages. He shook his head. "This is quite useless. It appears she married and had children. This is about their travels in Switzerland."

"How thrilling," Cordelia said ironically.

As if he seconded that emotion, Xander snored loudly in his hospital bed. Cordelia rolled her eyes.

"He doesn't usually snore," she offered, then blushed and stammered, "or so his, um, sister says."

Giles had never heard of a sister of Xander's before, but

whether or not Cordelia was an expert on his, ah, nocturnal habits was quite beyond the scope of the matter at hand. Anxiously, he glanced at the phone.

"If only Buffy would check in," he said.

Cordelia waved her hands at him. "You go back to the library and get the book, and I'll wait here in case she calls."

"Mmm. All right." He rose and spared an extra moment to gaze at Xander. "Youth is remarkably resilient," he murmured. Then he read Cordelia's blank stare and said, "The color's already returning to his cheeks."

"It's blood," she said bluntly, indicating an empty blood bag hooked into an IV in Xander's arm. "The nurse told me that was the last bag just when you were getting to the part about Lord Brian."

"Byron," Giles corrected automatically, then sighed. "Yes, Lord Brian indeed. Quite right."

"Go get the book," she urged.

He sighed. "I suppose I must. But do take care."

He left his books there and hurried out of the room.

Cordelia was a little shaken. All that talk about the Slayer dying . . . eeuu. It creeped her out. It must really creep out Giles. And Buffy, too, of course.

She rubbed her arms, suddenly cold. Xander might have died, if Buffy hadn't insisted they go look for him. That creeped her out worst of all.

About five minutes later, the phone rang. Cordelia picked it up.

"Oh, hi, Harmony," she said. "No, I'm still stuck here, can you believe it? His mother had to go pick up someone somewhere or something. Well, yes, he had a pretty nasty, ah, fall. A *sale*? I'm missing a *sale*? You're on your cell? Go to the petites right now. Go! If that leather jacket is marked down, you *have* to buy it for me. Of course I'll pay you back!"

CHAPTER THIRTEEN

The hospital phone was still busy. Xander must have a lot of worried relatives, or else maybe someone had knocked it off the hook.

Buffy sighed and got back in Cordelia's car.

The golden glow of the sinking sun glared against the windshield as Buffy braked the car in front of the building where Angel lived. She grabbed her Slayer's bag, hopped out, and scrambled down the stairs to pound on the door. It was the last place she could think of where Willow might be hiding out. Angel would have taken her in if she really needed a place—if he didn't know what else had happened.

Or maybe even if he did. Angel was a surprising person . . . make that vampire . . . make that person . . .

But when the heavy door scraped the floor as it opened, and she saw the bleary-eyed face of the dead man she loved, she knew she was out of luck again. Whatever Willow was going through, Buffy somehow knew that her chances of helping Willow were draining away with the last rays of the sun. She had maybe twenty minutes, and they might as well be twenty seconds. Or two.

"Sorry to wake you," she mumbled as she pushed past Angel into his dimly lit apartment and dropped her bag to the floor. She had long since grown used to the eclectic furnishings there, but it seemed as though each time she visited, she saw something new. Well, something old, but new to her.

Not this time. This time, everything seemed all too familiar.

"Buffy, what's wrong?" he asked.

"Willow," she whispered. Then she filled him in on everything that had happened up until that moment.

Buffy's eyes welled up as he came to her and tilted her head so she could lay it against his chest, a chest where she would never hear a heart beating. They'd been through so much together, suffered so much, and yet she still loved him. What else could she do? Love was like that.

"What's this shrine you found at her house?" Angel asked.

"I don't know," she admitted. "I was in such a rush that Giles and I didn't even have a chance to go over it. And I can't seem to locate him or even talk to him. I guess I should've hung around the hospital, for all the good I'm doing Willow." She sighed. "I guess I'll go back there."

"Can I see the things you took?" he asked.

Buffy reached for her bag, unzipped it, and pulled out the note first.

"Origami," Angel said. "An Asian art form."

She nodded. "I knew it was a word like that. All I could think of was rigatoni."

She showed him the disk on the chain around her neck.

He shook his head. "No idea what that is."

The withered little plant.

"Hmm," Angel murmured, and Buffy glanced up sharply to see if he realized how much he sounded like Giles. Apparently not.

"Looks like a bonsai tree," he said finally. "But it's been dead a while."

"How do you know all this stuff?" Buffy asked.

"I've traveled a lot," Angel replied.

"I never get to go anywhere," Buffy said, half-mocking herself.

Angel kissed her then, deeply and with a kind of gentle sympathy. "I'm sorry all this is happening," he whispered. "I wish I could be more help, but I've never heard of anything like it before. If Willow is a vampire—we don't know that, but if she is—she shouldn't be up and around during the day." He half-smiled. "Vampires don't go to school, Buffy."

Buffy stared at him.

"What did you say?" she demanded.

"I said . . ."

"Vampires don't go to school!" Buffy shouted. "Angel, that's it!"

He stared at her, stupefied.

"The things on Willow's desk aren't exactly the kind of souvenirs she would keep," Buffy said quickly. "Whatever, whoever she is now . . . that's who put those things there. I've been wasting my time looking in all the places *Willow* might go. She's changed now . . ."

The thought threw Buffy for a moment, stealing some of the joy of her realization. Her face became grim and her mind determined. "Origami. That dead bonsai tree was ripped from the ground." She slapped her forehead. "The Chia Pet garden! That's what it reminded me of."

Hastily, she explained about the Japanese friendship garden exhibit. "The real garden is still in Sunnydale," she said. "It may have some kind of weird connection to the one in Kobe. So maybe there's some extra vortex thingy there or something. And Willow as vampire is drawn there."

"Well, there aren't many other places in Sunnydale where you can get a bonsai tree," Angel said, nodding.

"In LA you can buy them at the mall," Buffy said, almost sadly. Suddenly she missed her old, normal life more than she ever had before. She was tired of all the weirdness. It seemed that the moment she thought she'd adjusted to her role as the

Slayer, something came along to change it. Up the stakes.

So to speak.

Angel glanced at the window.

Buffy said, "There are about eighteen more minutes of daylight left." She took a breath. "When you're the Slayer, eighteen minutes can be a lifetime."

Angel nodded. "Go. I'll come after you the second the sun goes down."

She kissed him lightly on the lips and looked away quickly so he wouldn't see her fear and worry. "See you soon."

"I'll hurry," he promised, but Buffy was already out the door and bounding up the steps.

A tiny slice of the sun was still visible on the horizon as she got into Cordelia's car. The sky was a garish pink on one end, and a deep, almost ghostly blue on the other.

Buffy put the car in gear, praying she wouldn't get stopped.

The disk clanked against the metal chain as if it were a time bomb sequenced for countdown.

Giles returned huffing and puffing with a leather book in his arms just as Xander closed the bathroom door and walked all by himself back to his bed.

The Watcher actually stumbled over his own feet and said, "Xander, what are you doing up?" Then, before Xander could answer, he glanced at Cordelia and said, "Has Buffy called?"

"Oops," Cordelia said, looking guilty. "I mean, no."

Xander looked curiously at his little lustbuddy and

wondered what the oops was about, but concentrated instead on Giles.

"Cor says you went off to get another book," he said, bobbing his head at that thing called *libro* by some—the ones who took Spanish—in Giles's arms.

"Um? Oh, yes. Yes." Giles was actually smiling. "It's just that I'm so delighted to see you up and about. Although I'm sure you're supposed to remain in bed."

"Yeah, well."

"He didn't like the bedpan," Cordelia offered helpfully.

"Thank you, Nurse Chase," Xander huffed, rolling his eyes. She did the same, and it looked like another fine evening with the Dueling Banjos except that they had more important things to talk about.

"The book," he urged Giles.

"The book," Giles concurred, and his smile grew. "As one might say, bingo."

Xander sat down and rubbed his hands. "Then bingo it is. And please read-o."

"Yes."

Giles read.

"In early Japan, executions were carried out by means of either strangulation or immolation, that is to say, burning. The spilling of blood revolted the fastidious Japanese mind. However, with the arrival of Buddhism, seppuku became the favored method, the victim voluntarily inserting a sword blade into his abdomen and slicing his bowels, thus causing

*a copious amount of bleeding (and, one must add, however
indelicately, pain of a truly unimaginable sort). If at all possible, the head of the condemned was summarily cut off with
another sword in order to spare him further agony. However,
to be decapitated without first freeing one's soul from the
body (for the Japanese believed that the soul resides within
the abdomen) was truly a dishonor."*

"And we couldn't have that," Xander quipped.

"Be quiet," Cordelia snapped. "Giles, keep reading. Please,"
she added sweetly.

*"Further regarding the ritual Magick of Ancient Japan,
it is considered possible to imprison a Spirit inside an inani-
mate object. One then says of the Spirit that it is 'bound' and
that the Object is 'alive.' Thus one says of a Bell into which
a Spirit has been bound,* Suzu ga imasu, *rather than* Suzu ga
arimasu. Imasu *being the verb for things that are alive, while*
arimasu *is used for the things which are not.*

*"In various versions of the legend of Sanno the Mountain
King, we read that his Sword is a living thing, which leads
one to assume a Spirit had been bound into it. Blood is prominently mentioned, specifically, the blooding of his enemy. The
story regarding Sanno's victorious battle with the evil Vampire Chirayoju generally includes the line,* and Chirayoju was
blooded, and thus vanquished."

"So it got out when Willow cut herself?" Xander said,
staring hard at Giles.

Giles returned his gaze. "It would appear so."

Xander ran his hands through his hair. "Listen, Giles, whatever happens, I'm not letting anyone put a stake through Willow. No way."

"Well, what I've been pondering is the uniqueness of this case," Giles began, and Xander wondered how many trails they were scheduled to meander down before they reached Giles's point. Because he had already reached his own conclusion: He'd lock Willow up like Oz—only, just for the rest of her natural life, instead of three nights a month—before he would ever allow her to be harmed.

"Yes, the pondering thing," Xander said, weary, pain-ridden, and very anxious.

Giles completely missed his impatience, or else was being very British and very polite about pretending not to notice it. "It seems to me that if the demon was extracted from one form, perhaps it can be done again."

"Okay, trap the vampire ghost. Got it," Xander said. "And we do that by . . . ?"

Giles smiled grimly. It was times like these he wished he was back in the land of tea, crumpets, and baked beans for breakfast. "I suppose we'll find that out after Cordelia and I have broken into the museum and had another look at that sword."

Fighting vertigo, Xander sat up. "Cordy, I never thought I'd say these words to you, but help me finish getting dressed."

"And I never thought I'd say this," Cordelia shot back, "but no way." She held her hand out to Giles. "Let's go."

"Hey, wait a minute," Xander protested.

Giles shook his head. "I'm terribly sorry, Xander, but you've got to stay here and get well." He gestured to the phone. "Besides, Buffy may call."

"Oh. Okay," Xander said, to Giles's surprise. "You're right. You two run along." He folded his hands and made a show of climbing back into bed. "I'm sitting here obediently, healing away. That's what I'm doing."

"Well, good," Giles said uncertainly.

As soon as they were out of range, Xander threw back his wafer-thin hospital blanket and climbed awkwardly out of bed. The room spun for a shorter period of time than the last time, and he figured that meant he was ready to put on his Robin cape.

He shuffled once more toward the little closet containing his clothes—his admittedly disgusting, blood-caked duds—and opted for his jeans and a scrub top he found hanging in his bathroom. Used? Covered with ebola virus?

Then it occurred to him to look for some scrub pants.

In a few minutes, he strolled out of the hospital and followed behind two hotties in outfits similar to his own. As they neared the parking lot, he made a show of groaning and turning back around.

One of them said, "Hey. Hi. What's the matter?" She stared at his face and he remembered he was kind of gross-looking.

He made a face. "I forgot that my roommate, Dr., ah,

Summers, has my car. Porsche. His is in the shop. His Beemer. I told him I had a double shift but we, ah, ran out of emergencies so I'm going home early because I'm still healing from my skiing accident." Inwardly, he winced at his unconvincing story.

The redhead looked impressed and said, "Oh, you're a doctor?"

"Yeah. I numb 'em." He shrugged casually. "I'll have to go call him. I just called the museum and told them I'd drop by to work on some lecture slides. On ebola. And numbing."

The hotties gave each other a let's-go-for-it look. The redhead said, "We can give you a lift, Doctor."

"We'd be happy to," added her little blond pal.

Xander said, "Thanks, ladies," and followed them to a Camry with a bumper sticker that read LOVE A NURSE.

But the ironic thing was, Xander was too sore and too exhausted to even consider it.

"Oh God, this thing is such a clunker," Cordelia wailed from the passenger side as she kept scanning Claire Silver's book of spells. "Giles, when are you going to get a real car?"

"Cordelia, I realize that as a young Southern Californian caught in the clutches of the obsession with—"

"Wait," Cordelia said, waving her hand. "There's a loose page stuck in the back of the book." She glanced at it. "Oh my God, Giles, listen!"

June 17, 1820

I have just learned something absolutely fascinating! A scroll has made its way to me from the actual Buddhist monastery on Mount Hiei, recording a number of events within the chronology of the Sword of Sanno. For indeed, such a sword exists, and resides there now!

The Emperor Kammu kept this sacred and dangerous object with him, housing it in the pavilion wherein dwelled the embodiment of his ancestor, Amaterasu-no-kami, the Sun Goddess.

But after widespread unrest (due to an unfair system of taxation and other social problems), the Emperor Kammu ordered the nation's capital moved from Nara to Kyoto. (Interestingly, this is when the current system of Japanese writing began to become codified, and there are many more documents preserved about magick spells from here than in the previous centuries.) At any rate, during this enormous undertaking, an earthquake occurred, and Emperor Kammu became concerned that this violent shifting of the earth had to do with the sword.

The Emperor sent the Sword of Sanno, with great pomp and ceremony, to the monastery, bidding them to protect it for all time. But to the head monk he wrote a remarkable and mystifying thing:

"I charge thee to do all thou canst to maintain the peace between thy patron kami, Lord Sanno, and the most dishonorable demon Chirayoju, both housed within the weapon. For thou alone keepest the secret, and as we have agreed, I shall tell no one else. For Lord Sanno's wrath would be terrible indeed, and no amount of atonement could ever satisfy the betrayal he must certainly feel by the actions of this most desperate Emperor."

From this I conclude that the Emperor bound Sanno within his own Sword.

"So there's someone else in the sword?" Cordelia asked. "Or is he the guy who's possessing Willow, or what?"

"I don't know," Giles confessed. "But we're there now, so . . ."

He slammed on the brakes.

"Good heavens, is that Xander?" he asked, pointing at a car pulled to the curb just ahead of them.

As if on cue, Xander straightened and waved at them.

CHAPTER FOURTEEN

As Tsukuyomi, the Moon God, glittered over the wintry landscape, Lord Chirayoju's hellish army marched swiftly and silently toward Emperor Kammu's palace. Once they had been sighted, runners burst into the Emperor's exquisite banquet hall with news of the invasion.

As the cold, exhausted men tumbled into the exalted company, the music stopped and all eyes looked to them. They lay prostrate until the Emperor gave them leave to speak. For daring to burst in as they had, it would have lain within his provenance to command them to take their own lives. One waited on the Emperor's invitation; one did not dare thrust oneself into his presence. But it was clear there was a crisis, or they would not have been so bold, and the Emperor quickly learned what was transpiring beyond his palace walls.

Sanno listened with glee as one of the runners answered the Emperor's calm and careful questions, the words tumbling out of the frightened soldier's mouth: "They are legions of demons, oh Great One, and vampires, and an angry mob of peasants. Their leader is a hideous being who floats on the lightest breeze. Its face glows green and slick, and it is nothing of Japan."

The court drew back in horror. Exquisite ladies turned to their warrior husbands and begged fate not to make them widows. Poetry-loving dandies clenched their fists inside their sleeves, fretting that they might be ordered to actually fight against such creatures.

After Emperor Kammu had finished with the runners' interviews, Sanno turned to him and said, "This is the evil Chinese *tengu* Chirayoju. It has sworn to drink your blood, but rest assured, most mighty sovereign, I shall protect you."

With his hand on the hilt of the sword in his belt, Kammu inclined his head in great thanks and said to Sanno, "My debt for your assistance will never be repaid. I will give your retinue weapons, soldiers, and horses."

"I have my own army, camping in the foothills," Sanno replied haughtily, "but I will accept your generous offer, for no army should ever turn down provisions."

Then Sanno clapped his hands and an icy winter wind whistled into the banquet hall. The assembled courtiers shook with cold, the oldest and youngest nearly turning blue, but Sanno did not seem to notice their discomfort.

He bellowed a fearsome battle cry, which was taken up by the wind, then shouted in ringing tones, "Come to me. It is time."

Carrying his words, the wind streamed in the opposite direction. Finding there a door of rice paper, it blasted through, leaving a gaping hole in its wake. In another instant, it burst through the very wall of the palace itself.

The Emperor noted the damage and was silent for a moment. Then he dared to say to the Mountain God, "It would be well if you would meet him outside my castle gates. Within, my people are defenseless."

Sanno glared at the Emperor. He thundered, "Am I not here to protect you, oh living god on this earth? Would you have my army expose itself to unnecessary harm and possibly fail in their mission? My troops will occupy this palace, and your courtiers must look to themselves."

Then Sanno bowed low, perhaps mockingly so, and added, "For your life must be preserved at all costs, Great Kammu."

"Then I shall share the danger," Kammu answered, rising and descending the dais where he sat with his Empress. "I go now to don my battle armor."

Sanno nodded, satisfied. For it was well that the Emperor joined the battle. In truth, the Mountain God's hatred for Chirayoju raged so fiercely that he did not care if Kammu's life was saved or lost. He did not care about the dishonor Kammu's death would cast on him. He only wanted the demon vampire dead. And the sight of Kammu at the head of his own army would inspire Sanno's warriors to fight more courageously.

As he left the banquet hall with every face lowered to the ground save Sanno's, the Emperor went not to the armory but to the pavilion wherein dwelled the form of Amaterasu, the Sun Goddess, who was the Emperor's ancestor. She stood on a pedestal in a beautiful, flowing gown of rose and scarlet, her mirror—part of the royal regalia—in her grasp.

Humbling himself on his knees, Kammu said to her, "Divine One, I fear that Lord Sanno has come not to protect our family, but with the sole purpose of vanquishing the Chinese demon that marches on us. I fear that in the heat of battle, the Mountain God will sacrifice whatever he must in order to kill this Chirayoju."

The room blazed with light as Amaterasu moved from her pedestal and stepped down from the platform, until she stood only one step higher than her descendant. She was so beautiful that it was difficult for Kammu to look upon her, so he kept his gaze lowered and stared at the floor.

"You are a wise man, Kammu," the Goddess said. "For indeed, Lord Sanno will take no care to curb his violent hatred of Lord Chirayoju. If one of our family stands between him and the demon, he would cut through that one as easily as his winds tear rice paper."

Troubled, Kammu listened, and became more troubled still as Amaterasu continued.

"My brother, Tsukuyomi, has told me that Lord Sanno's heart has changed for all time. His rage will remain after Lord Chirayoju's death, should he prevail in this war. He will never rest because Gemmyo, the Fujiwara daughter, has been taken from him. He will destroy the palace and all the land of Japan."

Kammu's blood ran cold. Summoning all the resolve in his warrior's heart, he said, "Divine Ancestor, I pray you to tell me how to stop both Lord Chirayoju and Lord Sanno."

Amaterasu's fiery presence cooled as she said gravely, "There is a way, but the rituals I reveal to you in my mirror must be precisely executed. In the chaos that will crash down upon this place, it will be most difficult."

"I will prevail," Kammu assured her.

"Does he carry an object of personal significance?" she asked.

"*Hai*," he said eagerly, "a great sword."

"A sword. That is the best answer that you could have given me." She lowered her head, and a golden sunbeam tear slid down her cheek. "However, it may be that you will fail, Emperor Kammu. In that case, you will die an excruciating, humiliating death. You will never see Heaven. And the world as you know it will end."

Kammu sighed, his heart heavy with dread. "But if I do not attempt it, all will surely be lost."

Amaterasu slowly nodded in agreement. More tears slid

to the floor, catching the mats aflame. For truly do the Divine Ancestors love the Emperors and their families.

At midnight, Chirayoju's army of peasants, devils, and vampires attacked the castle with savage ferocity.

Emperor Kammu's men, fierce warriors all, had never battled such terrifying opponents, but they bravely fought with swords and lances as from the battlements, and the archers let fly their flaming arrows.

Beside them, Sanno's army flung themselves headlong into the fray, as if they had no fear of death.

Fires blazed around the castle as the terrible invaders drew near, and the situation looked bleak indeed as rank after rank of Sanno and Kammu's combined armies fell beneath the onslaught.

Still, there was hope. Instructed by Sanno to string measures of rope low to the ground before the castle gates, the bloodthirsty *kappa* tripped and spilled the magick water in the bowl-like indentations in their heads. The human peasants of Chirayoju's army, sent ahead to absorb the arrows and lances of the Emperor's troops, were cut down like straw. Many of the *eta* vampires turned to dust as they were staked through the heart. And the *oni* were just as likely to turn on each other in the violent frenzy as on their nominal enemies.

Yet their leader, Chirayoju, seemed unconquerable. With its green, moldy face and taloned hands, it was a terrifying sight as it rose into the air and hurled volleys of fireballs into the castle courtyard.

Sanno answered in kind, and the two pummeled each other with fire and blazing whirlwinds. Sanno stamped the earth in fury. The ground shook so hard that trees were uprooted, waterfalls sprayed upward, and dragons threatened to escape from the cracks and fissures. The castle itself began to disintegrate. Timbers crashed to the castle floors. Kammu's favorite daughter was crushed to death, as were many others.

In desperation, realizing that the powerful demon and the equally powerful *kami* would soon lay waste to all of Nara, Kammu prayed to his Divine Ancestors and all the Heaven People, and suddenly the sky lightened a few degrees as Amaterasu showed her face far earlier than expected.

"Chirayoju!" Sanno called to his enemy. He pointed at the mountain range. "The sun will rise soon, and she will bring your death. Let us finish this. Surrender, and I will kill only you. Your vile followers may continue their miserable existence."

Sanno's challenge confirmed the Emperor's greatest fear about the Mountain God's real intentions. The thought that the remaining *oni* and *kappa* and vampire *eta* would be free to prey on his subjects was insupportable.

"Never!" Chirayoju shouted as it pounded the castle with more fire. More than two-thirds of the beautiful palace blazed, and Kammu's second-oldest daughter was burned to death in her chambers.

Emperor Kammu sat straight on his warhorse and lifted his hands. "Lord Chirayoju," he said, "it is as Lord Sanno has said.

The sky lightens. Soon you and your vampire warlords will burst into flame even as my palace and my child have burst into flame. I propose combat between the two of you. And I swear that I will offer my blood to you if you are the victor."

"What are you doing?" Sanno thundered at Kammu.

The Emperor lowered his voice and said, "My Divine Ancestor has revealed to me how you may kill it. I will arm you with the knowledge."

As reassurance, he spoke of some of the rituals and incantations that Amaterasu-*no-kami* had shown him in her mirror. But the Emperor did not reveal that he knew how to defeat the Mountain God as well.

Satisfied that he now held the upper hand, Sanno waved his banners and shouted to Chirayoju, "Demon lord, though you are a foul pestilence, yet are you powerful. I have pledged to the Emperor Kammu that I would protect his household. Yet with our combat, you and I are destroying his palace and killing his children. I, too, swear that if you defeat me, I will allow you to destroy me."

Chirayoju looked intrigued. As the monster hung in the air high above its followers, it looked toward the horizon. The mountaintops were dusted with the first purple washes of day. Perhaps it realized that if it did not defeat Sanno very soon, it would have to retreat, leaving its back vulnerable to every blow the Emperor and Sanno could deal.

At length it said, "I accept your challenge. I will come alone."

• • •

They met in the courtyard, the great Mountain God at one end, the fearsome vampire sorcerer at the other. The sky was still dark, but the divine light of the sun would soon lift the veils of night.

The Emperor had chanted over Sanno's sword, which was already an enchanted weapon, being the sword of a *kami*. But now it was even more powerful. If Sanno pierced Chirayoju straight through the heart, it would surely die.

Chirayoju faced the Mountain God without fear. This was but one minor deity; it was capable of devouring all of Heaven itself!

Mockingly, Chirayoju made an elaborate bow and thought, *Soon, this fool will die. And then not only shall I drink the blood of the weak-minded Emperor, but I shall devour Kammu completely.*

Also armed with a sword, Chirayoju assumed a battle stance.

Above them, in the parapets, the Emperor had donned clothes all of white. Around his head he wore a cloth inscribed with a character from the incantation the Goddess had taught him, the single word for the Life Force, which is *ki*.

He stood on sacred tatami mats blessed by the priests, and he poured ritual sake—rice wine—on the woven straw.

Below him, the two supernatural beings rushed at each other, brandishing their swords above their heads. The blades clanged, and sparks shot into the heavens like the lament-laden death songs of ancient dragons.

On the tatami before the Emperor lay his own sword. If he failed to stop them both, he planned to offer his own life to the gods, in the hope that they would protect his poor nation. As the Goddess had foretold, he would die an excruciating death, for he would slice open his own abdomen as atonement for his incompetence. The blood that gushed from his mortal wound would be the only blood of his that Chirayoju would enjoy.

But he prayed that this would not be his fate. He prayed that, instead, he would see Sanno victorious, and thus betrayed. He could not allow Sanno to walk the earth, for the Mountain God had become an evil thing, much like the demon he fought. Kammu's Divine Ancestor had assured him of this. And so she had revealed to him the sacred incantation, which would bind not only Chirayoju into the sword, but Lord Sanno as well.

"Chirayoju!" Sanno shouted. "I offer you an honorable death. Commit suicide with your blade, and I shall write a death poem for you."

Chirayoju sneered at Sanno and flew high into the air. "If your poetry sings like your sword, I would writhe in the spirit world to hear its discordant verses."

And so, as they charged each other in the courtyard below, Emperor Kammu prepared his tatami mat with salt and sake, and ran though his mind the phrases he must utter to bind them both into the steel.

As their swords clashed, the wind rose violently. The
earth shook, rolled, and trembled. Around Kammu, his castle
blazed. Though he would surely burn with it, he would not
move from this place until all was accomplished.

Softly, he whispered a poem of his own:

> *"Weep now, earth, air, fire,*
> *Tears for Kammu's dead children,*
> *Water, Earth's fourth soul."*

The Emperor Kammu would not falter.
He would bind them—or die.

CHAPTER FIFTEEN

There was no way anyone was sending Xander home, and that was that.

Now, that settled, he asked in a whisper, "Has it occurred to anyone that part of hanging out with the Slayer means getting a whole new education in petty crime?"

They watched as Cordelia approached the front door, nervously glancing back at them. Giles and Xander both urged her on. Finally, she began to pound on the door, screeching for help as loudly as she dared. They wanted the night watchman to come running, but they would rather not draw the attention of anyone working security at any nearby buildings. Not that there were many that could be deemed "nearby."

"Help me!" Cordelia cried. "Oh, please help!"

"For someone whose life has been in jeopardy several times, she's truly horrible at maintaining any kind of pretense," Giles whispered.

"Which is, y'know, a really, really bad thing," Xander replied with very little conviction.

They heard the locks ratcheting back. The door swung open and the night watchman appeared, a rather rotund individual in an ill-fitting dark blue uniform, holding a long nightstick in one hand.

"Miss, what is it?" he asked with genuine concern.

"Oh my God, help me, they're after me!" Cordelia said desperately, throwing herself at him more as if she were the first customer in line at the Macy's after-Thanksgiving sale than if her life were in danger. "Please! Two men were chasing me, I think they wanted . . . I don't know what they wanted, but you've got to help me! Really!"

"We're dead," Xander whispered. "This is never going to work. I've seen better acting on canceled daytime soaps."

Giles turned to regard him with one eyebrow raised.

"Which I never watch, and only ever saw while I was channel surfing, searching for the college squash . . . um, no, basketball games," Xander quickly corrected.

"Whatever we may think of her skills as a thespian, Cordelia's performance seems to be having the desired effect," Giles replied quietly.

Xander watched in awe as the night watchman patted

Cordelia's shoulder. She poured on the boo-hoo a little too thick, particularly since she had insisted she not be required to actually cry, as tears would ruin her newly applied mascara. Still, the guard seemed to be falling for it.

"Where'd these lowlifes come after you, darlin'?" the watchman asked.

"Over . . ." *Sniff.* ". . . over there," Cordelia said, and pointed off in the other direction, where a stand of trees separated the museum gate from the lawn.

Xander rolled his eyes. It was a sure bet the guy would wonder what she'd been doing over in a far dark corner of the grounds to begin with.

"All right, missy, don't you worry 'bout a thing," the middle-aged, potbellied watchman comforted her. "You go on inside now and call the police. I'm gonna have a look around. You lock up and wait by the door here for me to come back. Don't let anyone in but ol' Eddie, you hear?"

Cordelia whimpered in agreement and allowed Eddie to usher her into the museum, where she promptly slammed and locked the door. Xander stared in disbelief as the watchman started across the lawn as if the *Mission: Impossible* theme were playing in his head.

After a moment, he and Giles moved around the corner—Xander very gingerly—and tapped lightly on the door. Cordelia opened up quickly, they ducked in, and then she was twisting and sliding all the locks shut behind her.

"Well, that buys us about three minutes," Cordelia said archly. "Now what?"

"Hmm?" Giles asked, and glanced up innocently, with that I'm-sorry-was-planning-this-caper-supposed-to-be-my-idea? face.

"Oh, no," Xander said, wagging his finger at the Watcher. "Uh-uh. There'll be no *hmms*, do you understand, Giles? No *hmms*! Now. What do we do when he comes back?"

"Oh, well." Giles nodded, glanced away distractedly. "I suppose Cordelia should merely pretend to be too frightened to open the door. Cordelia, you might tell him he'll have to wait outside until the police arrive, just so that you can be sure of your safety."

"That's your plan?" Cordy asked. "For me to act like a stupid ditz?"

"What there is of it, yes." Giles lifted his chin as if daring them to call it a bad plan.

"That's a bad plan," Xander said. Cordelia looked pleased. "Not that you can't act like a stupid ditz, Cor. In fact, I've seen you do it."

Giles blinked, apparently surprised that the old lifting-the-chin-trick hadn't intimidated them.

"Yes, well, when you've developed a better plan, please do inform me," he said tartly, and turned to walk deeper into the museum toward the Japanese exhibits.

"See," Xander began, as he followed Giles, "my plan would have included making sure we didn't go to jail, which, in case you didn't know, is not some kind of modern slang for 'tropical paradise.'" He paused and caught his breath. "Are you getting this, Giles? Jail, bad!"

"Xander."

"Coming!"

A short time later, they stood staring at the Sword of Sanno.

"Fascinating."

"What is it, Mr. Spock?"

Giles sighed and glanced at Xander. He was not without a sense of humor himself, of course, but the boy did choose the oddest times to exercise his peculiar brand of levity.

"Take a look at this." Giles pointed at the large sword on the wall. "This is the sword that Willow cut herself on. The Sword of Sanno. There appear to be Oriental characters engraved in the guard."

With a pen, he indicated the metal plate that separated the blade from the hilt of the sword. "I wish I knew what these meant."

Then he looked a bit closer. The hilt itself was wound with braids of silk in a crisscross pattern that seemed to hold in place several small disks on either side.

"Look here," he said, more to himself than to Xander. Absently he listened for Cordelia's high-pitched cries, which would signal the return of Eddie the large watchman, but she was silent. In the silence, he fervently prayed that she had not forgotten her job.

"What am I looking at?" Xander asked.

"Well," Giles said, pointing at the hilt, "notice the silk braiding here, which seems designed to both hold and expose these round plates."

"Yeah," Xander said. "And I notice the same thing on just about all the other swords in here."

"Indeed," Giles admitted. "But those swords are *katana* or other, similar swords, all from a later period. Something this ancient would never have been treated in this way. It is a style that wasn't developed until much later. Also, the plates have markings similar to those on the guard."

Xander was silent. Giles turned to look at him.

"I thought you said you didn't know anything about Japanese history or culture or whatever," Xander said.

"Well, I recall very little from my schooling, but I did come to the exhibit. As did you." Xander just shrugged. "I've just finished reading Claire Silver's journals. In fact, we learned the most fascinating thing on the way over here. It seems that Sanno the Mountain God was also bound inside the sword."

"No kidding." Xander looked askance at the weapon. "He's in there *now*?"

"I'm not certain." Giles looked at him. "But I think so."

"Maybe those little disk things were added when he was, um, bound in. Maybe it happened later, so that's why all that extra stuff is from a later period."

"Perhaps," Giles said. "But if the enchantments were that powerful, Willow's simply cutting herself should not have been enough to allow Chirayoju to be set free. Though certainly, her blood would have been a partial catalyst, and Buffy did say that her state of mind was rather vulnerable. Still, if there was a binding spell, in fact, more than one, I don't understand how . . ."

"Hey, check this out," Xander said, and moved past Giles to point to the hilt. "It looks like one of the disks is missing. Here."

Giles stared at the spot where a disk had been. "Thank you, Xander, I believe you've just answered my question."

Xander blinked. "I have?"

"Now I've got to figure out how to remove that spirit from Willow and bind it again. We'll have to lure her here somehow," he said absently, deep in contemplation.

"Or we could just take the sword."

"No, wait!" Giles cried.

But it was too late. Xander had already reached for the sword on the wall, grabbed it by the hilt, and lifted it down.

"We're—," Xander began to say, but the sentence ended there, and the smile disappeared from his face. His eyes narrowed, his nostrils flared, he thrust his chest out as though he were trying to impress the girls. He lifted his chin with an arrogant flair, and for a moment Giles thought Xander was mocking him again.

Then he spoke.

"Free," he said.

But it wasn't Xander's voice. Not at all. It was deep and

resonant, as though it came from all around the room. It was filled with a power and a pride that made Giles want to drop his eyes to the floor in deference. He fought that urge, and instead stared right at Xander's face.

Xander's face. But Xander Harris was gone.

"Ahem," Giles cleared his throat nervously. "Sanno, I presume?"

Eyes that once were Xander's locked on Giles's face, and the Watcher felt his spine melt. If it wasn't for his memory of Xander's particularly foolish sense of humor, he might have shrunk from those eyes.

"I am Sanno, King of the Mountain," the spirit wearing Xander's flesh spoke to him. "Where is the vampire?"

"Well, I'm not quite sure, but you should know that . . ."

"No matter. I can smell it. Once and for all time, I will destroy it," Sanno thundered, and began to walk toward the back of the museum, toward a pair of French doors and away from the front, where Cordelia was now trying to hold off Eddie the watchman with her damsel-in-distress routine. In the shock of Xander's transformation, Giles had missed the watchman's return.

"Cordelia, a small change of plans. We've got to go!" Giles cried urgently. "Quickly!"

Giles heard her running down the hall, and turned to see her appear in the doorway. "Well, it's about ti—," she began, but didn't finish the sentence. Instead, she stood next to Giles and watched Xander, bearing in his right hand a sword Giles could barely have wielded with two, striding toward the French doors.

"The eternal war ends tonight!" Sanno declared, and crashed through the French doors, setting off numerous ear-shattering alarms.

Giles thought of Willow. "Yes," he whispered to himself. "That's precisely what I'm afraid of."

"We must hurry," Giles said at a trot. Cordelia fought to keep up. "We don't know where Willow is, and if we lose sight of Xander, we may never know. We'll be too late to do anything."

"Okay, yeah, but you aren't wearing heels!" Cordelia snapped as she watched the distant figure stride across the museum lawn. In the background, the security alarm had fallen silent. Eddie the watchman must have decided she was a psycho and told the police to go home.

The figure seemed to shimmer as it walked. It seemed bigger and taller than Xander, and yet, if she squinted, Xander was the only thing there. It was Xander they were following, but it wasn't.

She caught up to Giles and glommed on to him, trying like anything to step out of her shoes. With each step they took, her too-high heels sank about two inches into the lawn.

"Cordelia, please, take those wretched things off!" Giles pleaded.

"I'm sorry. I just need to stop for one second so I can get them off." She watched Xander up ahead and felt as if she might cry. "These are Ferragamos! Do you know how much they cost?"

Giles shook his head impatiently.

"A lot!" She added, "What's happened to Xander?"

"It appears he's been possessed by the Sword of Sanno, well, actually, by Sanno himself," Giles said anxiously as he watched the figure thunder away from them.

"Well, then why is he speaking English?" she asked, confused.

"I suppose Sanno has accessed all of Xander's knowledge, including the language center. Xander wouldn't be used to actually having to form the sounds required for ancient Japanese. Also, it must realize we wouldn't understand it otherwise. Fascinating, really," Giles replied.

"Oh, yeah, that'd be my response too," she said sarcastically as she yanked off her shoes, "but it's not. I mean, I know he's possessed, but how?"

"Cordelia, I'll try to explain later. We must hurry!"

"That's all I am to you guys," she said sadly. "The one you're going to explain everything to later—!"

"Cordelia, come!" Giles ordered, urging her along.

"—The one you talk to like she's a collie!"

She hurried after him, her precious shoes slung over her shoulder.

A cold wind kicked up around Giles and Cordelia, gathering in strength and pushing them forward. About twenty feet ahead, Xander turned and smiled at them.

"I thought to hurry you along," the booming voice told them. "So that you may witness the destruction of the vampire. It does not yet realize I have freed myself, but when it does—"

"You freed yourself?" Cordelia shouted at it. "Excuse me, but my boyfr—... the guy I... Xander Harris freed you, Mr. Sanno."

"I am *Sanno!*" the voice thundered. The figure lifted its arms and the wind blew so hard it almost lifted Giles from the earth. "The Mountain King." It lowered its arms and strutted. "I am the protector of the Land of the Rising Sun!"

Though she was losing her balance in the bitter gale, Cordelia was not about to capitulate. Giles found her scrappy behavior remarkably refreshing, as opposed to her penchant for superficiality.

"Well, well, um, you aren't in the Land of the Rising Sun, you're in the land of Sunnydale," Cordelia said. "And things are different here. We have our own person who destroys vampires." She waved him away. "So you can go home now."

"Silence!" Sanno bellowed. "Silence, mortal girl! *Baka no onna!*"

With a point of his fire, Cordelia was slammed to the ground and pinned there. She began to shriek and struggle, near tears.

Giles knelt on one knee and bowed. "Oh great and magickal warlord, *gomenasai*. Forgive the female," he said carefully. "She is very young and ignorant. She acts out of fear for the boy whose body you inhabit, knowing what is to come."

He hissed at Cordelia, "Apologize!"

"I'm sorry," she said meekly.

Sanno said, "Very well."

Immediately the wind stopped blowing. Blinking, Cordelia brushed her bangs from her eyes, waited a beat, then clumsily got to her feet. She looked drained.

"Thank you," she said.

Sanno turned and strutted away.

Cordelia raced over to Giles. "'What is to come'? I don't know what is to come. Do you?"

Giles gestured to the retreating figure. "Oh, my dear girl." He sighed. "I'm afraid he's going to fight Chirayoju."

Cordelia stared at Xander, and then at Giles. She said, "What? But that's Willow."

Giles sighed harder. "Precisely."

She cocked her head. "Willow and Xander are going to duke it out?"

"And other things. I imagine some magick will be involved." Gently he took her wrist. "Come along now. We must keep up."

"Magick?" she repeated, stumbling after him. "Why will there be magick?"

"Isn't there always?" he asked, trying to make a joke. But it wasn't at all funny.

"How do we know when one of them wins?"

He didn't want to answer her, but she shook him hard. "Giles!"

"Oh, well." He halted and looked at her sadly. "I suppose when one of them . . . loses." He swallowed, hating to say the words. "That is to say, when one of them dies."

CHAPTER SIXTEEN

The ruined Sunnydale Friendship Garden was not the weirdest thing Buffy had ever seen, but it was close. It was enormous, which both surprised and worried her: Why hadn't she ever seen it before? She'd lived in Sunnydale an entire year and she'd been sure she'd seen all its seven wonders—but this beat all of them by a mile.

The garden was sunk into the ground. She stood on the ridge above it and looked down on the skeletal trees and rotted humpbacked bridges as she scanned the area in the gray twilight. She flicked on her flashlight. The yellow beam flickered over stone lanterns and little red temple-things—*pagodas*, came the word, although she had no idea how she knew a thing like that when she couldn't even remember *origami*—and in the distance a large, darkened building made of wood with a gently curved tile roof. Wow. When this place was built, it had represented a lot of high hopes. And money.

Buffy looked up. The sun was peeking just above the horizon, dimming the landscape. Buffy heard no sounds, not even the chirping of crickets. That in itself was enough to give her the creeps.

But what she saw coming out of the building made her knees turn to water.

Willow was dressed in an elaborate Chinese robe and, over that, some kind of upper-body metal armor. She carried a spear, maybe a long sword, and she glanced up, apparently not noticing Buffy, then strode back into the building.

A light flickered in one of the open windows, as if from a candle.

Buffy swallowed hard and began to walk down a set of stone steps toward the building. Every sense was on alert: Her gaze darted left, right, as she tried very hard to look casual and unafraid.

To her right was a deep indentation that looked as though it might have been a pond or pool at one time. A wooden bridge rose over it, the center portion smashed, probably by vandals.

Buffy walked through the silent garden.

Then she thought she heard weeping.

She quickened her pace as she approached the building.

The weeping came from inside. It could only be Willow. Or so Buffy hoped.

There was a small wooden porch attached to the building. Carefully, aware that the wood could give way at any moment, Buffy stepped onto it and peered inside.

In the center of the bare, wood-floored room, Willow wept all alone, the tears splashing down her face. With a large, jade-green candle set in an ornate red candleholder before her, she was seated on a scarlet pillow, staring at the spear she had been carrying. On the floor nearby was a sword, a traditional Japanese *katana*, and Buffy didn't even want to know where or how Willow had come by all these things.

Not that she had time to think about it. Not while Willow was pointing the sharp tip of a spear directly at her own heart.

"Willow, no!" Buffy screamed, running toward her.

The floor beneath Buffy made a strange singing sound as she ran across it. It startled her, making her falter.

Willow's head jerked up. With a whiplike motion, she turned the spear around and pointed it at Buffy. Then she said, "Oh. It's only you." She wiped her face and stared with brutal hostility at the person who was supposed to be her best friend. The spear remained pointed at Buffy.

"Oh? It's only me?" Buffy echoed in astonishment.

"I thought you might be someone else." Her tears were gone. She was a different person.

Oh, yes, a very different person.

"Who were you expecting?" Buffy demanded, sliding her

hand into her Slayer's bag as discreetly as she could. "Pizza delivery? Cable guy?"

Willow pursed her lips. Then she smiled a cruel, knowing smile and patted a cushion across from her own. "I have within me a memory that in the past your childish humor amused me. Sit while I await the setting of the sun."

Buffy didn't move. Now that she had found Willow, with the sun at its last gasp, she didn't know what to do. Eerily, Willow continued to pat the cushion. Her smile broadened.

She gestured to the floor. "This is a 'Nightingale Floor.' A very ancient tradition, which I learned in Japan," she said. "The emperors installed them so that no one could sneak up on them. But of course I knew you were coming." She chuckled. "I could smell your blood. I cannot wait to taste of it."

"Willow," Buffy tried again. "Something very bad has happened to you. Let me take you to Giles so he can fix you."

"No one can 'fix' me." Willow raised her chin. "It is too late."

And then, for one awful moment, Willow's chin quivered and she reached toward Buffy with both her hands. She was trembling. "Stop it," she begged. "Buffy, stop *me*." Then she fell forward as if someone had shot her.

The sun had gone down. The night had fallen upon them all.

Buffy acted. She darted toward Willow over the strangely singing floor and grabbed away her spear. In one motion she cracked it over her knee and tossed the two pieces across the room.

"And what has that accomplished?" Willow asked, in a lower, deeper voice. "That was not the weapon you should fear."

"Okay," Buffy said slowly, glancing at the sword on the ground not far away, trying to buy time. Angel should be catching up to her any second. "And the weapon to be feared would be?"

"I am that weapon," Willow said.

Slowly she sat back up. The floor clinged and clanged. Buffy blinked. She could almost see another set of features superimposed over Willow's. A luminous green face with bloodred lips. Almond-shaped black eyes that bored into her. The face seemed covered with some kind of glowing growth, like mold or rotted wood. It was horrible.

Laughter boomed across the room even though Willow did not laugh.

The floor sang, though Buffy stood frozen.

"I am," Willow repeated.

She clapped her hands. Like arrows, vampires leaped into the room from every window and rushed Buffy. She realized they must have buried themselves in the garden the night before, to be so close so fast.

Instantly Buffy jumped to her feet and assumed a fighting stance. She kicked the first vamp to reach her in the face and scrambled to get a stake out of her bag, cursing herself for being caught off guard as another vampire grabbed her from behind. She thrust her body forward and down, flipping the vamp to the floor with a satisfying crack. She grabbed a stake and dispatched them both quickly, in twin clouds of dust.

The floor's song became a long screech of fury. The vampires descended upon her, a small army, and she punched and kicked, fully realizing for the first time that the other night at the Bronze, the vampires who had lain in wait for her had been sent by Willow. They had preferred death over her wrath.

But it wasn't her, that's what Buffy kept telling herself. It wasn't really Willow.

A girl vampire with bright red hair and an oversized St. Andrew's sweatshirt vaulted toward her with a savage snarl even as another fang-girl in a large sweater dove at her legs. For a moment, they had her.

Then Buffy moved. Her fists came up and she shattered the grip of the redhead. With the heels of her hands, she thrust the St. Andrew's girl's head back, then slammed the by-now-well-used stake deep into her chest.

As soon as the redhead had exploded, Buffy took care of the other one around her knees.

But there were more. There seemed to be no end to them. And even though she was holding her own so far, Buffy was growing tired.

Seated on her pillow, Willow watched, smiling. Buffy turned to her and held out a beseeching hand, just as Willow had earlier. Panting, she said, "Will, you can stop them."

Willow said slowly, as if the thought was just occurring to her, "Yes."

Hopefully, Buffy went on, "Yes, yes! Just tell them to stop. They'd do what you want. They're afraid of you."

Willow lowered her head. Buffy felt a surge of hope that her sweet, Smurfy buddy was battling the monster that had possessed her.

Then Willow threw back her head and laughed, spreading her arms wide. The features of the other being were laid over her face like a grotesque green plastic mask.

"They should fear me," Willow said, only it was not Willow's voice at all. It was a demon's, and it grated on Buffy's nerves like fingers on a blackboard. "As should you, Slayer."

It snapped its fingers and walked slowly toward Buffy. The other vampires released her and glided away, ringing the perimeter of the room like spectators at a wrestling match.

"You're tired," it said in a singsong voice, the floor echoing its hypnotic rhythm. "Very tired."

Buffy's eyes drooped. An ice-cold wind whipped up around her, sapping the energy from her muscles. Her legs quivered. Her knees began to buckle.

"Your heart is slowing. Your blood is congealing."

Buffy sagged. She could barely keep her eyes open.

Then Willow rose into the air with her arms spread as the wind slapped at Buffy. Her head brushed the ceiling and her hair streamed behind her. Balls of lightning tumbled from her fingertips and crackled as they smashed into the floor around Buffy, setting the floor on fire.

The singing floor began to scream.

The other vampires backed away from the growing flames of the tinderbox wood, looking at one another as if waiting for one of them to jump out a window, so the others could see if it was better to upset Willow or burn to death.

"Know me as the vampire sorcerer Chirayoju," Willow bellowed above the shriek of wind as it whipped the flames into a brilliant wall of death. "I have come forth from my prison at last. And as soon as you are no longer a threat to me, Slayer, I will rule this place."

"Sunnydale?" Buffy murmured. Now she was sweating from the heat, and suddenly she realized that the threat of the fire had distracted her long enough for Willow's hypnotic voice to begin to lose its effect on her. Her heart was not slowing, it was revving up like she was listening to thrash metal after two particularly thick espressos. And most definitely was her blood not congealing.

"Really, with all these special effects, you could do better," she went on, her voice stronger, her stance more assured. "Conquering Sunnydale would be nothing to brag about to the other vampire sorcerers in Vampire Sorcererland, believe me. They'd take your union card and laugh you right out of the club."

"Silence!" Chirayoju shrieked. It fell from the ceiling, aiming directly at Buffy.

Which would require, Buffy realized, that it pass through the wall of flame.

"Willow!" She shouted. "No!"

The body of her friend continued to plummet. Buffy took a deep breath and looked for a gap in the flames. She saw one about three feet to her left—the flames were only knee-high—and Buffy bounded over to the spot, making sure she still had her slayage equipment, and jumped over the fire. She felt the heat through the soles of her boots.

Chirayoju landed less than five feet from her and came at her with a series of roundhouse kicks. Buffy ducked them, giving as good as she got, then wincing as the monster cried out in pain, not in its own voice, but in Willow's.

"An interesting dilemma for you, eh?" Chirayoju said. "You must defeat me, but you do not want to kill your friend." It sneered at her, a morphing combination of its own features and Willow's. "You are weak."

"Oh?" Buffy stiff-armed Willow in her changing face. The thing inside her staggered backward. "How's that for weak?"

"You care for her," Chirayoju taunted her, coming at her. "I care for nothing and no one."

"You hear that, you guys? It doesn't care about you," Buffy called. She ticked a quick glance around the room. The other vampires had disappeared. No wonder. The entire building was engulfed in flames, the ceiling included. Any second now, the whole structure would cave in.

With a grunt of effort, Buffy launched herself at Chirayoju, forcing it back into the depths of the room. Yet Buffy's mind registered that Willow was in mortal danger from the flames.

She had no idea what to do. Chirayoju represented a threat far greater than just this tiny combat in a dead garden. Buffy had to stop it. But how to do that without sacrificing her best friend . . .

Above her, two wooden beams dislodged from the ceiling and crashed to the floor behind her. The floor groaned like a dying beast, and then it cracked open. Buffy staggered backward slightly. Another beam fell. Roof tiles shot through the weakened ceiling toward her and Chirayoju like bombs.

Suddenly she rushed at Chirayoju, grabbed the demon vampire around the waist, and dove with it out a window.

They rolled in the weeds and the dirt. Then Buffy flung it away from her and resumed her fighting stance.

It was then that she realized her Slayer's bag was still inside the burning building.

Chirayoju seemed to realize the same thing at the same time.

It grinned hideously.

"It ends," it said, advancing slowly as if savoring the moment of triumph. Smoke rose from its body. "You will be mine."

"Sorry, I've already got a Valentine."

Her mind raced as she scanned the area for a piece of wood, a branch, anything she could use as a weapon. Finally, in desperation, she reached inside her blouse and yanked the metal chain she wore around her neck. She held the cross before Chirayoju, having no idea if it would have any effect on a Chinese vampire sorcerer.

Chirayoju hissed and stopped short. Buffy almost cheered with relief. It was the same cross Angel had given her the night they met. She would have to thank him again for it. She would have to—

"Where did you get that?" the vampire demanded, gesturing to it.

"Does it matter?" she asked, feeling better as she caught her breath.

"It's mine! Give it back!" it shouted, balling its fists in frustration.

"Yours?" Buffy glanced at the chain. Along with the cross, the disk Willow had taken from the Sword of Sanno dangled from it.

Buffy grinned.

"Oh. *Yours*," she said. "Then come and get it."

Frenzied, screaming, Chirayoju flew at her.

For a heartbeat, Buffy froze. If Willow was really a vampire, just another hollow corpse filled with some kind of blood-sucking demon spirit—well, that'd be different. It wouldn't be Willow anymore. But as far as she could tell, whatever this Chirayoju was, it was inside the real flesh-and-blood Willow, and she was still in there too.

For the moment, Chirayoju seemed focused on the small disk she wore on a chain with her crucifix. Could she just give it up? Maybe . . .

Chirayoju lunged for her. The Slayer dropped her left shoulder, ducked it down, and came up under Willow's body, flipping Chirayoju over and back. Claws scrabbled for purchase on Buffy's blouse and arm, dragging deep, bloody furrows across the flesh of her upper biceps.

Buffy spun to face the vampire demon who possessed the body of her friend. The seething sting of the scratches on her arm gave her a new clarity: Staying alive was key. Part of the Slayer's job, actually. But unless she was willing to kill Willow, she would die.

Buffy took a deep breath. Then, silently, she apologized to Giles. To her mom. To Dad, wherever he was this week.

Because she knew she was about to fail in that primary task. Buffy Summers knew she was about to die.

Then, in that same moment of clarity, she recalled something that would save her life. Willow's hand. Or rather, her wrist. After Chirayoju had possessed her, Willow's fractured wrist had healed instantly. Almost miraculously.

Buffy smiled. She wasn't going to like hurting Willow, but at least now she knew that Willow would heal. She could defend herself without doing any lasting damage.

"All right, whatever the hell you are," Buffy snapped. "Come on, then. I want my friend back. If that means I have to keep inflicting pain until you decide to forfeit the game—well, let me tell you, I can go all night."

Chirayoju roared and rushed at her again. Willow's red-tinted locks flew back as the vampire sorcerer came at Buffy, more cautious this time, but no less savage.

"I have had entire nations on their knees before me,"

Chirayoju snarled. "The ancients whimpered in fear at the whisper of my name. So shall you."

The thing circled, looking for an opening. Buffy kept up her guard, and they faced each other down. She found it difficult to look at Willow's face, at the slack emptiness of her features, the hollowness of her eyes. Instead, she concentrated on the gossamer flickering of the grotesquely glowing green face that seemed to cling over Willow's like some sheer Halloween mask.

Only this wasn't Halloween.

Buffy knew from Halloween, and this was way worse.

"The ancients, huh?" Buffy asked, smiling. "Well, then, just for you, the Slayer's gonna have to reach way down deep inside and come up with a real old-school vampire butt-kicking."

That ghost mask stretched itself into a sickening smile. Buffy's stomach lurched as she saw Willow's mouth and cheeks move beneath it, lifted into a tiny smile themselves, as though the ghost mask were touching her face, twisting her features.

"Foolish girl," Chirayoju sneered. "You still do not grasp the truth of this conflict, do you? I have merely been testing you. This fragile shell I now wear has served me well, but it is weak and small.

"You, however, are the Slayer. Your body will be a much more suitable host for my magnificence."

"I could take that as a compliment," Buffy said. "But . . . no."

She shot forward in a high kick. It would have connected

well, a solid hit . . . if not for the wind. The wind that sprang up and tossed her through the air as though she were chaff in a summer breeze. Buffy landed painfully between a pair of squat pagodas. When she sat up, she had a hard time catching her breath.

Her left cheek was swollen and throbbing in pain, and she suspected the bone was bruised beneath the skin. Chirayoju wasn't like any vampire she'd ever fought. Maybe it was because she was holding back for Willow's sake, but she didn't think so. There was something so profoundly evil in this creature that it made it difficult for her to concentrate. Not merely evil, but consciously so.

Most vampires were simple predators, their evil confined to their lust for blood and death and terror. This was very, very different. The average bloodsucker barely considered what its prey was, what it might be thinking, what life it might live. Buffy sensed in Chirayoju a horrible intelligence. This ancient, savage thing knew exactly what effect its butchery would have on its victims' loved ones; it understood the questioning of reality that would come from an encounter with it.

Chirayoju was smart. The demon spirit was a vampire in more ways than one. It fed on blood, true. But Buffy realized that it fed on fear and despair as well.

And she wasn't about to give it that.

"Give yourself to me, Slayer," Chirayoju hissed, and seemed to float across the withered vegetation toward her.

Buffy looked up, felt the sharp pain of a torn muscle in her shoulder. She blew a strand of hair from her face with lips covered in bloody spittle. She was in rough shape, and she knew it.

She lowered her head as the vampire came for her. She reached for the concrete roof of the little pagoda in front of her and brought it up hard, with all her strength, in a blow that tore her shoulder muscle further. The concrete shattered on the side of Chirayoju's head with a crack. Blood sprayed, and Willow's skull gave way.

Chirayoju dropped to the dead garden.

Buffy's heart stopped. She couldn't breathe. Tears sprang to her eyes.

"Oh my God, Willow!" she whispered frantically. "I'm sorry."

She dropped to her knees in the soft, dead earth and reached for her friend. A hand whipped up from the ground and tangled in her hair, drawing her down, her face forced into the dirt and dead plants. The smell was rich and sweet and laced with rot.

"Now, Slayer," she heard it whisper, "your body will be mine. This form was useful to me, but you are so much more powerful. You aren't like other mortal girls."

Buffy threw an elbow back, slammed it into Willow's gut, then used her leverage to toss Chirayoju off her.

"I've been hearing that my whole life," she grunted, still trying to catch her breath. Buffy looked up at the ghastly double-vision face of her best friend.

Chirayoju's eyes bulged with rage. "You tempt my fury, girl."

"Yeah," Buffy agreed, getting to her feet. "I'm just kinda wacky like that. You and my mom should have a chat."

Wearing Willow's body, cloaked in an armored breast-plate, the vampire began to rise again.

C'mon, Buffy wanted to say. *Gimme a second to catch my breath, will ya?*

Chirayoju began to charge. Buffy set her legs, trying to convince her exhausted body that she was truly ready for another round. There was nothing else she could do.

Except to die before she could be possessed . . .

Then a shadow whipped past her and met Chirayoju head on. Claws ripped the air, ripped flesh, and Willow's body was flung backward to the earth.

Buffy blinked.

Angel stood over Chirayoju, his face twisted and feral. The back of his shirt was torn to shreds, and long, ragged wounds, stained crimson, were already healing.

"You're not going to touch her again," Angel said, his voice that low rumble Buffy knew so well—was so incredibly relieved to hear. "She might not want to do it, but if it comes to it, I'll kill that body you're in to keep you from getting to Buffy."

Buffy's relief evaporated. The Slayer's stomach lurched and a dagger of ice thrust itself into her chest. She reached out a hand as Angel advanced on the demon.

"Angel . . . ," she gasped. "No."

CHAPTER SEVENTEEN

G iles felt nauseous. Cordelia wasn't helping.

"Giles, what are we going to do?" Cordelia asked desperately.

Giles didn't tell her that she'd been asking the same question for the past four minutes, barely interrupting herself to breathe. Nor did he mention that his own mind was in as much turmoil as his stomach as he worked feverishly to answer that question.

But he did know that he'd been unnecessarily cold to Cordelia, and he regretted it.

"Cordelia, I must apologize." He sighed. "I've been terribly short with you, and I'm afraid it's because I'm feeling rather useless at the moment," he admitted sheepishly. "You see, I really don't know how to withdraw these spirits from Willow and Xander. I had hoped that if we kept up with Sanno—Xander—that I might be able to speak with it, to learn enough to stop this insanity."

Cordelia watched the receding figure of Xander. Giles followed her gaze. "And we're losing him, huh?" she said. "He's getting away from us."

"He's getting away from us," Giles agreed.

"Well, what about your books?" Cordelia asked hopefully. "There's gotta be something there, right? You've got the skinny on every nasty thing that's ever walked the earth."

"Well, perhaps not all the nasty things," Giles murmured, then looked at her. "Researching this could take all night, and this is happening right now. Not to mention that until we know where Xander—where Sanno—is going, we won't know where the battle is going to be fought." He looked glumly at the horizon, where Xander was fast disappearing.

Cordelia cocked her head at Giles and frowned.

"What did I say?" he asked.

"Well, only something clueless. I think." Cordelia hesitated, then went on. "You showed us yourself in the museum, Giles. If they're going to have it out, it'll be in that Japanese garden place. Don't you think?"

Giles paused, eyebrows raised. He looked far ahead, where Xander's possessed form melted into the night. It made sense.

If he recalled the layout of Sunnydale correctly, they did seem to be heading in that direction.

Which meant they didn't need to follow Xander at all. And suddenly, Giles had an idea or two about possession. It might even be worth giving an old-fashioned exorcism a try.

"I can see the Giles-mind in action," Cordelia declared hopefully. "Usually a frightening thing, but please tell me you've got something."

Giles spun, and turned to walk back the way they came.

"Wait. Where are you going?" Cordelia demanded.

"The library," Giles replied. "Come on, Cordelia, I'll need your help."

"But what about Xander?" she asked, glancing over her shoulder.

Giles stated the obvious. "We can't keep up."

She tried one more time. "But I've always been useless with research."

Giles gestured for her to follow him. "Well, it's time we changed that, then, isn't it?"

"We should get your car."

"Agreed." He kept walking.

In the library, Cordelia was too nervous for this sitting around and thumbing through books stuff. She shifted uncomfortably in her chair and said to Giles, "I don't even know how to spell exorcism."

"Look," he said excitedly as the fax machine rang.

He gestured for her to join him as the paper unspooled. With an excited flourish, he ripped it off.

"'Monsieur Giles, so sorry to hear of troubles in Sunnydale. I have fragments of Appendix 2a of Silver's *Spells*, published much later than your edition. Pages thirty-two through thirty-four only. She writes most excitedly of the sword's movement after the earthquake in Kobe. There was fear of escape of two spirits within. New enchantments were added, disks, I think, and the sword was put in Tokyo Museum. That is all I have at this time. You might try Heinrich Meyer-Dinkmann in Frankfurt, and of course you must have consulted Kobo at Tokyo University. Kindest regards, Henri Tourneur.'"

"All right, that's confirmation that the disks are wards," Giles said.

"All right," Cordelia agreed.

"Do keep looking." He gestured to the two-foot-tall stack of books he'd gathered on the table. "I'll try Meyer-Dinkmann. And it's e-x-o-r-c-i-s-m. I suggest you write it down."

"*Giles.*" She shook her head. "What I mean is I am not getting anywhere. I can't even see the words. All I see is Xander's face when we found him in the bushes. And in the hospital. And now." She swallowed hard. "I can't concentrate."

Giles put down his book and moved behind her. "But we must," he said gently. "I, too, am distracted. But this is what we can do to help him. It's all we can do."

"Then he's in big trouble," she muttered.

Giles was on the phone to Berlin.

"Guten Tag, hier spricht Giles," he began.

"Herr Giles! A pleasure!"

"That could be my job, if I spoke German," Cordelia muttered. "I *like* talking on the phone. But *no*, I have to look up *exorcism.*"

"Ja, ja, vielen Dank," Giles said, and hung up. "Well."

She looked up hopefully. "Yes?"

"Meyer-Dinkmann couldn't put his hands on it, but he's read more of Appendix 2a than Tourneur. It appears that there was an actual Incantation of Sanno, and it has all the details about how to bind spirits into swords." He looked dazed. "You know, Cordelia, this is rather how Miss Silver went about her research, only of course, everything was much slower in her day. Imagine what that woman could have accomplished given a fax, a telephone, and the vast resources of the Internet!"

"Yeah," Cordelia piped. "So where is the Incantation of Sanno?"

"Meyer-Dinkmann said it's online," Giles said enthusiastically. "He said he'd have, ah, downloaded the file for us, but his computer is temporarily down for an upgrade of some sort. But if I understand computers, we can simply search for the topic and see if we have any matches."

"Okay!" Cordelia said brightly, saved from the book stack. "Let's do it."

He moved his shoulders as he continued. "I haven't the

foggiest notion how to go about it, however. We need Willow."

"We need Willow," Cordelia agreed glumly.

Buffy and Angel caught Chirayoju off guard, and together were able to hurl the thing, in Willow's body, over the bony, upraised fingers of a dead cherry tree. Buffy fought to catch her breath as the monster landed in the dirt.

"We can't keep this up," Angel murmured to the girl he loved. "We have to finish it." He looked at her flushed, drawn face. "Buffy, we have to kill Willow."

Wildly the Slayer shook her head. "No. No way. Look, why don't you go? It hasn't torched me with that magick fire because it wants my bod. It can't kill me, I can't kill it. Stalemate. We could use some Giles-type help here."

Angel stared at her. "It may not want to kill you. That doesn't mean it won't. I'm not going anywhere."

Chirayoju rose to a standing position and brushed the dirt off its crimson robes with theatrical distaste. "I find this fighting style most plebeian," it said. Its right arm was crooked, and it limped as it moved forward.

Angel scrutinized Chirayoju's movements as it prepared to launch another attack, posturing like a martial arts master. Willow's body was badly injured. He knew Buffy couldn't stand to see her suffer, even if she wasn't Willow at the moment. But Angel would do whatever it took—including destroying Willow, who was *his* friend too—to make sure Buffy got out of this alive.

"Buffy, you know what must be done," *my love*, he added silently, pitying her. Wishing he could lift the burden of being the Chosen One from her shoulders for just five minutes. But that would do nothing. And she *was* the Chosen One. There was no way she could be anything less, not even for a heartbeat.

Looking very frightened and very young, she lifted her chin in defiance. Her eyes were huge in her face, but her jaw was set and hard. Her shoulders squared. "I won't do it."

"Then I will," Angel said firmly.

"No!" Buffy cried.

Chirayoju the vampire rose straight into the air and made fists of its hands, launching fireballs at them. Buffy and Angel rolled in opposite directions as the balls seemed to track them, then exploded into the earth as the two successfully eluded them. The dry brush and the brittle trees lit up like fireworks.

Buffy murmured, "Okay, maybe it doesn't want my bod."

She frowned as something occurred to her. "And how come you were so late, anyway?"

Another volley of fireballs careened toward them. Angel leaped on top of Buffy and rolled her out of the way. As she lay beneath him, he said, "Don't tell me you haven't noticed that the rest of Chirayoju's playmates kind of disappeared."

"Yeah. A likely excuse," she said as he let her up and she assumed a Slayer's fighting stance. "You probably went out for cigs."

"Gave 'em up," he assured her. "They take years off your life." Then he cried, "Look out!"

Chirayoju hurtled itself from the sky straight at Buffy.

"If you will not give yourself to me, then you will be eliminated! Choose, Slayer!"

Buffy jumped into the air and pummeled the vampire demon with a double kick, then flipped herself backward, catching herself at the last minute with her hands and pushing off them sideways, out of the way of Willow's body as it slammed hard on the ground.

"That answer your questions, Chumley?" Buffy asked. She got in a couple of quick kicks before Angel grabbed it by the shoulders and punched it hard, wincing as he heard a tiny gasp that sounded very much like Willow.

"Please," he heard, in Willow's voice. "Please."

"Stop!" Buffy shouted.

"It's a trick, Buffy," Angel called to her. "It's playing on your feelings. Don't listen to it."

"I'm allowing her to feel the pain," Chirayoju said, pulling itself away from Angel and focusing its attention on Buffy. It didn't even bother to look at him. "And it hurts, Slayer. It hurts more than you can imagine. Certainly more than *she* could—until now."

Tears welled in Buffy's eyes as she panted, fighting to catch her breath. She said unsteadily, "Hurt her any more, and I'll . . . I'll . . ."

Chirayoju laughed. "There is nothing you can do, is there? Except for one thing." It smiled. "I want your body, Slayer."

She sneered at it. "Sorry, I've got a steady."

Suddenly Chirayoju flew away from Buffy and focused its gaze on Angel. It said in a hypnotic voice, "You are now my slave, vampire. You will do as I say."

Buffy gaped as Angel's face grew slack and blank. His dark, intense eyes stared hard at the vampire demon. "You will begin to walk. You will walk until the sun comes up. And then you will die."

"No!" Buffy shouted.

Chirayoju smiled at Buffy in victory. It said, "Thus will he die, along with the girl whose body you are killing."

"Angel!" she cried.

"Don't worry, Buffy, you're not like other girls, and I'm not like other vampires!" Angel flew at Chirayoju and grabbed it around the neck. Angel bared his fangs, preparing to lower his mouth to Willow's throat, growling savagely.

Chirayoju said to Buffy, "I will let him kill her."

"Stop," Buffy said tiredly. "Okay. You win. Angel, let it go." Smiling grimly, she held out her hand. "Mr. Cheerios, congratulations. You've just won the big showcase on *Let's Make a Deal.*"

"No, Buffy," Angel said.

"Yes, Buffy," Buffy replied unhappily. She said to the vampire, "Let me say good-bye to him."

"No tricks," it said suspiciously as Angel glowered at it.

"No tricks," she assured it. "But I want something in return, or no deal."

"You dare—," it began.

"Shut up!" Buffy snapped. "You want my help? Then be quiet and listen. You don't attack him or Willow after you take me over. That's my condition."

It paused. Considered.

"That is your sole condition?"

"I'd like to make a list, but I figure that'd be pushing it," she retorted. Her heart was pounding. She was scared, but she wasn't about to let it know that. And there were worse things than being possessed by ancient Chinese demon vampires.

There was always math.

"Agreed," Chirayoju said. "I will not harm Weeping Willow, or the vampire you call your mate."

"Well, not my mate, exactly," she said, reddening as she glanced at Angel. "That sounds so . . . um, primitive."

Angel pleaded, "Buffy, don't do this."

She walked a short distance away as Angel reluctantly let the demon go. Buffy touched the chain around her neck, tried to find the clasp without being obvious about it, and gave it a yank as Angel caught up with her.

Protectively, desperately, he put his arms around her.

"Buffy, you don't know what it's like to be taken over by evil," he whispered. "I do. I can't let you go through with this."

"You don't have a choice, Angel," she said. "Please, just help me."

She lowered her gaze to her fist. "It has a jones for this little disk thingy. Willow accidently knocked it off the sword just before she cut herself. I figure it helped set Chirayoju free. When it saw it around my neck, it got all hyper."

She gathered the chain up in her fist and pressed it into his. Instantly, a look of pain crossed over his face. Her eyes widened and she glanced down, to see a small wisp of smoke trailing from his closed hand.

"Oh, the cross," she said, remembering that she had been wearing the silver cross he had given her the first night they met. "I'm so sorry."

"It's okay." He gave her a pained, crooked smile. "It's a good kind of hurt."

"Get it to Giles. He'll know what to do. He's like Scotty, you know, on *Star Trek*?" She paused. "Wow. You probably watched it when it first came on in the sixties."

But Angel wasn't swayed by her change of subject. "Buffy, please," he whispered. "Don't do it."

She gazed up at him fearfully. She wondered if she would ever be in Angel's arms again. She guessed he was wondering the same thing, because he looked very, very worried and held her too tight.

"Kiss me?" she whispered. "For luck?"

"I love you," he murmured.

Their lips met. She wanted to fling her arms around him, but she held the kiss, feeling his mouth against hers, a coolness in the fever of her terror. To be possessed by evil . . . she couldn't imagine a worse fate.

Except dying possessed by evil.

She was the first to pull away.

"Okay, Mr. Cheerios," she said jauntily, "I'm ready." She turned to face the monstrous evil as it glided up to her and grabbed up her hand. Its grip burned her as the cross must have burned Angel.

"Remember your promise," she said, swallowing hard. "No running in the halls."

"To the last, your weak and pointless jokes," it said.

"Next stop, Comedy Central," she replied unsteadily.

"Buffy," Angel said. "Buffy, stop. Don't go through with it."

It straightened her fingers and sliced at its own cheek. "My blood," it explained, smearing her hand against the wound.

"Willow's," Buffy said. "It's Will—" She inhaled deeply as something rammed hard through her chest, knocking her completely senseless.

Then she was surrounded by screaming—agonized and hopeless screaming. It went on and on until she thought she wouldn't be able to stand it for another second. Then it grew louder.

She heard Willow cry, "Buffy!"

Then she was burning up, standing inside a firestorm that ate away every inch of her being. She writhed as flames whooshed around her, burning through her lungs, her vocal cords, her ears.

She trembled, freezing, in utter silence. She looked left, right, but where she was, endless blackness stretched in all directions. She tried to move, but she was frozen to the . . .

to the . . .

to nothing.

She was utterly, vastly *nowhere*.

Somewhere, very far away, she heard a voice she once had known very well. With a laugh, it spoke:

"I have won."

CHAPTER EIGHTEEN

S top!" Angel roared.

Buffy stopped. Angel stood to bar her path and stared into her eyes. But she wasn't there. Everything that was Buffy had disappeared from her eyes; the spark that was her soul was missing. Still there, he knew . . . from painful experience. But buried as deep as the worst of secrets.

"I vowed to the Slayer that I would not attack you," Chirayoju said, Buffy's lips forming the vampire's words.

Vampire. Yes, but unlike any vampire Angel had ever faced. When it still wore its own flesh, Chirayoju must have been a great sorcerer. That was the only explanation Angel could imagine for the demon's power. It was essentially a ghost, a bodiless demon spirit that, when merged with a human host, made a vampire. Just like him. But nothing like him at all.

"Let her go," Angel demanded, aware that he also had to protect Willow, who was unconscious at his feet. Though Chirayoju's own magickal self-preservation had healed her almost completely of the wounds she had received while possessed, she was completely drained of energy.

Chirayoju smiled, and the way its grin twisted Buffy's face, it didn't look like Buffy anymore at all. *Which is good,* Angel thought. That would make it easier if he had to kill her. As if anything could make that easy.

The smile broadened, and suddenly a moldy green face seemed to shimmer into being, covering Buffy's features like a mask, though Angel could still see her through it.

This was Chirayoju's true face, then. Angel's lips curled back and his face changed as well, transforming into the savage face of the vampire within him. Chirayoju had made a mistake. If he'd kept using Buffy's face, Buffy's voice, Buffy's perfect mouth to speak, Angel didn't think he could ever have attacked.

But now he saw the face of the demon.

"I vowed I would not attack, but I said nothing about defending myself," Chirayoju declared. "Stand aside, Angelus . . . yes, I know your name. I plucked it from the Slayer's mind. Stand aside, or you will die your final death."

Without Buffy, he had nothing to live for, but Angel stood his ground. Chirayoju moved forward, prepared to attack, then stopped suddenly. The green ghost face shattered, and Buffy's eyes went wide. For a moment, Angel hoped that Buffy had driven the vampire out of her body, but no, the voice that came from her mouth was still not quite her own.

"I sense . . . something," Chirayoju said. "But it cannot be. Not here."

Then Angel sensed it too. A powerful new presence. He turned, ready to defend himself.

Then he saw who it was.

"Xander?" he called, staring at the new arrival. Xander had a huge old sword in his hands, and he marched into the dead garden with a wide grin on his face.

"What do you think you're doing?" Angel asked. "You're going to get yourself killed."

Xander swung the sword up, held it in battle position. It was a very heavy-looking weapon, and yet he moved it as though it were plastic. Angel looked more closely at Xander's face, at his strange smile. And then he knew.

This wasn't Xander any more than the other creature standing in the garden was Buffy. He didn't know who or what is was, but it wasn't the mortal who laughed and joked and called him Dead Boy.

"Another one?" he whispered to himself.

"Chirayoju!" Xander roared, or whatever was inside him did. "Once again you defile the sacred soil of the Land of the Rising Sun! And once again, you will fall beneath my sword. So swears Sanno, the King of the Mountain!"

A powerful wind sprang up suddenly and whipped at Angel. The gale was so strong it almost knocked him back, but he leaned into the wind, trying to figure out what his next move should be. These two were obviously bitter enemies.

"Foolish little god," Chirayoju snarled in return. "This is not Japan. The soil you stand on now may have been tilled by Japanese hands, but your nation—your mountain—is far from here. You stopped me once, but we have been locked in our bloody battle for many millennia now, and I have the measure of you, Sanno. You cannot defeat me here, on this dead patch of earth. Not when I wear the flesh of one who was already more than human!"

Chirayoju raised its right hand—Buffy's right hand—and laughed deeply. Cruelly. "Time to die, old spirit. The time has come for you to be washed from the earth forevermore!"

As Angel watched them posturing, circling, sizing each other up in the Eastern tradition of combat, he clutched the disk Buffy had slipped him. He realized he was trapped in a horrible dilemma: If he helped Xander, then Buffy might be killed, and vice versa.

Chirayoju's face changed yet again. The sparkle returned to Buffy's eyes for just a moment.

"Xander!" Buffy's voice cried. "No!"

Then it was gone, just as quickly. But Angel had seen it. And he knew that in her mind, in her soul, Buffy was fighting Chirayoju's control. For a moment, while the vampire spirit was distracted, she had taken her body back. She was fighting.

And when the Slayer fought, the Slayer won. In the end. That's why she was the Chosen One. Suddenly Angel had hope. It might be possible to keep them from killing each other after all.

"That's it, Buffy, come on!" he shouted, moving toward Chirayoju, bending against the gale force winds. "Push him out. Take your body back! You can do it!"

Chirayoju sprayed spheres of flame from its palms, and they sizzled through the air toward Xander . . . toward the Mountain King. But the king brought up his sword to stop the flames, and the fire seemed to be absorbed right into the metal.

The sword pointed toward Chirayoju as Sanno stepped forward. Angel jumped between them, eyes darting back and forth between the two ancient spirits.

"Stop," he said. "This battle serves neither one of you."

He turned to stare into Buffy's eyes, searching for her in there. Finding nothing.

"Out of the way, child," Chirayoju thundered, and raised its hands again.

Angel was about to protest when a blast of fire scorched his back. It had erupted from Sanno's hands, he realized as he arched with the pain. Then Chirayoju brought fire down upon him as well, and Angel fell to the ground, rolling in the dirt and the dead vegetation to douse the flames.

He grunted in pain as he stared up at Xander's face. The spirit that possessed him clearly enjoyed his own show of power and Angel's agony. It might be a battle of good versus evil, but he didn't think Sanno was much better than Chirayoju. Not after thousands of years of hatred. Sanno wanted to kill his enemy, and it didn't matter who died in the process. The Mountain King was arrogant and cruel, just like a vampire.

Any vampire.

The winds continued to howl all around Angel, kicking up dirt and uprooted plants. Angel slitted his eyes and began to sit up, wincing at the pain of his burns. But the pain was easy to ignore when he thought of what would happen if he didn't do something soon.

Then, over the gale, he heard someone calling his name.

"Angel!" Willow cried again, desperate to understand what was happening all around her. She ached all over, but that was starting to go away. What still hurt was inside: the memory of having been taken over by something not very nice. The brief flashes of reveling in cruelty, of laughing at Buffy and Angel as they had fought her . . .

Then Angel was there, coat flapping in the wind, ignoring the grit that stung her own face and arms. He moved to her and lifted her easily, then ran a few yards to the small gully where water had once run. They ducked behind the cracked wooden bridge that ran over the gully.

Willow didn't even have to ask what was happening. Part of her remembered. The rest of her just knew.

"Are you all right?" Angel asked.

There was an uncomfortable moment between them even as the battle raged not far away. Willow wondered how long that awkwardness would remain. Both of them were acutely aware that it wasn't all that long ago that Angel had been trying to take her life, rather than save it.

"I'm alive," Willow replied. "Alive is good."

"You remember how you got here?" Angel said quickly.

Willow nodded unhappily.

"Well, something like it's happened to Xander. That old Chinese vampire's greatest enemy, the guy who defeated him the first time, has taken control of Xander. Buffy's fighting for control of her body, but . . ."

Angel let his words trail off, and Willow felt a chill run all through her body. It was her fault. She'd been so obsessed with being more like Buffy . . . She should never have touched that sword!

But even as the thoughts entered her mind, she knew how foolish they were. There was no way she could have known what was going to happen. No, the only thing she had to concentrate on was how to save Buffy and Xander.

"They're going to kill each other," she said, softly enough that Angel couldn't have heard her over the wailing of the wind.

"Do you remember any of what was in its head?" Angel asked, shouting over the roar of the storm. "Can you think of any way to stop it?"

"No," Willow said, beginning to panic. She shook her head

as she stared at the bizarre sight of Buffy and Xander stalking each other, clearly about to launch another attack. She saw the shimmering ghost-faces of the vampire and the Mountain King floating over their features, and that comforted her a little, helped her remember they weren't really themselves.

She turned to Angel, frantic. "Can't you do something?" she demanded. "I mean, come on! I know it's in there, in you! Angelus is in there, and well, he's pretty nasty and you could stop them if you really wanted to! Stop them from killing each other. There's nobody else, Angel. It has to be you!"

Willow stared at him, her eyes pleading. When Angel glanced away, unable to meet her gaze, Willow sobbed loudly.

"I'm not Angelus anymore," he said. "And if I were, all I would do is kill them both, and that isn't really the outcome you're hoping for, is it?"

When she shook her head anxiously, he drawled, "Didn't think so."

"I'm sorry," Willow said meekly.

"Not as sorry as I am."

"So we just let them fight?" Willow asked, wide-eyed.

"What else can we do?" Angel said, turning back to stare at the two figures battling in the moonlight. "I might be able to affect the outcome of this battle, maybe even restrain one of them . . . but not both, Willow, don't you understand? The Mountain King isn't going to stop until Buffy's dead, and even if I could stop him, there'd still be Chirayoju to deal with."

"But what about when it's . . . when it's over?" Willow

persisted. "I mean, if the Mountain King kills Buffy, he might just go away, but if Chirayoju wins . . ."

Angel looked at her, and Willow knew she had never seen such sorrow in another person's eyes. "If she wins," Angel said grimly, "then I might just have to murder the one person I love in all the world."

Both of them turned at the sound of Chirayoju screeching in a voice that once had been Buffy's. The vampire sorcerer launched itself at Sanno. Twirling his sword over his head in great, swooping motions, Sanno charged at Chirayoju.

Then Chirayoju leaped into the air, shot flames at the Mountain King, executed a somersault, and landed on the other side of him. Fireballs erupted from the vampire's hands and burned the air as they spat at Sanno, but the Mountain King deflected them with the wide blade of his ancient sword. The orange light reflected off Buffy's features, giving her face combined with Chirayoju's ghastly mask a hellish cast.

Then the two immortal enemies rushed at each other again. Their battle had lasted for thousands of years. Each truly had the same measure of the other. But when the battle was to the death, Willow knew there could be only one victor.

As she watched, Buffy and Xander became a blur of fists and kicks and gouts of flame. Willow smelled burning flesh and singed hair. Sanno brought his sword down, slicing the air. The ugly blade missed Buffy's shoulder by inches, the top of her head by even less than that.

Angel turned to her, his eyes narrow and intense. He

reached out for Willow's hand and put something into her palm.

"Get this to Giles," the vampire whispered.

Willow looked down, saw the disk and the ancient crucifix, then stared hard at Angel. "What are you going to do?"

Angel smiled. "I'm going to try to keep them both alive." Then he was in motion. He turned and ran at Chirayoju . . . at Buffy . . . and dove at her, face shifting to the savage countenance of the vampire within.

Willow understood then, understood the words he hadn't spoken. He was going to try to keep Buffy and Xander alive, even if it meant his own final death.

But Willow wasn't about to argue. She knew that Angel was right. There was nothing else for them to do but look to Giles for answers. With a last glance at the fire that burned the air, the blood that spattered the dead garden, the blade that glinted in the light of the full moon, she turned and ran, bent over against the force of the wind.

She ran as if her life depended on it.

As if all their lives depended on it.

In fact, she ran like the devil.

Xander was paralyzed.

He could see. He could hear. But he could not move or feel or speak. Sanno had taken all of those abilities away from him. All he could do was rage in silence against the being that had invaded his body.

Somewhere inside his mind, thunder rolled across an entire world. Almost as if it were coming for him, somehow. As if it would roll over him and obliterate him forever . . . leaving Sanno alone in here, in his body. Somehow he knew that if he stopped fighting, if he just abandoned his body to Sanno, that thunder wouldn't just be in his head anymore. No. It would roll across the surface of the world, starting in Sunnydale. Then the King of the Mountain would be in charge, and anyone who didn't worship the King just might get rolled over too. Or struck by lightning. Or scorched by fire.

It was only that weird intuition that kept Xander from retreating completely. For if he could not control his body's actions, he certainly did not want to bear witness to them. Because his body moved, his arms swung a deadly blade. Sanno was trying to use him for vengeance, but that vengeance was going to cost Buffy her life.

Quietly, Xander realized that he hoped that Chirayoju would win. Then at least Xander would not have to live with the knowledge that he had been unable to stop himself from killing one of his best friends, a girl he cared very deeply for.

When Angel dove at Buffy, Xander felt the tiniest moment of triumph. Somehow, they would all get out of this alive. Or, at the very least, Buffy would. Angel wouldn't let anything bad happen to her.

Chirayoju collided with Angel, and the two crashed to the ground.

"Fool, fool!" Chirayoju shrieked. "What are you doing? I will burn you from the face of the earth!"

"You swore not to harm me," Angel reminded it as he grabbed at Chirayoju's punishing fists.

"What is his vow worth?" Sanno demanded as he approached them.

Then suddenly, Chirayoju's features vanished. Angel saw the light in Buffy's eyes. He heard Buffy's voice.

"Angel, stop me now," she whispered. "Kill me."

"Buffy, stay with me," he urged. "Fight him."

He grabbed her hands and threw them behind her back. Her chest pushed against his, and her breath was hot on his neck. He gave her a quick kiss, if only to keep her mind focused on who he was . . . and who she was.

Sanno's eyes lit up.

"The girl has overtaken him?" he asked.

"Yes, I think," Angel replied.

"Then this is the moment of triumph," Sanno declared. "Hold Chirayoju for me, boy. I'll cut off its head." At that precise moment, the light left Buffy's eyes and she was Chirayoju once more. The demon threw Angel off like a pesky mosquito and snarled at the Mountain King, blasting him backward with a wave of fire. Then, almost as an afterthought, it used the moment's respite to grab Angel around the neck.

"You would have done it, wouldn't you?" it demanded. It pushed Angel's head to one side and prepared to bite him.

"For that, I will destroy you, as certainly as I swore not to."

As Angel struggled, the monster's face congealed and formed over Buffy's. Its teeth lengthened and sharpened into fangs.

"Sanno is correct," it hissed. "My promises are worth nothing. Honor is for those who can afford it."

It smiled in anticipation of the kill, and lowered its teeth toward Angel's neck.

CHAPTER NINETEEN

Willow ran.

She'd expected pain. Aching lungs, bruises on top of bruises, weak and rubbery legs. And she knew the bruises were there, despite whatever healing magick Chirayoju had at its command. But for now, the pain was minimal, completely overwhelmed by fear and adrenaline. In fact, she felt great—alive. The wind whipped her long hair behind her as Willow sprinted across lawns and pavement, jumped low fences and hustled past silent houses, long since dark.

Tomorrow morning she was going to be a wreck. But right now, Willow was focused on only one thing—the only thing she could feel.

Freedom.

She was free. He was gone from her body. It was almost like the horrible flu she'd had in the eighth grade. She'd missed school for a whole week, couldn't even blow her nose her head was so stuffy. The sense of relief she'd felt when the flu was finally gone was only the tiniest fraction of the crazy glee that overwhelmed her now.

Willow ran.

She ran as fast as she could. After all the times that she had thought of Sunnydale as a tiny little burg that barely deserved mention on the map, after all the times she had walked practically all the way across town, now, for the first time, she cursed her hometown as being too big. The school wasn't far away, but it seemed as though she'd never get there.

Then she thought of what would happen if she didn't get there in time. She'd seen what Chirayoju was capable of—had felt it, in fact—and it was obvious that this Mountain King guy wasn't exactly a pushover. Angel was strong, but there was no way he could take both of them on without help. Particularly not while he was trying to keep Buffy and Xander alive.

Buffy. Xander.

Willow's adrenaline spiked even higher, but all the good feeling that came from her freedom disappeared almost instantly. It was her fault. She knew that any of her friends would have argued that with her, but none of them were with her at the moment. She was alone. As alone as she'd been the night she'd been mugged.

That's where it all started.

It was all her fault.

She'd wanted to be more like Buffy, wanted to be tough—a fighter. Wanted, in other words, to be anything but little Willow, everyone's favorite brainy Smurf. All that had somehow led to her becoming possessed by Chirayoju, though she didn't know exactly how. Still, it had to be true. When she cut her finger on that blade, somehow the vampire's captive spirit had sensed her, tasted her blood, felt how vulnerable she was. It had attacked her, violated her in ways much worse than any simple mugging.

And then Buffy had come and fought for her. Had been hurt. For her. Then she had done the thing that made Willow feel like throwing up. The thing that was even now gnawing a guilty little hole in her gut. Buffy had offered herself up to Chirayoju in Willow's place.

"Oh God, Buffy, I'm so sorry," Willow whispered.

Incredibly, though Willow was already at her top speed, she began to run even faster. The little disk clutched in her palm felt warm there, and she prayed that Giles would know what to do with it.

They were a team. She understood that now, more than ever. Each did his or her part, whatever they were called upon to do. Right now her job was to get this thing to Giles as quickly as possible. After that, it would be in Giles's hands.

"Please, please, please, please," she chanted under her breath as she ran. But Willow had no idea whom she was pleading with: her body, or Giles, or someone else who could make all this right. Maybe all of them.

Maybe anyone who'd listen.

Willow ran.

Her heart pumped so fast and hard that her chest constricted and she wondered if this was what a heart attack felt like. But when she glanced up again, she saw the school. She had never been happier to get to Sunnydale High.

Willow stumbled going up the front steps, catching her foot on the long Chinese robe in which she found herself dressed. She skinned her knee on the concrete. But she picked herself up and kept moving. The front door was locked, of course. Giles hadn't expected anyone to be following on his heels.

She pounded on the door and began to scream his name. Barely able to hear the sound of her own voice, Willow shrieked her throat raw. The side of her hand hurt, and she started to slap the door instead. Anything. Whatever it took.

The door opened. Cordelia stared at her.

"Oh my God, Willow, what's . . ."

Willow fell into Cordelia's stunned embrace, barely noticing the other girl's astonishment. Then Cordy hugged her a little, which surprised Cordy as much as it did Willow.

"What is it?" Cordelia asked, staring at her. "Your clothes. Is that armor? If you're here . . . oh my God, what's happened to Xander? And Buffy?"

"Still alive, I think," Willow panted, then moved past

Cordelia and started down the hallway toward the library. "But not for long if Giles can't do something."

Cordelia hurried up next to her and helped her along, gripping Willow's forearm and putting her other arm around her shoulders. "I think we may have something," Cordelia said simply.

"For all our sakes," Willow rasped, "you'd better."

In the library Cordelia looked up worriedly and said, "What was that? Are we having an earthquake?"

"Hmm, not a welcome thought, that. Seeing as the garden has a bit of a bad history with earthquakes," Giles muttered.

"Take a look at this," he added, showing her the fax. "Can you find this for us? On the, um, computer?"

Willow shrugged. "If it's on there, I can find it."

Giles picked up the sword disk and scrutinized it. It gleamed in his hand and he murmured, "It's a shame that simply replacing this old disk wouldn't bind them once again. Of course, we would also have to manage to get that sword from Sanno . . . Xander . . . somehow."

He must have felt both Cordelia's and Willow's eyes on him, for he looked up from the disk and cleared his throat.

"So, let's search."

"Let's search." Willow cracked her knuckles.

While she was working, Giles received another fax:

Giles-sensei,

My deepest apologies for my earlier behavior. It was very rude of me to criticize your methods of working with your Slayer. I feel a great bitterness in my soul that I failed in my own duty to Mariko-chan. It is difficult for me to accept responsibility for her death. My sense of powerlessness now colors my life, and I felt great jealousy when I spoke to you because your Slayer is alive. I am very ashamed.

As a token of my regret, I offer this: Intrigued by your studies, I have found the Legend of the Lost Slayer, as detailed on a scroll which was discovered late last year in Osaka. I am sending you the complete story, but the short version is this:

In 1612, there was a Watcher who was a samurai. Because he failed in his duty, he was ordered by his lord to commit *seppuku*. Where did his duty lie, to his Slayer, or his lord? He chose his lord, and his Slayer was left without help. She was killed three months later.

I think that your young American girl is fortunate to have such a caring Watcher as you, Giles-sensei. I thank you for this lesson, and again, I beg your pardon.

Kobo

Giles swallowed hard, moved by the old man's confession. There were many kinds of demons in the world, and many ways to be bound by them. In his own way, Kobo had been blooded.

• • •

A short time later, they were in Giles's ancient auto, trundling toward the site of the climax of this ancient battle. Willow only hoped that everyone was still alive.

"Y'know, Giles, I was thinking," she said, "I mean, if you can do this thing, put the demon into the sword, why can't we pull the demon out of Angel the same way?"

Giles ran a red light and Cordelia murmured, "Yay."

"It had crossed my mind. But we're not sure how well the spell will work. Even if it does, it may only be because we're using an object that's already enchanted. Not to mention that, of course, the only result of removing the very thing that makes Angel a vampire would be that Angel would no longer be immortal.

"But Buffy's not immortal," Willow said helpfully. "That wouldn't be too bad."

"What I mean, Willow, is that Angel would be dead."

"Okay, that would be bad."

"This is all so insane," Cordelia said suddenly. "Why do I keep getting myself involved with you people? I'm going to get myself killed!"

"You just can't help yourself?" Willow suggested helpfully.

Cordelia smiled weakly. "Maybe not. So, are you okay?" she asked.

Willow blinked. Surprised and happy that Cordelia would bother to ask. "I guess so," she answered. "Actually, I'm pretty much one big bruise, but I think I'll be all right. If I ever get over the guilt of having started all this."

Cordelia frowned and Giles shot Willow an angry glance.

"What's happened is no more your fault, Willow, than it is Buffy's fault that we all live on the Hellmouth," Giles said sharply.

Willow thought about that. "I don't know how Buffy does it," she replied. "I mean, she's got to live, right? She has to have a life, but she's constantly putting herself and everyone she loves in danger by being the Slayer. Not that she means to put us in danger," she added loyally.

Cordelia turned around in her seat to look at Willow. "We're in danger just living here. I'll never admit it if you tell her I said it, but I'd hate to think about what Sunnydale would be like if we didn't have the Slayer in town."

"Willow, Buffy merely does her best. That's all any of us can ask of her, or one another. Thus far, I think we've all done rather well," Giles said.

"Yeah." Willow nodded. "Thus far."

But she was comforted by their words. And she agreed with them. Buffy did her best to protect them all, but in the end it was their job to protect themselves. They all had to deal with living on the Hellmouth in their own way. They all had their own roles to play in the fight against darkness. It was a team effort.

"Thanks, you guys," she said.

Cordelia rolled her eyes and offered a little scowl in return, and Giles was already off elsewhere, deep in thought. Which was okay. They were doing what they did best.

Willow stared out her window at the stars.

Stared out and saw a reddish glow against the sky.

Beneath the car, the earth trembled.

The three looked at one another.

Cordelia said, "If it'll make this heap go faster, I'll get out and push."

CHAPTER TWENTY

Angel landed atop a granite pagoda, which shattered beneath him, sending a good-sized shard of stone tearing through his abdomen. He groaned loudly, rolled over, and tried in vain to sit up once more. His face had long since transformed into its more feral, vampiric appearance, and it felt like ice now to him, cold and dead.

Angel stared down at the shiny granite shard protruding from his belly, cursed under his breath, and gripped it with both hands. He yanked it out, roaring with the pain of it, and then held a hand over the hole. A ripple of pain passed through him as he forced himself to his knees, but Angel ignored it.

His own pain meant nothing as long as Buffy was in trouble. Right now, she was in very serious trouble.

"You think that little girl's body can stand up to the King of the Mountain?" Sanno roared through Xander's mouth, with a voice that didn't sound anything at all like Xander anymore.

With that, the Mountain King swept the great sword around once more and brought it down at an angle that would easily have decapitated Buffy. But Chirayoju was fast . . . Buffy was fast.

Only when Sanno laughed, as he did now, could Angel hear Xander inside him. That laugh was keeping him from killing the boy. That, and the fact that without Sanno, he didn't think he had a chance at all of defeating Chirayoju. Which was the dilemma, of course. He needed help to stop even one of them, but neither of them was interested in doing anything but killing each other.

"I have conquered foreign lands, Mountain King," Chirayoju thundered as it sent another ring of fire spouting at Xander. "When the bones of your host are ground into the earth, into the false garden of your homeland, I will be ruling nations!"

Using Xander's arms, Sanno brought up the sword, and the fire was turned harmlessly away, as if it were a weapon as solid as the blade. Which, in a magickal sense, Angel guessed it was.

They moved at each other again.

Angel tried to stand, tried to stop them, but a wave of pain overcame him, and he stumbled slightly. He needed just a few seconds to focus. To orient himself. But they were a few seconds he did not have.

Chirayoju's fist was aflame with a magickal blaze—Buffy's hand was on fire!—and it drove that burning fist into Xander's face, scorching flesh and boiling blood with a smell that made Angel's mouth water and made him want to retch all at the same time.

"No," Angel grunted, and started stalking toward them.

With a roar of pain and fury, Sanno drove his sword home. Its point punched through Buffy's shoulder just below the collarbone, and Angel wasn't sure, but he thought he saw her shirt tent out in the back, as though the blade has passed all the way through.

"No!" Angel screamed, and picked up speed, hand still clamped over his healing belly.

They stood that way, frozen for a second, maybe two. Then Sanno ripped the sword out, slamming his—Xander's—upper torso into Buffy's body and sending Chirayoju stumbling back, left arm hanging limply by her—its—side. Blood ran freely from the wound, and Angel stared at it as he approached. But already the blood was drying up. Already the wound was healing. By sorcery, or because Chirayoju was a vampire, he didn't know. But the speed of it was amazing.

He glanced at Sanno, saw that Xander's face was also healing, and with that amazement running through his mind, he launched himself the last few feet toward Buffy. In her eyes, Chirayoju's spirit burned. Her lips stretched into a disgusting laugh, and that ghostly face that the sorcerer had worn earlier returned, even as it reached out for Angel.

Angel clasped his fists together, brought them around from waist level and up into Buffy's face with all the strength he could summon. There was a loud crack, and Buffy's body flew backward several feet, her head snapped back and to one side.

"Well done, young one," a deep voice that was not Xander's said behind him.

Angel turned quickly as a powerful hand clamped on his shoulder. Behind him, the King of the Mountain grinned with Xander's face, but more and more, Sanno was taking over and Xander seemed almost to be disappearing into himself.

But then that smile disappeared, and for the first time Angel saw the true arrogance of an ancient god, or whatever manner of being this was that had once been called a god. He saw the cruelty and the conceit there, and Angel stiffened, prepared to fight again.

"*Arigato gozaimasu*," Sanno said. "I thank you, stripling. But now, keep out of my way!"

Then the King of the Mountain lifted Angel from the ground and threw him into the air. Angel landed hard on his back, and though his rage increased even further, a tiny spark of dread was born in his heart, a sort of hopelessness unlike anything he had ever known.

Somehow, he had to stop them both from fighting to the death. But he had no idea how to go about it.

"Come then, Mountain King, I will tear the throat from your host body, and drink down the boy's blood, and your spirit with it." Chirayoju sneered as it regained its footing, its guttural grunting twisting Buffy's perfect, soft mouth into something horrible, something Angel could barely stand to see.

"You will spill no more blood this night, vampire," Sanno declared, sword held at the ready.

"You're right," Chirayoju crowed, then slid toward Xander—toward the Mountain King—with the grace of a dancer, despite the arm that hung limply by its side . . . by Buffy's side.

Buffy's mouth contorted into a repulsive grin. "I won't spill a drop," it said from within her. "I wouldn't want to waste it. No, I will taste the blood of your host, and then I will gather the small army already in my thrall, and I will walk the night of this new land and my power will swell with each risen moon."

"You will walk only in the spirit world, parasite. I will see to that," Sanno proclaimed, and launched himself at the vampire again.

Chirayoju rushed to meet him.

Buffy was cold. She imagined she could remember what it was like to be buried in the frozen earth. To be dead, immobile in her own flesh. It must be something like this, she thought.

But of course she could not remember it. And she was grateful for that at least.

But this wasn't the same. Not exactly. For as she floated inside the limbo that was her own mind, she could see cracks in her prison. Glimpses of the outside. There were moments when she felt a phantom pain, the tingling of her fingers, the thudding of her heart. Moments when she saw through her own eyes and heard with her ears.

She gathered her energy, reached into the deepest reserves of her mind, into the fabric of everything that made her herself. Buffy Summers. The Chosen One.

The Slayer.

And when dawn finally broke, what was Chirayoju but another vampire? More powerful than others, maybe. Older. And there was that whole magick thing, sure. But he was still a vampire. Buffy knew what to do with vampires.

She focused her anger, her hatred, and her duty, concentrated on her revulsion and her thirst for vengeance until they became like some kind of mental weapon, a blade of her own. A blade that sliced from within. Then she surged up through her consciousness, and she attacked! Chirayoju screamed inside her mind.

"I hope it hurts, you son of a . . . ," she started to say.

With her own voice. Her own lips.

Then she was wrenched back down again, down away from the surface, away from the body that she'd successfully navigated through seventeen years of living in America.

Buffy should have given up then. She knew that. Every ounce of strength had gone into that last effort, and it had given her only a moment of triumph. No matter how strong she was, no matter how brave, no matter how persistent, even she might have lost all hope in that moment, were it not for one thing.

Chirayoju was afraid.

She didn't know quite what it feared. It had to do with the sword, and with the millennia it had spent as a captive inside the sword. But the King of the Mountain has already stabbed her—stabbed *it*—once, and there had been no reaction. But still, Chirayoju feared that sword, as if there was still some possibility that it might be trapped there again.

Chirayoju was afraid.

In the secret chambers of her mind, Buffy smiled.

As smoke from the burning Japanese farmhouse roiled toward the combatants, Chirayoju glared with hatred at the Mountain King and thought of the girl whose body it inhabited with loathing. She was fighting to reassert control of this form. For that she would pay.

While the ancient spirits raged, the fire from the farmhouse had spread. Flames raged around the battleground as the desiccated plants of the garden fed the blaze.

A wind whipped up, fanning the flames. Fireballs shot like arrows from Chirayoju's fingertips and were diverted by Sanno's sword, helping to spread the blaze ever faster.

As Angel watched, the winds whipped up and seemed to lift Chirayoju from the oval of garden that was not aflame, the patch of earth that had become the arena for this ancient battle. Buffy seemed to fly then, with the magick of the vampire sorcerer propelling her along. She hovered above the place where the tiny farmhouse had been, where the fire burned brightly.

Then she dropped into the flames.

"Buffy, no!" Angel screamed.

But it was only a moment before she reemerged, hair ablaze, skin blackened and smoking. Then the flames were out, and already Chirayoju's magick was working to repair the damage; new pink skin began to show through.

In Buffy's hand, Chirayoju held a long, gleaming *katana*. The sword reflected the light of the fire and of the full moon above. For a moment, Buffy's body just hung in the air.

Then the wind swept down with pummeling force and carried Chirayoju with it. It dropped to the earth in front of Xander . . . in front of Sanno, and the two spirits clashed swords.

"Buffy," Angel whispered.

Giles screeched to a halt. Before the car stopped rolling, Cordelia and Willow were out and running to the rise above the sunken garden.

"Oh my God!" Cordelia cried.

Silhouetted against the backdrop of fire, Xander and Buffy were fighting with swords. Metal clanged against metal as they savagely battled, hacking and slashing with every ounce of their supernatural energy.

Angel saw the three of them, waved, and began to run toward them.

"Willow! Cordelia! Help me," Giles called.

They both ran back to the car and took large sacks from him. Inside Willow's sack were salt, water, and white paper, all symbols of purity. Cordelia carried Claire Silver's book and a printout of the Incantation of Sanno. Giles brought a white bandanna on which he had written the Chinese character for the Japanese word for the life force: *ki*. And the disk.

Giles joined the girls at the crest and began pouring salt in a sacred circle. "Cover it with the paper," he said, and they quickly laid the pieces of paper inside the circle.

"They're blowing away!" Willow shouted, grabbing at the sheets as they were lifted by the wind and went sailing toward the fire.

"Here. Use rocks," Cordelia said, gathering some large pebbles and handing some to Willow. Impressed by Cordelia's quick thinking, Willow did as she said.

Once the paper lined the circle, the two girls stepped out and Giles sprinkled the water over the field of white.

Then he stepped into the circle and lifted the bandanna to the east and intoned, "Oh, great ancestors of the lords of Japan, I call upon you to cast the spirits forth from these mortal beings!" Bowing, he put the bandanna against his forehead and knotted the ends.

Angel ran up to Willow. "What's going on?" he asked, staring at them with a mixture of doubt and hope on his face.

"We're going to get the spirits out of Buffy and Xander," Willow explained. "Then we'll bind them in the sword with the disk."

"Great rulers, I call upon you to heed me!" Giles cried.

Xander rushed Buffy. She deflected his sword thrust and somersaulted over his head with a horrible, maniacal laugh.

"It's not working," Cordelia fretted. "It's not working!"

"Yet," Willow said hopefully.

Chirayoju faltered.

For a moment, Buffy felt as though she could break out of her prison and take her body back. She cried, "Yes!" and hoped that someone could hear her, sense her.

Help her.

Sanno looked at the crest of the hill. Willow swallowed as he seemed to stare through her at Giles.

"Mortals, do not interfere," he said.

"I have the ward," Giles told him. He held the disk high. "You can use it to bind the vampire and—"

"It is too late. It is unnecessary," Sanno said, but his attention was focused on the disk.

"He's lying," Angel murmured to Giles. "He was pretty interested in that when Buffy had it."

"Yes." Cordelia nodded. "He's lying for sure."

"How do you know?" Willow asked her.

Cordelia smiled grimly. "Believe me, I know when guys are being bogus. And that is *one* Mountain King who is not telling us the truth."

"Because it will bind him, too?" Willow asked hopefully.

They both looked at Giles, who murmured, "Perhaps. But we must get them out of Xander and Buffy before we deal with that issue."

Below them, the battle raged.

CHAPTER TWENTY-ONE

Giles shook his head and dropped his arms to his sides. "It isn't working!"

Angel stared at him, trying not to panic at the rage and helplessness that was welling up within him. All along, he'd been battling the feeling that he could do nothing to affect the outcome here. He'd fought at Buffy's side time and again, and nearly always he had felt secure in the knowledge that he had helped. He was a vampire, after all. He was strong and very hard to kill. The perfect companion for the Slayer, in an odd way.

But all night long, as the battle raged, the despair had grown greater in him as each moment ticked past. As each of his attacks was brushed aside by beings far more powerful than he. Angel could do nothing. He had held on to one small hope: that he could keep Xander and Buffy from killing each other long enough for Giles to arrive with a solution. He'd done that.

And now . . .

"What do you mean it isn't working?" Cordelia shrieked. "It's got to work! You're doing everything the book says to do! It's got to work!"

Giles ignored her now. He had begun chanting the Incantation of Sanno again, as if repetition was going to make it suddenly work when it hadn't been working before.

She stared down the small incline at Xander, slashing away at Buffy, fire burning from his hands and the wind making his hair sweep back off his forehead.

Cordelia didn't know exactly what it was she had with Xander. But she didn't want to lose him.

Not like this.

Cordelia Chase began to cry.

Without thinking, Willow stepped in close to Angel and reached for his hand. He clasped her fingers in his own without even glancing at her. Together they looked down at the two battling warriors, at the elements scorching and scouring the dead garden, and neither of them spoke a word.

Willow shivered and realized that she could barely recognize her friends from up here. They stood inside a circle, almost like an arena, made of blazing fire. The garden had long since given way to flames for the most part, and it was already starting to burn down to nothing but cinder and ash. There had been very little there to burn in the first place.

Xander and Buffy wore ugly, frightening masks, one white and the other sickly green, that shimmered just in front of their faces. Their bodies hadn't changed, not really, but just the way they carried themselves, the way they moved, they didn't look like Buffy and Xander anymore.

They weren't Buffy and Xander anymore.

Willow was over it being her fault. She had to be. No way could she have known what was going to happen when she touched that sword, when she was "blooded." And Willow had learned her lesson, no question about that. She'd learned that she should worry about being the best Willow she could be, and let Buffy worry about being Buffy.

If Buffy lived long enough to worry about being Buffy.

And that was it, wasn't it? That was why her heart hammered in her chest and her stomach felt like a ball of ice. Because the lesson wasn't over yet, was it?

It wasn't her fault. But that didn't make it any easier.

And she still felt useless.

Completely, and totally . . .

Willow stared at Xander and Buffy. Something was happening. Giles was finishing up his latest rendition of that radio-saturated top-ten hit, the Incantation of Sanno. And something was happening.

For a second, Buffy and Xander both faltered. The wind died. The flames fizzled. Then the moment was gone. Xander—Sanno—raised his sword and brought it down swiftly, but Chirayoju spun out of the way, using a move that Willow just *knew* the sorcerer had stolen from Buffy's mind. She had had enough information stolen during her own possession to know what it was like.

It was over. But for that moment . . . that split second . . .

"Am I hallucinating, or did something just . . . ," Giles muttered.

"Giles!" Willow shouted. "Do it again!"

Giles turned, opened his mouth to ask for elaboration, but when he saw the look on Willow's face—on all their faces—he began the chant again immediately.

For a stunning second, Buffy had been in charge. It wasn't so much that Chirayoju had gone as that it had been banished far back into her mind, just as she was now.

The vampire sorcerer controlled her body again. But it was anxious now, unfocused. Confused.

Buffy like confused.

All right, you evil SOB, she thought, *let's try this again.*

The Slayer concentrated her energies, reached out, and gathered up all the things that made her the Chosen One, every personal moment, every intimate memory. They were her weapons and her armor, all the things that made her *her*. Her individuality was her strength. It hadn't been enough before, when Chirayoju was filled with confidence, at the peak of its strength.

But she didn't think it was at the peak anymore. Some-one . . . Giles or Angel, maybe . . . someone was doing something to throw it off. And then there was that sword. Chirayoju was afraid of the sword, Buffy knew that. It had been trapped there before, and the thought of being . . .

. . . *oh boy, Cheerios. I am so not going to be your favorite girl after this,* she thought.

Gently this time, so that it would not sense her, she tried to glide upward, tried to inhabit her body. To see through her own eyes.

And suddenly she could see. Xander, with that ghostly face in front of his own, bringing that huge, razor-sharp sword around for another thrust.

"Chirayoju, you lose!" Buffy screamed with her mind.

And with her mouth! The words came out of her mouth! She had her body again, before the vampire sorcerer even knew that she had taken over. It would toss her back quickly, she knew. But she only needed a second to do what she needed to do.

"Do it, Xander!" she shouted. "Do it!"

Buffy threw her arms wide, left herself wide open for the falling blade, and waited for the cold rush of its point sliding through her chest and toward her heart.

Xander had been submerged completely. The King of the Mountain had taken him over and driven him under so far he had not even been aware of his possession. For him, it had been like a particularly deep sleep.

Seconds ago, he'd awakened in his own body, staring at Buffy, who was bruised and burned and . . . healing before his eyes, even as fire scorched her again. He'd felt the weight of the sword in his hands, felt the aches of his own bruises as he let the sword's point fall to the dirt so he wouldn't have to hold it up anymore.

"Buffy," he had whispered hoarsely, "what's . . ."

And then the Mountain King had surged up within him again.

But this time Xander didn't go away. This time he saw it all through his own eyes, though he was powerless to act. Powerless, that is, until the precise moment when Sanno began to bring the sword around into a thrust that would have cleaved Buffy's heart in two.

In that moment, Xander Harris had all the power he would ever need.

"No!" he roared, and his muscles were his own again.

Too late to stop the thrust, he could only redirect it. The blade impaled Buffy through the lower abdomen, sliced cleanly through. It was the second time she'd been stabbed with that sword, Xander seemed to recall from a horrible dream he'd been living only seconds earlier.

But this . . . this was different.

With Xander's mouth, Sanno, the King of the Mountain, screamed.

With Buffy's mouth, the vampire sorcerer Chirayoju wailed in agony.

Xander tried to move, but he was frozen. His entire body was locked in place, the blade stuck inside Buffy, and she wasn't moving either. It was, he thought, in a weird moment of clarity, like being electrocuted. Some kind of weird energy danced from Buffy to Xander and back again; a circuit had been set up between them.

No, Xander couldn't move his body, but neither could Sanno. Nobody was in the driver's seat now.

Buffy felt the pulling start, felt a horrible urge as blood rushed to the spot on her belly where the sword intruded. It was sucking at her, somehow. Inside her mind, Chirayoju screamed again, and then she knew what was happening.

The sword was dragging the vampire's spirit back to its prison. Dragging . . . but dragging at her as well. And if Chirayoju wouldn't let go, it would take Buffy instead.

Yessss! Chirayoju hissed inside her head.

I don't think so, Myron, Buffy thought. *You crashed this party, bud. I'm not going anywhere.*

"Oh my God!" Cordelia cried. "Look at them! They're, like, frozen, or something!"

"Buffy," Angel whispered.

Willow tried to breathe. "This is bad."

"Not necessarily," Giles began, interrupting his chanting for a moment.

Angel saw Buffy move, just a bit. Half an inch. Obscured

by smoke and what little remained of the fire. But when Giles stopped chanting, she—or Chirayoju—had started to move again.

When he turned on Giles, Angel was in full vamp mode.

"Giles, shut up and chant!"

He was relieved when Giles did as he demanded. He'd apologize later, if there was a later. For now, Angel thought he understood, just a little, of what Giles had been about to tell them.

"Come on." Angel grabbed Willow and Cordelia by their hands and started running down the incline toward the burning circle of embers that had been a garden, once upon a time.

"Angel!" Cordelia pulled on his wrist. "Angel!"

"What?" He tugged at them both to get them to keep up with him.

"I'm barefoot!" she screeched.

Angel reached around and grabbed both girls around the waist. Then, one under each arm, he sprinted across the ashes into the circle where Xander and Buffy were still joined, paralyzed in their weird portrait of battle. Of murder.

"Willow, get behind Xander!" Angel barked, putting them both down. "Cordelia, you get behind Buffy. When I tell you to pull, pull on them as hard as you can!"

Willow frowned, puzzled. "But won't that just start it all over again?" Willow asked.

Angel turned to meet her anxious gaze. "I'm going to be

holding the sword. If Giles's spell is working, which it seems to be, then maybe they'll be trapped with it."

Cordelia stared at him. *"Maybe?"*

"Just do it!" Angel said angrily. "It's the only chance they've got."

"Okay," Cordy agreed instantly. "Just . . . Willow, be gentle with Xander, okay?"

Angel held the disk in his hand and stared at the odd inscriptions. He had no idea if this was going to work, but no time to worry about what might happen if it didn't.

"Wait, Angel!" Willow wrung her hands and chewed her lower lip as she looked uncertainly up at him. "What if Chirayoju and Sanno are trying to escape? Won't they try to go into you?"

"I've already got a demon in me, Willow." He flashed her a self-mocking smile. "Remember? There isn't room for another."

"But what if the sword tries to pull you in too?" Cordelia asked.

Angel didn't want to think about that, and he didn't reply. He glanced at Willow, who always seemed so fragile, and saw so much strength there that he vowed never to underestimate the girl again. Then he glanced at Cordelia, and he realized that the same was true of her. As annoying as she could be, it was mostly just the way she had learned to be. But inside . . . well, she was here, wasn't she? Ready to do whatever it took.

"Ready?" he asked.

Both girls nodded.

"One . . . two . . . pull!"

Angel grabbed the blade, its edge slicing into his palms. Xander and Buffy were torn away from the circuit, falling to the ground with Willow and Cordelia. Angel felt the electricity of the magick surge through him, into him . . . tugging at him.

Chirayoju and Sanno were there, inside the blade, and they were fighting still. As they had been for millennia. As he figured they would be until the end of time. And he had no desire to join them in the land of their hatred, the world inside that blade.

Fighting the pull of the sword, Angel held it up by its blade and stared at the hilt. He took the disk and placed it back into the slot from which it had fallen. Just as he realized he had no way to hold it in place, he felt a sharp tug at his sleeve.

Buffy.

Really Buffy, this time. Weak, pale, trembling—holding on to the bloody wound at her belly, the wound that had not closed up completely when Chirayoju had been yanked so unceremoniously from her body—but Buffy just the same. She held up to him a piece of cloth she had torn from the bottom of her shirt. Angel smiled and tied it around the hilt of the sword, holding the disk in place.

Still, the blade seemed charged with the hatred that lived inside it.

• • •

Buffy just wanted to sleep for about six months. That, and have somebody sew up the wound in her gut. Every inch of her felt bruised, the wound stung sharply, and yet, oddly, the places where she had been seriously injured before Chirayoju's magick had healed her felt all tingly and new.

But it wasn't enough that she'd been put through the wringer physically. She'd also ruined a brand-new top.

Then Angel looked at her, his eyes searing with his concern for her, and nothing else seemed important.

"I'm okay," she said. "A quick trip to the ER, and I'll be doing backflips in no time. Now, give me that," she said, gesturing to the sword.

Angel handed her the heavy blade. Buffy held the Sword of Sanno with both hands above her right knee, took a breath, and then brought it down hard. Anyone else would have broken their leg. But Buffy Summers was the Slayer. The Chosen One.

The blade snapped in two.

"Now they'll be fighting forever," Willow said as she stepped up to where Buffy stood with Angel.

Xander and Cordy were right behind her, holding each other. "Sounds like another couple I know," Xander said drily.

So, *he* was back to normal.

"Angel." Giles panted as he rushed down the hill. "Thank God. You did it. You saved them."

"Buffy put the final kibosh on them," Angel said.

Willow pointed at Giles. "But if Giles hadn't kept chanting . . ."

Buffy reached out to Willow, took her hand, squeezed it, and then dropped it again. She looked around, got a bit dizzy, and held on to Angel for support.

"Looks like we all had a part to play tonight," Buffy said. "If any one of you hadn't been here, this might have turned out very differently."

"Yes." Giles pushed up his glasses and wiped the beads of perspiration from his brow. "It might have turned out to be the longest night mankind has ever known."

"It certainly feels that way." Cordelia sniffed. "I just want to go home and . . . by the way, Summers, where's my car?"

"I'm sure it's around here somewhere," Buffy replied, snuggling into Angel's embrace, wincing at the pain in her abdomen.

"Buffy." Willow reached for her friend. Buffy nodded back, giving her an I'm-going-to-be-fine look.

Xander cleared his throat. "Y'know, not that I'm not doing a little happy-to-be-alive dance—which, for those of you who don't know it, is generally done with little in the way of actual pirouettes—but I'm a little bothered by this whole Chirayoju thing."

"Only a little?" Willow looked at him, a small smile on her face.

"No, really," Xander argued. "I mean, don't we have enough *local* vampires? Now we have to start importing them?"

"C'mon, Xander, haven't you heard?" Buffy asked. "We

live on the Hellmouth. This is, like, Disney World for vamps."

"I'd hate to see Mickey," Willow muttered.

"You're missing the point, Will." Xander pointed at a certain young Slayer. "To the vampires, Buffy *is* Mickey."

And they went on that way, mixing their cartoon metaphors and generally making Buffy's headache worse, until they had to split up to get to Giles's and Cordelia's cars. Buffy paused and then took Willow aside, away from the others.

"Are you okay?" she asked, when she and her closest friend were out of earshot of the others.

"You've got a hole in your stomach, and you're asking me if *I'm* okay?"

Buffy looked at her gravely. "Will. Are you okay?"

Willow smiled sheepishly, shrugged a little Willow shrug, and nodded.

"I'll be all right," she replied. "I still think I should learn to fight a little better, but I doubt after the past week I'll ever start thinking that being the Slayer would be a *good* thing. No offense."

"None taken," Buffy said, grimacing in pain. "Besides, if I'm going to be laid up for a night or two, Giles may need a little help out on patrol. And you know Xander . . . he's a little distracted by that case of Cordy on the brain that he's come down with. Somebody's got to look out for him."

Willow grinned, then helped Buffy over to Giles's car.

In the back of Giles's ancient four-wheeled monster, on

the way to the emergency room, Buffy fell soundly asleep in Angel's arms, a bittersweet smile on her face.

Bittersweet because she knew, even as she drifted off, that in the morning he'd be gone. But not forever. Not even for long. It was the curse of the Slayer, and the gift of her love for Angel, that the night would always come again.

And in the front seat, next to Giles, Willow felt a curious lightening inside her, as if the heaviest of burdens had been lifted. Giles must have noticed, for he cocked his head, half taking his eyes off the road, and said quietly, "Willow?"

"You know," Willow said, "it's a lot of work and everything, fighting the forces of darkness on such a regular basis. But I think if we all stick together, we just might win."

Giles smiled. He was the luckiest of men.

And the most fortunate of Watchers.

"Bravo," he whispered, and drove on.

ABOUT THE AUTHORS

Nancy Holder has published more than seventy-eight books and more than two hundred short stories. She has received four Bram Stoker awards for her supernatural fiction. Among her books for Simon Pulse, she is the coauthor of the *New York Times* bestselling Wicked series and the Once upon a Time novels *The Rose Bride* and *Spirited*. She lives in San Diego with her daughter, Belle, their two cats, and their two Corgis. Visit her at www.nancyholder.com.

In addition to *One Thing or Your Mother*, **Kirsten Beyer** is the author of *Star Trek Voyager, String Theory: Fusion*; the Alias APO novel *Once Lost*; and contributed the short story "Isabo's Shirt" for the *Distant Shores Anthology*.

Kirsten has appeared in the Los Angeles productions of *Johnson over Jordan, This Old Planet*, and Harold Pinter's

The Ho _____ ple." She
also ap _____ miere of
Quills and has been ____ on *General Hospital* and *Passions*,
among many others.

Kirsten has undergraduate degrees in English literature
and theater arts, and a master's of fine arts from UCLA. She
lives in Los Angeles with her husband, David, and their very
fat cat, Owen.

Christopher Golden is the award-winning, bestselling author
of such novels as *Of Saints and Shadows*, *The Myth Hunters*, and
Soulless. A lifelong fan of the "team-up," Golden frequently col-
laborates with other writers on books, comic books, and scripts.
During his tenure with Buffy the Vampire Slayer, he wrote or
cowrote more than a dozen novels, several nonfiction companion
books, dozens of comics (including the comics-writing debuts
of Amber Benson and James Marsters), and both Buffy video
games. Golden was born and raised in Massachusetts, where he
still lives with his family. His original novels have been published in more than fourteen languages in countries around the
world. Please visit him at www.christophergolden.com.